OXFORD

JOHN MARC

MARY ELIZABETH BRADDON was born in London in October 1835, the youngest daughter of Henry Braddon (a feckless solicitor and writer on sporting subjects) and Fanny White, his Irish wife, who left him when Mary was 4 years old and brought her daughters up alone. In 1856 Braddon began producing magazine stories in an unsuccessful attempt to augment the family income, and in 1857, using the name Mary Seyton, she began a brief career as an actress, an experience on which she was to draw in several of her novels. In 1860 she wrote her first novel, *Three Times Dead* (later published as *The Trail of the Serpent*), met the publisher John Maxwell, and gave up the stage. From this point onwards Braddon's life and career became intertwined with Maxwell's. The first of their children was born in 1862 (they married in 1874, following the death of Maxwell's first wife), the year in which she had her first commercial success with *Lady Audley's Secret*. Partly as a result of the precariousness of Maxwell's publishing ventures, Braddon continued to produce fiction at an extraordinary rate throughout the rest of the nineteenth century as well as 'conducting' several magazines, including *Belgravia* (1866–76). One of the most notorious sensation novelists of the 1860s, Braddon later developed the satirical talents evident in some of her earlier work to produce sharply observed novels of contemporary social life. Several of Braddon's novels were adapted for the stage, and *Aurora Floyd* was made into a silent film in 1913. The last of her eighty novels was published posthumously in 1916, following her death in February 1915.

TORU SASAKI is an Associate Professor of Kyoto University, Japan. He has edited Hardy's *The Hand of Ethelberta* for Everyman Paperbacks, and (jointly with Norman Page) Wilkie Collins's novellas *Miss or Mrs?*, *The Haunted Hotel*, *The Guilty River* for Oxford World's Classics. He is also a contributor to *The Oxford Reader's Companion to Thomas Hardy* (forthcoming).

NORMAN PAGE is an Emeritus Professor of the University of Nottingham and the University of Alberta. His most recent book is *Auden and Isherwood: The Berlin Years* (1998). He has edited novels by Dickens, Hardy, Wilkie Collins, Mrs Henry Wood, and Oscar Wilde, and has recently completed *The Oxford Reader's Companion to Thomas Hardy* (forthcoming).

OXFORD WORLD'S CLASSICS

For almost 100 years Oxford World's Classics have brought readers closer to the world's great literature. Now with over 700 titles—from the 4,000-year-old myths of Mesopotamia to the twentieth century's greatest novels—the series makes available lesser-known as well as celebrated writing.

The pocket-sized hardbacks of the early years contained introductions by Virginia Woolf, T. S. Eliot, Graham Greene, and other literary figures which enriched the experience of reading. Today the series is recognized for its fine scholarship and reliability in texts that span world literature, drama and poetry, religion, philosophy and politics. Each edition includes perceptive commentary and essential background information to meet the changing needs of readers.

OXFORD WORLD'S CLASSICS

MARY ELIZABETH BRADDON

John Marchmont's Legacy

Edited with an Introduction and Notes by
TORU SASAKI *and* NORMAN PAGE

OXFORD
UNIVERSITY PRESS

OXFORD
UNIVERSITY PRESS

Great Clarendon Street, Oxford OX2 6DP

Oxford University Press is a department of the University of Oxford.
It furthers the University's objective of excellence in research, scholarship,
and education by publishing worldwide in

Oxford New York

Athens Auckland Bangkok Bogotá Buenos Aires Calcutta
Cape Town Chennai Dar es Salaam Delhi Florence Hong Kong Istanbul
Karachi Kuala Lumpur Madrid Melbourne Mexico City Mumbai
Nairobi Paris São Paulo Singapore Taipei Tokyo Toronto Warsaw

and associated companies in Berlin Ibadan

Oxford is a registered trade mark of Oxford University Press
in the UK and in certain other countries

Published in the United States
by Oxford University Press Inc., New York

Editorial matter © Toru Sasaki, Norman Page 1999

First published as an Oxford World's Classics paperback 1999

British Library Cataloguing in Publication Data
Data available

Library of Congress Cataloging in Publication Data
Data available
ISBN 0–19–283321–9

1 3 5 7 9 10 8 6 4 2

Typeset by RefineCatch Limited, Bungay, Suffolk
Printed in Great Britain by
Cox & Wyman Ltd., Reading, Berkshire

CONTENTS

INTRODUCTION

Readers who do not wish to learn details of the plot will prefer to treat the Introduction as an Afterword.

Sensation Novels of the 1860s

Wilkie Collins's *The Woman in White* was a tremendous publishing event of 1859–60. The circulation of *All the Year Round*, the weekly magazine in which it was serialized, rose even higher than during the run of Dickens's *A Tale of Two Cities*, the novel that immediately preceded it as a serial, and people thronged the street outside the magazine's office, waiting for the appearance of a new instalment. When it appeared in volume form, the entire first edition of 1,000 copies was sold out on the day of publication, and a fourth impression was printed within a month. It was even a social phenomenon. White became a popular colour for feminine dress, and a number of commodities named after the novel were produced: 'The Woman in White' bonnet, 'The Woman in White' perfume, and so on. This monumental success triggered the vogue of 'sensation novels'. Mrs Henry Wood quickly followed with *East Lynne* (1861), and Mary Elizabeth Braddon with *Lady Audley's Secret* (1862).

Such novels, of which these three writers were the chief exponents, were characterized by their liberal use of elements of crime, such as bigamy, fraud, blackmail, and murder, in addition to various 'sensational' ingredients such as insanity, adultery, and illegitimacy. Specifically, they dealt with crime within the family, secrets behind the façade of middle-class respectability. In this regard, the sensation novel may be thought of as modernized and domesticated Gothic fiction of the kind represented by Ann Radcliffe's *The Mysteries of Udolpho* (1794), which treats of horrors in sixteenth-century Italy. In a review of Braddon's *Aurora Floyd* (1863), the young Henry James astutely observed:

To Mr Collins belongs the credit of having introduced into fiction those most mysterious of mysteries, the mysteries which are at our own doors. This innovation gave a new impetus to the literature of horrors. It was

fatal to the authority of Mrs Radcliffe and her everlasting castle in the
Apennines. What are the Apennines to us, or we to the Apennines? Instead
of the terrors of 'Udolpho', we were treated to the terrors of the cheerful
country-house and the busy London lodgings. And there is no doubt that
these were infinitely the more terrible.[1]

These novels, supposedly appealing to physical sensations of terror
rather than to higher rational faculties, were deemed not only
inferior in aesthetic terms—Collins and Braddon create their effects,
according to James, 'without any imagination at all'—but also
morally corrupt and corrupting.

Sensation fiction drew censorious remarks from various quarters,
and one of the most vehement (as well as the most comprehensive)
attacks, published in a notably conservative journal, was penned by
an Oxford don, Henry Mansel, later Dean of St Paul's. Deploring
these 'morbid phenomena of literature,' he characterized sensation
novels as 'indications of a wide-spread corruption, of which they
are in part both the effect and the cause; called into existence to
supply the cravings of a diseased appetite, and contributing themselves to foster the disease, and to stimulate the want which they
supply'.[2] Clearly Mansel sees a vicious circle that involves the
'morally corrupt' public and the 'morally corrupt' novels. He is particularly distressed by 'Bigamy Novels', of which Braddon's *Lady
Audley* was the quintessential example. Noting that 'It is astonishing
how many of our modern writers have selected this interesting
breach of morality and law as the peg on which to hang a mystery
and a dénouement,'[3] he demands: 'to what does such a story naturally lead, but to the conclusion that, whatever a censorious world
may say to the contrary, female virtue has really very little to do
with the Seventh Commandment? Novelists of this school do their
best to inculcate as a duty the first two of the three stages towards
vice—"we first endure, then pity, then embrace"; and, in so doing,
they have assisted in no small degree to prepare the way for the
third.'[4]

Mansel is also concerned about the rise of what he calls the

---

[1] *Nation*, 9 Nov. 1865, repr. in Norman Page (ed.), *Wilkie Collins: The Critical
Heritage* (London: Routledge & Kegan Paul, 1974), 122–3.
[2] H. L. Mansel, 'Sensation Novels', *Quarterly Review*, 113 (Apr. 1863), 482–3.
[3] Ibid. 490.
[4] Ibid. 495.

'Newspaper Novel', which reflects the fact that the vogue of these 'corrupt' novels was aided by actual crimes and the sensational reporting of these events. After the abolition of the stamp duty on paper in 1855, newspapers had become cheap enough for a wider readership, and they covered, in lurid detail and with melodramatic exaggerations, the Yelverton bigamy-divorce trial of 1857-61, the Madeleine Smith murder trial of 1857, and various other notorious cases. The public was hungry for every little clue—there is 'something unspeakably disgusting in this ravenous appetite for carrion,'[5] remarks Mansel—and as *The Times* reviewer of *Lady Audley* puts it, 'the police and the newspaper offices are besieged by correspondents eager to propose new lines of inquiry. The secret which baffles the detectives, it is the province of the novelist to unravel' (18 November 1862).

These attacks on moral grounds, however, can be seen as a reaction on the part of the dominant conservative ideology against the threats that were posed by sensation novels. This was the period when there had been urgent debates about the laws governing marriage and divorce in England, culminating in the Matrimonial Causes Act of 1857 and the establishment of England's first Divorce Court in 1858. This law made divorce considerably easier where it had been extremely hard to obtain. Although it was still not equally available to both sexes (for wives were allowed to divorce their husbands on the ground of adultery only when that was compounded by other offences, such as cruelty and desertion), this was something of a minor social revolution, and the 'Bigamy Novels' palpably reflected, if mostly in an exploitative manner, these social changes for the betterment of women's position. Indeed, the subversive threats were most keenly felt where women were involved. As Elaine Showalter points out: 'The prominence of women, not just as consumers but also as creators of sensation fiction, was one of its most disturbing elements.'[6] In this connection, we might recall that the defendants in notorious trials of the period were frequently female, and that the courts were crowded by female spectators. The trial of Madeleine Smith, who poisoned her lover, fascinated middle-class women, and Mary S. Hartman suggests that they 'most probably found in the

    [5] Ibid. 502.
    [6] Elaine Showalter, 'Desperate Remedies: Sensation Novels of the 1860s', *Victorian Newsletter*, 49 (Spring 1976), 3.

trial a kind of vicarious outlet for their own frustrations'.[7] And, just as women figured conspicuously in these cases, so they did in sensation novels. There were a number of female characters of strong determination, whether good like Marian Halcombe in *The Woman in White*, or evil like Lucy Graham in *Lady Audley's Secret*, who could not be simply ruled by male domination. Although too much emphasis on their subversive quality may be misleading (for transgressions by women of powerful will were usually punished and contained), these novels certainly destabilized the traditional view of women.

This has a significant bearing upon James's comment on 'those most mysterious of mysteries, the mysteries which are at our own doors'. When Mansel makes a similar observation—'Proximity is, indeed, one great element of sensation'[8]—there is an underlying fear: facing tremendous changes in matters religious, social, and economic, unsettled Victorians turned to their homes for security, and when the home itself was threatened, the anxiety must have been all the stronger. No doubt orthodoxy was worried, for the undermining of the conventional idea of femininity was tantamount to the destruction of the sacred home. As Showalter observes, '[Lady Audley's] career and the careers of other sensation heroines of the 1860s make a strong statement about the way women confined to the home would take out their frustrations upon the family itself'.[9] It is, therefore—aside from their exciting narrative interests that 'electrify the nerves'—as representations of the women of the period that sensation novels draw our attention today; and *John Marchmont's Legacy* is no exception to this generalization.

Braddon's Novels Up To *John Marchmont's Legacy*

Mary Elizabeth Braddon (1835–1915) was the youngest daughter of a London solicitor, Henry Braddon. Besides being unfaithful to his wife, Fanny, he was financially irresponsible and went bankrupt. From about 1840 Fanny Braddon lived, with her three children, separately from him. After her brother Edward went to India and her

---

[7] Mary S. Hartman, 'Murder for Respectability: The Case of Madeleine Smith', *Victorian Studies*, 16 (June 1973), 399.

[8] Mansel, 'Sensation Novels', 488.

[9] Showalter, 'Desperate Remedies', 5.

older sister Maggie was married, Mary Elizabeth, in her attempt to support herself and her mother, first tried a career on the stage in Yorkshire (1857–60), then sought to earn a living by her pen. She wrote a comedietta called *The Loves of Arcadia*, which was successfully staged at a London theatre in March 1860. Another opportunity presented itself when C. H. Empson, a Yorkshire printer who had read her verse in a local paper, offered her ten pounds for a serial story: this became her first novel, *Three Times Dead, or the Secret of the Heath* (1860). Later, Braddon the successful author recalled this apprentice work: 'I gave loose to all my leanings to the violent in melodrama. Death stalked in ghastliest form across my pages; and villainy reigned triumphant till the Nemesis of the last chapter'.[10] Indeed, broadly melodramatic and filled with improbable coincidences, the novel traces the career of the villain, Ephraim East, who commits two murders and abets an aristocratic lady in another, then blackmails her into marrying him. The writing is very uneven, and half-successful attempts at Dickensian irony show that Braddon still has not found a true voice of her own.

At about that time she formed a relationship with John Maxwell, an energetic magazine-publisher, whom she had met in March 1860. They lived together from 1861, but were not able to marry until Maxwell's mentally disturbed wife died in 1874. Braddon's 'irregular' life, like George Eliot's, was often attacked when her books were reviewed. In February 1861, at the beginning of their partnership, Maxwell republished Braddon's first novel under the title of *The Trail of the Serpent*, with most of the places and characters renamed (for example, the protagonist, formerly Ephraim East, is now called Jebez North). This was something of a winner, and Maxwell wrote to her, reporting triumphantly that it had sold 1,000 copies in the first week after publication.[11] Interestingly, George Eliot was later to complain about this novel in a letter of 11 September 1866, shortly after the publication of her own *Felix Holt*: 'I sicken again with despondency under the sense that the most carefully written books lie, both outside and inside people's minds, deep undermost in a heap of trash. I suppose the reason my 6/- editions are never on the

---

[10] Braddon, 'My First Novel', *The Idler Magazine*, 3 (Feb. 1893), 25.

[11] See Robert Lee Wolff, *Nineteenth-Century Fiction: A Bibliographical Catalogue Based on the Collection Formed by Robert Lee Wolff*, 5 vols. (New York: Garland, 1981–6), i. 145. Maxwell's letter is dated 22 February 1861.

railway bookstalls is partly of the same kind that hinders the free distribution of Felix. They are not so attractive to the majority as "The Trail of the Serpent" . . .' In the context of our examination of the sensation novel, this letter commands our attention in two respects. First, despite her denigrating comment on Braddon's kind of fiction ('a heap of trash'), in *Felix Holt* Eliot herself incorporated sensational elements (notably in the form of Mrs Transome's guilty secret) that reveal the powerful influence of this popular genre. Secondly, it reminds us that the railway stall was also a target of Mansel's attack: 'keepers of bookstalls, as well as of refreshment-rooms, find an advantage in offering their customers something hot and strong'.[12]

Braddon soon started contributing a number of works to Maxwell's magazines: her second novel, *The Lady Lisle*, which appeared in *The Welcome Guest* (April–August 1861); stories, mostly sub-literary hackwork, to the *Halfpenny Journal*; and her third novel, *Lady Audley's Secret*, to *Robin Goodfellow* from July 1861. It was the signal success of the last that instantly placed her in the literary market as the rival of Wilkie Collins. Braddon was later to admit her debt to Collins in an interview, when she confessed that 'I always say that I owe "Lady Audley's Secret" to "The Woman in White." Wilkie Collins is assuredly my literary father. My admiration for "The Woman in White" inspired me with the idea of "Lady Audley" as a novel of construction and character.'[13]

An exhaustive enumeration of the similarities between *The Woman in White* and *Lady Audley* would be tedious, but it may be noted that Braddon reverses the main situation, choosing a female, instead of a male, perpetrator of crime, and that while in the former work Anne Catherick and Laura Fairlie are rescued out of asylums, in the latter Lucy Graham is put into one. Braddon, however, was not just cleverly imitating Collins; she was also expressing opposition to him. Lucy Graham, or Lady Audley, was clearly meant as a protest against the passive and angelic heroines of the period, such as Laura Fairlie. In a sense, here was a feminist rewriting of that famous precursor text. Meanwhile, there is no doubt that Braddon learned her lesson from Collins very well, for certainly *Lady Audley's*

[12] Mansel, 'Sensation Novels', 485.

[13] Joesph Hatton, 'Miss Braddon at Home: A Sketch and an Interview', *London Society*, 53 (Jan. 1888), 28.

Secret is much more tightly constructed than *Three Times Dead* or *The Lady Lisle*.

In January 1860 the publishers Smith & Elder had launched a high-quality literary monthly, *The Cornhill Magazine*, under the editorship of Thackeray. Its first issue contained, among other items, instalments of *Lovel the Widower* by the editor himself, *Roundabout Papers*, again by Thackeray, and *Framley Parsonage* by Trollope. The public keenly welcomed this publishing venture, which offered an instalment of a novel, short stories, poetry, and articles, all for one shilling—the same price as a single monthly part of a serialized novel published separately. Maxwell was eager to imitate the *Cornhill*'s popular success and, having secured George Augustus Sala as editor, started *Temple Bar* in December of the same year. Braddon was asked to contribute to this, and after publishing some poems and stories, she started *Aurora Floyd*, which ran from January 1862 to January 1863, thus overlapping with the serialization of *Lady Audley*, which finished in the *Sixpenny Magazine* in December 1862 (*Robin Goodfellow* having been discontinued in September 1861). *Aurora Floyd*, another bigamy novel, was again a great success, and before this serial reached its conclusion Braddon started publishing *John Marchmont's Legacy* in the same magazine in December 1862. Astonishingly enough, from March 1863 *John Marchmont* ran concurrently with yet another Braddon novel, *Eleanor's Victory*, serialized in *Once A Week*.

John Marchmont's Legacy

In order to understand Braddon's intentions in writing this novel, it is instructive to turn to her correspondence with Edward Bulwer-Lytton, whom she admired enormously and placed, along with Dickens, at the very top of the profession. Edward Bulwer-Lytton (1803–73), politician and writer, had achieved great popularity with such historical novels as *The Last Days of Pompeii* (1834), and had also worked hard to improve the lot of authors. With Dickens he had established a charitable scheme for needy authors, the Guild of Literature and Art, which Dickens believed would 'entirely change the status of the literary man in England'. Braddon sought guidance from him on the art of fiction-writing, and her surviving letters amply show how much she treasured his advice. (Charles Reade was another prominent writer of the period who gave her encouragement and counsel.) Braddon had no illusions about the commercial aspect of her imaginative creations; she was writing sensation novels, she admitted, because that was what the reading public wanted. That, however, was not all she cared about: 'I want to serve two masters. I want to be artistic & please you. I want to be sensational, & to please Mudie's [circulating library] subscribers' (May 1863). She expressed the hope that *John Marchmont* was 'better written' (13 April 1863) than *Lady Audley* or *Aurora Floyd*. And it is not simply the question of style that she was talking about, for Braddon was also seriously ambitious with respect to characterization: 'I have thought very much over what you said in your last letter with regard to a novel in which the story arises naturally out of the characters of the actors in it, as contrasted with a novel in which the actors are only mario-nettes, the slaves of the story. I fancied that in "John Marchmont" the story was made subordinate to the characters but even my kind-est reviewers tell me that it is not so and that the characters break down when the story begins' (17 January 1864). The critic in *The Times* (2 January 1864) must be one of those Braddon had in mind, for this reviewer states that *John Marchmont* 'may be pronounced the best' of her novels so far published, but adds that here, as in other sensation novels, 'when . . . the story begins . . . the force of character must give way to the exigencies of plot'. Indeed, criticism of this sort—that in the sensation novel the emphasis is always on plot at the expense of character—was frequently accorded to the fiction of Collins and Braddon.

Behind this argument lay what Henry James, in his essay 'The Art of Fiction' (1884), called 'an old-fashioned distinction between the novel of character and the novel of incident'. The use of this division (which survives even today) in the critical discussion of fiction became increasingly evident as sensation novels made their presence felt. Mansel, of course, had something to say about this: 'A sensation novel, as a matter of course, abounds in incident. Indeed, as a general rule, it consists of nothing else. Deep knowledge of human nature, graphic delineations of individual character . . . would be a hin-drance rather than a help to a work of this kind'.[14] George Henry Lewes was also irritated by the sensation novelists' abuse of 'striking

[14] Mansel, 'Sensation Novels', 486.

incidents', which in his opinion only disturb 'the natural evolution of their story' unless they 'serve to bring into focus the diffused rays of character and emotion'.[15] Lewes's view presumably parallels what Bulwer, whose letters to Braddon are almost totally lost, said to her.

Braddon was aware that her characterization in earlier novels had been weak, and she tried to make it stronger this time. She wrote to Bulwer: 'I am in hopes you will like "John Marchmont," the story I am now doing in "Temple Bar" better than "Aurora." I have tried to draw more original characters, or at least one character more original than any of my usual run of heroes & heroines' (May 1863).

When she says 'at least one character', Braddon no doubt has Olivia Arundel (later Olivia Marchmont) in mind. Mary Marchmont and Belinda Crawford are no more than conventional heroines, well qualified to become, successively, the wives of the upright, manly, and fairly conventional hero, but the portrait of Olivia is powerful and original, and it is no exaggeration to say that she dominates the novel, calling forth from the reader a complex reaction that blends sympathy and replusion. Concisely telling us that 'the life of this woman is told in these few words: she did her duty' (p. 66), Braddon explores Olivia's inner and outer worlds in a remarkable passage, as follows:

It was a fearfully monotonous, narrow, and uneventful life which Olivia Arundel led at Swampington Rectory. . . . The world outside that dull Lincolnshire town might be shaken by convulsions . . . but all those outer changes and revolutions made themselves but little felt in the quiet grass-grown streets, and the flat surrounding swamps, within whose narrow boundary Olivia Arundel had lived from infancy to womanhood; performing and repeating the same duties from day to day, with no other progress to mark the lapse of her existence than the slow alternation of the seasons, or the dark hollow circles which had lately deepened beneath her grey eyes, and the depressed lines about the corners of her firm lower-lip.

These outward tokens, beyond her own control, alone betrayed this woman's secret. She was weary of her life. She sickened under the dull burden which she had borne so long, and carried so patiently. The slow round of duty was loathsome to her. The horrible, narrow, unchanging existence, shut in by cruel walls, which bounded her on every side and kept her prisoner to herself, was odious to her. The powerful intellect revolted against the fetters that bound and galled it. The proud heart beat with murderous violence against the bonds that kept it captive. (p. 68)

This is a strong evocation of a painfully dull life, where the flatness of Olivia's daily activity is matched by the flat landscape. Her frustration and repression, the novel's imaginative core, are clearly expressed here, and Braddon goes on to show that Olivia's plight ultimately arises from the fact that she is a woman, and as such has not been given a role in life in which she can utilize and develop her talents: 'She ought to have been a great man', but the 'fetters that had bound Olivia's narrow life had eaten into her very soul, and cankered there' (p. 356). To be sure, Braddon's portrayal of Olivia may at times seem excessively melodramatic, at least by the canons of fictional realism: 'Olivia Marchmont grasped the trembling hands uplifted entreatingly to her, and held them in her own,—held them as if in a vice. She stood thus, with her stepdaughter pinioned in her grasp, and her eyes fixed upon the girl's face. Two streams of lurid light seemed to emanate from those dilated grey eyes; two spots of crimson blazed in the widow's hollow cheeks' (p. 161). One contemporary critic remarks of the latter portion of this passage that 'We doubt if, even at the Surrey Theatre, anything like it was ever delivered', but this reviewer is surely misguided in his comment that Olivia 'is but a creature of Miss Braddon's imagination, and that such a personage is as unreal as a hobgoblin'.[16]

Braddon did not like insincere philanthropy. She looked down upon the pomposity and affectations of her day, and was to show a marked dislike for self-righteous do-gooders in some of her later novels, most notably in *Rough Justice* (1898). But here Olivia is not the target of a clear-cut satire. Braddon's presentation of this character's moral nature is interesting in its complexity. On the one hand she tells us that Olivia's tragedy is that 'for all her goodness' (p. 67) —or, rather, 'even by reason of her goodness' (p. 68)—she is not loved. On the other hand, Olivia is 'not a good woman, in the commoner sense we attach to the phrase' (p. 69): she is 'a woman with a wicked heart steadfastly trying to do good, and to be good' (p. 83). The novel is clearly troubled about the question, what really is 'a good woman'? Consider, then, Olivia's essential predicament: the

---

[16] 'Sensation Novelists: Miss Braddon', *North British Review*, 43 (1865), 195.

torment she undergoes by virtue of her own uncontrollable passion for Edward, a man who appears to her to be foolish and frivolous, 'so little worthy of [her] sacrifice' (p. 165). The novelist takes pains to tell us that Olivia is in the wrong:

She was for ever weighing Edward Arundel against all the tortures she had endured for his sake, and for ever finding him wanting. He must have been a demigod if his perfections could have outweighed so much misery; and for this reason she was unjust to her cousin, and could not accept him for that which he really was,—a generous-hearted, candid, honourable young man (not a great man or a wonderful man),—a brave and honest-minded soldier, very well worthy of a good woman's love. (p. 147)

Apparently this authorial comment is meant to be taken straight. But given the very power of the portrait of Olivia, and the anxieties about the idea of a 'good woman', one is reluctant to make an easy judgement. Perhaps Edward is worthy of a good (but uninteresting) woman like Mary or Belinda, but not meant for a complicated person like Olivia? If Braddon is seen to be showing sympathetic under-standing towards Olivia, might it not be possible that the novelist, who must have shared with Olivia 'the powerful intellect' and the 'proud heart', was putting much of herself (including her sympathy) into this character, and then offering a kind of self-criticism (hence the authorial comment quoted above)?

Here it is tempting to hazard a biographical speculation. At one point in 1863, in a letter now lost, Bulwer must have criticized Braddon, as Robert Lee Wolff surmises, 'specifically for not taking seriously enough the jealous torments of Aurora's disappointed lover Bulstrode and her deceived husband Mellish'.[17] Braddon, in her reply, tried to explain why she 'failed to reach a higher tone' in these characters: 'I have begun to question the expediency of very deep emotion, & I think when one does that one must have pretty well passed beyond the power of feeling it. It is this feeling, or rather this incapacity for any strong feeling, that, I believe, causes the flippancy of tone which jars upon your sense of the dignity of art. I can't help looking down upon my heroes when they suffer, because I always have in my mind the memory of wasted suffering of my own.' She concludes that 'the faculty of writing a love story must die out with

[17] Robert Lee Wolff, *Sensational Victorian: The Life and Fiction of Mary Elizabeth Braddon* (New York: Garland, 1979), 156.

the first death of love' (May 1863).[18] Wolff suggests that this feeling 'must have stemmed from some earlier passionate love affair'.[19] Braddon obviously felt that she knew the pains of jealousy, and she deliberately did not elaborate them in her male characters. Her treatment of Olivia, however, is an entirely different matter, and one is tempted to think that in this serious attempt at characterization she must have probed the depths of her own feelings and then come up with this impressive portrait of Olivia. What Braddon hit upon might very well have been the situation of an intellectually acute woman hopelessly in love with a man of apparently unequal abilities. Olivia's 'wasted love' (p. 142) for Edward does seem to echo the novelist's own 'wasted suffering' (the phrase used in the letter quoted above).

Olivia is not understood by anyone, not even by her widowed father, who is 'afraid of his daughter' (p. 70)—except, that is, by Paul Marchmont, who takes advantage of her secret passion for Edward, and thus is able to involve her in his wicked scheme. This is the crux of the plot-development of the novel, and Braddon handles this part very well. Here 'the story arises naturally out of the character', as Bulwer recommended. But Braddon is on less sure ground with the imaginative creation of a villain: she has not been successful with a line of criminals from Ephraim East of *Three Times Dead* to Paul in this novel. She tries hard, particularly in the chapters dealing with Paul's last hours, but cannot quite bring it off. This section is by no means weak, but it lacks the psychological penetration Dickens displayed with Bill Sikes or Jonas Chuzzlewit.

Braddon, however, does better with the simple soldier-hero, Edward Arundel. It is clear from what he says to Mary—'You must never grow any older or more womanly . . . Remember that I always love you best when I think of you as the little girl in the shabby pinafore . . .' (p. 15)—that he cannot face mature sexuality. He is not sensitive, and cannot understand why Mary does not like the idea of her father's remarriage: he is 'dumbfounded by Mary's passionate sorrow' (p. 79). These two elements make it thoroughly convincing that Edward cannot comprehend, or even imagine, Olivia's sexual

---

[18] The source of all the quotations from Braddon's letters is Robert Lee Wolff, 'Devoted Disciple: The Letters of Mary Elizabeth Braddon to Sir Edward Bulwer-Lytton, 1862–1873', *Harvard Library Bulletin*, 22 (1974), 5–35, 129–61.

[19] Wolff, *Sensational Victorian*, 157.

yearning for him. Probably the most sensational incident of the novel occurs in the scene where Edward hears the cry of a baby in the boathouse that Paul uses as his studio. He is with Olivia, and when she tries violently to stop him from investigating this mystery, he attributes her wild behaviour to her madness, and thinks the child is hers. All this is psychologically credible, and again shows that the action of the story 'arises naturally out of the characters'.

The action of the novel covers a period of some seventeen years, from 1838 to 1855 (see the Appendix); in other words, though it begins a generation before the date at which the work was written and first published, it concludes within a few years of that time. This time-span is a necessary element in the structure because Edward first encounters Mary when she is no more than a child; like Jane Eyre, Maggie Tulliver, and many other Victorian heroines, Mary grows up as the narrative proceeds, and in due course marries and bears a child herself. But she remains, like Dickens's Amy Dorrit half-a-dozen years earlier, a child-woman—not least in the eyes of her husband, who tells her at one point, 'My own childish pet . . . You shall be sheltered, and protected, and hedged in on every side by your husband's love. . . . How strange it seems to me . . . that you should have been so womanly when you were a child, and yet are so childlike now that you are a woman!' (p. 208).

Before dismissing Edward as an unenlightened representative of a patriarchal society, however, we should bear in mind that the narrator endorses Edward's attitude towards Mary—or at least does not appear to call it seriously into question (see, for example, the final sentence of the novel). In this, as in so many other respects, Mary stands at the opposite pole from Olivia, who, for all her infatuation with Edward, would hardly have desired or accepted this kind of love. Nevertheless, Mary and Olivia share one thing, in both being motherless. As Lyn Pykett points out, all of Braddon's heroines share this lack of a mother; Pykett goes on to claim that 'As in so many nineteenth-century novels by women, the motherless heroine is both more vulnerable and more assertive than was the norm for a properly socialised woman'.[20]

Edward himself is not only the very model of an English gentleman but a professional soldier of the officer class, and the dating of

---

[20] Lyn Pkyett, *The Improper Feminine: The Women's Sensation Novel and the New Woman Writing* (London: Routledge, 1992), 87.

the action enables Braddon to dispatch him to India in the service of the East India Company for active service in the Afghan Wars of 1838–42. (It may be more than coincidence that Braddon's brother, another Edward, had also gone to India.) His absence is also a convenience to the narrative, since it allows Mary to grow up, and her father to come into his inheritance. Both this absence and the one near the end of the novel take the hero to pre-Mutiny India: the conclusion of the story in 1855 is within a couple of years of the outbreak of the Mutiny, with the ensuing transfer of the Company's powers to the British Crown—events that would still have been fresh in the minds of readers when serialization of the novel began at the end of 1862.

Though such off-stage events as the Afghan Wars, reinforced by references to such heroes of the day as Napier and Outram, are reminders of a larger public world, the action of the novel takes place in England, and very largely in the relatively isolated county of Lincolnshire. Marchmont Towers belongs in many respects to the tradition, derived by the sensation novel from Gothic fiction, of the ancient, lonely, and rather inaccessible mansion behind whose thick walls and heavy doors mysteries can be concealed and alarming events may take place. The introductory description of the house ('a little too dismal in its lonely grandeur') near the beginning of Chapter V associates it with 'Ancient tales of enchantment, dark German legends, wild Scottish fantasies, grim fragments of half-forgotten demonology, strange stories of murder, violence, mystery, and wrong . . .', while a later passage refers to it as 'this grim enchanted castle, where evil spirits seemed to hold possession' (p. 270).

As for the surrounding landscape, its desolation mirrors or objectifies the desolation of Olivia's inner life. Swampington Rectory (a loaded place-name), in the 'gloomy landscape' (p. 121) of Lincolnshire, 'fenny, misty, and flat always' (p. 54), offers no consoling natural beauty, no external solace for inner torment. Happier scenes, like Edward's childhood home in Devon and the pretty surroundings of Edward and Mary's brief honeymoon in Hampshire, are significantly located in other parts of England, more climatically favoured and more conventionally picturesque.

But the main action demands a severer setting, hostile as well as isolated. Two keywords in this novel are 'bleak' and 'dreary', and between them they may suggest the influence of two of the most celebrated of Braddon's contemporaries. Dickens's *Bleak House* (1853), ten years earlier, had been a precursor and almost a prototype of the sensation novel, and the most obviously 'sensational' portion of that novel is also set in a lonely mansion in Lincolnshire. In Sir Leicester Dedlock's ancestral home of Chesney Wold, as in Marchmont Towers, a proud and gifted woman compelled to suppress her passions lives a life of quiet despair, and the description of the Towers at the beginning of Chapter VI of *John Marchmont* ('The rain beats down') is strikingly reminiscent of a passage near the beginning of the second chapter of Dickens's novel ('The waters are out in Lincolnshire'). It must be said, though, that Olivia offers a much more convincing study of feminine psychology, more inward and more felt, than Dickens's glacial and stagey Lady Dedlock.

Tennyson, at the height of his fame in the 1860s, is an even more obvious presence in *John Marchmont's Legacy*. The epithet 'dreary', used so often in the novel, echoes throughout his well-known poem 'Mariana', and it is interesting to note that between the serial and volume versions of this novel a rather banal chapter-title was changed in order to incorporate a clear allusion to Tennyson's poem (see note on p. 77). (Mariana, like the same poet's Lady of Shalott, and like Braddon's Olivia, eats her heart out in physical and emotional isolation from the world of action and self-fulfilment.) In the next chapter a phrase of Braddon's echoes a line in Tennyson's later companion-poem 'Mariana in the South' ('When I shall cease to be all alone')—a quotation that in the original source appositely continues 'To live forgotten, and love forlorn'. Braddon's free adaptations suggest that she was quoting from memory, and she has clearly absorbed, and evidently wishes to reproduce in her own work, the spirit of these Tennysonian models. When Edward goes to Brittany in order to pick up the pieces of his shattered life, he follows in the footsteps of the hero of Tennyson's *Maud* (1855). And near the end of the novel, two more chapter-titles (XLI and XLIII) allude, respectively, to Tennyson's 'The Deserted House' and 'The Lotos-Eaters'.

Such poetic elements, like the Gothic strain, have a generalizing and distancing effect, but this is at the same time a novel resolutely of its own time: this tale of wickedness, crime, and madness is set not in the barbarous past or away from the centres of civilization but in a highly organized and technologically advanced society. There are, for example, many references to the railways (and to the well-thumbed text that minutely reflected their complex operations, Bradshaw's railway timetable); to newspapers (advertisements are placed in *The Times*); and to the postal service. An important plot-device involves the receipt of a letter which sends the hero on a journey and causes him to be seriously injured in a collision between a mail train to Exeter and a goods train carrying produce to London—powerful symbols of a highly organized modern society in which, as in the novels of Thomas Hardy, the patterns and rhythms of older modes of existence are rapidly being destroyed. All of this implies a chilling paradox: in the most advanced society the world had ever seen, horrors could still be perpetrated: what Conrad was later to call the darkness of man's heart remained a constant.

In *John Marchmont* Braddon continues, and develops, the themes and motifs which she dealt with in her previous novels. Like *Lady Audley's Secret* and *Aurora Floyd*, this is a 'bigamy novel', using the 'dead-but-not-dead' formula. (*Three Times Dead* and *The Lady Lisle* also contain these elements.) And just as Lady Audley's secret is madness, so is Olivia's—'My madness has been my love' (p. 429).

Drawing attention to the connection of *Lady Audley* with *John Marchmont*, Pykett observes that 'In each of these novels madness is used as a way of figuring the dangerous, improper feminine, which is both formed by and resists the management and control of the middle-class family and the self-regulation which is the internalisation of those broader social forms of control'. She goes on to remark that Olivia is 'in some ways an even more interesting representation [than Lady Audley] of the feminine and of madness, or indeed of the feminine as madness, since her insanity seems to be actively produced by the norms of respectable femininity.'[21] If *Aurora Floyd* is a story of jealousy, *John Marchmont* offers a variation on the theme: while Aurora is an object of jealousy, Olivia is motivated by that emotion. Moreover, Braddon seems to suggest that Olivia's sexual repression is even more dangerous than Aurora's abandonment.

There are also interesting similarities between *John Marchmont* and *Eleanor's Victory*, which was running simultaneously with this novel. The latter, also, has a theatrical background (no doubt reflecting the novelist's own early career), with its hero as a scene-painter,

---

[21] Ibid. 95.

and it contains an artist-villain. There is also the situation of a very young motherless girl deeply caring for her ineffectual father. In the same novel, one of the characters facetiously says, 'He might come in for the title himself, my dear, if seventeen of his first cousins, and first cousins once removed, would die' (ch. 53). This idea is treated more seriously in *John Marchmont*. Indeed, problems pertaining to inheritance figure largely in other Victorian novels: Dickens had treated them comically with Dick Swiveller in *The Old Curiosity Shop* (1841), and seriously in *Bleak House* (1853); in the years nearer Braddon's time, Collins used them in *The Woman in White* (1860) and *No Name* (1862), George Meredith in *Evan Harrington* (1860), and Trollope in *Orley Farm* (1862). *John Marchmont's Legacy* belongs to this group of novels, but we should be alert to the fact that the title of the novel refers not only to the property John Marchmont inherits, but also to the girl he bequeathes to Edward Arundel, as the novelist reminds us on several occasions (pp. 30, 151, 256, etc.).

Braddon knew how to tell a good story. Here she keeps the action going at an excellent pace; it slows down a little, perhaps, with Edward's courting of Belinda, but soon picks up with Olivia's emotional explosion. She had already mastered the art of writing a serial, and especially the divisions at the end of Chapters XIV and XXVIII (which respectively form the end of Volumes 1 and 2 in the 'three-decker' first edition) hold the reader in genuine suspense. Although there is no murder in this novel, it satisfies the generic requirements with kidnapping, blackmail, and other sensational elements. These Braddon uses well, as usual, and she is also capable of remarkable restraint where one might expect melodramatic excess. The description of the railway accident is a case in point: 'She prayed for him, hoping and believing everything; though at the hour in which she knelt, with the faint starlight shimmering upon her upturned face and clasped hands, Edward Arundel was lying, maimed and senseless, in the wretched waiting-room of a little railway-station in Dorsetshire . . .' (p. 216). Braddon always wrote very fast, and she was by no means a conscious stylist, but there is energy, vitality, and a remarkable individuality in her prose; Arnold Bennett calls this 'the sound vigour of the writing'[22] in her fiction, which is present in the above passage as in many other places in this novel.

[22] Arnold Bennett, *Fame and Fiction: An Enquiry into Certain Popularities* (London: Grant Richards, 1901), 27.

'It is a fact that there are thousands of tolerably educated English people who have never heard of Meredith, Hardy, Ibsen, Maeterlinck, Kipling, Barrie, Crockett; but you would travel far before you reached the zone where the name of Braddon failed of its recognition,'[23] wrote Bennett at the very end of Queen Victoria's reign. Braddon was an extremely popular writer with the general reading public, but her novels also fascinated a number of distinguished men of letters of the period. In 1868 Tennyson said to a guest that 'I am simply steeped in Miss Braddon—I am reading every word she ever wrote'.[24] Even Henry James, years after he published that perceptive but condescending review, wrote to her and confessed that 'I used to follow you ardently, and track you close, taking from your hands deep draughts of the happiest of anodynes'.[25] There seems to be every reason for the present-day reader to share the enjoyment of these great Victorians.

[23] Ibid. 24–5.

[24] Charles Tennyson, *Alfred Tennyson* (London: Macmillan, 1950), 377.

[25] In a letter dated 2 August 1911, quoted in Wolff, *Sensational Victorian*, 10.

NOTE ON THE TEXT

This edition of *John Marchmont's Legacy* is based on the first edition, in three volumes, published in 1863 by Tinsley Brothers. Established in 1854, the firm had offices at 18 Catherine Street, just off the Strand; it published works by (among others) Anthony Trollope, Harrison Ainsworth, Wilkie Collins, and Mrs Henry Wood, and became 'the chief producer of novels and light literature in London' (*DNB*).

Improperly, and somewhat confusingly, the second volume of the first edition bears on the title-page the words 'SECOND EDITION', and the third volume the words 'THIRD EDITION'. Mary Elizabeth Braddon's name does not appear on these title-pages, which bear only an ascription to 'the author of "Lady Audley's Secret," etc. etc. etc.'. In the present edition, a few obvious misprints have been silently corrected, and a small number of spellings that might distract the modern reader (for example, 'chesnut' for 'chestnut', 'seringa' for 'syringa', 'Harrowgate' for 'Harrogate') have been regularized.

Before volume publication, the novel had appeared as a serial in the London monthly magazine *Temple Bar* over a period of fourteen months, from December 1862 to January 1864. For its appearance as a serial, the novel was divided as follows (the chapter-numbering in the three-volume edition is given in parenthesis):

Chapters

1862			August	26–8 (II, 12–14)
December	1–3 (I, 1–3)		September	29–31 (III, 1–3)
			October	32–4 (III, 4–6)
1863			November	35–9 (III, 7–11)
January	4–6 (I, 4–6)		December	40–1 (III, 12–13)
February	7–10 (I, 7–10)			
March	11–13 (I, 11–13)		1864	
April	14–16 (I, 14–II, 2)		January	42–3, Epilogue
May	17–19 (II, 3–5)			(III, 14–15,
June	20–2 (II, 6–8)			Epilogue)
July	23–5 (II, 9–11)			

One chapter-title that was changed in the transition from serial to volume edition is indicated in the Explanatory Notes (p. 492).

The novel proved a commercial success, and Braddon's great popularity led to its reissue, along with many others from her fertile pen, in various formats much cheaper than the 'three-decker' primarily intended for the circulating libraries. Tinsley produced the second edition in December 1863, the third in February 1864, and the fourth—the first one-volume edition—in June 1864. The first cheap yellowback edition was published by Ward, Lock, & Tyler; as noted by Michael Sadleir in his bibliography (see item 3455), this is undated, but Chester W. Topp's *Victorian Yellowbacks and Paperbacks, 1849–1905*, vol. 2 (Denver: Hermitage Antiquarian Bookshop, 1995) states that it was published in September 1866. This is announced as a 'revised edition', and it is the basis of later reprints of the novel. Robert Lee Wolff's copy, an 1876 reissue by Ward, Lock, & Tyler (item 657b in Wolff's bibliography), is described on its title-page as a Stereotyped Edition. Stereotyped editions of this novel, all using the same plates as those of the revised edition, were later published, like a number of other Braddon titles, by other firms (John & Robert Maxwell; Spencer Blackett; Simpkin, Marshall, Hamilton, Kent, & Co.).

The textual changes in the 'revised edition' referred to above are mainly stylistic and do not significantly affect the content of the novel. Systematically, 'And' and 'But' at the beginning of a sentence are deleted; exclamation marks tend to be dropped; and the authorial 'I' is avoided—for example, 'I don't know' is turned into 'It is doubtful'. Three chapter-titles are changed: 'A Widow's Proposal' into 'A Widower's Wooing'; 'Mr Weston Refuses To Be Trampled On' into 'Mr Weston Refuses to be Trampled Upon'; and 'There is Confusion Worse Than Death' into 'A Modern Sardanapalus'.

In addition, passages are deleted at various points. The following is a list of the most substantial excisions (over 100 words) and other changes of interest:

pp. 54–5	'The rain beats down ... pertinacious honesty': present-tense verbs are changed to past tense throughout this passage.
p. 131	The reference to 'Mr Charles Kingsley' is omitted.

p. 136	The reference to 'simple Dinah Morris' is omitted.
p. 290	'I have said . . . same species': these two paragraphs are deleted.
pp. 302–3	'In his scrupulous . . . their value': these two paragraphs are deleted.
pp. 304–5	'It is . . . brother's blood': this paragraph is deleted.
p. 332	The reference to 'Professor Pepper' is omitted.
p. 336	'Academy in Trafalgar Square' is changed to 'Trafalgar Square', so that the reference is now to the National Gallery rather than the Royal Academy.
p. 337	'a modern Rubens or a new Raphael' is changed to 'a modern Claude or a new Salvator'.
pp. 345–6	'I heard a man . . . going': this passage is deleted.
pp. 357–9	'Little by little . . . the daughter he loved': this passage is deleted.
p. 385	'Amongst the later lines . . . to die young': this passage, including the quotation from Byron, is deleted.
p. 390	'last March' is changed to 'March '63'.
pp. 472–3	'Every superstition . . . loathsome phantoms': this paragraph is deleted.

Grateful thanks are due to Jennifer Carnell, Dr Chester W. Topp, the Harry Ransom Research Center, the University of Texas at Austin (which houses the Robert Lee Wolff Collection), and the Charles E. Young Research Library of the University of California at Los Angeles (which houses the Michael Sadleir Collection) for providing valuable information about the texts of this novel.

SELECT BIBLIOGRAPHY

Bibliographies

Sadleir, Michael, *XIX Century Fiction*, 2 vols. (Cambridge, 1951).
Wolff, Robert L., *Nineteenth-Century Fiction: A Bibliographical Catalogue*, 5 vols. (London and New York, 1981–6).

Biographies, Memoirs, and Letters

Maxwell, William B., *Time Gathered* (London, 1937).
Sadleir, Michael, *Things Past* (London, 1944).
Wolff, Robert L., 'Devoted Disciple: The Letters of Mary Elizabeth Braddon to Sir Edward Bulwer-Lytton, 1862–1873', *Harvard Library Bulletin*, 22: 1 (Jan. 1974), 1–35, and 22: 2 (Apr. 1974), 129–61.
—— *Sensational Victorian: The Life and Fiction of Mary Elizabeth Braddon* (New York, 1979).

Critical Studies of Braddon and General Studies of Sensation Fiction

Bennett, Arnold, 'Miss Braddon', in *Fame and Fiction: An Enquiry into Certain Popularities* (London, 1901), 23–33.
Brantlinger, Patrick, 'What Is "Sensational" About the Sensation Novel?', *Nineteenth Century Fiction*, 37 (1982), 1–28.
Casey, Ellen Miller, ' "Other People's Prudery": Mary Elizabeth Braddon', in Don Richard Cox (ed.), *Sexuality in Victorian Literature* (Tennessee, 1984).
Cvetkovich, Ann, *Mixed Feelings: Feminism, Mass Culture and Victorian Sensationalism* (New Brunswick, NJ, 1992).
Edwards, Philip D., *Some Mid-Victorian Thrillers: The Sensation Novel, Its Friends and Foes* (St Lucia, Queensland, 1971).
Fahnestock, Jeanne, 'Bigamy: The Rise and Fall of a Convention,' *Nineteenth Century Fiction*, 36 (1981–2), 47–71.
Flint, Kate, *The Woman Reader, 1837–1914* (Oxford, 1993).
Hughes, Winifred, *The Maniac in the Cellar: The Sensation Novel of the 1860s* (Princeton, 1980).
Kucich, John, *The Power of Lies: Transgression in Victorian Fiction* (Ithaca, NY, 1994).
Page, Norman, *Wilkie Collins: The Critical Heritage* (London, 1974).

Pykett, Lyn, *The Improper Feminine: The Woman's Sensation Novel and the New Woman Writing* (London, 1992).

—— *The Sensation Novel from 'The Woman in White' to 'The Moonstone'* (Plymouth, 1994).

Rance, Nicholas, *Wilkie Collins and other Sensation Novelists* (London, 1991).

Showalter, Elaine, 'Family Secrets and Domestic Subversion: Rebellion in the Novels of the Eighteen-sixties', in A. Wohl (ed.), *The Victorian Family: Structure and Stresses* (London, 1978).

Tillotson, Kathleen, 'The Lighter Reading of the Eighteen-sixties', Introduction to Wilkie Collins, *The Woman in White* (Boston, 1969).

Vicinus, Martha, '"Helpless and Unfriended": Nineteenth-Century Domestic Melodrama', *New Literary History*, 13 (1981), 127–43.

Further Reading in Oxford World's Classics

Braddon, Mary Elizabeth, *Aurora Floyd*, ed. P. D. Edwards.

—— *Lady Audley's Secret*, ed. David Skilton.

—— *The Doctor's Wife*, ed. Lyn Pykett.

Collins, Wilkie, *The Woman in White*, ed. John Sutherland.

A CHRONOLOGY OF
MARY ELIZABETH BRADDON

1835   Born 4 October in Frith Street, Soho, third child of Henry and Fanny Braddon.

*c.*1840   Her parents separate owing to her father's infidelity and financial irresponsibility.

1857–60 Goes on the provincial stage as 'Mary Seyton', working mainly in Yorkshire.

1860   Publishes *Three Times Dead*, her first novel.

1861   Begins to live with publisher John Maxwell, who cannot marry her since his wife is alive, and confined in a lunatic asylum; is stepmother to his five children.

1861–2   *Lady Audley's Secret* a great success.

1862   Bears the first of her children by Maxwell.

1862–3   *Aurora Floyd, John Marchmont's Legacy*.

1864   *The Doctor's Wife*.

1866   *The Lady's Mile. Belgravia Magazine* founded by Maxwell for Braddon, and conducted by her for a decade.

1868   Publishes her twentieth novel. Death of sister and mother.

1868–9   Nervous breakdown complicated by puerperal fever.

1873   Begins to write for the stage, with only modest success.

1874   Marries Maxwell on the death of his first wife.

1876   *Joshua Haggard's Daughter*.

1880   Publishes her fortieth novel.

1884   *Ishmael*.

1888   *The Fatal Three*.

1892   *The Venetians*.

1895   Death of John Maxwell

1896   Publishes her sixtieth novel.

1907   *Dead Love Has Chains*.

1915   Dies at Richmond, 4 February.

1916   *Mary*, her last novel and eighty-fifth book, is published.

JOHN MARCHMONT'S LEGACY

THIS STORY
IS DEDICATED
TO
MY MOTHER

CONTENTS

Contents

VOLUME III

VOLUME I

CHAPTER I

THE MAN WITH THE BANNER

THE history of Edward Arundel, second son of Christopher Arundel Dangerfield Arundel, of Dangerfield Park, Devonshire, began on a certain dark winter's night upon which the lad, still a school-boy, went with his cousin, Martin Mostyn, to witness a blank-verse tragedy at one of the London theatres.

There are few men who, looking back at the long story of their lives, cannot point to one page in the record of the past at which the actual history of life began. The page may come in the very middle of the book, perhaps; perhaps almost at the end. But let it come where it will, it is, after all, only the actual commencement. At an appointed hour in man's existence, the overture which has been going on ever since he was born is brought to a sudden close by the sharp vibration of the prompter's signal-bell; the curtain rises, and the drama of life begins. Very insignificant sometimes are the first scenes of the play,—common-place, trite, wearisome; but watch them closely, and interwoven with every word, dimly recognisable in every action, may be seen the awful hand of Destiny. The story has begun: already we, the spectators, can make vague guesses at the plot, and predicate the solemn climax; it is only the actors who are ignorant of the meaning of their several parts, and who are stupidly reckless of the obvious catastrophe.

The story of young Arundel's life began when he was a light-hearted, heedless lad of seventeen, newly escaped for a brief interval from the care of his pastors and masters.

The lad had come to London on a Christmas visit to his father's sister, a worldly-minded widow, with a great many sons and daughters, and an income only large enough to enable her to keep up the appearances of wealth essential to the family pride of one of the Arundels of Dangerfield.

Laura Arundel had married a Colonel Mostyn, of the East-India Company's service, and had returned from India after a wandering life of some years, leaving her dead husband behind her, and bringing away with her five daughters and three sons, most of whom had been born under canvas.

Mrs Mostyn bore her troubles bravely, and contrived to do more with her pension, and an additional income of four hundred a year from a small fortune of her own, than the most consummate womanly management can often achieve. Her house in Montague Square* was elegantly furnished, her daughters were exquisitely dressed, her sons sensibly educated, her dinners well cooked. She was not an agreeable woman; she was perhaps, if any thing, too sensible,—so very sensible as to be obviously intolerant of anything like folly in others. She was a good mother; but by no means an indulgent one. She expected her to succeed in life, and her daughters to marry rich men; and would have had little patience with any disappointment in either of these reasonable expectations. She was attached to her brother Christopher Arundel, and she was very well pleased to spend the autumn months at Dangerfield, where the hunting-breakfasts gave her daughters an excellent platform for the exhibition of charming demi-toilettes* and social and domestic graces, perhaps more dangerous to the susceptible hearts of rich young squires than the fascinations of a *valse à deux temps** or an Italian scena.*

But the same Mrs Mostyn, who never forgot to keep up her correspondence with the owner of Dangerfield Park, utterly ignored the existence of another brother, a certain Hubert Arundel, who had, perhaps, much more need of her sisterly friendship than the wealthy Devonshire squire. Heaven knows, the world seemed a lonely place to this younger son, who had been educated for the Church, and was fain to content himself with a scanty living in one of the dullest and dampest towns in fenny Lincolnshire. His sister might have very easily made life much more pleasant to the Rector of Swampington and his only daughter; but Hubert Arundel was a great deal too proud to remind her of this. If Mrs Mostyn chose to forget him,— the brother and sister had been loving friends and dear companions long ago, under the beeches at Dangerfield,—she was welcome to do so. She was better off than he was; and it is to be remarked, that if A's income is three hundred a year, and B's a thousand, the chances are as seven to three that B will forget any old intimacy that may have existed between himself and A. Hubert Arundel had been wild at college, and had put his autograph across so many oblong slips of blue paper, acknowledging value received that had been only half received, that by the time the claims of all the holders of these portentous morsels of stamped paper had been satisfied, the younger son's fortune had melted away, leaving its sometime possessor the happy owner of a pair of pointers, a couple of guns by crack makers, a good many foils, single-sticks, boxing-gloves, wire masks, basket helmets, leathern leg-guards, and other paraphernalia, a complete set of the old *Sporting Magazine*, from 1792 to the current year, bound in scarlet morocco, several boxes of very bad cigars, a Scotch terrier, and a pipe of undrinkable port.

Of all these possessions, only the undrinkable port now remained to show that Hubert Arundel had once had a decent younger son's fortune, and had succeeded most admirably in making ducks and drakes of it. The poor about Swampington believed in the sweet red wine, which had been specially concocted for Israelitish dealers in jewelry, cigars, pictures, wines, and specie. The Rector's pensioners smacked their lips over the mysterious liquid, and confidently affirmed that it did them more good than all the doctor's stuff the parish apothecary could send them. Poor Hubert Arundel was well content to find that at least this scanty crop of corn had grown up from the wild oats he had sown at Cambridge. The wine pleased the poor creatures who drank it, and was scarcely likely to do them any harm; and there was a reasonable prospect that the last bottle would by-and-by pass out of the rectory cellars, and with it the last token of that bitterly regretted past.

I have no doubt that Hubert Arundel felt the sting of his only sister's neglect, as only a poor and proud man can feel such an insult; but he never let any confession of this sentiment escape his lips; and when Mrs Mostyn, being seized with a fancy for doing this forgotten brother a service, wrote him a letter of insolent advice, winding up with an offer to procure his only child a situation as nursery governess, the Rector of Swampington only crushed the missive in his strong hand, and flung it into his study-fire, with a muttered exclamation that sounded terribly like an oath.

'A *nursery* governess!' he repeated, savagely; 'yes; an underpaid drudge, to teach children their A B C, and mend their frocks and make their pinafores. I should like Mrs Mostyn to talk to my little Livy for half an hour. I think my girl would have put the lady down so completely by the end of that time, that we should never hear any more about nursery governesses.'

He laughed bitterly as he repeated the obnoxious phrase; but his laugh changed to a sigh.

Was it strange that the father should sigh as he remembered how he had seen the awful hand of Death fall suddenly upon younger and stronger men than himself? What if he were to die, and leave his only child unmarried? What would become of her, with her dangerous gifts, with her fatal dowry of beauty and intellect and pride?

'But she would never do any thing wrong,' the father thought. 'Her religious principles are strong enough to keep her right under any circumstances, in spite of any temptation. Her sense of duty is more powerful than any other sentiment. She would never be false to that; she would never be false to that.'

In return for the hospitality of Dangerfield Park, Mrs Mostyn was in the habit of opening her doors to either Christopher Arundel or his sons, whenever any one of the three came to London. Of course she infinitely preferred seeing Arthur Arundel, the eldest son and heir, seated at her well-spread table, and flirting with one of his pretty cousins, than to be bored with his rackety younger brother, a noisy lad of seventeen, with no better prospects than a commission in her Majesty's service, and a hundred and fifty pounds a year to eke out his pay; but she was, notwithstanding, graciously pleased to invite Edward to spend his Christmas holidays in her comfortable household; and it was thus it came to pass that on the 29th of December, in the year 1838, the story of Edward Arundel's life began in a stage-box at Drury Lane Theatre.

The box had been sent to Mrs Mostyn by the fashionable editor of a fashionable newspaper; but that lady and her daughters being previously engaged, had permitted the two boys to avail themselves of the editorial privilege.

The tragedy was the dull production of a distinguished literary amateur, and even the great actor who played the principal character could not make the performance particularly enlivening. He certainly failed in impressing Mr Edward Arundel, who flung himself back in his chair and yawned dolefully during the earlier part of the entertainment.

'It ain't particularly jolly, is it, Martin?' he said naïvely. 'Let's go out and have some oysters, and come in again just before the pantomime* begins.'

'Mamma made me promise that we wouldn't leave the theatre till we left for good, Ned,' his cousin answered; 'and then we're to go straight home in a cab.'

Edward Arundel sighed.

'I wish we hadn't come till half-price,* old fellow,' he said drearily. 'If I'd known it was to be a tragedy, I wouldn't have come away from the Square in such a hurry. I wonder why people write tragedies, when nobody likes them.'

He turned his back to the stage, and folded his arms upon the velvet cushion of the box preparatory to indulging himself in a deliberate inspection of the audience. Perhaps no brighter face looked upward that night towards the glare and glitter of the great chandelier than that of the fair-haired lad in the stage-box. His candid blue eyes beamed with a more radiant sparkle than any of the myriad lights in the theatre; a nimbus of golden hair shone about his broad white forehead; glowing health, careless happiness, truth, good-nature, honesty, boyish vivacity, and the courage of a young lion,— all were expressed in the fearless smile, the frank yet half-defiant gaze. Above all, this lad of seventeen looked especially what he was,—a thorough gentleman. Martin Mostyn was prim and effeminate, precociously tired of life, precociously indifferent to everything but his own advantage; but the Devonshire boy's talk was still fragrant with the fresh perfume of youth and innocence, still gay with the joyous recklessness of early boyhood. He was as impatient for the noisy pantomime overture, and the bright troops of fairies in petticoats of spangled muslin, as the most inveterate cockney cooling his snub-nose against the iron railing of the gallery. He was as ready to fall in love with the painted beauty of the ill-paid ballet-girls, as the veriest child in the wide circle of humanity about him. Fresh, untainted, unsuspicious, he looked out at the world, ready to believe in everything and everybody.

'How you do fidget, Edward!' whispered Martin Mostyn peevishly; 'why don't you look at the stage? It's capital fun.'

'Fun!'

'Yes; I don't mean the tragedy you know, but the supernumeraries.* Did you ever see such an awkward set of fellows in all your life? There's a man there with weak legs and a heavy banner, that I've been watching all the evening. He's more fun than all the rest of it put together.'

Mr Mostyn, being of course much too polite to point out the man in question, indicated him with a twitch of his light eyebrows; and Edward Arundel, following that indication, singled out the banner-holder from a group of soldiers in medieval dress, who had been standing wearily enough upon one side of the stage during a long, strictly private and confidential dialogue between the princely hero of the tragedy and one of his accommodating satellites. The lad uttered a cry of surprise as he looked at the weak-legged banner-holder.

Mr Mostyn turned upon his cousin with some vexation.

'I can't help it, Martin,' exclaimed young Arundel; 'I can't be mistaken—yes—poor fellow, to think that he should come to this!—you haven't forgotten him, Martin, surely?'

'Forgotten what—forgotten whom? My dear Edward, what *do* you mean?'

'John Marchmont, the poor fellow who used to teach us mathematics at Vernon's; the fellow the governor sacked because——'

'Well, what of him?'

'The poor chap with the banner!' exclaimed the boy, in a breathless whisper; 'don't you see, Martin? didn't you recognise him? It's Marchmont, poor old Marchmont, that we used to chaff, and that the governor sacked because he had a constitutional cough, and wasn't strong enough for his work.'

'Oh, yes, I remember him well enough,' Mr Mostyn answered, indifferently. 'Nobody could stand his cough, you know; and he was a vulgar fellow, into the bargain.'

'He wasn't a vulgar fellow,' said Edward indignantly;—'there, there's the curtain down again;—he belonged to a good family in Lincolnshire, and was heir-presumptive to a stunning fortune. I've heard him say so twenty times.'

Martin Mostyn did not attempt to repress an involuntary sneer, which curled his lips as his cousin spoke.

'Oh, I dare say you've heard *him* say so, my dear boy,' he murmured superciliously,

'Ah, and it was true,' cried Edward; 'he wasn't a fellow to tell lies; perhaps he'd have suited Mr Vernon better if he had been. He had bad health, and was weak, and all that sort of thing; but he wasn't a snob. He showed me a signet-ring that he used to wear on his watch-chain——'

'A *silver* watch-chain,' simpered Mr Mostyn, 'just like a carpenter's.'

'Don't be such a supercilious cad, Martin. He was very kind to me, poor Marchmont; and I know I was always a nuisance to him, poor old fellow; for you know I never could get on with Euclid.* I'm sorry to see him here. Think, Martin, what an occupation for him! I don't suppose he gets more than nine or ten shillings a week for it.'

'A shilling a night is, I believe, the ordinary remuneration of a stage-soldier. They pay as much for the real thing as for the sham, you see; the defenders of our country risk their lives for about the same consideration. Where are you going, Ned?'

Edward Arundel had left his place, and was trying to undo the door of the box.

'To see if I can get at this poor fellow.'

'You persist in declaring, then, that the man with the weak legs is our old mathematical drudge? Well, I shouldn't wonder. The fellow was coughing all through the five acts, and that's uncommonly like Marchmont. You're surely not going to renew your acquaintance with him?'

But young Arundel had just succeeded in opening the door, and he left the box without waiting to answer his cousin's question. He made his way very rapidly out of the theatre, and fought manfully through the crowds who were waiting about the pit and gallery doors, until he found himself at the stage-entrance. He had often looked with reverent wonder at the dark portal; but he had never before essayed to cross the sacred threshold. But the guardian of the gate to this theatrical paradise, inhabited by fairies at a guinea a week, and baronial retainers at a shilling a night, is ordinarily a very inflexible individual, not to be corrupted by any mortal persuasion, and scarcely corruptible by the more potent influence of gold or silver. Poor Edward's half-a-crown had no effect whatever upon the stern door-keeper, who thanked him for his donation, but told him that it was against his orders to let anybody go upstairs.

'But I want to see some one so particularly,' the boy said eagerly. 'Don't you think you could manage it for me, you know? He's an old friend of mine,—one of the supernu—what's-its-names?' added

Edward, stumbling over the word. 'He carried a banner in the tragedy, you know; and he's got such an awful cough, poor chap.'

'Ze man who garried ze panner vith a gough,' said the doorkeeper reflectively. He was an elderly German, and had kept guard at that classic doorway for half-a-century or so; 'Parking Cheremiah.'

'Barking Jeremiah!'

'Yes, sir. They gall him Parking pecause he's berbetually goughin' his poor veag head off; And they gall him Cheremiah pecause he's alvays belangholy,'

'Oh, do let me see him,' cried Mr Edward Arundel. 'I know you can manage it; so do, that's a good fellow. I tell you he's a friend of mine, and quite a gentleman too. Bless you, there isn't a move in mathematics he isn't up to; and he'll come into a fortune some of these days—'

'Yaase,' interrupted the door-keeper, sarcastically, 'Zey bake von of him pegause off dad.'

'And can I see him?'

'I phill dry and vind him vor you. Here, you Chim,' said the doorkeeper, addressing a dirty youth, who had just nailed an official announcement of the next morning's rehearsal upon the back of a stony-hearted swing-door, which was apt to jam the fingers of the uninitiated,—' vot is ze name off yat zuber vith ze pad gough, ze man zay gall Parking.'

'Oh, that's Morti-more.'

'To you know if he's on in ze virsd zene?'

'Yes. He's one of the demons; but the scene's just over. Do you want him?'

'You gan dake ub zis young chendleman's gard do him, and dell him to slib town here if he has kod a vaid,' said the door-keeper.

Mr Arundel handed his card to the dirty boy.

'He'll come to me fast enough, poor fellow,' he muttered. 'I usen't to chaff him as the others did, and I'm glad I didn't, now.'

Edward Arundel could not easily forget that one brief scrutiny in which he had recognised the wasted face of the schoolmaster's hack, who had taught him mathematics only two years before. Could there be anything more piteous than that degrading spectacle? The feeble frame, scarcely able to sustain that paltry one-sided banner of calico and tinsel; the two rude daubs of coarse vermilion upon the hollow cheeks; the black smudges that were meant for eyebrows; the wretched scrap of horsehair glued upon the pinched chin in dismal mockery of a beard; and through all this the pathetic pleading of large hazel eyes, bright with the unnatural lustre of disease, and saying perpetually, more plainly than words can speak, 'Do not look at me; do not despise me; do not even pity me. It won't last long.'

The fresh-hearted schoolboy was still thinking of this, when a wasted hand was laid lightly and tremulously on his arm, and looking up he saw a man in a hideous mask and a tight-fitting suit of scarlet and gold standing by his side.

'I'll take off my mask in a minute, Arundel,' said a faint voice, that sounded hollow and muffled within a cavern of pasteboard and wickerwork. 'It was very good of you to come round; very, very good!'

'I was so sorry to see you here, Marchmont; I knew you in a moment, in spite of the disguise.'

The supernumerary had struggled out of his huge head-gear by this time, and laid the fabric of papier-mâché and tinsel carefully aside upon a shelf. He had washed his face before putting on the mask, for he was not called upon to appear before a British public in martial semblance any more upon that evening. The pale wasted face was interesting and gentlemanly, not by any means handsome, but almost womanly in its softness of expression. It was the face of a man who had not yet seen his thirtieth birthday; who might never live to see it, Edward Arundel thought mournfully.

'Why do you do this, Marchmont?' the boy asked bluntly.

'Because there was nothing else left for me to do,' the stage-demon answered with a sad smile. 'I can't get a situation in a school, for my health won't suffer me to take one; or it won't suffer any employer to take me, for fear of my falling ill upon his hands, which comes to the same thing; so I do a little copying for the law-stationers, and this helps out that, and I get on as well as I can. I wouldn't so much mind if it wasn't for—'

He stopped suddenly, interrupted by a paroxysm of coughing.

'If it wasn't for whom, old fellow?'

'My poor little girl; my poor little motherless Mary.'

Edward Arundel looked grave, and perhaps a little ashamed of himself. He had forgotten until this moment that his old tutor had been left a widower at four-and-twenty, with a little daughter to support out of his scanty stipend.

'Don't be down-hearted, old fellow,' the lad whispered, tenderly;

'perhaps I shall be able to help you, you know. And the little girl can go down to Dangerfield; I know my mother would take care of her, and will keep her there till you get strong and well. And then you might start a fencing-room, or a shooting-gallery, or something of that sort, at the West End; and I'd come to you, and bring lots of fellows to you, and you'd get on capitally, you know.'

Poor John Marchmont, the asthmatic supernumerary, looked perhaps the very last person in the world whom it could be possible to associate with a pair of foils, or a pistol and a target; but he smiled faintly at his old pupil's enthusiastic talk.

'You were always a good fellow, Arundel,' he said, gravely. 'I don't suppose I shall ever ask you to do me a service; but if, by-and-by, this cough makes me knock under, and my little Polly should be left— I—I think you'd get your mother to be kind to her,—wouldn't you, Arundel?'

A picture rose before the supernumerary's weary eyes as he said this; the picture of a pleasant lady whose description he had often heard from the lips of a loving son, a rambling old mansion, wide-spreading lawns, and long arcades of oak and beeches leading away to the blue distance. If this Mrs Arundel, who was so tender and compassionate and gentle to every red-cheeked cottage-girl who crossed her pathway,—Edward had told him this very often,—would take compassion also upon this little one! If she would only condescend to see the child, the poor pale neglected flower, the fragile lily, the frail exotic blossom, that was so cruelly out of place upon the bleak pathways of life!

'If that's all that troubles you,' young Arundel cried eagerly, 'you may make your mind easy, and come and have some oysters. We'll take care of the child. I'll adopt her, and my mother shall educate her, and she shall marry a duke. Run away, now, old fellow, and change your clothes, and come and have oysters, and stout out of the pewter.'

Mr Marchmont shook his head.

'My time's just up,' he said; 'I'm on in the next scene. It was very kind of you to come round, Arundel; but this isn't exactly the best place for you. Go back to your friends, my dear boy, and don't think any more of me. I'll write to you some day about little Mary.'

'You'll do nothing of the kind,' exclaimed the boy. 'You'll give me your address instanter, and I'll come to see you the first thing to-morrow morning, and you'll introduce me to little Mary; and if she and I are not the best friends in the world, I shall never again boast of my successes with lovely woman. What's the number, old fellow?'

Mr Arundel had pulled out a smart morocco pocket-book and a gold pencil-case.

'Twenty-seven, Oakley Street, Lambeth. But I'd rather you wouldn't come, Arundel; your friends wouldn't like it.'

'My friends may go hang themselves. I shall do as I like, and I'll be with you to breakfast, sharp ten.'

The supernumerary had no time to remonstrate. The progress of the music, faintly audible from the lobby in which this conversation had taken place, told him that his scene was nearly on.

'I can't stop another moment. Go back to your friends, Arundel. Good night. God bless you!'

'Stay; one word. The Lincolnshire property—'

'Will never come to me, my boy,' the demon answered sadly, through his mask; for he had been busy re-investing himself in that demoniac guise. 'I tried to sell my reversion, but the Jews almost laughed in my face when they heard me cough. Good night.'

He was gone, and the swing-door slammed in Edward Arundel's face. The boy hurried back to his cousin, who was cross and dissatisfied at his absence. Martin Mostyn had discovered that the ballet-girls were all either old or ugly, the music badly chosen, the pantomime stupid, the scenery a failure. He asked a few supercilious questions about his old tutor, but scarcely listened to Edward's answers; and was intensely aggravated with his companion's pertinacity in sitting out the comic business—in which poor John Marchmont appeared and re-appeared; now as a well-dressed passenger carrying a parcel, which he deliberately sacrificed to the felonious propensities of the clown; now as a policeman, now as a barber, now as a chemist, now as a ghost; but always buffeted, or cajoled, or bonneted, or imposed upon; always piteous, miserable, and long-suffering; with arms that ached from carrying a banner through five acts of blank-verse weariness, with a head that had throbbed under the weight of a ponderous edifice of pasteboard and wicker, with eyes that were sore with the evil influence of blue-fire* and gunpowder smoke, with a throat that had been poisoned by sulphurous vapours, with bones that were stiff with the playful pummelling of clown and pantaloon; and all for—a shilling a night!

CHAPTER II

LITTLE MARY

POOR John Marchmont had given his address unwillingly enough to his old pupil. The lodging in Oakley Street was a wretched back-room upon the second-floor of a house whose lower regions were devoted to that species of establishment commonly called a 'ladies' wardrobe.' The poor gentleman, the teacher of mathematics, the law-writer, the Drury-Lane supernumerary, had shrunk from any exposure of his poverty; but his pupil's imperious good-nature had overridden every objection, and John Marchmont awoke upon the morning after the meeting at Drury-Lane to the rather embarrassing recollection that he was to expect a visitor to breakfast with him.

How was he to entertain this dashing, high-spirited young school-boy, whose lot was cast in the pleasant pathways of life, and who was no doubt accustomed to see at his matutinal meal such luxuries as John Marchmont had only beheld in the fairy-like realms of comestible beauty exhibited to hungry foot-passengers behind the plate-glass windows of Italian warehouses?

'He has hams stewed in Madeira, and Perigord pies,* I dare say, at his Aunt Mostyn's,' John thought, despairingly. 'What can I give him to eat?'

But John Marchmont, after the manner of the poor, was apt to over-estimate the extravagance of the rich. If he could have seen the Mostyn breakfast then preparing in the lower regions of Montague Square, he might have been considerably relieved; for he would have only beheld mild infusions of tea and coffee—in silver vessels, certainly—four French rolls hidden under a glistening damask napkin, six triangular fragments of dry toast, cut from a stale half-quartern, four new-laid eggs, and about half a pound of bacon cut into rashers of transcendental delicacy. Widow ladies who have daughters to marry do not plunge very deep into the books of Messrs Fortnum and Mason.*

'He used to like hot rolls when I was at Vernon's,' John thought, rather more hopefully; 'I wonder whether he likes hot rolls still?'

Pondering thus, Mr Marchmont dressed himself,—very neatly, very carefully; for he was one of those men whom even poverty cannot rob of man's proudest attribute, his individuality. He made no noisy protest against the humiliations to which he was compelled to submit; he uttered no boisterous assertions of his own merit; he urged no clamorous demand to be treated as a gentleman in his day of misfortune; but in his own mild, undemonstrative way he did assert himself, quite as effectually as if he had raved all day upon the hardship of his lot, and drunk himself mad and blind under the pressure of his calamities. He never abandoned the habits which had been peculiar to him from his childhood. He was as neat and orderly in his second-floor-back as he had been seven or eight years before in his simple apartments at Cambridge. He did not recognise that association which most men perceive between poverty and shirt-sleeves, or poverty and beer. He was content to wear threadbare cloth, but adhered most obstinately to a prejudice in favour of clean linen. He never acquired those lounging vagabond habits peculiar to some men in the day of trouble. Even amongst the supernumeraries of Drury Lane, he contrived to preserve his self-respect; if they nicknamed him Barking Jeremiah, they took care only to pronounce that playful sobriquet when the gentleman-super was safely out of hearing. He was so polite in the midst of his reserve, that the person who could wilfully have offended him must have been more unkindly than any of her Majesty's servants. It is true, that the great tragedian, on more than one occasion, apostrophised the weak-kneed banner-holder as 'BEAST,' when the super's cough had peculiarly disturbed his composure; but the same great man gave poor John Marchmont a letter to a distinguished physician, compassionately desiring the relief of the same pulmonary affection. If John Marchmont had not been prompted by his own instincts to struggle against the evil influences of poverty, he would have done battle sturdily for the sake of one who was ten times dearer to him than himself,

If he *could* have become a swindler or a reprobate,—it would have been about as easy for him to become either as to have burst at once, and without an hour's practice, into a full-blown Léotard* or Olmar,*—his daughter's influence would have held him back as securely as if the slender arms twined tenderly about him had been chains of adamant forged by an enchanter's power.

How could he be false to his little one, this helpless child, who had been confided to him in the darkest hour of his existence; the hour in which his wife had yielded to the many forces arrayed against her in life's battle, and had left him alone in the world to fight for his little girl?

'If I were to die, I think Arundel's mother would be kind to her,' John Marchmont thought, as he finished his careful toilet. 'Heaven knows, I have no right to ask or expect such a thing; but Polly will be rich by-and-by, perhaps, and will be able to repay them.'

A little hand knocked lightly at the door of his room while he was thinking this, and a childish voice said,

'May I come in, papa?'

The little girl slept with one of the landlady's children, in a room above her father's. John opened the door, and let her in. The pale wintry sunshine, creeping in at the curtainless window near which Mr Marchmont sat, shone full upon the child's face as she came towards him. It was a small, pale face, with singularly delicate features, a tiny straight nose, a pensive mouth, and large thoughtful hazel eyes. The child's hair fell loosely upon her shoulders; not in those cork-screw curls so much affected by mothers in the humbler walks of life, nor yet in those crisp undulations lately adopted in Belgravian* nurseries; but in soft silken masses, only curling at the extreme end of each tress. Miss Marchmont—she was always called Miss Marchmont in that Oakley Street household—wore her brown-stuff frock and scanty diaper pinafore as neatly as her father wore his threadbare coat and darned linen. She was very pretty, very lady-like, very interesting; but it was impossible to look at her without a vague feeling of pain, that was difficult to understand. You knew, by-and-by, why you were sorry for this little girl. She had never been a child. That divine period of perfect innocence,—innocence of all sorrow and trouble, falsehood and wrong,—that bright holiday-time of the soul, had never been hers. The ruthless hand of poverty had snatched away from her the gift which God had given her in her cradle; and at eight years old she was a woman,—a woman invested with all that is most beautiful amongst womanly attributes—love, tenderness, compassion, carefulness for others, unselfish devotion, uncomplaining patience, heroic endurance. She was a woman by reason of all these virtues ; but she was no longer a child. At three years old she had bidden farewell for ever to the ignorant selfishness, the animal enjoyment of childhood, and had learned what it was to be sorry for poor papa and mamma; and from that first time of awakening to the sense of pity and love, she had never ceased to be the comforter of the helpless young husband who was so soon to be left wifeless.

John had been compelled to leave his child, in order to get a living for her and for himself in the hard service of Mr Laurence Vernon, the principal of the highly select and expensive academy at which Edward Arundel and Martin Mostyn had been educated. But he had left her in good hands; and when the bitter day of his dismissal came, he was scarcely as sorry as he ought to have been for the calamity which brought him back to his little Mary. It is impossible for any words of mine to tell how much he loved the child; but take into consideration his hopeless poverty, his sensitive and reserved nature, his utter loneliness, the bereavement that had cast a shadow upon his youth, and you will perhaps understand an affection that was almost morbid in its intensity, and which was reciprocated most fully by its object. The little girl loved her father *too much*. When he was with her, she was content to sit by his side, watching him as he wrote; proud to help him, if even by so much as wiping his pens or handing him his blotting-paper; happy to wait upon him, to go out marketing for him, to prepare his scanty meals, to make his tea, and arrange and re-arrange every object in the slenderly furnished second-floor back-room. They talked sometimes of the Lincolnshire fortune,— the fortune which *might* come to Mr Marchmont, if three people, whose lives when Mary's father had last heard of them, were each worth three times his own feeble existence, would be so obliging as to clear the way for the heir-at-law, by taking an early departure to the churchyard. A more practical man than John Marchmont would have kept a sharp eye upon these three lives, and by some means or other contrived to find out whether number one was consumptive, or number two dropsical, or number three apoplectic; but John was utterly incapable of any such Machiavellian proceeding. I think he sometimes beguiled his weary walks between Oakley Street and Drury Lane by the dreaming of such childish day-dreams as I should be almost ashamed to set down upon this sober page. The three lives might all happen to be riding in the same express upon the occasion of a terrible collision; but the poor fellow's gentle nature shrank appalled before the vision he had invoked. He could not sacrifice a whole train-full of victims, even for little Mary. He contented himself with borrowing a 'Times' newspaper now and then, and looking at the top of the second column, with the faint hope that he should see his own name in large capitals, coupled with the announcement that by applying somewhere he might hear of something to his advantage. He contented himself with this, and with talking about the future to little Mary in the dim firelight. They spent long hours in the shadowy room, only lighted by the faint flicker of a pitiful handful of coals; for the commonest dip-candles* are sevenpence-halfpenny a pound, and were dearer, I dare say, in the year '38. Heaven knows what splendid castles in the air these two simple-hearted creatures built for each other's pleasure by that comfortless hearth. I believe that, though the father made a pretence of talking of these things only for the amusement of his child, he was actually the more childish of the two. It was only when he left that fire-lit room, and went back into the hard, reasonable, commonplace world, that he remembered how foolish the talk was, and how it was impossible—yes, impossible—that he, the law-writer and supernumerary, could ever come to be master of Marchmont Towers.

Poor little Mary was in this less practical than her father. She carried her day-dreams into the street, until all Lambeth was made glorious by their supernal radiance. Her imagination ran riot in a vision of a happy future, in which her father would be rich and powerful. I am sorry to say that she derived most of her ideas of grandeur from the New Cut.* She furnished the drawing-room at Marchmont Towers from the splendid stores of an upholsterer in that thoroughfare. She laid flaming Brussels carpets upon the polished oaken floors which her father had described to her, and hung cheap satin damask of gorgeous colours before the great oriel windows. She put gilded vases of gaudy artificial flowers on the high carved mantel-pieces in the old rooms, and hung a disreputable gray parrot—for sale at a greengrocer's, and given to the use of bad language—under the stone colonnade at the end of the western wing. She appointed the tradespeople who should serve the faraway Lincolnshire household; the small matter of distance could, of course, never stand in the way of her gratitude and benevolence. Her papa would employ the civil greengrocer who gave such excellent halfpennyworths of watercresses; the kid butterman who took such pains to wrap up a quarter of a pound of the best eighteenpenny fresh butter for the customer whom he always called 'little lady;' the considerate butcher who never cut *more* than the three-quarters of a pound of rump-steak, which made an excellent dinner for Mr

Marchmont and his little girl. Yes, all these people should be rewarded when the Lincolnshire property came to Mary's papa. Miss Marchmont had some thoughts of building a shop close to Marchmont Towers for the accommodating butcher, and of adopting the greengrocer's eldest daughter for her confidante and companion. Heaven knows how many times the little girl narrowly escaped being run over while walking the material streets in some ecstatic reverie such as this; but Providence was very careful of the motherless girl, and she always returned safely to Oakley Street with her pitiful little purchases of tea and sugar, butter and meat. You will say, perhaps, that at least these foolish day-dreams were childish; but I maintain still, that Mary's soul had long ago bade adieu to infancy, and that even in these visions she was womanly; for she was always thoughtful of others rather than of herself, and there was a great deal more of the practical business of life mingled with the silvery web of her fancies than there should have been so soon after her eighth birthday. At times, too, an awful horror would quicken the pulses of her loving heart as she heard the hacking sound of her father's cough; and a terrible dread would seize her,—the fear that John Marchmont might never live to inherit the Lincolnshire fortune. The child never said her prayers without adding a little extempore supplication, that she might die when her father died. It was a wicked prayer, perhaps; and a clergyman might have taught her that her life was in the hands of Providence; and that it might please Him who had created her to doom her to many desolate years of loneliness; and that it was not for her, in her wretched and helpless ignorance, to rebel against His divine will. I think if the Archbishop of Canterbury had driven from Lambeth Palace to Oakley Street to tell little Mary this, he would have taught her in vain; and that she would have fallen asleep that night with the old prayer upon her lips, the fond foolish prayer that the bonds which love had woven so firmly might never be roughly broken by death.

Miss Marchmont heard the story of last night's meeting with great pleasure, though it must be owned she looked a little grave when she was told that the generous-hearted school-boy was coming to breakfast; but her gravity was only that of a thoughtful housekeeper, who ponders ways and means, and even while you are telling her the number and quality of your guests, sketches out a rough ground-plan of her dishes, considers the fish in season, and the soups most fitting to precede them, and balances the contending advantages of Palestine and Julienne or Hare and Italian.*

'A "nice" breakfast you say, papa,' she said, when her father had finished speaking; 'then we must have watercresses, *of course*.'

'And hot rolls, Polly dear. Arundel was always fond of hot rolls.'

'And hot rolls, four for threepence-halfpenny in the Cut.'—(I am ashamed to say that this benighted child talked as deliberately of the 'Cut' as she might have done of the 'Row.')*—'There'll be one left for tea, papa; for we could never eat four rolls. They'll take *such* a lot of butter, though.'

The little housekeeper took out an antediluvian bead-purse, and began to examine her treasury. Her father handed all his money to her, as he would have done to his wife; and Mary doled him out the little sums he wanted,—money for half an ounce of tobacco, money for a pint of beer. There were no penny papers* in those days, or what a treat an occasional 'Telegraph' would have been to poor John Marchmont!

Mary had only one personal extravagance. She read novels,— dirty, bloated, ungainly volumes,—which she borrowed from a snuffy old woman in a little back street, who charged her the smallest hire ever known in the circulating-library business, and who admired her as a wonder of precocious erudition. The only pleasure the child knew in her father's absence was the perusal of these dingy pages; she neglected no duty, she forgot no tender office of ministering care for the loved one who was absent; but when all the little duties had her finished, how delicious it was to sit down to 'Madeleine the Deserted,' or 'Cosmo the Pirate,' and to lose herself far away in illimitable regions, peopled by wandering princesses in white satin, and gentlemanly bandits, who had been stolen from their royal fathers' halls by vengeful hordes of gipsies. During these early years of poverty and loneliness, John Marchmont's daughter stored up, in a mind that was morbidly sensitive rather than strong, a terrible amount of dim poetic sentiment; the possession of which is scarcely, perhaps, the best or safest dower for a young lady who has life's journey all before her.

At half-past nine o'clock, all the simple preparations necessary for the reception of a visitor had been completed by Mr Marchmont and his daughter. All vestiges of John's bed had disappeared; leaving, it is true, rather a suspicious-looking mahogany chest of drawers to mark the spot where once a bed had been. The window had been opened, the room aired and dusted, a bright little fire burned in the shining grate, and the most brilliant of tin tea-kettles hissed upon the hob. The white table-cloth was darned in several places; but it was a remnant of the small stock of linen with which John had begun married life; and the Irish damask asserted its superior quality, in spite of many darns, as positively as Mr Marchmont's good blood asserted itself in spite of his shabby coat. A brown teapot full of strong tea, a plate of French rolls, a pat of fresh butter, and a broiled haddock, do not compose a very epicurean repast; but Mary Marchmont looked at the humble breakfast as a prospective success.

'We could have haddocks every day at Marchmont Towers, couldn't we, papa?' she said naïvely.

But the little girl was more than delighted when Edward Arundel dashed up the narrow staircase, and burst into the room, fresh, radiant, noisy, splendid, better dressed even than the waxen preparations of elegant young gentlemen exhibited at the portal of a great outfitter in the New Cut, and yet not at all like either of those red-lipped types of fashion. How delighted the boy declared himself with every thing! He had driven over in a cabriolet,* and he was awfully hungry, he informed his host. The rolls and watercresses disappeared before him as if by magic; little Mary shivered at the slashing cuts he made at the butter; the haddock had scarcely left the gridiron before it was no more.

'This is ten times better than Aunt Mostyn's skinny breakfasts,' the young gentleman observed candidly. 'You never get enough with her. Why does she say, "You won't take another egg, will you, Edward?" if she wants me to have one? You should see our hunting-breakfasts at Dangerfield, Marchmont. Four sorts of claret, and no end of Moselle and champagne. You shall go to Dangerfield some day, to see my mother, Miss Mary.'

He called her 'Miss Mary,' and seemed rather shy of speaking to her. Her womanliness impressed him in spite of himself. He had a fancy that she was old enough to feel the humiliation of her father's position, and to be sensitive upon the matter of the two-pair back; and he was sorry the moment after he had spoken of Dangerfield.

'What a snob I am!' he thought; 'always bragging of home.'

But Mr Arundel was not able to stop very long in Oakley Street, for the supernumerary had to attend a rehearsal at twelve o'clock; so at half past eleven John Marchmont and his pupil went out together, and little Mary was left alone to clear away the breakfast, and perform the rest of her household duties.

She had plenty of time before her, so she did not begin at once, but sat upon a stool near the fender, gazing dreamily at the low fire.

'How good and kind he is!' she thought; 'just like Cosmo,—only Cosmo was dark; or like Reginald Ravenscroft,—but then he was dark too. I wonder why the people in novels are always dark? How kind he is to papa! Shall we ever go to Dangerfield, I wonder, papa and I? Of course I wouldn't go without papa.'

CHAPTER III

ABOUT THE LINCOLNSHIRE PROPERTY

WHILE Mary sat absorbed in such idle visions as these, Mr Marchmont and his old pupil walked towards Waterloo Bridge together.

'I'll go as far as the theatre with you, Marchmont,' the boy said; 'it's my holidays now, you know, and I can do as I like. I am going to a private tutor in another month, and he's to prepare me for the army. I want you to tell me all about that Lincolnshire property, old boy. Is it anywhere near Swampington?'

'Yes; within nine miles.'

'Goodness gracious me! Lord bless my soul! what an extraordinary coincidence! My uncle Hubert's Rector of Swampington—such a hole! I go there sometimes to see him and my cousin Olivia. Isn't she a stunner, though! Knows more Greek and Latin than I, and more mathematics than you. Could eat our heads off at any thing.'

John Marchmont did not seem very much impressed by the coincidence that appeared so extraordinary to Edward Arundel; but, in order to oblige his friend, he explained very patiently and lucidly how it was that only three lives stood between him and the possession of Marchmont Towers, and all lands and tenements appertaining thereto.

'The estate's a very large one,' he said finally; 'but the idea of *my* ever getting it is, of course, too preposterous.'

'Good gracious me! I don't see that at all,' exclaimed Edward with extraordinary vivacity. 'Let me see, old fellow; if I understand your story right, this is how the case stands: your first cousin is the present possessor of Marchmont Towers; he has a son, fifteen years of age, who may or may not marry; only one son, remember. But he has also an uncle—a bachelor uncle, and your uncle, too—who, by the terms of your grandfather's will, must get the property before you can succeed to it. Now, this uncle is an old man: so of course *he'll* die soon. The present possessor himself is a middle-aged man; so I shouldn't think *he* can be likely to last long. I dare say he drinks too much port, or hunts, or something of that sort; goes to sleep after dinner, and does all manner of apoplectic things, I'll be bound. Then there's the son, only fifteen, and not yet marriageable; consumptive,

I dare say. Now, will you tell me the chances are not six to six he dies unmarried? So you see, my dear old boy, you're sure to get the fortune; for there's nothing to keep you out of it, except—'

'Except three lives, the worst of which is better than mine. It's kind of you to look at it in this sanguine way, Arundel; but I wasn't born to be a rich man. Perhaps, after all, Providence has used me better than I think. I mightn't have been happy at Marchmont Towers. I'm a shy, awkward, humdrum fellow. If it wasn't for Mary's sake—'

'Ah, to be sure!' cried Edward Arundel. 'You're not going to forget all about—Miss Marchmont!' He was going to say 'little Mary,' but had checked himself abruptly at the sudden recollection of the earnest hazel eyes that had kept wondering watch upon his ravages at the breakfast-table. 'I'm sure Miss Marchmont's born to be an heiress. I never saw such a little princess.'

'What!' demanded John Marchmont sadly, 'in a darned pinafore and a threadbare frock?'

The boy's face flushed, almost indignantly, as his old master said this.

'You don't think I'm such a snob as to admire a lady'—he spoke thus of Miss Mary Marchmont, yet midway between her eighth and ninth birthday—'the less because she isn't rich? But of course your daughter will have the fortune by-and-by, even if—'

He stopped, ashamed of his want of tact; for he knew John would divine the meaning of that sudden pause.

'Even if I should die before Philip Marchmont,' the teacher of mathematics answered, quietly. 'As far as that goes, Mary's chance is as remote as my own. The fortune can only come to her in the event of Arthur dying without issue, or, having issue, failing to cut off the entail, I believe they call it.'

'Arthur! that's the son of the present posessor?'

'Yes. If I and my poor little girl, who is delicate like her mother, should die before either of these three men, there is another who will stand in my shoes, and will look out perhaps more eagerly than I have done for his chances of getting the property.'

'Another!' exclaimed Mr Arundel. 'By Jove, Marchmont, it's the most complicated affair I ever heard of. It's worse than those sums you used to set me in barter: "If A. sells B. 999 Stilton cheeses at 9½*d.* a pound," and all that sort of thing, you know. Do make me understand it, old fellow, if you can.'

John Marchmont sighed.

'It's a wearisome story, Arundel,' he said. 'I don't know why I should bore you with it.'

'But you don't bore me with it,' cried the boy energetically. 'I'm awfully interested in it, you know; and I could walk up and down here all day talking about it.'

The two gentlemen had passed the Surrey toll-gate of Waterloo Bridge by this time. The South-Western Terminus had not been built in the year '38, and the bridge was about the quietest thoroughfare any two companions confidentially inclined could have chosen. The shareholders knew this, to their cost.

Perhaps Mr Marchmont might have been beguiled into repeating the old story, which he had told so often in the dim firelight to his little girl; but the great clock of St Paul's boomed forth the twelve ponderous strokes that told the hour of noon, and a hundred other steeples upon either side of the water made themselves clamorous with the same announcement.

'I must leave you, Arundel,' the supernumerary said hurriedly; he had just remembered that it was time for him to go and be browbeaten by a truculent stage-manager. 'God bless you, my dear boy! It was very good of you to want to see me, and the sight of your fresh face has made me very happy. I *should* like you to understand all about the Lincolnshire property. God knows there's small chance of its ever coming to me or to my child; but when I am dead and gone, Mary will be left alone in the world, and it would be some comfort to me to know that she was not without *one* friend—generous and disinterested like you, Arundel,—who, if the chance *did* come, would see her righted.'

'And so I would,' cried the boy eagerly. His face flushed, and his eyes fired. He was a preux chevalier* already, in thought, going forth to do battle for a hazel-eyed mistress.

'I'll *write* the story, Arundel,' John Marchmont said; 'I've no time to tell it, and you mightn't remember it either. Once more, goodbye; once more, God bless you!'

'Stop!' exclaimed Edward Arundel, flushing a deeper red than before,—he had a very boyish habit of blushing,—'stop, dear old boy. You must borrow this of me, please. I've lots of them. I should only spend it on all sorts of bilious things; or stop out late and get tipsy. You shall pay me with interest when you get Marchmont Towers. I shall come and see you again soon. Good-bye.'

The lad forced some crumpled scrap of paper into his old tutor's hand, bolted through the toll-bar, and jumped into a cabriolet, whose high-stepping charger was dawdling along Lancaster Place.

The supernumerary hurried on to Drury Lane as fast as his weak legs could carry him. He was obliged to wait for a pause in the rehearsal before he could find an opportunity of looking at the parting gift which his old pupil had forced upon him. It was a crumpled and rather dirty five-pound note, wrapped round two half-crowns, a shilling, and half-a-sovereign.

The boy had given his friend the last remnant of his slender stock of pocket-money. John Marchmont turned his face to the dark wing that sheltered him, and wept silently. He was of a gentle and rather womanly disposition, be it remembered; and he was in that weak state of health in which a man's eyes are apt to moisten, in spite of himself, under the influence of any unwonted emotion.

He employed a part of that afternoon in writing the letter which he had promised to send to his boyish friend:—

'My DEAR ARUNDEL,

'My purpose in writing to you to-day is so entirely connected with the future welfare of my beloved and only child, that I shall carefully abstain from any subject not connected with her interests. I say nothing, therefore, respecting your conduct of this morning, which, together with my previous knowledge of your character, has decided me upon confiding to you the doubts and fears which have long tormented me upon the subject of my darling's future.

'I am a doomed man, Arundel! The doctors have told me this; but they have told me also that, though I can never escape the sentence of death which was passed upon me long ago, I may live for some years if I live the careful life which only a rich man can lead. If I go on carrying banners and breathing sulphur, I cannot last long. My little girl will be left penniless, but not quite friendless; for there are humble people, relatives of her poor mother, who would help her kindly, I am sure, in their own humble way. The trials which I fear for my orphan girl are not so much the trials of poverty as the dangers of wealth. If the three men who, on my death, would alone stand between Mary and the Lincolnshire property die childless, my poor darling will become the only obstacle in the pathway of a man whom, I will freely own to you, I distrust.

'My father, John Marchmont, was the third of four brothers. The eldest, Philip, died leaving one son, also called Philip, and the present possessor of Marchmont Towers. The second, Marmaduke, is still alive, a bachelor. The third, John, left four children, of whom I alone survive. The fourth, Paul, left a son and two daughters. The son is an artist, exercising his profession now in London; one of the daughters is married to a parish surgeon, who practises at Stanfield, in Lincolnshire; the other is an old maid, and entirely dependent upon her brother.

'It is this man, Paul Marchmont the artist, whom I fear.

'Do not think me weak, or foolishly suspicious, Arundel, when I tell you that the very thought of this man brings the cold sweat upon my forehead, and seems to stop the beating of my heart. I know that this is a prejudice, and an unworthy one. I do not believe Paul Marchmont is a good man; but I can assign no sufficient reason for my hatred and terror of him. It is impossible for you, a frank and careless boy, to realise the feelings of a man who looks at his only child, and remembers that she may soon be left, helpless and defenceless, to fight the battle of life with a bad man. Sometimes I pray to God that the Marchmont property may never come to my child after my death; for I cannot rid myself of the thought—may Heaven forgive me for its unworthiness!—that Paul Marchmont would leave no means untried, however foul, to wrest the fortune from her. I dare say worldly people would laugh at me for writing this letter to you, my dear Arundel; but I address myself to the best friend I have,—the only creature I know whom the influence of a bad man is never likely to corrupt. *Noblesse oblige!* I am not afraid that Edward Dangerfield Arundel will betray any trust, however foolish, that may have been confided to him.

'Perhaps, in writing to you thus, I may feel something of that blind hopefulness—amid the shipwreck of all that commonly gives birth to hope—which the mariner cast away upon some desert island feels, when he seals his simple story in a bottle, and launches it upon the waste of waters that close him in on every side. Before my little girl is four years older, you will be a man, Arundel—with a man's intellect, a man's courage, and, above all, a man's keen sense of honour. So long as my darling remains poor, her humble friends will be strong enough to protect her; but if ever Providence should think fit to place her in a position of antagonism to Paul Marchmont,—for he

would look upon any one as an enemy who stood between him and
fortune,—she would need a far more powerful protector than any
she could find amongst her poor mother's relatives. Will *you* be that
protector, Edward Arundel? I am a drowning man, you see, and
catch at the frailest straw that floats past me. I believe in you,
Edward, as much as I distrust Paul Marchmont. If the day ever
comes in which my little girl should have to struggle with this man,
will you help her to fight the battle? It will not be an easy one.

'Subjoined to this letter I send you an extract from the copy of my
grandfather's will, which will explain to you how he left his property.
Do not lose either the letter or the extract. If you are willing to
undertake the trust which I confide to you to-day, you may have need
to refer to them after my death. The legacy of a child's helplessness
is the only bequest which I can leave to the only friend I have.

'JOHN MARCHMONT.

'27, OAKLEY STREET, LAMBETH,
    '*December* 30*th*, 1838.

'EXTRACT FROM THE WILL OF PHILIP MARCHMONT, SENIOR, OF MARCHMONT TOWERS

'"I give and devise all that my estate known as Marchmont Towers
and appurtenances thereto belonging to the use of my eldest son
Philip Marchmont during his natural life without impeachment of
waste and from and after his decease then to the use of my grandson
Philip the first son of my said son Philip during the term of his
natural life without impeachment of waste and after the decease of
my said grandson Philip to the use of the first and every other son of
my said grandson severally and successively according to their
respective seniority in tail and for default of such issue to the use of
all and every the daughters and daughter of my said grandson Philip
as tenants in common in tail with cross remainders between or
amongst them in tail and if all the daughters of my said grandson
Philip except one shall die without issue or if there shall be but one
such daughter then to the use of such one or only daughter in tail
and in default of such issue then to the use of the second and every
other son of my said eldest son severally and successively according
to his respective seniority in tail and in default of such issue to the
use of all and every the daughters and daughter of my said eldest son
Philip as tenants in common in tail with cross remainders between or

amongst them in tail and in default of such issue to the use of my
second son Marmaduke and his assigns during the term of his natural life without impeachment of waste and after his decease to the
use of the first and every son of my said son Marmaduke severally
and successively according to their respective seniorities in tail and
for default of such issue to the use of all and every the daughters and
daughter of my said son Marmaduke as tenants in common in tail
with cross remainders between or amongst them in tail and if all the
daughters of my said son Marmaduke except one shall die without
issue or if there shall be but one such daughter then to the use of
such one or only daughter in tail and in default of such issue then to
the use of my third son John during the term of his natural life
without impeachment of waste and from and after his decease then
to the use of my grandson John the first son of my said son John
during the term of his natural life without impeachment of waste
and after the decease of my said grandson John to the use of the first
and every other son of my said grandson John severally and successively according to their respective seniority in tail and for default of
such issue to the use of all and every the daughters and daughter of
my said grandson John as tenants in common in tail with cross
remainders between or among them in tail and if all the daughters of
my said grandson John except one shall die without issue or if there
shall be but one such daughter" [*This, you will see, is my little Mary*]
"then to the use of such one or only daughter in tail and in default
of such issue then to the use of the second and every other son of
my said third son John severally and successively according to his
respective seniority in tail and in default of such issue to the use of
all and every the daughters and daughter of my said third son John as
tenants in common in tail with cross remainders between or amongst
them in tail and in default of such issue to the use of my fourth son
Paul during the term of his natural life without impeachment of
waste and from and after his decease then to the use of my grandson
Paul the son of my said son Paul during his natural life without
impeachment of waste and after the decease of my said grandson Paul
to the use of the first and every other son of my said grandson severally and successively according to their respective seniority in tail and
for default of such issue to the use of all and every the daughters and
daughter of my said grandson Paul as tenants in common in tail with
cross remainders between or amongst them in tail and if all the

daughters of my said grandson Paul except one shall die without issue or if there shall be but one such daughter then to the use of such one or only daughter in tail and in default of such issue then to the use of the second and every other son of my said fourth son Paul severally and successively according to his respective seniority in tail and in default of such issue to the use of all and every the daughters and daughter of my said fourth son Paul as tenants in common in tail with cross remainders between or amongst them in tail," &c. &c.

'P.S.—Then comes what the lawyers call a general devise to trustees, to preserve the contingent remainders before devised from being destroyed; but what that means, perhaps you can get somebody to tell you. I hope it may be some legal jargon to preserve my *very* contingent remainder.'

The tone of Edward Arundel's answer to this letter was more characteristic of the writer than in harmony with poor John's solemn appeal.

'You dear, foolish old Marchmont,' the lad wrote, 'of course I shall take care of Miss Mary; and my mother shall adopt her, and she shall live at Dangerfield, and be educated with my sister Letitia, who has the jolliest French governess, and a German maid for conversation; and don't let Paul Marchmont try on any of his games with me, that's all! But what do you mean, you ridiculous old boy, by talking about dying, and drowning, and shipwrecked mariners, and catching at straws, and all that sort of humbug, when you know very well that you'll live to inherit the Lincolnshire property, and that I'm coming to you every year to shoot, and that you're going to build a tennis-court,—of course there *is* a billiard-room,—and that you're going to have a stud of hunters, and be master of the hounds, and no end of bricks to

'Your ever devoted Roman countryman and lover,

'EDGARDO?

'42, MONTAGUE SQUARE,
'*December* 31*st*, 1838.

'P.S.—By-the-bye, don't you think a situation in a lawyer's office would suit you better than the TRDL?* If you do, I think I could manage it. A happy new year to Miss Mary!'

It was thus that Mr Edward Arundel accepted the solemn trust which his friend confided to him in all simplicity and good faith. Mary Marchmont herself was not more innocent in the ways of the world outside Oakley Street, the Waterloo Road, and the New Cut, than was the little girl's father; nothing seemed more natural to him than to intrust the doubtful future of his only child to the bright-faced handsome boy, whose early boyhood had been unblemished by a mean sentiment or a dishonourable action. John Marchmont had spent three years in the Berkshire Academy at which Edward and his cousin, Martin Mostyn, had been educated; and young Arundel, who was far behind his kinsman in the comprehension of a problem in algebra, had been wise enough to recognise that paradox which Martin Mostyn could not understand—a gentleman in a shabby coat. It was thus that a friendship had arisen between the teacher of mathematics and his handsome pupil; and it was thus that an unreasoning belief in Edward Arundel had sprung up in John's simple mind.

'If my little girl were certain of inheriting the fortune,' Mr Marchmont thought, 'I might find many who would be glad to accept my trust, and to serve her well and faithfully. But the chance is such a remote one. I cannot forget how the Jews laughed at me two years ago, when I tried to borrow money upon my reversionary interest. No! I must trust this brave-hearted boy, for I have no one else to confide in; and who else is there who would not ridicule my fear of my cousin Paul?'

Indeed, Mr Marchmont had some reason to be considerably ashamed of his antipathy to the young artist working for his bread, and for the bread of his invalid mother and unmarried sister, in that bitter winter of '38; working patiently and hopefully, in despite of all discouragement, and content to live a joyless and monotonous life in a dingy lodging near Fitzroy Square. I can find no excuse for John Marchmont's prejudice against an industrious and indefatigable young man, who was the sole support of two helpless women. Heaven knows, if to be adored by two women is any evidence of a man's virtue, Paul must have been the best of men; for Stephanie Marchmont, and her daughter Clarisse, regarded the artist with a reverential idolatry that was not without a tinge of romance. I can assign no reason, then, for John's dislike of his cousin. They had been schoolfellows at a wretched suburban school, where the children of poor people were boarded, lodged, and educated all the year round for a pitiful stipend of something under twenty pounds. One of the special points of the prospectus was the announcement that there were no holidays; for the jovial Christmas gatherings of merry faces, which are so delightful to the wealthy citizens of Bloomsbury or Tyburnia,* take another complexion in poverty-stricken households, whose scantily-stocked larders can ill support the raids of rawboned lads clamorous for provender. The two boys had met at a school of this calibre, and had never met since. They may not have been the best friends, perhaps, at the classical academy; but their quarrels were by no means desperate. They may have rather freely discussed their several chances of the Lincolnshire property; but I have no romantic story to tell of a stirring scene in the humble schoolroom—no exciting record of deadly insult and deep vows of vengeance. No inkstand was ever flung by one boy into the face of the other; no savage blow from a horsewhip ever cut a fatal scar across the brow of either of the cousins. John Marchmont would have been almost as puzzled to account for his objection to his kinsman, as was the nameless gentleman who so naïvely confessed his dislike of Dr Fell. I fear that a great many of our likings and dislikings are too apt to be upon the Dr Fell* principle. Mr Wilkie Collins's Basil* could not tell *why* he fell madly in love with the lady whom it was his evil fortune to meet in an omnibus; nor why he entertained an uncomfortable feeling about the gentleman who was to be her destroyer. David Copperfield* disliked Uriah Heep even before he had any substantial reason for objecting to the evil genius of Agnes Wickfield's father. The boy disliked the snake-like schemer of Canterbury because his eyes were round and red, and his hands clammy and unpleasant to the touch. Perhaps John Marchmont's reasons for his aversion to his cousin were about as substantial as those of Master Copperfield. It may be that the schoolboy disliked his comrade because Paul Marchmont's handsome grey eyes were a little too near together; because his thin and delicately chiselled lips were a thought too tightly compressed; because his cheeks would fade to an awful corpse-like whiteness under circumstances which would have brought the rushing life-blood, hot and red, into another boy's face; because he was silent and suppressed when it would have been more natural to be loud and clamorous; because he could smile under provocations that would have made another frown; because, in short, there was that about him which, let it be found where it will, always gives birth to suspicion,—MYSTERY!

So the cousins had parted, neither friends nor foes, to tread their separate roads in the unknown country, which is apt to seem barren and desolate enough to travellers who foot it in hobnailed boots considerably the worse for wear; and as the iron hand of poverty held John Marchmont even further back than Paul upon the hard road which each had to tread, the quiet pride of the teacher of mathematics most effectually kept him out of his kinsman's way. He had only heard enough of Paul to know that he was living in London, and working hard for a living; working as hard as John himself, perhaps; but at least able to keep afloat in a higher social position than the law-stationer's hack and the banner-holder of Drury Lane.

But Edward Arundel did not forget his friends in Oakley Street. The boy made a morning call upon his father's solicitors, Messrs Paulette, Paulette, and Mathewson, of Lincoln's Inn Fields, and was so extremely eloquent in his needy friend's cause, as to provoke the good-natured laughter of one of the junior partners, who declared that Mr Edward Arundel ought to wear a silk gown* before he was thirty. The result of this interview was, that before the first month of the new year was out, John Marchmont had abandoned the classic banner and the demoniac mask to a fortunate successor, and had taken possession of a hard-seated, slim-legged stool in one of the offices of Messrs. Paulette, Paulette, and Mathewson, as copying and out-door clerk, at a salary of thirty shillings a week.

So little Mary entered now upon a golden age, in which her evenings were no longer desolate and lonely, but spent pleasantly with her father in the study of such learning as was suited to her years, or perhaps rather to her capacity, which was far beyond her years; and on certain delicious nights, to be remembered ever afterwards, John Marchmont took his little girl to the gallery of one or other of the transpontine* theatres; and I am sorry to say that my heroine—for she is to be my heroine by-and-by—sucked oranges, ate Abernethy biscuits, and cooled her delicate nose against the iron railing of the gallery, after the manner of the masses when they enjoy the British Drama.

But all this time John Marchmont was utterly ignorant of one rather important fact in the history of those three lives which he was apt to speak of as standing between him and Marchmont Towers.

Young Arthur Marchmont, the immediate heir of the estate, had been shot to death upon the 1st of September, 1838, without blame to anyone or anything but his own boyish carelessness, which had induced him to scramble through a hedge with his fowling-piece, the costly present of a doting father, loaded and on full-cock. This melancholy event, which had been briefly recorded in all the newspapers, had never reached the knowledge of poor John Marchmont, who had no friends to busy themselves about his interests, or to rush eagerly to carry him any intelligence affecting his prosperity. Nor had he read the obituary notice respecting Marmaduke Marchmont, the bachelor, who had breathed his last stertorous breath in a fit of apoplexy exactly one twelvemonth before the day upon which Edward Arundel breakfasted in Oakley Street.

CHAPTER IV

GOING AWAY

EDWARD ARUNDEL went from Montague Square straight into the household of the private tutor of whom he had spoken, there to complete his education, and to be prepared for the onerous duties of a military life. From the household of this private tutor he went at once into a cavalry regiment; after sundry examinations,* which were not nearly so stringent in the year one thousand eight hundred and forty, as they have since become. Indeed, I think the unfortunate young cadets who are educated upon the high-pressure system, and who are expected to give a synopsis of Portuguese political intrigue during the eighteenth century, a scientific account of the currents of the Red Sea, and a critical disquisition upon the comedies of Aristophanes as compared with those of Pedro Calderon de la Barca,* not forgetting to glance at the effect of different ages and nationalities upon the respective minds of the two playwrights, within a given period of, say half-an-hour,—would have envied Mr Arundel for the easy manner in which he obtained his commission in a distinguished cavalry regiment. Mr Edward Arundel therefore inaugurated the commencement of the year 1840 by plunging very deeply into the books of a crack military-tailor in New Burlington Street, and by a visit to Dangerfield Park; where he went to make his adieux before sailing for India, whither his regiment had just been ordered.

I do not doubt that Mrs Arundel was very sorrowful at this sudden parting with her yellow-haired younger son. The boy and his mother walked together in the wintry sunset under the leafless beeches at Dangerfield, and talked of the dreary voyage that lay before the lad; the arid plains and cruel jungles far away; perils by sea and perils by land; but across them all, Fame waving her white beckoning arms to the young soldier, and crying, 'Come, conqueror that shall be! come, through trial and danger, through fever and famine,—come to your rest upon my blood-stained lap!' Surely this boy, being only just eighteen years of age, may be forgiven if he is a little romantic, a little over eager and impressionable, a little too confident that the next thing to going out to India as a sea-sick subaltern in a great transport-ship is coming home with the reputation of a Clive.* Perhaps he may be forgiven, too, if, in his fresh enthusiasm, he sometimes forgot the shabby friend whom he had helped little better than a twelvemonth before, and the earnest hazel eyes that had shone upon him in the pitiful Oakley Street chamber. I do not say that he was utterly unmindful of his old teacher of mathematics. It was not in his nature to forget anyone who had need of his services; for this boy, so eager to be a soldier, was of the chivalrous temperament, and would have gone out to die for his mistress, or his friend, if need had been. He had received two or three grateful letters from John Marchmont; and in these letters the lawyer's clerk had spoken pleasantly of his new life, and hopefully of his health, which had improved considerably, he said, since his resignation of the tragic banner and the pantomimic mask. Neither had Edward quite forgotten his promise of enlisting Mrs Arundel's sympathies in aid of the motherless little girl. In one of these wintry walks beneath the black branches at Dangerfield, the lad had told the sorrowful story of his well-born tutor's poverty and humiliation.

'Only think, mother!' he cried at the end of the little history. 'I saw the poor fellow carrying a great calico flag, and marching about at the heel of a procession, to be laughed at by the costermongers in the gallery; and I know that he belongs to a capital Lincolnshire family, and will come in for no end of money if he only lives long enough. But if he should die, mother, and leave his little girl destitute, you'll look after her, won't you?'

I don't know whether Mrs Arundel quite entered into her son's ideas upon the subject of adopting Mary Marchmont, or whether she had any definite notion of bringing the little girl home to Dangerfield for the natural term of her life, in the event of the child being left an orphan. But she was a kind and charitable lady, and she scarcely cared to damp her boy's spirits by holding forth upon the doubtful wisdom of his adopting, or promising to adopt, any stray orphans who might cross his pathway.

'I hope the little girl may not lose her father, Edward,' she said gently. 'Besides, dear, you say that Mr Marchmont tells you he has humble friends, who would take the child if anything happened to him. He does not wish us to adopt the little girl; he only asks us to interest ourselves in her fate.'

'And you will do that, mother darling?' cried the boy. 'You will take an interest in her, won't you? You couldn't help doing so, if you were to see her. She's not like a child, you know,—not a bit like Letitia. She's as grave and quiet as you are, mother,—or graver, I think; and she looks like a lady, in spite of her poor, shabby pinafore and frock.'

'Does she wear shabby frocks?' said the mother, 'I could help her in that matter, at all events, Ned. I might send her a great trunk-full of Letitia's things: she outgrows them before they have been worn long enough to be shabby.'

The boy coloured, and shook his head.

'It's very kind of you to think of it, mother dear; but I don't think that would quite answer,' he said.

'Why not?'

'Because, you see, John Marchmont is a gentleman; and, you know, though he's so dreadfully poor now, he *is* heir to Marchmont Towers. And though he didn't mind doing any thing in the world to earn a few shillings a week, he mightn't like to take cast-off clothes.'

So nothing more was to be said or done upon the subject.

Edward Arundel wrote his humble friend a pleasant letter, in which he told John that he had enlisted his mother's sympathy in Mary's cause, and in which he spoke in very glowing terms of the Indian expedition that lay before him.

'I wish I could come to say good-bye to you and Miss Mary before I go,' he wrote; 'but that's impossible. I go straight from here to Southampton by coach at the end of this month, and the *Auckland* sails on the 2nd of February. Tell Miss Mary I shall bring her home all kinds of pretty presents from Afghanistan,*—ivory fans, and Cashmere shawls, and Chinese puzzles, and embroidered slippers with turned-up toes, and diamonds, and attar-of-roses, and suchlike; and remember that I expect you to write to me, and to give me the earliest news of your coming into the Lincolnshire property.'

John Marchmont received this letter in the middle of January. He gave a despondent sigh as he refolded the boyish epistle, after reading it to his little girl.

'We haven't so many friends, Polly,' he said, 'that we should be indifferent to the loss of this one.'

Mary Marchmont's cheek grew paler at her father's sorrowful speech. That imaginative temperament, which was, as I have said, almost morbid in its intensity, presented every object to the little girl in a light in which things are looked at by very few children. Only these few words, and her fancy roamed far away to that cruel land whose perils her father had described to her. Only these few words, and she was away in the rocky Bolan Pass,* under hurricanes of drifting snow; she saw the hungry soldiers fighting with savage dogs for the possession of foul carrion. She had heard all the perils and difficulties which had befallen the Army of the Indus in the year '39,* and the womanly heart ached with the pain of those cruel memories.

'He will go to India and be killed, papa dear,' she said. 'Oh! why, why do they let him go? His mother can't love him, can she? She would never let him go, if she did.'

John Marchmont was obliged to explain to his daughter that motherly love must not go so far as to deprive a nation of its defenders; and that the richest jewels which Cornelia* can give to her country are those ruby life-drops which flow from the hearts of her bravest and brightest sons. Mary was no political economist; she could not reason upon the necessity of chastising Persian insolence, or checking Russian encroachments upon the far-away shores of the Indus. Was Edward Arundel's bright head, with its aureola of yellow hair, to be cloven asunder by an Afghan renegade's sabre, because the young Shah of Persia had been contumacious?

Mary Marchmont wept silently that day over a three-volume novel, while her father was away serving writs upon wretched insolvents, in his capacity of out-door clerk to Messrs Paulette, Paulette, and Mathewson.

The young lady no longer spent her quiet days in the two-pair back. Mr Marchmont and his daughter had remained faithful to Oakley Street and the proprietress of the ladies' wardrobe, who was a good, motherly creature; but they had descended to the grandeur of the first floor, whose gorgeous decorations Mary had glanced at furtively in the days gone by, when the splendid chambers were occupied by an elderly and reprobate commission-agent, who seemed utterly indifferent to the delights of a convex mirror, surmounted by a maimed eagle, whose dignity was somewhat impaired by the loss of a wing; but which bijou appeared, to Mary, to be a fitting adornment for the young Queen's* palace in St James's Park.

But neither the eagle nor the third volume of a thrilling romance could comfort Mary upon this bleak January day. She shut her book, and stood by the window, looking out into the dreary street, that seemed so blotted and dim under the falling snow.

'It snowed in the Pass of Bolan,' she thought; 'and the treacherous Indians harassed the brave soldiers, and killed their camels. What will become of him in that dreadful country? Shall we ever see him again?'

Yes, Mary, to your sorrow! Indian scimitars will let him go scatheless; famine and fever will pass him by; but the hand which points to that far-away day on which you and he are to meet, will never fail or falter in its purpose until the hour of your meeting comes.

We have no need to dwell upon the preparations which were made for the young soldier's departure from home, nor on the tender farewells between the mother and her son.

Mr Arundel was a country gentleman *pur et simple*; a hearty, broad-shouldered squire, who had no thought above his farm and his dog-kennel, or the hunting of the red deer with which his neighbourhood abounded. He sent his younger son to India as coolly as he had sent the elder to Oxford. The boy had little to inherit, and must be provided for in a gentlemanly manner. Other younger sons of the House of Arundel had fought and conquered in the Honourable East India Company's service; and was Edward any better than they, that there should be sentimental whining because the lad was going away to fight his way to fortune, if he could? Mr Arundel went even further than this, and declared that Master Edward was a lucky dog to be going out at such a time, when there was plenty of fighting, and a very fair chance of speedy promotion for a good soldier.

He gave the young cadet his blessing, reminded him of the limit of such supplies as he was to expect from home, bade him keep clear of the brandy-bottle and the dice-box; and having done this, believed that he had performed his duty as an Englishman and a father.

If Mrs Arundel wept, she wept in secret, loth to discourage her son by the sight of those natural, womanly tears. If Miss Letitia Arundel was sorry to lose her brother, she mourned with most praiseworthy discretion, and did not forget to remind the young traveller that she expected to receive a muslin frock, embroidered with beetle-wings, by an early mail. And as Algernon Fairfax Dangerfield Arundel, the heir, was away at college, there was no one else to mourn. So Edward left the home of his forefathers by a branch-coach, which started from the 'Arundel Arms' in time to meet the 'Telegraph' at Exeter; and no noisy lamentations shook the sky above Dangerfield Park—no mourning voices echoed through the spacious rooms. The old servants were sorry to lose the younger-born, whose easy, genial temperament had made him an especial favourite; but there was a certain admixture of joviality with their sorrow, as there generally is with all mourning in the basement; and the strong ale, the famous Dangerfield October, went faster upon that 31st of January than on any day since Christmas.

I doubt if any one at Dangerfield Park sorrowed as bitterly for the departure of the boyish soldier as a romantic young lady, of nine years old, in Oakley Street, Lambeth; whose one sentimental day-dream—half-childish, half-womanly—owned Edward Arundel as its centre figure.

So the curtain falls on the picture of a brave ship sailing eastward, her white canvas strained against the cold grey February sky, and a little girl weeping over the tattered pages of a stupid novel in a shabby London lodging.

CHAPTER V

MARCHMONT TOWERS

THERE is a lapse of three years and a half between the acts; and the curtain rises to reveal a widely-different picture:—the picture of a noble mansion in the flat Lincolnshire country; a stately pile of building, standing proudly forth against a background of black woodland; a noble building, supported upon either side by an octagon tower, whose solid masonry is half-hidden by the ivy which clings about the stonework, trailing here and there, and flapping restlessly with every breath of wind against the narrow casements.

A broad stone terrace stretches the entire length of the grim façade, from tower to tower; and three flights of steps lead from the terrace to the broad lawn, which loses itself in a vast grassy flat, only broken by a few clumps of trees and a dismal pool of black water, but called by courtesy a park. Grim stone griffins surmount the terrace-steps, and griffins' heads and other architectural monstrosities, worn and moss-grown, keep watch and ward over every door and window, every archway and abutment—frowning threat and defiance upon the daring visitor who approaches the great house by this, the formidable chief entrance.

The mansion looks westward: but there is another approach, a low archway on the southern side, which leads into a quadrangle, where there is a quaint little door under a stone portico, ivy-covered like the rest; a comfortable little door of massive oak, studded with knobs of rusty iron,—a door generally affected by visitors familiar with the house.

This is Marchmont Towers,—a grand and stately mansion, which had been a monastery in the days when England and the Pope were friends and allies; and which had been bestowed upon Hugh Marchmont, gentleman, by his Sovereign Lord and Most Christian Majesty the King Henry VIII, of blessed memory, and by that gentleman-commoner extended and improved at considerable outlay. This is Marchmont Towers,—a splendid and a princely habitation truly, but perhaps scarcely the kind of dwelling one would choose for the holy resting-place we call home. The great mansion is a little too dismal in its lonely grandeur: it lacks shelter when the dreary winds come sweeping across the grassy flats in the bleak winter weather; it lacks shade when the western sun blazes on every window-pane in the stifling summer evening. It is at all times rather too stony in its aspect; and is apt to remind one almost painfully of every weird and sorrowful story treasured in the storehouse of memory. Ancient tales of enchantment, dark German legends, wild Scottish fancies, grim fragments of half-forgotten demonology, strange stories of murder, violence, mystery, and wrong, vaguely intermingle in the stranger's mind as he looks, for the first time, at Marchmont Towers.

But of course these feelings wear off in time. So invincible is the power of custom, that we might make ourselves comfortable in the Castle of Otranto,* after a reasonable sojourn within its mysterious walls: familiarity would breed contempt for the giant helmet,* and all the other grim apparitions of the haunted dwelling. The commonplace and ignoble wants of every-day life must surely bring disenchantment with them. The ghost and the butcher's boy cannot well exist contemporaneously; and the avenging shade can scarcely continue to lurk beneath the portal which is visited by the matutinal milkman. Indeed, this is doubtless the reason that the most restless and impatient spirit, bent on early vengeance and immediate retribution, will yet wait until the shades of night have fallen before he reveals himself, rather than run the risk of an ignominious encounter with the postman or the parlour-maid. Be it how it might, the phantoms of Marchmont Towers were not intrusive. They may have perambulated the long tapestried corridors, the tenantless chambers, the broad black staircase of shining oak; but, happily, no dweller in the mansion was ever scared by the sight of their pale faces. All the dead-and-gone beauties, and soldiers, and lawyers, and parsons, and simple country-squires of the Marchmont race may have descended from their picture-frames to hold a witches' sabbath in the old mansion; but as the Lincolnshire servants were hearty eaters and heavy sleepers, the ghosts had it all to themselves. I believe there was one dismal story attached to the house,—the story of a Marchmont of the time of Charles I, who had murdered his coachman in a fit of insensate rage; and it was even asserted, upon the authority of an old housekeeper, that John Marchmont's grandmother, when a young woman and lately come as a bride to the Towers, had beheld the murdered coachman stalk into her chamber, ghastly and blood-bedabbled, in the dim summer twilight. But as this story was not particularly romantic, and possessed none of the elements likely to insure popularity,—such as love, jealousy, revenge, mystery, youth, and beauty,—it had never been very widely disseminated.

I should think that the new owner of Marchmont Towers—new within the last six months—was about the last person in Christendom to be hypercritical, or to raise fanciful objections to his dwelling; for inasmuch as he had come straight from a wretched transpontine lodging to this splendid Lincolnshire mansion, and had at the same time exchanged a stipend of thirty shillings a week for an income of eleven thousand a year (derivable from lands that spread far away, over fenny flats and low-lying farms, to the solitary seashore), he had ample reason to be grateful to Providence, and well pleased with his new abode.

Yes; Philip Marchmont, the childless widower, had died six months before, at the close of the year '43, of a broken heart,—his old servants said, broken by the loss of his only and idolised son; after which loss he had never been known to smile. He was one of those undemonstrative men who can take a great sorrow quietly, and only—die of it. Philip Marchmont lay in a velvet-covered coffin, above his son's, in the stone recess set apart for them in the Marchmont vault beneath Kemberling Church, three miles from the Towers; and John reigned in his stead. John Marchmont, the supernumerary, the banner-holder of Drury Lane, the patient, conscientious copying and outdoor clerk of Lincoln's Inn, was now sole owner of the Lincolnshire estate, sole master of a household of well-trained old servants, sole proprietor of a very decent country-gentleman's stud, and of chariots, barouches, chaises, phaetons,* and other vehicles—a little shabby and out of date it may be, but very comfortable to a man for whom an omnibus ride had long been a treat and a rarity. Nothing had been touched or disturbed since Philip Marchmont's death. The rooms he had used were still the occupied apartments; the chambers he had chosen to shut up were still kept with locked doors; the servants who had served him waited upon his successor, whom they declared to be a quiet, easy gentleman, far too wise to interfere with old servants, every one of whom knew the ways of the house a great deal better than he did, though he was the master of it.

There was, therefore, no shadow of change in the stately mansion.

The dinner-bell still rang at the same hour; the same tradespeople left the same species of wares at the low oaken door; the old house-keeper, arranging her simple *menu*, planned her narrow round of soups and roasts, sweets and made-dishes, exactly as she had been wont to do, and had no new tastes to consult. A grey-haired bachelor, who had been own-man* to Philip, was now own-man to John. The carriage which had conveyed the late lord every Sunday to morning and afternoon service at Kemberling conveyed the new lord, who sat in the same seat that his predecessor had occupied in the great family-pew, and read his prayers out of the same book,—a noble crimson, morocco-covered volume, in which George, our most gracious King and Governor, and all manner of dead-and-gone princes and princesses were prayed for.

The presence of Mary Marchmont made the only change in the old house; and even that change was a very trifling one. Mary and her father were as closely united at Marchmont Towers as they had been in Oakley Street. The little girl clung to her father as tenderly as ever—more tenderly than ever perhaps; for she knew something of that which the physicians had said, and she knew that John Marchmont's lease of life was not a long one. Perhaps it would be better to say that he had no lease at all. His soul was a tenant on sufferance in its frail earthly habitation, receiving a respite now and again, when the flicker of the lamp was very low—every chance breath of wind threatening to extinguish it for ever. It was only those who knew John Marchmont very intimately who were fully acquainted with the extent of his danger. He no longer bore any of those fatal outward signs of consumption, which fatigue and deprivation had once made painfully conspicuous. The hectic flush and the unnatural brightness of the eyes had subsided; indeed, John seemed much stronger and heartier than of old; and it is only great medical practitioners who can tell to a nicety what is going on *inside* a man, when he presents a very fair exterior to the unprofessional eye. But John was decidedly better than he had been. He might live three years, five, seven, possibly even ten years; but he must live the life of a man who holds himself perpetually upon his defence against death; and he must recognise in every bleak current of wind, in every chilling damp, or perilous heat, or over-exertion, or ill-chosen morsel of food, or hasty emotion, or sudden passion, an insidious ally of his dismal enemy.

Mary Marchmont knew all this,—or divined it, perhaps, rather than knew it, with the child-woman's subtle power of divination, which is even stronger than the actual woman's; for her father had done his best to keep all sorrowful knowledge from her. She knew that he was in danger; and she loved him all the more dearly, as the one precious thing which was in constant peril of being snatched away. The child's love for her father has not grown any less morbid in its intensity since Edward Arundel's departure for India; nor has Mary become more childlike since her coming to Marchmont Towers, and her abandonment of all those sordid cares, those pitiful every-day duties, which had made her womanly.

It may be that the last lingering glamour of childhood had for ever faded away with the realisation of the day-dream which she had carried about with her so often in the dingy transpontine thorough-fares around Oakley Street. Marchmont Towers, that fairy palace, whose lighted windows had shone upon her far away across a cruel forest of poverty and trouble, like the enchanted castle which appears to the lost wanderer of the child's story, was now the home of the father she loved. The grim enchanter Death, the only magician of our modern histories, had waved his skeleton hand, more powerful than the star-gemmed wand of any fairy godmother, and the obstacles which had stood between John Marchmont and his inheritance had one by one been swept away.

But was Marchmont Towers quite as beautiful as that fairy palace of Mary's day-dream? No, not quite—not quite. The rooms were handsome,—handsomer and larger, even, than the rooms she had dreamed of; but perhaps none the better for that. They were grand and gloomy and magnificent; but they were not the sunlit chambers which her fancy had built up, and decorated with such shreds and patches of splendour as her narrow experience enabled her to devise. Perhaps it was rather a disappointment to Miss Marchmont to discover that the mansion was completely furnished, and that there was no room in it for any of those splendours which she had so often contemplated in the New Cut. The parrot at the greengrocer's was a vulgar bird, and not by any means admissible in Lincolnshire. The carrying away and providing for Mary's favourite tradespeople was not practicable; and John Marchmont had demurred to her proposal of adopting the butcher's daughter.

There is always something to be given up even when our brightest visions are realised; there is always some one figure (a low one perhaps) missing in the fullest sum of earthly happiness. I dare say if Alnaschar* had married the Vizier's daughter, he would have found her a shrew, and would have looked back yearningly to the humble days in which he had been an itinerant vendor of crockery-ware.

If, therefore, Mary Marchmont found her sunlit fancies not quite realised by the great stony mansion that frowned upon the fenny countryside, the wide grassy flat, the black pool, with its dismal shelter of weird pollard-willows, whose ugly reflections, distorted on the bosom of the quiet water, looked like the shadows of hump-backed men;—if these things did not compose as beautiful a picture as that which the little girl had carried so long in her mind, she had no more reason to be sorry than the rest of us, and had been no more foolish than other dreamers. I think she had built her airy castle too much after the model of a last scene in a pantomime, and that she expected to find spangled waters twinkling in perpetual sunshine, revolving fountains, ever-expanding sunflowers, and gilded clouds of rose-coloured gauze,—every thing except the fairies, in short,—at Marchmont Towers. Well, the dream was over: and she was quite a woman now, and very grateful to Providence when she remembered that her father had no longer need to toil for his daily bread, and that he was luxuriously lodged, and could have the first physicians in the land at his beck and call.

'Oh, papa, it is so nice to be rich!' the young lady would exclaim now and then, in a fleeting transport of enthusiasm. 'How good we ought to be to the poor people, when we remember how poor we once were!'

And the little girl did not forget to be good to the poor about Kemberling and Marchmont Towers. There were plenty of poor, of course—free-and-easy pensioners, who came to the Towers for brandy, and wine, and milk, and woollen stuffs, and grocery, precisely as they would have gone to a shop, except that there was to be no bill. The housekeeper doled out her bounties with many short homilies upon the depravity and ingratitude of the recipients, and gave tracts of an awful and denunciatory nature to the pitiful petitioners—tracts interrogatory, and tracts fiercely imperative; tracts that asked, 'Where are you going?' 'Why are you wicked?' 'What will become of you?' and other tracts which cried, 'Stop, and think!' 'Pause, while there is time!' 'Sinner, consider!' 'Evil-doer, beware!' Perhaps it may not be the wisest possible plan to begin the work of reformation by frightening, threatening, and otherwise disheartening the wretched sinner to be reformed. There is a certain sermon in the New Testament, containing sacred and comforting words which were spoken upon a mountain near at hand to Jerusalem, and spoken to an auditory amongst which there must have been many sinful creatures; but there is more of blessing than cursing in that sublime discourse, and it might be rather a tender father pleading gently with his wayward children that an offended Deity dealing out denunciation upon a stubborn and refractory race. But the authors of the tracts may have never read this sermon, perhaps; and they may take their ideas of composition from that comforting service which we read on Ash-Wednesday,* cowering in fear and trembling in our pews, and calling down curses upon ourselves and our neighbours. Be it as it might, the tracts were not popular amongst the pensioners of Marchmont Towers. They infinitely preferred to hear Mary read a chapter in the New Testament, or some pretty patriarchal story of primitive obedience and faith. The little girl would discourse upon the Scripture histories in her simple, old-fashioned manner; and many a stout Lincolnshire farm-labourer was content to sit over his hearth, with a pipe of shag-tobacco and a mug of fettled* beer while Miss Marchmont read and expounded the history of Abraham and Isaac, or Joseph and his brethren.

'It's joost loike a story-book to hear her,' the man would say to his wife; 'and yet she brings it all hoame, too, loike. If she reads about Abraham, she'll say, maybe, "That's joost how you gave your only son to be a soldier, you know, Muster Moggins;"—she allus says Muster Moggins;—"you gave un into God's hands, and you troosted God would take care of un; and whatever cam' to un would be the best, even if it was death." That's what she'll say, bless her little heart! so gentle and tender loike. The wust o' chaps couldn't but listen to her.'

Mary Marchmont's morbidly sensitive nature adapted her to all charitable offices. No chance word in her simple talk ever inflicted a wound upon the listener. She had a subtle and intuitive comprehension of other people's feelings, derived from the extreme susceptibility of her own. She had never been vulgarised by the associations of poverty; for her self-contained nature took no colour from the things that surrounded her, and she was only at Marchmont Towers that which she had been from the age of six—a little lady, grave and gentle, dignified, discreet, and wise.

There was one bright figure missing out of the picture which Mary had been wont of late years to make of the Lincolnshire mansion, and that was the figure of the yellow-haired boy who had breakfasted upon haddocks and hot rolls in Oakley Street. She had imagined Edward Arundel an inhabitant of that fair Utopia. He would live with them; or, if he could not live with them, he would be with them as a visitor,—often—almost always. He would leave off being a soldier, for of course her papa could give him more money than he could get by being a soldier—(you see that Mary's experience of poverty had taught her to take a mercantile and sordid view of military life)—and he would come to Marchmont Towers, and ride, and drive, and play tennis (what was tennis? she wondered), and read three-volume novels all day long. But that part of the dream was at least broken. Marchmont Towers was Mary's home, but the young soldier was far away; in the Pass of Bolan, perhaps,—Mary had a picture of that cruel rocky pass almost always in her mind,—or cutting his way through a black jungle, with the yellow eyes of hungry tigers glaring out at him through the rank tropical foliage; or dying of thirst and fever under a scorching sun, with no better pillow than the neck of a dead camel, with no more tender watcher than the impatient vulture flapping her wings above his head, and waiting till he, too, should be carrion. What was the good of wealth, if it could not bring this young soldier home to a safe shelter in his native land? John Marchmont smiled when his daughter asked this question, and implored her father to write to Edward Arundel, recalling him to England.

'God knows how glad I should be to have the boy here, Polly!' John said, as he drew his little girl closer to his breast,—she sat on his knee still, though she was thirteen years of age. 'But Edward has a career before him, my dear, and could not give it up for an inglorious life in this rambling old house. It isn't as if I could hold out any inducement to him: you know, Polly, I can't; for I mustn't leave any money away from my little girl.'

'But he might have half my money, papa, or all of it,' Mary added piteously. 'What could I do with money, if——?'

She didn't finish the sentence; she never could complete any such sentence as this; but her father knew what she meant.

So six months had passed since a dreary January day upon which John Marchmont had read, in the second column of the 'Times,' that he could hear of something greatly to his advantage by applying to a certain solicitor, whose offices were next door but one to those of Messrs. Paulette, Paulette, and Mathewson's. His heart began to beat very violently when he read that advertisement in the supplement, which it was one of his duties to air before the fire in the clerks' office; but he showed no other sign of emotion. He waited until he took the papers to his employer; and as he laid them at Mr Mathewson's elbow, murmured a respectful request to be allowed to go out for half-an-hour, upon his own business.

'Good gracious me, Marchmont!' cried the lawyer; 'what can you want to go out for at this time in the morning? You've only just come; and there's that agreement between Higgs and Sandyman must be copied before——'

'Yes, I know, sir. I'll be back in time to attend to it; but I—I think I've come into a fortune, sir; and I should like to go and see about it.'

The solicitor turned in his revolving library-chair, and looked aghast at his clerk. Had this Marchmont—always rather unnaturally reserved and eccentric—gone suddenly mad? No; the copying-clerk stood by his employer's side, grave, self-possessed as ever, with his forefinger upon the advertisement.

'Marchmont—John—call—Messrs Tindal and Trollam—' gasped Mr Mathewson. 'Do you mean to tell me it's *you*?'

'Yes, sir.'

'Egad, I'll go with you!' cried the solicitor, hooking his arm through that of his clerk, snatching his hat from an adjacent stand, and dashing through the outer office, down the great staircase, and into the next door but one before John Marchmont knew where he was.

John had not deceived his employer. Marchmont Towers was his, with all its appurtenances. Messrs Paulette, Paulette, and Mathewson took him in hand, much to the chagrin of Messrs Tindal and Trollam, and proved his identity in less than a week. On a shelf above the high wooden desk at which John had sat, copying law-papers, with a weary hand and an aching spine, appeared two bran-new deed-boxes, inscribed, in white letters, with the name and address of JOHN MARCHMONT, ESQ., MARCHMONT TOWERS. The copying-clerk's sudden accession to fortune was the talk of all the *employés* in 'The Fields.'* Marchmont Towers was exaggerated into half Lincolnshire, and a tidy slice of Yorkshire; eleven thousand a year was expanded into an annual million. Everybody expected *largesse* from the legatee. How fond people had been of the quiet clerk, and how magnanimously they had concealed their sentiments during his poverty, lest they should wound him, as they urged, 'which' they knew he was sensitive; and how expansively they now dilated on their long-suppressed emotions! Of course, under these circumstances, it is hardly likely that everybody could be satisfied; so it is a small thing to say that the dinner which John gave—by his late employers' suggestion (he was about the last man to think of giving a dinner)—at the 'Albion Tavern,' to the legal staff of Messrs Paulette, Paulette, and Mathewson, and such acquaintance of the legal profession as they should choose to invite, was a failure; and that gentlemen who were pretty well used to dine upon liver and bacon, or beefsteak and onions, or the joint, vegetables, bread, cheese, and celery for a shilling, turned up their noses at the turbot, murmured at the paucity of green fat in the soup, made light of red mullet and ortolans, objected to the flavour of the truffles, and were contemptuous about the wines.

John knew nothing of this. He had lived a separate and secluded existence; and his only thought now was of getting away to Marchmont Towers, which had been familiar to him in his boyhood, when he had been wont to go there on occasional visits to his grandfather. He wanted to get away from the turmoil and confusion of the big, heartless city, in which he had endured so much; he wanted to carry away his little girl to a quiet country home, and live and die there in peace. He liberally rewarded all the good people about Oakley Street who had been kind to little Mary; and there was weeping in the regions of the Ladies' Wardrobe when Mr Marchmont and his daughter went away one bitter winter's morning in a cab, which was to carry them to the hostelry whence the coach started for Lincoln.

It is strange to think how far those Oakley-street days of privation and endurance seem to have receded in the memories of both father and daughter. The impalpable past fades away, and it is difficult for John and his little girl to believe that they were once so poor and desolate. It is Oakley Street now that is visionary and unreal. The stately county families bear down upon Marchmont Towers in great lumbering chariots, with brazen crests upon the hammer-cloths,* and sulky coachmen in Brown-George wigs.* The county mammas patronise and caress Miss Marchmont—what a match she will be for one of the county sons by-and-by!—the county daughters discourse with Mary about her poor, and her fancy-work, and her piano. She is getting on slowly enough with her piano, poor little girl! under the tuition of the organist of Swampington, who gives lessons to that part of the county. And there are solemn dinners now and then at Marchmont Towers—dinners at which Miss Mary appears when the cloth has been removed, and reflects in silent wonder upon the change that has come to her father and herself. Can it be true that she has ever lived in Oakley Street, whither came no more aristocratic visitors than her Aunt Sophia, who was the wife of a Berkshire farmer, and always brought hogs' puddings, and butter, and home-made bread, and other rustic delicacies to her brother-in-law; or Mrs Brigsome, the washerwoman, who made a morning-call every Monday, to fetch John Marchmont's shabby shirts? The shirts were not shabby now; and it was no longer Mary's duty to watch them day by day, and manipulate them tenderly when the linen grew frayed at the sharp edges of the folds, or the buttonholes gave signs of weakness. Corson, Mr Marchmont's own-man, had care of the shirts now: and John wore diamond-studs and a black-satin waistcoat, when he gave a dinner-party. They were not very lively, those Lincolnshire dinner-parties; though the dessert was a sight to look upon, in Mary's eyes. The long shining table, the red and gold and purple Indian china, the fluffy woollen d'oyleys, the sparkling cutglass, the sticky preserved ginger and guava-jelly, and dried orange rings and chips, and all the stereotyped sweetmeats, were very grand and beautiful, no doubt; but Mary had seen livelier desserts in Oakley Street, though there had been nothing better than a brown-paper bag of oranges from the Westminster Road, and a bottle of two-and-twopenny Marsala from a licensed victualler's in the Borough, to promote conviviality.

CHAPTER VI

THE YOUNG SOLDIER'S RETURN

THE rain beats down upon the battlemented roof of Marchmont Towers this July day, as if it had a mind to flood the old mansion. The flat waste of grass, and the lonely clumps of trees, are almost blotted out by the falling rain. The low grey sky shuts out the distance. This part of Lincolnshire—fenny, misty, and flat always—seems flatter and mistier than usual to-day. The rain beats hopelessly upon the leaves in the wood behind Marchmont Towers, and splashes into great pools beneath the trees, until the ground is almost hidden by the fallen water, and the trees seem to be growing out of a black lake. The land is lower behind Marchmont Towers, and slopes down gradually to the bank of a dismal river, which straggles through the Marchmont property at a snail's pace, to gain an impetus farther on, until it hurries into the sea somewhere northward of Grimsby. The wood is not held in any great favour by the household at the Towers; and it has been a pet project of several Marchmonts to level and drain it, but a project not very easily to be carried out. Marchmont Towers is said to be unhealthy, as a dwelling-house, by reason of this wood, from which miasmas rise in certain states of the weather; and it is on this account that the back of the house—the eastern front, at least, as it is called—looking to the wood is very little used.

Mary Marchmont sits at a window in the western drawing-room, watching the ceaseless falling of the rain upon this dreary summer afternoon. She is little changed since the day upon which Edward Arundel saw her in Oakley Street. She is taller, of course, but her figure is as slender and childish as ever: it is only her face in which the earnestness of premature womanhood reveals itself in a grave and sweet serenity very beautiful to contemplate. Her soft brown eyes have a pensive shadow in their gentle light; her mouth is even more pensive. It has been said of Jane Grey, of Mary Stuart, of Marie Antoinette, Charlotte Corday, and other fated women, that in the gayest hours of their youth they bore upon some feature, or in some expression, the shadow of the End—an impalpable, indescribable presage of an awful future, vaguely felt by those who looked upon them.

Is it thus with Mary Marchmont? Has the solemn hand of Destiny set that shadowy brand upon the face of this child, that even in her prosperity, as in her adversity, she should be so utterly different from all other children? Is she already marked out for some womanly martyrdom—already set apart for more than common suffering?

She sits alone this afternoon, for her father is busy with his agent. Wealth does not mean immunity from all care and trouble; and Mr Marchmont has plenty of work to get through, in conjunction with his land-steward, a hard-headed Yorkshireman, who lives at Kemberling, and insists on doing his duty with pertinacious honesty.

The large brown eyes looked wistfully out at the dismal waste and the falling rain. There was a wretched equestrian making his way along the carriage-drive.

'Who can come to see us on such a day?' Mary thought. 'It must be Mr Gormby, I suppose;'—the agent's name was Gormby. 'Mr Gormby never cares about the wet; but then I thought he was with papa. Oh, I hope it isn't anybody coming to call.'

But Mary forgot all about the struggling equestrian the next moment. She had some morsel of fancy-work upon her lap, and picked it up and went on with it, setting slow stitches, and letting her thoughts wander far away from Marchmont Towers—to India, I am afraid; or to that imaginary India which she had created for herself out of such images as were to be picked up in the 'Arabian Nights.' She was roused suddenly by the opening of a door at the farther end of the room, and by the voice of a servant, who mumbled a name which sounded something like Mr Armenger.

She rose, blushing a little, to do honour to one of her father's county acquaintance, as she thought; when a fair-haired gentleman dashed in, very much excited and very wet, and made his way towards her.

'I *would* come, Miss Marchmont,' he said,—'I would come, though the day was so wet. Everybody vowed I was mad to think of it, and it was as much as my poor brute of a horse could do to get over the ten miles of swamp between this and my uncle's house; but I would come! Where's John? I want to see John. Didn't I always tell him he'd come into the Lincolnshire property? Didn't I always say so, now? You should have seen Martin Mostyn's face—he's got a capital berth in the War Office, and he's such a snob!—when I told him the news: it was as long as my arm! But I must see John, dear old fellow! I long to congratulate him.'

Mary stood with her hands clasped, and her breath coming quickly. The blush had quite faded out, and left her unusually pale. But Edward Arundel did not see this: young gentlemen of four-and-twenty are not very attentive to every change of expression in little girls of thirteen.

'Oh, is it you, Mr Arundel? Is it really you?'

She spoke in a low voice, and it was almost difficult to keep the rushing tears back while she did so. She had pictured him so often in peril, in famine, in sickness, in death, that to see him here, well, happy, light-hearted, cordial, handsome, and brave, as she had seen him four-and-a-half years before in the two-pair back in Oakley Street, was almost too much for her to bear without the relief of tears. But she controlled her emotion as bravely as if she had been a woman of twenty.

'I am so glad to see you,' she said quietly; 'and papa will be so glad too! It is the only thing we want, now we are rich; to have you with us. We have talked of you so often; and I—we—have been so unhappy sometimes, thinking that——'

'That I should be killed, I suppose?'

'Yes; or wounded very, very badly. The battles in India have been dreadful, have they not?'

Mr Arundel smiled at her earnestness.

'They have not been exactly child's play,' he said, shaking back his chestnut hair and smoothing his thick moustache. He was a man now, and a very handsome one; something of that type which is known in this year of grace as 'swell';* but brave and chivalrous withal, and not afflicted with any impediment in his speech. 'The men who talk of the Afghans as a chicken-hearted set of fellows are rather out of their reckoning. The Indians can fight, Miss Mary, and fight like the devil; but we can lick 'em!'

He walked over to the fireplace—where, upon this chilly wet day, there was a fire burning—and began to shake himself dry. Mary, following him with her eyes, wondered if there was such another soldier in all Her Majesty's dominions, and how soon he would be made General-in-Chief of the Army of the Indus.

'Then you've not been wounded at all, Mr Arundel?' she said, after a pause.

'Oh, yes, I've been wounded; I got a bullet in my shoulder from an Afghan musket, and I'm home on sick-leave.'

This time he saw the expression of her face, and interpreted her look of alarm.

'But I'm not ill, you know, Miss Marchmont,' he said, laughing. 'Our fellows are very glad of a wound when they feel home-sick. The 8th come home before long, all of 'em; and I've a twelvemonth's leave of absence; and we're pretty sure to be ordered out again by the end of that time, as I don't believe there's much chance of quiet over there.'

'You will go out again!——'

Edward Arundel smiled at her mournful tone.

'To be sure, Miss Mary. I have my captaincy to win, you know; I'm only a lieutenant, as yet.'

It was only a twelvemonth's reprieve, after all, then, Mary thought. He would go back again—to suffer, and to be wounded, and to die, perhaps. But then, on the other hand, there was a twelve-month's respite; and her father might in that time prevail upon the young soldier to stay at Marchmont Towers. It was such inexpress-ible happiness to see him once more, to know that he was safe and well, that Mary could scarcely do otherwise than see all things in a sunny light just now.

She ran to John Marchmont's study to tell him of the coming of this welcome visitor; but she wept upon her father's shoulder before she could explain who it was whose coming had made her so glad. Very few friendships had broken the monotony of her solitary exist-ence; and Edward Arundel was the only chivalrous image she had ever known, out of her books.

John Marchmont was scarcely less pleased than his child to see the man who had befriended him in his poverty. Never has more heart-felt welcome been given than that which greeted Edward Arundel at Marchmont Towers.

'You will stay with us, of course, my dear Arundel,' John said; 'you will stop for September and the shooting. You know you promised you'd make this your shooting-box; and we'll build the tennis-court. Heaven knows, there's room enough for it in the great quadrangle; and there's a billiard-room over this, though I'm afraid the table is out of order. But we can soon set that right, can't we, Polly?'

'Yes, yes, papa; out of my pocket-money, if you like.'

Mary Marchmont said this in all good faith. It was sometimes difficult for her to remember that her father was really rich, and had no need of help out of her pocket-money. The slender savings in her little purse had often given him some luxury that he would not otherwise have had, in the time gone by.

'You got my letter, then?' John said; 'the letter in which I told you——'

'That Marchmont Towers was yours. Yes, my dear old boy. That letter was amongst a packet my agent brought me half-an-hour before I left Calcutta. God bless you, dear old fellow; how glad I was to hear of it! I've only been in England a fortnight. I went straight from Southampton to Dangerfield to see my father and mother, stayed there little over ten days, and then offended them all by running away. I reached Swampington yesterday, slept at my uncle Hubert's, paid my respects to my cousin Olivia, who is,—well, I've told you what she is,— and rode over here this morning, much to the annoyance of the inhabitants of the Rectory. So, you see, I've been doing nothing but offending people for your sake, John; and for yours, Miss Mary. By-the-by, I've brought you such a doll!'

A doll! Mary's pale face flushed a faint crimson. Did he think her still a child, then, this soldier; did he think her only a silly child, with no thought above a doll, when she would have gone out to India, and braved every peril of that cruel country, to be his nurse and comfort in fever and sickness, like the brave Sisters of Mercy she had read of in some of her novels?

Edward Arundel saw that faint crimson glow lighting up in her face.

'I beg your pardon, Miss Marchmont,' he said. 'I was only joking; of course you are a young lady now, almost grown up, you know. Can you play chess?'

'No, Mr Arundel.'

'I am sorry for that; for I have brought you a set of chessmen that once belonged to Dost Mahommed Khan.* But I'll teach you the game, if you like?'

'Oh, yes, Mr Arundel; I should like it very, very much.'

The young soldier could not help being amused by the little girl's earnestness. She was about the same age as his sister Letitia; but, oh, how widely different to that bouncing and rather wayward young lady, who tore the pillow-lace upon her muslin frocks, rumpled her long ringlets, rasped the skin off the sharp points of her elbows by repeated falls upon the gravel-paths at Dangerfield, and tormented a long-suffering Swiss attendant, half-lady's-maid, half-governess, from morning till night. No fold was awry in Mary Marchmont's simple black-silk frock; no plait disarranged in the neat cambric tucker* that encircled the slender white throat. Intellect here reigned supreme. Instead of the animal spirits of a thoughtless child, there was a woman's loving carefulness for others, a woman's unselfishness and devotion.

Edward Arundel did not understand all this, but I think he had a dim comprehension of the greater part of it.

'She is a dear little thing,' he thought, as he watched her clinging to her father's arm; and then he began to talk about Marchmont Towers, and insisted upon being shown over the house; and, perhaps for the first time since the young heir had shot himself to death upon a bright September morning in a stubble-field within earshot of the park, the sound of merry laughter echoed through the long corridors, and resounded in the unoccupied rooms.

Edward Arundel was in raptures with everything. 'There never was such a dear old place,' he said. '"Gloomy?" "dreary?" "draughty?" pshaw! Cut a few logs out of that wood at the back there, pile 'em up in the wide chimneys, and set a light to 'em, and Marchmont Towers would be like a baronial mansion at Christmas-time.' He declared that every dingy portrait he looked at was a Rubens or a Velasquez, or a Vandyke, a Holbein, or a Lely.*

'Look at that fur border to the old woman's black-velvet gown, John; look at the colouring of the hands! Do you think anybody but Peter Paul could have painted that? Do you see that girl with the blue-satin stomacher* and the flaxen ringlets?—one of your ancestresses, Miss Mary, and very like you. If that isn't in Sir Peter Lely's best style,—his earlier style, you know, before he was spoiled by royal patronage, and got lazy,—I know nothing of painting.'

The young soldier ran on in this manner, as he hurried his host from room to room; now throwing open windows to look out at the wet prospect; now rapping against the wainscot to find secret hiding-places behind sliding panels; now stamping on the oak-flooring in the hope of discovering a trap-door. He pointed out at least ten eligible sites for the building of the tennis-court; he suggested more alterations and improvements than a builder could have completed in a lifetime. The place brightened under the influence of his presence, as a landscape lights up under a burst of sudden sunshine breaking through a dull grey sky.

Mary Marchmont did not wait for the removal of the table-cloth that evening, but dined with her father and his friend in a snug oak-panelled chamber, half-breakfast-room, half-library, which opened out of the western drawing-room. How different Edward Arundel was to all the rest of the world, Miss Marchmont thought; how gay, how bright, how genial, how happy! The county families, mustered in their fullest force, couldn't make such mirth amongst them as this young soldier created in his single person.

The evening was an evening in fairy-land. Life was sometimes like the last scene in a pantomime, after all, with rose-coloured cloud and golden sunlight.

One of the Marchmont servants went over to Swampington early the next day to fetch Mr Arundel's portmanteaus from the Rectory; and after dinner upon that second evening, Mary Marchmont took her seat opposite Edward, and listened reverently while he explained to her the moves upon the chessboard.

'So you don't know my cousin Olivia?' the young soldier said by-and-by. 'That's odd! I should have thought she would have called upon you long before this.'

Mary Marchmont shook her head.

'No,' she said; 'Miss Arundel has never been to see us; and I should so like to have seen her, because she would have told me about you. Mr Arundel has called one or twice upon papa; but I have never seen him. He is not our clergyman, you know; Marchmont Towers belongs to Kemberling parish.'

'To be sure; and Swampington is ten miles off. But, for all that, I should have thought Olivia would have called upon you. I'll drive you over to-morrow, if John thinks me whip enough to trust you with me, and you shall see Livy. The Rectory's such a queer old place!'

Perhaps Mr Marchmont was rather doubtful as to the propriety of committing his little girl to Edward Arundel's charioteership for a ten-mile drive upon a wretched road. Be it as it might, a lumbering barouche, with a pair of over-fed horses, was ordered next morning, instead of the high, old-fashioned gig* which the soldier had proposed driving; and the safety of the two young people was confided to a sober old coachman, rather sulky at the prospect of a drive to Swampington so soon after the rainy weather.

It does not rain always, even in this part of Lincolnshire; and the July morning was bright and pleasant, the low hedges fragrant with starry opal-tinted wild roses and waxen honeysuckle, the yellowing corn waving in the light summer breeze. Mary assured her companion that she had no objection whatever to the odour of cigar-smoke; so Mr Arundel lolled upon the comfortable cushions of the barouche, with his back to the horses, smoking cheroots, and talking gaily, while Miss Marchmont sat in the place of state opposite to him. A happy drive; a drive in a fairy chariot through regions of fairyland, for ever and for ever to be remembered by Mary Marchmont.

They left the straggling hedges and the yellowing corn behind them by-and-by, as they drew near the outskirts of Swampington. The town lies lower even than the surrounding country, flat and low as that country is. A narrow river crawls at the base of a half-ruined wall, which once formed part of the defences of the place. Black barges lie at anchor here; and a stone bridge, guarded by a toll-house, spans the river. Mr Marchmont's carriage lumbered across this bridge, and under an archway, low, dark, stony, and grim, into a narrow street of solid, well-built houses, low, dark, stony, and grim, like the archway, but bearing the stamp of reputable occupation. I believe the grass grew, and still grows, in this street, as it does in all the other streets and in the market-place of Swampington. They are all pretty much in the same style, these streets,—all stony, narrow, dark, and grim; and they wind and twist hither and thither, and in and out, in a manner utterly bewildering to the luckless stranger, who, seeing that they are all alike, has no landmarks for his guidance.

There are two handsome churches, both bearing an early date in the history of Norman supremacy: one crowded into an inconvenient corner of a back street, and choked by the houses built up round about it; the other lying a little out of the town, upon a swampy waste looking towards the sea, which flows within a mile of Swampington. Indeed, there is no lack of water in that Lincolnshire borough. The river winds about the outskirts of the town: unexpected creeks and inlets meet you at every angle; shallow pools lie here and there about the marshy suburbs; and in the dim distance the low line of the grey sea meets the horizon.

But perhaps the positive ugliness of the town is something redeemed by a vague air of romance and old-world mystery which pervades it. It is an exceptional place, and somewhat interesting thereby. The great Norman church upon the swampy waste, the scattered tombstones, bordered by the low and moss-grown walls, make a picture which is apt to dwell in the minds of those who look upon it, although it is by no means a pretty picture. The Rectory lies close to the churchyard; and a wicket-gate opens from Mr Arundel's garden into a narrow pathway, leading across a patch of tangled grass and through a lane of sunken and lop-sided tombstones, to the low vestry door. The Rectory itself is a long irregular building, to which one incumbent after another has built the additional chamber, or chimney, or porch, or bow-window, necessary for his accommodation. There is very little garden in front of the house, but a patch of lawn and shrubbery and a clump of old trees at the back.

'It's not a pretty house, is it, Miss Marchmont?' asked Edward, as he lifted his companion out of the carriage.

'No, not very pretty,' Mary answered; 'but I don't think any thing is pretty in Lincolnshire. Oh, there's the sea!' she cried, looking suddenly across the marshes to the low grey line in the distance. 'How I wish we were as near the sea at Marchmont Towers!'

The young lady had something of a romantic passion for the wide-spreading ocean. It was an unknown region, that stretched far away, and was wonderful and beautiful by reason of its solemn mystery. All her Corsair stories were allied to that far, fathomless deep. The white sail in the distance was Conrad's, perhaps; and he was speeding homeward to find Medora* dead in her lonely watch-tower, with fading flowers upon her breast. The black hull yonder, with dirty canvas spread to the faint breeze, was the bark of some terrible pirate bound on rapine and ravage. (She was a coal-barge, I have no doubt, sailing Londonward with her black burden.) Nymphs and Lurleis,* Mermaids and Mermen, and tiny water-babies with silvery tails, for ever splashing in the sunshine, were all more or less associated with the long grey line towards which Mary Marchmont looked with solemn, yearning eyes.

'We'll drive down to the seashore some morning, Polly,' said Mr Arundel. He was beginning to call her Polly, now and then, in the easy familiarity of their intercourse. 'We'll spend a long day on the sands, and I'll smoke cheroots while you pick up shells and seaweed.'

Miss Marchmont clasped her hands in silent rapture. Her face was irradiated by the new light of happiness. How good he was to her, this brave soldier, who must undoubtedly be made Commander-in-Chief of the Army of the Indus in a year or so!

Edward Arundel led his companion across the flagged way between the iron gate of the Rectory garden and a half-glass door leading into the hall. Out of this simple hall, only furnished with a couple of chairs, a barometer, and an umbrella-stand, they went, without announcement, into a low, old-fashioned room, half-study, half-parlour, where a young lady was sitting at a table writing.

She rose as Edward opened the door, and came to meet him.

'At last!' she said; 'I thought your rich friends engrossed all your attention.'

She paused, seeing Mary.

'This is Miss Marchmont, Olivia,' said Edward; 'the only daughter of my old friend. You must be very fond of her, please; for she is a dear little girl, and I know she means to love you.'

Mary lifted her soft brown eyes to the face of the young lady, and then dropped her eyelids suddenly, as if half-frightened by what she had seen there.

What was it? What was it in Olivia Arundel's handsome face from which those who looked at her so often shrank, repelled and disappointed? Every line in those perfectly-modelled features was beautiful to look at; but, as a whole, the face was not beautiful. Perhaps it was too much like a marble mask, exquisitely chiselled, but wanting in variety of expression. The handsome mouth was rigid; the dark grey eyes had a cold light in them. The thick bands of raven-black hair were drawn tightly off a square forehead, which was the brow of an intellectual and determined man rather than of a woman. Yes; womanhood was the something wanted in Olivia Arundel's face. Intellect, resolution, courage, are rare gifts; but they are not the gifts whose tokens we look for most anxiously in a woman's face. If Miss Arundel had been a queen, her diadem would have become her nobly; and she might have been a very great queen: but Heaven help the wretched creature who had appealed from minor tribunals to *her* mercy! Heaven help delinquents of every kind whose last lingering hope had been in her compassion!

Perhaps Mary Marchmont vaguely felt something of all this. At any rate, the enthusiasm with which she had been ready to regard Edward Arundel's cousin cooled suddenly beneath the winter in that pale, quiet face.

Miss Arundel said a few words to her guest; kindly enough; but rather too much as if she had been addressing a child of six. Mary, who was accustomed to be treated as a woman, was wounded by her manner.

'How different she is from Edward!' thought Miss Marchmont. 'I shall never like her as I like him.'

'So this is the pale-faced child who is to have Marchmont Towers by-and-by,' thought Miss Arundel; 'and these rich friends are the people for whom Edward stays away from us.'

The lines about the rigid mouth grew harder, the cold light in the grey eyes grew colder, as the young lady thought this.

It was thus that these two women met: while one was but a child in years; while the other was yet in the early bloom of womanhood: these two, who were predestined to hate each other, and inflict suffering upon each other in the days that were to come. It was thus that they thought of one another; each with an unreasonable dread, an undefined aversion gathering in her breast.

Six weeks passed, and Edward Arundel kept his promise of shooting the partridges on the Marchmont preserves. The wood behind the Towers, and the stubbled corn-fields on the home-farm, bristled with game. The young soldier heartily enjoyed himself through that delicious first week in September; and came home every afternoon, with a heavy game-bag and a light heart, to boast of his prowess before Mary and her father.

The young man was by this time familiar with every nook and corner of Marchmont Towers; and the builders were already at work at the tennis-court which John had promised to erect for his friend's pleasure. The site ultimately chosen was a bleak corner of the eastern front, looking to the wood; but, as Edward declared the spot in every way eligible, John had no inclination to find fault with his friend's choice. There was other work for the builders; for Mr Arundel had taken a wonderful fancy to a ruined boat-house upon the brink of the river; and this boat-house was to be rebuilt and restored, and made into a delightful pavilion, in the upper chambers of which Mary might sit with her father in the hot summer weather, while Mr Arundel kept a couple of trim wherries in the recesses below.

So, you see, the young man made himself very much at home, in his own innocent, boyish fashion, at Marchmont Towers. But as he had brought life and light to the old Lincolnshire mansion, nobody was inclined to quarrel with him for any liberties which he might choose to take: and every one looked forward sorrowfully to the dark days before Christmas, at which time he was under a promise to return to Dangerfield Park; there to spend the remainder of his leave of absence.

CHAPTER VII

OLIVIA

WHILE busy workmen were employed at Marchmont Towers, hammering at the fragile wooden walls of the tennis-court,—while Mary Marchmont and Edward Arundel wandered, with the dogs at their heels, amongst the rustle of the fallen leaves in the wood behind the great gaunt Lincolnshire mansion,—Olivia, the Rector's daughter, sat in her father's quiet study, or walked to and fro in the gloomy streets of Swampington, doing her duty day by day.

Yes, the life of this woman is told in these few words: she did her duty. From the earliest age at which responsibility can begin, she had done her duty, uncomplainingly, unswervingly, as it seemed to those who watched her.

She was a good woman. The bishop of the diocese had specially complimented her for her active devotion to that holy work which falls somewhat heavily upon the only daughter of a widowed rector. All the stately dowagers about Swampington were loud in their praises of Olivia Arundel. Such devotion, such untiring zeal in a young person of three-and-twenty years of age, were really most laudable, these solemn elders said, in tones of supreme patronage; for the young saint of whom they spoke wore shabby gowns, and was the portionless daughter of a poor man who had let the world slip by him, and who sat now amid the dreary ruins of a wasted life, looking yearningly backward, with hollow regretful eyes, and bewailing the chances he had lost. Hubert Arundel loved his daughter; loved her with that sorrowful affection we feel for those who suffer for our sins, whose lives have been blighted by our follies.

Every shabby garment which Olivia wore was a separate reproach to her father; every deprivation she endured stung him as cruelly as if she had turned upon him and loudly upbraided him for his wasted life and his squandered patrimony. He loved her; and he watched her day after day, doing her duty to him as to all others; doing her duty for ever and for ever; but when he most yearned to take her to his heart, her own cold perfections arose, and separated him from the child he loved. What was he but a poor, vacillating, erring creature; weak, supine, idle, epicurean; unworthy to approach this girl, who never seemed to sicken of the hardness of her life, who never grew weary of well-doing?

But how was it that, for all her goodness, Olivia Arundel won so small a share of earthly reward? I do not allude to the gold and jewels and other worldly benefits with which the fairies in our children's story-books reward the benevolent mortals who take compassion upon them when they experimentalise with human nature in the guise of old women; but I speak rather of the love and gratitude, the tenderness and blessings, which usually wait upon the footsteps of those who do good deeds. Olivia Arundel's charities were never ceasing; her life was one perpetual sacrifice to her father's parishioners. There was no natural womanly vanity, no simple girlish fancy, which this woman had not trodden under foot, and trampled out in the hard pathway she had chosen for herself.

The poor people knew this. Rheumatic men and women, crippled and bed-ridden, knew that the blankets which covered them had been bought out of money that would have purchased silk dresses for the Rector's handsome daughter, or luxuries for the frugal table at the Rectory. They knew this. They knew that, through frost and snow, through storm and rain, Olivia Arundel would come to sit beside their dreary hearths, their desolate sick-beds, and read holy books to them; sublimely indifferent to the foul weather without, to the stifling atmosphere within, to dirt, discomfort, poverty, inconvenience; heedless of all, except the performance of the task she had set herself.

People knew this; and they were grateful to Miss Arundel, and submissive and attentive in her presence; they gave her such return as they were able to give for the benefits, spiritual and temporal, which she bestowed upon them: but they did not love her.

They spoke of her in reverential accents, and praised her whenever her name was mentioned; but they spoke with tearless eyes and unfaltering voices. Her virtues were beautiful, of course, as virtue in the abstract must always be; but I think there was a want of individuality in her goodness, a lack of personal tenderness in her kindness, which separated her from the people she benefited.

Perhaps there was something almost chilling in the dull monotony of Miss Arundel's benevolence. There was no blemish of mortal weakness upon the good deeds she performed; and the recipients of her bounties, seeing her so far off, grew afraid of her, even by reason of her goodness, and *could* not love her.

She made no favourites amongst her father's parishioners. Of all the school-children she had taught, she had never chosen one curly-headed urchin for a pet. She had no good days and bad days; she was never foolishly indulgent or extravagantly cordial. She was always the same,—Church-of-England charity personified; meting out all mercies by line and rule; doing good with a note-book and a pencil in her hand; looking on every side with calm, scrutinising eyes; rigidly just, terribly perfect.

It was a fearfully monotonous, narrow, and uneventful life which Olivia Arundel led at Swampington Rectory. At three-and-twenty years of age she could have written her history upon a few pages. The world outside that dull Lincolnshire town might be shaken by convulsions, and made irrecognisable by repeated change; but all those outer changes and revolutions made themselves but little felt in the quiet grass-grown streets, and the flat surrounding swamps, within whose narrow boundary Olivia Arundel had lived from infancy to womanhood; performing and repeating the same duties from day to day, with no other progress to mark the lapse of her existence than the slow alternation of the seasons, and the dark hollow circles which had lately deepened beneath her grey eyes, and the depressed lines about the corners of her firm lower-lip.

These outward tokens, beyond her own control, alone betrayed this woman's secret. She was weary of her life. She sickened under the dull burden which she had borne so long, and carried so patiently. The slow round of duty was loathsome to her. The horrible, narrow, unchanging existence, shut in by cruel walls, which bounded her on every side and kept her prisoner to herself, was odious to her. The powerful intellect revolted against the fetters that bound and galled it. The proud heart beat with murderous violence against the bonds that kept it captive.

'Is my life always to be this—always, always, always?' The passionate nature burst forth sometimes, and the voice that had so long been stifled cried aloud in the black stillness of the night, 'Is it to go on for ever and for ever; like the slow river that creeps under the broken wall? O my God! is the lot of other women never to be mine? Am I never to be loved and admired; never to be sought and chosen?

Is my life to be all of one dull, grey, colourless monotony; without one sudden gleam of sunshine, without one burst of rainbow-light?'

How shall I anatomise this woman, who, gifted with no womanly tenderness of nature, unendowed with that pitiful and unreasoning affection which makes womanhood beautiful, yet tried, and tried unceasingly, to do her duty, and to be good; clinging, in the very blindness of her soul, to the rigid formulas of her faith, but unable to seize upon its spirit? Some latent comprehension of the want in her nature made her only the more scrupulous in the performance of those duties which she had meted out for herself. The holy sentences she had heard, Sunday after Sunday, feebly read by her father, haunted her perpetually, and would not be put away from her. The tenderness in every word of those familiar gospels was a reproach to the want of tenderness in her own heart. She could be good to her father's parishioners, and she could make sacrifices for them; but she could not love them, any more than they could love her.

That divine and universal pity, that spontaneous and boundless affection, which is the chief loveliness of womanhood and Christianity, had no part in her nature. She could understand Judith* with the Assyrian general's gory head held aloft in her uplifted hand; but she could not comprehend that diviner mystery of sinful Magdalene* sitting at her Master's feet, with the shame and love in her face half hidden by a veil of drooping hair.

No; Olivia Arundel was not a good woman, in the commoner sense we attach to the phrase. It was not natural to her to be gentle and tender, to be beneficent, compassionate, and kind, as it is to the women we are accustomed to call 'good.' She was a woman who was for ever fighting against her nature; who was for ever striving to do right; for ever walking painfully upon the difficult road mapped out for her; for ever measuring herself by the standard she had set up for her self-abasement. And who shall say that such a woman as this, if she persevere unto the end, shall not wear a brighter crown than her more gentle sisters,—the starry circlet of a martyr?

If she persevere unto the end! But was Olivia Arundel the woman to do this? The deepening circles about her eyes, the hollowing cheeks, and the feverish restlessness of manner which she could not always control, told how terrible the long struggle had become to her. If she could have died then,—if she had fallen beneath the weight of her burden,—what a record of sin and anguish might have remained unwritten in the history of woman's life! But this woman was one of those who can suffer, and yet not die. She bore her burden a little longer; only to fling it down by-and-by, and to abandon herself to the eager devils who had been watching for her so untiringly.

Hubert Arundel was afraid of his daughter. The knowledge that he had wronged her,—wronged her even before her birth by the foolish waste of his patrimony, and wronged her through life by his lack of energy in seeking such advancement as a more ambitious man might have won,—the knowledge of this, and of his daughter's superior virtues, combined to render the father ashamed and humiliated by the presence of his only child. The struggle between this fear and his remorseful love of her was a very painful one; but fear had the mastery, and the Rector of Swampington was content to stand aloof, mutely watchful of his daughter, wondering feebly whether she was happy, striving vainly to discover that one secret, that keystone of the soul, which must exist in every nature, however outwardly commonplace.

Mr Arundel had hoped that his daughter would marry, and marry well, even at Swampington; for there were rich young landowners who visited at the Rectory. But Olivia's handsome face won her few admirers, and at three-and-twenty Miss Arundel had received no offer of marriage. The father reproached himself for this. It was he who had blighted the life of his penniless girl; it was his fault that no suitors came to woo his motherless child. Yet many dowerless maidens have been sought and loved; and I do not think it was Olivia's lack of fortune which kept admirers at bay. I believe it was rather that inherent want of tenderness which chilled and dispirited the timid young Lincolnshire squires.

Had Olivia ever been in love ? Hubert Arundel constantly asked himself this question. He did so because he saw that some blighting influence, even beyond the poverty and dulness of her home, had fallen upon the life of his only child. What was it ? What was it? Was it some hopeless attachment, some secret tenderness, which had never won the sweet return of love for love?

He would no more have ventured to question his daughter upon this subject than he would have dared to ask his fair young Queen, newly married* in those days, whether she was happy with her handsome husband.

Miss Arundel stood by the Rectory gate in the early September

evening, watching the western sunlight on the low sea-line beyond
the marshes. She was wearied and worn out by a long day devoted to
visiting amongst her parishioners; and she stood with her elbow
leaning on the gate, and her head resting on her hand, in an attitude
peculiarly expressive of fatigue. She had thrown off her bonnet,
and her black hair was pushed carelessly from her forehead. Those
masses of hair had not that purple lustre, nor yet that wandering
glimmer of red gold, which gives peculiar beauty to some raven
tresses. Olivia's hair was long and luxuriant; but it was of that dead,
inky blackness, which is all shadow. It was dark, fathomless, inscrutable, like herself. The cold grey eyes looked thoughtfully seaward.
Another day's duty had been done. Long chapters of Holy Writ had
been read to troublesome old women afflicted with perpetual coughs;
stifling, airless cottages had been visited; the dull, unvarying track
had been beaten by the patient feet, and the yellow sun was going
down upon another joyless day. But did the still evening hour bring
peace to that restless spirit? No; by the rigid compression of the lips,
by the feverish lustre in the eyes, by the faint hectic flush in the oval
cheeks, by every outward sign of inward unrest, Olivia Arundel was
not at peace! The listlessness of her attitude was merely the listlessness of physical fatigue. The mental struggle was not finished with
the close of the day's work.

The young lady looked up suddenly as the tramp of a horse's
hoofs, slow and lazy-sounding on the smooth road, met her ear. Her
eyes dilated, and her breath went and came more rapidly; but she did
not stir from her weary attitude.

The horse was from the stables at Marchmont Towers, and the
rider was Mr Arundel. He came smiling to the Rectory gate, with the
low sunshine glittering in his chestnut hair, and the light of careless,
indifferent happiness irradiating his handsome face.

'You must have thought I'd forgotten you and my uncle, my dear
Livy,' he said, as he sprang lightly from his horse. 'We've been so
busy with the tennis-court, and the boat-house, and the partridges,
and goodness knows what besides at the Towers, that I couldn't get
the time to ride over till this evening. But to-day we dined early, on
purpose that I might have the chance of getting here. I come upon an
important mission, Livy, I assure you.'

'What do you mean?'

There was no change in Miss Arundel's voice when she spoke to her cousin; but there was a change, not easily to be defined, in her face when she looked at him. It seemed as if that weary hopelessness of expression which had settled on her countenance lately grew more weary, more hopeless, as she turned towards this bright young soldier, glorious in the beauty of his own light-heartedness. It may have been merely the sharpness of contrast which produced this effect. It may have been an actual change arising out of some secret hidden in Olivia's breast.

'What do you mean by an important mission, Edward?' she said.

She had need to repeat the question; for the young man's attention had wandered from her, and he was watching his horse as the animal cropped the tangled herbage about the Rectory gate.

'Why, I've come with an invitation to a dinner at Marchmont Towers. There's to be a dinner-party; and, in point of fact, it's to be given on purpose for you and my uncle. John and Polly are full of it. You'll come, won't you, Livy?'

Miss Arundel shrugged her shoulders, with an impatient sigh.

'I hate dinner-parties,' she said ; 'but, of course, if papa accepts Mr Marchmont's invitation, I cannot refuse to go. Papa must choose for himself.'

There had been some interchange of civilities between Marchmont Towers and Swampington Rectory during the six weeks which had passed since Mary's introduction to Olivia Arundel; and this dinner-party was the result of John's simple desire to do honour to his friend's kindred.

'Oh, you must come, Livy,' Mr Arundel exclaimed. 'The tennis-court is going on capitally. I want you to give us your opinion again. Shall I take my horse round to the stables? I am going to stop an hour or two, and ride back by moonlight.'

Edward Arundel took the bridle in his hand, and the cousins walked slowly round by the low garden-wall to a dismal and rather dilapidated stable-yard at the back of the Rectory, where Hubert Arundel kept a wall-eyed white horse, long-legged, shallow-chested, and large-headed, and a fearfully and wonderfully made phaëton, with high wheels and a mouldy leathern hood.

Olivia walked by the young soldier's side with that air of hopeless indifference that had so grown upon her very lately. Her eyelids drooped with a look of sullen disdain; but the grey eyes glanced furtively now and again at her companion's handsome face. He was very handsome. The glitter of reddish gold in his hair, and the light in his fearless blue eyes; the careless grace peculiar to the kind of man we call 'a swell;' the gay *insouciance* of an easy, candid, generous nature,— all combined to make Edward Arundel singularly attractive. These spoiled children of nature demand our admiration, in very spite of ourselves. These beautiful, useless creatures call upon us to rejoice in their valueless beauty, like the flaunting poppies in the cornfield, and the gaudy wild-flowers in the grass.

The darkness of Olivia's face deepened after each furtive glance she cast at her cousin. Could it be that this girl, to whom nature had given strength but denied grace, envied the superficial attractions of the young man at her side? She did envy him; she envied him that sunny temperament which was so unlike her own; she envied him that wondrous power of taking life lightly. Why should existence be so bright and careless to him; while to her it was a terrible fever-dream, a long sickness, a never-ceasing battle?

'Is my uncle in the house?' Mr Arundel asked, as he strolled from the stable into the garden with his cousin by his side.

'No; he has been out since dinner,' Olivia answered; 'but I expect him back every minute. I came out into the garden,—the house seemed so hot and stifling to-night, and I have been sitting in close cottages all day.'

'Sitting in close cottages !' repeated Edward. 'Ah, to be sure; visiting your rheumatic old pensioners, I suppose. How good you are, Olivia!'

'Good!'

She echoed the word in the very bitterness of a scorn that could not be repressed.

'Yes; everybody says so. The Millwards were at Marchmont Towers the other day, and they were talking of you, and praising your goodness, and speaking of your schools, and your blanket-associations, and your invalid-societies, and your mutual-help clubs, and all your plans for the parish. Why, you must work as hard as a prime-minister, Livy, by their account; you, who are only a few years older than I.'

Only a few years! She started at the phrase, and bit her lip.

'I was three-and-twenty last month,' she said.

'Ah, yes; to be sure. And I'm one-and-twenty. Then you're only two years older than I, Livy. But, then, you see, you're so clever, that you seem much older than you are. You'd make a fellow feel rather afraid of you, you know. Upon my word you do, Livy.'

Miss Arundel did not reply to this speech of her cousin's. She was walking by his side up and down a narrow gravelled pathway, bordered by a hazel-hedge; she had gathered one of the slender twigs, and was idly stripping away the fluffy buds.

'What do you think, Livy?' cried Edward suddenly, bursting out laughing at the end of the question. 'What do you think? It's my belief you've made a conquest.'

'What do you mean?'

'There you go; turning upon a fellow as if you could eat him. Yes, Livy; it's no use your looking savage. You've made a conquest; and of one of the best fellows in the world, too. John Marchmont's in love with you.'

Olivia Arundel's face flushed a vivid crimson to the roots of her black hair.

'How dare you come here to insult me, Edward Arundel?' she cried passionately.

'Insult you? Now, Livy dear, that's too bad, upon my word,' remonstrated the young man. 'I come and tell you that as good a man as ever breathed is over head and ears in love with you, and that you may be mistress of one of the finest estates in Lincolnshire if you please, and you turn round upon me like no end of furies.'

'Because I hate to hear you talk nonsense,' answered Olivia, her bosom still heaving with that first outburst of emotion, but her voice suppressed and cold. 'Am I so beautiful, or so admired or beloved, that a man who has not seen me half a dozen times should fall in love with me? Do those who know me estimate me so much, or prize me so highly, that a stranger should think of me? You *do* insult me, Edward Arundel, when you talk as you have talked to-night.'

She looked out towards the low yellow light in the sky with a black gloom upon her face, which no reflected glimmer of the sinking sun could illumine; a settled darkness, near akin to the utter blackness of despair.

'But, good heavens, Olivia, what do you mean?' cried the young man. 'I tell you something that I think a good joke, and you go and make a tragedy out of it. If I'd told Letitia that a rich widower had fallen in love with her, she'd think it the finest fun in the world.'

'I'm not your sister Letitia.'

'No; but I wish you'd half as good a temper as she has, Livy. However, never mind; I'll say no more. If poor old Marchmont has fallen in love with you, that's his look-out. Poor dear old boy, he's let out the secret of his weakness half a dozen ways within these last few days. It's Miss Arundel this, and Miss Arundel the other; so unselfish, so accomplished, so ladylike, so good! That's the way he goes on, poor simple old dear; without having the remotest notion that he's making a confounded fool of himself.'

Olivia tossed the rumpled hair from her forehead with an impatient gesture of her hand.

'Why should this Mr Marchmont think all this of me?' she said, 'when—' she stopped abruptly.

'When—what, Livy?'

'When other people don't think it.'

'How do you know what other people think? You haven't asked them, I suppose?'

The young soldier treated his cousin in very much the same free-and-easy manner which he displayed towards his sister Letitia. It would have been almost difficult for him to recognise any degree in his relationship to the two girls. He loved Letitia better than Olivia; but his affection for both was of exactly the same character.

Hubert Arundel came into the garden, wearied out, like his daughter, while the two cousins were walking under the shadow of the neglected hazels. He declared his willingness to accept the invitation to Marchmont Towers, and promised to answer John's ceremonious note the next day.

'Cookson, from Kemberling, will be there, I suppose,' he said, alluding to a brother parson, 'and the usual set? Well, I'll come, Ned, if you wish it. You'd like to go, Olivia?'

'If you like, papa.'

There was a duty to be performed now—the duty of placid obedience to her father; and Miss Arundel's manner changed from angry impatience to grave respect. She owed no special duty, be it remembered, to her cousin. She had no line or rule by which to measure her conduct to him.

She stood at the gate nearly an hour later, and watched the young man ride away in the dim moonlight. If every separate tramp of his horse's hoofs had struck upon her heart, it could scarcely have given her more pain than she felt as the sound of those slow footfalls died away in the distance.

'O my God,' she cried, 'is this madness to undo all that I have done? Is this folly to be the climax of my dismal life? Am I to die for the love of a frivolous, fair-haired boy, who laughs in my face when he tells me that his friend has pleased to "take a fancy to me"?'

She walked away towards the house; then stopping, with a sudden shiver, she turned, and went back to the hazel-alley she had paced with Edward Arundel.

'Oh, my narrow life!' she muttered between her set teeth; 'my narrow life! It is that which has made me the slave of this madness. I love him because he is the brightest and fairest thing I have ever seen. I love him because he brings me all I have ever known of a more beautiful world than that I live in. Bah! why do I reason with myself?' she cried, with a sudden change of manner. 'I love him because I am mad.'

She paced up and down the hazel-shaded pathway till the moon-light grew broad and full, and every ivy-grown gable of the Rectory stood sharply out against the vivid purple of the sky. She paced up and down, trying to trample the folly within her under her feet as she went; a fierce, passionate, impulsive woman, fighting against her mad love for a bright-faced boy.

'Two years older—only two years!' she said; 'but he spoke of the difference between us as if it had been half a century. And then I am so clever, that I seem older than I am; and he is afraid of me! Is it for this that I have sat night after night in my father's study, poring over the books that were too difficult for him? What have I made of myself in my pride of intellect? What reward have I won for my patience?'

Olivia Arundel looked back at her long life of duty—a dull, dead level, unbroken by one of those monuments which mark the desert of the past; a desolate flat, unlovely as the marshes between the low Rectory wall and the shimmering grey sea.

CHAPTER VIII

'MY LIFE IS COLD, AND DARK, AND DREARY'*

MR RICHARD PAULETTE, of that eminent legal firm, Paulette, Paulette, and Mathewson, coming to Marchmont Towers on business, was surprised to behold the quiet ease with which the sometime copying-clerk received the punctilious country gentry who came to sit at his board and do him honour.

Of all the legal fairy-tales, of all the parchment-recorded romances, of all the poetry run into affidavits, in which the solicitor had ever been concerned, this story seemed the strangest. Not so very strange in itself, for such romances are not uncommon in the history of a lawyer's experience; but strange by reason of the tranquil manner in which John Marchmont accepted his new position, and did the honours of his house to his late employer.

'Ah, Paulette,' Edward Arundel said, clapping the solicitor on the back, 'I don't suppose you believed me when I told you that my friend here was heir-presumptive to a handsome fortune.'

The dinner-party at the Towers was conducted with that stately grandeur peculiar to such solemnities. There was the usual round of country-talk and parish-talk; the hunting squires leading the former section of the discourse, the rectors and rectors' wives supporting the latter part of the conversation. You heard on one side that Martha Harris' husband had left off drinking, and attended church morning and evening ; and on the other that the old grey fox that had been hunted nine seasons between Crackbin Bottom and Hollowcraft Gorse had perished ignobly in the poultry-yard of a recusant farmer. While your left ear became conscious of the fact that little Billy Smithers had fallen into a copper of scalding water, your right received the dismal tidings that all the young partridges had been drowned by the rains after St Swithin,* and that there were hardly any of this year's birds, sir, and it would be a very blue look-out for next season.

Mary Marchmont had listened to gayer talk in Oakley Street than any that was to be heard that night in her father's drawing-rooms, except indeed when Edward Arundel left off flirting with some pretty girls in blue, and hovered near her side for a little while, quizzing the company. Heaven knows the young soldier's jokes were commonplace enough; but Mary admired him as the most brilliant and accomplished of wits.

'How do you like my cousin, Polly?' he asked at last.

'Your cousin, Miss Arundel?'

'Yes.'

'She is very handsome.'

'Yes, I suppose so,' the young man answered carelessly. 'Everybody says that Livy's handsome; but it's rather a cold style of beauty, isn't it? A little too much of the Pallas Athenë* about it for my taste. I like those girls in blue, with the crinkly auburn hair,—there's a touch of red in it in the light,—and the dimples. You've a dimple, Polly, when you smile.'

Miss Marchmont blushed as she received this information, and her brown eyes wandered away, looking very earnestly at the pretty girls in blue. She looked at them with a strange interest, eager to discover what it was that Edward admired.

'But you haven't answered my question, Polly,' said Mr Arundel. 'I am afraid you have been drinking too much wine, Miss Marchmont, and muddling that sober little head of yours with the fumes of your papa's tawny port. I asked you how you liked Olivia.'

Mary blushed again.

'I don't know Miss Arundel well enough to like her—yet,' she answered timidly.

'But shall you like her when you've known her longer? Don't be jesuitical,* Polly. Likings and dislikings are instantaneous and instinctive. I liked you before I'd eaten half a dozen mouthfuls of the roll you buttered for me at that breakfast in Oakley Street, Polly. You don't like my cousin Olivia, miss; I can see that very plainly. You're jealous of her.'

'Jealous of her!'

The bright colour faded out of Mary Marchmont's face, and left her ashy pale.

'Do *you* like her, then?' she asked.

But Mr Arundel was not such a coxcomb as to catch at the secret so naïvely betrayed in that breathless question.

'No, Polly,' he said, laughing; 'she's my cousin, you know, and I've known her all my life; and cousins are like sisters. One likes to tease and aggravate them, and all that; but one doesn't fall in love with them. But I think I could mention somebody who thinks a great deal of Olivia.'

'Who?'

'Your papa.'

Mary looked at the young soldier in utter bewilderment.

'Papa!' she echoed.

'Yes, Polly. How would you like a step-mamma? How would you like your papa to marry again?'

Mary Marchmont started to her feet, as if she would have gone to her father in the midst of all those spectators. John was standing near Olivia and her father, talking to them, and playing nervously with his slender watch-chain when he addressed the young lady.

'My papa—marry again!' gasped Mary. 'How dare you say such a thing, Mr Arundel?'

Her childish devotion to her father arose in all its force; a flood of passionate emotion that overwhelmed her sensitive nature. Marry again! marry a woman who would separate him from his only child! Could he ever dream for one brief moment of such a horrible cruelty?

She looked at Olivia's sternly handsome face, and trembled. She could almost picture that very woman standing between her and her father, and putting her away from him. Her indignation quickly melted into grief. Indignation, however intense; was always short-lived in that gentle nature.

'Oh, Mr Arundel !' she said, piteously appealing to the young man, 'papa would never, never, never marry again,—would he?'

'Not if it was to grieve you, Polly, I dare say,' Edward answered soothingly.

He had been dumbfounded by Mary's passionate sorrow. He had expected that she would have been rather pleased, than otherwise, at the idea of a young stepmother,—a companion in those vast lonely rooms, an instructress and a friend as she grew to womanhood.

'I was only talking nonsense, Polly darling,' he said. 'You mustn't make yourself unhappy about any absurd fancies of mine. I think your papa admires my cousin Olivia; and I thought, perhaps, you'd be glad to have a stepmother.'

'Glad to have any one who'd take papa's love away from me?' Mary said plaintively. 'Oh, Mr Arundel, how could you think so?'

In all their familiarity the little girl had never learned to call her father's friend by his Christian name, though he had often told her to do so. She trembled to pronounce that simple Saxon name, which was so beautiful and wonderful because it was his: but when she read a very stupid novel, in which the hero was a namesake of Mr Arundel's, the vapid pages seemed to be phosphorescent with light wherever the name appeared upon them.

I scarcely know why John Marchmont lingered by Miss Arundel's chair. He had heard her praises from every one. She was a paragon of goodness, an uncanonised saint, for ever sacrificing herself for the benefit of others. Perhaps he was thinking that such a woman as this would be the best friend he could win for his little girl. He turned from the county matrons, the tender, kindly, motherly creatures, who would have been ready to take little Mary to the loving shelter of their arms, and looked to Olivia Arundel—this cold, perfect bene-factress of the poor—for help in his difficulty.

'She, who is so good to all her father's parishioners, could not refuse to be kind to my poor Mary?' he thought.

But how was he to win this woman's friendship for his darling? He asked himself this question even in the midst of the frivolous people about him, and with the buzz of their conversation in his ears. He was perpetually tormenting himself about his little girl's future, which seemed more dimly perplexing now than it had ever appeared in Oakley Street, when the Lincolnshire property was a far-away dream, perhaps never to be realised. He felt that his brief lease of life was running out; he felt as if he and Mary had been standing upon a narrow tract of yellow sand, very bright, very pleasant under the sunshine, but with the slow-coming tide rising like a wall about them, and creeping stealthily onward to overwhelm them.

Mary might gather bright-coloured shells and wet seaweed in her childish ignorance; but he, who knew that the flood was coming, could but grow sick at heart with the dull horror of that hastening doom. If the black waters had been doomed to close over them both, the father might have been content to go down under the sullen waves, with his daughter clasped to his breast. But it was not to be so. He was to sink in that unknown stream while she was left upon the tempest-tossed surface, to be beaten hither and thither, feebly bat-tling with the stormy billows.

Could John Marchmont be a Christian, and yet feel this horrible dread of the death which must separate him from his daughter? I fear this frail, consumptive widower loved his child with an intensity of affection that is scarcely reconcilable with Christianity. Such great passions as these must be put away before the cross can be taken up, and the troublesome path followed. In all love and kindness towards his fellow-creatures, in all patient endurance of the pains and troubles that befel himself, it would have been difficult to find a more single-hearted follower of Gospel-teaching than John Marchmont; but in his affection for his motherless child he was a very Pagan. He set up an idol for himself, and bowed down before it. Doubtful and fearful of the future, he looked hopelessly forward. He *could* not trust his orphan child into the hands of God; and drop away himself into the fathomless darkness, serene in the belief that she would be cared for and protected. No; he could not trust. He could be faithful for himself; simple and confiding as a child; but not for her. He saw the gloomy rooks louring black in the distance; the pitiless waves beating far away yonder, impatient to devour the frail boat that was so soon to be left alone upon the waters. In the thick darkness of the future he could see no ray of light, except one,—a new hope that had lately risen in his mind; the hope of winning some noble and perfect woman to be the future friend of his daughter.

The days were past in which, in his simplicity, he had looked to Edward Arundel as the future shelter of his child. The generous boy had grown into a stylish young man, a soldier, whose duty lay far away from Marchmont Towers. No; it was to a good woman's guardianship the father must leave his child.

Thus the very intensity of his love was the one motive which led John Marchmont to contemplate the step that Mary thought such a cruel and bitter wrong to her.

It was not till long after the dinner-party at Marchmont Towers that these ideas resolved themselves into any positive form, and that John began to think that for his daughter's sake he might be led to contemplate a second marriage. Edward Arundel had spoken the truth when he told his cousin that John Marchmont had repeatedly mentioned her name; but the careless and impulsive young man had been utterly unable to fathom the feeling lurking in his friend's mind. It was not Olivia Arundel's handsome face which had won John's admiration; it was the constant reiteration of her praises upon every side which had led him to believe that this woman, of all others, was the one whom he would do well to win for his child's friend and guardian in the dark days that were to come.

The knowledge that Olivia's intellect was of no common order, together with the somewhat imperious dignity of her manner, strengthened this belief in John Marchmont's mind. It was not a good woman only whom he must seek in the friend he needed for his child; it was a woman powerful enough to shield her in the lonely path she would have to tread; a woman strong enough to help her, perhaps, by-and-by to do battle with Paul Marchmont.

So, in the blind paganism of his love, John refused to trust his child into the hands of Providence, and chose for himself a friend and guardian who should shelter his darling. He made his choice with so much deliberation, and after such long nights and days of earnest thought, that he may be forgiven if he believed he had chosen wisely.

Thus it was that in the dark November days, while Edward and Mary played chess by the wide fireplace in the western drawing-room, or ball in the newly-erected tennis-court, John Marchmont sat in his study examining his papers, and calculating the amount of money at his own disposal, in serious contemplation of a second marriage.

Did he love Olivia Arundel? No. He admired her and respected her, and he firmly believed her to be the most perfect of women. No impulse of affection had prompted the step he contemplated taking. He had loved his first wife truly and tenderly; but he had never suffered very acutely from any of those torturing emotions which form the several stages of the great tragedy called Love.

But had he ever thought of the likelihood of his deliberate offer being rejected by the young lady who had been the object of such careful consideration? Yes; he had thought of this, and was prepared to abide the issue. He should, at least, have tried his uttermost to secure a friend for his darling.

With such unloverlike feelings as these the owner of Marchmont Towers drove into Swampington one morning, deliberately bent upon offering Olivia Arundel his hand. He had consulted with his land-steward, and with Messrs Paulette, and had ascertained how far he could endow his bride with the goods of this world. It was not much that he could give her, for the estate was strictly entailed; but there would be his own savings for the brief term of his life, and if he lived only a few years these savings might accumulate to a considerable amount, so limited were the expenses of the quiet Lincolnshire household; and there was a sum of money, something over nine thousand pounds, left him by Philip Marchmont, senior. He had something, then, to offer to the woman he sought to make his wife; and, above all, he had a supreme belief in Olivia Arundel's utter disinterestedness. He had seen her frequently since the dinner-party, and had always seen her the same,—grave, reserved, dignified; patiently employed in the strict performance of her duty.

He found Miss Arundel sitting in her father's study, busily cutting out coarse garments for her poor. A newly-written sermon lay open on the table. Had Mr Marchmont looked closely at the manuscript, he would have seen that the ink was wet, and that the writing was Olivia's. It was a relief to this strange woman to write sermons sometimes—fierce denunciatory protests against the inherent wickedness of the human heart. Can you imagine a woman with a wicked heart steadfastly trying to do good, and to be good? It is a dark and horrible picture; but it is the only true picture of the woman whom John Marchmont sought to win for his wife.

The interview between Mary's father and Olivia Arundel was not a very sentimental one; but it was certainly the very reverse of commonplace. John was too simple-hearted to disguise the purpose of his wooing. He pleaded, not for a wife for himself, but a mother for his orphan child. He talked of Mary's helplessness in the future, not of his own love in the present. Carried away by the egotism of his one affection, he let his motives appear in all their nakedness. He spoke long and earnestly; he spoke until the blinding tears in his eyes made the face of her he looked at seem blotted and dim.

Miss Arundel watched him as he pleaded; sternly, unflinchingly. But she uttered no word until he had finished; and then, rising suddenly, with a dusky flush upon her face, she began to pace up and down the narrow room. She had forgotten John Marchmont. In the strength and vigour of her intellect, this weak-minded widower, whose one passion was a pitiful love for his child, appeared to her so utterly insignificant, that for a few moments she had forgotten his presence in that room—his very existence, perhaps. She turned to him presently, and looked him full in the face.

'You do not love me, Mr Marchmont?' she said.

'Pardon me,' John stammered; 'believe me, Miss Arundel, I respect, I esteem you so much, that—'

'That you choose me as a fitting friend for your child. I understand. I am not the sort of woman to be loved. I have long comprehended that. My cousin Edward Arundel has often taken the trouble to tell me as much. And you wish me to be your wife in order that you may have a guardian for your child? It is very much the same thing as engaging a governess; only the engagement is to be more binding.'

'Miss Arundel,' exclaimed John Marchmont, 'forgive me! You misunderstand me; indeed you do. Had I thought that I could have offended you—'

'I am not offended. You have spoken the truth where another man would have told a lie. I ought to be flattered by your confidence in me. It pleases me that people should think me good, and worthy of their trust.'

She broke into a sigh as she finished speaking.

'And you will not reject my appeal?'

'I scarcely know what to do,' answered Olivia, pressing her hand to her forehead.

She leaned against the angle of the deep casement window, looking out at the garden, desolate and neglected in the bleak winter weather. She was silent for some minutes. John Marchmont did not interrupt her; he was content to wait patiently until she should choose to speak.

'Mr Marchmont,' she said at last, turning upon poor John with an abrupt vehemence that almost startled him, 'I am three-and-twenty; and in the long, dull memory of the three-and-twenty years that have made my life, I cannot look back upon one joy—no, so help me Heaven, not one!' she cried passionately. 'No prisoner in the Bastille, shut in a cell below the level of the Seine, and making companions of rats and spiders in his misery, ever led a life more hopelessly narrow, more pitifully circumscribed, than mine has been. These grass-grown streets have made the boundary of my existence. The flat fenny country round me is not flatter or more dismal than my life. You will say that I should take an interest in the duties which I do; and that they should be enough for me. Heaven knows I have tried to do so; but my life is hard. Do you think there has been nothing in all this to warp my nature? Do you think, after hearing this, that I am the woman to be a second mother to your child?'

She sat down as she finished speaking, and her hands dropped listlessly in her lap. The unquiet spirit raging in her breast had been stronger than herself, and had spoken. She had lifted the dull veil through which the outer world beheld her, and had showed John Marchmont her natural face.

'I think you are a good woman, Miss Arundel,' he said earnestly. 'If I had thought otherwise, I should not have come here to-day. I want a good woman to be kind to my child; kind to her when I am dead and gone,' he added, in a lower voice.

Olivia Arundel sat silent and motionless, looking straight before her out into the black dulness of the garden. She was trying to think out the dark problem of her life.

Strange as it may seem, there was a certain fascination for her in John Marchmont's offer. He offered her something, no matter what; it would be a change. She had compared herself to a prisoner in the Bastille; and I think she felt very much as such a prisoner might have felt upon his gaoler's offering to remove him to Vincennes.* The new prison might be worse than the old one, perhaps; but it would be different. Life at Marchmont Towers might be more monotonous, more desolate, than at Swampington; but it would be a new monotony, another desolation. Have you never felt, when suffering the hideous throes of toothache, that it would be a relief to have the earache or the rheumatism; that variety even in torture would be agreeable?

Then, again, Olivia Arundel, though unblest with many of the charms of womanhood, was not entirely without its weaknesses. To marry John Marchmont would be to avenge herself upon Edward Arundel. Alas! she forgot how impossible it is to inflict a dagger-thrust upon him who is guarded by the impenetrable armour of indifference. She saw herself the mistress of Marchmont Towers, waited upon by liveried servants, courted, not patronised by the country gentry; avenged upon the mercenary aunt who had slighted her, who had bade her go out and get her living as a nursery govern-ess. She saw this; and all that was ignoble in her nature arose, and urged her to snatch the chance offered her—the one chance of lifting herself out of the horrible obscurity of her life. The ambition which might have made her an empress lowered its crest, and cried, 'Take this; at least it is something.' But, through all, the better voices which she had enlisted to do battle with the natural voice of her soul cried, 'This is a temptation of the devil; put it away from thee.'

But this temptation came to her at the very moment when her life had become most intolerable; too intolerable to be borne, she thought. She knew now, fatally, certainly, that Edward Arundel did not love her; that the one only day-dream she had ever made for herself had been a snare and a delusion. The radiance of that foolish dream had been the single light of her life. That taken away from her, the darkness was blacker than the blackness of death; more horrible than the obscurity of the grave.

In all the future she had not one hope: no, not one. She had loved Edward Arundel with all the strength of her soul; she had wasted a world of intellect and passion upon this bright-haired boy. This foolish, grovelling madness had been the blight of her life. But for this, she might have grown out of her natural self by force of her conscientious desire to do right; and might have become, indeed, a good and perfect woman. If her life had been a wider one, this wasted love would, perhaps, have shrunk into its proper insignificance; she would have loved, and suffered, and recovered; as so many of us recover from this common epidemic. But all the volcanic forces of an impetuous nature, concentrated into one narrow focus, wasted themselves upon this one feeling, until that which should have been a sentiment became a madness.

To think that in some far-away future time she might cease to love Edward Arundel, and learn to love somebody else, would have seemed about as reasonable to Olivia as to hope that she could have new legs and arms in that distant period. She could cut away this fatal passion with a desperate stroke, it may be, just as she could cut off her arm; but to believe that a new love would grow in its place was quite as absurd as to believe in the growing of a new arm. Some cork monstrosity might replace the amputated limb; some sham and simulated affection might succeed the old love.

Olivia Arundel thought of all these things, in about ten minutes by the little skeleton clock* upon the mantel-piece, and while John Marchmont fidgeted rather nervously, with a pair of gloves in the crown of his hat, and waited for some definite answer to his appeal. Her mind came back at last, after all its passionate wanderings, to the rigid channel she had so laboriously worn for it, — the narrow groove of duty. Her first words testified this.

'If I accept this responsibility, I will perform it faithfully,' she said, rather to herself than to Mr Marchmont.

'I am sure you will, Miss Arundel,' John answered eagerly; 'I am sure you will. You mean to undertake it, then? you mean to consider my offer? May I speak to your father? may I tell him that I have spoken to you? may I say that you have given me a hope of your ultimate consent?'

'Yes, yes,' Olivia said, rather impatiently; 'speak to my father; tell him anything you please. Let him decide for me; it is my duty to obey him.'

There was a terrible cowardice in this. Olivia Arundel shrank from marrying a man she did not love, prompted by no better desire than the mad wish to wrench herself away from her hated life. She wanted to fling the burden of responsibility in this matter away from her. Let another decide, let another urge her to do this wrong; and let the wrong be called a sacrifice.

So for the first time she set to work deliberately to cheat her own conscience. For the first time she put a false mark upon the standard she had made for the measurement of her moral progress.

She sank into a crouching attitude on a low stool by the fire-place, in utter prostration of body and mind, when John Marchmont had left her. She let her weary head fall heavily against the carved oaken shaft that supported the old-fashioned mantel-piece, heedless that her brow struck sharply against the corner of the wood-work.

If she could have died then, with no more sinful secret than a woman's natural weakness hidden in her breast; if she could have died then, while yet the first step upon the dark pathway of her life was untrodden,—how happy for herself, how happy for others! How miserable a record of sin and suffering might have remained unwritten in the history of woman's life!

She sat long in the same attitude. Once, and once only, two solitary tears gathered in her eyes, and rolled slowly down her pale cheeks.

'Will you be sorry when I am married, Edward Arundel?' she murmured; 'will you be sorry?'

CHAPTER IX

'WHEN SHALL I CEASE TO BE ALL ALONE?'

HUBERT ARUNDEL was not so much surprised as might have been anticipated at the proposal made him by his wealthy neighbour. Edward had prepared his uncle for the possibility of such a proposal by sundry jocose allusions and arch hints upon the subject of John Marchmont's admiration for Olivia. The frank and rather frivolous young man thought it was his cousin's handsome face that had captivated the master of Marchmont Towers, and was quite unable to fathom the hidden motive underlying all John's talk about Miss Arundel.

The Rector of Swampington, being a simple-hearted and not very far-seeing man, thanked God heartily for the chance that had befallen his daughter. She would be well off and well cared for, then, by the mercy of Providence, in spite of his own shortcomings, which had left her with no better provision for the future than a pitiful Policy of Assurance upon her father's life. She would be well provided for henceforward, and would live in a handsome house; and all those noble qualities which had been dwarfed and crippled in a narrow sphere would now expand, and display themselves in unlooked-for grandeur.

'People have called her a good girl,' he thought; 'but how could they ever know her goodness, unless they had seen, as I have, the deprivations she has borne so uncomplainingly?'

John Marchmont, being newly instructed by his lawyer, was able to give Mr Arundel a very clear statement of the provision he could make for his wife's future. He could settle upon her the nine thousand pounds left him by Philip Marchmont. He would allow her five hundred a year pin-money during his lifetime; he would leave her his savings at his death; and he would effect an insurance upon his life for her benefit. The amount of these savings would, of course, depend upon the length of John's life; but the money would accumulate very quickly, as his income was eleven thousand a year, and his expenditure was not likely to exceed three.

The Swampington living was worth little more than three hundred and fifty pounds a year; and out of that sum Hubert Arundel and his daughter had done treble as much good for the numerous poor of the parish as ever had been achieved by any previous Rector or his family. Hubert and his daughter had patiently endured the most grinding poverty, the burden ever falling heavier on Olivia, who had the heroic faculty of endurance as regards all physical discomfort. Can it be wondered, then, that the Rector of Swampington thought the prospect offered to his child a very brilliant one? Can it be wondered that he urged his daughter to accept this altered lot?

He did urge her, pleading John Marchmont's cause a great deal more warmly than the widower had himself pleaded.

'My darling,' he said, 'my darling girl! if I can live to see you mistress of Marchmont Towers, I shall go to my grave contented and happy. Think, my dear, of the misery from which this marriage will save you. Oh, my dear girl, I can tell you now what I never dared tell you before; I can tell you of the long, sleepless nights I have passed thinking of you, and of the wicked wrongs I have done you. Not wilful wrongs, my love,' the Rector added, with the tears gathering in his eyes; 'for you know how dearly I have always loved you. But a father's responsibility towards his children is a very heavy burden. I have only looked at it in this light lately, my dear,—now that I've let the time slip by, and it is too late to redeem the past. I've suffered very much, Olivia; and all this has seemed to separate us, somehow. But that's past now, isn't it, my dear? and you'll marry this Mr Marchmont. He appears to be a very good, conscientious man, and I think he'll make you happy.'

The father and daughter were sitting together after dinner in the dusky November twilight, the room only lighted by the fire, which was low and dim. Hubert Arundel could not see his daughter's face as he talked to her; he could only see the black outline of her figure sharply defined against the grey window behind her, as she sat opposite to him. He could see by her attitude that she was listening to him, with her head drooping and her hands lying idle in her lap.

She was silent for some little time after he had finished speaking; so silent that he feared his words might have touched her too painfully, and that she was crying.

Heaven help this simple-hearted father! She had scarcely heard three consecutive words that he had spoken, but had only gathered dimly from his speech that he wanted her to accept John Marchmont's offer.

Every great passion is a supreme egotism. It is not the object which we hug so determinedly; it is not the object which coils itself about our weak hearts: it is our own madness we worship and cleave to, our own pitiable folly which we refuse to put away from us. What is Bill Sykes'* broken nose or bull-dog visage to Nancy? The creature she loves and will not part from is not Bill, but her own love for Bill,—the one delusion of a barren life; the one grand selfishness of a feeble nature.

Olivia Arundel's thoughts had wandered far away while her father had spoken so piteously to her. She had been thinking of her cousin Edward, and had been asking herself the same question over and over again. Would he be sorry? would he be sorry if she married John Marchmont?

But she understood presently that her father was waiting for her to speak; and, rising from her chair, she went towards him, and laid her hand upon his shoulder.

'I am afraid I have not done my duty to you, papa,' she said.

Latterly she had been for ever harping upon this one theme,—her duty! That word was the keynote of her life; and her existence had latterly seemed to her so inharmonious, that it was scarcely strange she should repeatedly strike that leading note in the scale.

'My darling,' cried Mr Arundel, 'you have been all that is good!'

'No, no, papa; I have been cold, reserved, silent.'

'A little silent, my dear,' the Rector answered meekly; 'but you have not been happy. I have watched you, my love, and I know you have not been happy. But that is not strange. This place is so dull, and your life has been so fatiguing. How different that would all be at Marchmont Towers!'

'You wish me to marry Mr Marchmont, then, papa?'

'I do, indeed, my love. For your own sake, of course,' the Rector added deprecatingly.

'You really wish it?'

'Very, very much, my dear.'

'Then I will marry him, papa.'

She took her hand from the Rector's shoulder, and walked away from him to the uncurtained window, against which she stood with her back to her father, looking out into the grey obscurity.

I have said that Hubert Arundel was not a very clever or far-seeing person; but he vaguely felt that this was not exactly the way in which a brilliant offer of marriage should be accepted by a young lady who was entirely fancy-free, and he had an uncomfortable apprehension that there was something hidden under his daughter's quiet manner.

'But, my dear Olivia,' he said nervously, 'you must not for a moment suppose that I would force you into this marriage, if it is in any way repugnant to yourself. You—you may have formed some prior attachment—or, there may be somebody who loves you, and has loved you longer than Mr Marchmont, who—'

His daughter turned upon him sharply as he rambled on.

'Somebody who loves me!' she echoed. 'What have you ever seen that should make you think any one loved me?'

The harshness of her tone jarred upon Mr Arundel, and made him still more nervous.

'My love, I beg your pardon. I have seen nothing. I—'

'Nobody loves me, or has ever loved me,—but you,' resumed Olivia, taking no heed of her father's feeble interruption. 'I am not the sort of woman to be loved; I feel and know that. I have an aquiline nose, and a clear skin, and dark eyes, and people call me handsome; but nobody loves me, or ever will, so long as I live.'

'But Mr Marchmont, my dear,—surely he loves and admires you?' remonstrated the Rector.

'Mr Marchmont wants a governess and *chaperone* for his daughter, and thinks me a suitable person to fill such a post; that is all the *love* Mr Marchmont has for me. No, papa; there is no reason I should shrink from this marriage. There is no one who will be sorry for it; no one! I am asked to perform a duty towards this little girl, and I am prepared to perform it faithfully. That is my part of the bargain. Do I commit a sin in marrying John Marchmont in this spirit, papa?'

She asked the question eagerly, almost breathlessly; as if her decision depended upon her father's answer.

'A sin, my dear! How can you ask such a question?'

'Very well, then; if I commit no sin in accepting this offer, I will accept it.'

It was thus Olivia paltered with her conscience, holding back half the truth. The question she should have asked was this, 'Do I commit a sin in marrying one man, while my heart is racked by a mad passion for another?'

Miss Arundel could not visit her poor upon the day after this interview with her father. Her monotonous round of duty seemed more than ever abhorrent to her. She wandered across the dreary marshes, down by the lonely seashore, in the grey November fog.

She stood for a long time, shivering with the cold dampness of the atmosphere, but not even conscious that she was cold, looking at a dilapidated boat that lay upon the rugged beach. The waters before her and the land behind her were hidden by a dense veil of mist. It seemed as if she stood alone in the world,—utterly isolated, utterly forgotten.

'O my God!' she murmured, 'if this boat at my feet could drift me away to some desert island, I could never be more desolate than I am, amongst the people who do not love me.'

Dim lights in distant windows were gleaming across the flats when she returned to Swampington, to find her father sitting alone and dispirited at his frugal dinner. Miss Arundel took her place quietly at the bottom of the table, with no trace of emotion upon her face.

'I am sorry I stayed out so long, papa,' she said; 'I had no idea it was so late.'

'Never mind, my dear, I know you have always enough to occupy you. Mr Marchmont called while you were out. He seemed very anxious to hear your decision, and was delighted when he found that it was favourable to himself.'

Olivia dropped her knife and fork, and rose from her chair suddenly, with a strange look, which was almost terror, in her face.

'It is quite decided, then?' she said.

'Yes, my love. But you are not sorry, are you?'

'Sorry! No; I am glad.'

She sank back into her chair with a sigh of relief. She *was* glad. The prospect of this strange marriage offered a relief from the horrible oppression of her life.

'Henceforward to think of Edward Arundel will be a sin,' she thought. 'I have not won another man's love; but I shall be another man's wife.'

CHAPTER X

MARY'S STEPMOTHER

PERHAPS there was never a quieter courtship than that which followed Olivia's acceptance of John Marchmont's offer. There had been no pretence of sentiment on either side; yet I doubt if John had been much more sentimental during his early love-making days, though he had very tenderly and truly loved his first wife. There were few sparks of the romantic or emotional fire in his placid nature. His love for his daughter, though it absorbed his whole being, was a silent and undemonstrative affection; a thoughtful and almost fearful devotion, which took the form of intense but hidden anxiety for his child's future, rather than any outward show of tenderness.

Had his love been of a more impulsive and demonstrative character, he would scarcely have thought of taking such a step as that he now contemplated, without first ascertaining whether it would be agreeable to his daughter.

But he never for a moment dreamt of consulting Mary's will upon this important matter. He looked with fearful glances towards the dim future, and saw his darling, a lonely figure upon a barren landscape, beset by enemies eager to devour her; and he snatched at this one chance of securing her a protectress, who would be bound to her by a legal as well as a moral tie; for John Marchmont meant to appoint his second wife the guardian of his child. He thought only of this; and he hurried on his suit at the Rectory, fearful lest death should come between him and his loveless bride, and thus deprive his darling of a second mother.

This was the history of John Marchmont's marriage. It was not till a week before the day appointed for the wedding that he told his daughter what he was about to do. Edward Arundel knew the secret, but he had been warned not to reveal it to Mary.

The father and daughter sat together late one evening in the first week of December, in the great western drawing-room. Edward had gone to a party at Swampington, and was to sleep at the Rectory; so Mary and her father were alone.

It was nearly eleven o'clock; but Miss Marchmont had insisted upon sitting up until her father should retire to rest. She had always sat up in Oakley Street, she had remonstrated, though she was much younger then. She sat on a velvet-covered hassock at her father's feet, with her loose hair falling over his knee, as her head lay there in loving abandonment. She was not talking to him; for neither John nor Mary were great talkers; but she was with him—that was quite enough.

Mr Marchmont's thin fingers twined themselves listlessly in and out of the fair curls upon his knee. Mary was thinking of Edward and the party at Swampington. Would he enjoy himself very, very much? Would he be sorry that she was not there? It was a grown-up party, and she wasn't old enough for grown-up parties yet. Would the pretty girls in blue be there? and would he dance with them?

Her father's face was clouded by a troubled expression, as he looked absently at the red embers in the low fireplace. He spoke presently, but his observation was a very commonplace one. The opening speeches of a tragedy are seldom remarkable for any ominous or solemn meaning. Two gentlemen meet each other in a street very near the footlights, and converse rather flippantly about the aspect of affairs in general; there is no hint of bloodshed and agony till we get deeper into the play.

So Mr Marchmont, bent upon making rather an important communication to his daughter, and for the first time feeling very fearful as to how she would take it, began thus:

'You really ought to go to bed earlier, Polly dear; you've been looking very pale lately, and I know such hours as these must be bad for you.'

'Oh, no, papa dear,' cried the young lady; 'I'm always pale; that's natural to me. Sitting up late doesn't hurt me, papa. It never did in Oakley Street, you know.'

John Marchmont shook his head sadly.

'I don't know that,' he said. 'My darling had to suffer many evils through her father's poverty. If you had some one who loved you, dear, a lady, you know,—for a man does not understand these sort of things,—your health would be looked after more carefully, and—and—your education—and—in short, you would be altogether happier; wouldn't you, Polly darling?'

He asked the question in an almost piteously appealing tone. A terrible fear was beginning to take possession of him. His daughter might be grieved at this second marriage. The very step which he had taken for her happiness might cause her loving nature pain and sorrow. In the utter cowardice of his affection he trembled at the thought of causing his darling any distress in the present, even for her own welfare,—even for her future good; and he *knew* that the step he was about to take would secure that. Mary started from her reclining position, and looked up into her father's face.

'You're not going to engage a governess for me, papa?' she cried eagerly. 'Oh, please don't. We are so much better as it is. A governess would keep me away from you, papa; I know she would. The Miss Llandels, at Impley Grange, have a governess; and they only come down to dessert for half an hour, or go out for a drive sometimes, so that they very seldom see their papa. Lucy told me so; and they said they'd give the world to be always with their papa, as I am with you. Oh, pray, pray, papa darling, don't let me have a governess.'

The tears were in her eyes as she pleaded to him. The sight of those tears made him terribly nervous.

'My own dear Polly,' he said, 'I'm not going to engage a governess. I—; Polly, Polly dear, you must be reasonable. You mustn't grieve your poor father. You are old enough to understand these things now, dear. You know what the doctors have said. I may die, Polly, and leave you alone in the world.'

She clung closely to her father, and looked up, pale and trembling, as she answered him.

'When you die, papa, I shall die too. I could never, never live without you.'

'Yes, yes, my darling, you would. You will live to lead a happy life, please God, and a safe one; but if I die, and leave you very young, very inexperienced, and innocent, as I may do, my dear, you must not be without a friend to watch over you, to advise, to protect you. I have thought of this long and earnestly, Polly; and I believe that what I am going to do is right.'

'What you are going to do!' Mary cried, repeating her father's words, and looking at him in sudden terror. 'What do you mean, papa? What are you going to do? Nothing that will part us! O papa, papa, you will never do anything to part us!'

'No, Polly darling,' answered Mr Marchmont. 'Whatever I do, I do for your sake, and for that alone. I'm going to be married, my dear.'

Mary burst into a low wail, more pitiful than any ordinary weeping.

'O papa, papa,' she cried, 'you never will, you never will!'

The sound of that piteous voice for a few moments quite unmanned John Marchmont; but he armed himself with a desperate courage. He determined not to be influenced by this child to relinquish the purpose which he believed was to achieve her future welfare.

'Mary, Mary dear,' he said reproachfully, 'this is very cruel of you. Do you think I haven't consulted your happiness before my own? Do you think I shall love you less because I take this step for your sake? You are very cruel to me, Mary.'

The little girl rose from her kneeling attitude, and stood before her father, with the tears streaming down her white cheeks, but with a certain air of resolution about her. She had been a child for a few moments; a child, with no power to look beyond the sudden pang of that new sorrow which had come to her. She was a woman now, able to rise superior to her sorrow in the strength of her womanhood.

'I won't be cruel, papa,' she said; 'I was selfish and wicked to talk like that. If it will make you happy to have another wife, papa, I'll not be sorry. No, I won't be sorry, even if your new wife separates us—a little.'

'But, my darling,' John remonstrated, 'I don't mean that she should separate us at all. I wish you to have a second friend, Polly; some one who can understand you better than I do, who may love you perhaps almost as well.' Mary Marchmont shook her head; she could not realise this possibility. 'Do you understand me, my dear?' her father continued earnestly. 'I want you to have some one who will be a mother to you; and I hope—I am sure that Olivia—'

Mary interrupted him by a sudden exclamation, that was almost like a cry of pain.

'Not Miss Arundel!' she said. 'O papa, it is not Miss Arundel you're going to marry!'

Her father bent his head in assent.

'What is the matter with you, Mary?' he said, almost fretfully, as he saw the look of mingled grief and terror in his daughter's face. 'You are really quite unreasonable to-night. If I am to marry at all, who should I choose for a wife? Who could be better than Olivia

Arundel? Everybody knows how good she is. Everybody talks of her goodness.'

In these two sentences Mr Marchmont made confession of a fact he had never himself considered. It was not his own impulse, it was no instinctive belief in her goodness, that had led him to choose Olivia Arundel for his wife. He had been influenced solely by the reiterated opinions of other people.

'I know she is very good, papa,' Mary cried; 'but, oh, why, why do you marry her? Do you love her so very, very much?'

'Love her!' exclaimed Mr Marchmont naïvely; 'no, Polly dear; you know I never loved any one but you.'

'Why do you marry her then?'

'For your sake, Polly; for your sake.'

'But don't then, papa; oh, pray, pray don't. I don't want her. I don't like her. I could never be happy with her.'

'Mary! Mary!'

'Yes, I know it's very wicked to say so, but it's true, papa; I never, never, never could be happy with her. I know she is good, but I don't like her. If I did anything wrong, I should never expect her to forgive me for it; I should never expect her to have mercy upon me. Don't marry her, papa; pray, pray don't marry her.'

'Mary,' said Mr Marchmont resolutely, 'this is very wrong of you. I have given my word, my dear, and I cannot recall it. I believe that I am acting for the best. You must not be childish now, Mary. You have been my comfort ever since you were a baby; you mustn't make me unhappy now.'

Her father's appeal went straight to her heart. Yes, she had been his help and comfort since her earliest infancy, and she was not unused to self-sacrifice: why should she fail him now ? She had read of martyrs, patient and holy creatures, to whom suffering was glory; she would be a martyr, if need were, for his sake. She would stand steadfast amid the blazing faggots, or walk unflinchingly across the white-hot ploughshare, for his sake, for his sake.

'Papa, papa,' she cried, flinging herself upon her father's neck, 'I will not make you sorry. I will be good and obedient to Miss Arundel, if you wish it.'

Mr Marchmont carried his little girl up to her comfortable bed-chamber, close at hand to his own. She was very calm when she bade him good night, and she kissed him with a smile upon her face; but all through the long hours before the late winter morning Mary Marchmont lay awake, weeping silently and incessantly in her new sorrow; and all through the same weary hours the master of that noble Lincolnshire mansion slept a fitful and troubled slumber, rendered hideous by confused and horrible dreams, in which the black shadow that came between him and his child, and the cruel hand that thrust him for ever from his darling, were Olivia Arundel's.

But the morning light brought relief to John Marchmont and his child. Mary arose with the determination to submit patiently to her father's choice, and to conceal from him all traces of her foolish and unreasoning sorrow. John awoke from troubled dreams to believe in the wisdom of the step he had taken, and to take comfort from the thought that in the far-away future his daughter would have reason to thank and bless him for the choice he had made.

So the few days before the marriage passed away—miserably short days, that flitted by with terrible speed; and the last day of all was made still more dismal by the departure of Edward Arundel, who left Marchmont Towers to go to Dangerfield Park, whence he was most likely to start once more for India.

Mary felt that her narrow world of love was indeed crumbling away from her. Edward was lost, and to-morrow her father would belong to another. Mr Marchmont dined at the Rectory upon that last evening; for there were settlements to be signed, and other matters to be arranged; and Mary was alone—quite alone—weeping over her lost happiness.

'This would never have happened,' she thought, 'if we hadn't come to Marchmont Towers. I wish papa had never had the fortune; we were so happy in Oakley Street,—so very happy. I wouldn't mind a bit being poor again, if I could be always with papa.'

Mr Marchmont had not been able to make himself quite comfortable in his mind, after that unpleasant interview with his daughter in which he had broken to her the news of his approaching marriage. Argue with himself as he might upon the advisability of the step he was about to take, he could not argue away the fact that he had grieved the child he loved so intensely. He could not blot away from his memory the pitiful aspect of her terror-stricken face as she had turned it towards him when he uttered the name of Olivia Arundel.

No; he had grieved and distressed her. The future might reconcile her to that grief, perhaps, as a bygone sorrow which she had been allowed to suffer for her own ultimate advantage. But the future was a long way off: and in the meantime there was Mary's altered face, calm and resigned, but bearing upon it a settled look of sorrow, very close at hand; and John Marchmont could not be otherwise than unhappy in the knowledge of his darling's grief.

I do not believe that any man or woman is ever suffered to take a fatal step upon the roadway of life without receiving ample warning by the way. The stumbling-blocks are placed in the fatal path by a merciful hand; but we insist upon clambering over them, and surmounting them in our blind obstinacy, to reach that shadowy something beyond, which we have in our ignorance appointed to be our goal. A thousand ominous whispers in his own breast warned John Marchmont that the step he considered so wise was not a wise one: and yet, in spite of all these subtle warnings, in spite of the ever-present reproach of his daughter's altered face, this man, who was too weak to trust blindly in his God, went on persistently upon his way, trusting, with a thousand times more fatal blindness, in his own wisdom.

He could not be content to confide his darling and her altered fortunes to the Providence which had watched over her in her poverty, and sheltered her from every harm. He could not trust his child to the mercy of God; but he cast her upon the love of Olivia Arundel.

A new life began for Mary Marchmont after the quiet wedding at Swampington Church. The bride and bridegroom went upon a brief honeymoon excursion far away amongst snow-clad Scottish mountains and frozen streams, upon whose bloomless margins poor John shivered dismally. I fear that Mr Marchmont, having been, by the hard pressure of poverty, compelled to lead a Cockney life for the better half of his existence, had but slight relish for the grand and sublime in nature. I do not think he looked at the ruined walls* which had once sheltered Macbeth and his strong-minded partner with all the enthusiasm which might have been expected of him. He had but one idea about Macbeth, and he was rather glad to get out of the neighbourhood associated with the warlike Thane; for his memories of the past presented King Duncan's murderer as a very stern and uncompromising gentleman, who was utterly intolerant of banners held awry, or turned with the blank and ignoble side towards the audience, and who objected vehemently to a violent fit of coughing on the part of any one of his guests during the blank barmecide feast* of pasteboard and Dutch metal* with which he was wont to entertain them. No; John Marchmont had had quite enough of Macbeth, and rather wondered at the hot enthusiasm of other red-nosed tourists, apparently indifferent to the frosty weather.

I fear that the master of Marchmont Towers would have preferred Oakley Street, Lambeth, to Princes Street,* Edinburgh; for the nipping and eager airs* of the Modern Athens* nearly blew him across the gulf between the new town and the old. A visit to the Calton Hill* produced an attack of that chronic cough which had so severely tormented the weak-kneed supernumerary in the draughty corridors of Drury Lane. Melrose and Abbotsford* fatigued this poor feeble tourist; he tried to be interested in the stereotyped round of associations beloved by other travellers, but he had a weary craving for rest, which was stronger than any hero-worship; and he discovered, before long, that he had done a very foolish thing in coming to Scotland in December and January, without having consulted his physician as to the propriety of such a step.

But above all personal inconvenience, above all personal suffering, there was one feeling ever present in his heart—a sick yearning for the little girl he had left behind him; a mournful longing to be back with his child. Already Mary's sad forebodings had been in some way realised; already his new wife had separated him, unintentionally of course, from his daughter. The aches and pains he endured in the bleak Scottish atmosphere reminded him only too forcibly of the warnings he had received from his physicians. He was seized with a panic, almost, when he remembered his own imprudence. What if he had needlessly curtailed the short span of his life? What if he were to die soon—before Olivia had learned to love her stepdaughter; before Mary had grown affectionately familiar with her new guardian? Again and again he appealed to his wife, imploring her to be tender to the orphan child, if he should be snatched away suddenly.

'I know you will love her by-and-by, Olivia,' he said; 'as much as I do, perhaps; for you will discover how good she is, how patient and unselfish. But just at first, and before you know her very well, you will be kind to her, won't you, Olivia? She has been used to great indulgence; she has been spoiled, perhaps; but you'll remember all that, and be very kind to her?'

'I will try and do my duty,' Mrs Marchmont answered. 'I pray that I never may do less.'

There was no tender yearning in Olivia Marchmont's heart towards the motherless girl. She herself felt that such a sentiment was wanting, and comprehended that it should have been there. She would have loved her stepdaughter in those early days, if she could have done so; but *she could not*—she could not. All that was tender or womanly in her nature had been wasted upon her hopeless love for Edward Arundel. The utter wreck of that small freight of affection had left her nature warped and stunted, soured, disappointed, unwomanly.

How was she to love this child, this hazel-haired, dove-eyed girl, before whom woman's life, with all its natural wealth of affection, stretched far away, a bright and fairy vista? How was *she* to love her,—she, whose black future was unchequered by one ray of light; who stood, dissevered from the past, alone in the dismal, dreamless monotony of the present?

'No,' she thought; 'beggars and princes can never love one another. When this girl and I are equals,—when she, like me, stands alone upon a barren rock, far out amid the waste of waters, with not one memory to hold her to the past, with not one hope to lure her onward to the future, with nothing but the black sky above and the black waters around,—*then* we may grow fond of each other.'

But always more or less steadfast to the standard she had set up for herself, Olivia Marchmont intended to do her duty to her step-daughter. She had not failed in other duties, though no glimmer of love had brightened them, no natural affection had made them pleasant. Why should she fail in this?

If this belief in her own power should appear to be somewhat arrogant, let it be remembered that she had set herself hard tasks before now, and had performed them. Would the new furnace through which she was to pass be more terrible than the old fires? She had gone to God's altar with a man for whom she had no more love than she felt for the lowest or most insignificant of the miserable sinners in her father's flock. She had sworn to honour and obey him, meaning at least faithfully to perform that portion of her vow; and on the night before her loveless bridal she had grovelled, white, writhing, mad, and desperate, upon the ground, and had plucked out of her lacerated heart her hopeless love for another man.

Yes; she had done this. Another woman might have spent that bridal eve in vain tears and lamentations, in feeble prayers, and such weak struggles as might have been evidenced by the destruction of a few letters, a tress of hair, some fragile foolish tokens of a wasted love. She would have burnt five out of six letters, perhaps, that helpless, ordinary sinner, and would have kept the sixth, to hoard away hidden among her matrimonial trousseau; she would have thrown away fifteen–sixteenths of that tress of hair, and would have kept the sixteenth portion,—one delicate curl of gold, slender as the thread by which her shattered hopes had hung,—to be wept over and kissed in the days that were to come. An ordinary woman would have played fast and loose with love and duty; and so would have been true to neither.

But Olivia Arundel did none of these things. She battled with her weakness as St George battled with the fiery dragon. She plucked the rooted serpent from her heart, reckless as to how much of that desperate heart was to be wrenched away with its roots. A cowardly woman would have killed herself, perhaps, rather than endure this mortal agony. Olivia Arundel killed more than herself; she killed the passion that had become stronger than herself.

'Alone she did it;' unaided by any human sympathy or compassion, unsupported by any human counsel, not upheld by her God; for the religion she had made for herself was a hard creed, and the many words of tender comfort which must have been familiar to her were unremembered in that long night of anguish.

It was the Roman's stern endurance, rather than the meek faithfulness of the Christian, which upheld this unhappy girl under her torture. She did not do this thing because it pleased her to be obedient to her God. She did not do it because she believed in the mercy of Him who inflicted the suffering, and looked forward hopefully, even amid her passionate grief, to the day when she should better comprehend that which she now saw so darkly. No; she fought the terrible fight, and she came forth out of it a conqueror, by reason of her own indomitable power of suffering, by reason of her own extraordinary strength of will.

But she did conquer. If her weapon was the classic sword and not the Christian cross, she was nevertheless a conqueror. When she stood before the altar and gave her hand to John Marchmont, Edward Arundel was dead to her. The fatal habit of looking at him as the one centre of her narrow life was cured. In all her Scottish wanderings, her thoughts never once went back to him; though a hundred chance words and associations tempted her, though a thousand memories assailed her, though some trick of his face in the faces of other people, though some tone of his voice in the voices of strangers, perpetually offered to entrap her. No; she was steadfast.

Dutiful as a wife as she had been dutiful as a daughter, she bore with her husband when his feeble health made him a wearisome companion. She waited upon him when pain made him fretful, and her duties became little less arduous than those of a hospital nurse. When, at the bidding of the Scotch physician who had been called in at Edinburgh, John Marchmont turned homewards, travelling slowly and resting often on the way, his wife was more devoted to him than his experienced servant, more watchful than the best-trained sick-nurse. She recoiled from nothing, she neglected nothing; she gave him full measure of the honour and obedience which she had promised upon her wedding-day. And when she reached Marchmont Towers upon a dreary evening in January, she passed beneath the solemn portal of the western front, carrying in her heart the full determination to hold as steadfastly to the other half of her bargain, and to do her duty to her stepchild.

Mary ran out of the western drawing-room to welcome her father and his wife. She had cast off her black dresses in honour of Mr Marchmont's marriage, and she wore some soft, silken fabric, of a pale shimmering blue, which contrasted exquisitely with her soft, brown hair, and her fair, tender face. She uttered a cry of mingled alarm and sorrow when she saw her father, and perceived the change that had been made in his looks by the northern journey; but she checked herself at a warning glance from her stepmother, and bade that dear father welcome, clinging about him with an almost desperate fondness. She greeted Olivia gently and respectfully.

'I will try to be very good, mamma,' she said, as she took the passive hand of the lady who had come to rule at Marchmont Towers.

'I believe you will, my dear,' Olivia answered, kindly.

She had been startled a little as Mary addressed her by that endearing corruption of the holy word mother. The child had been so long motherless, that she felt little of that acute anguish which some orphans suffer when they have to look up in a strange face and say 'mamma.' She had taught herself the lesson of resignation, and she was prepared to accept this stranger as her new mother, and to look up to her and obey her hence-forward. No thought of her own future position, as sole owner of that great house and all appertain-ing to it, ever crossed Mary Marchmont's mind, womanly as that mind had become in the sharp experiences of poverty. If her father had told her that he had cut off the entail, and settled Marchmont Towers upon his new wife, I think she would have submitted meekly to his will, and would have seen no injustice in the act. She loved him blindly and confidingly. Indeed, she could only love after one fash-ion. The organ of veneration must have been abnormally developed in Mary Marchmont's head. To believe that any one she loved was otherwise than perfect, would have been, in her creed, an infidelity against love. Had any one told her that Edward Arundel was not eminently qualified for the post of General-in-Chief of the Army of the Indus; or that her father could by any possible chance be guilty of a fault or folly: she would have recoiled in horror from the treasonous slanderer.

A dangerous quality, perhaps, this quality of guilelessness which thinketh no evil, which cannot be induced to see the evil under its very nose. But surely, of all the beautiful and pure things upon this earth, such blind confidence is the purest and most beautiful. I knew a lady, dead and gone,—alas for this world, which could ill afford to lose so good a Christian!—who carried this trustfulness of spirit, this utter incapacity to believe in wrong, through all the strife and turmoil of a troubled life, unsullied and unlessened, to her grave. She was cheated and imposed upon, robbed and lied to, by people who loved her, perhaps, while they wronged her,—for to know her was to love her. She was robbed systematically by a confidential servant for years, and for years refused to believe those who told her of his delinquencies. She *could* not believe that people were wicked. To the day of her death she had faith in the scoundrels and scamps who had profited by her sweet compassion and untiring benevol-ence; and indignantly defended them against those who dared to say that they were anything more than 'unfortunate.' To go to her was to go to a never-failing fountain of love and tenderness. To know her goodness was to understand the goodness of God; for her love approached the Infinite, and might have taught a sceptic the possibility of Divinity. Three-score years and ten of worldly experience left her an accomplished lady, a delightful companion; but in guilelessness a child.

So Mary Marchmont, trusting implicitly in those she loved, submitted to her father's will, and prepared to obey her stepmother. The new life at the Towers began very peacefully; a perfect harmony reigned in the quiet household. Olivia took the reins of management with so little parade, that the old housekeeper, who had long been paramount in the Lincolnshire mansion, found herself superseded before she knew where she was. It was Olivia's nature to govern. Her strength of will asserted itself almost unconsciously. See took possession of Mary Marchmont as she had taken possession of her schoolchildren at Swampington, making her own laws for the government of their narrow intellects. She planned a routine of study that was actually terrible to the little girl, whose education had hitherto been conducted in a somewhat slip-slop manner by a weakly-indulgent father. She came between Mary and her one amusement,—the reading of novels. The half-bound romances were snatched ruthlessly from this young devourer of light literature, and sent back to the shabby circulating library at Swampington. Even the gloomy old oak book-cases in the library at the Towers, and the Abbotsford edition of the Waverley Novels, were forbidden to poor Mary; for, though Sir Walter Scott's morality is irreproachable, it will not do for a young lady to be weeping over Lucy Ashton or Amy Robsart* when she should be consulting her terrestrial globe, and informing herself as to the latitude and longitude of the Fiji Islands.

So a round of dry and dreary lessons began for poor Miss Marchmont, and her brain grew almost dazed under that continuous and pelting shower of hard facts which many worthy people consider the one sovereign method of education. I have said that her mind was far in advance of her years; Olivia perceived this, and set her tasks in advance of her mind: in order that the perfection attained by a sort of steeple-chase of instruction might not be lost to her. If Mary learned difficult lessons with surprising rapidity, Mrs Marchmont plied her with even yet more difficult lessons, thus keeping the spur perpetually in the side of this heavily-weighted racer on the road to learning. But it must not be thought that Olivia wilfully tormented or oppressed her stepdaughter. It was not so. In all this, John Marchmont's second wife implicitly believed that she was doing her duty to the child committed to her care. She fully believed that this dreary routine of education was wise and right, and would be for Mary's ultimate advantage. If she caused Miss Marchmont to get up at abnormal hours on bleak wintry mornings, for the purpose of wrestling with a difficult variation by Hertz or Schubert,* she herself rose also, and sat shivering by the piano, counting the time of the music which her stepdaughter played.

Whatever pains and trouble she inflicted on Mary, she most unshrinkingly endured herself. She waded through the dismal slough of learning side by side with the younger sufferer: Roman emperors, mediæval schisms, early British manufactures, Philippa of Hainault, Flemish woollen stuffs, Magna Charta, the side-real heavens, Luther, Newton, Huss, Galileo, Calvin, Loyola, Sir Robert Walpole, Cardinal Wolsey, conchology, Arianism in the Early Church, trial by jury, Habeas Corpus, zoology, Mr Pitt, the American war, Copernicus, Confucius, Mahomet, Harvey, Jenner, Lycurgus, and Catherine of Aragon; through a very diabolical dance of history, science, theology, philosophy, and instruction of all kinds, did this devoted priestess lead her hapless victim, struggling onward towards that distant altar at which Pallas Athenë waited, pale and inscrutable, to receive a new disciple.

But Olivia Marchmont did not mean to be unmerciful; she meant to be good to her stepdaughter. She did not love her; but, on the other hand, she did not dislike her. Her feelings were simply negative. Mary understood this, and the submissive obedience she rendered to her stepmother was untempered by affection. So for nearly two years these two people led a monotonous life, unbroken by any more important event than a dinner party at Marchmont Towers, or a brief visit to Harrogate or Scarborough.

This monotonous existence was not to go on for ever. The fatal day, so horribly feared by John Marchmont; was creeping closer and closer. The sorrow which had been shadowed in every childish dream, in every childish prayer, came at last; and Mary Marchmont was left an orphan.

Poor John had never quite recovered the effects of his winter excursion to Scotland; neither his wife's devoted nursing, nor his physician's care, could avail for ever; and, late in the autumn of the second year of his marriage, he sank, slowly and peacefully enough as regards physical suffering, but not without bitter grief of mind.

In vain Hubert Arundel talked to him; in vain did he himself pray for faith and comfort in this dark hour of trial. He *could* not bear to leave his child alone in the world. In the foolishness of his love, he would have trusted in the strength of his own arm to shield her in the battle; yet he could not trust her hopefully to the arm of God. He prayed for her night and day during the last week of his illness; while she was praying passionately, almost madly, that he might be spared to her, or that she might die with him. Better for her, according to all mortal reasoning, if she had. Happier for her, a thousand times, if she could have died as she wished to die, clinging to her father's breast.

The blow fell at last upon those two loving hearts. These were the awful shadows of death that shut his child's face from John Marchmont's fading sight. His feeble arms groped here and there for her in that dim and awful obscurity.

Yes, this was death. The narrow tract of yellow sand had little by little grown narrower and narrower. The dark and cruel waters were closing in; the feeble boat went down into the darkness: and Mary stood alone, with her dead father's hand clasped in hers,—the last feeble link which bound her to the Past,—looking blankly forward to an unknown Future.

CHAPTER XI

THE DAY OF DESOLATION

YES; the terrible day had come. Mary Marchmont roamed hither and thither in the big gaunt rooms, up and down the long dreary corridors, white and ghostlike in her mute anguish, while the under-taker's men were busy in her father's chamber, and while John's widow sat in the study below, writing business letters, and making all necessary arrangements for the funeral.

In those early days no one attempted to comfort the orphan. There was something more terrible than the loudest grief in the awful quiet of the girl's anguish. The wan eyes, looking wearily out of a white haggard face, that seemed drawn and contracted as if by some hideous physical torture, were tearless. Except the one long wail of despair which had burst from her lips in the awful moment of her father's death agony, no cry of sorrow, no utterance of pain, had given relief to Mary Marchmont's suffering.

She suffered, and was still.* She shrank away from all human companionship; she seemed specially to avoid the society of her stepmother. She locked the door of her room upon all who would have intruded on her, and flung herself upon the bed, to lie there in a dull stupor for hour after hour. But when the twilight was grey in the desolate corridors, the wretched girl wandered out into the gallery on which her father's room opened, and hovered near that solemn death-chamber; fearful to go in, fearful to encounter the watchers of the dead, lest they should torture her by their hackneyed expressions of sympathy, lest they should agonise her by their commonplace talk of the lost.

Once during that brief interval, while the coffin still held terrible tenancy of the death-chamber, the girl wandered in the dead of the night, when all but the hired watchers were asleep, to the broad landing of the oaken staircase, and into a deep recess formed by an embayed window that opened over the great stone porch which shel-tered the principal entrance to Marchmont Towers.

The window had been left open; for even in the bleak autumn weather the atmosphere of the great house seemed hot and oppres-sive to its living inmates, whose spirits were weighed down by a vague sense of the Awful Presence in that Lincolnshire mansion. Mary had wandered to this open window, scarcely knowing whither she went, after remaining for a long time on her knees by the threshold of her father's room, with her head resting against the oaken panel of the door,—not praying; why should she pray now, unless her prayers could have restored the dead? She had come out upon the wide staircase, and past the ghostly pictured faces, that looked grimly down upon her from the oaken wainscot against which they hung; she had wandered here in the dim grey light—there was light somewhere in the sky, but only a shadowy and uncertain glimmer of fading starlight or coming dawn—and she stood now with her head resting against one of the angles of the massive stonework, looking out of the open window.

The morning which was already glimmering dimly in the eastern sky behind Marchmont Towers was to witness poor John's funeral. For nearly six days Mary Marchmont had avoided all human companionship: for nearly six days she had shunned all human sympathy and comfort. During all that time she had never eaten, except when forced to do so by her stepmother; who had visited her from time to time, and had insisted upon sitting by her bedside while she took the food that had been brought to her. Heaven knows how often the girl had slept during those six dreary days; but her feverish slumbers had brought her very little rest or refreshment. They had brought her nothing but cruel dreams, in which her father was still alive; in which she felt his thin arms clasped round her neck, his faint and fitful breath warm upon her cheek.

A great clock in the stables struck five while Mary Marchmont stood looking out of the Tudor window. The broad grey flat before the house stretched far away, melting into the shadowy horizon. The pale stars grew paler as Mary looked at them; the black-water pools began to glimmer faintly under the widening patch of light in the eastern sky. The girl's senses were bewildered by her suffering, and her head was light and dizzy.

Her father's death had made so sudden and terrible a break in her existence, that she could scarcely believe the world had not come to an end, with all the joys and sorrows of its inhabitants. Would there be anything more after tomorrow? she thought; would the blank days and nights go monotonously on when the story that had given them a meaning and a purpose had come to its dismal end? Surely not;

surely, after those gaunt iron gates, far away across the swampy waste that was called a park, had closed upon her father's funeral train, the world would come to an end, and there would be no more time or space. I think she really believed this in the semi-delirium into which she had fallen within the last hour. She believed that all would be over; and that she and her despair would melt away into the emptiness that was to engulf the universe after her father's funeral.

Then suddenly the full reality of her grief flashed upon her with horrible force. She clasped her hands upon her forehead, and a low faint cry broke from her white lips.

It was *not* all over. Time and space would *not* be annihilated. The weary, monotonous, workaday world would still go on upon its course. *Nothing* would be changed. The great gaunt stone mansion would still stand, and the dull machinery of its interior would still go on: the same hours; the same customs; the same inflexible routine. John Marchmont would be carried out of the house that had owned him master, to lie in the dismal vault under Kemberling Church; and the world in which he had made so little stir would go on without him. The easy-chair in which he had been wont to sit would be wheeled away from its corner by the fireplace in the western drawing-room. The papers in his study would be sorted and put away, or taken possession of by strange hands. Cromwells and Napoleons die, and the earth reels for a moment, only to be 'alive and bold' again in the next instant, to the astonishment of poets, and the calm satisfaction of philosophers; and ordinary people eat their breakfasts while the telegram lies beside them upon the table, and while the ink in which Mr Reuter's* message is recorded is still wet from the machine in Printing-house Square.*

Anguish and despair more terrible than any of the tortures she had felt yet took possession of Mary Marchmont's breast. For the first time she looked out at her own future. Until now she had thought only of her father's death. She had despaired because he was gone; but she had never contemplated the horror of her future life,—a life in which she was to exist without him. A sudden agony, that was near akin to madness, seized upon this girl, in whose sensitive nature affection had always had a morbid intensity. She shuddered with a wild dread at the prospect of that blank future; and as she looked out at the wide stone steps below the window from which she was leaning, for the first time in her young life the idea of self-destruction flashed across her mind.

She uttered a cry, a shrill, almost unearthly cry, that was notwithstanding low and feeble, and clambered suddenly upon the broad stone sill of the Tudor casement. She wanted to fling herself down and dash her brains out upon the stone steps below; but in the utter prostration of her state she was too feeble to do this, and she fell backwards and dropped in a heap upon the polished oaken flooring of the recess, striking her forehead as she fell. She lay there unconscious until nearly seven o'clock, when one of the women-servants found her, and carried her off to her own room, where she suffered herself to be undressed and put to bed.

Mary Marchmont did not speak until the good-hearted Lincolnshire housemaid had laid her in her bed, and was going away to tell Olivia of the state in which she had found the orphan girl.

'Don't tell my stepmother anything about me, Susan,' she said; 'I think I was mad last night.'

This speech frightened the housemaid, and she went straight to the widow's room. Mrs Marchmont, always an early riser, had been up and dressed for some time, and went at once to look at her stepdaughter.

She found Mary very calm and reasonable. There was no trace of bewilderment or delirium in her manner; and when the principal doctor of Swampington came a couple of hours afterwards to look at the young heiress, he declared that there was no cause for any alarm. The young lady was sensitive, morbidly sensitive, he said, and must be kept very quiet for a few days, and watched by some one whose presence would not annoy her. If there was any girl of her own age whom she had ever shown a predilection for, that girl would be the fittest companion for her just now. After a few days, it would be advisable that she should have change of air and change of scene. She must not be allowed to brood continuously on her father's death. The doctor repeated this last injunction more than once. It was most important that she should not give way too perpetually to her grief.

So Mary Marchmont lay in her darkened room while her father's funeral train was moving slowly away from the western entrance. It happened that the orphan girl's apartments looked out into the quadrangle; so she heard none of the subdued sounds which attended the departure of that solemn procession. In her weakness she had grown submissive to the will of others. She thought this feebleness and exhaustion gave warning of approaching death. Her prayers would be granted, after all. This anguish and despair would be but of brief duration, and she would ere long be carried to the vault under Kemberling Church; to lie beside her father in the black stillness of that solemn place.

Mrs Marchmont strictly obeyed the doctor's injunctions. A girl of seventeen, the daughter of a small tenant farmer near the Towers, had been a special favourite with Mary, who was not apt to make friends amongst strangers. This girl, Hester Pollard, was sent for, and came willingly and gladly to watch her young patroness. She brought her needlework with her, and sat near the window busily employed, while Mary lay shrouded by the curtains of the bed. All active services necessary for the comfort of the invalid were performed by Olivia or her own special attendant—an old servant who had lived with the Rector ever since his daughter's birth, and had only left him to follow that daughter to Marchmont Towers after her marriage. So Hester Pollard had nothing to do but to keep very quiet, and patiently await the time when Mary might be disposed to talk to her. The farmer's daughter was a gentle, unobtrusive creature, very well fitted for the duty imposed upon her.

CHAPTER XII

PAUL

OLIVIA MARCHMONT sat in her late husband's study while John's funeral train was moving slowly along under the misty October sky. A long stream of carriages followed the stately hearse, with its four black horses, and its voluminous draperies of rich velvet, and nodding plumes that were damp and heavy with the autumn atmosphere. The unassuming master of Marchmont Towers had won for himself a quiet popularity amongst the simple country gentry, and the best families in Lincolnshire had sent their chiefs to do honour to his burial, or at the least their empty carriages to represent them at that mournful ceremonial. Olivia sat in her dead husband's favourite chamber. Her head lay back upon the cushion of the roomy morocco-covered arm-chair in which he had so often sat. She had been working hard that morning, and indeed every morning since John Marchmont's death, sorting and arranging papers, with the aid of Richard Paulette, the Lincoln's Inn solicitor, and James Gormby, the land-steward. She knew that she had been left sole guardian of her step-daughter, and executrix to her husband's will; and she had lost no time in making herself acquainted with the business details of the estate, and the full nature of the responsibilities intrusted to her.

She was resting now. She had done all that could be done until after the reading of the will. She had attended to her stepdaughter. She had stood in one of the windows of the western drawing-room, watching the departure of the funeral *cortège*; and now she abandoned herself for a brief space to that idleness which was so unusual to her.

A fire burned in the low grate at her feet, and a rough cur—half shepherd's dog, half Scotch deer-hound, who had been fond of John, but was not fond of Olivia—lay at the further extremity of the hearth-rug, watching her suspiciously.

Mrs Marchmont's personal appearance had not altered during the two years of her married life. Her face was thin and haggard; but it had been thin and haggard before her marriage. And yet no one could deny that the face was handsome, and the features beautifully chiselled. But the grey eyes were hard and cold, the line of the faultless eyebrows gave a stern expression to the countenance; the thin lips were rigid and compressed. The face wanted both light and colour. A sculptor copying it line by line would have produced a beautiful head. A painter must have lent his own glowing tints if he wished to represent Olivia Marchmont as a lovely woman.

Her pale face looked paler, and her dead black hair blacker, against the blank whiteness of her widow's cap. Her mourning dress clung closely to her tall, slender figure. She was little more than twenty-five, but she looked a woman of thirty. It had been her misfortune to look older than she was from a very early period in her life.

She had not loved her husband when she married him, nor had she ever felt for him that love which in most womanly natures grows out of custom and duty. It was not in her nature to love. Her passionate idolatry of her boyish cousin had been the one solitary affection that had ever held a place in her cold heart. All the fire of her nature had been concentrated in this one folly, this one passion, against which only heroic endurance had been able to prevail.

Mrs Marchmont felt no grief, therefore, at her husband's loss. She had felt the shock of his death, and the painful oppression of his dead presence in the house. She had faithfully nursed him through many illnesses; she had patiently tended him until the very last; she had done her duty. And now, for the first time, she had leisure to contemplate the past, and look forward to the future.

So far this woman had fulfilled the task which she had taken upon herself; she had been true and loyal to the vow she had made before God's altar, in the church of Swampington. And now she was free. No, not quite free; for she had a heavy burden yet upon her hands; the solemn charge of her stepdaughter during the girl's minority. But as regarded marriage-vows and marriage-ties she was free.

She was free to love Edward Arundel again.

The thought came upon her with a rush and an impetus, wild and strong as the sudden uprising of a whirlwind, or the loosing of a mountain-torrent that had long been bound. She was a wife no longer. It was no longer a sin to think of the bright-haired soldier, fighting far away. She was free. When Edward returned to England by-and-by, he would find her free once more; a young widow,— young, handsome, and rich enough to be no bad prize for a younger son. He would come back and find her thus; and then—and then—!

She flung one of her clenched hands up into the air, and struck it on her forehead in a sudden paroxysm of rage. What then? Would he love her any better then than he had loved her two years ago? No; he would treat her with the same cruel indifference, the same common-place cousinly friendliness, with which he had mocked and tortured her before. Oh, shame! Oh, misery! Was there no pride in women, that there could be one among them fallen so low as her; ready to grovel at the feet of a fair-haired boy, and to cry aloud, 'Love me, love me! or be pitiful, and strike me dead!'

Better that John Marchmont should have lived for ever, better that Edward Arundel should die far away upon some Eastern battle-field, before some Afghan fortress, than that he should return to inflict upon her the same tortures she had writhed under two years before.

'God grant that he may never come back!' she thought. 'God grant that he may marry out yonder, and live and die there! God keep him from me for ever and for ever in this weary world!'

And yet in the next moment, with the inconsistency which is the chief attribute of that madness we call love, her thoughts wandered away dreamily into visions of the future; and she pictured Edward Arundel back again at Swampington, at Marchmont Towers. Her soul burst its bonds and expanded, and drank in the sunlight of gladness: and she dared to think that it *might* be so—there *might* be happiness yet for her. He had been a boy when he went back to India,—careless, indifferent. He would return a man,—graver, wiser, altogether changed: changed so much as to love her perhaps.

She knew that, at least, no rival had shut her cousin's heart against her, when she and he had been together two years before. He had been indifferent to her; but he had been indifferent to others also. There was comfort in that recollection. She had questioned him very sharply as to his life in India and at Dangerfield, and she had dis-covered no trace of any tender memory of the past, no hint of a cherished dream of the future. His heart had been empty: a boyish, unawakened heart: a temple in which the niches were untenanted, the shrine unhallowed by the presence of a goddess.

Olivia Marchmont thought of these things. For a few moments, if only for a few moments, she abandoned herself to such thoughts as these. She let herself go. She released the stern hold which it was her habit to keep upon her own mind; and in those bright moments of delicious abandonment the glorious sunshine streamed in upon her narrow life, and visions of a possible future expanded before her like a fairy panorama, stretching away into realms of vague light and splendour. It was *possible*; it was at least possible.

But, again, in the next moment the magical panorama collapsed and shrivelled away, like a burning scroll; the fairy picture, whose gorgeous colouring she had looked upon with dazzled eyes, almost blinded by its overpowering glory, shrank into a handful of black ashes, and was gone. The woman's strong nature reasserted itself; the iron will rose up, ready to do battle with the foolish heart.

'I *will* not be fooled a second time,' she cried. 'Did I suffer so little when I blotted that image out of my heart? Did the destruction of my cruel Juggernaut* cost me so small an agony that I must needs be ready to elevate the false god again, and crush out my heart once more under the brazen wheels of his chariot? *He will never love me!*'

She writhed; this self-sustained and resolute woman writhed in her anguish as she uttered those five words, 'He will never love me!' She knew that they were true; that of all the changes that Time could bring to pass, it would never bring such a change as that. There was not one element of sympathy between herself and the young soldier; they had not one thought in common. Nay, more; there was an absolute antagonism between them, which, in spite of her love, Olivia fully recognised. Over the gulf that separated them no coincidence of thought or fancy, no sympathetic emotion, ever stretched its electric chain to draw them together in mysterious union. They stood aloof, divided by the width of an intellectual universe. The woman knew this, and hated herself for her folly, scorning alike her love and its object; but her love was not the less because of her scorn. It was a madness, an isolated madness, which stood alone in her soul, and fought for mastery over her better aspirations, her wiser thoughts. We are all familiar with strange stories of wise and great minds which have been ridden by some hobgoblin fancy, some one horrible monomania; a bleeding head upon a dish, a grinning skeleton playing hide-and-seek in the folds of the bed-curtains; some devilry or other before which the master-spirit shrank and dwindled until the body withered and the victim died.

Had Olivia Marchmont lived a couple of centuries before, she would have gone straight to the nearest old crone, and would have boldly accused the wretched woman of being the author of her misery.

'You harbour a black cat and other noisome vermin, and you prowl about muttering to yourself o' nights,' she might have said. 'You have been seen to gather herbs, and you make strange and uncanny signs with your palsied old fingers. The black cat is the devil, your colleague; and the rats under your tumble-down roof are his imps, your associates. It is *you* who have instilled this horrible madness into my soul; for it *could* not come of itself.'

And Olivia Marchmont, being resolute and strong-minded, would not have rested until her tormentor had paid the penalty of her foul work at a stake in the nearest market-place.

And indeed some of our madnesses are so mad, some of our follies are so foolish, that we might almost be forgiven if we believed that there was a company of horrible crones meeting somewhere on an invisible Brocken,* and making incantations for our destruction. Take up a newspaper and read its hideous revelations of crime and folly; and it will be scarcely strange if you involuntarily wonder whether witchcraft is a dark fable of the middle ages, or a dreadful truth of the nineteenth century. Must not some of these miserable creatures whose stories we read be *possessed*; possessed by eager, relentless demons, who lash and goad them onward, until no black abyss of vice, no hideous gulf of crime, is black or hideous enough to content them?

Olivia Marchmont might have been a good and great woman. She had all the elements of greatness. She had genius, resolution, an indomitable courage, an iron will, perseverance, self-denial, temperance, chastity. But against all these qualities was set a fatal and foolish love for a boy's handsome face and frank and genial manner. If Edward Arundel had never crossed her path, her unfettered soul might have taken the highest and grandest flight; but, chained down, bound, trammelled by her love for him, she grovelled on the earth like some maimed and wounded eagle, who sees his fellows afar off, high in the purple empyrean, and loathes himself for his impotence.

'What do I love him for?' she thought. 'Is it because he has blue eyes and chestnut hair, with wandering gleams of golden light in it? Is it because he has gentlemanly manners, and is easy and pleasant, genial and light-hearted? Is it because he has a dashing walk, and the air of a man of fashion? It must be for some of these attributes, surely; for I know nothing more in him. Of all the things he has ever said, I can remember nothing—and I remember his smallest words,

Heaven help me!—that any sensible person could think worth repeating. He is brave, I dare say, and generous; but what of that? He is neither braver nor more generous than other men of his rank and position.'

She sat lost in such a reverie as this while her dead husband was being carried to the roomy vault set apart for the owners of Marchmont Towers and their kindred; she was absorbed in some such thoughts as these, when one of the grave, grey-headed old servants brought her a card upon a heavy salver emblazoned with the Marchmont arms.

Olivia took the card almost mechanically. There are some thoughts which carry us a long way from the ordinary occupations of every-day life, and it is not always easy to return to the dull jog-trot routine. The widow passed her left hand across her brow before she looked at the name inscribed upon the card in her right.

'Mr Paul Marchmont.'

She started as she read the name. Paul Marchmont! She remembered what her husband had told her of this man. It was not much; for John's feelings on the subject of his cousin had been of so vague a nature that he had shrunk from expounding them to his stern, practical wife. He had told her, therefore, that he did not very much care for Paul, and that he wished no intimacy ever to arise between the artist and Mary; but he had said nothing more than this.

'The gentleman is waiting to see me, I suppose?' Mrs Marchmont said.

'Yes, ma'am. The gentleman came to Kemberling by the 11.5 train from London, and has driven over here in one of Harris's flys.'*

'Tell him I will come to him immediately. Is he in the drawing-room?'

'Yes, ma'am.'

The man bowed and left the room. Olivia rose from her chair and lingered by the fireplace with her foot on the fender, her elbow resting on the carved oak chimneypiece.

'Paul Marchmont! He has come to the funeral, I suppose. And he expects to find himself mentioned in the will, I dare say. I think, from what my husband told me, he will be disappointed in that. Paul Marchmont! If Mary were to die unmarried, this man or his sisters would inherit Marchmont Towers.'

There was a looking-glass over the mantelpiece; a narrow, oblong glass, in an old-fashioned carved ebony frame, which was inclined forward. Olivia looked musingly in this glass, and smoothed the heavy bands of dead-black hair under her cap.

'There are people who would call me handsome,' she thought, as she looked with a moody frown at her image in the glass; 'and yet I have seen Edward Arundel's eyes wander away from my face, even while I have been talking to him, to watch the swallows skimming by in the sun, or the ivy-leaves flapping against the wall.'

She turned from the glass with a sigh, and went out into a dusky corridor. The shutters of all the principal rooms and the windows upon the grand staircase were still closed; the wide hall was dark and gloomy, and drops of rain spattered every now and then upon the logs that smouldered on the wide old-fashioned hearth. The misty October morning had heralded a wet day.

Paul Marchmont was sitting in a low easy-chair before a blazing fire in the western drawing-room, the red light full upon his face. It was a handsome face, or perhaps, to speak more exactly, it was one of those faces that are generally called 'interesting.' The features were very delicate and refined, the pale greyish-blue eyes were shaded by long brown lashes, and the small and rather feminine mouth was overshadowed by a slender auburn moustache, under which the rosy tint of the lips was very visible. But it was Paul Marchmont's hair which gave a peculiarity to a personal appearance that might otherwise have been in no way out of the common. This hair, fine, silky, and luxuriant, was *white*, although its owner could not have been more than thirty-seven years of age.

The uninvited guest rose as Olivia Marchmont entered the room.

'I have the honour of speaking to my cousin's widow?' he said, with a courteous smile.

'Yes, I am Mrs Marchmont.'

Olivia seated herself near the fire. The wet day was cold and cheerless. Mrs Marchmont shivered as she extended her long thin hand to the blaze.

'And you are doubtless surprised to see me here, Mrs Marchmont?' the artist said, leaning upon the back of his chair in the easy attitude of a man who means to make himself at home. 'But believe me, that although I never took advantage of a very friendly letter written to me by poor John——'

Paul Marchmont paused for a moment, keeping sharp watch upon the widow's face; but no sorrowful expression, no evidence of emotion, was visible in that inflexible countenance.

'Although, I repeat, I never availed myself of a sort of general invitation to come and shoot his partridges, or borrow money of him, or take advantage of any of those other little privileges generally claimed by a man's poor relations, it is not to be supposed, my dear Mrs Marchmont, that I was altogether forgetful of either Marchmont Towers or its owner, my cousin. I did not come here, because I am a hard-working man, and the idleness of a country house would have been ruin to me. But I heard sometimes of my cousin from neighbours of his.'

'Neighbours!' repeated Olivia, in a tone of surprise.

'Yes; people near enough to be called neighbours in the country. My sister lives at Stanfield. She is married to a surgeon who practises in that delightful town. You know Stanfield, of course?'

'No, I have never been there. It is five-and-twenty miles from here.'

'Indeed! too far for a drive, then. Yes, my sister lives at Stanfield. John never knew much of her in his adversity, and therefore may be forgiven if he forgot her in his prosperity. But she did not forget him. We poor relations have excellent memories. The Stanfield people have so little to talk about, that it is scarcely any wonder if they are inquisitive about the affairs of the grand country gentry round about them. I heard of John through my sister; I heard of his marriage through her,'—he bowed to Olivia as he said this,—'and I wrote immediately to congratulate him upon that happy event,'— he bowed again here;—'and it was through Lavinia Weston, my sister, that I heard of poor John's death, one day before the announcement appeared in the columns of the "Times." I am sorry to find that I am too late for the funeral. I could have wished to have paid my cousin the last tribute of esteem that one man can pay another.'

'You would wish to hear the reading of the will?' Olivia said, interrogatively.

Paul Marchmont shrugged his shoulders, with a low, careless laugh; not an indecorous laugh,— nothing that this man did or said ever appeared ill-advised or out of place. The people who disliked him were compelled to acknowledge that they disliked him unreasonably, and very much on the Doctor-Fell principle; for it was impossible to take objection to either his manners or his actions.

'That important legal document can have very little interest for me, my dear Mrs Marchmont,' he said gaily. 'John can have had nothing to leave me. I am too well acquainted with the terms of my grandfather's will to have any mercenary hopes in coming to Marchmont Towers.'

He stopped, and looked at Olivia's impassible face.

'What on earth could have induced this woman to marry my cousin?' he thought. 'John could have had very little to leave his widow.'

He played with the ornaments at his watch-chain, looking reflectively at the fire for some moments.

'Miss Marchmont,—my cousin, Mary Marchmont, I should say,—bears her loss pretty well, I hope?'

Olivia shrugged her shoulders.

'I am sorry to say that my stepdaughter displays very little Christian resignation,' she said.

And then a spirit within her arose and whispered, with a mocking voice, 'What resignation do *you* show beneath *your* affliction,—you, who should be so good a Christian? How have *you* learned to school your rebellious heart?'

'My cousin is very young,' Paul Marchmont said, presently.

'She was fifteen last July.'

'Fifteen! Very young to be the owner of Marchmont Towers and an income of eleven thousand a year,' returned the artist. He walked to one of the long windows, and drawing aside the edge of the blind, looked out upon the terrace and the wide flats before the mansion. The rain dripped and splashed upon the stone steps; the rain-drops hung upon the grim adornments of the carved balustrade, soaking into moss-grown escutcheons and half-obliterated coats-of-arms. The weird willows by the pools far away, and a group of poplars near the house, looked gaunt and black against the dismal grey sky.

Paul Marchmont dropped the blind, and turned away from the gloomy landscape with a half-contemptuous gesture. 'I don't know that I envy my cousin, after all,' he said: 'the place is dreary as Tennyson's Moated Grange.'*

There was the sound of wheels on the carriage-drive before the terrace, and presently a subdued murmur of hushed voices in the hall. Mr Richard Paulette, and the two medical men who had attended John Marchmont, had returned to the Towers, for the reading of the will. Hubert Arundel had returned with them; but the other followers in the funeral train had departed to their several homes. The undertaker and his men had come back to the house by the side-entrance, and were making themselves very comfortable in the servants'-hall after the fulfilment of their mournful duties.

The will was to be read in the dining-room; and Mr Paulette and the clerk who had accompanied him to Marchmont Towers were already seated at one end of the long carved-oak table, busy with their papers and pens and ink, assuming an importance the occasion did not require. Olivia went out into the hall to speak to her father.

'You will find Mr Marchmont's solicitor in the dining-room,' she said to Paul, who was looking at some of the old pictures on the drawing-room walls.

A large fire was blazing in the wide grate at the end of the dining-room. The blinds had been drawn up. There was no longer need that the house should be wrapped in darkness. The Awful Presence had departed; and such light as there was in the gloomy October sky was free to enter the rooms, which the death of one quiet, unobtrusive creature had made for a time desolate.

There was no sound in the room but the low voices of the two doctors talking of their late patient in undertones near the fireplace, and the occasional fluttering of the papers under the lawyer's hand. The clerk, who sat respectfully a little way behind his master, and upon the very edge of his ponderous morocco-covered chair, had been wont to give John Marchmont his orders, and to lecture him for being tardy with his work a few years before, in the Lincoln's Inn office. He was wondering now whether he should find himself remembered in the dead man's will, to the extent of a mourning-ring or an old-fashioned silver snuff-box.

Richard Paulette looked up as Olivia and her father entered the room, followed at a little distance by Paul Marchmont, who walked at a leisurely pace, looking at the carved doorways and the pictures against the wainscot, and appearing, as he had declared himself, very little concerned in the important business about to be transacted.

'We shall want Miss Marchmont here, if you please,' Mr Paulette said, as he looked up from his papers.

'Is it necessary that she should be present?' Olivia asked.

'Very necessary.'

'But she is ill; she is in bed.'

'It is most important that she should be here when the will is read. Perhaps Mr Bolton'—the lawyer looked towards one of the medical men—'will see. He will be able to tell us whether Miss Marchmont can safely come downstairs.'

Mr Bolton, the Swampington surgeon who had attended Mary that morning, left the room with Olivia. The lawyer rose and warmed his hands at the blaze, talking to Hubert Arundel and the London physician as he did so. Paul Marchmont, who had not been introduced to any one, occupied himself entirely with the pictures for a little time; and then, strolling over to the fireplace, fell into conversation with the three gentlemen, contriving, adroitly enough, to let them know who he was. The lawyer looked at him with some interest,—a professional interest, no doubt; for Mr Paulette had a copy of old Philip Marchmont's will in one of the japanned deed-boxes inscribed with poor John's name. He knew that this easy-going, pleasant-mannered, white-haired gentleman was the Paul Marchmont named in that document, and stood next in succession to Mary. Mary might die unmarried, and it was as well to be friendly and civil to a man who was at least a possible client.

The four gentlemen stood upon the broad Turkey hearth-rug for some time, talking of the dead man, the wet weather, the cold autumn, the dearth of partridges, and other very safe topics of conversation. Olivia and the Swampington doctor were a long time absent; and Richard Paulette, who stood with his back to the fire, glanced every now and then towards the door.

It opened at last, and Mary Marchmont came into the room, followed by her stepmother.

Paul Marchmont turned at the sound of the opening of that ponderous oaken door, and for the first time saw his second cousin, the young mistress of Marchmont Towers. He started as he looked at her, though with a scarcely perceptible movement, and a change came over his face. The feminine pinky hue in his cheeks faded suddenly, and left them white. It had been a peculiarity of Paul Marchmont's, from his boyhood, always to turn pale with every acute emotion.

What was the emotion which had now blanched his cheeks? Was he thinking, 'Is *this* fragile creature the mistress of Marchmont

Towers? Is *this* frail life all that stands between me and eleven thousand a year?'

The light which shone out of that feeble earthly tabernacle did indeed seem a frail and fitful flame, likely to be extinguished by any rude breath from the coarse outer world. Mary Marchmont was deadly pale; black shadows encircled her wistful hazel eyes. Her new mourning-dress, with its heavy trimmings of lustreless crape, seemed to hang loose upon her slender figure; her soft brown hair, damp with the water with which her burning forehead had been bathed, fell in straight lank tresses about her shoulders. Her eyes were tearless, her mouth terribly compressed. The rigidity of her face betokened the struggle by which her sorrow was repressed. She sat in an easy-chair which Olivia indicated to her, and with her hands lying on the white handkerchief in her lap, and her swollen eyelids drooping over her eyes, waited for the reading of her father's will. It would be the last, the very last, she would ever hear of that dear father's words. She remembered this, and was ready to listen attentively; but she remembered nothing else. What was it to her that she was sole heiress of that great mansion, and of eleven thousand a year? She had never in her life thought of the Lincolnshire fortune with any reference to herself or her own pleasures; and she thought of it less than ever now.

The will was dated, February 4th, 1844, exactly two months after John's marriage. It had been made by the master of Marchmont Towers without the aid of a lawyer, and was only witnessed by John's housekeeper; and by Corson the old valet, a confidential servant who had attended upon Mr Marchmont's predecessor.

Richard Paulette began to read; and Mary, for the first time since she had take her seat near the fire, lifted her eyes, and listened breathlessly, with faintly tremulous lips. Olivia sat near her step-daughter; and Paul Marchmont stood in a careless attitude at one corner of the fireplace, with his shoulders resting against the massive oaken chimneypiece. The dead man's will ran thus:

'I John Marchmont of Marchmont Towers declare this to be my last will and testament Being persuaded that my end is approaching I feel my dear little daughter Mary will he left unprotected by any natural guardian My young friend Edward Arundel I had hoped when in my poverty would have been a friend and adviser to her if not a protector but her tender years and his position in life must place this now out of the question and I may die before a fond hope which I have long cherished can be realised and which may now never be realised I now desire to make my will more particularly to provide as well as I am permitted for the guardianship and care of my dear little Mary during her minority Now I will and desire that my wife Olivia shall act as guardian adviser and mother to my dear little Mary and that she place herself under the charge and guardianship of my wife And as she will be an heiress of very considerable property I would wish her to be guided by the advice of my said wife in the management of her property and particularly in the choice of a husband As my dear little Mary will be amply provided for on my death I make no provision for her by this my will but I direct my executrix to present to her a diamond-ring which I wish her to wear in memory of her loving father so that she may always have me in her thoughts and particularly of these my wishes as to her future life until she shall be of age and capable of acting on her own judgment I also request my executrix to present my young friend Edward Arundel also with a diamond-ring of the value of at least one hundred guineas as a slight tribute of the regard and esteem which I have ever entertained for him ... As to all the property as well real as personal over which I may at the time of my death have any control and capable of claiming or bequeathing I give devise and bequeath to my wife Olivia absolutely And I appoint my said wife sole executrix of this my will and guardian of my dear little Mary'

There were a few very small legacies, including a mourning-ring to the expectant clerk; and this was all. Paul Marchmont had been quite right; nobody could be less interested than himself in this will.

But he was apparently very much interested in John's widow and daughter. He tried to enter into conversation with Mary, but the girl's piteous manner seemed to implore him to leave her unmolested; and Mr Bolton approached his patient almost immediately after the reading of the will, and in a manner took possession of her. Mary was very glad to leave the room once more, and to return to the dim chamber where Hester Pollard sat at needlework. Olivia left her step daughter to the care of this humble companion, and went back to the long dining-room, where the gentlemen still hung listlessly over the fire, not knowing very well what to do with themselves.

Mrs Marchmont could not do less than invite Paul to stay a few

days at the Towers. She was virtually mistress of the house during
Mary's minority, and on her devolved all the troubles, duties, and
responsibilities attendant on such a position. Her father was going to
stay with her till the end of the week; and he therefore would be able
to entertain Mr Marchmont. Paul unhesitatingly accepted the
widow's hospitality. The old place was picturesque and interesting,
he said; there were some genuine Holbeins in the hall and dining-
room, and one good Lely in the drawing-room. He would give himself a couple of days' holiday, and go to Stanfield by an early train on
Saturday.

'I have not seen my sister for a long time,' he said; 'her life is dull
enough and hard enough, Heaven knows, and she will be glad to see
me upon my way back to London.'

Olivia bowed. She did not persuade Mr Marchmont to extend his
visit. The common courtesy she offered him was kept within the
narrowest limits. She spent the best part of the time in the dead
man's study during Paul's two-days' stay, and left the artist almost
entirely to her father's companionship.

But she was compelled to appear at dinner, and she took her
accustomed place at the head of the table. Paul therefore had some
opportunity of sounding the depths of the strangest nature he had
ever tried to fathom. He talked to her very much, listening with
unvarying attention to every word she uttered. He watched her—
but with no obtrusive gaze—almost incessantly; and when he went
away from Marchmont Towers, without having seen Mary since
the reading of the will, it was of Olivia he thought; it was the
recollection of Olivia which interested as much as it perplexed
him.

The few people waiting for the London train looked at the artist
as he strolled up and down the quiet platform at Kemberling
Station, with his head bent and his eyebrows slightly contracted. He
had a certain easy, careless grace of dress and carriage, which
harmonised well with his delicate face, his silken silvery hair, his
carefully-trained auburn moustache, and rosy, womanish mouth. He
was a romantic-looking man. He was the beau-ideal of the hero in a
young lady's novel. He was a man whom schoolgirls would have
called 'a dear.' But it had been better, I think, for any helpless wretch
to be in the bull-dog hold of the sturdiest Bill Sykes ever loosed
upon society by right of his ticket-of-leave,* than in the power of

Paul Marchmont, artist and teacher of drawing, of Charlotte Street, Fitzroy Square.

He was thinking of Olivia as he walked slowly up and down the bare platform, only separated by a rough wooden paling from the flat open fields in the outskirts of Kemberling.

'The little girl is as feeble as a pale February butterfly,' he thought; 'a puff of frosty wind might wither her away. But that woman, that woman—how handsome she is, with her accurate profile and iron mouth; but what a raging fire there is hidden somewhere in her breast, and devouring her beauty by day and night! If I wanted to paint the sleeping scene in *Macbeth*, I'd ask her to sit for the Thane's wicked wife. Perhaps she has some bloody secret as deadly as the murder of a grey-headed Duncan upon her conscience, and leaves her bedchamber in the stillness of the night to walk up and down those long oaken corridors at the Towers, and wring her hands and wail aloud in her sleep. Why did she marry John Marchmont? His life gave her little more than a fine house to live in; his death leaves her with nothing but ten or twelve thousand pounds in the Three per Cents. What is her mystery—what is her secret, I wonder? for she must surely have one.'

Such thoughts as these filled his mind as the train carried him away from the lonely little station, and away from the neighbourhood of Marchmont Towers, within whose stony walls Mary lay in her quiet chamber, weeping for her dead father, and wishing—God knows in what utter singleness of heart!—that she had been buried in the vault by his side.

CHAPTER XIII
OLIVIA'S DESPAIR

THE life which Mary and her stepmother led at Marchmont Towers after poor John's death was one of those tranquil and monotonous existences that leave very little to be recorded, except the slow progress of the weeks and months, the gradual changes of the seasons. Mary bore her sorrows quietly, as it was her nature to bear all things. The doctor's advice was taken, and Olivia removed her stepdaughter to Scarborough soon after the funeral. But the change of scene was slow to effect any change in the state of dull despairing sorrow into which the girl had fallen. The sea-breezes brought no colour into her pale cheeks. She obeyed her stepmother's behests unmurmuringly, and wandered wearily by the dreary seashore in the dismal November weather, in search of health and strength. But wherever she went, she carried with her the awful burden of her grief; and in every changing cadence of the low winter winds, in every varying murmur of the moaning waves, she seemed to hear her dead father's funeral dirge.

I think that, young as Mary Marchmont was, this mournful period was the grand crisis of her life. The past, with its one great affection, had been swept away from her, and as yet there was no friendly figure to fill the dismal blank of the future. Had any kindly matron, any gentle Christian creature been ready to stretch out her arms to the desolate orphan, Mary's heart would have melted, and she would have crept to the shelter of that womanly embrace, to nestle there for ever. But there was no one. Olivia Marchmont obeyed the letter of her husband's solemn appeal, as she had obeyed the letter of those Gospel sentences that had been familiar to her from her childhood, but was utterly unable to comprehend its spirit. She accepted the charge intrusted to her. She was unflinching in the performance of her duty; but no one glimmer of the holy light of motherly love and tenderness, the semi-divine compassion of womanhood, ever illumined the dark chambers of her heart. Every night she questioned herself upon her knees as to her rigid performance of the level round of duty she had allotted to herself; every night—scrupulous and relentless as the hardest judge who ever pronounced sentence upon a criminal—she took note of her own shortcomings, and acknowledged her deficiencies.

But, unhappily, this self-devotion of Olivia's pressed no less heavily upon Mary than on the widow herself. The more rigidly Mrs Marchmont performed the duties which she understood to be laid upon her by her dead husband's last will and testament, the harder became the orphan's life. The weary treadmill of education worked on, when the young student was well-nigh fainting upon every step in that hopeless revolving ladder of knowledge. If Olivia, on communing with herself at night, found that the day just done had been too easy for both mistress and pupil, the morrow's allowance of Roman emperors and French grammar was made to do penance for yesterday's shortcomings.

'This girl has been intrusted to my care, and one of my first duties is to give her a good education,' Olivia Marchmont thought. 'She is inclined to be idle; but I must fight against her inclination, whatever trouble the struggle entails upon myself. The harder the battle, the better for me if I am conqueror.'

It was only thus that Olivia Marchmont could hope to be a good woman. It was only by the rigid performance of hard duties, the patient practice of tedious rites, that she could hope to attain that eternal crown which simpler Christians seem to win so easily.

Morning and night the widow and her stepdaughter read the Bible together; morning and night they knelt side by side to join in the same familiar prayers; yet all these readings and all these prayers failed to bring them any nearer together. No tender sentence of inspiration, not the words of Christ himself, ever struck the same chord in these two women's hearts, bringing both into sudden unison. They went to church three times upon every dreary Sunday,— dreary from the terrible uniformity which made one day a mechanical repetition of another,—and sat together in the same pew; and there were times when some solemn word, some sublime injunction, seemed to fall with a new meaning upon the orphan girl's heart; but if she looked at her stepmother's face, thinking to see some ray of that sudden light which had newly shone into her own mind reflected *there*, the blank gloom of Olivia's countenance seemed like a dead wall, across which no glimmer of radiance ever shone.

They went back to Marchmont Towers in the early spring. People imagined that the young widow would cultivate the society of her husband's old friends, and that morning callers would be welcome at the Towers, and the stately dinner-parties would begin again, when Mrs Marchmont's year of mourning was over. But it was not so; Olivia closed her doors upon almost all society, and devoted herself entirely to the education of her stepdaughter. The gossips of Swampington and Kemberling, the county gentry who had talked of her piety and patience, her unflinching devotion to the poor of her father's parish, talked now of her self-abnegation, the sacrifices she made for her stepdaughter's sake, the noble manner in which she justified John Marchmont's confidence in her goodness. Other women would have intrusted the heiress's education to some hired governess, people said; other women would have been upon the look-out for a second husband; other women would have grown weary of the dulness of that lonely Lincolnshire mansion, the monotonous society of a girl of sixteen. They were never tired of lauding Mrs Marchmont as a model for all stepmothers in time to come.

Did she sacrifice much, this woman, whose spirit was a raging fire, who had the ambition of a Semiramis, the courage of a Boadicea,* the resolution of a Lady Macbeth? Did she sacrifice much in resigning such provincial gaieties as might have adorned her life,—a few dinner-parties, an occasional county ball, a flirtation with some ponderous landed gentleman or hunting squire?

No; these things would very soon have grown odious to her— more odious than the monotony of her empty life, more wearisome even than the perpetual weariness of her own spirit. I said, that when she accepted a new life by becoming the wife of John Marchmont, she acted in the spirit of a prisoner, who is glad to exchange his old dungeon for a new one. But, alas! the novelty of the prison-house had very speedily worn off, and that which Olivia Arundel had been at Swampington Rectory, Olivia Marchmont was now in the gaunt country mansion,—a wretched woman, weary of herself and all the world, devoured by a slow-consuming and perpetual fire.

This woman was, for two long melancholy years, Mary Marchmont's sole companion and instructress. I say sole companion advisedly; for the girl was not allowed to become intimate with the younger members of such few county families as still called occasionally at the Towers, lest she should become empty-headed and frivolous by their companionship. Alas, there was little fear of Mary becoming empty-headed! As she grew taller, and more slender, she seemed to get weaker and paler; and her heavy head drooped wearily under the load of knowledge which it had been made to carry, like some poor sickly flower oppressed by the weight of the dew-drops, which would have revivified a hardier blossom.

Heaven knows to what end Mrs Marchmont educated her step-daughter! Poor Mary could have told the precise date of any event in universal history, ancient or modern; she could have named the exact latitude and longitude of the remotest island in the least navigable ocean, and might have given an accurate account of the manners and customs of its inhabitants, had she been called upon to do so. She was alarmingly learned upon the subject of tertiary and old red sandstone, and could have told you almost as much as Mr Charles Kingsley* himself about the history of a gravel-pit,—though I doubt if she could have conveyed her information in quite such a pleasant manner; she could have pointed out every star in the broad heavens above Lincolnshire, and could have told the history of its discovery; she knew the hardest names that science had given to the familiar field-flowers she met in her daily walks;—yet I cannot say that her conversation was any the more brilliant because of this, or that her spirits grew lighter under the influence of this general mental illumination.

But Mrs Marchmont did most earnestly believe that this laborious educational process was one of the duties she owed her step-daughter; and when, at seventeen years of age, Mary emerged from the struggle, laden with such intellectual spoils as I have described above, the widow felt a quiet satisfaction as she contemplated her work, and said to herself, 'In this, at least, I have done my duty.'

Amongst all the dreary mass of instruction beneath which her health had very nearly succumbed, the girl had learned one thing that was a source of pleasure to herself; she had learned to become a very brilliant musician. She was not a musical genius, remember; for no such vivid flame as the fire of genius had ever burned in her gentle breast; but all the tenderness of her nature, all the poetry of a hyper-poetical mind, centred in this one accomplishment, and, con-demned to perpetual silence in every other tongue, found a new and glorious language here. The girl had been forbidden to read Byron and Scott; but she was not forbidden to sit at her piano, when the day's toils were over, and the twilight was dusky in her quiet room, playing dreamy melodies by Beethoven and Mozart, and making her

own poetry to Mendelssohn's wordless songs.* I think her soul must
have shrunk and withered away altogether had it not been for this
one resource, this one refuge, in which her mind regained its elas-
ticity, springing up, like a trampled flower, into new life and beauty.

Olivia was well pleased to see the girl sit hour after hour at her
piano. She had learned to play well and brilliantly herself, mastering
all difficulties with the proud determination which was a part of her
strong nature; but she had no special love for music. All things that
compose the poetry and beauty of life had been denied to this
woman, in common with the tenderness which makes the chief loveliness of womankind. She sat by the piano and listened while Mary's
slight hands wandered over the keys, carrying the player's soul away
into trackless regions of dreamland and beauty; but she heard
nothing in the music except so many chords, so many tones and
semitones, played in such or such a time.

It would have been scarcely natural for Mary Marchmont,
reserved and self-contained though she had been ever since her
father's death, to have had no yearning for more genial companionship than that of her stepmother. The girl who had kept watch in her
room, by the doctor's suggestion, was the one friend and confidante
whom the young mistress of Marchmont Towers fain would have
chosen. But here Olivia interposed, sternly forbidding any intimacy
between the two girls. Hester Pollard was the daughter of a small
tenant-farmer, and no fit associate for Mrs Marchmont's stepdaughter. Olivia thought that this taste for obscure company was the
fruit of Mary's early training—the taint left by those bitter, debasing
days of poverty, in which John Marchmont and his daughter had
lived in some wretched Lambeth lodging.

'But Hester Pollard is fond of me, mamma,' the girl pleaded; 'and
I feel so happy at the old farm house! They are all so kind to me
when I go there,—Hester's father and mother, and little brothers
and sisters, you know; and the poultry-yard, and the pigs and horses,
and the green pond, with the geese cackling round it, remind me of
my aunt's, in Berkshire. I went there once with poor papa for a day
or two; it was *such* a change after Oakley Street.'

But Mrs Marchmont was inflexible upon this point. She would
allow her stepdaughter to pay a ceremonial visit now and then to
Farmer Pollard's, and to be entertained with cowslip-wine and
pound-cake in the low, old-fashioned parlour, where all the polished

mahogany chairs were so shining and slippery that it was a marvel how anybody ever contrived to sit down upon them. Olivia allowed such solemn visits as these now and then, and she permitted Mary to renew the farmer's lease upon sufficiently advantageous terms, and to make occasional presents to her favourite, Hester. But all stolen visits to the farmyard, all evening rambles with the farmer's daughter in the apple orchard at the back of the low white farmhouse, were sternly interdicted; and though Mary and Hester were friends still, they were fain to be content with a chance meeting once in the course of a dreary interval of months, and a silent pressure of the hand.

'You mustn't think that I am proud of my money, Hester,' Mary said to her friend, 'or that I forget you now that we see each other so seldom. Papa used to let me come to the farm whenever I liked; but papa had seen a great deal of poverty. Mamma keeps me almost always at home at my studies; but she is very good to me, and of course I am bound to obey her; papa wished me to obey her.'

The orphan girl never for a moment forgot the terms of her father's will. *He* had wished her to obey; what should she do, then, but be obedient? Her submission to Olivia's lightest wish was only a part of the homage which she paid to that beloved father's memory.

It was thus she grew to early womanhood; a child in gentle obedience and docility; a woman by reason of that grave and thoughtful character which had been peculiar to her from her very infancy. It was in a life such as this, narrow, monotonous, joyless, that her seventeenth birthday came and went, scarcely noticed, scarcely remembered, in the dull uniformity of the days which left no track behind them; and Mary Marchmont was a woman,—a woman with all the tragedy of life before her; infantine in her innocence and inexperience of the world outside Marchmont Towers.

The passage of time had been so long unmarked by any break in its tranquil course, the dull routine of life had been so long undisturbed by change, that I believe the two women thought their lives would go on for ever and ever. Mary, at least, had never looked beyond the dull horizon of the present. Her habit of castle-building had died out with her father's death. What need had she to build castles, now that he could no longer inhabit them? Edward Arundel, the bright boy she remembered in Oakley Street, the dashing young officer who had come to Marchmont Towers, had dropped back into the chaos of the past. Her father had been the keystone in the arch of Mary's existence: he was gone, and a mass of chaotic ruins alone remained of the familiar visions which had once beguiled her. The world had ended with John's Marchmont's death, and his daughter's life since that great sorrow had been at best only a passive endurance of existence. They had heard very little of the young soldier at Marchmont Towers. Now and then a letter from some member of the family at Dangerfield had come to the Rector of Swampington. The warfare was still raging far away in the East, cruel and desperate battles were being fought, and brave Englishmen were winning loot and laurels, or perishing under the scimitars of Sikhs and Afghans, as the case might be. Squire Arundel's youngest son was not doing less than his duty, the letters said. He had gained his captaincy, and was well spoken of by great soldiers, whose very names were like the sound of the war-trumpet to English ears.

Olivia heard all this. She sat by her father, sometimes looking over his shoulder at the crumpled letter, as he read aloud to her of her cousin's exploits. The familiar name seemed to be all ablaze with lurid light as the widow's greedy eyes devoured it. How common-place the letters were! What frivolous nonsense Letitia Arundel intermingled with the news of her brother!—'You'll be glad to hear that my grey pony has got the better of his lameness. Papa gave a hunting-breakfast on Tuesday week. Lord Mountlitchcombe was present; but the hunting-men are very much aggravated about the frost, and I fear we shall have no crocuses. Edward has got his captaincy, papa told me to tell you. Sir Charles Napier and Major Outram have spoken very highly of him; but he—Edward, I mean— got a sabre-cut on his left arm, besides a wound on his forehead, and was laid up for nearly a month. I daresay you remember old Colonel Tollesly, at Halburton Lodge? He died last November; and has left all his money to ——' and the young lady ran on thus, with such gossip as she thought might be pleasing to her uncle; and there were no more tidings of the young soldier, whose life-blood had so nearly been spilt for his country's glory.

Olivia thought of him as she rode back to Marchmont Towers. She thought of the sabre-cut upon his arm, and pictured him wounded and bleeding, lying beneath the canvas-shelter of a tent, comfortless, lonely, forsaken.

'Better for me if he had died,' she thought; 'better for me if I were to hear of his death to-morrow!'

And with the idea the picture of such a calamity arose before her so vividly and hideously distinct, that she thought for one brief moment of agony, 'This is not a fancy, it is a presentiment; it is second sight; the thing will occur.'

She imagined herself going to see her father as she had gone that morning. All would be the same: the low grey garden-wall of the Rectory; the ceaseless surging of the sea; the prim servant-maid; the familiar study, with its litter of books and papers; the smell of stale cigar-smoke; the chintz curtains flapping in the open window; the dry leaves fluttering in the garden without. There would be nothing changed except her father's face, which would be a little graver than usual. And then, after a little hesitation—after a brief preamble about the uncertainty of life, the necessity for looking always beyond this world, the horrors of war,—the dreadful words would be upon his lips, when she would read all the hideous truth in his face, and fall prone to the ground, before he could say, 'Edward Arundel is dead!'

Yes; she felt all the anguish. It would be this—this sudden paralysis of black despair. She tested the strength of her endurance by this imaginary torture,—scarcely imaginary, surely, when it seemed so real,—and asked herself a strange question: 'Am I strong enough to bear this, or would it be less terrible to go on, suffering for ever—for ever abased and humiliated by the degradation of my love for a man who does not care for me?'

So long as John Marchmont had lived, this woman would have been true to the terrible victory she had won upon the eve of her bridal. She would have been true to herself and to her marriage-vow; but her husband's death, in setting her free, had cast her back upon the madness of her youth. It was no longer a sin to think of Edward Arundel. Having once suffered this idea to arise in her mind, her idol grew too strong for her, and she thought of him by night and day.

Yes; she thought of him for ever and ever. The narrow life to which she doomed herself, the self-immolation which she called duty, left her a prey to this one thought. Her work was not enough for her. Her powerful mind wasted and shrivelled for want of worthy employment. It was like one vast roll of parchment whereon half the wisdom of the world might have been inscribed, but on which was only written over and over again, in maddening repetition, the name of Edward Arundel. If Olivia Marchmont could have gone to America, and entered herself amongst the feminine professors of law or medicine,—if she could have turned field-preacher, like simple Dinah Morris,* or set up a printing-press in Bloomsbury, or even written a novel,—I think she might have been saved. The superabundant energy of her mind would have found a new object. As it was, she did none of these things. She had only dreamt one dream, and by force of perpetual repetition the dream had become a madness.

But the monotonous life was not to go on for ever. The dull, grey, leaden sky was to be illumined by sudden bursts of sunshine, and swept by black thunder-clouds, whose stormy violence was to shake the very universe for these two solitary women.

John Marchmont had been dead nearly three years. Mary's humble friend, the farmer's daughter, had married a young trades-man in the village of Kemberling, a mile and a half from the Towers. Mary was a woman now, and had seen the last of the Roman emperors and all the dry-as-dust studies of her early girlhood. She had nothing to do but accompany her stepmother hither and thither amongst the poor cottagers about Kemberling and two or three other small parishes within a drive of the Towers, 'doing good,' after Olivia's fashion, by line and rule. At home the young lady did what she pleased, sitting for hours together at her piano, or wading through gigantic achievements in the way of embroidery-work. She was even allowed to read novels now, but only such novels as were especially recommended to Olivia, who was one of the patronesses of a book-club at Swampington: novels in which young ladies fell in love with curates, and didn't marry them: novels in which everybody suffered all manner of misery, and rather liked it: novels in which, if the heroine did marry the man she loved—and this happy conclu-sion was the exception, and not the rule—the smallpox swept away her beauty, or a fatal accident deprived him of his legs, or eyes, or arms before the wedding-day.

The two women went to Kemberling Church together three times every Sunday. It was rather monotonous—the same church, the same rector and curate, the same clerk, the same congregation, the same old organ-tunes and droning voices of Lincolnshire charity-children, the same sermons very often. But Mary had grown accustomed to monotony. She had ceased to hope or care for anything since her father's death, and was very well contented to be let alone, and allowed to dawdle through a dreary life which was utterly without aim or purpose. She sat opposite her stepmother on one particular afternoon in the state-pew at Kemberling, which was lined with faded red baize, and raised a little above the pews of meaner worshippers; she was sitting with her listless hands lying in her lap, looking thoughtfully at her stepmother's stony face, and listening to the dull droning of the rector's voice above her head. It was a sunny afternoon in early June, and the church was bright with a warm yellow radiance; one of the old diamond-paned windows was open, and the tinkling of a sheep-bell far away in the distance, and the hum of bees in the churchyard, sounded pleasantly in the quiet of the hot atmosphere.

The young mistress of Marchmont Towers felt the drowsy influence of that tranquil summer weather creeping stealthily upon her. The heavy eyelids drooped over her soft brown eyes, those wistful eyes which had so long looked wearily out upon a world in which there seemed so little joy. The rector's sermon was a very long one this warm afternoon, and there was a low sound of snoring somewhere in one of the shadowy and sheltered pews beneath the galleries. Mary tried very hard to keep herself awake. Mrs Marchmont had frowned darkly at her once or twice already, for to fall asleep in church was a dire iniquity in Olivia's rigid creed; but the drowsiness was not easily to be conquered, and the girl was sinking into a peaceful slumber in spite of her stepmother's menacing frowns, when the sound of a sharp footfall on one of the gravel pathways in the churchyard aroused her attention.

Heaven knows why she should have been awoke out of her sleep by the sound of that step. It was different, perhaps, to the footsteps of the Kemberling congregation. The brisk, sharp sound of the tread striking lightly but firmly on the gravel was not compatible with the shuffling gait of the tradespeople and farmers' men who formed the greater part of the worshippers at that quiet Lincolnshire church. Again, it would have been a monstrous sin in that tranquil place for any one member of the congregation to disturb the devotions of the rest by entering at such a time as this. It was a stranger, then, evidently. What did it matter? Miss Marchmont scarcely cared to lift her eyelids to see who or what the stranger was; but the intruder let in such a flood of June sunshine when he pushed open the ponderous oaken door under the church-porch, that she was dazzled by that sudden burst of light, and involuntarily opened her eyes.

The stranger let the door swing softly to behind him, and stood beneath the shadow of the porch, not caring to advance any further, or to disturb the congregation by his presence.

Mary could not see him very plainly at first. She could only dimly define the outline of his tall figure, the waving masses of chestnut hair tinged with gleams of gold; but little by little his face seemed to grow out of the shadow, until she saw it all,—the handsome patrician features, the luminous blue eyes, the amber moustache,—the face which, in Oakley Street eight years ago, she had elected as her type of all manly perfection, her ideal of heroic grace.

Yes; it was Edward Arundel. Her eyes lighted up with an unwonted rapture as she looked at him; her lips parted; and her breath came in faint gasps. All the monotonous years, the terrible agonies of sorrow, dropped away into the past; and Mary Marchmont was conscious of nothing except the unutterable happiness of the present.

The one friend of her childhood had come back. The one link, the almost forgotten link, that bound her to every day-dream of those foolish early days, was united once more by the presence of the young soldier. All that happy time, nearly five years ago,—that happy time in which the tennis-court had been built, and the boat-house by the river restored,—those sunny autumn days before her father's second marriage,—returned to her. There was pleasure and joy in the world, after all; and then the memory of her father came back to her mind, and her eyes filled with tears. How sorry Edward would be to see his old friend's empty place in the western drawing-room; how sorry for her, and for her loss! Olivia Marchmont saw the change in her stepdaughter's face, and looked at her with stern amazement. But, after the first shock of that delicious surprise, Mary's training asserted itself. She folded her hands,—they trembled a little, but Olivia did not see that,—and waited patiently, with her eyes cast down and a faint flush lighting up her pale cheeks, until the sermon was finished, and the congregation began to disperse. She was not impatient. She felt as if she could have waited thus peacefully and contentedly for ever, knowing that the only friend she had on earth was near her.

Olivia was slow to leave her pew; but at last she opened the door and went out into the quiet aisle, followed by Mary, out under the shadowy porch and into the gravel-walk in the churchyard, where Edward Arundel was waiting for the two ladies.

John Marchmont's widow uttered no cry of surprise when she saw her cousin standing a little way apart from the slowly-dispersing Kemberling congregation. Her dark face faded a little, and her heart seemed to stop its pulsation suddenly, as if she had been turned into stone; but this was only for a moment. She held out her hand to Mr Arundel in the next instant, and bade him welcome to Lincolnshire.

'I did not know you were in England,' she said.

'Scarcely any one knows it yet,' the young man answered; 'and I have not even been home. I came to Marchmont Towers at once.'

He turned from his cousin to Mary, who was standing a little behind her stepmother.

'Dear Polly,' he said, taking both her hands in his, 'I was so sorry for you, when I heard ——'

He stopped, for he saw the tears welling up to her eyes. It was not his allusion to her father's death that had distressed her. He had called her Polly, the old familiar name, which she had never heard since that dead father's lips had last spoken it.

The carriage was waiting at the gate of the churchyard, and Edward Arundel went back to Marchmont Towers with the two ladies. He had reached the house a quarter of an hour after they had left it for afternoon church, and had walked over to Kemberling.

'I was so anxious to see you, Polly,' he said, 'after all this long time, that I had no patience to wait until you and Livy came back from church.'

Olivia started as the young man said this. It was Mary Marchmont whom he had come to see, then—not herself. Was *she* never to be anything? Was she to be for ever insulted by this humiliating indifference? A dark flush came over her face, as she drew her head up with the air of an offended empress, and looked angrily at her cousin. Alas! he did not even see that indignant glance. He was bending over Mary, telling her, in a low tender voice, of the grief he had felt at learning the news of her father's death.

Olivia Marchmont looked with an eager, scrutinising gaze at her stepdaughter. Could it be possible that Edward Arundel might ever come to love this girl? *Could* such a thing be possible? A hideous depth of horror and confusion seemed to open before her with the thought. In all the past, amongst all things she had imagined, amongst all the calamities she had pictured to herself, she had never thought of anything like this. Would such a thing ever come to pass? Would she ever grow to hate this girl—this girl, who had been intrusted to her by her dead husband—with the most terrible hatred that one woman can feel towards another?

In the next moment she was angry with herself for the abject folly of this new terror. She had never yet learned to think of Mary as a woman. She had never thought of her otherwise than as the pale childlike girl who had come to her meekly, day after day, to recite difficult lessons, standing in a submissive attitude before her, and rendering obedience to her in all things. Was it likely, was it possible, that this pale-faced girl would enter into the lists against her in the great battle of her life? Was it likely that she was to find her adversary and her conqueror here, in the meek child who had been committed to her charge?

She watched her stepdaughter's face with a jealous, hungry gaze. Was it beautiful? No! The features were delicate; the brown eyes soft and dovelike, almost lovely, now that they were irradiated by a new light, as they looked shyly up at Edward Arundel. But the girl's face was wan and colourless. It lacked the splendour of beauty. It was only after you had looked at Mary for a very long time that you began to think her rather pretty.

The five years during which Edward Arundel had been away had made little alteration in him. He was rather taller, perhaps; his amber moustache thicker; his manner more dashing than of old. The mark of a sabre-cut under the clustering chestnut curls upon the temple gave him a certain soldierly dignity. He seemed a man of the world now, and Mary Marchmont was rather afraid of him. He was so different to the Lincolnshire squires, the bashful younger sons who were to be educated for the Church: he was so dashing, so elegant, so splendid! From the waving grace of his hair to the tip of the polished boot peeping out of his well-cut trouser (there were no pegtops* in 1847, and it was *le genre** to show very little of the boot), he was a creature to be wondered at, to be almost reverenced, Mary thought. She could not help admiring the cut of his coat, the easy *nonchalance* of his manner, the waxed ends of his curved moustache, the dangling toys of gold and enamel that jingled at his watch-chain, the waves of perfume that floated away from his cambric handkerchief. She was childish enough to worship all these external attributes in her hero.

'Shall I invite him to Marchmont Towers?' Olivia thought; and while she was deliberating upon this question, Mary Marchmont cried out, 'You will stop at the Towers, won't you, Mr Arundel, as you did when poor papa was alive?'

'Most decidedly, Miss Marchmont,' the young man answered. 'I mean to throw myself upon your hospitality as confidingly as I did a long time ago in Oakley Street, when you gave me hot rolls for my breakfast.'

Mary laughed aloud—perhaps for the first time since her father's death. Olivia bit her lip. She was of so little account, then, she thought, that they did not care to consult her. A gloomy shadow spread itself over her face. Already, already she began to hate this pale-faced, childish orphan girl, who seemed to be transformed into a new being under the spell of Edward Arundel's presence.

But she made no attempt to prevent his stopping at the Towers, though a word from her would have effectually hindered his coming. A dull torpor of despair took possession of her; a black apprehension paralysed her mind. She felt that a pit of horror was opening before her ignorant feet. All that she had suffered was as nothing to what she was about to suffer. Let it be, then! What could she do to keep this torture away from her? Let it come, since it seemed that it must come in some shape or other.

She thought all this, while she sat back in a corner of the carriage watching the two faces opposite to her, as Edward and Mary, seated with their backs to the horses, talked together in low confidential tones, which scarcely reached her ear. She thought all this during the short drive between Kemberling and Marchmont Towers; and when the carriage drew up before the low Tudor portico, the dark shadow had settled on her face. Her mind was made up. Let Edward Arundel come; let the worst come. She had struggled; she had tried to do her duty; she had striven to be good. But her destiny was stronger than herself, and had brought this young soldier over land and sea, safe out of every danger, rescued from every peril, to be her destruction. I think that in this crisis of her life the last faint ray of Christian light faded out of this lost woman's soul, leaving utter darkness and desolation. The old landmarks, dimly descried in the weary desert, sank for ever down into the quicksands, and she was left alone,—alone with her despair. Her jealous soul prophesied the evil which she dreaded. This man, whose indifference to her was almost an insult, would fall in love with Mary Marchmont,—with Mary Marchmont, whose eyes lit up into new beauty under the glances of his, whose pale face blushed into faint bloom as he talked to her. The girl's undisguised admiration would flatter the young man's vanity, and he would fall in love with her out of very frivolity and weakness of purpose.

'He is weak and vain, and foolish and frivolous, I daresay,' Olivia thought; 'and if I were to fling myself upon my knees at his feet, and tell him that I loved him, he would be flattered and grateful, and would be ready to return my affection. If I could tell him what this girl tells him in every look and word, he would be as pleased with me as he is with her.'

Her lip curled with unutterable scorn as she thought this. She was so despicable to herself by the deep humiliation of her wasted love, that the object of that foolish passion seemed despicable also. She was for ever weighing Edward Arundel against all the tortures she had endured for his sake, and for ever finding him wanting. He must have been a demigod if his perfections could have outweighed so much misery; and for this reason she was unjust to her cousin, and could not accept him for that which he really was,—a generous-hearted, candid, honourable young man (not a great man or a wonderful man),—a brave and honest-minded soldier, very well worthy of a good woman's love.

Mr Arundel stayed at the Towers, occupying the room which had been his in John Marchmont's lifetime; and a new existence began for Mary. The young man was delighted with his old friend's daughter. Among all the Calcutta belles whom he had danced with at Government-House balls and flirted with upon the Indian race-course, he could remember no one as fascinating as this girl, who seemed as childlike now, in her early womanhood, as she had been womanly while she was a child. Her naïve tenderness for himself bewitched and enraptured him. Who could have avoided being charmed by that pure and innocent affection, which was as freely given by the girl of eighteen as it had been by the child, and was unchanged in character by the lapse of years? The young officer had been so much admired and caressed in Calcutta, that perhaps, by reason of his successes, he had returned to England heart-whole; and he abandoned himself, without any *arrière-pensée*,* to the quiet happiness which he felt in Mary Marchmont's society. I do not say that he was intoxicated by her beauty, which was by no means of the intoxicating order, or that he was madly in love with her. The gentle fascination of her society crept upon him before he was aware of its influence. He had never taken the trouble to examine his own feelings; they were disengaged,—as free as butterflies to settle upon which flower might seem the fairest; and he had therefore no need to put himself under a course of rigorous self-examination. As yet he believed that the pleasure he now felt in Mary's society was the same order of enjoyment he had experienced five years before, when he had taught her chess, and promised her long rambles by the seashore.

They had no long rambles now in solitary lanes and under flowering hedgerows beside the waving green corn. Olivia watched them with untiring eyes. The tortures to which a jealous woman may condemn herself are not much greater than those she can inflict upon others. Mrs Marchmont took good care that her ward and her cousin were not *too* happy. Wherever they went, she went also; whenever they spoke, she listened; whatever arrangement was most likely to please them was opposed by her. Edward was not coxcomb enough to have any suspicion of the reason of this conduct on his cousin's part. He only smiled and shrugged his shoulders; and attributed her watchfulness to an overstrained sense of her responsibility, and the necessity of *surveillance*.

'Does she think me such a villain and a traitor,' he thought, 'that she fears to leave me alone with my dead friend's orphan daughter, lest I should whisper corruption into her innocent ear? How little these good women know of us, after all! What vulgar suspicions and narrow-minded fears influence them against us! Are they honourable and honest towards one another, I wonder, that they can entertain such pitiful doubts of our honour and honesty?'

So, hour after hour, and day after day, Olivia Marchmont kept watch and ward over Edward and Mary. It seems strange that love could blossom in such an atmosphere; it seems strange that the cruel gaze of those hard grey eyes did not chill the two innocent hearts, and prevent their free expansion. But it was not so; the egotism of love was all-omnipotent. Neither Edward nor Mary was conscious of the evil light in the glance that so often rested upon them. The universe narrowed itself to the one spot of earth upon which these two stood side by side.

Edward Arundel had been more than a month at Marchmont Towers when Olivia went, upon a hot July evening, to Swampington, on a brief visit to the Rector,—a visit of duty. She would doubtless have taken Mary Marchmont with her; but the girl had been suffering from a violent headache throughout the burning summer day, and had kept her room. Edward Arundel had gone out early in the morning upon a fishing excursion to a famous trout-stream seven or eight miles from the Towers, and was not likely to return until after nightfall. There was no chance, therefore, of a meeting between Mary and the young officer, Olivia thought—no chance of any confidential talk which she would not be by to hear.

Did Edward Arundel love the pale-faced girl, who revealed her devotion to him with such childlike unconsciousness? Olivia Marchmont had not been able to answer that question. She had sounded the young man several times upon his feelings towards her stepdaughter; but he had met her hints and insinuations with perfect frankness, declaring that Mary seemed as much a child to him now as she had appeared nearly nine years before in Oakley Street, and that the pleasure he took in her society was only such as he might have felt in that of any innocent and confiding child.

'Her simplicity is so bewitching, you know, Livy,' he said; 'she looks up in my face, and trusts me with all her little secrets, and tells me her dreams about her dead father, and all her foolish, innocent fancies, as confidingly as if I were some playfellow of her own age and sex. She's so refreshing after the artificial belles of a Calcutta ballroom, with their stereotyped fascinations and their complete manual of flirtation, the same for ever and ever. She is such a pretty little spontaneous darling, with her soft, shy, brown eyes, and her low voice, which always sounds to me like the cooing of the doves in the poultry-yard.'

I think that Olivia, in the depth of her gloomy despair, took some comfort from such speeches as these. Was this frank expression of regard for Mary Marchmont a token of *love*? No; not as the widow understood the stormy madness. Love to her had been a dark and terrible passion, a thing to be concealed, as monomaniacs have sometimes contrived to keep the secret of their mania, until it burst forth at last, fatal and irrepressible, in some direful work of wreck and ruin.

So Olivia Marchmont took an early dinner alone, and drove away from the Towers at four o'clock on a blazing summer afternoon, more at peace perhaps than she had been since Edward Arundel's coming. She paid her dutiful visit to her father, sat with him for some time, talked to the two old servants who waited upon him, walked two or three times up and down the neglected garden, and then drove back to the Towers.

The first object upon which her eyes fell as she entered the hall was Edward Arundel's fishing-tackle lying in disorder upon an oaken bench near the broad arched door that opened out into the quadrangle. An angry flush mounted to her face as she turned upon the servant near her.

'Mr Arundel has come home?' she said.

'Yes, ma'am, he came in half an hour ago; but he went out again almost directly with Miss Marchmont.'

'Indeed! I thought Miss Marchmont was in her room?'

'No, ma'am; she came down to the drawing-room about an hour after you left. Her head was better, ma'am, she said.'

'And she went out with Mr Arundel? Do you know which way they went?'

'Yes, ma'am; I heard Mr Arundel say he wanted to look at the old boat-house by the river.'

'And they have gone there?'

'I think so, ma'am.'

'Very good; I will go down to them. Miss Marchmont must not stop out in the night-air. The dew is falling already.'

The door leading into the quadrangle was open; and Olivia swept across the broad threshold, haughty and self-possessed, very stately-looking in her long black garments. She still wore mourning for her dead husband. What inducement had she ever had to cast off that sombre attire; what need had she to trick herself out in gay colours? What loving eyes would be charmed by her splendour? She went out of the door, across the quadrangle, under a stone archway, and into the low stunted wood, which was gloomy even in the summer-time. The setting sun was shining upon the western front of the Towers; but here all seemed cold and desolate. The damp mists were rising from the sodden ground beneath the tree; the frogs were croaking down by the river-side. With her small white teeth set, and her breath coming in fitful gasps, Olivia Marchmont hurried to the water's edge, winding in and out between the trees, tearing her black dress amongst the brambles, scorning all beaten paths, heedless where she trod, so long as she made her way speedily to the spot she wanted to reach.

At last the black sluggish river and the old boat-house came in sight, between a long vista of ugly distorted trunks and gnarled branches of pollard oak and willow. The building was dreary and dilapidated-looking, for the improvements commenced by Edward Arundel five years ago had never been fully carried out; but it was sufficiently substantial, and bore no traces of positive decay. Down by the water's edge there was a great cavernous recess for the shelter of the boats, and above this there was a pavilion, built of brick and stone, containing two decent-sized chambers, with latticed windows overlooking the river. A flight of stone steps with an iron balustrade led up to the door of this pavilion, which was supported upon the solid side-walls of the boat-house below.

In the stillness of the summer twilight Olivia heard the voices of those whom she came to seek. They were standing down by the edge of the water, upon a narrow pathway that ran along by the sedgy brink of the river, and only a few paces from the pavilion. The door of the boat-house was open; a long-disused wherry lay rotting upon the damp and mossy flags. Olivia crept into the shadowy recess. The door that faced the river had fallen from its rusty hinges, and the slimy woodwork lay in ruins upon the shore. Sheltered by the stone archway that had once been closed by this door, Olivia listened to the voices beside the still water.

Mary Marchmont was standing close to the river's edge; Edward stood beside her, leaning against the trunk of a willow that hung over the water.

'My childish darling,' the young man murmured, as if in reply to something his companion had said, 'and so you think, because you are simple-minded and innocent, I am not to love you. It is your innocence I love, Polly dear,—let me call you Polly, as I used five years ago,—and I wouldn't have you otherwise for all the world. Do you know that sometimes I am almost sorry I ever came back to Marchmont Towers?'

'Sorry you came back?' cried Mary, in a tone of alarm. 'Oh, why do you say that, Mr Arundel?'

'Because you are heiress to eleven thousand a year, Mary, and the Moated Grange behind us; and this dreary wood, and the river,—the river is yours, I daresay, Miss Marchmont;—and I wish you joy of the possession of so much sluggish water and so many square miles of swamp and fen.'

'But what then?' Mary asked wonderingly.

'What then? Do you know, Polly darling, that if I ask you to marry me people will call me a fortune-hunter, and declare that I came to Marchmont Towers bent upon stealing its heiress's innocent heart, before she had learned the value of the estate that must go along with it? God knows they'd wrong me, Polly, as cruelly as ever an honest man was wronged; for, so long as I have money to pay my tailor and tobacconist,—and I've more than enough for both of them,—I want nothing further of the world's wealth. What should I do with all this swamp and fen, Miss Marchmont—with all that horrible complication of expired leases to be renewed, and income-taxes to be appealed against, that rich people have to endure? If you were not rich, Polly, I ——'

He stopped and laughed, striking the toe of his boot amongst the weeds, and knocking the pebbles into the water. The woman crouching in the shadow of the archway listened with whitened cheeks and glaring eyes; listened as she might have listened to the sentence of her death, drinking in every syllable, in her ravenous desire to lose no breath that told her of her anguish.

'If I were not rich!' murmured Mary; 'what if I were not rich?'

'I should tell you how dearly I love you, Polly, and ask you to be my wife by-and-by.'

The girl looked up at him for a few moments in silence, shyly at first, and then more boldly, with a beautiful light kindling in her eyes.

'I love you dearly too, Mr Arundel,' she said at last; 'and I would rather you had my money than any one else in the world; and there was something in papa's will that made me think—'

'There was something that made you think he would wish this, Polly,' cried the young man, clasping the trembling little figure to his breast. 'Mr Paulette sent me a copy of the will, Polly, when he sent my diamond-ring; and I think there were some words in it that hinted at such a wish. Your father said he left me this legacy, darling,—I have his letter still,—the legacy of a helpless girl. God knows I will try to be worthy of such a trust, Mary dearest; God knows I will be faithful to my promise, made nine years ago.'

The woman listening in the dark archway sank down upon the damp flags at her feet, amongst the slimy rotten wood and rusty iron nails and broken bolts and hinges. She sat there for a long time, not unconscious, but quite motionless, her white face leaning against the moss-grown arch, staring blankly out of the black shadows. She sat there and listened, while the lovers talked in low tender murmurs of the sorrowful past and of the unknown future; that beautiful untrodden region, in which they were to go hand in hand through all the long years of quiet happiness between the present moment and the grave. She sat and listened till the moonlight faintly shimmered upon the water, and the footsteps of the lovers died away upon the narrow pathway by which they went back to the house.

Olivia Marchmont did not move until an hour after they had gone. Then she raised herself with an effort, and walked with stiffened limbs slowly and painfully to the house, and to her own room, where she locked her door, and flung herself upon the ground in the darkness.

Mary came to her to ask why she did not come to the drawing-room, and Mrs Marchmont answered, with a hoarse voice, that she was ill, and wished to be alone. Neither Mary, nor the old woman-servant who had been Olivia's nurse long ago, and who had some little influence over her, could get any other answer than this.

CHAPTER XIV
DRIVEN AWAY

MARY MARCHMONT and Edward Arundel were happy. They were happy; and how should they guess the tortures of that desperate woman, whose benighted soul was plunged in a black gulf of horror by reason of their innocent love? How should these two—very children in their ignorance of all stormy passions, all direful emotions—know that in the darkened chamber where Olivia Marchmont lay, suffering under some vague illness, for which the Swampington doctor was fain to prescribe quinine, in utter unconsciousness as to the real nature of the disease which he was called upon to cure,—how should they know that in that gloomy chamber a wicked heart was abandoning itself to all the devils that had so long held patient watch for this day?

Yes; the struggle was over. Olivia Marchmont flung aside the cross she had borne in dull, mechanical obedience, rather than in Christian love and truth. Better to have been sorrowful Magdalene, forgiven for her love and tears, than this cold, haughty, stainless woman, who had never been able to learn the sublime lessons which so many sinners have taken meekly to heart. The religion which was wanting in the vital principle of Christianity, the faith which showed itself only in dogged obedience, failed this woman in the hour of her agony. Her pride arose; the defiant spirit of the fallen angel asserted its gloomy grandeur.

'What have I done that I should suffer like this?' she thought. 'What am I that an empty-headed soldier should despise me, and that I should go mad because of his indifference? Is this the recompense for my long years of obedience? Is this the reward Heaven bestows upon me for my life of duty!'

She remembered the histories of other women,—women who had gone their own way and had been happy; and a darker question arose in her mind; almost the question which Job asked in his agony.

'Is there neither truth nor justice in the dealings of God?' she thought. 'Is it useless to be obedient and submissive, patient and untiring? Has all my life been a great mistake, which is to end in confusion and despair?'

And then she pictured to herself the life that might have been hers if Edward Arundel had loved her. How good she would have been! The hardness of her iron nature would have been melted and subdued. By force of her love and tenderness for him, she would have learned to be loving and tender to others. Her wealth of affection for him would have overflowed in gentleness and consideration for every creature in the universe. The lurking bitterness which had lain hidden in her heart ever since she had first loved Edward Arundel, and first discovered his indifference to her; and the poisonous envy of happier women, who had loved and were beloved,—would have been blotted away. Her whole nature would have undergone a wondrous transfiguration, purified and exalted by the strength of her affection. All this might have come to pass if he had loved her,—if he had only loved her. But a pale-faced child had come between her and this redemption; and there was nothing left for her but despair.

Nothing but despair? Yes; perhaps something further,—revenge.

But this last idea took no tangible shape. She only knew that, in the black darkness of the gulf into which her soul had gone down, there was, far away somewhere, one ray of lurid light. She only knew this as yet, and that she hated Mary Marchmont with a mad and wicked hatred. If she could have thought meanly of Edward Arundel,—if she could have believed him to be actuated by mercenary motives in his choice of the orphan girl,—she might have taken some comfort from the thought of his unworthiness, and of Mary's probable sorrow in the days to come. But she *could* not think this. Little as the young soldier had said in the summer twilight beside the river, there had been that in his tones and looks which had convinced the wretched watcher of his truth. Mary might have been deceived by the shallowest pretender; but Olivia's eyes devoured every glance; Olivia's greedy ears drank in every tone; and she *knew* that Edward Arundel loved her stepdaughter.

She knew this, and she hated Mary Marchmont. What had she done, this girl, who had never known what it was to fight a battle with her own rebellious heart? what had she done, that all this wealth of love and happiness should drop into her lap unsought,—comparatively unvalued, perhaps?

John Marchmont's widow lay in her darkened chamber thinking over these things; no longer fighting the battle with her own heart, but utterly abandoning herself to her desperation,—reckless hardened, impenitent.

Edward Arundel could not very well remain at the Towers while the reputed illness of his hostess kept her to her room. He went over to Swampington, therefore, upon a dutiful visit to his uncle; but rode to the Towers every day to inquire very particularly after his cousin's progress, and to dawdle on the sunny western terrace with Mary Marchmont.

Their innocent happiness needs little description. Edward Arundel retained a good deal of that boyish chivalry which had made him so eager to become the little girl's champion in the days gone by. Contact with the world had not much sullied the freshness of the young man's spirit. He loved his innocent, childish companion with the purest and truest devotion; and he was proud of the recollection that in the day of his poverty John Marchmont had chosen *him* as the future shelterer of this tender blossom.

'You must never grow any older or more womanly, Polly,' he said sometimes to the young mistress of Marchmont Towers. 'Remember that I always love you best when I think of you as the little girl in the shabby pinafore, who poured out my tea for me one bleak December morning in Oakley Street.'

They talked a great deal of John Marchmont. It was such a happiness to Mary to be able to talk unreservedly of her father to some one who had loved and comprehended him.

'My stepmamma was very good to poor papa, you know, Edward,' she said, 'and of course he was very grateful to her; but I don't think he ever loved her quite as he loved you. You were the friend of his poverty, Edward; he never forgot that.'

Once, as they strolled side by side together upon the terrace in the warm summer noontide, Mary Marchmont put her little hand through her lover's arm, and looked up shyly in his face.

'Did papa say that, Edward?' she whispered; 'did he really say that?'

'Did he really say what, darling?'

'That he left me to you as a legacy?'

'He did indeed, Polly,' answered the young man. 'I'll bring you the letter to-morrow.'

And the next day he showed Mary Marchmont the yellow sheet of letter-paper and the faded writing, which had once been black and wet under her dead father's hand. Mary looked through her tears at the old familiar Oakley-street address, and the date of the very day upon which Edward Arundel had breakfasted in the shabby lodging. Yes—there were the words: 'The legacy of a child's helplessness is the only bequest I can leave to the only friend I have.'

'And you shall never know what it is to be helpless while I am near you, Polly darling,' the soldier said, as he refolded his dead friend's epistle. 'You may defy your enemies henceforward, Mary—if you have any enemies. O, by-the-bye, you have never heard any thing of that Paul Marchmont, I suppose?'

'Papa's cousin—Mr Marchmont the artist?'

'Yes.'

'He came to the reading of papa's will.'

'Indeed! and did you see much of him?'

'Oh, no, very little. I was ill, you know,' the girl added, the tears rising to her eyes at the recollection of that bitter time,—'I was ill, and I didn't notice any thing. I know that Mr Marchmont talked to me a little; but I can't remember what he said.'

'And he has never been here since?'

'Never.'

Edward Arundel shrugged his shoulders. This Paul Marchmont could not be such a designing villain, after all, or surely he would have tried to push his acquaintance with his rich cousin!

'I dare say John's suspicion of him was only one of the poor fellow's morbid fancies,' he thought. 'He was always full of morbid fancies.'

Mrs Marchmont's rooms were in the western front of the house; and through her open windows she heard the fresh young voices of the lovers as they strolled up and down the terrace. The cavalry officer was content to carry a watering-pot full of water, for the refreshment of his young mistress's geraniums in the stone vases on the balustrade, and to do other under-gardener's work for her pleasure. He talked to her of the Indian campaign; and she asked a hundred questions about midnight marches and solitary encampments, fainting camels, lurking tigers in the darkness of the jungle, intercepted supplies of provisions, stolen ammunition, and all the other details of the war.

Olivia arose at last, before the Swampington surgeon's saline draughts and quinine mixtures had subdued the fiery light in her eyes, or cooled the raging fever that devoured her. She arose because she could no longer lie still in her desolation knowing that, for two hours in each long summer's day, Edward Arundel and Mary Marchmont could be happy together in spite of her. She came down stairs, therefore, and renewed her watch—chaining her step-daughter to her side, and interposing herself for ever between the lovers.

The widow arose from her sick-bed an altered woman, as it appeared to all who knew her. A mad excitement seemed to have taken sudden possession of her. She flung off her mourning garments, and ordered silks and laces, velvets and satins, from a London milliner; she complained of the absence of society, the monotonous dulness of her Lincolnshire life; and, to the surprise of every one, sent out cards of invitation for a ball at the Towers in honour of Edward Arundel's return to England. She seemed to be seized with a desire to do something, she scarcely cared what, to disturb the even current of her days.

During the brief interval between Mrs Marchmont's leaving her room and the evening appointed for the ball, Edward Arundel found no very convenient opportunity of informing his cousin of the engagement entered into between himself and Mary. He had no wish to hurry this disclosure; for there was something in the orphan girl's childishness and innocence that kept all definite ideas of an early marriage very far away from her lover's mind. He wanted to go back to India, and win more laurels, to lay at the feet of the mistress of Marchmont Towers. He wanted to make a name for himself; which should cause the world to forget that he was a younger son,—a name that the vilest tongue would never dare to blacken with the epithet of fortune-hunter.

The young man was silent therefore, waiting for a fitting opportunity in which to speak to Mary's stepmother. Perhaps he rather dreaded the idea of discussing his attachment with Olivia; for she had looked at him with cold angry eyes, and a brow as black as thunder, upon those occasions on which she had sounded him as to his feelings for Mary.

'She wants poor Polly to marry some grandee, I dare say,' he thought, 'and will do all she can to oppose my suit. But her trust will cease with Mary's majority; and I don't want my confiding little darling to marry me until she is old enough to choose for herself, and to choose wisely. She will be one-and-twenty in three years; and what are three years? I would wait as long as Jacob* for my pet, and

serve my fourteen years' apprenticeship under Sir Charles Napier,*
and be true to her all the time.'

Olivia Marchmont hated her stepdaughter. Mary was not slow to
perceive the change in the widow's manner towards her. It had
always been cold, and sometimes severe; but it was now almost
abhorrent. The girl shrank appalled from the sinister light in her
stepmother's gray eyes, as they followed her unceasingly, dogging
her footsteps with a hungry and evil gaze. The gentle girl wondered
what she had done to offend her guardian, and then, being unable to
think of any possible delinquency by which she might have incurred
Mrs Marchmont's displeasure, was fain to attribute the change in
Olivia's manner to the irritation consequent upon her illness, and
was thus more gentle and more submissive than of old; enduring
cruel looks, returning no answer to bitter speeches, but striving to
conciliate the supposed invalid by her sweetness and obedience.

But the girl's amiability only irritated the despairing woman. Her
jealousy fed upon every charm of the rival who had supplanted her.
That fatal passion fed upon Edward Arundel's every look and tone,
upon the quiet smile which rested on Mary's face as the girl sat over
her embroidery, in meek silence, thinking of her lover. The self-
tortures which Olivia Marchmont inflicted upon herself were so
horrible to bear, that she turned, with a mad desire for relief, upon
those she had the power to torture. Day by day, and hour by hour,
she contrived to distress the gentle girl, who had so long obeyed her,
now by a word, now by a look, but always with that subtle power of
aggravation which some women possess in such an eminent
degree—until Mary Marchmont's life became a burden to her, or
would have so become, but for that inexpressible happiness, of which
her tormentor could not deprive her,—the joy she felt in her knowledge of Edward Arundel's love.

She was very careful to keep the secret of her stepmother's altered
manner from the young soldier. Olivia was his cousin, and he had
said long ago that she was to love her. Heaven knows she had tried to
do so, and had failed most miserably; but her belief in Olivia's goodness was still unshaken. If Mrs Marchmont was now irritable, capricious, and even cruel, there was doubtless some good reason for the
alteration in her conduct; and it was Mary's duty to be patient. The
orphan girl had learned to suffer quietly when the great affliction
of her father's death had fallen upon her; and she suffered so quietly

now, that even her lover failed to perceive any symptoms of her distress. How could she grieve him by telling him of her sorrows, when his very presence brought such unutterable joy to her?

So, on the morning of the ball at Marchmont Towers,—the first entertainment of the kind that had been given in that grim Lincolnshire mansion since young Arthur Marchmont's untimely death,—Mary sat in her room, with her old friend Farmer Pollard's daughter, who was now Mrs Jobson, the wife of the most prosperous carpenter in Kemberling. Hester had come up to the Towers to pay a dutiful visit to her young patroness; and upon this particular occasion Olivia had not cared to prevent Mary and her humble friend spending half an hour together. Mrs Marchmont roamed from room to room upon this day, with a perpetual restlessness. Edward Arundel was to dine at the Towers, and was to sleep there after the ball. He was to drive his uncle over from Swampington, as the Rector had promised to show himself for an hour or two at his daughter's entertainment. Mary had met her stepmother several times that morning, in the corridors and on the staircase; but the widow had passed her in silence, with a dark face, and a shivering, almost abhorrent gesture.

The bright July day dragged itself out at last, with hideous slowness for the desperate woman, who could not find peace or rest in all those splendid rooms, on all that grassy flat, dry and burning under the blazing summer sun. She had wandered out upon the waste of barren turf; with her head bared to the hot sky, and had loitered here and there by the still pools, looking gloomily at the black tideless water, and wondering what the agony of drowning was like. Not that she had any thought of killing herself. No: the idea of death was horrible to her; for after her death Edward and Mary would be happy. Could she ever find rest in the grave, knowing this? Could there be any possible extinction that would blot out her jealous fury? Surely the fire of her hate—it was no longer love, but hate, that raged in her heart—would defy annihilation, eternal by reason of its intensity. When the dinner-hour came, and Edward and his uncle arrived at the Towers, Olivia Marchmont's pale face was lit up with eyes that flamed like fire; but she took her accustomed place very quietly, with her father opposite to her, and Mary and Edward upon either side.

'I'm sure you're ill, Livy,' the young man said; 'you're pale as death, and your hand is dry and burning. I'm afraid you've not been obedient to the Swampington doctor.'

Mrs Marchmont shrugged her shoulders with a short contemptuous laugh.

'I am well enough,' she said. 'Who cares whether I am well or ill?'

Her father looked up at her in mute surprise. The bitterness of her tone startled and alarmed him; but Mary never lifted her eyes. It was in such a tone as this that her stepmother had spoken constantly of late.

But two or three hours afterwards, when the flats before the house were silvered by the moonlight, and the long ranges of windows glittered with the lamps within, Mrs Marchmont emerged from her dressing-room another creature, as it seemed.

Edward and his uncle were walking up and down the great oaken banqueting-hall, which had been decorated and fitted up as a ball-room for the occasion, when Olivia crossed the wide threshold of the chamber. The young officer looked up with an involuntary expression of surprise. In all his acquaintance with his cousin, he had never seen her thus. The gloomy black-robed woman was transformed into a Semiramis. She wore a voluminous dress of a deep claret-coloured velvet, that glowed with the warm hues of rich wine in the lamplight. Her massive hair was coiled in a knot at the back of her head, and diamonds glittered amidst the thick bands that framed her broad white brow. Her stern classical beauty was lit up by the unwonted splendour of her dress, and asserted itself as obviously as if she had said, 'Am I a woman to be despised for the love of a pale-faced child?'

Mary Marchmont came into the room a few minutes after her stepmother. Her lover ran to welcome her, and looked fondly at her simple dress of shadowy white crape, and the pearl circlet that crowned her soft brown hair. The pearls she wore upon this night had been given to her by her father on her fourteenth birthday.

Olivia watched the young man as he bent over Mary Marchmont. He wore his uniform to-night for the special gratification of his young mistress, and he was looking down with a tender smile at her childish admiration of the bullion* ornaments upon his coat, and the decoration he had won in India.

The widow looked from the two lovers to an antique glass upon an ebony bureau in a niche opposite to her, which reflected her own face,—her own face, more beautiful than she had ever seen it before, with a feverish glow of vivid crimson lighting up her hollow cheeks.

'I might have been beautiful if he had loved me,' she thought; and then she turned to her father, and began to talk to him of his parishioners, the old pensioners upon her bounty, whose little histories were so hatefully familiar to her. Once more she made a feeble effort to tread the old hackneyed pathway, which she had toiled upon with such weary feet; but she could not,—she could not. After a few minutes she turned abruptly from the Rector, and seated herself in a recess of the window, from which she could see Edward and Mary.

But Mrs Marchmont's duties as hostess soon demanded her attention. The county families began to arrive; the sound of carriage-wheels seemed perpetual upon the crisp gravel-drive before the western front; the names of half the great people in Lincolnshire were shouted by the old servants in the hall. The band in the music-gallery struck up a quadrille, and Edward Arundel led the youthful mistress of the mansion to her place in the dance.

To Olivia that long night seemed all glare and noise and confusion. She did the honours of the ballroom, she received her guests, she meted out due attention to all; for she had been accustomed from her earliest girlhood to the stereotyped round of country society. She neglected no duty; but she did all mechanically, scarcely knowing what she said or did in the feverish tumult of her soul.

Yet, amidst all the bewilderment of her senses, in all the confusion of her thoughts, two figures were always before her. Wherever Edward Arundel and Mary Marchmont went, her eyes followed them—her fevered imagination pursued them. Once, and once only, in the course of that long night she spoke to her stepdaughter.

'How often do you mean to dance with Captain Arundel, Miss Marchmont?' she said.

But before Mary could answer, her stepmother had moved away upon the arm of a portly country squire, and the girl was left in sorrowful wonderment as to the reason of Mrs Marchmont's angry tone.

Edward and Mary were standing in one of the deep embayed windows of the banqueting-hall, when the dancers began to disperse, long after supper. The girl had been very happy that evening, in spite of her stepmother's bitter words and disdainful glances. For almost the first time in her life, the young mistress of Marchmont Towers had felt the contagious influence of other people's happiness. The brilliantly-lighted ballroom, the fluttering dresses of the dancers, the joyous music, the low sound of suppressed laughter, the bright faces which smiled at each other upon every side, were as new as any thing in fairyland to this girl, whose narrow life had been overshadowed by the gloomy figure of her stepmother, for ever interposed between her and the outer world. The young spirit arose and shook off its fetters, fresh and radiant as the butterfly that escapes from its chrysalis-shell. The new light of happiness illumined the orphan's delicate face, until Edward Arundel began to wonder at her loveliness, as he had wondered once before that night at the fiery splendour of his cousin Olivia.

'I had no idea Olivia was so handsome, or you so pretty, my darling,' he said, as he stood with Mary in the embrasure of the window. 'You look like Titania,* queen of the fairies, Polly, with your cloudy draperies and crown of pearls.'

The window was open, and Captain Arundel looked wistfully at the broad flagged quadrangle beautified by the light of the full summer moon. He glanced back into the room; it was nearly empty now; and Mrs Marchmont was standing near the principal doorway, bidding the last of her guests good-night.

'Come into the quadrangle, Polly,' he said, 'and take a turn with me under the colonnade, It was a cloister once, I dare say, in the good old days before Harry the Eighth was king; and cowled monks have paced up and down under its shadow, muttering mechanical aves and paternosters, as the beads of their rosaries dropped slowly through their shrivelled old fingers. Come out into the quadrangle, Polly; all the people we know or care about are gone; and we'll go out and walk in the moonlight as true lovers ought.'

The soldier led his young companion across the threshold of the window, and out into a cloister-like colonnade that ran along one side of the house. The shadows of the Gothic pillars were black upon the moonlit flags of the quadrangle, which was as light now as in the day; but a pleasant obscurity reigned in the sheltered colonnade.

'I think this little bit of pre-Lutheran masonry is the best of all your possessions, Polly,' the young man said, laughing. 'By-and-by, when I come home from India a general,—as I mean to do, Miss Marchmont, before I ask you to become Mrs Arundel,—I shall stroll up and down here in the still summer evenings, smoking my cheroots. You will let me smoke out of doors, won't you, Polly? But suppose I should leave some of my limbs on the banks of the Sutlej,* and come limping home to you with a wooden leg, would you have me then, Mary; or would you dismiss me with ignominy from your sweet presence, and shut the doors of your stony mansion upon myself and my calamities? I'm afraid, from your admiration of my gold epaulettes and silk sash, that glory in the abstract would have very little attraction for you.'

Mary Marchmont looked up at her lover with widely-opened and wondering eyes, and the clasp of her hand tightened a little upon his arm.

'There is nothing that could ever happen to you that would make me love you less *now*,' she said naïvely. 'I dare say at first I liked you a little because you were handsome, and different to every one else I had ever seen. You were so very handsome, you know,' she added apologetically; 'but it was not because of that *only* that I loved you. I loved you because papa told me you were good and generous, and his true friend when he was in cruel need of a friend. Yes; you were his friend at school, when your cousin, Martin Mostyn, and the other pupils sneered at him and ridiculed him. How can I ever forget that, Edward? How can I ever love you enough to repay you for that?' In the enthusiasm of her innocent devotion, she lifted her pure young brow, and the soldier bent down and kissed that white throne of all virginal thoughts, as the lovers stood side by side, half in the moonlight, half in the shadow.

Olivia Marchmont came into the embrasure of the open window, and took her place there to watch them.

She came again to the torture. From the remotest end of the long banqueting-room she had seen the two figures glide out into the moonlight. She had seen them, and had gone on with her courteous speeches, and had repeated her formula of hospitality, with the fire in her heart devouring and consuming her. She came again, to watch and to listen, and to endure her self-imposed agonies—as mad and foolish in her fatal passion as some besotted wretch who should come willingly to the wheel upon which his limbs had been well-nigh broken, and supplicate for a renewal of the torture. She stood rigid and motionless in the shadow of the arched window, hiding herself, as she had hidden in the dark cavernous recess by the river; she stood and listened to all the childish babble of the lovers as they loitered up and down the vaulted cloister. How she despised them, in the haughty superiority of an intellect which might have planned a revolution, or saved a sinking state! What bitter scorn curled her lip, as their foolish talk fell upon her ear! They talked like Florizel and Perdita, like Romeo and Juliet, like Paul and Virginia;* and they talked a great deal of nonsense, no doubt—soft harmonious foolishness, with little more meaning in it than there is in the cooing of doves, but tender and musical, and more than beautiful, to each other's ears. A tigress, famished and desolate, and but lately robbed of her whelps, would not be likely to listen very patiently to the communing of a pair of prosperous ringdoves. Olivia Marchmont listened with her brain on fire, and the spirit of a murderess raging in her breast. What was she that she should be patient? All the world was lost to her. She was thirty years of age, and she had never yet won the love of any human being. She was thirty years of age, and all the sublime world of affection was a dismal blank for her. From the outer darkness in which she stood, she looked with wild and ignorant yearning into that bright region which her accursed foot had never trodden, and saw Mary Marchmont wandering hand-in-hand with the only man *she* could have loved—the only creature who had ever had the power to awake the instinct of womanhood in her soul.

She stood and waited until the clock in the quadrangle struck the first quarter after three: the moon was fading out, and the colder light of early morning glimmered in the eastern sky.

'I musn't keep you out here any longer, Polly,' Captain Arundel said, pausing near the window. 'It's getting cold, my dear, and it's high time the mistress of Marchmont should retire to her stony bower. Good-night, and God bless you, my darling! I'll stop in the quadrangle and smoke a cheroot before I go to my room. Your stepmamma will be wondering what has become of you, Mary, and we shall have a lecture upon the proprieties to-morrow; so, once more, good-night.'

He kissed the fair young brow under the coronal of pearls, stopped to watch Mary while she crossed the threshold of the open window, and then strolled away into the flagged court, with his cigarcase in his hand.

Olivia Marchmont stood a few paces from the window when her

stepdaughter entered the room, and Mary paused involuntarily, terrified by the cruel aspect of the face that frowned upon her: terrified by something that she had never seen before,—the horrible darkness that overshadows the souls of the lost.

'Mamma!' the girl cried, clasping her hands in sudden affright— 'mamma! why do you look at me like that? Why have you been so changed to me lately? I cannot tell you how unhappy I have been. Mamma, mamma! what have I done to offend you?'

Olivia Marchmont grasped the trembling hands uplifted entreatingly to her, and held them in her own,—held them as if in a vice. She stood thus, with her stepdaughter pinioned in her grasp, and her eyes fixed upon the girl's face. Two streams of lurid light seemed to emanate from those dilated gray eyes; two spots of crimson blazed in the widow's hollow cheeks.

'*What* have you done?' she cried. 'Do you think I have toiled for nothing to do the duty which I promised my dead husband to perform for your sake? Has all my care of you been so little, that I am to stand by now and be silent, when I see what you are? Do you think that I am blind, or deaf; or besotted; that you defy me and outrage me, day by day, and hour by hour, by your conduct?'

'Mamma, mamma! what do you mean?'

'Heaven knows how rigidly you have been educated; how carefully you have been secluded from all society, and sheltered from every influence, lest harm or danger should come to you. I have done my duty, and I wash my hands of you. The debasing taint of your mother's low breeding reveals itself in your every action. You run after my cousin Edward Arundel, and advertise your admiration of him, to himself, and every creature who knows you. You fling yourself into his arms, and offer him yourself and your fortune; and in your low cunning you try to keep the secret from me, your protectress and guardian, appointed by the dead father whom you pretend to have loved so dearly.'

Olivia Marchmont still held her stepdaughter's wrists in her iron grasp. The girl stared wildly at her with her trembling lips apart. She began to think that the widow had gone mad.

'I blush for you—I am ashamed of you!' cried Olivia. It seemed as if the torrent of her words burst forth almost in spite of herself. 'There is not a village girl in Kemberling, there is not a scullerymaid in this house, who would have behaved as you have done. I have watched you, Mary Marchmont, remember, and I know all. I know your wanderings down by the river-side. I heard you—yes, by the Heaven above me!—I heard you offer yourself to my cousin.'

Mary drew herself up with an indignant gesture, and over the whiteness of her face there swept a sudden glow of vivid crimson that faded as quickly as it came. Her submissive nature revolted against her stepmother's horrible tyranny. The dignity of innocence arose and asserted itself against Olivia's shameful upbraiding.

'If I offered myself to Edward Arundel, mamma,' she said, 'it was because we love each other very truly, and because I think and believe papa wished me to marry his old friend.'

'Because *we* love each other very truly!' Olivia echoed in a tone of unmitigated scorn. 'You can answer for Captain Arundel's heart, I suppose, then, as well as for your own? You must have a tolerably good opinion of yourself, Miss Marchmont, to be able to venture so much. Bah!' she cried suddenly, with a disdainful gesture of her head; 'do you think your pitiful face has won Edward Arundel? Do you think he has not had women fifty times your superior, in every quality of mind and body, at his feet out yonder in India? Are you idiotic and besotted enough to believe that it is anything but your fortune this man cares for? Do you know the vile things people will do, the lies they will tell, the base comedies of guilt and falsehood they will act, for the love of eleven thousand a year? And you think that he loves you! Child, dupe, fool! are you weak enough to be deluded by a fortune-hunter's pretty pastoral flatteries? Are you weak enough to be duped by a man of the world, worn out and jaded, no doubt, as to the world's pleasures—in debt perhaps, and in pressing need of money, who comes here to try and redeem his fortunes by a marriage with a semi-imbecile heiress?'

Olivia Marchmont released her hold of the shrinking girl, who seemed to have become transfixed to the spot upon which she stood, a pale statue of horror and despair.

The iron will of the strong and resolute woman rode roughshod over the simple confidence of the ignorant girl. Until this moment, Mary Marchmont had believed in Edward Arundel as implicitly as she had trusted in her dead father. But now, for the first time, a dreadful region of doubt opened before her; the foundations of her world reeled beneath her feet. Edward Arundel a fortune-hunter! This woman, whom she had obeyed for five weary years, and who had acquired that ascendancy over her which a determined and vigorous nature must always exercise over a morbidly sensitive disposition, told her that she had been deluded. This woman laughed aloud in bitter scorn of her credulity. This woman, who could have no possible motive for torturing her, and who was known to be scrupulously conscientious in all her dealings, told her, as plainly as the most cruel words could tell a cruel truth, that her own charms could not have won Edward Arundel's affection.

All the beautiful day-dreams of her life melted away from her. She had never questioned herself as to her worthiness of her lover's devotion. She had accepted it as she accepted the sunshine and the starlight—as something beautiful and incomprehensible, that came to her by the beneficence of God, and not through any merits of her own. But as the fabric of her happiness dwindled away, the fatal spell exercised over the girl's weak nature by Olivia's violent words evoked a hundred doubts. How should he love her? why should he love her in preference to every other woman in the world? Set any woman to ask herself this question, and you fill her mind with a thousand suspicions, a thousand jealous doubts of her lover, though he were the truest and noblest in the universe.

Olivia Marchmont stood a few paces from her stepdaughter, watching her while the black shadow of doubt blotted every joy from her heart, and utter despair crept slowly into her innocent breast. The widow expected that the girl's self-esteem would assert itself— that she would contradict and defy the traducer of her lover's truth; but it was not so. When Mary spoke again, her voice was low and subdued, her manner as submissive as it had been two or three years before, when she had stood before her stepmother, waiting to repeat some difficult lesson.

'I dare say you are right, mamma,' she said in a low dreamy tone, looking not at her stepmother, but straight before her into vacancy, as if her tearless eyes were transfixed by the vision of all her shattered hopes, filling with wreck and ruin the desolate foreground of a blank future. 'I dare say you are right, mamma; it was very foolish of me to think that Edward—that Captain Arundel could care for me, for—for—my own sake; but if—if he wants my fortune, I should wish him to have it. The money will never be any good to me, you know, mamma; and he was so kind to papa in his poverty—so kind!

I will never, never believe anything against him;—but I couldn't expect him to love me. I shouldn't have offered to be his wife; I ought only to have offered him my fortune.'

She heard her lover's footstep in the quadrangle without, in the stillness of the summer morning, and shivered at the sound. It was less than a quarter of an hour since she had been walking with him up and down that cloistered way, in which his footsteps were echoing with a hollow sound; and now ——. Even in the confusion of her anguish, Mary Marchmont could not help wondering, as she thought in how short a time the happiness of a future might be swept away into chaos.

'Good-night, mamma,' she said presently, with an accent of weariness. She did not look at her stepmother (who had turned away from her now, and had walked towards the open window), but stole quietly from the room, crossed the hall, and went up the broad staircase to her own lonely chamber. Heiress though she was, she had no special attendant of her own: she had the privilege of summoning Olivia's maid whenever she had need of assistance; but she retained the simple habits of her early life, and very rarely troubled Mrs Marchmont's grim and elderly Abigail.*

Olivia stood looking out into the stony quadrangle. It was broad daylight now; the cocks were crowing in the distance, and a skylark singing somewhere in the blue heaven, high up above Marchmont Towers. The faded garlands in the banqueting-room looked wan in the morning sunshine; the lamps were burning still, for the servants waited until Mrs Marchmont should have retired, before they entered the room. Edward Arundel was walking up and down the cloister, smoking his second cigar.

He stopped presently, seeing his cousin at the window.

'What, Livy!' he cried, 'not gone to bed yet?'

'No; I am going directly.'

'Mary has gone, I hope?'

'Yes; she has gone. Good-night.'

'Good *morning*, my dear Mrs Marchmont,' the young man answered, laughing. 'If the partridges were in, I should be going out shooting, this lovely morning, instead of crawling ignominiously to bed, like a worn-out reveller who has drunk too much sparkling hock. I like the still best, by-the-bye,—the Johannisberger, that poor John's predecessor imported from the Rhine. But I suppose there is no help for it, and I must go to bed in the face of all that eastern glory. I should be mounting for a gallop on the race-course, if I were in Calcutta. But I'll go to bed, Mrs Marchmont, and humbly await your breakfast-hour. They're stacking the new hay in the meadows beyond the park. Don't you smell it?'

Olivia shrugged her shoulders with an impatient frown. Good heavens! how frivolous and senseless this man's talk seemed to her! She was plunging her soul into an abyss of sin and ruin for his sake; and she hated him, and rebelled against him, because he was so little worthy of the sacrifice.

'Good morning,' she said abruptly; 'I'm tired to death.'

She moved away, and left him.

Five minutes afterwards, he went up the great oak-staircase after her, whistling a serenade from *Fra Diavolo** as he went. He was one of those people to whom life seems all holiday. Younger son though he was, he had never known any of the pitfalls of debt and difficulty into which the junior members of rich families are so apt to plunge headlong in early youth, and from which they emerge enfeebled and crippled, to endure an after-life embittered by all the shabby miseries which wait upon aristocratic pauperism. Brave, honourable, and simple-minded, Edward Arundel had fought the battle of life like a good soldier, and had carried a stainless shield when the fight was thickest, and victory hard to win. His sunshiny nature won him friends, and his better qualities kept them. Young men trusted and respected him; and old men, gray in the service of their country, spoke well of him. His handsome face was a pleasant decoration at any festival; his kindly voice and hearty laugh at a dinner-table were as good as music in the gallery at the end of the banqueting-chamber.

He had that freshness of spirit which is the peculiar gift of some natures; and he had as yet never known sorrow, except, indeed, such tender and compassionate sympathy as he had often felt for the calamities of others.

Olivia Marchmont heard her cousin's cheery tenor voice as he passed her chamber. 'How happy he is!' she thought. 'His very happiness is one insult the more to me.'

The widow paced up and down her room in the morning sunshine, thinking of the things she had said in the banqueting-hall below, and of her stepdaughter's white despairing face. What had she done? What was the extent of the sin she had committed? Olivia

Marchmont asked herself these two questions. The old habit of self-examination was not quite abandoned yet. She sinned, and then set herself to work to try and justify her sin.

'How should he love her!' she thought. 'What is there in her pale unmeaning face that should win the love of a man who despises me?'

She stopped before a cheval-glass, and surveyed herself from head to foot, frowning angrily at her handsome image, hating herself for her despised beauty. Her white shoulders looked like stainless marble against the rich ruby darkness of her velvet dress. She had snatched the diamond ornaments from her head, and her long black hair fell about her bosom in thick waveless tresses.

'I am handsomer than she is, and cleverer; and I love him better, ten thousand times, than she loves him,' Olivia Marchmont thought, as she turned contemptuously from the glass. 'Is it likely, then, that he cares for anything but her fortune? Any other woman in the world would have argued as I argued to-night. Any woman would have believed that she did her duty in warning this besotted girl against her folly. What do I know of Edward Arundel that should lead me to think him better or nobler than other men? and how many men sell themselves for the love of a woman's wealth! Perhaps good may come of my mad folly, after all; and I may have saved this girl from a life of misery by the words I have spoken to-night.'

The devils—for ever lying in wait for this woman, whose gloomy pride rendered her in some manner akin to themselves—may have laughed at her as she argued thus with herself.

She lay down at last to sleep, worn out by the excitement of the long night, and to dream horrible dreams. The servants, with the exception of one who rose betimes to open the great house, slept long after the unwonted festival. Edward Arundel slumbered as heavily as any member of that wearied household; and thus it was that there was no one in the way to see a shrinking, trembling figure creep down the sunlit-staircase, and steal across the threshold of the wide hall door.

There was no one to see Mary Marchmont's silent flight from the gaunt Lincolnshire mansion, in which she had known so little real happiness. There was no one to comfort the sorrow-stricken girl in her despair and desolation of spirit. She crept away, like some escaped prisoner, in the early morning, from the house which the law called her own.

And the hand of the woman whom John Marchmont had chosen to be his daughter's friend and counsellor was the hand which drove that daughter from the shelter of her home. The voice of her whom the weak father had trusted in, fearful to confide his child into the hands of God, but blindly confident in his own judgment—was the voice which had uttered the lying words, whose every syllable had been as a separate dagger thrust in the orphan girl's lacerated heart. It was her father,—her father, who had placed this woman over her, and had entailed upon her the awful agony that drove her out into an unknown world, careless whither she went in her despair.

END OF VOL. I

CHAPTER XV

MARY'S LETTER

IT was past twelve o'clock when Edward Arundel strolled into the dining-room. The windows were open, and the scent of the mignionette upon the terrace was blown in upon the warm summer breeze.

Mrs Marchmont was sitting at one end of the long table, reading a newspaper. She looked up as Edward entered the room. She was pale, but not much paler than usual. The feverish light had faded out of her eyes, and they looked dim and heavy.

'Good morning, Livy,' the young man said. 'Mary is not up yet, I suppose ?'

'I believe not.'

'Poor little girl! A long rest will do her good after her first ball. How pretty and fairy-like she looked in her white gauze dress, and with that circlet of pearls round her hair! Your taste, I suppose, Olivia? She looked like a snow-drop among all the other gaudy flowers,—the roses and tiger-lilies, and peonies and dahlias. That eldest Miss Hickman is handsome, but she's so terribly conscious of her attractions. That little girl from Swampington with the black ringlets is rather pretty; and Laura Filmer is a jolly, dashing girl; she looks you full in the face, and talks to you about hunting with as much gusto as an old whipper-in.* I don't think much of Major Hawley's three tall sandy-haired daughters; but Fred Hawley's a capital fellow: it's a pity he's a civilian. In short, my dear Olivia, take it altogether, I think your ball was a success, and I hope you'll give us another in the hunting-season.'

Mrs Marchmont did not condescend to reply to her cousin's meaningless rattle. She sighed wearily, and began to fill the tea-pot from the old-fashioned silver urn. Edward loitered in one of the windows, whistling to a peacock that was stalking solemnly backwards and forwards upon the stone balustrade.

'I should like to drive you and Mary down to the sea-shore, Livy, after breakfast. Will you go?'

Mrs Marchmont shook her head.

'I am a great deal too tired to think of going out to-day,' she said ungraciously.

'And I never felt fresher in my life,' the young man responded, laughing; 'last night's festivities seem to have revivified me. I wish Mary would come down,' he added, with a yawn; 'I could give her another lesson in billiards, at any rate. Poor little girl, I am afraid she'll never make a cannon.'

Captain Arundel sat down to his breakfast, and drank the cup of tea poured out for him by Olivia. Had she been a sinful woman of another type, she would have put arsenic into the cup perhaps, and so have made an end of the young officer and of her own folly. As it was, she only sat by, with her own untasted breakfast before her, and watched him while he ate a plateful of raised pie, and drank his cup of tea, with the healthy appetite which generally accompanies youth and a good conscience. He sprang up from the table directly he had finished his meal, and cried out impatiently, 'What can make Mary so lazy this morning? she is usually such an early riser.'

Mrs Marchmont rose as her cousin said this, and a vague feeling of uneasiness took possession of her mind. She remembered the white face which had blanched beneath the angry glare of her eyes, the blank look of despair that had come over Mary's countenance a few hours before.

'I will go and call her myself,' she said. 'N—no; I'll send Barbara.' She did not wait to ring the bell, but went into the hall, and called sharply, 'Barbara! Barbara!'

A woman came out of a passage leading to the housekeeper's room, in answer to Mrs Marchmont's call; a woman of about fifty years of age, dressed in gray stuff, and with a grave inscrutable face, a wooden countenance that gave no token of its owner's character. Barbara Simmons might have been the best or the worst of women, a Mrs Fry or a Mrs Brownrigg,* for any evidence her face afforded against either hypothesis.

'I want you to go up-stairs, Barbara, and call Miss Marchmont,' Olivia said. 'Captain Arundel and I have finished breakfast.'

The woman obeyed, and Mrs Marchmont returned to the dining-room, where Edward was trying to amuse himself with the 'Times' of the previous day.

Ten minutes afterwards Barbara Simmons came into the room carrying a letter on a silver waiter. Had the document been a death-warrant, or a telegraphic announcement of the landing of the French at Dover, the well-trained servant would have placed it upon a salver before presenting it to her mistress.

'Miss Marchmont is not in her room, ma'am,' she said; 'the bed has not been slept on; and I found this letter, addressed to Captain Arundel, upon the table.'

Olivia's face grew livid; a horrible dread rushed into her mind. Edward snatched the letter which the servant held towards him.

'Mary not in her room! What, in Heaven's name, can it mean?' he cried.

He tore open the letter. The writing was not easily decipherable for the tears which the orphan girl had shed over it.

'MY OWN DEAR EDWARD,—I have loved you so dearly and so foolishly, and you have been so kind to me, that I have quite forgotten how unworthy I am of your affection. But I am forgetful no longer. Something has happened which has opened my eyes to my own folly,—I know now that you did not love me; that I had no claim to your love; no charms or attractions such as so many other women possess, and for which you might have loved me. I know this now, dear Edward, and that all my happiness has been a foolish dream; but do not think that I blame any one but myself for what has happened. Take my fortune: long ago, when I was a little girl, I asked my father to let me share it with you. I ask you now to take it all, dear friend; and I go away for ever from a house in which I have learnt how little happiness riches can give. Do not be unhappy about me. I shall pray for you always,—always remembering your goodness to my dead father; always looking back to the day upon which you came to see us in our poor lodging. I am very ignorant of all worldly business, but I hope the law will let me give you Marchmont Towers, and all my fortune, whatever it may be. Let Mr Paulette see this latter part of my letter, and let him fully understand that I abandon all my rights to you from this day. Good-bye, dear friend; think of me sometimes, but never think of me sorrowfully.

'MARY MARCHMONT.'

This was all. This was the letter which the heart-broken girl had written to her lover. It was in no manner different from the letter she might have writen to him nine years before in Oakley Street. It was as childish in its ignorance and inexperience; as womanly in its tender self-abnegation.

Edward Arundel stared at the simple lines like a man in a dream, doubtful of his own identity, doubtful of the reality of the world about him, in his hopeless wonderment. He read the letter line by line again and again, first in dull stupefaction, and muttering the words mechanically as he read them, then with the full light of their meaning dawning gradually upon him.

Her fortune! He had never loved her! She had discovered her own folly! What did it all mean? What was the clue to the mystery of this letter, which had stunned and bewildered him, until the very power of reflection seemed lost? The dawning of that day had seen their parting, and the innocent face had been lifted to his, beaming with love and trust. And now—? The letter dropped from his hand, and fluttered slowly to the ground. Olivia Marchmont stooped to pick it up. Her movement aroused the young man from his stupor, and in that moment he caught the sight of his cousin's livid face.

He started as if a thunderbolt had burst at his feet. An idea, sudden as some inspired revelation, rushed into his mind.

'Read that letter, Olivia Marchmont!' he said.

The woman obeyed. Slowly and deliberately she read the childish epistle which Mary had written to her lover. In every line, in every word, the widow saw the effect of her own deadly work; she saw how deeply the poison, dropped from her own envenomed tongue, had sunk into the innocent heart of the girl.

Edward Arundel watched her with flaming eyes. His tall soldierly frame trembled in the intensity of his passion. He followed his cousin's eyes along the lines in Mary Marchmont's letter, waiting till she should come to the end. Then the tumultuous storm of indignation burst forth, until Olivia cowered beneath the lightning of her cousin's glance.

Was this the man she had called frivolous? Was this the boyish red-coated dandy she had despised? Was this the curled and perfumed representative of swelldom, whose talk never soared to higher flights than the description of a day's snipe-shooting, or a run with the Burleigh fox-hounds? The wicked woman's eyelids drooped over her averted eyes; she turned away, shrinking from this fearless accuser.

'This mischief is some of *your* work, Olivia Marchmont!' Edward
Arundel cried. 'It is you who have slandered and traduced me to my
dead friend's daughter! Who else would dare accuse a Dangerfield
Arundel of baseness? who else would be vile enough to call my
father's son a liar and a traitor? It is you who have whispered shameful insinuations into this poor child's innocent ear! I scarcely need
the confirmation of your ghastly face to tell me this. It is you who
have driven Mary Marchmont from the home in which you should
have sheltered and protected her! You envied her, I suppose,—
envied her the thousands which might have ministered to your
wicked pride and ambition;—the pride which has always held you
aloof from those who might have loved you; the ambition that has
made you a soured and discontented woman, whose gloomy face
repels all natural affection. You envied the gentle girl whom your
dead husband committed to your care, and who should have been
most sacred to you. You envied her, and seized the first occasion
upon which you might stab her to the very core of her tender heart.
What other motive could you have had for doing this deadly wrong?
None, so help me Heaven!'

No other motive! Olivia Marchmont dropped down in a heap on
the ground near her cousin's feet; not kneeling, but grovelling upon
the carpeted floor, writhing convulsively, with her hands twisted one
in the other, and her head falling forward on her breast. She uttered
no syllable of self-justification or denial. The pitiless words rained
down upon her provoked no reply. But in the depths of her heart
sounded the echo of Edward Arundel's words: 'The pride which has
always held you aloof from those who might have loved you; . . . a
discontented woman, whose gloomy face repels all natural affection.'

'O God!' she thought, 'he *might* have loved me, then! He might
have loved me, if I could have locked my anguish in my own heart,
and smiled at him and flattered him.'

And then an icy indifference took possession of her. What did it
matter that Edward Arundel repudiated and hated her? He had
never loved her. His careless friendliness had made as wide a gulf
between them as his bitterest hate could ever make. Perhaps, indeed,
his new-born hate would be nearer to love than his indifference had
been, for at least he would think of her now, if he thought ever so
bitterly.

'Listen to me, Olivia Marchmont,' the young man said, while the woman still crouched upon the ground near his feet, self-confessed in the abandonment of her despair. 'Wherever this girl may have gone, driven hence by your wickedness, I will follow her. My answer to the lie you have insinuated against me shall be my immediate marriage with my old friend's orphan child. *He* knew me well enough to know how far I was above the baseness of a fortune-hunter and he wished that I should be his daughter's husband. I should be a coward and a fool were I to be for one moment influenced by such a slander as that which you have whispered in Mary Marchmont's ear. It is not the individual only whom you traduce. You slander, the cloth I wear, the family to which I belong; and my best justification will be the contempt in which I hold your infamous insinuations. When you hear that I have squandered Mary Marchmont's fortune, or cheated the children I pray God she may live to bear me, it will be time enough for you to tell the world that your kinsman Edward Dangerfield Arundel is a swindler and a traitor.'

He strode out into the hall, leaving his cousin on the ground; and she heard his voice outside the dining-room door making inquiries of the servants.

They could tell him nothing of Mary's flight. Her bed had not been slept in; nobody had seen her leave the house; it was most likely, therefore, that she had stolen away very early, before the servants were astir.

Where had she gone? Edward Arundel's heart beat wildly as he asked himself that question. He remembered how often he had heard of women, as young and innocent as Mary Marchmont, who had rushed to destroy themselves in a tumult of agony and despair. How easily this poor child, who believed that her dream of happiness was for ever broken, might have crept down through the gloomy wood to the edge of the sluggish river, to drop into the weedy stream, and hide her sorrow under the quiet water. He could fancy her, a new Ophelia,* pale and pure as the Danish prince's slighted love, floating past the weird branches of the willows, borne up for a while by the current, to sink in silence amongst the shadows farther down the stream.

He thought of these things in one moment, and in the next dismissed the thought. Mary's letter breathed the spirit of gentle resignation rather than of wild despair. 'I shall always pray for you; I shall always remember you,' she had written. Her lover remembered how much sorrow the orphan girl had endured in her brief life. He looked back to her childish days of poverty and self-denial; her early loss of her mother; her grief at her father's second marriage; the shock of that beloved father's death. Her sorrows had followed each other in gloomy succession, with only narrow intervals of peace between them. She was accustomed, therefore, to grief. It is the soul untutored by affliction, the rebellious heart that has never known calamity, which becomes mad and desperate, and breaks under the first blow. Mary Marchmont had learned the habit of endurance in the hard school of sorrow.

Edward Arundel walked out upon the terrace, and re-read the missing girl's letter. He was calmer now, and able to face the situation with all its difficulties and perplexities. He was losing time perhaps in stopping to deliberate; but it was no use to rush off in reckless haste, undetermined in which direction he should seek for the lost mistress of Marchmont Towers. One of the grooms was busy in the stables saddling Captain Arundel's horse, and in the mean time the young man went out alone upon the sunny terrace to deliberate upon Mary's letter.

Complete resignation was expressed in every line of that childish epistle. The heiress spoke most decisively as to her abandonment of her fortune and her home. It was clear, then, that she meant to leave Lincolnshire; for she would know that immediate steps would be taken to discover her hiding-place, and bring her back to Marchmont Towers.

Where was she likely to go in her inexperience of the outer world? where but to those humble relations of her dead mother's, of whom her father had spoken in his letter to Edward Arundel, and with whom the young man knew she had kept up an occasional correspondence, sending them many little gifts out of her pocket-money. These people were small tenant-farmers, at a place called Marlingford, in Berkshire. Edward knew their name and the name of the farm.

'I'll make inquiries at the Kemberling station to begin with,' he thought. 'There's a through train from the north that stops at Kemberling at a little before six. My poor darling may have easily caught that, if she left the house at five.'

Captain Arundel went back into the hall, and summoned Barbara Simmons. The woman replied with rather a sulky air to his numerous questions; but she told him that Miss Marchmont had left her ball-dress upon the bed, and had put on a gray cashmere dress trimmed with black ribbon, which she had worn as half-mourning for her father; a black straw bonnet, with a crape veil, and a silk mantle trimmed with crape. She had taken with her a small carpet-bag, some linen,—for the linen-drawer of her wardrobe was open, and the things scattered confusedly about,—and the little morocco case in which she kept her pearl ornaments, and the diamond ring left her by her father.

'Had she any money?' Edward asked.

'Yes, sir; she was never without money. She spent a good deal amongst the poor people she visited with my mistress; but I dare say she may have had between ten and twenty pounds in her purse.'

'She will go to Berkshire,' Edward Arundel thought: 'the idea of going to her humble friends would be the first to present itself to her mind. She will go to her dead mother's sister, and give her all her jewels, and ask for shelter in the quiet farmhouse. She will act like one of the heroines in the old-fashioned novels she used to read in Oakley Street, the simple-minded damsels of those innocent story-books, who think nothing of resigning a castle and a coronet, and going out into the world to work for their daily bread in a white satin gown, and with a string of pearls to bind their dishevelled locks.'

Captain Arundel's horse was brought round to the terrace-steps, as he stood with Mary's letter in his hand, waiting to hurry away to the rescue of his sorrowful love.

'Tell Mrs Marchmont that I shall not return to the Towers till I bring her stepdaughter with me,' he said to the groom; and then, without stopping to utter another word, he shook the rein on his horse's neck, and galloped away along the gravelled drive leading to the great iron gates of Marchmont Towers.

Olivia heard his message, which had been spoken in a clear loud voice, like some knightly defiance, sounding trumpet-like at a castle-gate. She stood in one of the windows of the dining-room, hidden by the faded velvet curtain, and watched her cousin ride away, brave and handsome as any knight-errant of the chivalrous past, and as true as Bayard* himself.

CHAPTER XVI

A NEW PROTECTOR

CAPTAIN ARUNDEL's inquiries at the Kemberling station resulted in an immediate success. A young lady—a young woman, the railway official called her—dressed in black, wearing a crape veil over her face, and carrying a small carpet-bag in her hand, had taken a second-class ticket for London, by the 5.50, a parliamentary train,* which stopped at almost every station on the line, and reached Euston Square at half-past twelve.

Edward looked at his watch. It was ten minutes to two o'clock. The express did not stop at Kemberling; but he would be able to catch it at Swampington at a quarter past three. Even then, however, he could scarcely hope to get to Berkshire that night.

'My darling girl will not discover how foolish her doubts have been until to-morrow,' he thought. 'Silly child! has my love so little the aspect of truth that she *can* doubt me?'

He sprang on his horse again, flung a shilling to the railway porter who had held the bridle, and rode away along the Swampington road. The clocks in the gray old Norman turrets were striking three as the young man crossed the bridge, and paid his toll at the little toll-house by the stone archway.

The streets were as lonely as usual in the hot July afternoon; and the long line of sea beyond the dreary marshes was blue in the sunshine. Captain Arundel passed the two churches, and the low-roofed rectory, and rode away to the outskirts of the town, where the station glared in all the brilliancy of new red bricks, and dazzling stuccoed chimneys, athwart a desert of waste ground.

The express-train came tearing up to the quiet platform two minutes after Edward had taken his ticket; and in another minute the clanging bell pealed out its discordant signal, and the young man was borne, with a shriek and a whistle, away upon the first stage of his search for Mary Marchmont.

It was nearly seven o'clock when he reached Euston Square; and he only got to the Paddington station in time to hear that the last train for Marlingford had just started. There was no possibility of his reaching the little Berkshire village that night. No mail-train stopped within a reasonable distance of the obscure station. There was no help for it, therefore, Captain Arundel had nothing to do but to wait for the next morning.

He walked slowly away from the station, very much disheartened by this discovery.

'I'd better sleep at some hotel up this way,' he thought, as he strolled listlessly in the direction of Oxford Street, 'so as to be on the spot to catch the first train to-morrow morning. What am I to do with myself all this night, racked with uncertainty about Mary?'

He remembered that one of his brother officers was staying at the hotel in Covent Garden where Edward himself stopped, when business detained him in London for a day or two.

'Shall I go and see Lucas?' Captain Arundel thought. 'He's a good fellow, and won't bore me with a lot of questions, if he sees I've something on my mind. There may be some letters for me at E——'s. Poor little Polly!'

He could never think of her without something of that pitiful tenderness which he might have felt for a young and helpless child, whom it was his duty and privilege to protect and succour. It may be that there was little of the lover's fiery enthusiasm mingled with the purer and more tender feelings with which Edward Arundel regarded his dead friend's orphan daughter; but in place of this there was a chivalrous devotion, such as woman rarely wins in these degenerate modern days.

The young soldier walked through the lamp-lit western streets thinking of the missing girl; now assuring himself that his instinct had not deceived him, and that Mary must have gone straight to the Berkshire farmer's house, and in the next moment seized with a sudden terror that it might be otherwise: the helpless girl might have gone out into a world of which she was as ignorant as a child, determined to hide herself from all who had ever known her. If it should be thus: if, on going down to Marlingford, he obtained no tidings of his friend's daughter, what was he to do? Where was he to look for her next?

He would put advertisements in the papers, calling upon his betrothed to trust him and return to him. Perhaps Mary Marchmont was, of all people in this world, the least likely to look into a newspaper; but at least it would be doing something to do this, and

Edward Arundel determined upon going straight off to Printing-House Square, to draw up an appeal to the missing girl.

It was past ten o'clock when Captain Arundel came to this determination, and he had reached the neighbourhood of Covent Garden and of the theatres. The staring play-bills adorned almost every threshold, and fluttered against every door-post; and the young soldier, going into a tobacconist's to fill his cigar-case, stared abstractedly at a gaudy blue-and-red announcement of the last dramatic attraction to be seen at Drury Lane. It was scarcely strange that the Captain's thoughts wandered back to his boyhood, that shadowy time, far away behind his later days of Indian warfare and glory, and that he remembered the December night upon which he had sat with his cousin in a box at the great patent theatre,* watching the consumptive supernumerary struggling under the weight of his banner. From the box at Drury Lane to the next morning's breakfast in Oakley Street, was but a natural transition of thought; but with that recollection of the humble Lambeth lodging, with the picture of a little girl in a pinafore sitting demurely at her father's table, and meekly waiting on his guest, an idea flashed across Edward Arundel's mind, and brought the hot blood into his face.

What if Mary had gone to Oakley Street? Was not this even more likely than that she should seek refuge with her kinsfolk in Berkshire? She had lived in the Lambeth lodging for years, and had only left that plebeian shelter for the grandeur of Marchmont Towers. What more natural than that she should go back to the familiar habitation, dear to her by reason of a thousand associations with her dead father? What more likely than that she should turn instinctively, in the hour of her desolation, to the humble friends whom she had known in her childhood?

Edward Arundel was almost too impatient to wait while the smart young damsel behind the tobacconist's counter handed him change for the half-sovereign which he had just tendered her. He darted out into the street, and shouted violently to the driver of a passing hansom,—there are always loitering hansoms in the neighbourhood of Covent Garden,—who was, after the manner of his kind, looking on any side rather than that upon which Providence had sent him a fare.

'Oakley Street, Lambeth,' the young man cried. 'Double fare if you get there in ten minutes.'

The tall raw-boned horse rattled off at that peculiar pace common to his species, making as much noise upon the pavement as if he had been winning a metropolitan Derby, and at about twenty minutes past nine drew up, smoking and panting, before the dimly lighted windows of the Ladies' Wardrobe, where a couple of flaring tallow-candles illuminated the splendour of a foreground of dirty artificial flowers, frayed satin shoes, and tarnished gilt combs; a middle distance of blue gauzy tissue, embroidered with beetles' wings; and a background of greasy black silk. Edward Arundel flung back the doors of the hansom with a bang, and leaped out upon the pavement. The proprietress of the Ladies' Wardrobe was lolling against the door-post, refreshing herself with the soft evening breezes from the roads of Westminster and Waterloo, and talking to her neighbour.

'Bless her pore dear innercent 'art!' the woman was saying; 'she's cried herself to sleep at last. But you never hear any think so pitiful as she talked to me at fust, sweet love!—and the very picture of my own poor Eliza Jane, as she looked. You might have said it was Eliza Jane come back to life, only paler and more sickly like, and not that beautiful fresh colour, and ringlets curled all round in a crop, as Eliza Ja—'

Edward Arundel burst in upon the good woman's talk, which rambled on in an unintermitting stream, unbroken by much punctuation.

'Miss Marchmont is here,' he said; 'I know she is. Thank God, thank God! Let me see her please, directly. I am Captain Arundel, her father's friend, and her affianced husband. You remember me, perhaps? I came here nine years ago to breakfast, one December morning. I can recollect you perfectly, and I know that you were always good to my poor friend's daughter. To think that I should find her here! You shall be well rewarded for your kindness to her. But take me to her; pray take me to her at once!'

The proprietress of the wardrobe snatched up one of the candles that guttered in a brass flat-candlestick upon the counter, and led the way up the narrow staircase. She was a good lazy creature, and she was so completely borne down by Edward's excitement, that she could only mutter disjointed sentences, to the effect that the gentleman had brought her heart into her mouth, and that her legs felt all of a jelly; and that her poor knees was a'most giving way under her, and other incoherent statements concerning the physical effect of the mental shocks she had that day received.

She opened the door of that shabby sitting-room upon the first-floor, in which the crippled eagle brooded over the convex mirror, and stood aside upon the threshold while Captain Arundel entered the room. A tallow candle was burning dimly upon the table, and a girlish form lay upon the narrow horsehair sofa, shrouded by a woollen shawl.

'She went to sleep about half-an-hour ago, sir,' the woman said, in a whisper; 'and she cried herself to sleep, pore lamb, I think. I made her some tea, and got her a few creases and a French roll, with a bit of best fresh;* but she wouldn't touch nothin', or only a few spoonfuls of the tea, just to please me. What is it that's drove her away from her 'ome, sir, and such a good 'ome too? She showed me a diamont ring as her pore par gave her in his will. He left me twenty pound, pore gentleman,—which he always acted like a gentleman bred and born; and Mr Pollit, the lawyer, sent his clerk along with it and his compliments,—though I'm sure I never looked for nothink, having always had my rent faithful to the very minute: and Miss Mary used to bring it down to me so pretty, and—'

But the whispering had grown louder by this time, and Mary Marchmont awoke from her feverish sleep, and lifted her weary head from the hard horsehair pillow and looked about her, half forgetful of where she was, and of what had happened within the last eighteen hours of her life. Her eyes wandered here and there, doubtful as to the reality of what they looked upon, until the girl saw her lover's figure, tall and splendid in the humble apartment, a tender half-reproachful smile upon his face, and his handsome blue eyes beaming with love and truth. She saw him, and a faint shriek broke from her tremulous lips, as she rose and fell upon his breast.

'You love me, then, Edward,' she cried; 'you do love me!'

'Yes, my darling, as truly and tenderly as ever woman was loved upon this earth.'

And then the soldier sat down upon the hard bristly sofa, and with Mary's head still resting upon his breast, and his strong hand straying amongst her disordered hair, he reproached her for her foolishness, and comforted and soothed her; while the proprietress of the apartment stood, with the brass candlestick in her hand, watching the young lovers and weeping over their sorrows, as if she had been witnessing a scene in a play. Their innocent affection was unrestrained by the good woman's presence; and when Mary had smiled upon her lover, and assured him that she would never, never, never doubt him again, Captain Arundel was fain to kiss the soft-hearted landlady in his enthusiasm, and to promise her the handsomest silk dress that had ever been seen in Oakley Street, amongst all the faded splendours of silk and satin that ladies'-maids brought for her consideration.

'And now my darling, my foolish run-away Polly, what is to be done with you?' asked the young soldier. 'Will you go back to the Towers to-morrow morning?'

Mary Marchmont clasped her hands before her face, and began to tremble violently.

'Oh, no, no, no!' she cried; 'don't ask me to do that, don't ask me to go back, Edward. I can never go back to that house again, while—'

She stopped suddenly, looking piteously at her lover.

'While my cousin Olivia Marchmont lives there,' Captain Arundel said with an angry frown. 'God knows it's a bitter thing for me to think that your troubles should come from any of my kith and kin, Polly. She has used you very badly, then, this woman? She has been very unkind to you?'

'No, no! never before last night. It seems so long ago; but it was only last night, was it? Until then she was always kind to me. I didn't love her, you know, though I tried to do so for papa's sake, and out of gratitude to her for taking such trouble with my education; but one can be grateful to people without loving them, and I never grew to love her. But last night—last night—she said such cruel things to me—such cruel things. O Edward, Edward!' the girl cried suddenly, clasping her hands and looking imploringly at Captain Arundel, 'were the cruel things she said true? Did I do wrong when I offered to be your wife?'

How could the young man answer this question except by clasping his betrothed to his heart? So there was another little love-scene, over which Mrs Pimpernel,—the proprietress's name was Pimpernel —wept fresh tears, murmuring that the Capting was the sweetest young man, sweeter than Mr Macready in Claude Melnock; and that the scene altogether reminded her of that 'cutting' episode where the proud mother went on against the pore young man, and Miss Faucit* came out so beautiful. They are a play-going population in Oakley Street, and compassionate and sentimental like all true playgoers.

'What shall I do with you, Miss Marchmont?' Edward Arundel asked gaily, when the little love-scene was concluded. 'My mother and sister are away, at a German watering-place, trying some un-pronounceable Spa for the benefit of poor Letty's health. Reginald is with them, and my father's alone at Dangerfield. So I can't take you down there, as I might have done if my mother had been at home; I don't much care for the Mostyns, or you might have stopped in Montague Square. There are no friendly friars nowadays who will marry Romeo and Juliet at half-an-hour's notice. You must live a fortnight* somewhere, Polly: where shall it be?'

'Oh, let me stay here, please,' Miss Marchmont pleaded; 'I was always so happy here!'

'Lord love her precious heart!' exclaimed Mrs Pimpernel, lifting up her hands in a rapture of admiration. 'To think as she shouldn't have a bit of pride, after all the money as her pore par come into! To think as she should wish to stay in her old lodgin's, where everythink shall be done to make her comfortable; and the air back and front is very 'ealthy, though you might not believe it, and the Blind School and Bedlam* hard by, and Kennington Common only a pleasant walk, and beautiful and open this warm summer weather.'

'Yes, I should like to stop here, please,' Mary murmured. Even in the midst of her agitation, overwhelmed as she was by the emotions of the present, her thoughts went back to the past, and she remem-bered how delightful it would be to go and see the accommodating butcher, and the greengrocer's daughter, the kind butterman who had called her 'little lady,' and the disreputable gray parrot. How delightful it would be to see these humble friends, now that she was grown up, and had money wherewith to make them presents in token of her gratitude!

'Very well, then, Polly,' Captain Arundel said, 'you'll stay here. And Mrs ——'

'Pimpernel,' the landlady suggested.

'Mrs Pimpernel will take as good care of you as if you were Queen of England, and the welfare of the nation depended upon your safety. And I'll stop at my hotel in Covent Garden; and I'll see Richard Paulette,—he's my lawyer as well as yours, you know, Polly,—and tell him something of what has happened, and make arrangements for our immediate marriage.'

'Our marriage!'

Mary Marchmont echoed her lover's last words, and looked up at him almost with a bewildered air. She had never thought of an early marriage with Edward Arundel as the result of her flight from Lincolnshire. She had a vague notion that she would live in Oakley Street for years, and that in some remote time the soldier would come to claim her.

'Yes, Polly darling, Olivia Marchmont's conduct has made me decide upon a very bold step. It is evident to me that my cousin hates you; for what reason, Heaven only knows, since you can have done nothing to provoke her hate. When your father was a poor man, it was to me he would have confided you. He changed his mind afterwards, very naturally, and chose another guardian for his orphan child. If my cousin had fulfilled this trust, Mary, I would have deferred to her authority, and would have held myself aloof until your minority was passed, rather than ask you to marry me without your stepmother's consent. But Olivia Marchmont has forfeited her right to be consulted in this matter. She has tortured you and traduced me by her poisonous slander. If you believe in me, Mary, you will consent to be my wife. My justification lies in the future. You will not find that I shall sponge upon your fortune, my dear, or lead an idle life because my wife is a rich woman.'

Mary Marchmont looked up with shy tenderness at her lover.

'I would rather the fortune were yours than mine, Edward,' she said. 'I will do whatever you wish; I will be guided by you in every thing.'

It was thus that John Marchmont's daughter consented to become the wife of the man she loved, the man whose image she had associated since her childhood with all that was good and beautiful in mankind. She knew none of those pretty stereotyped phrases, by means of which well-bred young ladies can go through a graceful fencing-match of hesitation and equivocation, to the anguish of a doubtful and adoring suitor. She had no notion of that delusive negative, that bewitching feminine 'no,' which is proverbially understood to mean 'yes.' Weary courses of Roman Emperors, South-Sea Islands, Sidereal Heavens, Tertiary and Old Red Sandstone, had very ill-prepared this poor little girl for the stern realities of life.

'I will be guided by you, dear Edward,' she said; 'my father wished me to be your wife; and if I did not love you, it would please me to obey him.'

It was eleven o'clock when Captain Arundel left Oakley Street. The hansom had been waiting all the time, and the driver, seeing that his fare was young, handsome, dashing, and what he called 'milingtary-like,' demanded an enormous sum when he landed the soldier before the portico of the hotel in Covent Garden.

Edward took a hasty breakfast the next morning, and then hurried off to Lincoln's-Inn Fields. But here a disappointment awaited him. Richard Paulette had started for Scotland upon a piscatorial excursion. The elder Paulette was an octogenarian, who lived in the south of France, and kept his name in the business as a fiction, by means of which elderly and obstinate country clients were deluded into the belief that the solicitor who conducted their affairs was the same legal practitioner who had done business for their fathers and grandfathers before them. Mathewson, a grim man, was away amongst the Yorkshire wolds, superintending the foreclosure of certain mortgages upon a bankrupt baronet's estate. A confidential clerk, who received clients, and kept matters straight during the absence of his employers, was very anxious to be of use to Captain Arundel: but it was not likely that Edward could sit down and pour his secrets into the bosom of a clerk, however trustworthy a personage that employé might be.

The young man's desire had been that his marriage with Mary Marchmont should take place at least with the knowledge and approbation of her dead father's lawyer: but he was impatient to assume the only title by which he might have a right to be the orphan girl's champion and protector; and he had therefore no inclination to wait until the long vacation* was over, and Messrs Paulette and Mathewson returned from their northern wanderings. Again, Mary Marchmont suffered from a continual dread that her stepmother would discover the secret of her humble retreat, and would follow her and reassume authority over her.

'Let me be your wife before I see her again, Edward,' the girl pleaded innocently, when this terror was uppermost in her mind. 'She could not say cruel things to me if I were your wife. I know it is wicked to be so frightened of her; because she was always good to me until that night: but I cannot tell you how I tremble at the thought of being alone with her at Marchmont Towers. I dream sometimes that I am with her in the gloomy old house, and that we two are alone there, even the servants all gone, and you far away in India, Edward,—at the other end of the world.'

It was as much as her lover could do to soothe and reassure the trembling girl when these thoughts took possession of her. Had he been less sanguine and impetuous, less careless in the buoyancy of his spirits, Captain Arundel might have seen that Mary's nerves had been terribly shaken by the scene between her and Olivia, and all the anguish which had given rise to her flight from Marchmont Towers. The girl trembled at every sound. The shutting of a door, the noise of a cab stopping in the street below, the falling of a book from the table to the floor, startled her almost as much as if a gunpowder-magazine had exploded in the neighbourhood. The tears rose to her eyes at the slightest emotion. Her mind was tortured by vague fears, which she tried in vain to explain to her lover. Her sleep was broken by dismal dreams, foreboding visions of shadowy evil.

For a little more than a fortnight Edward Arundel visited his betrothed daily in the shabby first-floor in Oakley Street, and sat by her side while she worked at some fragile scrap of embroidery, and talked gaily to her of the happy future; to the intense admiration of Mrs Pimpernel, who had no greater delight than to assist in the pretty little sentimental drama that was being enacted on her first-floor.

Thus it was that, on a cloudy and autumnal August morning, Edward Arundel and Mary Marchmont were married in a great empty-looking church in the parish of Lambeth, by an indifferent curate, who shuffled through the service at railroad speed, and with far less reverence for the solemn rite than he would have displayed had he known that the pale-faced girl kneeling before the altar-rails was undisputed mistress of eleven thousand a-year. Mrs Pimpernel, the pew-opener, and the registrar, who was in waiting in the vestry, and was beguiled thence to give away the bride, were the only witnesses to this strange wedding. It seemed a dreary ceremonial to Mrs Pimpernel, who had been married at the same church five-and-twenty years before, in a cinnamon satin spencer,* and a coal-scuttle bonnet, and with a young person in the dressmaking line in attendance upon her as bridesmaid.

It *was* rather a dreary wedding, no doubt. The drizzling rain dripped ceaselessly in the street without, and there was a smell of damp plaster in the great empty church. The melancholy street-cries sounded dismally from the outer world, while the curate was hurrying through those portentous words which were to unite Edward

Arundel and Mary Marchmont until the final day of earthly separation. The girl clung shivering to her lover, her husband now, as they went into the vestry to sign their names in the marriage-register. Throughout the service she had expected to hear a footstep in the aisle behind her, and Olivia Marchmont's cruel voice crying out to forbid the marriage.

'I am your wife now, Edward, am I not?' she said, when she had signed her name in the register.

'Yes, my darling, for ever and for ever.'

'And nothing can part us now?'

'Nothing but death, my dear.'

In the exuberance of his spirits, Edward Arundel spoke of the King of Terrors as if he had been a mere nobody, whose power to change or mar the fortunes of mankind was so trifling as to be scarcely worth mentioning.

The vehicle in waiting to carry the mistress of Marchmont Towers upon the first stage of her bridal tour was nothing better than a hack cab.* The driver's garments exhaled stale tobacco-smoke in the moist atmosphere, and in lieu of the flowers which are wont to bestrew the bridal path of an heiress, Miss Marchmont trod upon damp and mouldy straw. But she was happy,—happy, with a fearful apprehension that her happiness could not be real,—a vague terror of Olivia's power to torture and oppress her, which even the presence of her lover-husband could not altogether drive away. She kissed Mrs Pimpernel, who stood upon the edge of the pavement, crying bitterly, with the slippery white lining of a new silk dress, which Edward Arundel had given her for the wedding, gathered tightly round her.

'God bless you, my dear!' cried the honest dealer in frayed satins and tumbled gauzes; 'I couldn't take this more to heart if you was my own Eliza Jane going away with the young man as she was to have married, and as is now a widower with five children, two in arms, and the youngest brought up by hand. God bless your pretty face, my dear; and oh, pray take care of her, Captain Arundel, for she's a tender flower, sir, and truly needs your care. And it's but a trifle, my own sweet young missy, for the acceptance of such as you, but it's given from a full heart, and given humbly.'

The latter part of Mrs Pimpernel's speech bore relation to a hard newspaper parcel, which she dropped into Mary's lap. Mrs Arundel opened the parcel presently, when she had kissed her humble friend for the last time, and the cab was driving towards Nine Elms, and found that Mrs Pimpernel's wedding-gift was a Scotch shepherdess in china, with a great deal of gilding about her tartan garments, very red legs, a hat and feathers, and curly sheep. Edward put this article of *virtù** very carefully away in his carpet-bag; for his bride would not have the present treated with any show of disrespect.

'How good of her to give it me!' Mary said; 'it used to stand upon the back-parlour chimney-piece when I was a little girl; and I was so fond of it. Of course I am not fond of Scotch shepherdesses now, you know, dear; but how should Mrs Pimpernel know that? She thought it would please me to have this one.'

'And you'll put it in the western drawing-room at the Towers, won't you, Polly?' Captain Arundel asked, laughing.

'I won't put it anywhere to be made fun of, sir,' the young bride answered, with some touch of wifely dignity; 'but I'll take care of it, and never have it broken or destroyed; and Mrs Pimpernel shall see it, when she comes to the Towers,—if I ever go back there,' she added, with a sudden change of manner.

'*If* you ever go back there!' cried Edward. 'Why, Polly, my dear, Marchmont Towers is your own house. My cousin Olivia is only there upon sufferance, and her own good sense will tell her she has no right to stay there, when she ceases to be your friend and pro-tectress. She is a proud woman, and her pride will surely never suffer her to remain where she must feel she can be no longer welcome.'

The young wife's face turned white with terror at her husband's words.

'But I could never ask her to go, Edward,' she said. 'I wouldn't turn her out for the world. She may stay there for ever if she likes. I never have cared for the place since papa's death; and I couldn't go back while she is there, I'm so frightened of her, Edward, I'm so frightened of her.'

The vague apprehension burst forth in this childish cry. Edward Arundel clasped his wife to his breast, and bent over her, kissing her pale forehead, and murmuring soothing words, as he might have done to a child.

'My dear, my dear,' he said, 'my darling Mary, this will never do; my own love, this is so very foolish.'

'I know, I know, Edward; but I can't help it, I can't indeed; I was frightened of her long ago; frightened of her even the first day I saw her, the day you took me to the Rectory. I was frightened of her when papa first told me he meant to marry her; and I am frightened of her now; even now that I am your wife, Edward, I'm frightened of her still.'

Captain Arundel kissed away the tears that trembled on his wife's eyelids; but she had scarcely grown quite composed even when the cab stopped at the Nine Elms railway station. It was only when she was seated in the carriage with her husband, and the rain cleared away as they advanced farther into the heart of the pretty pastoral country, that the bride's sense of happiness and safety in her husband's protection, returned to her. But by that time she was able to smile in his face, and to look forward with delight to a brief sojourn in that pretty Hampshire village, which Edward had chosen for the scene of his honeymoon.

'Only a few days of quiet happiness, Polly,' he said; 'a few days of utter forgetfulness of all the world except you; and then I must be a man of business again, and write to your stepmother and my father and mother, and Messrs Paulette and Mathewson, and all the people who ought to know of our marriage.'

CHAPTER XVII

PAUL'S SISTER

OLIVIA MARCHMONT shut herself once more in her desolate chamber, making no effort to find the runaway mistress of the Towers; indifferent as to what the slanderous tongues of her neighbours might say of her; hardened, callous, desperate.

To her father, and to any one else who questioned her about Mary's absence,—for the story of the girl's flight was soon whispered abroad, the servants at the Towers having received no injunctions to keep the matter secret,—Mrs Marchmont replied with such an air of cold and determined reserve as kept the questioners at bay ever afterwards.

So the Kemberling people, and the Swampington people, and all the country gentry within reach of Marchmont Towers, had a mystery and a scandal provided for them, which afforded ample scope for repeated discussion, and considerably relieved the dull monotony of their lives. But there were some questioners whom Mrs Marchmont found it rather difficult to keep at a distance; there were some intruders who dared to force themselves upon the gloomy woman's solitude, and who *would* not understand that their presence was abhorrent to her.

These people were a surgeon and his wife, who had newly settled at Kemberling; the best practice in the village falling into the market by reason of the death of a steady-going, gray-headed old practitioner, who for many years had shared with one opponent the responsibility of watching over the health of the Lincolnshire village.

It was about three weeks after Mary Marchmont's flight when these unwelcome guests first came to the Towers.

Olivia sat alone in her dead husband's study,—the same room in which she had sat upon the morning of John Marchmont's funeral,—a dark and gloomy chamber, wainscoted with blackened oak, and lighted only by a massive stone-framed Tudor window looking out into the quadrangle, and overshadowed by that cloistered colonnade beneath whose shelter Edward and Mary had walked upon the morning of the girl's flight. This wainscoted study was an apartment which most women, having all the rooms in Marchmont Towers at their disposal, would have been likely to avoid; but the gloom of the chamber harmonised with that horrible gloom which had taken possession of Olivia's soul, and the widow turned from the sunny western front, as she turned from all the sunlight and gladness in the universe, to come here, where the summer radiance rarely crept through the diamond-panes of the window, where the shadow of the cloister shut out the glory of the blue sky.

She was sitting in this room,—sitting near the open window, in a high-backed chair of carved and polished oak, with her head resting against the angle of the embayed window, and her handsome profile thrown into sharp relief by the dark green-cloth curtain, which hung in straight folds from the low ceiling to the ground, and made a sombre background to the widow's figure. Mrs Marchmont had put away all the miserable gewgaws and vanities which she had ordered from London in a sudden excess of folly or caprice, and had reassumed her mourning-robes of lustreless black. She had a book in her hand,—some new and popular fiction, which all Lincolnshire was eager to read; but although her eyes were fixed upon the pages before her, and her hand mechanically turned over leaf after leaf at regular intervals of time, the fashionable romance was only a weary repetition of phrases, a dull current of words, always intermingled with the images of Edward Arundel and Mary Marchmont, which arose out of every page to mock the hopeless reader.

Olivia flung the book away from her at last, with a smothered cry of rage.

'Is there no cure for this disease?' she muttered. 'Is there no relief except madness or death?'

But in the infidelity which had arisen out of her despair this woman had grown to doubt if either death or madness could bring her oblivion of her anguish. She doubted the quiet of the grave; and half-believed that the torture of jealous rage and slighted love might mingle even with that silent rest, haunting her in her coffin, shutting her out of heaven, and following her into a darker world, there to be her torment everlastingly. There were times when she thought madness must mean forgetfulness; but there were other moments when she shuddered, horror-stricken, at the thought that, in the wandering brain of a mad woman, the image of that grief which had caused the shipwreck of her senses might still hold its place, distorted and exaggerated,—a gigantic unreality, ten thousand times more terrible than the truth. Remembering the dreams which disturbed her broken sleep,—those dreams which, in their feverish horror, were little better than intervals of delirium,—it is scarcely strange if Olivia Marchmont thought thus.

She had not succumbed without many struggles to her sin and despair. Again and again she had abandoned herself to the devils at watch to destroy her, and again and again she had tried to extricate her soul from their dreadful power; but her most passionate endeavours were in vain. Perhaps it was that she did not strive aright; it was for this reason, surely, that she failed so utterly to arise superior to her despair; for otherwise that terrible belief attributed to the Calvinists, that some souls are foredoomed to damnation, would be exemplified by this woman's experience. She could not forget. She could not put away the vengeful hatred that raged like an all-devouring fire in her breast, and she cried in her agony, 'There is no cure for this disease!'

I think her mistake was in this, that she did not go to the right Physician. She practised quackery with her soul, as some people do with their bodies; trying their own remedies, rather than the simple prescriptions of the Divine Healer of all woes. Self-reliant, and scornful of the weakness against which her pride revolted, she trusted to her intellect and her will to lift her out of the moral slough into which her soul had gone down. She said:

'I am not a woman to go mad for the love of a boyish face; I am not a woman to die for a foolish fancy, which the veriest schoolgirl might be ashamed to confess to her companion. I am not a woman to do this, and I *will* cure myself of my folly.'

Mrs Marchmont made an effort to take up her old life, with its dull round of ceaseless duty, its perpetual self-denial. If she had been a Roman Catholic, she would have gone to the nearest convent, and prayed to be permitted to take such vows as might soonest set a barrier between herself and the world; she would have spent the long weary days in perpetual and secret prayer; she would have worn deeper indentations upon the stones already hollowed by faithful knees. As it was, she made a routine of penance for herself, after her own fashion: going long distances on foot to visit her poor, when she might have ridden in her carriage; courting exposure to rain and foul weather; wearing herself out with unnecessary fatigue, and returning footsore to her desolate home, to fall fainting into the strong arms of her grim attendant, Barbara.

But this self-appointed penance could not shut Edward Arundel and Mary Marchmont from the widow's mind. Walking through a fiery furnace their images would have haunted her still, vivid and palpable even in the agony of death. The fatigue of the long weary walks made Mrs Marchmont wan and pale; the exposure to storm and rain brought on a tiresome, hacking cough, which worried her by day and disturbed her fitful slumbers by night. No good whatever seemed to come of her endeavours; and the devils who rejoiced at her weakness and her failure claimed her as their own. They claimed her as their own; and they were not without terrestrial agents, working patiently in their service, and ready to help in securing their bargain.

The great clock in the quadrangle had struck the half-hour after three; the atmosphere of the August afternoon was sultry and oppressive. Mrs Marchmont had closed her eyes after flinging aside her book, and had fallen into a doze: her nights were broken and wakeful, and the hot stillness of the day had made her drowsy.

She was aroused from this half-slumber by Barbara Simmons, who came into the room carrying two cards upon a salver,—the same old-fashioned and emblazoned salver upon which Paul Marchmont's card had been brought to the widow nearly three years before. The Abigail stood halfway between the door and the window by which the widow sat, looking at her mistress's face with a glance of sharp scrutiny.

'She's changed since he came back, and changed again since he went away,' the woman thought; 'just as she always changed at the Rectory at his coming and going. Why didn't he take to her, I wonder? He might have known her fancy for him, if he'd had eyes to watch her face, or ears to listen to her voice. She's handsomer than the other one, and cleverer in book-learning; but she keeps 'em off— she seems allers to keep 'em off.'

I think Olivia Marchmont would have torn the very heart out of this waiting-woman's breast, had she known the thoughts that held a place in it: had she known that the servant who attended upon her, and took wages from her, dared to pluck out her secret, and to speculate upon her suffering.

The widow awoke suddenly, and looked up with an impatient frown. She had not been awakened by the opening of the door, but by that unpleasant sensation which almost always reveals the presence of a stranger to a sleeper of nervous temperament.

'What is it, Barbara?' she asked; and then, as her eyes rested on the cards, she added, angrily, 'Haven't I told you that I would not see any callers to-day? I am worn out with my cough, and feel too ill to see any one.'

'Yes, Miss Livy,' the woman answered;—she called her mistress by this name still, now and then, so familiar had it grown to her during the childhood and youth of the Rector's daughter;—'I didn't forget that, Miss Livy: I told Richardson you was not to be disturbed. But the lady and gentleman said, if you saw what was wrote upon the back of one of the cards, you'd be sure to make an exception in their favour. I think that was what the lady said. She's a middle-aged lady, very talkative and pleasant-mannered,' added the grim Barbara, in nowise relaxing the stolid gravity of her own manner as she spoke.

Olivia snatched the cards from the salver.

'Why do people worry me so?' she cried, impatiently. 'Am I not to be allowed even five minutes' sleep without being broken in upon by some intruder or other?'

Barbara Simmons looked at her mistress's face. Anxiety and sadness dimly showed themselves in the stolid countenance of the lady's-maid. A close observer, penetrating below that aspect of wooden solemnity which was Barbara's normal expression, might have discovered a secret: the quiet waiting-woman loved her mistress with a jealous and watchful affection, that took heed of every change in its object.

Mrs Marchmont examined the two cards, which bore the names of Mr and Mrs Weston, Kemberling. On the back of the lady's card these words were written in pencil:

'Will Mrs Marchmont be so good as to see Lavinia Weston, Paul Marchmont's younger sister, and a connection of Mrs M.'s?'

Olivia shrugged her shoulders, as she threw down the card.

'Paul Marchmont! Lavinia Weston!' she muttered; 'yes, I remember he said something about a sister married to a surgeon at Stanfield. Let these people come to me, Barbara.'

The waiting-woman looked doubtfully at her mistress.

'You'll maybe smooth your hair, and freshen yourself up a bit, before ye see the folks, Miss Livy,' she said, in a tone of mingled suggestion and entreaty. 'Ye've had a deal of worry lately, and it's made ye look a little fagged and haggard-like. I'd not like the Kemberling folks to say as you was ill.'

Mrs Marchmont turned fiercely upon the Abigail.

'Let me alone!' she cried. 'What is it to you, or to any one, how I look? What good have my looks done me, that I should worry myself about them?' she added, under her breath. 'Show these people in here, if they want to see me.'

'They've been shown into the western drawing-room, ma'am;— Richardson took 'em in there.'

Barbara Simmons fought hard for the preservation of appearances. She wanted the Rector's daughter to receive these strange people, who had dared to intrude upon her, in a manner befitting the dignity of John Marchmont's widow. She glanced furtively at the disorder of the gloomy chamber. Books and papers were scattered here and there; the hearth and low fender were littered with heaps of torn letters,—for Olivia Marchmont had no tenderness for the memorials of the past, and indeed took a fierce delight in sweeping away the unsanctified records of her joyless, loveless life. The high-backed oaken chairs had been pushed out of their places; the green-cloth cover had been drawn half off the massive table, and hung in trailing folds upon the ground. A book flung here; a shawl there; a handkerchief in another place; an open secretaire, with scattered documents and uncovered inkstand,—littered the room, and bore mute witness of the restlessness of its occupant. It needed no very subtle psychologist to read aright those separate tokens of a disordered mind; of a weary spirit which had sought distraction in a dozen occupations, and had found relief in none. It was some vague sense of this that caused Barbara Simmons's anxiety. She wished to keep strangers out of this room, in which her mistress, wan, haggard, and weary-looking, revealed her secret by so many signs and tokens. But before Olivia could make any answer to her servant's suggestion, the door, which Barbara had left ajar, was pushed open by a very gentle hand, and a sweet voice said, in cheery chirping accents,

'I am sure I may come in; may I not, Mrs Marchmont? The impression my brother Paul's description gave me of you is such a very pleasant one, that I venture to intrude uninvited, almost forbidden, perhaps.'

The voice and manner of the speaker were so airy and self-possessed, there was such a world of cheerfulness and amiability in every tone, that, as Olivia Marchmont rose from her chair, she put her hand to her head, dazed and confounded, as if by the too boisterous carolling of some caged bird. What did they mean, these accents of gladness, these clear and untroubled tones, which sounded shrill, and almost discordant, in the despairing woman's ears? She stood, pale and worn, the very picture of all gloom and misery, staring hopelessly at her visitor; too much abandoned to her grief to remember, in that first moment, the stern demands of pride. She stood still; revealing, by her look, her attitude, her silence, her abstraction, a whole history to the watchful eyes that were looking at her.

Mrs Weston lingered on the threshold of the chamber in a pretty half-fluttering manner; which was charmingly expressive of a struggle between a modest poor-relation-like diffidence and an earnest desire to rush into Olivia's arms. The surgeon's wife was a delicate-looking little woman, with features that seemed a miniature and feminine reproduction of her brother Paul's, and with very light hair,—hair so light and pale that, had it turned as white as the artist's in a single night, very few people would have been likely to take heed of the change. Lavinia Weston was eminently what is generally called a *lady-like* woman. She always conducted herself in that especial and particular manner which was exactly fitted to the occasion. She adjusted her behaviour by the nicest shades of colour and hair-breadth scale of measurement. She had, as it were, made for herself a homoepathic system of good manners, and could mete out politeness and courtesy in the veriest globules, never administering either too much or too little. To her husband she was a treasure beyond all price; and if the Lincolnshire surgeon, who was a fat, solemn-faced man, with a character as level and monotonous as the flats and fens of his native county, was henpecked, the feminine autocrat held the reins of government so lightly, that her obedient subject was scarcely aware how very irresponsible his wife's authority had become.

As Olivia Marchmont stood confronting the timid hesitating figure of the intruder, with the width of the chamber between them, Lavinia Weston, in her crisp muslin-dress and scarf, her neat bonnet and bright ribbons and primly-adjusted gloves, looked something like an adventurous canary who had a mind to intrude upon the den of a hungry lioness. The difference, physical and moral, between the timid bird and the savage forest-queen could be scarcely wider than that between the two women.

But Olivia did not stand for ever embarrassed and silent in her visitor's presence. Her pride came to her rescue. She turned sternly upon the polite intruder.

'Walk in, if you please, Mrs Weston,' she said, 'and sit down. I was denied to you just now because I have been ill, and have ordered my servants to deny me to every one.'

'But, my dear Mrs Marchmont,' murmured Lavinia Weston in soft, almost dove-like accents, 'if you have been ill, is not your illness another reason for seeing us, rather than for keeping us away from you? I would not, of course, say a word which could in any way be calculated to give offence to your regular medical attendant,—you have a regular medical attendant, no doubt; from Swampington, I dare say,—but a doctor's wife may often be useful when a doctor is himself out of place. There are little nervous ailment—depression of spirits, mental uneasiness—from which women, and sensitive women, suffer acutely, and which perhaps a woman's more refined nature alone can thoroughly comprehend. You are not looking well, my dear Mrs Marchmont. I left my husband in the drawing-room, for I was so anxious that our first meeting should take place without witnesses. Men think women sentimental when they are only impulsive. Weston is a good simple-hearted creature, but he knows as much about a woman's mind as he does of an Aeolian harp.* When the strings vibrate, he hears the low plaintive notes, but he has no idea whence the melody comes. It is thus with us, Mrs Marchmont. These medical men watch us in the agonies of hysteria; they hear our sighs, they see our tears, and in their awkwardness and ignorance they prescribe commonplace remedies out of the pharmacopoeia. No, dear Mrs Marchmont, you do not look well. I fear it is the mind, the mind, which has been over-strained. Is it not so?'

Mrs Weston put her head on one side as she asked this question, and smiled at Olivia with an air of gentle insinuation. If the doctor's wife wished to plumb the depths of the widow's gloomy soul, she had an advantage here; for Mrs Marchmont was thrown off her guard by the question, which had been perhaps asked hap-hazard, or it may be with a deeply considered design. Olivia turned fiercely upon the polite questioner.

'I have been suffering from nothing but a cold which I caught the other day,' she said; 'I am not subject to any fine-ladylike hysteria, I can assure you, Mrs Weston.'

The doctor's wife pursed up her lips into a sympathetic smile, not at all abashed by this rebuff. She had seated herself in one of the high-backed chairs, with her muslin skirt spread out about her. She looked a living exemplification of all that is neat and prim and commonplace, in contrast with the pale, stern-faced woman, standing rigid and defiant in her long black robes.

'How very chy-arming!' exclaimed Mrs Weston. 'You are really *not* nervous. Dee-ar me; and from what my brother Paul said, I should have imagined that any one so highly organised must be rather nervous. But I really fear I am impertinent, and that I presume upon our very slight relationship. It *is* a relationship, is it not, although such a very slight one?'

'I have never thought of the subject,' Mrs Marchmont replied coldly. 'I suppose, however, that my marriage with your brother's cousin—'

'And *my* cousin—'

'Made a kind of connexion between us. But Mr Marchmont gave me to understand that you lived at Stanfield, Mrs Weston.'

'Until last week, positively until last week,' answered the surgeon's wife. 'I see you take very little interest in village gossip, Mrs Marchmont, or you would have heard of the change at Kemberling.'

'What change?'

'My husband's purchase of poor old Mr Dawnfield's practice. The dear old man died a month ago,—you heard of his death, of course,—and Mr Weston negotiated the purchase with Mrs Dawnfield in less than a fortnight. We came here early last week, and already we are making friends in the neighbourhood. How strange that you should not have heard of our coming!'

'I do not see much society,' Olivia answered indifferently, 'and I hear nothing of the Kemberling people.'

'Indeed!' cried Mrs Weston; 'and we hear so much of Marchmont Towers at Kemberling.'

She looked full in the widow's face as she spoke, her stereotyped smile subsiding into a look of greedy curiosity; a look whose intense eagerness could not be concealed.

That look, and the tone in which her last sentence had been

spoken, said as plainly as the plainest words could have done, 'I have heard of Mary Marchmont's flight.'

Olivia understood this; but in the passionate depth of her own madness she had no power to fathom the meanings or the motives of other people. She revolted against this Mrs Weston, and disliked her because the woman intruded upon her in her desolation; but she never once thought of Lavinia Weston's interest in Mary's movements; she never once remembered that the frail life of that orphan girl only stood between this woman's brother and the rich heritage of Marchmont Towers.

Blind and forgetful of everything in the hideous egotism of her despair, what was Olivia Marchmont but a fitting tool, a plastic and easily-moulded instrument, in the hands of unscrupulous people, whose hard intellects had never been beaten into confused shapelessness in the fiery furnace of passion?

Mrs Weston had heard of Mary Marchmont's flight; but she had heard half a dozen different reports of that event, as widely diversified in their details as if half a dozen heiresses had fled from Marchmont Towers. Every gossip in the place had a separate story as to the circumstances which had led to the girl's running away from her home. The accounts vied with each other in graphic force and minute elaboration; the conversations that had taken place between Mary and her stepmother, between Edward Arundel and Mrs Marchmont, between the Rector of Swampington and nobody in particular, would have filled a volume, as related by the gossips of Kemberling; but as everybody assigned a different cause for the terrible misunderstanding at the Towers, and a different direction for Mary's flight,—and as the railway official at the station, who could have thrown some light on the subject, was a stern and moody man, who had little sympathy with his kind, and held his tongue persistently,—it was not easy to get very near the truth. Under these circumstances, then, Mrs Weston determined upon seeking information at the fountain-head, and approaching the cruel stepmother, who, according to some of the reports, had starved and beaten her dead husband's child.

'Yes, dear Mrs Marchmont,' said Lavinia Weston, seeing that it was necessary to come direct to the point if she wished to wring the truth from Olivia; 'yes, we hear of everything at Kemberling; and I need scarcely tell you, that we heard of the sad trouble which you have had to endure since your ball—the ball that is spoken of as the most chy-arming entertainment remembered in the neighbourhood for a long time. We heard of this sad girl's flight.'

Mrs Marchmont looked up with a dark frown, but made no answer.

'Was she—it really is such a very painful question, that I almost shrink from—but was Miss Marchmont at all—eccentric—a little mentally deficient? Pray pardon me, if I have given you pain by such a question; but ——'

Olivia started, and looked sharply at her visitor. 'Mentally deficient? No!' she said. But as she spoke her eyes dilated, her pale cheeks grew paler, her upper lip quivered with a faint convulsive movement. It seemed as if some idea presented itself to her with a sudden force that almost took away her breath.

'*Not* mentally deficient!' repeated Lavinia Weston; 'dee-ar me! It's a great comfort to hear that. Of course Paul saw very little of his cousin, and he was not therefore in a position to judge,—though his opinions, however rapidly arrived at; are generally so *very* accurate;—but he gave me to understand that he thought Miss Marchmont appeared a little—just a little—weak in her intellect. I am very glad to find he was mistaken.'

Olivia made no reply to this speech. She had seated herself in her chair by the window; she looked straight before her into the flagged quadrangle, with her hands lying idle in her lap. It seemed as if she were actually unconscious of her visitor's presence, or as if, in her scornful indifference, she did not even care to affect any interest in that visitor's conversation.

Lavinia Weston returned again to the attack.

'Pray, Mrs Marchmont, do not think me intrusive or impertinent,' she said pleadingly, 'if I ask you to favour me with the true particulars of this sad event. I am sure you will be good enough to remember that my brother Paul, my sister, and myself are Mary Marchmont's nearest relatives on her father's side, and that we have therefore some right to feel interested in her?'

By this very polite speech Lavinia Weston plainly reminded the widow of the insignificance of her own position at Marchmont Towers. In her ordinary frame of mind Olivia would have resented the ladylike slight, but to-day she neither heard nor heeded it; she was brooding with a stupid, unreasonable persistency over the words 'mental deficiency,' 'weak intellect.' She only roused herself by a great effort to answer Mrs Weston's question, when that lady had repeated it in very plain words.

'I can tell you nothing about Miss Marchmont's flight,' she said, coldly, 'except that she chose to run away from her home. I found reason to object to her conduct upon the night of the ball; and the next morning she left the house, assigning no reason—to me, at any rate—for her absurd and improper behaviour.'

'She assigned no reason to *you* my dear Mrs Marchmont; but she assigned a reason to somebody, I infer, from what you say?'

'Yes; she wrote a letter to my cousin, Captain Arundel.'

'Telling him the reason of her departure?'

'I don't know—I forget. The letter told nothing clearly; it was wild and incoherent.'

Mrs Weston sighed,—a long-drawn, desponding sigh.

'Wild and incoherent!' she murmured, in a pensive tone. 'How grieved Paul will be to hear of this! He took such an interest in his cousin—a delicate and fragile-looking young creature, he told me. Yes, he took a very great interest in her, Mrs Marchmont, though you may perhaps scarcely believe me when I say so. He kept himself purposely aloof from this place; his sensitive nature led him to abstain from even revealing his interest in Miss Marchmont. His position, you must remember, with regard to this poor dear girl, is a very delicate—I may say a very painful—one.'

Olivia remembered nothing of the kind. The value of the Marchmont estates; the sordid worth of those wide-stretching farms, spreading far-away into Yorkshire; the pitiful, closely-calculated revenue, which made Mary a wealthy heiress,—were so far from the dark thoughts of this woman's desperate heart, that she no more suspected Mrs Weston of any mercenary design in coming to the Towers, than of burglarious intentions with regard to the silver spoons in the plate-room. She only thought that the surgeon's wife was a tiresome woman, against whose pertinacious civility her angry spirit chafed and rebelled, until she was almost driven to order her from the room.

In this cruel weariness of spirit Mrs Marchmont gave a short impatient sigh, which afforded a sufficient hint to such an accomplished tactician as her visitor.

'I know I have tired you, my dear Mrs Marchmont,' the doctor's wife said, rising and arranging her muslin scarf as she spoke, in token of her immediate departure. 'I am so sorry to find you a sufferer from that nasty hacking cough; but of course you have the best advice,—Mr Barlow from Swampington I think you said?'—Olivia had said nothing of the kind;—'and I trust the warm weather will prevent the cough taking any hold of your chest. If I might venture to suggest flannels—so many young women quite ridicule the idea of flannels—but, as the wife of a humble provincial practitioner, I have learned their value. Good-bye, dear Mrs Marchmont. I may come again, may I not, now that the ice is broken, and we are so well acquainted with each other? Good-bye.'

Olivia could not refuse to take at least *one* of the two plump and tightly-gloved hands which were held out to her with an air of frank cordiality; but the widow's grasp was loose and nerveless, and, inasmuch as two consentient parties are required to the shaking of hands as well as to the getting up of a quarrel, the salutation was not a very hearty one.

The surgeon's pony must have been weary of standing before the flight of shallow steps leading to the western portico, when Mrs Weston took her seat by her husband's side in the gig, which had been newly painted and varnished since the worthy couple's hegira* from Stanfield.

The surgeon was not an ambitious man, nor a designing man; he was simply stupid and lazy—lazy although, in spite of himself, he led an active and hard-working life; but there are many square men whose sides are cruelly tortured by the pressure of the round holes into which they are ill-advisedly thrust, and if our destinies were meted out to us in strict accordance with our temperaments, Mr Weston should have been a lotus-eater. As it was, he was content to drudge on, mildly complying with every desire of his wife; doing what she told him, because it was less trouble to do the hardest work at her bidding than to oppose her. It would have been surely less painful for Macbeth* have finished that ugly business of the murder than to have endured my lady's black contemptuous scowl, and the bitter scorn and contumely concentrated in those four words, 'Give *me* the daggers.'

Mr Weston asked one or two commonplace questions about his wife's interview with John Marchmont's widow; but, slowly apprehending that Lavinia did not care to discuss the matter, he relapsed into meek silence, and devoted all his intellectual powers to the task of keeping the pony out of the deeper ruts in the rugged road between Marchmont Towers and Kemberling High Street.

'What is the secret of that woman's life?' thought Lavinia Weston during that homeward drive. 'Has she ill-treated the girl, or is she plotting in some way or other to get hold of the Marchmont fortune? Pshaw! that's impossible. And yet she may be making a purse, some-how or other, out of the estate. Anyhow, there is bad blood between the two women.'

CHAPTER XVIII

A STOLEN HONEYMOON

THE village to which Edward Arundel took his bride was within a few miles of Winchester. The young soldier had become familiar with the place in his early boyhood, when he had gone to spend a part of one bright midsummer holiday at the house of a schoolfellow; and had ever since cherished a friendly remembrance of the winding trout-streams, the rich verdure of the valleys, and the sheltering hills that shut in the pleasant little cluster of thatched cottages, the pretty white-walled villas, and the grey old church.

But to Mary, whose experiences of town and country were limited to the dingy purlieus of Oakley Street and the fenny flats of Lincolnshire, this Hampshire village seemed a rustic paradise, which neither trouble nor sorrow could ever approach. She had trembled at the thought of Olivia's coming in Oakley Street; but here she seemed to lose all terror of her stern stepmother,—here, sheltered and protected by her young husband's love, she fancied that she might live life out happy and secure.

She told Edward this one sunny morning, as they sat by the young man's favourite trout-stream. Captain Arundel's fishing-tackle lay idle on the turf at his side, for he had been beguiled into forgetfulness of a ponderous trout he had been watching and finessing with for upwards of an hour, and had flung himself at full length upon the mossy margin of the water, with his uncovered head lying in Mary's lap.

The childish bride would have been content to sit for ever thus in that rural solitude, with her fingers twisted in her husband's chestnut curls, and her soft eyes keeping timid watch upon his handsome face,—so candid and unclouded in its careless repose. The undulating meadow-land lay half-hidden in a golden haze, only broken here and there by the glitter of the brighter sunlight that lit up the waters of the wandering streams that intersected the low pastures. The massive towers of the cathedral, the grey walls of St Cross, loomed dimly in the distance; the bubbling plash of a mill-stream sounded like some monotonous lullaby in the drowsy summer atmosphere. Mary looked from the face she loved to the fair landscape about her, and a tender solemnity crept into her mind—a reverent love and admiration for this beautiful earth, which was almost akin to awe.

'How pretty this place is, Edward!' she said. 'I had no idea there were such places in all the wide world. Do you know, I think I would rather be a cottage-girl here than an heiress in Lincolnshire. Edward, if I ask you a favour, will you grant it?'

She spoke very earnestly, looking down at her husband's upturned face; but Captain Arundel only laughed at her question, without even caring to lift the drowsy eyelids that drooped over his blue eyes.

'Well, my pet, if you want anything short of the moon, I suppose your devoted husband is scarcely likely to refuse it. Our honeymoon is not a fortnight old yet, Polly dear; you wouldn't have me turn tyrant quite as soon as this. Speak out, Mrs Arundel, and assert your dignity as a British matron. What is the favour I am to grant?'

'I want you to live here always, Edward darling,' pleaded the girlish voice. 'Not for a fortnight or a month, but for ever and ever. I have never been happy at Marchmont Towers. Papa died there, you know, and I cannot forget that. Perhaps that ought to have made the place sacred to me, and so it has; but it is sacred like papa's tomb in Kemberling Church, and it seems like profanation to be happy in it, or to forget my dead father even for a moment. Don't let us go back there, Edward. Let my stepmother live there all her life. It would seem selfish and cruel to turn her out of the house she has so long been mistress of. Mr Gormby will go on collecting the rents, you know, and can send us as much money as we want; and we can take that pretty house we saw to let on the other side of Milldale,—the house with the rookery, and the dovecotes, and the sloping lawn leading down to the water. You know you don't like Lincolnshire, Edward, any more than I do, and there's scarcely any trout-fishing near the Towers.'

Captain Arundel opened his eyes, and lifted himself out of his reclining position before he answered his wife.

'My own precious Polly,' he said, smiling fondly at the gentle childish face turned in such earnestness towards his own; 'my runaway little wife, rich people have their duties to perform as well as poor people; and I am afraid it would never do for you to hide in this out-of-the-way Hampshire village, and play absentee from stately Marchmont and all its dependencies. I love that pretty, infantine, unworldly spirit of yours, my darling; and I sometimes wish we were two grown-up babes in the wood, and could wander about gathering wild flowers, and eating black-berries and hazel-nuts, until the shades of evening closed in, and the friendly robins came to bury us. Don't fancy I am tired of our honeymoon, Polly, or that I care for Marchmont Towers any more than you do; but I fear the non-residence plan would never answer. The world would call my little wife eccentric, if she ran away from her grandeur; and Paul Marchmont the artist,—of whom your poor father had rather a bad opinion, by the way,—would be taking out a statute of lunacy* against you.'

'Paul Marchmont!' repeated Mary. 'Did papa dislike Mr Paul Marchmont?'

'Well, poor John had a sort of a prejudice against the man, I believe; but it was only a prejudice, for he freely confessed that he could assign no reason for it. But whatever Mr Paul Marchmont may be, you must live at the Towers, Mary, and be Lady Bountiful-in-chief in your neighbourhood, and look after your property, and have long interviews with Mr Gormby, and become altogether a woman of business; so that when I go back to India——'

Mary interrupted him with a little cry:

'Go back to India!' she exclaimed. 'What do you mean, Edward?'

'I mean, my darling, that my business in life is to fight for my Queen and country, and not to sponge upon my wife's fortune. You don't suppose I'm going to lay down my sword at seven and twenty years of age, and retire upon my pension? No, Polly; you remember what Lord Nelson said on the deck of the *Victory* at Trafalgar. That saying can never be so hackneyed as to lose its force. I must do my duty, Polly—I must do my duty, even if duty and love pull different ways, and I have to leave my darling, in the service of my country.'

Mary clasped her hands in despair, and looked piteously at her lover-husband, with the tears streaming down her pale cheeks.

'O Edward,' she cried, 'how cruel you are; how very, very cruel you are to me! What is the use of my fortune if you won't share it with me, if you won't take it all; for it is yours, my dearest—it is all yours? I remember the words in the Marriage Service, "with all my goods I thee endow." I have given you Marchmont Towers, Edward; nobody in the world can take it away from you. You never, never, never could be so cruel as to leave me! I know how brave and good you are, and I am proud to think of your noble courage and all the brave deeds you did in India. But you *have* fought for your country, Edward; you *have* done your duty. Nobody can expect more of you; nobody shall take you from me. O my darling, my husband, you promised to shelter and defend me while our lives last! You won't leave me—you won't leave me, will you?'

Edward Arundel kissed the tears away from his wife's pale face, and drew her head upon his bosom.

'My love,' he said tenderly, 'you cannot tell how much pain it gives me to hear you talk like this. What can I do? To give up my profession would be to make myself next kin to a pauper. What would the world say of me, Mary? Think of that. This runaway marriage would be a dreadful dishonour to me, if it were followed by a life of lazy dependence on my wife's fortune. Nobody can dare to slander the soldier who spends the brightest years of his life in the service of his country. You would not surely have me be less than true to myself, Mary darling? For my honour's sake, I must leave you.'

'O no, no, no!' cried the girl, in a low wailing voice. Unselfish and devoted as she had been in every other crisis of her young life, she could not be reasonable or self-denying here; she was seized with despair at the thought of parting with her husband. No, not even for his honour's sake could she let him go. Better that they should both die now, in this early noontide of their happiness.

'Edward, Edward,' she sobbed, clinging convulsively about the young man's neck, 'don't leave me—don't leave me!'

'Will you go with me to India, then, Mary?'

She lifted her head suddenly, and looked her husband in the face, with the gladness in her eyes shining through her tears, like an April sun through a watery sky.

'I would go to the end of the world with you, my own darling,' she said; 'the burning sands and the dreadful jungles would have no terrors for me, if I were with you, Edward.'

Captain Arundel smiled at her earnestness.

'I won't take you into the jungle, my love,' he answered, playfully; 'or if I do, your palki* shall be well guarded, and all ravenous beasts kept at a respectful distance from my little wife. A great many ladies go to India with their husbands, Polly, and come back very little the worse for the climate or the voyage; and except your money, there is no reason you should not go with me.'

'Oh, never mind my money; let anybody have that.'

'Polly,' cried the soldier, very seriously, 'we must consult Richard Paulette as to the future. I don't think I did right in marrying you during his absence; and I have delayed writing to him too long, Polly. Those letters must be written this afternoon.'

'The letter to Mr Paulette and to your father?'

'Yes; and the letter to my cousin Olivia.'

Mary's face grew sorrowful again, as Captain Arundel said this.

'*Must* you tell my stepmother of our marriage?' she said.

'Most assuredly, my dear. Why should we keep her in ignorance of it? Your father's will gave her the privilege of advising you, but not the power to interfere with your choice, whatever that choice might be. You were your own mistress, Mary, when you married me. What reason have you to fear my cousin Olivia?'

'No reason, perhaps,' the girl answered, sadly; 'but I do fear her. I know I am very foolish, Edward, and you have reason to despise me,—you who are so brave. But I could never tell you how I tremble at the thought of being once more in my stepmother's power. She said cruel things to me, Edward. Every word she spoke seemed to stab me to the heart; but it isn't that only. There's something more than that; something that I can't describe, that I can't understand; something which tells me that she hates me.'

'Hates you, darling?'

'Yes, Edward; yes, she hates me. It wasn't always so, you know. She used to be only cold and reserved, but lately her manner has changed. I thought that she was ill, perhaps, and that my presence worried her. People often wish to be alone, I know, when they are ill. O Edward I have seen her shrink from me, and shudder if her dress brushed against mine, as if I had been some horrible creature. What have I done, Edward, that she should hate me?'

Captain Arundel knitted his brows, and set himself to work out this womanly problem; but he could make nothing of it. Yes, what Mary had said was perfectly true: Olivia hated her. The young man had seen that upon the morning of the girl's flight from Marchmont Towers; he had seen vengeful fury and vindictive passion raging in the dark face of John Marchmont's widow. But what reason could the woman have for her hatred of this innocent girl? Again and again Olivia's cousin asked himself this question; and he was so far away from the truth at last, that he could only answer it by imagining the lowest motive for the widow's bad feeling. 'She envies my poor little girl her fortune and position,' he thought.

'But you won't leave me alone with my stepmother, will you, Edward?' Mary said, recurring to her old prayer. 'I am not afraid of her, nor of anybody or anything in the world, while you are with me,—how should I be?—but I think if I were to be alone with her again, I should die. She would speak to me again as she spoke upon the night of the ball, and her bitter taunts would kill me. I *could* not bear to be in her power again, Edward.'

'And you shall not, my darling,' answered the young man, enfolding the slender, trembling figure in his strong arms. 'My own childish pet, you shall never be exposed to any woman's insolence or tyranny. You shall be sheltered and protected, and hedged in on every side by your husband's love. And when I go to India, you shall sail with me, my pearl. Mary, look up and smile at me, and let's have no more talk of cruel stepmothers. How strange it seems to me, Polly dear, that you should have been so womanly when you were a child, and yet are so childlike now you are a woman!'

The mistress of Marchmont Towers looked doubtfully at her husband, as if she feared her childishness might be displeasing to him.

'You don't love me any the less because of that, do you, Edward?' she asked timidly.

'Because of what, my treasure?'

'Because I am so—childish?'

'Polly,' cried the young man, 'do you think Jupiter liked Hebe any the less because she was fresh and innocent as the nectar she served out to him? If he had, my dear, he'd have sent for Clotho, or Atropos,* or some one or other of the elderly maiden ladies of Hades, to wait upon him as cupbearer. I wouldn't have you otherwise than you are, Polly, by so much as one thought.'

The girl looked up at her husband in a rapture of innocent affection.

'I am too happy, Edward,' she said, in a low, awe-stricken whisper—'I am too happy! So much happiness can never last.'

Alas! the orphan girl's experience of this life had early taught her the lesson which some people learn so late. She had learnt to distrust the equal blue of a summer sky, the glorious splendour of the blazing sunlight. She was accustomed to sorrow; but these brief glimpses of perfect happiness filled her with a dim sense of terror. She felt like some earthly wanderer who had strayed across the threshold of Paradise. In the midst of her delight and admiration, she trembled for the moment in which the ruthless angels, bearing flaming swords, should drive her from the celestial gates.

'It can't last, Edward,' she murmured.

'Can't last, Polly!' cried the young man; 'why, my dove is transformed all at once into a raven. We have outlived our troubles, Polly, like the hero and heroine in one of your novels; and what is to prevent our living happy ever afterwards, like them? If you remember, my dear, no sorrows or trials ever fall to the lot of people *after* marriage. The persecutions, the separations, the estrangements, are all ante-nuptial. When once your true novelist gets his hero and heroine up to the altar-rails in real earnest,—he gets them into the church sometimes, and then forbids the banns, or brings a former wife, or a rightful husband, pale and denouncing, from behind a pillar, and drives the wretched pair out again, to persecute them through three hundred pages more before he lets them get back again,—but when once the important words are spoken and the knot tied, the story's done, and the happy couple get forty or fifty years' wedded bliss, as a set-off against the miseries they have endured in the troubled course of a twelvemouth's courtship. That's the sort of thing, isn't it, Polly?'

The clock of St Cross, sounding faintly athwart the meadows, struck three as the young man finished speaking.

'Three o'clock, Polly!' he cried; 'we must go home, my pet. I mean to be businesslike today.'

Upon each day in that happy honeymoon holiday Captain Arundel had made some such declaration with regard to his intention of being businesslike; that is to say, setting himself deliberately to the task of writing those letters which should announce and explain his marriage to the people who had a right to hear of it. But the soldier had a dislike to all letter-writing, and a special horror of any epistolary communication which could come under the denomination of a business-letter; so the easy summer days slipped by,—the delicious drowsy noontides, the soft and dreamy twilight, the tender moonlit nights,—and the Captain put off the task for which he had no fancy, from after breakfast until after dinner, and from after dinner until after breakfast; always beguiled away from his open travelling-desk by a word from Mary, who called him to the window to look at a pretty child on the village green before the inn, or at the blacksmith's dog, or the tinker's donkey, or a tired Italian organ-boy who had strayed into that out-of-the-way nook, or at the smart butcher from Winchester, who rattled over in a pony-cart twice a week to take orders from the gentry round about, and to insult and defy the local purveyor, whose stock-in-trade generally seemed to consist of one leg of mutton and a dish of pig's fry.

The young couple walked slowly through the meadows, crossing rustic wooden bridges that spanned the winding stream, loitering to look down into the clear water at the fish which Captain Arundel pointed out, but which Mary could never see;—that young lady always fixing her eyes upon some long trailing weed afloat in the transparent water, while the silvery trout indicated by her husband glided quietly away to the sedgy bottom of the stream. They lingered by the water-mill, beneath whose shadow some children were fishing; they seized upon every pretext for lengthening that sunny homeward walk, and only reached the inn as the village clocks were striking four, at which hour Captain Arundel had ordered dinner.

But after the simple little repast, mild and artless in its nature as the fair young spirit of the bride herself; after the landlord, sympathetic yet respectful, had in his own person attended upon his two guests; after the pretty rustic chamber had been cleared of all evidence of the meal that had been eaten, Edward Arundel began seriously to consider the business in hand.

'The letters must be written, Polly,' he said, seating himself at a table near the open window. Trailing branches of jasmine and honey-suckle made a framework round the diamond-paned casement; the perfumed blossoms blew into the room with every breath of the warm August breeze, and hung trembling in the folds of the chintz curtains. Mr Arundel's gaze wandered dreamily away through this open window to the primitive picture without,—the scattered cottages upon the other side of the green, the cattle standing in the pond, the cackling geese hurrying homeward across the purple ridge of common, the village gossips loitering beneath the faded sign that hung before the low white tavern at the angle of the road. He looked at all these things as he flung his leathern desk upon the table, and made a great parade of unlocking and opening it.

'The letters must be written,' he repeated, with a smothered sigh. 'Did you ever notice a peculiar property in stationery, Polly?'

Mrs Edward Arundel only opened her brown eyes to their widest extent, and stared at her husband.

'No, I see you haven't,' said the young man. 'How should you, you fortunate Polly? You've never had to write any business-letters yet, though you are an heiress. The peculiarity of all stationery, my dear, is, that it is possessed of an intuitive knowledge of the object for which it is to be used. If one has to write an unpleasant letter, Polly, it might go a little smoother, you know; one might round one's paragraphs, and spell the difficult words—the "believes" and "receives," the "tills" and "untils," and all that sort of thing—better with a pleasant pen, an easygoing, jolly, soft-nibbed quill, that would seem to say, "Cheer up, old fellow! I'll carry you through it; we'll get to 'your very obedient servant' before you know where you are," and so on. But, bless your heart, Polly! let a poor unbusinesslike fellow try to write a business-letter, and everything goes against him. The pen knows what he's at, and jibs, and stumbles, and shies about the paper, like a broken-down screw;* the ink turns thick and lumpy; the paper gets as greasy as a London pavement after a fall of snow, till a poor fellow gives up, and knocks under to the force of circumstances. You see if my pen doesn't splutter, Polly, the moment I address Richard Paulette.'

Captain Arundel was very careful in the adjustment of his sheet of paper, and began his letter with an air of resolution.

'White Hart Inn, Milldale, near Winchester,
'August 14th

'MY DEAR SIR,'

He wrote as much as this with great promptitude, and then, with his elbow on the table, fell to staring at his pretty young wife and drumming his fingers on his chin. Mary was sitting opposite her husband at the open window, working, or making a pretence of being occupied with some impossible fragment of Berlin wool-work,* while she watched her husband.

'How pretty you look in that white frock, Polly!' said the soldier; 'you call those things frocks, don't you. And that blue sash, too,—you ought always to wear white, Mary, like your namesakes abroad who are *vouée au blanc** by their faithful mothers, and who are a blessing to the laundresses for the first seven or fourteen years of their lives. What shall I say to Paulette? He's such a jolly fellow, there oughtn't to be much difficulty about the matter. "My dear sir," seems absurdly stiff; "my dear Paulette,"—that's better,—"I write this to inform you that your client, Miss Mary March——" What's that, Polly?'

It was the postman, a youth upon a pony, with the afternoon letters from London. Captain Arundel flung down his pen and went to the window. He had some interest in this young man's arrival, as he had left orders that such letters as were addressed to him at the hotel in Covent Garden should be forwarded to him at Milldale.

'I daresay there's a letter from Germany, Polly,' he said eagerly. 'My mother and Letitia are capital correspondents; I'll wager anything there's a letter, and I can answer it in the one I'm going to write this evening, and that'll be killing two birds with one stone. I'll run down to the postman, Polly.'

Captain Arundel had good reason to go after his letters, for there seemed little chance of those missives being brought to him. The youthful postman was standing in the porch drinking ale out of a ponderous earthenware mug, and talking to the landlord, when Edward went down.

'Any letters for me, Dick?' the Captain asked. He knew the Christian name of almost every visitor or hanger-on at the little inn, though he had not stayed there an entire fortnight, and was as popular and admired as if he had been some free-spoken young squire to whom all the land round about belonged.

''Ees, sir,' the young man answered, shuffling off his cap; 'there be two letters for ye.'

He handed the two packets to Captain Arundel, who looked doubtfully at the address of the uppermost, which, like the other, had been re-directed by the people at the London hotel. The original address of this letter was in a handwriting that was strange to him; but it bore the postmark of the village from which the Dangerfield letters were sent.

The back of the inn looked into an orchard, and through an open door opposite to the porch Edward Arundel saw the low branches of the trees, and the ripening fruit red and golden in the afternoon sunlight. He went out into this orchard to read his letters, his mind a little disturbed by the strange handwriting upon the Dangerfield epistle.

The letter was from his father's housekeeper, imploring him most earnestly to go down to the Park without delay. Squire Arundel had been stricken with paralysis, and was declared to be in imminent danger. Mrs and Miss Arundel and Mr Reginald were away in Germany. The faithful old servant implored the younger son to lose no time in hurrying home, if he wished to see his father alive.

The soldier leaned against the gnarled grey trunk of an old apple-tree, and stared at this letter with a white awe-stricken face.

What was he to do? He must go to his father, of course. He must go without a moment's delay. He must catch the first train that would carry him westward from Southampton. There could be no question as to his duty. He must go; he must leave his young wife.

His heart sank with a sharp thrill of pain, and with perhaps some faint shuddering sense of an unknown terror, as he thought of this.

'It was lucky I didn't write the letters,' he reflected; 'no one will guess the secret of my darling's retreat. She can stay here till I come back to her. God knows I shall hurry back the moment my duty sets me free. These people will take care of her. No one will know where to look for her. I'm very glad I didn't write to Olivia. We were so happy this morning! Who could think that sorrow would come between us so soon?'

Captain Arundel looked at his watch. It was a quarter to six o'clock, and he knew that an express left Southampton for the west at eight. There would be time for him to catch that train with the help of a sturdy pony belonging to the landlord of the White Hart, which would rattle him over to the station in an hour and a half. There would be time for him to catch the train; but, oh! how little time to comfort his darling—how little time to reconcile his young wife to the temporary separation!

He hurried back to the porch, briefly explained to the landlord what had happened, ordered the pony and gig to be got ready immediately, and then went very, very slowly upstairs, to the room in which his young wife sat by the open window waiting for his return.

Mary looked up at his face as he entered the room, and that one glance told her of some new sorrow.

'Edward,' she cried, starting up from her chair with a look of terror, 'my stepmother has come.'

Even in his trouble the young man smiled at his foolish wife's all-absorbing fear of Olivia Marchmont.

'No, my darling,' he said; 'I wish to heaven our worst trouble were the chance of your father's widow breaking in upon us. Something has happened, Mary; something very sorrowful, very serious for me. My father is ill, Polly dear, dangerously ill, and I must go to him.'

Mary Arundel drew a long breath. Her face had grown very white, and the hands that were linked tightly round her husband's arm trembled a little.

'I will try to bear it,' she said; 'I will try to bear it.'

'God bless you, my darling!' the soldier answered fervently, clasping his young wife to his breast. 'I know you will. It will be a very short parting, Mary dearest. I will come back to you directly I have seen my father. If he is worse, there will be little need for me to stop at Dangerfield; if he is better, I can take you back there with me. My own darling love, it is very bitter for us to be parted thus; but I know that you will bear it like a heroine. Won't you, Polly?'

'I will try to bear it, dear.'

She said very little more than this, but clung about her husband, not with any desperate force, not with any clamorous and tumultuous grief, but with a half-despondent resignation; as a drowning man, whose strength is well-nigh exhausted, may cling, in his hopelessness, to a spar, which he knows he must presently abandon.

Mary Arundel followed her husband hither and thither while he made his brief and hurried preparations for the sudden journey; but although she was powerless to assist him,—for her trembling hands let fall everything she tried to hold, and there was a mist before her eyes, which distorted and blotted the outline of every object she looked at,—she hindered him by no noisy lamentations, she distressed him by no tears. She suffered, as it was her habit to suffer, quietly and uncomplainingly.

The sun was sinking when she went with Edward downstairs to the porch, before which the landlord's pony and gig were in waiting, in custody of a smart lad who was to accompany Mr Arundel to Southampton. There was no time for any protracted farewell. It was better so, perhaps, Edward thought. He would be back so soon, that the grief he felt in this parting—and it may be that his suffering was scarcely less than Mary's—seemed wasted anguish, to which it would have been sheer cowardice to give way. But for all this the soldier very nearly broke down when he saw his childish wife's piteous face, white in the evening sunlight, turned to him in mute appeal, as if the quivering lips would fain have entreated him to abandon all and to remain. He lifted the fragile figure in his arms,—alas! it had never seemed so fragile as now,—and covered the pale face with passionate kisses and fast-dropping tears.

'God bless and defend you, Mary! God keep——'

He was ashamed of the huskiness of his voice, and putting his wife suddenly away from him, he sprang into the gig, snatched the reins from the boy's hand, and drove away at the pony's best speed. The old-fashioned vehicle disappeared in a cloud of dust; and Mary, looking after her husband with eyes that were as yet tearless, saw nothing but glaring light and confusion, and a pastoral landscape that reeled and heaved like a stormy sea.

It seemed to her, as she went slowly back to her room, and sat down amidst the disorder of open portmanteaus and overturned hatboxes, which the young man had thrown here and there in his hurried selection of the few things necessary for him to take on his hasty journey—it seemed as if the greatest calamity of her life had now befallen her. As hopelessly as she had thought of her father's death, she now thought of Edward Arundel's departure. She could not see beyond the acute anguish of this separation. She could not realise to herself that there was no cause for all this terrible sorrow; that the parting was only a temporary one; and that her husband would return to her in a few days at the furthest. Now that she was alone, now that the necessity for heroism was past, she abandoned herself utterly to the despair that had held possession of her soul from the moment in which Captain Arundel had told her of his father's illness.

The sun went down behind the purple hills that sheltered the western side of the little village. The tree-tops in the orchard below the open window of Mrs Arundel's bedroom grew dim in the grey twilight. Little by little sound of voices in the rooms below died away into stillness. The fresh rosy-cheeked country girl who had waited upon the young husband and wife, came into the sitting-room with a pair of wax-candles in old-fashioned silver candlesticks, and lingered in the room for a little time, expecting to receive some order from the lonely watcher. But Mary had locked the door of her bedchamber, and sat with her head upon the sill of the open window, looking out into the dim orchard. It was only when the stars glimmered in the tranquil sky that the girl's blank despair gave way before a sudden burst of tears, and she flung herself down beside the white-curtained bed to pray for her young husband. She prayed for him in an ecstatic fervour of love and faith, carried away by the new hopefulness that arose out of her ardent supplications, and picturing him going triumphant on his course, to find his father out of danger,—restored to health, perhaps,—and to return to her before the stars glimmered through the darkness of another summer's night. She prayed for him, hoping and believing everything; though at the hour in which she knelt, with the faint starlight shimmering upon her upturned face and clasped hands, Edward Arundel was lying, maimed and senseless, in the wretched waiting-room of a little railway-station in Dorsetshire, watched over by an obscure country surgeon, while the frightened officials scudded here and there in search of some vehicle in which the young man might be conveyed to the nearest town.

There had been one of those accidents which seem terribly common on every line of railway, however well managed. A signalman had mistaken one train for another; a flag had been dropped too soon; and the down-express had run into a heavy luggage-train blundering up from Exeter with farm-produce for the London markets. Two men had been killed, and a great many passengers hurt; some very seriously. Edward Arundel's case was perhaps one of the most serious amongst these.

CHAPTER XIX

SOUNDING THE DEPTHS

LAVINIA WESTON spent the evening after her visit to Marchmont Towers at her writing-desk, which, like everything else appertaining to her, was a model of neatness and propriety; perfect in its way, although it was no marvellous specimen of walnut-wood and burnished gold, no elegant structure of papier-mâché and mother-of-pearl, but simply a schoolgirl's homely rosewood desk, bought for fifteen shillings or a guinea.

Mrs Weston had administered the evening refreshment of weak tea, stale bread, and strong butter to her meek husband, and had dismissed him to the surgery, a sunken and rather cellar-like apartment opening out of the prim second-best parlour, and approached from the village street by a side-door. The surgeon was very well content to employ himself with the preparation of such draughts and boluses* as were required by the ailing inhabitants of Kemberling, while his wife sat at her desk in the room above him. He left his gallipots* and pestle and mortar once or twice in the course of the evening, to clamber ponderously up the three or four stairs leading to the sitting-room, and stare through the keyhole of the door at Mrs Weston's thoughtful face, and busy hand gliding softly over the smooth note-paper. He did this in no prying or suspicious spirit, but out of sheer admiration for his wife.

'What a mind she has!' he murmured rapturously, as he went back to his work; 'what a mind!'

The letter which Lavinia Weston wrote that evening was a very long one. She was one of those women who write long letters upon every convenient occasion. To-night she covered two sheets of note-paper with her small neat handwriting. Those two sheets contained a detailed account of the interview that had taken place that day between the surgeon's wife and Olivia; and the letter was addressed to the artist, Paul Marchmont.

Perhaps it was in consequence of the receipt of this letter that Paul Marchmont arrived at his sister's house at Kemberling two days after Mrs Weston's visit to Marchmont Towers. He told the surgeon that he came to Lincolnshire for a few days' change of air, after a long spell of very hard work; and George Weston, who looked upon his brother-in-law as an intellectual demi-god, was very well content to accept any explanation of Mr Marchmont's visit.

'Kemberling isn't a very lively place for you, Mr Paul,' he said apologetically,—he always called his wife's brother Mr Paul,—'but I dare say Lavinia will contrive to make you comfortable. She persuaded me to come here when old Dawnfield died; but I can't say she acted with her usual tact, for the business ain't as good as my Stanfield practice; but I don't tell Lavinia so.'

Paul Marchmont smiled.

'The business will pick up by-and-by, I daresay,' he said. 'You'll have the Marchmont Towers family to attend to in good time, I suppose.'

'That's what Lavinia said,' answered the surgeon. ' "Mrs John Marchmont can't refuse to employ a relation," she says; "and, as first-cousin to Mary Marchmont's father, I ought"—meaning herself, you know—"to have some influence in that quarter." But then, you see, the very week we come here the gal goes and runs away; which rather, as one may say, puts a spoke in our wheel, you know.'

Mr George Weston rubbed his chin reflectively as he concluded thus. He was a man given to spending his leisure-hours—when he had any leisure, which was not very often—in tavern parlours, where the affairs of the nation were settled and unsettled every evening over sixpenny glasses of hollands* and water; and he regretted his removal from Stanfield, which had been as the uprooting of all his dearest associations. He was a solemn man, who never hazarded an opinion lightly,—perhaps because he never had an opinion to hazard,—and his stolidity won him a good deal of respect from strangers; but in the hands of his wife he was meeker than the doves that cooed in the pigeon-house behind his dwelling, and more plastic than the knob of white wax upon which industrious Mrs Weston was wont to rub her thread when engaged in the mysteries of that elaborate and terrible science which women paradoxically call *plain* needlework.

Paul Marchmont presented himself at the Towers upon the day after his arrival at Kemberling. His interview with the widow was a very long one. He had studied every line of his sister's letter; he had weighed every word that had fallen from Olivia's lips and had been recorded by Lavinia Weston; and taking the knowledge thus obtained as his starting-point, he took his dissecting-knife and went to work at an intellectual autopsy. He anatomised the wretched woman's soul. He made her tell her secret, and bare her tortured breast before him; now wringing some hasty word from her impatience, now entrapping her into some admission,—if only so much as a defiant look, a sudden lowering of the dark brows, an involuntary compression of the lips. He *made* her reveal herself to him. Poor Rosencranz and Guildenstern were sorry blunderers in that art which is vulgarly called pumping, and were easily put out by a few quips and quaint retorts from the mad Danish prince; but Paul Marchmont *would* have played upon Hamlet more deftly than ever mortal musician played upon pipe or recorder,* and would have fathomed the remotest depths of that sorrowful and erratic soul. Olivia writhed under the torture of that polite inquisition, for she knew that her secrets were being extorted from her; that her pitiful folly—that folly which she would have denied even to herself, if possible—was being laid bare in all its weak foolishness. She knew this; but she was compelled to smile in the face of her bland inquisitor; to respond to his commonplace expressions of concern about the protracted absence of the missing girl, and meekly to receive his suggestions respecting the course it was her duty to take. He had the air of responding to *her* suggestions, rather than of himself dictating any particular line of conduct. He affected to believe that he was only agreeing with some understood ideas of hers, while he urged his own views upon her.

'Then we are quite of one mind in this, my dear Mrs Marchmont,' he said at last; 'this unfortunate girl must not be suffered to remain away from her legitimate home any longer than we can help. It is our duty to find and bring her back. I need scarcely say that you, being bound to her by every tie of affection, and having, beyond this, the strongest claim upon her gratitude for your devoted fulfilment of the trust confided in you,—one hears of these things, Mrs Marchmont, in a country village like Kemberling,—I need scarcely say that you are the most fitting person to win the poor child back to a sense of her duty—if she *can* be won to such a sense.' Paul Marchmont added, after a sudden pause and a thoughtful sigh, 'I sometimes fear——'

He stopped abruptly, waiting until Olivia should question him.

'You sometimes fear——?'

'That—that the error into which Miss Marchmont has fallen is the result of a mental rather than of a moral deficiency.'

'What do you mean?'

'I mean this, my dear Mrs Marchmont,' answered the artist, gravely; 'one of the most powerful evidences of the soundness of a man's brain is his capability of assigning a reasonable motive for every action of his life. No matter how unreasonable the action in itself may seem, if the motive for that action can be demonstrated. But the moment a man acts *without* motive, we begin to take alarm and to watch him. He is eccentric; his conduct is no longer amenable to ordinary rule; and we begin to trace his eccentricities to some weakness or deficiency in his judgment or intellect. Now, I ask you what motive Mary Marchmont can have had for running away from this house?'

Olivia quailed under the piercing scrutiny of the artist's cold grey eyes, but she did not attempt to reply to his question.

'The answer is very simple,' he continued, after that long scrutiny; 'the girl could have had no cause for flight; while, on the other hand, every reasonable motive that can be supposed to actuate a woman's conduct was arrayed against her. She had a happy home, a kind stepmother. She was within a few years of becoming undisputed mistress of a very large estate. And yet, immediately after having assisted at a festive entertainment, to all appearance as gay and happy as the gayest and happiest there, this girl runs away in the dead of the night, abandoning the mansion which is her own property, and assigning no reason whatever for what she does. Can you wonder, then, if I feel confirmed in an opinion that I formed upon the day on which I heard the reading of my cousin's will?'

'What opinion?'

'That Mary Marchmont is as feeble in mind as she is fragile in body.'

He launched this sentence boldly, and waited for Olivia's reply. He had discovered the widow's secret. He had fathomed the cause of her jealous hatred of Mary Marchmont; but even *he* did not yet understand the nature of the conflict in the desperate woman's breast. She could not be wicked all at once. Against every fresh sin she made a fresh struggle, and she would not accept the lie which the artist tried to force upon her.

'I do not think that there is any deficiency in my stepdaughter's intellect,' she said, resolutely.

She was beginning to understand that Paul Marchmont wanted to ally himself with her against the orphan heiress, but as yet she did not understand why he should do so. She was slow to comprehend feelings that were utterly foreign to her own nature. There was so little of mercenary baseness in this strange woman's soul, that had the flame of a candle alone stood between her and the possession of Marchmont Towers, I doubt she would have cared to waste a breath upon its extinction. She had lived away from the world, and out of the world; and it was difficult for her to comprehend the mean and paltry wickednesses which arise out of the worship of Baal.*

Paul Marchmont recoiled a little before the straight answer which the widow had given him.

'You think Miss Marchmont strong-minded, then, perhaps?' he said.

'No; not strong-minded.'

'My dear Mrs Marchmont, you deal in paradoxes,' exclaimed the artist. 'You say that your stepdaughter is neither weak-minded nor strong-minded?'

'Weak enough, perhaps, to be easily influenced by other people; weak enough to believe anything my cousin Edward Arundel might choose to tell her; but not what is generally called deficient in intellect.'

'You think her perfectly able to take care of herself?'

'Yes ; I think so'

'And yet this running away looks almost as if——. But I have no wish to force any unpleasant belief upon you, my dear madam. I think—as you yourself appear to suggest—that the best thing we can do is to get this poor girl home again as quickly as possible. It will never do for the mistress of Marchmont Towers to be wandering about the world with Mr Edward Arundel. Pray pardon me, Mrs Marchmont, if I speak rather disrespectfully of your cousin; but I really cannot think that the gentleman has acted very honourably in this business.'

Olivia, was silent. She remembered the passionate indignation of the young soldier, the angry defiance hurled at her, as Edward Arundel galloped away from the gaunt western façade. She remembered these things, and involuntarily contrasted them with the smooth blandness of Paul Marchmont's talk, and the deadly purpose lurking beneath it—of which deadly purpose some faint suspicion was beginning to dawn upon her.

If she could have thought Mary Marchmont mad,—if she could have thought Edward Arundel base, she would have been glad; for then there would have been some excuse for her own wickedness. But she could not think so. She slipped little by little down into the black gulf; now dragged by her own mad passion; now lured yet further downward by Paul Marchmont.

Between this man and eleven thousand a year the life of a fragile girl was the solitary obstacle. For three years it had been so, and for three years Paul Marchmont had waited—patiently, as it was his habit to wait—the hour and the opportunity for action. The hour and opportunity had come, and this woman, Olivia Marchmont, only stood in his way. She must become either his enemy or his tool, to be baffled or to be made useful. He had now sounded the depths of her nature, and he determined to make her his tool.

'It shall be my business to discover this poor child's hiding-place,' he said; 'when that is found I will communicate with you, and I know you will not refuse to fulfil the trust confided to you by your late husband. You will bring your stepdaughter back to this house, and henceforward protect her from the dangerous influence of Edward Arundel.'

Olivia looked at the speaker with an expression which seemed like terror. It was as if she said,—

'Are you the devil, that you hold out this temptation to me, and twist my own passions to serve your purpose?'

And then she paltered with her conscience.

'Do you consider that it is my duty to do this?' she asked.

'My dear Mrs Marchmont, most decidedly.'

'I will do it, then. I—I—wish to do my duty.'

'And you can perform no greater act of charity than by bringing this unhappy girl back to a sense of *her* duty. Remember, that her reputation, her future happiness, may fall a sacrifice to this foolish conduct, which, I regret to say, is very generally known in the neighbourhood. Forgive me if I express my opinion too freely; but I cannot help thinking, that if Mr Arundel's intentions had been strictly honourable, he would have written to you before this, to tell you that his search for the missing girl had failed; or, in the event of his finding her, he would have taken the earliest opportunity of bringing her back to her own home. My poor cousin's somewhat unprotected position, her wealth, and her inexperience of the world, place her at the mercy of a fortune-hunter; and Mr Arundel has himself to thank if his conduct gives rise to the belief that he wishes to compromise this girl in the eyes of the scandalous, and thus make sure of your consent to a marriage which would give him command of my cousin's fortune.'

Olivia Marchmont's bosom heaved with the stormy beating of her heart. Was she to sit calmly by and hold her peace while this man slandered the brave young soldier, the bold, reckless, generous-hearted lad, who had shone upon her out of the darkness of her life, as the very incarnation of all that is noble and admirable in mankind? Was she to sit quietly by and hear a stranger lie away her kinsman's honour, truth and manhood?

Yes, she must do so. This man had offered her a price for her truth and her soul. He was ready to help her to the revenge she longed for. He was ready to give her his aid in separating the innocent young lovers, whose pure affection had poisoned her life, whose happiness was worse than the worst death to her. She kept silent, therefore, and waited for Paul to speak again.

'I will go up to Town to-morrow, and set to work about this business,' the artist said, as he rose to take leave of Mrs Marchmont. 'I do not believe that I shall have much difficulty in finding the young lady's hiding-place. My first task shall be to look for Mr Arundel. You can perhaps give me the address of some place in London where your cousin is in the habit of staying?'

'I can.'

'Thank you; that will very much simplify matters. I shall write you immediate word of any discovery I make, and will then leave all the rest to you. My influence over Mary Marchmont as an entire stranger could be nothing. Yours, on the contrary, must be unbounded. It will be for you to act upon my letter.'

Olivia Marchmont waited for two days and nights for the promised letter. Upon the third morning it came. The artist's epistle was very brief:

'MY DEAR MRS MARCHMONT,—I have made the necessary

discovery. Miss Marchmont is to be found at the White Hart Inn, Milldale, near Winchester. May I venture to urge your proceeding there in search of her without delay?

'Yours very faithfully,
'PAUL MARCHMONT.

'*Charlotte Street, Fitzroy Square,*
'*Aug.* 15th.'

CHAPTER XX

RISEN FROM THE GRAVE

THE rain dripped ceaselessly upon the dreary earth under a grey November sky,—a dull and lowering sky, that seemed to brood over this lower world with some menace of coming down to blot out and destroy it. The express-train, rushing headlong across the wet flats of Lincolnshire, glared like a meteor in the gray fog; the dismal shriek of the engine was like the cry of a bird of prey. The few passengers who had chosen that dreary winter's day for their travels looked despondently out at the monotonous prospect, seeking in vain to descry some spot of hope in the joyless prospect; or made futile attempts to read their newspapers by the dim light of the lamp in the roof of the carriage. Sulky passengers shuddered savagely as they wrapped themselves in huge woollen rugs or ponderous coverings made from the skins of wild beasts. Melancholy passengers drew grotesque and hideous travelling-caps over their brows, and, coiling themselves in the corner of their seats, essayed to sleep away the weary hours. Everything upon this earth seemed dismal and damp, cold and desolate, incongruous and uncomfortable.

But there was one first-class passenger in that Lincolnshire express who made himself especially obnoxious to his fellows by the display of an amount of restlessness and superabundant energy quite out of keeping with the lazy despondency of those about him.

This was a young man with a long tawny beard and a white face,— a very handsome face, though wan and attenuated, as if with some terrible sickness, and somewhat disfigured by certain strappings of plaister, which were bound about a patch of his skull a little above the left temple. This young man had one side of the carriage to himself; and a sort of bed had been made up for him with extra cushions, upon which he lay at full length, when he was still, which was never for very long together. He was enveloped almost to the chin in voluminous railway-rugs, but, in spite of these coverings, shuddered every now and then, as if with cold. He had a pocket-pistol* amongst his travelling paraphernalia, which he applied occasionally to his dry lips. Sometimes drops of perspiration broke suddenly out upon his forehead, and were brushed away by a tremulous hand, that was scarcely strong enough to hold a cambric handkerchief. In short, it was sufficiently obvious to every one that this young man with the tawny beard had only lately risen from a sick-bed, and had risen therefrom considerably before the time at which any prudent medical practitioner would have given him licence to do so.

It was evident that he was very, very ill, but that he was, if anything, more ill at ease in mind than in body; and that some terrible gnawing anxiety, some restless care, some horrible uncertainty or perpetual foreboding of trouble, would not allow him to be at peace. It was as much as the three fellow-passengers who sat opposite to him could do to bear with his impatience, his restlessness, his short half-stifled moans, his long weary sighs; the horror of his fidgety feet shuffled incessantly upon the cushions; the suddenly convulsive jerks with which he would lift himself upon his elbow to stare fiercely into the dismal fog outside the carriage window; the groans that were wrung from him as he flung himself into new and painful positions; the frightful aspect of physical agony which came over his face as he looked at his watch,—and he drew out and consulted that ill-used chronometer, upon an average, once in a quarter of an hour; his impatient crumpling of the crisp leaves of a new 'Bradshaw,'* which he turned over ever and anon, as if, by perpetual reference to that mysterious time-table, he might hasten the advent of the hour at which he was to reach his destination. He was, altogether, a most aggravating and exasperating travelling companion; and it was only out of Christian forbearance with the weakness of his physical state that his irritated fellow-passengers refrained from uniting themselves against him, and casting him bodily out of the window of the carriage; as a clown sometimes flings a venerable but tiresome pantaloon through a square trap or pitfall, lurking, undreamed of, in the façade of an honest tradesman's dwelling.

The three passengers had, in divers manners, expressed their sympathy with the invalid traveller; but their courtesies had not been responded to with any evidence of gratitude or heartiness. The young man had answered his companions in an absent fashion, scarcely deigning to look at them as he spoke;—speaking altogether with the air of some sleep-walker, who roams hither and thither absorbed in a dreadful dream, making a world for himself; and peopling it with horrible images unknown to those about him.

Had he been ill?—Yes, very ill. He had had a railway accident, and then brain-fever. He had been ill for a long time.

Somebody asked him how long.

He shuffled about upon the cushions, and groaned aloud at this question, to the alarm of the man who had asked it.

'How long?' he cried, in a fierce agony of mental or bodily uneasiness;—' how long? Two months,—three months,—ever since the 15th of August.'

Then another passenger, looking at the young man's very evident sufferings from a commercial point of view, asked him whether he had had any compensation.

'Compensation!' cried the invalid. 'What compensation?'

'Compensation from the Railway Company. I hope you've a strong case against them, for you've evidently been a terrible sufferer.'

It was dreadful to see the way in which the sick man writhed under this question.

'Compensation!' he cried. 'What compensation can they give me for an accident that shut me in a living grave for three months, that separated me from ——? You don't know what you're talking about, sir,' he added suddenly; 'I can't think of this business patiently; I can't be reasonable. If they'd hacked *me* to pieces, I shouldn't have cared. I've been under a red-hot Indian sun, when we fellows couldn't see the sky above us for the smoke of the cannons and the flashing of the sabres about our heads, and I'm not afraid of a little cutting and smashing more or less; but when I think what others may have suffered through —— I'm almost mad, and——!'

He couldn't say any more, for the intensity of his passion had shaken him as a leaf is shaken by a whirlwind; and he fell back upon the cushions, trembling in every limb, and groaning aloud. His fellow passengers looked at each other rather nervously, and two out of the three entertained serious thoughts of changing carriages when the express stopped midway between London and Lincoln.

But they were reassured by-and-by; for the invalid, who was Captain Edward Arundel, or that pale shadow of the dashing young cavalry officer which had risen from a sick-bed, relapsed into silence, and displayed no more alarming symptoms than that perpetual restlessness and disquietude which is cruelly wearying even to the strongest nerves. He only spoke once more, and that was when the short day, in which there had been no actual daylight, was closing in, and the journey nearly finished, when he startled his companions by crying out suddenly,—

'O my God! will this journey never come to an end? Shall I never be put out of this horrible suspense?'

The journey, or at any rate Captain Arundel's share of it, came to an end almost immediately afterwards, for the train stopped at Swampington; and while the invalid was staggering feebly to his feet, eager to scramble out of the carriage, his servant came to the door to assist and support him.

'You seem to have borne the journey wonderful, sir,' the man said respectfully, as he tried to rearrange his master's wrappings, and to do as much as circumstances, and the young man's restless impatience, would allow of being done for his comfort.

'I have suffered the tortures of the infernal regions, Morrison,' Captain Arundel ejaculated, in answer to his attendant's congratulatory address. 'Get me a fly directly; I must go to the Towers at once.'

'Not to-night, sir, surely?' the servant remonstrated, in a tone of alarm. 'Your Mar and the doctors said you *must* rest at Swampington for a night.'

'I'll rest nowhere till I've been to Marchmont Towers,' answered the young soldier passionately. 'If I must walk there,—if I'm to drop down dead on the road,—I'll go. If the cornfields between this and the Towers were a blazing prairie or a raging sea, I'd go. Get me a fly, man; and don't talk to me of my mother or the doctors. I'm going to look for my wife. Get me a fly.'

This demand for a commonplace hackney vehicle sounded rather like an anti-climax, after the young man's talk of blazing prairies and raging seas; but passionate reality has no ridiculous side, and Edward Arundel's most foolish words were sublime by reason of their earnestness.

'Get me a fly, Morrison,' he said, grinding his heel upon the platform in the intensity of his impatience. 'Or, stay; we should gain more in the end if you were to go to the George—it's not ten minutes' walk from here; one of the porters will take you—the people there know me, and they'll let you have some vehicle, with a pair of horses and a clever driver. Tell them it's for an errand of life and death, and that Captain Arundel will pay them three times their usual price, or six times, if they wish. Tell them anything, so long as you get what we want.'

The valet, an old servant of Edward Arundel's father, was carried away by the young man's mad impetuosity. The vitality of this broken-down invalid, whose physical weakness contrasted strangely with his mental energy, bore down upon the grave man-servant like an avalanche, and carried him whither it would. He was fain to abandon all hope of being true to the promises which he had given to Mrs Arundel and the medical men, and to yield himself to the will of the fiery young soldier.

He left Edward Arundel sitting upon a chair in the solitary waiting-room, and hurried after the porter who had volunteered to show him the way to the George Inn, the most prosperous hotel in Swampington.

The valet had good reason to be astonished by his young master's energy and determination; for Mary Marchmont's husband was as one rescued from the very jaws of death. For eleven weeks after that terrible concussion upon the South-Western Railway, Edward Arundel had lain in a state of coma,—helpless, mindless; all the story of his life blotted away, and his brain transformed into as blank a page as if he had been an infant lying on his mother's knees. A fractured skull had been the young Captain's chief share in those injuries which were dealt out pretty freely to the travellers in the Exeter mail on the 15th of August; and the young man had been conveyed to Dangerfield Park, whilst his father's corpse lay in stately solemnity in one of the chief rooms, almost as much a corpse as that dead father.

Mrs Arundel's troubles had come, as the troubles of rich and prosperous people often do come, in a sudden avalanche, that threatened to overwhelm the tender-hearted matron. She had been summoned from Germany to attend her husband's deathbed; and she was called away from her faithful watch beside that deathbed, to hear tidings of the accident that had befallen her younger son.

Neither the Dorsetshire doctor who attended the stricken traveller upon his homeward journey, and brought the strong man, helpless as a child, to claim the same tender devotion that had watched over his infancy, nor the Devonshire doctors who were summoned to Dangerfield, gave any hope of their patient's recovery. The sufferer might linger for years, they said; but his existence would be only a living death, a horrible blank, which it was a cruelty to wish prolonged. But when a great London surgeon appeared upon the scene, a new light, a wonderful gleam of hope, shone in upon the blackness of the mother's despair.

This great London surgeon, who was a very unassuming and matter-of-fact little man, and who seemed in a great hurry to earn his fee and run back to Savile Row by the next express, made a brief examination of the patient, asked a very few sharp and trenchant questions of the reverential provincial medical practitioners, and then declared that the chief cause of Edward Arundel's state lay in the fact that a portion of the skull was depressed,—a splinter pressed upon the brain

The provincial practitioners opened their eyes very wide; and one of them ventured to mutter something to the effect that he had thought as much for a long time. The London surgeon further stated, that until the pressure was removed from the patient's brain, Captain Edward Arundel would remain in precisely the same state as that into which he had fallen immediately upon the accident. The splinter could only be removed by a very critical operation, and this operation must be deferred until the patient's bodily strength was in some measure restored.

The surgeon gave brief but decisive directions to the provincial medical men as to the treatment of their patient during this inter-regnum, and then departed, after promising to return as soon as Captain Arundel was in a fit state for the operation. This period did not arrive till the first week in November, when the Devonshire doctors ventured to declare their patient's shattered frame in a great measure renovated by their devoted attention, and the tender care of the best of mothers.

The great surgeon came. The critical operation was performed, with such eminent success as to merit a very long description, which afterwards appeared in the Lancet;* and slowly, like the gradual lifting of a curtain, the black shadows passed away from Edward Arundel's mind, and the memory of the past returned to him.

It was then that he raved madly about his young wife, perpetually demanding that she might be summoned to him; continually declaring that some great misfortune would befall her if she were not brought to his side, that, even in his feebleness, he might defend and protect her. His mother mistook his vehemence for the raving of delirium. The doctors fell into the same error, and treated him for brain-fever. It was only when the young soldier demonstrated to them that he could, by making an effort over himself be as reasonable as they were, that he convinced them of their mistake. Then he begged to be left alone with his mother; and, with his feverish hands clasped in hers, asked her the meaning of her black dress, and the reason why his young wife had not come to him. He learned that his mother's mourning garments were worn in memory of his dead father. He learned also, after much bewilderment and passionate questioning, that no tidings of Mary Marchmont had ever come to Dangerfield.

It was then that the young man told his mother the story of his marriage: how that marriage had been contracted in haste, but with no real desire for secrecy ; how he had, out of mere idleness, put off writing to his friends until that last fatal night; and how, at the very moment when the pen was in his hand and the paper spread out before him, the different claims of a double duty had torn him asunder, and he had been summoned from the companionship of his bride to the deathbed of his father.

Mrs Arundel tried in vain to set her son's mind at rest upon the subject of his wife's silence.

'No, mother!' he cried; 'it is useless talking to me. You don't know my poor darling. She has the courage of a heroine, as well as the simplicity of a child. There has been some foul play at the bottom of this; it is treachery that has kept my wife from me. She would have come here on foot, had she been free to come. I know whose hand is in this business. Olivia Marchmont has kept my poor girl a prisoner; Olivia Marchmont has set herself between me and my darling!'

'But you don't know this, Edward. I'll write to Mr Paulette ; he will be able to tell us what has happened.'

The young man writhed in a sudden paroxysm of mental agony.

'Write to Mr Paulette!' he exclaimed 'No, mother; there shall be no delay, no waiting for return-posts. That sort of torture would kill me in a few hours. No, mother; I will go to my wife by the first train that will take me on my way to Lincolnshire.'

'You will go! You, Edward in your state!'

There was a terrible outburst of remonstrance and entreaty on the part of the poor mother. Mrs Arundel went down upon her knees before her son, imploring him not to leave Dangerfield till his strength was recovered; imploring him to let her telegraph a summons to Richard Paulette; to let her go herself to Marchmont Towers in search of Mary; to do anything rather than carry out the one mad purpose that he was bent on,—the purpose of going himself to look for his wife.

The mother's tears and prayers were vain; no adamant was ever firmer than the young soldier.

'She is my wife, mother,' he said; 'I have sworn to protect and cherish her; and I have reason to think she has fallen into merciless hands. If I die upon the road, I must go to her. It is not a case in which I can do my duty by proxy. Every moment I delay is a wrong to that poor helpless girl. Be reasonable, dear mother, I implore you; I should suffer fifty times more by the torture of suspense if I stayed here, than I can possibly suffer in a railroad journey from here to Lincolnshire.'

The soldier's strong will triumphed over every opposition. The provincial doctors held up their hands, and protested against the madness of their patient; but without avail. All that either Mrs Arundel or the doctors could do, was to make such preparations and arrangements as would render the weary journey easier; and it was under the mother's superintendence that the aircushions, the brandy-flasks, the hartshorn, sal-volatile,* and railway-rugs, had been provided for the Captain's comfort.

It was thus that, after a blank interval of three months, Edward Arundel, like some creature newly risen from the grave, returned to Swampington, upon his way to Marchmont Towers.

The delay seemed endless to this restless passenger, sitting in the empty waiting-room of the quiet Lincolnshire station, though the ostler and stable-boys at the 'George' were bestirring themselves with good-will, urged on by Mr Morrison's promises of liberal reward for their trouble, and though the man who was to drive the carriage lost no time in arraying himself for the journey. Captain Arundel looked at his watch three times while he sat in that dreary Swampington waiting-room. There was a clock over the mantel-piece, but he would not trust to that.

'Eight o'clock!' he muttered. 'It will be ten before I get to the Towers, if the carriage doesn't come directly.'

He got up, and walked from the waiting-room to the platform, and from the platform to the door of the station. He was so weak as to be obliged to support himself with his stick; and even with that help he tottered and reeled sometimes like a drunken man. But, in his eager impatience, he was almost unconscious of his own weakness.

'Will it never come?' he muttered. 'Will it never come?'

At last, after an intolerable delay, as it seemed to the young man, the carriage-and-pair from the George Inn rattled up to the door of the station with Mr Morrison upon the box, and a postillion loosely balanced upon one of the long-legged, long-backed, bony grey horses. Edward Arundel got into the vehicle before his valet could alight to assist him.

'Marchmont Towers !' he cried to the postillion; 'and a five-pound note if you get there in less than an hour.'

He flung some money to the officials who had gathered about the door to witness his departure, and who had eagerly pressed forward to render him that assistance which, even in his weakness, he disdained.

These men looked gravely at each other as the carriage dashed off into the fog, blundering and reeling as it went along the narrow half-made road, that led from the desert patch of waste ground upon which the station was built into the high-street of Swampington.

'Marchmont Towers!' said one of the men, in a tone that seemed to imply that there was something ominous even in the name of the Lincolnshire mansion. 'What does *he* want at Marchmont Towers, I wonder?'

'Why, don't you know who he is, mate?' responded the other man, contemptuously.

'No.'

'He's Parson Arundel's nevy,—the young officer that some folks said ran away with the poor young miss oop at the Towers.'

'My word! is he now? Why, I shouldn't ha' known him.'

'No; he's a'most like the ghost of what he was, poor young chap. I've heerd as he was in that accident as happened last August on the Sou'-Western.'

The railway official shrugged his shoulders.

'It's all a queer story,' he said. 'I can't make out naught about it; but I know *I* shouldn't care to go up to the Towers after dark.'

Marchmont Towers had evidently fallen into rather evil repute amongst these simple Lincolnshire people.

The carriage in which Edward Arundel rode was a superannuated old chariot, whose uneasy springs rattled and shook the sick man to pieces. He groaned aloud every now and then from sheer physical agony; and yet I almost doubt if he knew that he suffered, so superior in its intensity was the pain of his mind to every bodily torture. Whatever consciousness he had of his racked and aching limbs was as nothing in comparison to the racking anguish of suspense, the intolerable agony of anxiety, which seemed multiplied by every moment. He sat with his face turned towards the open window of the carriage, looking out steadily into the night. There was nothing before him but a blank darkness and thick fog, and a flat country blotted out by the falling rain; but he strained his eyes until the pupils dilated painfully, in his desire to recognise some landmark in the hidden prospect.

'*When* shall I get there?' he cried aloud, in a paroxysm of rage and grief. 'My own one, my pretty one, my wife, when shall I get to you?'

He clenched his thin hands until the nails cut into his flesh. He stamped upon the floor of the carriage. He cursed the rusty, creaking springs, the slow-footed horses, the pools of water through which the wretched animals floundered pastern-deep. He cursed the dark-ness of the night, the stupidity of the postillion, the length of the way,—everything, and anything, that kept him back from the end which he wanted to reach.

At last the end came. The carriage drew up before the tall iron gates, behind which stretched, dreary and desolate as some patch of common-land, that melancholy waste which was called a park.

A light burned dimly in the lower window of the lodge,—a little spot that twinkled faintly red and luminous through the darkness and the rain; but the iron gates were as closely shut as if Marchmont Towers had been a prison-house. Edward Arundel was in no humour to linger long for the opening of those gates. He sprang from the carriage, reckless of the weakness of his cramped limbs, before the valet could descend from the rickety box-seat, or the postillion could get off his horse, and shook the wet and rusty iron bars with his own wasted hands. The gates rattled, but resisted the concussion; they had evidently been locked for the night. The young man seized an iron ring, dangling at the end of a chain, which hung beside one of the stone pillars, and rang a peal that resounded like an alarm-signal through the darkness. A fierce watchdog far away in the distance howled dismally at the summons, and the dissonant shriek of a pea-cock sounded across the flat.

The door of the lodge was opened about five minutes after the bell had rung, and an old man peered out into the night, holding a candle shaded by his feeble hand, and looking suspiciously towards the gate.

'Who is it?' he said.

'It is I, Captain Arundel. Open the gate, please.'

The man, who was very old, and whose intellect seemed to have grown as dim and foggy as the night itself, reflected for a few moments, and then mumbled,—

'Cap'en Arundel! Ay, to be sure, to be sure. Parson Arundel's nevy; ay, ay.'

He went back into the lodge, to the disgust and aggravation of the young soldier, who rattled fiercely at the gate once more in his impatience. But the old man emerged presently, as tranquil as if the blank November night had been some sun-shiny noontide in July, carrying a lantern and a bunch of keys, one of which he proceeded in a leisurely manner to apply to the great lock of the gate.

'Let me in!' cried Edward Arundel. 'Man alive! do you think I came down here to stand all night staring through these iron bars? Is Marchont Towers a prison, that you shut your gates as if they were never to be opened until the Day of Judgment?'

The old man responded with a feeble, chirpy laugh, an audible grin, senile and conciliatory.

'We've no need to keep t' geates open arter dark,' he said; 'folk doan't coome to the Toowers arter dark.'

He had succeeded by this time in turning the key in the lock; one of the gates rolled slowly back upon its rusty hinges, creaking and groaning as if in hoarse protest against all visitors to the Towers; and Edward Arundel entered the dreary domain which John Marchmont had inherited from his kinsman.

The postillion turned his horses from the highroad without the gates into the broad drive leading up to the mansion. Far away, across the wet flats, the broad western front of that gaunt stone dwelling-place frowned upon the travellers, its black grimness only relieved by two or three dim red patches, that told of lighted windows and human habitation. It was rather difficult to associate friendly flesh and blood with Marchmont Towers on this dark November night.

The nervous traveller would have rather expected to find diabolical denizens lurking within those black and stony walls; hideous enchantments beneath that rain bespattered roof; weird and incarnate horrors brooding by deserted hearths, and fearful shrieks of souls in perpetual pain breaking upon the stillness of the night.

Edward Arundel had no thought of these things. He knew that the place was darksome and gloomy, and that, in very spite of himself, he had always been unpleasantly impressed by it; but he knew nothing more. He only wanted to reach the house without delay, and to ask for the young wife whom he had parted with upon a balmy August evening three months before. He wanted this passionately, almost madly; and every moment made his impatience wilder, his anxiety more intense. It seemed as if all the journey from Dangerfield Park to Lincolnshire was as nothing compared to the space that still lay between him and Marchmont Towers.

'We've done it in doublequick time, sir,' the postillion said, complacently pointing to the steaming sides of his horses. 'Master 'll gie it to me for driving the beasts like this.'

Edward Arundel looked at the panting animals. They had brought him quickly, then, though the way had seemed so long.

'You shall have a five-pound note, my lad,' he said, 'if you get me up to yonder house in five minutes.'

He had his hand upon the door of the carriage, and as leaning against it for support, while he tried to recover enough strength with which to clamber into the vehicle, when his eye was caught by some white object flapping in the rain against the stone pillar of the gate, and made dimly visible in a flickering patch of light from the lodge-keeper's lantern.

'What's that?' he cried, pointing to this white spot upon the moss-grown stone.

The old man slowly raised his eyes to the spot towards which the soldier's finger pointed.

'That?' he mumbled. 'Ay, to be sure, to be sure. Poor young lady! That's the printed bill as they stook oop. It's the printed bill, to be sure, to be sure. I'd a'most forgot it. It ain't been much good, anyhow; and I'd a'most forgot it.'

'The printed bill! the young lady!' gasped Edward Arundel, in a hoarse, choking voice.

He snatched the lantern from the lodge-keeper's hand with a force that sent the old man reeling and tottering several paces backward; and, rushing to the stone pillar, held the light up above his head, on a level with the white placard which had attracted his notice. It was damp and dilapidated at the edges; but that which was printed upon it was as visible to the soldier as though each commonplace character had been a fiery sign inscribed upon a blazing scroll.

This was the announcement which Edward Arundel read upon the gate-post of Marchmont Towers:—

'ONE HUNDRED POUNDS REWARD.—Whereas Miss Mary Marchmont left her home on Wednesday last, October 17th, and has not since been heard of, this is to give notice that the above reward will be given to any one who shall afford such information as will lead to her recovery if she be alive, or to the discovery of her body if she be dead. The missing young lady is eighteen years of age, rather below the middle height, of fair complexion, light-brown hair, and hazel eyes. When she left her home, she had on a grey silk dress, grey shawl, and straw bonnet. She was last seen near the river-side upon the afternoon of Wednesday, the 17th instant.

'*Marchmont Towers, October 20th,* 1848.'

CHAPTER XXI

FACE TO FACE

IT is not easy to imagine a lion-hearted you cavalry officer, whose soldiership in the Punjab had won the praises of a Napier and an Outram,* fainting away like a heroine of romance at the coming of evil tidings; but Edward Arundel, who had risen from a sick-bed to take a long and fatiguing journey in utter defiance of the doctors, was not strong enough to bear the dreadful welcome that greeted him upon the gate-post at Marchmont Towers.

He staggered, and would have fallen, had not the extended arms of his father's confidential servant been luckily opened to receive and support him. But he did not lose his senses.

'Get me into the carriage, Morrison,' he cried. 'Get me up to that house. They've tortured and tormented my wife while I've been lying like a log on my bed at Dangerfield. For God's sake, get me up there as quick as you can!'

Mr Morrison had read the placard on the gate across his young master's shoulder. He lifted the Captain into the carriage, shouted to the postillion to drive on, and took his seat by the young man's side.

'Begging you pardon, Mr Edward,' he said, gently; 'but the young lady may be found by this time. That bill's been sticking there for upwards of a month, you see, sir, and it isn't likely but what Miss Marchmont has been found between that time and this.'

The invalid passed his hand across his forehead, down which the cold sweat rolled in great beads.

'Give me some brandy,' he whispered; 'pour some brandy down my throat, Morrison, if you've any compassion upon me; I must get strength somehow for the struggle that lies before me.'

The valet took a wicker-covered flask from his pocket, and put the neck of it to Edward Arundel's lips.

'She may be found, Morrison,' muttered the young man, after drinking a long draught of the fiery spirit; he would willingly have drunk living fire itself, in his desire to obtain unnatural strength in this crisis. 'Yes; you're right there. She may be found. But to think that she should have been driven away! To think that my poor, help-less, tender girl should have been driven a second time from the home that is her own! Yes; her own by every law and every right. Oh, the relentless devil, the pitiless devil!—what can be the motive of her conduct? Is it madness, or the infernal cruelty of a fiend incarnate?'

Mr Morrison thought that his young master's brain had been disordered by the shock he had just undergone, and that this wild talk was mere delirium.

'Keep your heart up, Mr Edward,' he murmured, soothingly; 'you may rely upon it, the young lady has been found.'

But Edward was in no mind to listen to any mild consolatory remarks from his valet. He had thrust his head out of the carriage-window and his eyes were fixed upon the dimly-lighted casements of the western drawing-room.

'The room in which John and Polly and I used to sit together when first I came from India,' he murmured. 'How happy we were!—how happy we were!'

The carriage stopped before the stone portico, and the young man got out once more, assisted by his servant. His breath came short and quick now that he stood upon the threshold. He pushed aside the servant who opened the familiar door at the summons of the clanging bell, and strode into the hall. A fire burned on the wide hearth; but the atmosphere of the great stone-paved chamber was damp and chilly.

Captain Arundel walked straight to the door of the western drawing-room. It was there that he had seen lights in the windows; it was there that he expected to find Olivia Marchmont.

He was not mistaken. A shaded lamp burnt dimly on a table near the fire. There was a low invalid-chair beside this table, an open book upon the floor, and an Indian shawl, one he had sent to his cousin, flung carelessly upon the pillows. The neglected fire burned low in the old-fashioned grate, and above the dull-red blaze stood the figure of a woman, tall, dark, and gloomy of aspect.

It was Olivia Marchmont, in the mourning-robes that she had worn, with but one brief intermission, ever since her husband's death. Her profile was turned towards the door by which Edward Arundel entered the room; her eyes were bent steadily upon the low heap of burning ashes in the grate. Even in that doubtful light the young man could see that her features were sharpened, and that a settled frown had contracted her straight black brows.

In her fixed attitude, in her air of deathlike tranquillity, this woman resembled some sinful vestal sister,* set, against her will, to watch a sacred fire, and brooding moodily over her crimes.

She did not hear the opening of the door; she had not even heard the trampling of the horses' hoofs, or the crashing of the wheels upon the gravel before the house. There were times when her sense of external things was, as it were, suspended and absorbed in the intensity of her obstinate despair.

'Olivia!' said the soldier.

Mrs Marchmont looked up at the sound of that accusing voice, for there was something in Edward Arundel's simple enunciation of her name which seemed like an accusation or a menace. She looked up, with a great terror in her face, and stared aghast at her unexpected visitor. Her white cheeks, her trembling lips, and dilated eyes could not have more palpably expressed a great and absorbing horror, had the young man standing quietly before her been a corpse newly risen from its grave.

'Olivia Marchmont,' said Captain Arundel, after a brief pause, 'I have come here to look for my wife.'

The woman pushed her trembling hands across her forehead, brushing the dead black hair from her temples, and still staring with the same unutterable horror at the face of her cousin. Several times she tried to speak; but the broken syllables died away in her throat in hoarse, inarticulate mutterings. At last, with a great effort, the words came.

'I—I—never expected to see you,' she said; 'I heard that you were very ill; I heard that you——'

'You heard that I was dying,' interrupted Edward Arundel; 'or that, if I lived, I should drag out the rest of my existence in hopeless idiocy. The doctors thought as much a week ago, when one of them, cleverer than the rest I suppose, had the courage to perform an operation that restored me to consciousness. Sense and memory came back to me by degrees. The thick veil that had shrouded the past was rent asunder; and the first image that came to me was the image of my young wife, as I had seen her upon the night of our parting. For more than three months I had been dead. I was suddenly restored to life. I asked those about me to give me tidings of my wife. Had she sought me out?—had she followed me to Dangerfield? No! They could tell me nothing. They thought that I was delirious, and tried to soothe me with compassionate speeches, merciful falsehoods, promising me that I should see my darling. But I soon read the secret of their scared looks. I saw pity and wonder mingled in my mother's face, and I entreated her to be merciful to me, and to tell me the truth. She had compassion upon me, and told me all she knew, which was very little. She had never heard from my wife. She had never heard of any marriage between Mary Marchmont and me. The only communication which she had received from any of her Lincolnshire relations had been a letter from my uncle Hubert, in reply to one of hers telling him of my hopeless state.

'This was the shock that fell upon me when life and memory came back. I could not bear the imprisonment of a sick-bed. I felt that for the second time I must go out into the world to look for my darling; and in defiance of the doctors, in defiance of my poor mother, who thought that my departure from Dangerfield was a suicide, I am here. It is here that I come first to seek for my wife. I might have stopped in London to see Richard Paulette; I might sooner have gained tidings of my darling. But I came here; I came here without stopping by the way, because an uncontrollable instinct and an unreasoning impulse tells me that it is here I ought to seek her. I am here, her husband, her only true and legitimate defender; and woe be to those who stand between me and my wife!'

He had spoken rapidly in his passion; and he stopped, exhausted by his own vehemence, and sank heavily into a chair near the lamplit table.

Then for the first time that night Olivia Marchmont plainly saw her cousin's face, and saw the terrible change that had transformed the handsome young soldier, since the bright August morning on which he had gone forth from Marchmont Towers. She saw the traces of a long and wearisome illness sadly visible in his waxen-hued complexion, his hollow cheeks, the faded lustre of his eyes, his dry and pallid lips. She saw all this, the woman whose one great sin had been to love this man wickedly and madly, in spite of her better self, in spite of her womanly pride; she saw the change in him that had altered him from a young Apollo to a shattered and broken invalid. And did any revulsion of feeling arise in her breast? Did any corresponding transformation in her own heart bear witness to the baseness of her love?

No; a thousand times, no! There was no thrill of disgust, how transient soever; not so much as one passing shudder of painful surprise, one pang of womanly regret. No! In place of these, a passionate yearning arose in this woman's haughty soul; a flood of sudden tenderness rushed across the black darkness of her mind. She fain would have flung herself upon her knees, in loving self-abasement, at the sick man's feet. She fain would have cried aloud, amid a tempest of passionate sobs,—

'O my love, my love! you are dearer to me a hundred times by this cruel change. It was *not* your bright-blue eyes and waving chestnut hair,—it was not your handsome face, your brave, soldier-like bearing that I loved. My love was not so base as that. I inflicted a cruel outrage upon myself when I thought that I was the weak fool of a handsome face. Whatever *I* have been, my love, at least, has been pure. My love is pure, though I am base. I will never slander that again, for I know now that it is immortal.'

In the sudden rush of that flood-tide of love and tenderness, all these thoughts welled into Olivia Marchmont's mind. In all her sin and desperation she had never been so true a woman as now; she had never, perhaps, been so near being a good woman. But the tender emotion was swept out of her breast the next moment by the first words of Edward Arundel.

'Why do you not answer my question?' he said.

She drew herself up in the erect and rigid attitude that had become almost habitual to her. Every trace of womanly feeling faded out of her face, as the sunlight disappears behind the sudden darkness of a thundercloud.

'What question?' she asked, with icy indifference.

'The question I have come to Lincolnshire to ask—the question I have perilled my life, perhaps, to ask,' cried the young man. 'Where is my wife?'

The widow turned upon him with a horrible smile.

'I never heard that you were married,' she said. 'Who is your wife?'

'Mary Marchmont, the mistress of this house.'

Olivia opened her eyes, and looked at him in half-sardonic surprise.

'Then it was not a fable ?' she said.

'What was not a fable?'

'The unhappy girl spoke the truth when she said that you had married her at some out-of-the-way church in Lambeth.'

'The truth! Yes!' cried Edward Arundel. 'Who should dare to say that she spoke other than the truth? Who should dare to disbelieve her?'

Olivia Marchmont smiled again,—that same strange smile which was almost too horrible for humanity, and yet had a certain dark and gloomy grandeur of its own. Satan, the star of the morning,* may have so smiled despairing defiance upon the Archangel Michael.

'Unfortunately,' she said, 'no one believed the poor child. Her story was such a very absurd one, and she could bring forward no shred of evidence in support of it.'

'O my God!' ejaculated Edward Arundel, clasping his hands above his head in a paroxysm of rage and despair; 'I see it all—I see it all! My darling has been tortured to death. Woman!' he cried, 'are you possessed by a thousand fiends? Is there no one sentiment of womanly compassion left in your breast? If there is one spark of womanhood in your nature, I appeal to that; I ask you what has happened to my wife?'

'My wife! my wife!' The reiteration of that familiar phrase was to Olivia Marchmont like the perpetual thrust of a dagger aimed at an open wound. It struck every time upon the same tortured spot, and inflicted the same agony.

'The placard upon the gates of this place can tell you as much as I can,' she said.

The ghastly whiteness of the soldier's face told her that he had seen the placard of which she spoke.

'She has not been found, then?' he said, hoarsely.

'No.'

'How did she disappear?'

'As she disappeared upon the morning on which you followed her. She wandered out of the house, this time leaving no letter, nor message, nor explanation of any kind whatever. It was in the middle of the day that she went out; and for some time her absence caused no alarm. But, after some hours, she was waited for and watched for very anxiously. Then a search was made.'

'Where?'

'Wherever she had at any time been in the habit of walking,—in the park; in the wood; along the narrow path by the water; at Pollard's farm; at Hester's house at Kemberling,—in every place where it might be reasonably imagined there was the slightest chance of finding her.'

'And all this was without result?'

'It was.'

'*Why* did she leave this place? God help you, Olivia Marchmont, if it was your cruelty that drove her away!'

The widow took no notice of the threat implied in these words. Was there anything upon earth that she feared now? No—nothing. Had she not endured the worst long ago, in Edward Arundel's contempt? She had no fear of a battle with this man; or with any other creature in the world; or with the whole world arrayed and banded together against her, if need were. Amongst all the torments of those black depths to which her soul had gone down, there was no such thing as fear. That cowardly baseness is for the happy and prosperous, who have something to lose. This woman was by nature dauntless and resolute as the hero of some classic story; but in her despair she had the desperate and reckless courage of a starving wolf. The hand of death was upon her; what could it matter how she died?

'I am very grateful to you, Edward Arundel,' she said, bitterly, 'for the good opinion you have always had of me. The blood of the Dangerfield Arundels must have had some drop of poison intermingled with it, I should think, before it could produce so vile a creature as myself; and yet I have heard people say that my mother was a good woman.'

The young man writhed impatiently beneath the torture of his cousin's deliberate speech. Was there to be no end to this unendurable delay? Even now,—now that he was in this house, face to face with the woman he had come to question—it seemed as if he *could* not get tidings of his wife.

So, often in his dreams, he had headed a besieging-party against the Afghans, with the scaling-ladders reared against the wall; he had seen the dark faces grinning down upon him—all savage glaring eyes and fierce glistening teeth—and heard the voices of his men urging him on to the encounter, but had felt himself paralysed and helpless, with his sabre weak as a withered reed in his nerveless hand.

'For God's sake, let there be no quarrelling with phrases between you and me, Olivia!' he cried. 'If you or any other living being have injured my wife, the reckoning between us shall be no light one. But there will be time enough to talk of that by-and-by. I stand before you, newly risen from a grave in which I have lain for more than three months, as dead to the world, and to every creature I have ever loved or hated, as if the Funeral Service had been read over my coffin. I come to demand from you an account of what has happened during that interval. If you palter or prevaricate with me, I shall know that it is because you fear to tell me the truth.'

'Fear!'

'Yes; you have good reason to fear, if you have wronged Mary Arundel. Why did she leave this house?'

'Because she was not happy in it, I suppose. She chose to shut herself up in her own room, and to refuse to be governed, or advised, or consoled. I tried to do my duty to her; yes,' cried Olivia March-mont, suddenly raising her voice, as if she had been vehemently contradicted;—'yes, I did try to do my duty to her. I urged her to listen to reason; I begged her to abandon her foolish falsehood about a marriage with you in London.'

'You disbelieved in that marriage?'

'I did,' answered Olivia.

'You lie!' cried Edward Arundel. 'You knew the poor child had spoken the truth. You knew her—you knew me—well enough to know that I should not have detained her away from her home an hour, except to make her my wife—except to give myself the strong-est right to love and defend her.'

'I knew nothing of the kind, Captain Arundel; you and Mary Marchmont had taken good care to keep your secrets from me. I knew nothing of your plots, your intentions. *I* should have con-sidered that one of the Dangerfield Arundels would have thought his honour sullied by such an act as a stolen marriage with an heiress, considerably under age, and nominally in the guardianship of her stepmother. I did, therefore, disbelieve the story Mary Marchmont told me. Another person, much more experienced than I, also dis-believed the unhappy girl's account of her absence.'

'Another person! What other person?'

'Mr Marchmont.'

'Mr Marchmont!'

'Yes; Paul Marchmont,—my husband's first-cousin.'

A sudden cry of rage and grief broke from Edward Arundel's lips.

'O my God!' he exclaimed, 'there was some foundation for the warning in John Marchmont's letter, after all. And I laughed at him; I laughed at my poor friend's fears.'

The widow looked at her kinsman in mute wonder.

'Has Paul Marchmont been in this house?' he asked.

'Yes.'

'When was he here?'

'He has been here often; he comes here constantly. He has been living at Kemberling for the last three months.'

'Why?'

'For his own pleasure, I suppose,' Olivia answered haughtily. 'It is no business of mine to pry into Mr Marchmont's motives.'

Edward Arundel ground his teeth in an access of ungovernable passion. It was not against Olivia, but against himself this time that he was enraged. He hated himself for the arrogant folly, the obstinate presumption, with which he had ridiculed and slighted John Marchmont's vague fears of his kinsman Paul.

'So this man has been here,—is here constantly,' he muttered. 'Of course, it is only natural that he should hang about the place. And you and he are staunch allies; I suppose?' he added, turning upon Olivia.

'Staunch allies! Why?'

'Because you both hate my wife.'

'What do you mean?'

'You both hate her. You, out of a base envy of her wealth; because of her superior rights, which made you a secondary person in this house, perhaps,—there is nothing else for which you *could* hate her. Paul Marchmont, because she stands between him and a fortune. Heaven help her! Heaven help my poor, gentle, guileless darling! Surely Heaven must have had some pity upon her when her husband was not by!'

The young man dashed the blinding tears from his eyes. They were the first that he had shed since he had risen from that which many people had thought his dying-bed, to search for his wife.

But this was no time for tears or lamentations. Stern determination took the place of tender pity and sorrowful love. It was a time for resolution and promptitude.

'Olivia Marchmont,' he said, 'there has been some foul play in this business. My wife has been missing a month; yet when I asked my mother what had happened at this house during my illness, she could tell me nothing. Why did you not write to tell her of Mary's flight?'

'Because Mrs Arundel has never done me the honour to cultivate any intimacy between us. My father writes to his sister-in-law sometimes; I scarcely ever write to my aunt. On the other hand, your mother had never seen Mary Marchmont, and could not be expected to take any great interest in her proceedings. There was, therefore, no reason for my writing a special letter to announce the trouble that had befallen me.'

'You might have written to my mother about my marriage. You might have applied to her for confirmation of the story which you disbelieved.'

Olivia Marchmont smiled.

'Should I have received that confirmation?' she said. 'No. I saw your mother's letters to my father. There was no mention in those letters of any marriage; no mention whatever of Mary Marchmont. This in itself was enough to confirm my disbelief. Was it reasonable to imagine that you would have married, and yet have left your mother in total ignorance of the fact?'

'O God, help me!' cried Edward Arundel, wringing his hands. 'It seems as if my own folly, my own vile procrastination, have brought this trouble upon my wife. Olivia Marchmont, have pity upon me. If you hate this girl, your malice must surely have been satisfied by this time. She has suffered enough. Pity me, and help me; if you have any human feeling in your breast. She left this house because her life here had grown unendurable; because she saw herself doubted, disbelieved, widowed in the first month of her marriage, utterly desolate and friendless. Another woman might have borne up against all this misery. Another woman would have known how to assert herself, and to defend herself even in the midst of her sorrow and desolation. But my poor darling is a child; a baby in ignorance of the world. How should *she* protect herself against her enemies? Her only instinct was to run away from her persecutors,—to hide herself from those whose pretended doubts flung the horror of dishonour upon her. I can understand all now; I can understand. Olivia Marchmont, this man Paul has a strong reason for being a villain. The motives that have induced you to do wrong must be very small in comparison to his. He plays an infamous game, I believe; but he plays for a high stake.'

A high stake! Had not *she* perilled her soul upon the casting of this die? Had *she* not flung down her eternal happiness in that fatal game of hazard?

'Help me, then, Olivia,' said Edward, imploringly; 'help me to find my wife; and atone for all that you have ever done amiss in the past. It is not too late.'

His voice softened as he spoke. He turned to her, with his hands clasped, waiting anxiously for her answer. Perhaps this appeal was the last cry of her good angel, pleading against the devils for her redemption. But the devils had too long held possession of this woman's breast. They arose, arrogant and unpitying, and hardened her heart against that pleading voice.

'How much he loves her!' thought Olivia Marchmont; 'how dearly he loves her! For her sake he humiliates himself to me.'

Then, with no show of relenting in her voice or manner, she said deliberately:

'I can only tell you again what I told you before. The placard you saw at the park-gates can tell you as much as I can. Mary March- mont ran away. She was sought for in every direction, but without success. Mr Marchmont, who is a man of the world, and better able to suggest what is right in such a case as this, advised that Mr Paulette should be sent for. He was accordingly communicated with. He came, and instituted a fresh search. He also caused a bill to be printed and distributed through the country. Advertisements were inserted in the "Times" and other papers. For some reason—I forget what reason—Mary Marchmont's name did not appear in these advertisements. They were so worded as to render the publication of the name unnecessary.'

Edward Arundel pushed his hand across his forehead.

'Richard Paulette has been here?' he murmured, in a low voice.

He had every confidence in the lawyer; and a deadly chill came over him at the thought that the cool, hard-headed solicitor had failed to find the missing girl.

'Yes; he was here two or three days.'

'And he could do nothing?'

'Nothing, except what I have told you.'

The young man thrust his hand into his breast to still the cruel beating of his heart. A sudden terror had taken possession of him,— a horrible dread that he should never look upon his young wife's face again. For some minutes there was a dead silence in the room, only broken once or twice by the falling of some ashes on the hearth. Captain Arundel sat with his face hidden behind his hand. Olivia still stood as she had stood when her cousin entered the room, erect and gloomy, by the old-fashioned chimney-piece.

'There was something in that placard,' the soldier said at last, in a hoarse, altered voice,—'there was something about my wife having been seen last by the water-side. Who saw her there?'

'Mr Weston, a surgeon of Kemberling,—Paul Marchmont's brother-in-law.'

'Was she seen by no one else?'

'Yes; she was seen at about the same time—a little sooner or later, we don't know which—by one of Farmer Pollard's men.'

'And she has never been seen since?'

'Never; that is to say, we can hear of no one who has seen her.'

'At what time in the day was she seen by this Mr Weston?'

'At dusk; between five and six o'clock.'

Edward Arundel put his hand suddenly to his throat, as if to check some choking sensation that prevented his speaking.

'Olivia,' he said, 'my wife was last seen by the river-side. Does any one think that, by any unhappy accident, by any terrible fatality, she lost her way after dark, and fell into the water? or that—O God, that would be too horrible!—does any one suspect that she drowned herself?'

'Many things have been said since her disappearance,' Olivia Marchmont answered. 'Some people say one thing, some another.'

'And it has been said that she—that she was drowned?'

'Yes; many people have said so. The river was dragged while Mr Paulette was here, and after he went away. The men were at work with the drags for more than a week.'

'And they found nothing?'

'Nothing.'

'Was there any other reason for supposing that—that my wife fell into the river?'

'Only one reason.'

'What was that?'

'I will show you,' Olivia Marchmont answered.

She took a bunch of keys from her pocket and went to an old-fashioned bureau or cabinet upon the other side of the room. She unlocked the upper part of this bureau, opened one of the drawers, and took from it something which she brought to Edward Arundel.

This something was a little shoe; a little shoe of soft bronzed leather, stained and discoloured with damp and moss, and trodden down upon one side, as if the wearer had walked a weary way in it, and had been unaccustomed to so much walking.

Edward Arundel remembered, in that brief childishly-happy honeymoon at the little village near Winchester, how often he had laughed at his young wife's propensity for walking about damp meadows in such delicate little slippers as were better adapted to the requirements of a ball-room. He remembered the slender foot, so small that he could take it in his hand; the feeble little foot that had grown tired in long wanderings by the Hampshire trout-streams, but which had toiled on in heroic self-abnegation so long as it was the will of the sultan to pedestrianise.

'Was this found by the river-side?' he asked, looking piteously at the slipper which Mrs Marchmont had put into his hand.

'Yes; it was found amongst the rushes on the shore, a mile below the spot at which Mr Weston saw my stepdaughter.'

Edward Arundel put the little shoe into his bosom.

'I'll not believe it,' he cried suddenly; 'I'll not believe that my darling is lost to me. She was too good, far too good, to think of suicide; and Providence would never suffer my poor lonely child to be led away to a dreary death upon that dismal river-shore. No, no; she fled away from this place because she was too wretched here. She went away to hide herself amongst those whom she could trust, until her husband came to claim her. I will believe anything in the world except that she is lost to me. And I will not believe that, I will never believe that, until I look down at her corpse; until I lay my hand on her cold breast, and feel that her true heart has ceased beating. As I went out of this place four months ago to look for her, I will go again now. My darling, my darling, my innocent pet, my childish bride; I will go to the very end of the world in search of you.'

The widow ground her teeth as she listened to her kinsman's passionate words. Why did he for ever goad her to blacker wickedness by this parade of his love for Mary? Why did he force her to remember every moment how much cause she had to hate this pale-faced girl?

Captain Arundel rose, and walked a few paces, leaning on his stick as he went.

'You will sleep here to-night, of course?' Olivia Marchmont said.

'Sleep here!'

His tone expressed plainly enough that the place was abhorrent to him.

'Yes; where else should you stay?'

'I meant to have stopped at the nearest inn.'

'The nearest inn is at Kemberling.'

'That would suit me well enough,' the young man answered indifferently; 'I must be in Kemberling early to-morrow, for I must see Paul Marchmont. I am no nearer the comprehension of my wife's flight by anything that you have told me. It is to Paul Marchmont that I must look next. Heaven help him if he tries to keep the truth from me.'

'You will see Mr Marchmont here as easily as at Kemberling,' Olivia answered; 'he comes here every day.'

'What for?'

'He has built a sort of painting-room down by the river-side, and he paints there whenever there is light.'

'Indeed!' cried Edward Arundel; 'he makes himself at home at Marchmont Towers, then?'

'He has a right to do so, I suppose,' answered the widow indifferently. 'If Mary Marchmont is dead, this place and all belonging to it is his. As it is, I am only here on sufferance.'

'He has taken possession, then?'

'On the contrary, he shrinks from doing so.'

'And, by the Heaven above us, he does wisely,' cried Edward Arundel. 'No man shall seize upon that which belongs to my darling. No foul plot of this artist-traitor shall rob her of her own. God knows how little value *I* set upon her wealth; but I will stand between her and those who try to rob her, until my last gasp. No, Olivia; I'll not stay here; I'll accept no hospitality from Mr Marchmont. I suspect him too much.'

He walked to the door; but before he reached it the widow went to one of the windows, and pushed aside the blind.

'Look at the rain,' she said; 'hark at it; don't you hear it, drip, drip, drip upon the stone? I wouldn't turn a dog out of doors upon such a night as this; and you—you are so ill—so weak. Edward Arundel, do you hate me so much that you refuse to share the same shelter with me, even for a night?'

There is nothing so difficult of belief to a man, who is not a coxcomb, as the simple fact that he is beloved by a woman whom he does not love, and has never wooed by word or deed. But for this, surely Edward Arundel must, in that sudden burst of tenderness, that one piteous appeal have discovered a clue to his cousin's secret.

He discovered nothing; he guessed nothing. But he was touched by her tone, even in spite of his utter ignorance of its meaning, and he replied, in an altered manner,

'Certainly, Olivia, if you really wish it, I will stay. Heaven knows I have no desire that you and I should be ill friends. I want your help; your pity, perhaps. I am quite willing to believe that any cruel things you said to Mary arose from an outbreak of temper. I cannot think that you could be base at heart. I will even attribute your disbelief of the statement made by my poor girl as to our marriage to the narrow prejudices learnt in a small country town. Let us be friends, Olivia.'

He held out his hand. His cousin laid her cold fingers in his open palm, and he shuddered as if he had come in contact with a corpse. There was nothing very cordial in the salutation. The two hands seemed to drop asunder, lifeless and inert; as if to bear mute witness that between these two people there was no possibility of sympathy or union.

But Captain Arundel accepted his cousin's hospitality. Indeed he had need to do so; for he found, that his valet had relied upon his master's stopping at the Towers, and had sent the carriage back to Swampington. A tray with cold meat and wine was brought into the drawing-room for the young soldier's refreshment. He drank a glass of Madeira, and made some pretence of eating a few mouthfuls, out of courtesy to Olivia; but he did this almost mechanically. He sat silent and gloomy, brooding over the terrible shock that he had so newly received; brooding over the hidden things that had happened in that dreary interval, during which he had been as powerless to defend his wife from trouble as a dead man.

Again and again the cruel thought returned to him, each time with a fresh agony,—that if he had written to his mother, if he had told her the story of his marriage, the things which had happened could never have come to pass. Mary would have been sheltered and protected by a good and loving woman. This thought, this horrible self-reproach, was the bitterest thing the young man had to bear.

'It is too great a punishment,' he thought; 'I am too cruelly punished for having forgotten everything in my happiness with my darling.'

The widow sat in her low easy-chair near the fire, with her eyes fixed upon the burning coals; the grate had been replenished, and the light of the red blaze shone full upon Olivia Marchmont's haggard face. Edward Arundel, aroused for a few moments out of his gloomy abstraction, was surprised at the change which an interval of a few months had made in his cousin. The gloomy shadow which he had often seen on her face had become a fixed expression; every line had deepened, as if by the wear and tear of ten years, rather than by the progress of a few months. Olivia Marchmont had grown old before her time. Nor was this the only change. There was a look, undefined and undefinable, in the large luminous grey eyes, unnaturally luminous now, which filled Edward Arundel with a vague sense of terror; a terror which he would not—which he dared not—attempt to analyse. He remembered Mary's unreasoning fear of her stepmother, and he now scarcely wondered at that fear. There was something almost weird and unearthly in the aspect of the woman sitting opposite to him by the broad hearth: no vestige of colour in her gloomy face, a strange light burning in her eyes, and her black draperies falling round her in straight, lustreless folds.

'I fear you have been ill, Olivia,' the young man said, presently.

Another sentiment had arisen in his breast side by side with that vague terror,—a fancy that perhaps there was some reason why his cousin should be pitied.

'Yes,' she answered indifferently; as if no subject of which Captain Arundel could have spoken would have been of less concern to her,— 'yes, I have been very ill.'

'I am sorry to hear it.'

Olivia looked up at him and smiled. Her smile was the strangest he had ever seen upon a woman's face.

'I am very sorry to hear it. What has been the matter with you?'

'Slow fever, Mr Weston said.'

'Mr Weston?'

'Yes; Mr Marchmont's brother-in-law. He has succeeded to Mr

Dawnfield's practice at Kemberling. He attended me, and he attended my stepdaughter.'

'My wife was ill, then?'

'Yes; she had brain-fever: she recovered from that, but she did not recover strength. Her low spirits alarmed me, and I considered it only right—Mr Marchmont suggested also—that a medical man should be consulted.'

'And what did this man, this Mr Weston, say?'

'Very little; there was nothing the matter with Mary, he said. He gave her a little medicine, but only in the desire of strengthening her nervous system. He could give her no medicine that would have any very good effect upon her spirits, while she chose to keep herself obstinately apart from every one.'

The young man's head sank upon his breast. The image of his desolate young wife arose before him; the image of a pale, sorrowful girl, holding herself apart from her persecutors, abandoned, lonely, despairing. Why had she remained at Marchmont Towers? Why had she ever consented to go there, when she had again and again expressed such terror of her stepmother? Why had she not rather followed her husband down to Devonshire, and thrown herself upon his relatives for protection? Was it like this girl to remain quietly here in Lincolnshire, when the man she loved with such innocent devotion was lying between life and death in the west?

'She is such a child,' he thought,—'such a child in her ignorance of the world. I must not reason about her as I would about another woman.'

And then a sudden flush of passionate emotion rose to his face, as a new thought flashed into his mind. What if this helpless girl had been detained by force at Marchmont Towers?

'Olivia,' he cried, 'whatever baseness this man, Paul Marchmont, may be capable of, you at least must be superior to any deliberate sin. I have all my life believed in you, and respected you, as a good woman. Tell me the truth, then, for pity's sake. Nothing that you can tell me will fill up the dead blank that the horrible interval since my accident has made in my life. But you can give me some help. A few words from you may clear away much of this darkness. How did you find my wife? How did you induce her to come back to this place? I know that she had an unreasonable dread of returning here.'

'I found her through the agency of Mr Marchmont,' Olivia

answered, quietly. 'I had some difficulty in inducing her to return here ; but after hearing of your accident—'

'How was the news of that broken to her?'

'Unfortunately she saw a paper that had happened to be left in her way.'

'By whom?'

'By Mr Marchmont.'

'Where was this?'

'In Hampshire.'

'Indeed! Then Paul Marchmont went with you to Hampshire?'

'He did. He was of great service to me in this crisis. After seeing the paper, my stepdaughter was seized with brain-fever. She was unconscious when we brought her back to the Towers. She was nursed by my old servant Barbara, and had the highest medical care. I do not think that anything more could have been done for her.'

'No,' answered Edward Arundel, bitterly; 'unless you could have loved her.'

'We cannot force our affections,' the widow said, in a hard voice.

Another voice in her breast seemed to whisper; 'Why do you reproach me for not having loved this girl? If you had loved *me*, the whole world could have been different.'

'Olivia Marchmont,' said Captain Arundel, 'by your own avowal there has never been any affection for this orphan girl in your heart. It is not my business to dwell upon the fact, as something almost unnatural under the peculiar circumstances through which that helpless child was cast upon your protection. It is needless to try to understand why you have hardened your heart against my poor wife. Enough that it is so. But I may still believe that, whatever your feelings may be towards your dead husband's daughter, you would not be guilty of any deliberate act of treachery against her. I can afford to believe this of you; but I cannot believe it of Paul Marchmont. That man is my wife's natural enemy. If he has been here during my illness, he has been here to plot against her. When he came here, he came to attempt her destruction. She stands between him and this estate. Long ago, when I was a careless schoolboy, my poor friend, John Marchmont, told me that, if ever the day came upon which Mary's interests should be opposed to the interests of her cousin, that man would be a dire and bitter enemy; so much the more terrible because in all appearance her friend. The day came; and I, to whom the orphan girl had been left as a sacred legacy was not by to defend her. But I have risen from a bed that many have thought a bed of death; and I come to this place with one indomitable resolution paramount in my breast,—the determination to find my wife, and to bring condign punishment upon the man who has done her wrong.'

Captain Arundel spoke in a low voice; but his passion was all the more terrible because of the suppression of those common outward evidences by which anger ordinarily betrays itself. He relapsed into thoughtful silence.

Olivia made no answer to anything that he had said. She sat looking at him steadily, with an admiring awe in her face. How splendid he was—this young hero—even in his sickness and feebleness! How splendid, by reason of the grand courage, the chivalrous devotion, that shone out of his blue eyes!

The clock struck eleven while the cousins sat opposite to each other,—only divided, physically, by the width of the tapestried hearth-rug; but, oh, how many weary miles asunder in spirit!—and Edward Arundel rose, startled from his sorrowful reverie.

'If I were a strong man,' he said, 'I would see Paul Marchmont to-night. But I must wait till to-morrow morning. At what time does he come to his painting-room?'

'At eight o'clock, when the mornings are bright; but later when the weather is dull.'

'At eight o'clock! I pray Heaven the sun may shine early to-morrow! I pray Heaven I may not have to wait long before I find myself face to face with that man! Good-night, Olivia.'

He took a candle from a table near the door, and lit it almost mechanically. He found Mr Morrison waiting for him, very sleepy and despondent, in a large bedchamber in which Captain Arundel had never slept before,—a dreary apartment, decked out with the faded splendours of the past; a chamber in which the restless sleeper might expect to see a phantom lady in a ghostly sacque,* cowering over the embers, and spreading her transparent hands above the red light.

'It isn't particular comfortable, after Dangerfield,' the valet muttered in a melancholy voice; 'and all I 'ope, Mr Edward, is, that the sheets are not damp. I've been a stirrin' of the fire and puttin' on fresh coals for the last hour. There's a bed for me in the dressin' room, within call.'

Captain Arundel scarcely heard what his servant said to him. He was standing at the door of the spacious chamber, looking out into a long low-roofed corridor, in which he had just encountered Barbara, Mrs Marchmont's confidential attendant—the wooden-faced, in-scrutable-looking woman, who, according to Olivia, had watched and ministered to his wife.

'Was that the tenderest face that looked down upon my darling as she lay on her sick-bed?' he thought. 'I had almost as soon have had a ghoul to watch by my poor dear's pillow.'

CHAPTER XXII

THE PAINTING-ROOM BY THE RIVER

EDWARD ARUNDEL lay awake through the best part of that November night, listening to the ceaseless dripping of the rain upon the terrace, and thinking of Paul Marchmont. It was of this man that he must demand an account of his wife. Nothing that Olivia had told him had in any way lessened this determination. The little slipper found by the water's edge; the placard flapping on the moss-grown pillar at the entrance to the park; the story of a possible suicide, or a more probable accident;—all these things were as nothing beside the young man's suspicion of Paul Marchmont. He had pooh-poohed John's dread of his kinsman as weak and unreasonable; and now, with the same unreason, he was ready to condemn this man, whom he had never seen, as a traitor and a plotter against his young wife.

He lay tossing from side to side all that night, weak and feverish, with great drops of cold perspiration rolling down his pale face, sometimes falling into a fitful sleep, in whose distorted dreams Paul Marchmont was for ever present, now one man, now another. There was no sense of fitness in these dreams; for sometimes Edward Arundel and the artist were wrestling together with newly-sharpened daggers in their eager hands, each thirsting for the other's blood; and in the next moment they were friends, and had been friendly—as it seemed—for years.

The young man woke from one of these last dreams, with words of good-fellowship upon his lips, to find the morning light gleaming through the narrow openings in the damask window-curtains, and Mr Morrison laying out his master's dressing apparatus upon the carved oak toilette-table.

Captain Arundel dressed himself as fast as he could, with the assistance of the valet, and then made his way down the broad staircase, with the help of his cane, upon which he had need to lean pretty heavily, for he was as weak as a child.

'You had better give me the brandy-flask, Morrison,' he said. 'I am going out before breakfast. You may as well come with me, by-the-by; for I doubt if I could walk as far as I want to go, without the help of your arm.'

In the hall Captain Arundel found one of the servants. The western door was open, and the man was standing on the threshold looking out at the morning. The rain had ceased; but the day did not yet promise to be very bright, for the sun gleamed like a ball of burnished copper through a pale November mist.

'Do you know if Mr Paul Marchmont has gone down to the boat-house?' Edward asked.

'Yes, sir,' the man answered; 'I met him just now in the quadrangle. He'd been having a cup of coffee with my mistress.'

Edward started. They were friends, then, Paul Marchmont and Olivia!—friends, but surely not allies! Whatever villainy this man might be capable of committing, Olivia must at least be guiltless of any deliberate treachery?

Captain Arundel took his servant's arm and walked out into the quadrangle, and from the quadrangle to the low-lying woody swamp, where the stunted trees looked grim and weird-like in their leafless ugliness. Weak as the young man was, he walked rapidly across the sloppy ground, which had been almost flooded by the continual rains. He was borne up by his fierce desire to be face to face with Paul Marchmont. The savage energy of his mind was stronger than any physical debility. He dismissed Mr Morrison as soon as he was within sight of the boat-house, and went on alone, leaning on his stick, and pausing now and then to draw breath, angry with himself for his weakness.

The boat-house, and the pavilion above it, had been patched up by some country workmen. A handful of plaster here and there, a little new brickwork, and a mended window-frame bore witness of this. The ponderous old-fashioned wooden shutters had been repaired, and a good deal of the work which had been begun in John Marchmont's lifetime had now, in a certain rough manner, been completed. The place, which had hitherto appeared likely to fall into utter decay, had been rendered weather-tight and habitable; the black smoke creeping slowly upward from the ivy-covered chimney, gave evidence of occupation. Beyond this, a large wooden shed, with a wide window fronting the north, had been erected close against the boat-house. This rough shed Edward Arundel at once understood to be the painting-room which the artist had built for himself.

He paused a moment outside the door of this shed. A man's

voice—a tenor voice, rather thin and metallic in quality was singing a scrap of Rossini upon the other side of the frail woodwork.

Edward Arundel knocked with the handle of his stick upon the door. The voice left off singing, to say 'Come in.'

The soldier opened the door, crossed the threshold, and stood face to face with Paul Marchmont in the bare wooden shed. The painter had dressed himself for his work. His coat and waistcoat lay upon a chair near the door. He had put on a canvas jacket, and had drawn a loose pair of linen trousers over those which belonged to his usual costume. So far as this paint-besmeared coat and trousers went, nothing could have been more slovenly than Paul Marchmont's appearance; but some tincture of foppery exhibited itself in the black velvet smoking-cap, which contrasted with and set off the silvery whiteness of his hair, as well as in the delicate curve of his amber moustache. A moustache was not a very common adornment in the year 1848. It was rather an eccentricity affected by artists, and permitted as the wild caprice of irresponsible beings, not amenable to the laws that govern rational and respectable people.

Edward Arundel sharply scrutinised the face and figure of the artist. He cast a rapid glance round the bare whitewashed walls of the shed, trying to read even in those bare walls some chance clue to the painter's character. But there was not much to be gleaned from the details of that almost empty chamber. A dismal, black-looking iron stove, with a crooked chimney, stood in one corner. A great easel occupied the centre of the room. A sheet of tin, nailed upon a wooden shutter, swung backwards and forwards against the northern window, blown to and fro by the damp wind that crept in through the crevices in the framework of the roughly-fashioned casement. A heap of canvases were piled against the walls, and here and there a half-finished picture—a lurid Turneresque* landscape; a black stormy sky; or a rocky mountain-pass, dyed blood-red by the setting sun—was propped up against the whitewashed background. Scattered scraps of water-colour, crayon, old engravings, sketches torn and tumbled, bits of rockwork and foliage, lay littered about the floor; and on a paint-stained deal-table of the roughest and plainest fashion were gathered the colour-tubes and palettes, the brushes and sponges and dirty cloths, the greasy and sticky tin-cans, which form the paraphernalia of an artist. Opposite the northern window was the moss-grown stone-staircase leading up to the pavilion over the boat-house. Mr Marchmont had built his painting-room against the side of the pavilion, in such a manner as to shut in the staircase and doorway which formed the only entrance to it. His excuse for the awkwardness of this piece of architecture was the impossibility of otherwise getting the all-desirable northern light for the illumination of his rough studio.

This was the chamber in which Edward Arundel found the man from whom he came to demand an account of his wife's disappearance. The artist was evidently quite prepared to receive his visitor. He made no pretence of being taken off his guard, as a meaner pretender might have done. One of Paul Marchmont's theories was, that as it is only a fool who would use brass where he could as easily employ gold, so it is only a fool who tells a lie when he can conveniently tell the truth.

'Captain Arundel, I believe?' he said, pushing a chair forward for his visitor. 'I am sorry to say I recognise you by your appearance of ill health. Mrs Marchmont told me you wanted to see me. Does my meerschaum* annoy you? I'll put it out if it does. No? Then, if you'll allow me, I'll go on smoking. Some people say tobacco-smoke gives a tone to one's pictures. If so, mine ought to be Rembrandts in depth of colour.'

Edward Arundel dropped into the chair that had been offered to him. If he could by any possibility have rejected even this amount of hospitality from Paul Marchmont, he would have done so; but he was a great deal too weak to stand, and he knew that his interview with the artist must be a long one.

'Mr Marchmont,' he said, 'if my cousin Olivia told you that you might expect to see me here to-day, she most likely told you a great deal more. Did she tell you that I looked to you to account to me for the disappearance of my wife?'

Paul Marchmont shrugged his shoulders, as who should say, 'This young man is an invalid. I must not suffer myself to be aggravated by his absurdity.' Then taking his meerschaum from his lips, he set it down, and seated himself at a few paces from Edward Arundel on the lowest of the moss-grown steps leading up to the pavilion.

'My dear Captain Arundel,' he said, very gravely, 'your cousin did repeat to me a great deal of last night's conversation. She told me that you had spoken of me with a degree of violence, natural enough perhaps to a hot-tempered young soldier, but in no manner justified by our relations. When you call upon me to account for the disappearance of Mary Marchmont, you act about as rationally as if you declared me answerable for the pulmonary complaint that carried away her father. If, on the other hand, you call upon me to assist you in the endeavour to fathom the mystery of her disappearance, you will find me ready and willing to aid you to the very uttermost. It is to my interest as much as to yours that this mystery should be cleared up.'

'And in the meantime you take possession of this estate?'

'No, Captain Arundel. The law would allow me to do so; but I decline to touch one farthing of the revenue which this estate yields, or to commit one act of ownership, until the mystery of Mary Marchmont's disappearance, or of her death, is cleared up.'

'The mystery of her death?' said Edward Arundel; 'you believe, then, that she is dead?'

'I anticipate nothing; I think nothing,' answered the artist; 'I only wait. The mysteries of life are so many and so incomprehensible,— the stories, which are every day to be read by any man who takes the trouble to look through a newspaper, are so strange, and savour so much of the improbabilities of a novel-writer's first wild fiction,— that I am ready to believe everything and anything. Mary Marchmont struck me, from the first moment in which I saw her, as sadly deficient in mental power. Nothing she could do would astonish me. She may be hiding herself away from us, prompted only by some eccentric fancy of her own. She may have fallen into the power of designing people. She may have purposely placed her slipper by the water-side, in order to give the idea of an accident or a suicide; or she may have dropped it there by chance, and walked barefoot to the nearest railway-station. She acted unreasonably before when she ran away from Marchmont Towers; she may have acted unreasonably again.'

'You do not think, then, that she is dead?'

'I hesitate to form any opinion; I positively decline to express one.'

Edward Arundel gnawed savagely at the ends of his moustache. This man's cool imperturbability, which had none of the studied smoothness of hypocrisy, but which seemed rather the plain candour of a thorough man of the world, who had no wish to pretend to any sentiment he did not feel, baffled and infuriated the passionate young soldier. Was it possible that this man, who met him with such cool self-assertion, who in no manner avoided any discussion of Mary Marchmont's disappearance,—was it possible that he could have had any treacherous and guilty part in that calamity? Olivia's manner looked like guilt; but Paul Marchmont's seemed the personification of innocence. Not angry innocence, indignant that its purity should have been suspected; but the matter-of-fact, commonplace innocence of a man of the world, who is a great deal too clever to play any hazardous and villainous game.

'You can perhaps answer me this question, Mr Marchmont,' said Edward Arundel. 'Why was my wife doubted when she told the story of her marriage?'

The artist smiled, and rising from his seat upon the stone step, took a pocket-book from one of the pockets of the coat that he had been wearing.

'I *can* answer that question,' he said, selecting a paper from amongst others in the pocket-book. 'This will answer it.'

He handed Edward Arundel the paper, which was a letter folded lengthways, and indorsed, 'From Mrs Arundel, August 31st.' Within this letter was another paper, indorsed, 'Copy of letter to Mrs Arundel, August 28th.'

'You had better read the copy first,' Mr Marchmont said, as Edward looked doubtfully at the inner paper.

The copy was very brief, and ran thus:

'Marchmont Towers, August 28, 1848.

'MADAM,—I have been given to understand that your son, Captain Arundel, within a fortnight of his sad accident, contracted a secret marriage with a young lady, whose name I, for several reasons, prefer to withhold. If you can oblige me by informing me whether there is any foundation for this statement, you will confer a very great favour upon

'Your obedient servant,
'PAUL MARCHMONT.'

The answer to this letter, in the hand of Edward Arundel's mother, was equally brief:

'Dangerfield Park, August 31, 1848

'SIR,—In reply to your inquiry, I beg to state that there can be no foundation whatever for the report to which you allude. My son is too honourable to contract a secret marriage; and although his present unhappy state renders it impossible for me to receive the assurance from his own lips, my confidence in his high principles justifies me in contradicting any such report as that which forms the subject of your letter.

> 'I am, sir,
>
> 'Yours obediently,
>
> 'LETITIA ARUNDEL.'

The soldier stood, mute and confounded, with his mother's letter in is hand. It seemed as if every creature had been against the helpless girl whom he had made his wife. Every hand had been lifted to drive her from the house that was her own; to drive her out upon the world, of which she was ignorant, a wanderer and an outcast; perhaps to drive her to a cruel death.

'You can scarcely wonder if the receipt of that letter confirmed me in my previous belief that Mary Marchmont's story of a marriage arose out of the weakness of a brain, never too strong, and at that time very much enfeebled by the effect of a fever.'

Edward Arundel was silent. He crushed his mother's letter in his hand. Even his mother—even his mother—that tender and compassionate woman, whose protection he had so freely promised, ten years before, in the lobby of Drury Lane, to John Marchmont's motherless child,—even she, by some hideous fatality, had helped to bring grief and shame upon the lonely girl. All this story of his young wife's disappearance seemed enveloped in a wretched obscurity, through whose thick darkness he could not penetrate. He felt himself encompassed by a web of mystery, athwart which it was impossible to cut his way to the truth. He asked question after question, and received answers which seemed freely given; but the story remained as dark as ever. What did it all mean? What was the clue to the mystery? Was this man, Paul Marchmont,—busy amongst his unfinished pictures, and bearing in his every action, in his every word, the stamp of an easy-going, free-spoken soldier of fortune,— likely to have been guilty of any dark and subtle villainy against the missing girl? He had disbelieved in the marriage; but he had had some reason for his doubt of a fact that could not very well be welcome to him.

The young man rose from his chair, and stood irresolute, brooding over these things.

'Come, Captain Arundel,' cried Paul Marchmont, heartily, 'believe me, though I have not much superfluous sentimentality left in my composition after a pretty long encounter with the world, still I can truly sympathise with your regret for this poor silly child. I hope, for your sake, that she still lives, and is foolishly hiding herself from us all. Perhaps, now you are able to act in the business, there may be a better chance of finding her. I am old enough to be your father, and am ready to give you the help of any knowledge of the world which I may have gathered in the experience of a lifetime. Will you accept my help?'

Edward Arundel paused for a moment, with his head still bent, and his eyes fixed upon the ground. Then suddenly lifting his head, he looked full in the artist's face as he answered him.

'No!' he cried. 'Your offer may be made in all good faith, and if so, I thank you for it; but no one loves this missing girl as I love her; no one has so good a right as I have to protect and shelter her. I will look for my wife, alone, unaided; except by such help as I pray that God may give me.'

CHAPTER XXIII

IN THE DARK

EDWARD ARUNDEL walked slowly back to the Towers, shaken in body, perplexed in mind, baffled, disappointed, and most miserable; the young husband, whose married life had been shut within the compass of a brief honeymoon, went back to that dark and gloomy mansion within whose encircling walls Mary had pined and despaired.

'Why did she stop here?' he thought; 'why didn't she come to me? I thought her first impulse would have brought her to me. I thought my poor childish love would have set out on foot to seek her husband, if need were.'

He groped his way feebly and wearily amidst the leafless wood, and through the rotting vegetation decaying in oozy slime beneath the black shelter of the naked trees. He groped his way towards the dismal eastern front of the great stone dwelling-house, his face always turned towards the blank windows, that stared down at him from the discoloured walls.

'Oh, if they could speak!' he exclaimed, almost beside himself in his perplexity and desperation; 'if they could speak! If those cruel walls could find a voice, and tell me what my darling suffered within their shadow! If they could tell me why she despaired, and ran away to hide herself from her husband and protector! *If* they could speak!'

He ground his teeth in a passion of sorrowful rage.

'I should gain as much by questioning yonder stone wall as by talking to my cousin, Olivia Marchmont,' he thought, presently. 'Why is that woman so venomous a creature in her hatred of my innocent wife? Why is it that, whether I threaten, or whether I appeal, I can gain nothing from her—nothing? She baffles me as completely by her measured answers, which seem to reply to my questions, and which yet tell me nothing, as if she were a brazen image set up by the dark ignorance of a heathen people, and dumb in the absence of an impostor-priest. She baffles me, question her how I will. And Paul Marchmont, again,—what have I learned from him? Am I a fool, that people can prevaricate and lie to me like this? Has my brain no sense, and my arm no strength, that I cannot wring the truth from the false throats of these wretches?'

The young man gnashed his teeth again in the violence of his rage.

Yes, it was like a dream; it was like nothing but a dream. In dreams he had often felt this terrible sense of impotence wrestling with a mad desire to achieve something or other. But never before in his waking hours had the young soldier experienced such a sensation.

He stopped, irresolute, almost bewildered, looking back at the boat-house, a black spot far away down by the sedgy brink of the slow river, and then again turning his face towards the monotonous lines of windows in the eastern frontage of Marchmont Towers.

'I let that man play with me to-day,' he thought; 'but our reckoning is to come. We have not done with each other yet.'

He walked on towards the low archway leading into the quadrangle.

The room which had been John Marchmont's study, and which his widow had been wont to occupy since his death, looked into this quadrangle. Edward Arundel saw his cousin's dark head bending over a book, or a desk perhaps, behind the window.

'Let her beware of me, if she has done any wrong to my wife!' he thought. 'To which of these people am I to look for an account of my poor lost girl? To which of these two am I to look! Heaven guide me to find the guilty one; and Heaven have mercy upon that wretched creature when the hour of reckoning comes; for I will have none.'

Olivia Marchmont, looking through the window, saw her kinsman's face while this thought was in his mind. The expression which she saw there was so terrible, so merciless, so sublime in its grand and vengeful beauty, that her own face blanched even to a paler hue than that which had lately become habitual to it.

'Am I afraid of him?' she thought, as she pressed her forehead against the cold glass, and by a physical effort restrained the convulsive trembling that had suddenly shaken her frame. 'Am I afraid of him? No; what injury can he inflict upon me worse than that which he has done me from the very first? If he could drag me to a scaffold, and deliver me with his own hands into the grasp of the hangman, he would do me no deeper wrong than he has done me from the hour of my earliest remembrance of him. He could inflict no new pangs, no sharper tortures, than I have been accustomed to suffer at his hands. He does not love me. He has never loved me. He never will love me. *That* is my wrong; and it is for that I take my revenge!'

She lifted her head, which had rested in a sullen attitude against the glass, and looked at the soldier's figure slowly advancing towards the western side of the house.

Then, with a smile,—the same horrible smile which Edward Arundel had seen light up her face on the previous night,—she muttered between her set teeth:—

'Shall I be sorry because this vengeance has fallen across my pathway? Shall I repent, and try to undo what I have done? Shall I thrust myself between others and Mr Edward Arundel? Shall *I* make myself the ally and champion of this gallant soldier, who seldom speaks to me except to insult and upbraid me? Shall *I* take justice into my hands, and interfere for my kinsman's benefit? No; he has chosen to threaten me; he has chosen to believe vile things of me. From the first his indifference has been next kin to insolence. Let him take care of himself.'

Edward Arundel took no heed of the grey eyes that watched him with such a vengeful light in their fixed gaze. He was still thinking of his missing wife, still feeling, to a degree that was intolerably painful, that miserable dream-like sense of helplessness and prostration.

'What am I to do?' he thought. 'Shall I be for ever going backwards and forwards between my Cousin Olivia and Paul Marchmont; for ever questioning them, first one and then the other, and never getting any nearer to the truth?'

He asked himself this question, because the extreme anguish, the intense anxiety, which he had endured, seemed to have magnified the smallest events, and to have multiplied a hundred-fold the lapse of time. It seemed as if he had already spent half a lifetime in his search after John Marchmont's lost daughter.

'O my friend, my friend!' he thought, as some faint link of association, some memory thrust upon him by the aspect of the place in which he was, brought back the simple-minded tutor who had taught him mathematics eighteen years before,—'my poor friend, if this girl had not been my love and my wife, surely the memory of your trust in me would be enough to make me a desperate and merciless avenger of her wrongs.'

He went into the hall, and from the hall to the tenantless western drawing-room,—a dreary chamber, with its grim and faded splendour, its stiff, old-fashioned furniture; a chamber which, unadorned by the presence of youth and innocence, had the aspect of belonging to a day that was gone, and people that were dead. So might have looked one of those sealed-up chambers in the buried cities of Italy,* when the doors were opened, and eager living eyes first looked in upon the habitations of the dead.

Edward Arundel walked up and down the empty drawing-room. There were the ivory chessmen that he had brought from India, under a glass shade on an inlaid table in a window. How often he and Mary had played together in that very window; and how she had always lost her pawns, and left bishops and knights undefended, while trying to execute impossible manoeuvres with her queen! The young man paced slowly backwards and forward across the old-fashioned bordered carpet, trying to think what he should do. He must form some plan of action in his own mind, he thought. There was foul work somewhere, he most implicitly believed; and it was for him to discover the motive of the treachery, and the person of the traitor.

Paul Marchmont! Paul Marchmont!

His mind always travelled back to this point. Paul Marchmont was Mary's natural enemy. Paul Marchmont was therefore surely the man to be suspected, the man to be found out and defeated.

And yet, if there was any truth in appearances, it was Olivia who was most inimical to the missing girl; it was Olivia whom Mary had feared; it was Olivia who had driven John Marchmont's orphan-child from her home once, and who might, by the same power to tyrannise and torture a weak and yielding nature, have so banished her again.

Or these two, Paul and Olivia, might both hate the defenceless girl, and might have between them plotted a wrong against her.

'Who will tell me the truth about my lost darling?' cried Edward Arundel. 'Who will help me to look for my missing love?'

His lost darling; his missing love. It was thus that the young man spoke of his wife. That dark thought which had been suggested to him by the words of Olivia, by the mute evidence of the little bronze slipper picked up near the river-brink, had never taken root, or held even a temporary place in his breast. He would not—nay, more, he could not—think that his wife was dead. In all his confused and miserable dreams that dreary November night, no dream had ever shown him *that*. No image of death had mingled itself with the distorted shadows that had tormented his sleep. No still white face had looked up at him through a veil of murky waters. No moaning sob of a rushing stream had mixed its dismal sound with the many voices of his slumbers. No; he feared all manner of unknown sorrows; he looked vaguely forward to a sea of difficulty, to be waded across in blindness and bewilderment before he could clasp his rescued wife in his arms; but he never thought that she was dead.

Presently the idea came to him that it was outside Marchmont Towers,—away, beyond the walls of this grim, enchanted castle, where evil spirits seemed to hold possession,—that he should seek for the clue to his wife's hiding-place.

'There is Hester, that girl who was fond of Mary,' he thought; 'she may be able to tell me something, perhaps. I will go to her.'

He went out into the hall to look for his servant, the faithful Morrison, who had been eating a very substantial breakfast with the domestics of the Towers—'the sauce to meat' being a prolonged discussion of the facts connected with Mary Marchmont's disappearance and her relations with Edward Arundel—and who came, radiant and greasy from the enjoyment of hot buttered cakes and Lincolnshire bacon, at the sound of his master's voice.

'I want you to get me some vehicle, and a lad who will drive me a few miles, Morrison,' the young soldier said; 'or you can drive me yourself, perhaps?'

'Certainly, Master Edward; I have driven your pa often, when we was travellin' together. I'll go and see if there's a phee-aton or a shay that will suit you, sir; something that goes easy on its springs.'

'Get anything,' muttered Captain Arundel, 'so long as you can get it without loss of time.'

All fuss and anxiety upon the subject of his health worried the young man. He felt his head dizzied with weakness and excitement; his arm—that muscular right arm, which had done him good service two years before in an encounter with a tigress—was weaker than the jewel-bound wrist of a woman. But he chafed against anything like consideration of his weakness; he rebelled against anything that seemed likely to hinder him in that one object upon which all the powers of his mind were bent.

Mr Morrison went away with some show of briskness, but dropped into a very leisurely pace as soon as he was fairly out of his master's sight. He went straight to the stables, where he had a pleasant gossip with the grooms and hangers-on, and amused himself further by inspecting every bit of horseflesh in the Marchmont stables, prior to selecting a quiet grey cob which he felt himself capable of driving, and an old-fashioned gig with a yellow body and black and yellow wheels, bearing a strong resemblance to a monstrous wooden wasp.

While the faithful attendant to whom Mrs Arundel had delegated the care of her son was thus employed, the soldier stood in the stone hall, looking out at the dreary wintry landscape, and pining to hurry away across the dismal swamps to the village in which he hoped to hear tidings of her he sought. He was lounging in a deep oaken window-seat, looking hopelessly at that barren prospect, that monotonous expanse of flat morass and leaden sky, when he heard a footstep behind him; and turning round saw Olivia's confidential servant, Barbara Simmons, the woman who had watched by his wife's sick-bed,—the woman whom he had compared to a ghoul.

She was walking slowly across the hall towards Olivia's room, whither a bell had just summoned her. Mrs Marchmont had lately grown fretful and capricious, and did not care to be waited upon by any one except this woman, who had known her from her childhood, and was no stranger to her darkest moods.

Edward Arundel had determined to appeal to every living creature who was likely to know anything of his wife's disappearance, and he snatched the first opportunity of questioning this woman.

'Stop, Mrs Simmons,' he said, moving away from the window; 'I want to speak to you; I want to talk to you about my wife.'

The woman turned to him with a blank face, whose expressionless stare might mean either genuine surprise or an obstinate determination not to understand anything that might be said to her.

'Your wife, Captain Arundel!' she said, in cold measured tones, but with an accent of astonishment.

'Yes; my wife. Mary Marchmont, my lawfully-wedded wife. Look here, woman,' cried Edward Arundel; 'if you cannot accept the word of a soldier, and an honourable man, you can perhaps believe the evidence of your eyes.'

He took a morocco memorandum-book from his breast-pocket. It was full of letters, cards, banknotes, and miscellaneous scraps of paper carelessly stuffed into it, and amongst them Captain Arundel found the certificate of his marriage, which he had put away at random upon his wedding morning, and which had lain unheeded in his pocket-book ever since.

'Look here,' he cried, spreading the document before the waiting-woman's eyes, and pointing with a shaking hand, to the lines. 'You believe that, I suppose?'

'O yes, sir,' Barbara Simmons answered, after deliberately reading the certificate. 'I have no reason to disbelieve it; no wish to disbelieve it.'

'No ; I suppose not,' muttered Edward Arundel, 'unless you too are leagued with Paul Marchmont.'

The woman did not flinch at this hinted accusation, but answered the young man in that slow and emotionless manner which no change of circumstance seemed to have power to alter.

'I am leagued with no one, sir,' she said, coldly. 'I serve no one except my mistress, Miss Olivia—I mean Mrs Marchmont.'

The study-bell rang for the second time while she was speaking.

'I must go to my mistress now, sir,' she said. 'You heard her ringing for me.'

'Go, then, and let me see you as you come back. I tell you I must and will speak to you. Everybody in this house tries to avoid me. It seems as if I was not to get a straight answer from any one of you. But I *will* know all that is to be known about my lost wife. Do you hear, woman? I will know!'

'I will come back to you directly, sir,' Barbara Simmons answered quietly.

The leaden calmness of this woman's manner irritated Edward Arundel beyond all power of expression. Before his cousin Olivia's gloomy coldness he had been flung back upon himself as before an iceberg; but every now and then some sudden glow of fiery emotion had shot up amid that frigid mass, lurid and blazing, and the iceberg had been transformed into an angry and passionate woman, who might, in that moment of fierce emotion, betray the dark secrets of her soul. But *this* woman's manner presented a passive barrier, athwart which the young soldier was as powerless to penetrate as he would have been to walk through a block of solid stone.

Olivia was like some black and stony castle, whose barred windows bade defiance to the besieger, but behind whose narrow casements transient flashes of light gleamed fitfully upon the watchers without, hinting at the mysteries that were hidden within the citadel.

Barbara Simmons resembled a blank stone wall, grimly confronting the eager traveller, and giving no indication whatever of the unknown country on the other side.

She came back almost immediately, after being only a few moments in Olivia's room,—certainly not long enough to consult with her mistress as to what she was to say or to leave unsaid,—and presented herself before Captain Arundel.

'If you have any questions to ask, sir, about Miss Marchmont—about your wife—I shall be happy to answer them,' she said.

'I have a hundred questions to ask,' exclaimed the young man; 'but first answer me this one plainly and truthfully—Where do you think my wife has gone? What do you think has become of her?'

The woman was silent for a few moments, and then answered very gravely,—

'I would rather not say what I think, sir.'

'Why not?'

'Because I might say that which would make you unhappy.'

'Can anything be more miserable to me than the prevarication which I meet with on every side?' cried Edward Arundel. 'If you or any one else will be straightforward with me—remembering that I come to this place like a man who has risen from the grave, depending wholly on the word of others for the knowledge of that which is more vital to me than anything upon this earth—that person will be the best friend I have found since I rose from my sick-bed to come hither. You can have had no motive—if you are not in Paul Marchmont's pay—for being cruel to my poor girl. Tell me the truth, then; speak, and speak fearlessly.'

'I have no reason to fear, sir,' answered Barbara Simmons, lifting her faded eyes to the young man's eager face, with a gaze that seemed to say, 'I have done no wrong, and I do not shrink from justifying myself.' 'I have no reason to fear, sir; I was piously brought up, and have done my best always to do my duty in the state of life in which Providence has been pleased to place me. I have not had a particularly happy life, sir; for thirty years ago I lost all that made me happy, in them that loved me, and had a claim to love me. I have attached myself to my mistress; but it isn't for me to expect a lady like her would stoop to make me more to her or nearer to her than I have a right to be as a servant.'

There was no accent of hypocrisy or cant in any one of these deliberately-spoken words. It seemed as if in this speech the woman had told the history of her life; a brief, unvarnished history of a barren life, out of which all love and sunlight had been early swept away, leaving behind a desolate blank, that was not destined to be filled up by any affection from the young mistress so long and patiently served.

'I am faithful to my mistress, sir,' Barbara Simmons added, presently; 'and I try my best to do my duty to her. I owe no duty to any one else.'

'You owe a duty to humanity,' answered Edward Arundel. 'Woman, do you think duty is a thing to be measured by line and rule? Christ came to save the lost sheep of the children of Israel; but was He less pitiful to the Canaanitish woman* when she carried her sorrows to His feet? You and your mistress have made hard precepts for yourselves, and have tried to live by them. You try to circumscribe the area of your Christian charity, and to do good within given limits. The traveller who fell among thieves* would have died of his wounds, for any help he might have had from you, if he had lain beyond your radius. Have you yet to learn that Christianity is cosmopolitan, illimitable, inexhaustible, subject to no laws of time or space? The duty you owe to your mistress is a duty that she buys and pays for—a matter of sordid barter, to be settled when you take your wages; the duty you owe to every miserable creature in your pathway is a sacred debt, to be accounted for to God.'

As the young soldier spoke thus, carried away by his passionate agitation, suddenly eloquent by reason of the intensity of his feeling, a change came over Barbara's face. There was no very palpable evidence of emotion in that stolid countenance; but across the wooden blankness of the woman's face flitted a transient shadow, which was like the shadow of fear.

'I tried to do my duty to Miss Marchmont as well as to my mistress,' she said. 'I waited on her faithfully while she was ill. I sat up with her six nights running; I didn't take my clothes off for a week. There are folks in the house who can tell you as much.'

'God knows I am grateful to you, and will reward you for any pity you may have shown my poor darling,' the young man answered, in a more subdued tone; 'only, if you pity me, and wish to help me, speak out, and speak plainly. What do you think has become of my lost girl?'

'I cannot tell you, sir. As God looks down upon me and judges me, I declare to you that I know no more than you know. But I think——'

'You think what?'

'That you will never see Miss Marchmont again.'

Edward Arundel started as violently as if, of all sentences, this was the last he had expected to hear pronounced. His sanguine temperament, fresh in its vigorous and untainted youth, could not grasp the thought of despair. He could be mad with passionate anger against the obstacles that separated him from his wife; but he could not believe those obstacles to be insurmountable. He could not doubt the power of his own devotion and courage to bring him back his lost love.

'Never—see her—again!'

He repeated these words as if they had belonged to a strange language, and he were trying to make out their meaning.

'You think,' he gasped hoarsely, after a long pause,—'you think—that—she is—dead?'

'I think that she went out of this house in a desperate state of mind. She was seen—not by me, for I should have thought it my duty to stop her if I had seen her so—she was seen by one of the servants crying and sobbing awfully as she went away upon that last afternoon.'

'And she was never seen again?'

'Never by me.'

'And—you—you think she went out of this house with the intention of—of—destroying herself?'

The words died away in a hoarse whisper, and it was by the motion of his white lips that Barbara Simmons perceived what the young man meant.

'I do, sir.'

'Have you any—particular reason for thinking so?'

'No reason beyond what I have told you, sir.'

Edward Arundel bent his head, and walked away to hide his blanched face. He tried instinctively to conceal this mental suffering, as he had sometimes hidden physical torture in an Indian hospital, prompted by the involuntary impulse of a brave man. But though the woman's words had come upon him like a thunderbolt, he had no belief in the opinion they expressed. No; his young spirit wrestled against and rejected the awful conclusion. Other people might think what they chose; but he knew better than they. His wife was *not* dead. His life had been so smooth, so happy, so prosperous, so unclouded and successful, that it was scarcely strange he should be sceptical of calamity,—that his mind should be incapable of grasping the idea of a catastrophe so terrible as Mary's suicide.

'She was intrusted to me by her father,' he thought. 'She gave her faith to me before God's altar. She *cannot* have perished body and soul; she *cannot* have gone down to destruction for want of my arm outstretched to save her. God is too good to permit such misery.'

The young soldier's piety was of the simplest and most unquestioning order, and involved an implicit belief that a right cause must always be ultimately victorious. With the same blind faith in which he had often muttered a hurried prayer before plunging in amidst the mad havoc of an Indian battle-field, confident that the justice of Heaven would never permit heathenish Afghans to triumph over Christian British gentlemen, he now believed that, in the darkest hour of Mary Marchmont's life, God's arm had held her back from the dread horror—the unatonable offence—of self-destruction.

'I thank you for having spoken frankly to me,' he said to Barbara Simmons; 'I believe that you have spoken in good faith. But I do not think my darling is for ever lost to me. I anticipate trouble and anxiety, disappointment, defeat for a time,—for a long time, perhaps; but I *know* that I shall find her in the end. The business of my life henceforth is to look for her.'

Barbara's dull eyes held earnest watch upon the young man's countenance as he spoke. Anxiety and even fear were in that gaze, palpable to those who knew how to read the faint indications of the woman's stolid face.

CHAPTER XXIV

THE PARAGRAPH IN THE NEWSPAPER

MR MORRISON brought the gig and pony to the western porch while Captain Arundel was talking to his cousin's servant, and presently the invalid was being driven across the flat between the Towers and the high-road to Kemberling.

Mary's old favourite, Farmer Pollard's daughter, came out of a low rustic shop as the gig drew up before her husband's door. This good-natured, tender-hearted Hester, advanced to matronly dignity under the name of Mrs Jobson, carried a baby in her arms, and wore a white dimity* hood, that made a penthouse over her simple rosy face. But at the sight of Captain Arundel nearly all the rosy colour disappeared from the country-woman's plump cheeks, and she stared aghast at the unlooked-for visitor, almost ready to believe that, if anything so substantial as a pony and gig could belong to the spiritual world, it was the phantom only of the soldier that she looked upon.

'O sir!' she said; 'O Captain Arundel, is it really you?'

Edward alighted before Hester could recover from the surprise occasioned by his appearance.

'Yes, Mrs Jobson,' he said. 'May I come into your house? I wish to speak to you.'

Hester curtseyed, and stood aside to allow her visitor to pass her. Her manner was coldly respectful, and she looked at the young officer with a grave, reproachful face, which was strange to him. She ushered her guest into a parlour at the back of the shop; a prim apartment, splendid with varnished mahogany, shell-work boxes—bought during Hester's honeymoon-trip to a Lincolnshire watering-place—and voluminous achievements in the way of crochet-work; a gorgeous and Sabbath-day chamber, looking across a stand of geraniums into a garden that was orderly and trimly kept even in this dull November weather.

Mrs Jobson drew forward an uneasy easy-chair, covered with horsehair, and veiled by a crochet-work representation of a peacock embowered among roses. She offered this luxurious seat to Captain Arundel, who, in his weakness, was well content to sink down upon the slippery cushions.

'I have come here to ask you to help me in my search for my wife, Hester,' Edward Arundel said, in a scarcely audible voice.

It is not given to the bravest mind to be utterly independent and defiant of the body; and the soldier was beginning to feel that he had very nearly run the length of his tether, and must soon submit himself to be prostrated by sheer physical weakness.

'Your wife!' cried Hester eagerly. 'O sir, is that true?'

'Is what true?'

'That poor Miss Mary was your lawful wedded wife?'

'She was,' replied Edward Arundel sternly, 'my true and lawful wife. What else should she have been, Mrs Jobson?'

The farmer's daughter burst into tears.

'O sir,' she said, sobbing violently as she spoke,—'O sir, the things that was said against that poor dear in this place and all about the Towers! The things that was said! It makes my heart bleed to think of them; it makes my heart ready to break when I think what my poor sweet young lady must have suffered. And it set me against you, sir; and I thought you was a bad and cruel-hearted man!'

'What did they say?' cried Edward. 'What did they dare to say against her or against me?'

'They said that you had enticed her away from her home, sir, and that—that—there had been no marriage; and that you had deluded that poor innocent dear to run away with you; and that you'd deserted her afterwards, and the railway accident had come upon you as a punishment like; and that Mrs Marchmont had found poor Miss Mary all alone at a country inn, and had brought her back to the Towers.'

'But what if people did say this?' exclaimed Captain Arundel. 'You could have contradicted their foul slanders; you could have spoken in defence of my poor helpless girl.'

'Me, sir!'

'Yes. You must have heard the truth from my wife's own lips.'

Hester Jobson burst into a new flood of tears as Edward Arundel said this.

'O no, sir,' she sobbed; 'that was the most cruel thing of all. I never could get to see Miss Mary; they wouldn't let me see her.'

'Who wouldn't let you?'

'Mrs Marchmont and Mr Paul Marchmont. I was laid up, sir, when the report first spread about that Miss Mary had come home.

Things was kept very secret, and it was said that Mrs Marchmont was dreadfully cut up by the disgrace that had come upon her stepdaughter. My baby was born about that time, sir; but as soon as ever I could get about, I went up to the Towers, in the hope of seeing my poor dear miss. But Mrs Simmons, Mrs Marchmont's own maid, told me that Miss Mary was ill, very ill, and that no one was allowed to see her except those that waited upon her and that she was used to. And I begged and prayed that I might be allowed to see her, sir, with the tears in my eyes; for my heart bled for her, poor darling dear, when I thought of the cruel things that was said against her, and thought that, with all her riches and her learning, folks could dare to talk of her as they wouldn't dare talk of a poor man's wife like me. And I went again and again, sir; but it was no good; and, the last time I went, Mrs Marchmont came out into the hall to me, and told me that I was intrusive and impertinent, and that it was me, and such as me, as had set all manner of scandal afloat about her stepdaughter. But I went again, sir, even after that; and I saw Mr Paul Marchmont, and he was very kind to me, and frank and free-spoken,—almost like you, sir; and he told me that Mrs Marchmont was rather stern and unforgiving towards the poor young lady,—he spoke very kind and pitiful of poor Miss Mary,—and that he would stand my friend, and he'd contrive that I should see my poor dear as soon as ever she picked up her spirits a bit, and was more fit to see me; and I was to come again in a week's time, he said.'

'Well; and when you went——?'

'When I went, sir,' sobbed the carpenter's wife, 'it was the 18th of October, and Miss Mary had run away upon the day before, and every body at the Towers was being sent right and left to look for her. I saw Mrs Marchmont for a minute that afternoon; and she was as white as a sheet, and all of a tremble from head to foot, and she walked about the place as if she was out of her mind like.'

'Guilt,' thought the young soldier; 'guilt of some sort. God only knows what that guilt has been!'

He covered his face with his hands, and waited to hear what more Hester Jobson had to tell him. There was no need of questioning here—no reservation or pevarication. With almost as tender regret as he himself could have felt, the carpenter's wife told him all that she knew of the sad story of Mary's disappearance.

'Nobody took much notice of me, sir, in the confusion of the place,'

Mrs Jobson continued; 'and there is a parlour-maid at the Towers called Susan Rose, that had been a schoolfellow with me ten years before, and I got her to tell me all about it. And she said that poor dear Miss Mary had been weak and ailing ever since she had recovered from the brain-fever, and that she had shut herself up in her room, and had seen no one except Mrs Marchmont, and Mr Paul, and Barbara Simmons; but on the 17th Mrs Marchmont sent for her, asking her to come to the study. And the poor young lady went; and then Susan Rose thinks that there was high words between Mrs Marchmont and her stepdaughter; for as Susan was crossing the hall poor Miss came out of the study, and her face was all smothered in tears, and she cried out, as she came into the hall, "I can't bear it any longer. My life is too miserable; my fate is too wretched!" And then she ran upstairs, and Susan Rose followed up to her room and listened outside the door; and she heard the poor dear sobbing and crying out again and again, "O papa, papa! If you knew what I suffer! O papa, papa, papa!"—so pitiful, that if Susan Rose had dared she would have gone in to try and comfort her; but Miss Mary had always been very reserved to all the servants, and Susan didn't dare intrude upon her. It was late that evening when my poor young lady was missed, and the servants sent out to look for her.'

'And you, Hester,—you knew my wife better than any of these people,—where do you think she went?'

Hester Jobson looked piteously at the questioner.

'O sir!' she cried; 'O Captain Arundel, don't ask me; pray, pray don't ask me.'

'You think like these other people,—you think that she went away to destroy herself?'

'O sir, what can I think, what can I think except that? She was last seen down by the water-side, and one of her shoes was picked up amongst the rushes; and for all there's been such a search made after her, and a reward offered, and advertisements in the papers, and everything done that mortal could do to find her, there's been no news of her, sir,—not a trace to tell of her being living; not a creature to come forward and speak to her being seen by them after that day. What can I think, sir, what can I think, except—'

'Except that she threw herself into the river behind Marchmont Towers.'

'I've tried to think different, sir; I've tried to hope I should see that poor sweet lamb again; but I can't, I can't. I've worn mourning for these three last Sundays, sir; for I seemed to feel as if it was a sin and a disrespectfulness towards her to wear colours, and sit in the church where I have seen her so often, looking so meek and beautiful, Sunday after Sunday.'

Edward Arundel bowed his head upon his hands and wept silently. This woman's belief in Mary's death afflicted him more than he dared confess to himself. He had defied Olivia and Paul Marchmont, as enemies, who tried to force a false conviction upon him; but he could neither doubt nor defy this honest, warm-hearted creature, who wept aloud over the memory of his wife's sorrows. He could not doubt her sincerity; but he still refused to accept the belief which on every side was pressed upon him. He still refused to think that his wife was dead.

'The river was dragged for more than a week,' he said, presently, 'and my wife's body was never found.'

Hester Jobson shook her head mournfully.

'That's a poor sign, sir,' she answered; 'the river's full of holes, I've heard say. My husband had a fellow-'prentice who drowned himself in that river seven year ago, and *his* body was never found.'

Edward Arundel rose and walked towards the door.

'I do not believe that my wife is dead,' he cried. He held out his hand to the carpenter's wife. 'God bless you!' he said. 'I thank you from my heart for your tender feeling towards my lost girl.'

He went out to the gig, in which Mr Morrison waited for him, rather tired of his morning's work.

'There is an inn a little way farther along the street, Morrison,' Captain Arundel said. 'I shall stop there.'

The man stared at his master.

'And not go back to Marchmont Towers, Mr Edward?'

'No.'

Edward Arundel had held Nature in abeyance for more than four-and-twenty hours, and this outraged Nature now took her revenge by flinging the young man prostrate and powerless upon his bed at the simple Kemberling hostelry, and holding him prisoner there for three dreary days; three miserable days, with long, dark interminable evenings, during which the invalid had no better employment than to lie brooding over his sorrows, while Mr Morrison read the

'Times' newspaper in a monotonous and droning voice, for his sick master's entertainment.

How that helpless and prostrate prisoner, bound hand and foot in the stern grasp of retaliative Nature, loathed the leading-articles, the foreign correspondence, in the leviathan journal! How he sickened at the fiery English of Printing-House Square, as expounded by Mr Morrison! The sound of the valet's voice was like the unbroken flow of a dull river. The great names that surged up every now and then upon that sluggish tide of oratory made no impression upon the sick man's mind. What was it to him if the glory of England were in danger, the freedom of a mighty people wavering in the balance? What was it to him if famine-stricken Ireland* were perishing, and the far-away Indian possessions menaced by contumacious and treacherous Sikhs?* What was it to him if the heavens were shrivelled like a blazing scroll, and the earth reeling on its shaken foundations? What had he to do with any catastrophe except that which had fallen upon his innocent young wife?

'O my broken trust!' he muttered sometimes, to the alarm of the confidential servant; 'O my broken trust!'

But during the three days in which Captain Arundel lay in the best chamber at the Black Bull—the chief inn of Kemberling, and a very splendid place of public entertainment long ago, when all the northward-bound coaches had passed through that quiet Lincolnshire village—he was not without a medical attendant to give him some feeble help in the way of drugs and doctor's stuff, in the battle which he was fighting with offended Nature. I don't know but that the help, however well intended, may have gone rather to strengthen the hand of the enemy; for in those days—the year '48 is very long ago when we take the measure of time by science—country practitioners were apt to place themselves upon the side of the disease rather than of the patient, and to assist grim Death in his siege, by lending the professional aid of purgatives and phlebotomy.

On this principle Mr George Weston, the surgeon of Kemberling, and the submissive and well-tutored husband of Paul Marchmont's sister, would fain have set to work with the prostrate soldier, on the plea that the patient's skin was hot and dry, and his white lips parched with fever. But Captain Arundel protested vehemently against any such treatment.

'You shall not take an ounce of blood out of my veins,' he said, 'or give me one drop of medicine that will weaken me. What I want is strength; strength to get up and leave this intolerable room, and go about the business that I have to do. As to fever,' he added scornfully, 'as long as I have to lie here and am hindered from going about the business of my life, every drop of my blood will boil with a fever that all the drugs in Apothecaries' Hall* would have no power to subdue. Give me something to strengthen me. Patch me up somehow or other, Mr Weston, if you can. But I warn you that, if you keep me long here, I shall leave this place either a corpse or a madman.'

The surgeon, drinking tea with his wife and brother-in-law half an hour afterwards, related the conversation that had taken place between himself and his patient, breaking up his narrative with a great many 'I said's' and 'said he's,' and with a good deal of rambling commentary upon the text.

Lavinia Weston looked at her brother while the surgeon told his story.

'He is very desperate about his wife, then, this dashing young captain?' Mr Marchmont said, presently.

'Awful,' answered the surgeon; 'regular awful. I never saw anything like it. Really it was enough to cut a man up to hear him go on so. He asked me all sorts of questions about the time when she was ill and I attended upon her, and what did she say to me, and did she seem very unhappy, and all that sort of thing. Upon my word, you know, Mr Paul,—of course I am very glad to think of your coming into the fortune, and I'm very much obliged to you for the kind promises you've made to me and Lavinia; but I almost felt as if I could have wished the poor young lady hadn't drowned herself.'

Mrs Weston shrugged her shoulders, and looked at her brother.

'*Imbecile!*' she muttered.

She was accustomed to talk to her brother very freely in rather school-girl French before her husband, to whom that language was as the most recondite of tongues, and who heartily admired her for superior knowledge.

He sat staring at her now, and eating bread-and-butter with a simple relish, which in itself was enough to mark him out as a man to be trampled upon.

On the fourth day after his interview with Hester, Edward Arundel was strong enough to leave his chamber at the Black Bull.

'I shall go to London by to-night's mail, Morrison,' he said to his servant; 'but before I leave Lincolnshire, I must pay another visit to Marchmont Towers. You can stop here, and pack my portmanteau while I go.'

A rumbling old fly—looked upon as a splendid equipage by the inhabitants of Kemberling—was furnished for Captain Arundel's accommodation by the proprietor of the Black Bull; and once more the soldier approached that ill-omened dwelling-place which had been the home of his wife.

He was ushered without any delay to the study in which Olivia spent the greater part of her time.

The dusky afternoon was already closing in. A low fire burned in the old-fashioned grate, and one lighted wax-candle stood upon an open davenport, before which the widow sat amid a confusion of torn papers, cast upon the ground about her.

The open drawers of the davenport,* the littered scraps of paper and loosely-tied documents, thrust, without any show of order, into the different compartments of the desk, bore testimony to that state of mental distraction which had been common to Olivia Marchmont for some time past. She herself, the gloomy tenant of the Towers, sat with her elbow resting on her desk, looking hopelessly and absently at the confusion before her.

'I am very tired,' she said, with a sigh, as she motioned her cousin to a chair. 'I have been trying to sort my papers, and to look for bills that have to be paid, and receipts. They come to me about everything. I am very tired.'

Her manner was changed from that stern defiance with which she had last confronted her kinsman to an air of almost piteous feebleness. She rested her head on her hand, repeating, in a low voice,

'Yes, I am very tired.'

Edward Arundel looked earnestly at her faded face, so faded from that which he remembered it in its proud young beauty, that, in spite of his doubt of this woman, he could scarcely refrain from some touch of pity for her.

'You are ill, Olivia,' he said.

'Yes, I am ill; I am worn out; I am tired of my life. Why does not God have pity upon me, and take the bitter burden away? I have carried it too long.'

She said this not so much to her cousin as to herself. She was like Job in his despair, and cried aloud to the Supreme Himself in a gloomy protest against her anguish.

'Olivia,' said Edward Arundel very earnestly, 'what is it that makes you unhappy? Is the burden that you carry a burden on your conscience? Is the black shadow upon your life a guilty secret? Is the cause of your unhappiness that which I suspect it to be? Is it that, in some hour of passion, you consented to league yourself with Paul Marchmont against my poor innocent girl? For pity's sake, speak, and undo what you have done. You cannot have been guilty of a crime. There has been some foul play, some conspiracy, some suppression; and my darling has been lured away by the machinations of this man. But he could not have got her into his power without your help. You hated her,—Heaven alone knows for what reason,—and in an evil hour you helped him, and now you are sorry for what you have done. But it is not too late, Olivia; Olivia, it is surely not too late. Speak, speak, woman, and undo what you have done. As you hope for mercy and forgiveness from God, undo what you have done. I will exact no atonement from you. Paul Marchmont, this smooth traitor, this frank man of the world, who defied me with a smile,—he only shall be called upon to answer for the wrong done against my darling. Speak, Olivia, for pity's sake,' cried the young man, casting himself upon his knees at his cousin's feet. 'You are of my own blood; you must have some spark of regard for me; have compassion upon me, then, or have compassion upon your own guilty soul, which must perish everlastingly if you withhold the truth. Have pity, Olivia, and speak!'

The widow had risen to her feet, recoiling from the soldier as he knelt before her, and looking at him with an awful light in the eyes that alone gave life to her corpse-like face.

Suddenly she flung her arms up above her head, stretching her wasted hands towards the ceiling.

'By the God who has renounced and abandoned me,' she cried, 'I have no more knowledge than you have of Mary Marchmont's fate. From the hour in which she left this house, upon the 17th of October, until this present moment, I have neither seen her nor heard of her. If I have lied to you, Edward Arundel,' she added, dropping her extended arms, and turning quietly to her cousin,—'if I have lied to you in saying this, may the tortures which I suffer be doubled to me,—if in the infinite of suffering there is any anguish worse than that I now endure.'

Edward Arundel paused for a little while, brooding over this strange reply to his appeal. Could he disbelieve his cousin?

It is common to some people to make forcible and impious asseverations of an untruth shamelessly, in the very face of an insulted Heaven. But Olivia Marchmont was a woman who, in the very darkest hour of her despair, knew no wavering from her faith in the God she had offended.

'I cannot refuse to believe you, Olivia,' Captain Arundel said presently. 'I do believe in your solemn protestations, and I no longer look for help from you in my search for my lost love. I absolve you from all suspicion of being aware of her fate *after* she left this house. But so long as she remained beneath this roof she was in your care, and I hold you responsible for the ills that may have then befallen her. You, Olivia, must have had some hand in driving that unhappy girl away from her home.'

The widow had resumed her seat by the open davenport. She sat with her head bent, her brows contracted, her mouth fixed and rigid, her left hand trifling absently with the scattered papers before her.

'You accused me of this once before, when Mary Marchmont left this house,' she said sullenly.

'And you were guilty then,' answered Edward.

'I cannot hold myself answerable for the actions of others. Mary Marchmont left this time, as she left before, of her own free will.'

'Driven away by your cruel words.'

'She must have been very weak,' answered Olivia, with a sneer, 'if a few harsh words were enough to drive her away from her own house.'

'You deny, then, that you were guilty of causing this poor deluded child's flight from this house?'

Olivia Marchmont sat for some moments in moody silence; then suddenly raising her head, she looked her cousin full in the face.

'I do,' she exclaimed; 'if any one except herself is guilty of an act which was her own, I am not that person.'

'I understand,' said Edward Arundel; 'it was Paul Marchmont's hand that drove her out upon the dreary world. It was Paul Marchmont's brain that plotted against her. You were only a minor instrument; a willing tool, in the hands of a subtle villain. But he shall answer; he shall answer!'

The soldier spoke the last words between his clenched teeth. Then with his chin upon his breast, he sat thinking over what he had just heard.

'How was it?' he muttered; 'how was it? He is too consummate a villain to use violence. His manner the other morning told me that the law was on his side. He had done nothing to put himself into my power, and he defied me. How was it, then? By what means did he drive my darling to her despairing flight?'

As Captain Arundel sat thinking of these things, his cousin's idle fingers still trifled with the papers on the desk; while, with her chin resting on her other hand, and her eyes fixed upon the wall before her, she stared blankly at the reflection of the flame of the candle on the polished oaken panel. Her idle fingers, following no design, strayed here and there among the scattered papers, until a few that lay nearest the edge of the desk slid off the smooth morocco, and fluttered to the ground.

Edward Arundel, as absent-minded as his cousin, stooped involuntarily to pick up the papers. The uppermost of those that had fallen was a slip cut from a country newspaper, to which was pinned an open letter, a few lines only. The paragraph in the newspaper slip was marked by double ink-lines drawn round it by a neat penman. Again almost involuntarily, Edward Arundel looked at this marked paragraph. It was very brief:

'We regret to be called upon to state that another of the sufferers in the accident which occurred last August on the South-Western Railway has expired from injuries received upon that occasion. Captain Arundel, of the HEICS,* died on Friday night at Dangerfield Park, Devon, the seat of his elder brother.'

The letter was almost as brief as the paragraph:

'Kemberling, October 17th.

'MY DEAR MRS MARCHMONT,—The enclosed has just come to hand. Let us hope it is not true. But, in case of the worst, it should be shown to Miss Marchmont *immediately*. Better that she should hear the news from you than from a stranger.

'Yours sincerely,
'PAUL MARCHMONT.'

'I understand everything now,' said Edward Arundel, laying these two papers before his cousin; 'it was with this printed lie that you and Paul Marchmont drove my wife to despair—perhaps to death. My darling, my darling,' cried the young man, in a burst of uncontrollable agony, 'I refused to believe that you were dead; I refused to believe that you were lost to me. I can believe it now; I can believe it now.'

CHAPTER XXV

EDWARD ARUNDEL'S DESPAIR

Yes; Edward Arundel could believe the worst now. He could believe now that his young wife, on hearing tidings of his death, had rushed madly to her own destruction; too desolate, too utterly unfriended and miserable, to live under the burden of her sorrows.

Mary had talked to her husband in the happy, loving confidence of her bright honeymoon; she had talked to him of her father's death, and the horrible grief she had felt; the heart-sickness, the eager yearning to be carried to the same grave, to rest in the same silent sleep.

'I think I tried to throw myself from the window upon the night before papa's funeral,' she had said; 'but I fainted away. I know it was very wicked of me. But I was mad. My wretchedness had driven me mad.'

He remembered this. Might not this girl, this helpless child, in the first desperation of her grief, have hurried down to that dismal river, to hide her sorrows for ever under its slow and murky tide?

Henceforward it was with a new feeling that Edward Arundel looked for his missing wife. The young and hopeful spirit which had wrestled against conviction, which had stubbornly preserved its own sanguine fancies against the gloomy forebodings of others, had broken down before the evidence of that false paragraph in the country newspaper. That paragraph was the key to the sad mystery of Mary Arundel's disappearance. Her husband could understand now why she ran away, why she despaired; and how, in that desperation and despair, she might have hastily ended her short life.

It was with altered feelings, therefore, that he went forth to look for her. He was no longer passionate and impatient, for he no longer believed that his young wife lived to yearn for his coming, and to suffer for the want of his protection; he no longer thought of her as a lonely and helpless wanderer driven from her rightful home, and in her childish ignorance straying farther and farther away from him who had the right to succour and to comfort her. No; he thought of her now with sullen despair at his heart; he thought of her now in utter hopelessness; he thought of her with a bitter and agonising regret, which we only feel for the dead.

But this grief was not the only feeling that held possession of the young soldier's breast. Stronger even than his sorrow was his eager yearning for vengeance, his savage desire for retaliation.

'I look upon Paul Marchmont as the murderer of my wife,' he said to Olivia, on that November evening on which he saw the paragraph in the newspaper; 'I look upon that man as the deliberate destroyer of a helpless girl; and he shall answer to me for her life. He shall answer to me for every pang she suffered, for every tear she shed. God have mercy upon her poor erring soul, and help me to my vengeance upon her destroyer.'

He lifted his eyes to heaven as he spoke, and a solemn shadow overspread his pale face, like a dark cloud upon a winter landscape.

I have said that Edward Arundel no longer felt a frantic impatience to discover his wife's fate. The sorrowful conviction which at last had forced itself upon him left no room for impatience. The pale face he had loved was lying hidden somewhere beneath those dismal waters. He had no doubt of that. There was no need of any other solution to the mystery of his wife's disappearance. That which he had to seek for was the evidence of Paul Marchmont's guilt.

The outspoken young soldier, whose nature was as transparent as the stainless soul of a child, had to enter into the lists with a man who was so different from himself, that it was almost difficult to believe the two individuals belonged to the same species.

Captain Arundel went back to London, and betook himself forthwith to the office of Messrs Paulette, Paulette, and Mathewson. He had the idea, common to many of his class, that all lawyers, whatever claims they might have to respectability, are in a manner past-masters in every villainous art; and, as such, the proper people to deal with a villain.

'Richard Paulette will be able to help me,' thought the young man; 'Richard Paulette saw through Paul Marchmont, I dare say.'

But Richard Paulette had very little to say about the matter. He had known Edward Arundel's father, and he had known the young soldier from his early boyhood, and he seemed deeply grieved to witness his client's distress; but he had nothing to say against Paul Marchmont.

'I cannot see what right you have to suspect Mr Marchmont of any guilty share in your wife's disappearance,' he said. 'Do not think I defend him because he is our client. You know that we are rich enough, and honourable enough, to refuse the business of any man whom we thought a villain. When I was in Lincolnshire, Mr Marchmont did everything that a man could do to testify his anxiety to find his cousin.'

'Oh, yes,' Edward Arundel answered bitterly; 'that is only consistent with the man's diabolical artifice; *that* was a part of his scheme. He wished to testify that anxiety, and he wanted you as a witness to his conscientious search after my—poor—lost girl.' His voice and manner changed for a moment as he spoke of Mary.

Richard Paulette shook his head.

'Prejudice, prejudice, my dear Arundel,' he said; 'this is all prejudice upon your part, I assure you. Mr Marchmont behaved with perfect honesty and candour. "I won't tell you that I'm sorry to inherit this fortune," he said, "because if I did you wouldn't believe me—what man in his senses *could* believe that a poor devil of a landscape painter would regret coming into eleven thousand a year?—but I am very sorry for this poor little girl's unhappy fate." And I believe,' added Mr Paulette, decisively, 'that the man was heartily sorry.'

Edward Arundel groaned aloud.

'O God! this is too terrible,' he muttered. 'Everybody will believe in this man rather than in me. How am I to be avenged upon the wretch who caused my darling's death?'

He talked for a long time to the lawyer, but with no result. Richard Paulette considered the young man's hatred of Paul Marchmont only a natural consequence of his grief for Mary's death.

'I can't wonder that you are prejudiced against Mr Marchmont,' he said; 'it's natural; it's only natural; but, believe me, you are wrong. Nothing could be more straightforward, and even delicate, than his conduct. He refuses to take possession of the estate, or to touch a farthing of the rents. "No," he said, when I suggested to him that he had a right to enter in possession,—"no; we will not shut the door against hope. My cousin may be hiding herself somewhere; she may return by-and-by. Let us wait a twelve-month. If, at the end of that time, she does not return, and if in the interim we receive no tidings from her, no evidence of her existence, we may reasonably conclude that she is dead; and I may fairly consider myself the rightful owner of Marchmont Towers. In the mean time, you will act as if you were still Mary Marchmont's agent, holding all moneys as in trust for her, but to be delivered up to me at the expiration of a year from the day on which she disappeared." I do not think anything could be more straightforward than that,' added Richard Paulette, in conclusion.

'No,' Edward answered, with a sigh; 'it *seems* very straightforward. But the man who could strike at a helpless girl by means of a lying paragraph in a newspaper—'

'Mr Marchmont may have believed in that paragraph.'

Edward Arundel rose, with a gesture of impatience.

'I came to you for help, Mr Paulette,' he said; 'but I see you don't mean to help me. Good day.'

He left the office before the lawyer could remonstrate with him. He walked away, with passionate anger against all the world raging in his breast.

'Why, what a smooth-spoken, false-tongued world it is!' he thought. 'Let a man succeed in the vilest scheme, and no living creature will care to ask by what foul means he may have won his success. What weapons can I use against this Paul Marchmont, who twists truth and honesty to his own ends, and masks his basest treachery under an appearance of candour?'

From Lincoln's Inn Fields Captain Arundel drove over Waterloo Bridge to Oakley Street. He went to Mrs Pimpernel's establishment, without any hope of the glad surprise that had met him there a few months before. He believed implicitly that his wife was dead, and wherever he went in search of her he went in utter hopelessness, only prompted by the desire to leave no part of his duty undone.

The honest-hearted dealer in cast-off apparel wept bitterly when she heard how sadly the Captain's honeymoon had ended. She would have been content to detain the young soldier all day, while she bemoaned the misfortunes that had come upon him; and now, for the first time, Edward heard of dismal forebodings, and horrible dreams, and unaccountable presentiments of evil, with which this honest woman had been afflicted on and before his wedding-day, and of which she had made special mention at the time to divers friends and acquaintances.

'I never shall forget how shivery-like I felt as the cab drove off, with that pore dear a-lookin' and smilin' at me out of the winder. I says to Mrs Polson, as her husband is in the shoemakin' line, two doors further down,—I says, "I do hope Capting Harungdell's lady will get safe to the end of her journey." I felt the cold shivers a-creepin' up my back just azackly like I did a fortnight before my pore Jane died, and I couldn't get it off my mind as somethink was goin' to happen.'

From London Captain Arundel went to Winchester, much to the disgust of his valet, who was accustomed to a luxuriously idle life at Dangerfield Park, and who did not by any means relish this desultory wandering from place to place. Perhaps there was some faint ray of hope in the young man's mind, as he drew near to that little village-inn beneath whose shelter he had been so happy with his childish bride. If she had *not* committed suicide; if she had indeed wandered away, to try and bear her sorrows in gentle Christian resignation; if she had sought some retreat where she might be safe from her tormentors,—would not every instinct of her loving heart have led her here?—here, amid these low meadows and winding streams, guarded and surrounded by the pleasant shelter of grassy hill-tops, crowned by waving trees?—here, where she had been so happy with the husband of her choice?

But, alas! that newly-born hope, which had made the soldier's heart beat and his cheek flush, was as delusive as many other hopes that lure men and women onward in their weary wanderings upon this earth. The landlord of the White Hart Inn answered Edward Arundel's question with stolid indifference.

No; the young lady had gone away with her ma, and a gentleman who came with her ma. She had cried a deal, poor thing, and had seemed very much cut up. (It was from the chambermaid Edward heard this.) But her ma and the gentleman had seemed in a great hurry to take her away. The gentleman said that a village inn wasn't the place for her, and he said he was very much shocked to find her there; and he had a fly got ready, and took the two ladies away in it to the George, at Winchester, and they were to go from there to London; and the young lady was crying when she went away, and was as pale as death, poor dear.

This was all that Captain Arundel gained by his journey to Milldale. He went across country to the farming people near Reading, his wife's poor relations. But they had heard nothing of her. They had wondered, indeed, at having no letters from her, for she had been very kind to them. They were terribly distressed when they were told of her disappearance.

This was the forlorn hope. It was all over now. Edward Arundel could no longer struggle against the cruel truth. He could do nothing now but avenge his wife's sorrows. He went down to Devonshire, saw his mother, and told her the sad story of Mary's flight. But he could not rest at Dangerfield, though Mrs Arundel implored him to stay long enough to recruit his shattered health. He hurried back to London, made arrangements with his agent for being bought out of his regiment by his brother officers, and then, turning his back upon the career that had been far dearer to him than his life, he went down to Lincolnshire once more, in the dreary winter weather, to watch and wait patiently, if need were, for the day of retribution.

There was a detached cottage, a lonely place enough, between Kemberling and Marchmont Towers, that had been to let for a long time, being very much out of repair, and by no means inviting in appearance. Edward Arundel took this cottage. All necessary repairs and alterations were executed under the direction of Mr Morrison, who was to remain permanently in the young man's service. Captain Arundel had a couple of horses brought down to his new stable, and hired a country lad, who was to act as groom under the eye of the factotum. Mr Morrison and this lad, with one female servant, formed Edward's establishment.

Paul Marchmont lifted his auburn eyebrows when he heard of the new tenant of Kemberling Retreat. The lonely cottage had been christened Kemberling Retreat by a sentimental tenant; who had ultimately levanted,* leaving his rent three quarters in arrear. The artist exhibited a gentlemanly surprise at this new vagary of Edward Arundel's, and publicly expressed his pity for the foolish young man.

'I am so sorry that the poor fellow should sacrifice himself to a romantic grief for my unfortunate cousin,' Mr Marchmont said, in the parlour of the Black Bull, where he condescended to drop in now and then with his brother-in-law, and to make himself popular amongst the magnates of Kemberling, and the tenant-farmers, who looked to him as their future, if not their actual, landlord. 'I am really sorry for the poor lad. He's a handsome, high-spirited fellow, and I'm sorry he's been so weak as to ruin his prospects in the Company's service. Yes; I am heartily sorry for him.'

Mr Marchmont discussed the matter very lightly in the parlour of the Black Bull, but he kept silence as he walked home with the surgeon; and Mr George Weston, looking askance at his brother-in-law's face, saw that something was wrong, and thought it advisable to hold his peace.

Paul Marchmont sat up late that night talking to Lavinia after the surgeon had gone to bed. The brother and sister conversed in subdued murmurs as they stood close together before the expiring fire, and the faces of both were very grave, indeed, almost apprehensive.

'He must be terribly in earnest,' Paul Marchmont said, 'or he would never have sacrificed his position. He has planted himself here, close upon us, with a determination of watching us. We shall have to be very careful.'

It was early in the new year that Edward Arundel completed all his arrangements, and took possession of Kemberling Retreat. He knew that, in retiring from the East India Company's service, he had sacrificed the prospect of a brilliant and glorious career, under some of the finest soldiers who ever fought for their country. But he had made this sacrifice willingly—as an offering to the memory of his lost love; as an atonement for his broken trust. For it was one of his most bitter miseries to remember that his own want of prudence had been the first cause of all Mary's sorrows. Had he confided in his mother,—had he induced her to return from Germany to be present at his marriage, and to accept the orphan girl as a daughter,—Mary need never again have fallen into the power of Olivia Marchmont. His own imprudence, his own rashness, had flung this poor child, helpless and friendless, into the hands of the very man against whom John Marchmont had written a solemn warning,—a warning that it should have been Edward's duty to remember. But who could have calculated upon the railway accident; and who could have foreseen a separation in the first blush of the honeymoon? Edward Arundel had trusted in his own power to protect his bride from every ill that might assail her. In the pride of his youth and strength he had forgotten that he was not immortal, and the last idea that could have entered his mind was the thought that he should be stricken down by a sudden calamity, and rendered even more helpless than the girl he had sworn to shield and succour.

The bleak winter crept slowly past, and the shrill March winds were loud amidst the leafless trees in the wood behind Marchmont Towers. This wood was open to any foot-passenger who might choose to wander that way; and Edward Arundel often walked upon the bank of the slow river, and past the boat-house, beneath whose shadow he had wooed his young wife in the bright summer that was gone. The place had a mournful attraction for the young man, by reason of the memory of the past, and a different and far keener fascination in the fact of Paul Marchmont's frequent occupation of his roughly-built painting-room.

In a purposeless and unsettled frame of mind, Edward Arundel kept watch upon the man he hated, scarcely knowing why he watched, or for what he hoped, but with a vague belief that something would be discovered; that some accident might come to pass which would enable him to say to Paul Marchmont,

'It was by your treachery my wife perished; and it is you who must answer to me for her death.'

Edward Arundel had seen nothing of his cousin Olivia during that dismal winter. He had held himself aloof from the Towers,—that is to say, he had never presented himself there as a guest, though he had been often on horseback and on foot in the wood by the river. He had not seen Olivia, but he had heard of her through his valet, Mr Morrison, who insisted on repeating the gossip of Kemberling for the benefit of his listless and indifferent master.

'They do say as Mr Paul Marchmont is going to marry Mrs John Marchmont, sir,' Mr Morrison said, delighted at the importance of his information. 'They say as Mr Paul is always up at the Towers visitin' Mrs John, and that she takes his advice about everything as she does, and that she's quite wrapped up in him like.'

Edward Arundel looked at his attendant with unmitigated surprise.

'My cousin Olivia marry Paul Marchmont!' he exclaimed. 'You should be wiser than to listen to such foolish gossip, Morrison. You know what country people are, and you know they can't keep their tongues quiet.'

Mr Morrison took this reproach as a compliment to his superior intelligence.

'It ain't oftentimes as I listens to their talk, sir,' he said; 'but if I've heard this said once, I've heard it twenty times; and I've heard it at the Black Bull, too, Mr Edward, where Mr Marchmont fre*quents* sometimes with his sister's husband; and the landlord told me as it had been spoken of once before his face, and he didn't deny it.'

Edward Arundel pondered gravely over this gossip of the Kemberling people. It was not so very improbable, perhaps, after all. Olivia only held Marchmont Towers on sufferance. It might be that, rather than be turned out of her stately home, she would accept the hand of its rightful owner. She would marry Paul Marchmont, perhaps, as she had married his cousin,—for the sake of a fortune and a position. She had grudged Mary her wealth, and now she sought to become a sharer in that wealth.

'Oh, the villainy, the villainy!' cried the soldier. 'It is all one base fabric of treachery and wrong. A marriage between these two will be only a part of the scheme. Between them they have driven my darling to her death, and they will now divide the profits of their guilty work.'

The young man determined to discover whether there had been any foundation for the Kemberling gossip. He had not seen his cousin since the day of his discovery of the paragraph in the newspaper, and he went forthwith to the Towers, bent on asking Olivia the straight question as to the truth of the reports that had reached his ears.

He walked over to the dreary mansion. He had regained his strength by this time, and he had recovered his good looks; but something of the brightness of his youth was gone; something of the golden glory of his beauty had faded. He was no longer the young Apollo, fresh and radiant with the divinity of the skies. He had suffered; and suffering had left its traces on his countenance. That smiling hopefulness, that supreme confidence in a bright future, which is the virginity of beauty, had perished beneath the withering influence of affliction.

Mrs Marchmont was not to be seen at the Towers. She had gone down to the boat-house with Mr Paul Marchmont and Mrs Weston, the servant said.

'I will see them together,' Edward Arundel thought. 'I will see if my cousin dares to tell me that she means to marry this man.'

He walked through the wood to the lonely building by the river. The March winds were blowing among the leafless trees, ruffling the black pools of water that the rain had left in every hollow; the smoke from the chimney of Paul Marchmont's painting-room struggled hopelessly against the wind, and was beaten back upon the roof from which it tried to rise. Everything succumbed before that pitiless north-easter.

Edward Arundel knocked at the door of the wooden edifice erected by his foe. He scarcely waited for the answer to his summons, but lifted the latch, and walked across the threshold, uninvited, unwelcome.

There were four people in the painting-room. Two or three seemed to have been talking together when Edward knocked at the door; but the speakers had stopped simultaneously and abruptly, and there was a dead silence when he entered.

Olivia Marchmont was standing under the broad northern window; the artist was sitting upon one of the steps leading up to the pavilion; and a few paces from him, in an old cane-chair near the easel, sat George Weston, the surgeon, with his wife leaning over the back of his chair. It was at this man that Edward Arundel looked longest, riveted by the strange expression of his face. The traces of intense agitation have a peculiar force when seen in a usually stolid countenance. Your mobile faces are apt to give an exaggerated record of emotion. We grow accustomed to their changeful expression, their vivid betrayal of every passing sensation. But this man's was one of those faces which are only changed from their apathetic stillness by some moral earthquake, whose shock arouses the most impenetrable dullard from his stupid imperturbability. Such a shock had lately affected George Weston, the quiet surgeon of Kemberling, the submissive husband of Paul Marchmont's sister. His face was as white as death; a slow trembling shook his ponderous frame; with one of his big fat hands he pulled a cotton handkerchief from his pocket, and tremulously wiped the perspiration from his bald forehead. His wife bent over him, and whispered a few words in his ear; but he shook his head with a piteous gesture, as if to testify his inability to comprehend her. It was impossible for a man to betray more obvious signs of violent agitation than this man betrayed.

'It's no use, Lavinia,' he murmured hopelessly, as his wife whispered to him for the second time; 'it's no use, my dear; I can't get over it.'

Mrs Weston cast one rapid, half-despairing, half-appealing glance at her brother, and in the next moment recovered herself, by an effort only such as great women, or wicked women, are capable of.

'Oh, you men!' she cried, in her liveliest voice; 'oh, you men! What big silly babies, what nervous creatures you are! Come, George, I won't have you giving way to this foolish nonsense, just because an extra glass or so of Mrs Marchmont's very fine old port has happened to disagree with you. You must not think we are a drunkard, Mr Arundel,' added the lady, turning playfully to Edward, and patting her husband's clumsy shoulder as she spoke; 'we are only a poor village surgeon, with a limited income, and a very weak head, and quite unaccustomed to old light port. Come, Mr George Weston, walk out into the open air, sir, and let us see if the March wind will bring you back your senses.'

And without another word Lavinia Weston hustled her husband, who walked like a man in a dream, out of the painting-room, and closed the door behind her.

Paul Marchmont laughed as the door shut upon his brother-in-law.

'Poor George!' he said, carelessly; 'I thought he helped himself to the port a little too liberally. He never could stand a glass of wine; and he's the most stupid creature when he is drunk.'

Excellent as all this by-play was, Edward Arundel was not deceived by it.

'The man was not drunk,' he thought; 'he was frightened. What could have happened to throw him into that state? What mystery are these people hiding amongst themselves; and what should *he* have to do with it?'

'Good evening, Captain Arundel,' Paul Marchmont said. 'I congratulate you on the change in your appearance since you were last in this place. You seem to have quite recovered* the effects of that terrible railway accident.'

Edward Arundel drew himself up stiffly as the artist spoke to him.

'We cannot meet except as enemies, Mr Marchmont,' he said. 'My cousin has no doubt told you what I said of you when I discovered the lying paragraph which you caused to be shown to my wife.'

'I only did what any one else would have done under the circumstances,' Paul Marchmont answered quietly. 'I was deceived by a penny-a-liner's* false report. How should I know the effect that report would have upon my unhappy cousin?'

'I cannot discuss this matter with you,' cried Edward Arundel, his voice tremulous with passion; 'I am almost mad when I think of it. I am not safe; I dare not trust myself. I look upon you as the deliberate assassin of a helpless girl; but so skilful an assassin, that nothing less than the vengeance of God can touch you. I cry aloud to Him night and day, in the hope that He will hear me and avenge my wife's death. I cannot look to any earthly law for help: but I trust in God; I put my trust in God.'

There are very few positive and consistent atheists in this world. Mr Paul Marchmont was a philosopher of the infidel school, a student of Voltaire and the brotherhood of the Encyclopedia,* and a believer in those liberal days before the Reign of Terror, when Frenchmen, in coffee-houses, discussed the Supreme under the soubriquet of Mons. l'Etre; but he grew a little paler as Edward Arundel, with kindling eyes and uplifted hand, declared his faith in a Divine Avenger.

The sceptical artist may have thought,

'What if there should be some reality in the creed so many weak fools confide in? What if there *is* a God who cannot abide iniquity?'

'I came here to look for you, Olivia,' Edward Arundel said presently. 'I want to ask you a question. Will you come into the wood with me?'

'Yes, if you wish it,' Mrs Marchmont answered quietly.

The cousins went out of the painting-room together, leaving Paul Marchmont alone. They walked on for a few yards in silence.

'What is the question you came here to ask me?' Olivia asked abruptly.

'The Kemberling people have raised a report about you which I should fancy would be scarcely agreeable to yourself,' answered Edward. 'You would hardly wish to benefit by Mary's death, would you, Olivia?'

He looked at her searchingly as he spoke. Her face was at all times so expressive of hidden cares, of cruel mental tortures, that there was little room in her countenance for any new emotion. Her cousin looked in vain for any change in it now.

'Benefit by her death!' she exclaimed. 'How should I benefit by her death?'

'By marrying the man who inherits this estate. They say you are going to marry Paul Marchmont.'

Olivia looked at him with an expression of surprise.

'Do they say that of me?' she asked. 'Do people say that?'

'They do. Is it true, Olivia?'

The widow turned upon him almost fiercely.

'What does it matter to you whether it is true or not? What do you care whom I marry, or what becomes of me?'

'I care this much,' Edward Arundel answered, 'that I would not have your reputation lied away by the gossips of Kemberling. I should despise you if you married this man. But if you do not mean to marry him, you have no right to encourage his visits; you are trifling with your own good name. You should leave this place, and by that means give the lie to any false reports that have arisen about you.'

'Leave this place!' cried Olivia Marchmont, with a bitter laugh. 'Leave this place! O my God, if I could; if I could go away and bury myself somewhere at the other end of the world, and forget,—and forget!' She said this as if to herself; as if it had been a cry of despair wrung from her in despite of herself; then, turning to Edward Arundel, she added, in a quieter voice, 'I can never leave this place till I leave it in my coffin. I am a prisoner here for life.'

She turned from him, and walked slowly away, with her face towards the dying sunlight in the low western sky.

CHAPTER XXVI

EDWARD'S VISITORS

PERHAPS no greater sacrifice had ever been made by an English gentleman than that which Edward Arundel willingly offered up as an atonement for his broken trust, as a tribute to his lost wife. Brave, ardent, generous, and sanguine, this young soldier saw before him a brilliant career in the profession which he loved. He saw glory and distinction beckoning to him from afar, and turned his back upon those shining sirens. He gave up all, in the vague hope of, sooner or later, avenging Mary's wrongs upon Paul Marchmont.

He made no boast, even to himself, of that which he had done. Again and again memory brought back to him the day upon which he breakfasted in Oakley Street, and walked across Waterloo Bridge with the Drury Lane supernumerary. Every word that John Marchmont had spoken; every look of the meek and trusting eyes, the pale and thoughtful face; every pressure of the thin hand which had grasped his in grateful affection, in friendly confidence,—came back to Edward Arundel after an interval of nearly ten years, and brought with it a bitter sense of self-reproach.

'He trusted his daughter to me,' the young man thought. 'Those last words in the poor fellow's letter are always in my mind: "The only bequest which I can leave to the only friend I have is the legacy of a child's helplessness." And I have slighted his solemn warning: and I have been false to my trust.'

In his scrupulous sense of honour, the soldier reproached himself as bitterly for that imprudence, out of which so much evil had arisen, as another man might have done after a wilful betrayal of his trust. He could not forgive himself. He was for ever and ever repeating in his own mind that one brief phase which is the universal chorus of erring men's regret: 'If I had acted differently, if I had done otherwise, this or that would not have come to pass.' We are perpetually wandering amid the hopeless deviations of a maze, finding pitfalls and precipices, quicksands and morasses, at every turn in the painful way; and we look back at the end of our journey to discover a straight and pleasant roadway by which, had we been wise enough to choose it, we might have travelled safely and comfortably to our destination.

But Wisdom waits for us at the goal instead of accompanying us upon our journey. She is a divinity whom we meet very late in life; when we are too near the end of our troublesome march to derive much profit from her counsels. We can only retail them to our juniors, who, not getting them from the fountain-head, have very small appreciation of their value.

The young captain of East Indian cavalry suffered very cruelly from the sacrifice which he had made. Day after day, day after day, the slow, dreary, changeless, eventless, and unbroken life dragged itself out; and nothing happened to bring him any nearer to the purpose of this monotonous existence; no promise of even ultimate success rewarded his heroic self-devotion. Afar, he heard of the rush and clamour of war, of dangers and terror, of conquest and glory. His own regiment was in the thick of the strife, his brothers in arms were doing wonders. Every mail brought some new record of triumph and glory.

The soldier's heart sickened as he read the story of each new encounter; his heart sickened with that terrible yearning,—that yearning which seems physically palpable in its perpetual pain; the yearning with which a child at a hard school, lying broad awake in the long, gloomy, rush-lit bedchamber in the dead of the silent night, remembers the soft resting-place of his mother's bosom; the yearning with which a faithful husband far away from home sighs for the presence of the wife he loves. Even with such a heart-sickness as this Edward Arundel pined to be amongst the familiar faces yonder in the East,—to hear the triumphant yell of his men as they swarmed after him through the breach in an Afghan wall,—to see the dark heathens blanch under the terror of Christian swords.

He read the records of the war again and again, again and again, till every scene arose before him,—a picture, flaming and lurid, grandly beautiful, horribly sublime. The very words of those newspaper reports seemed to blaze upon the paper on which they were written, so palpable were the images which they evoked in the soldier's mind. He was frantic in his eager impatience for the arrival of every mail, for the coming of every new record of that Indian warfare. He was like a devourer of romances, who reads a thrilling story link by link, and who is impatient for every new chapter of the fiction. His dreams were of nothing but battle and victory, danger, triumph, and death; and he often woke in the morning exhausted by the excitement of those visionary struggles, those phantom terrors.

His sabre hung over the chimney-piece in his simple bedchamber. He took it down sometimes, and drew it from the sheath. He could have almost wept aloud over that idle sword. He raised his arm, and the weapon vibrated with a whirring noise as he swept the glittering steel in a wide circle through the empty air. An infidel's head should have been swept from his vile carcass in that rapid circle of the keen-edged blade. The soldier's arm was as strong as ever, his wrist as supple, his muscular force unwasted by mental suffering. Thank Heaven for that! But after that brief thanksgiving his arm dropped inertly, and the idle sword fell out of his relaxing grasp.

'I seem a craven to myself,' he cried; 'I have no right to be here—I have no right to be here while those other fellows are fighting for their lives out yonder. O God, have mercy upon me! My brain gets dazed sometimes; and I begin to wonder whether I am most bound to remain here and watch Paul Marchmont, or to go yonder and fight for my country and my Queen.'

There were many phases in this mental fever. At one time the young man was seized with a savage jealousy of the officer who had succeeded to his captaincy. He watched this man's name, and every record of his movements, and was constantly taking objection to his conduct. He was grudgingly envious of this particular officer's triumphs, however small. He could not feel generously towards this happy successor, in the bitterness of his own enforced idleness.

'What opportunities this man has!' he thought; '*I* never had such chances.'

It is almost impossible for me to faithfully describe the tortures which this monotonous existence inflicted upon the impetuous young man. It is the speciality of a soldier's career that it unfits most men for any other life. They cannot throw off the old habitudes. They cannot turn from the noisy stir of war to the tame quiet of every-day life; and even when they fancy themselves wearied and worn out, and willingly retire from service, their souls are stirred by every sound of the distant contest, as the war-steed is aroused by the blast of a trumpet. But Edward Arundel's career had been cut suddenly short at the very hour in which it was brightest with the promise of future glory. It was as if a torrent rushing madly down a mountain-side had been dammed up, and its waters bidden to stagnate upon a level plain. The rebellious waters boiled and foamed in a sullen fury. The soldier could not submit himself contentedly to his fate. He might strip off his uniform, and accept sordid coin as the price of the epaulettes he had won so dearly; but he was at heart a soldier still. When he received the sum which had been raised amongst his juniors as the price of his captaincy, it seemed to him almost as if he had sold his brother's blood.

It was summer-time now. Ten months had elapsed since his marriage with Mary Marchmont, and no new light had been thrown upon the disappearance of his young wife. No one could feel a moment's doubt as to her fate. She had perished in that lonely river which flowed behind Marchmont Towers, and far away down to the sea.

The artist had kept his word, and had as yet taken no step towards entering into possession of the estate which he inherited by his cousin's death. But Mr Paul Marchmont spent a great deal of time at the Towers, and a great deal more time in the painting-room by the riverside, sometimes accompanied by his sister, sometimes alone.

The Kemberling gossips had grown by no means less talkative upon the subject of Olivia and the new owner of Marchmont Towers. On the contrary, the voices that discussed Mrs Marchmont's conduct were a great deal more numerous than heretofore; in other words, John Marchmont's widow was 'talked about.' Everything is said in this phrase. It was scarcely that people said bad things of her; it was rather that they talked more about her than any woman can suffer to be talked of with safety to her fair fame. They began by saying that she was going to marry Paul Marchmont; they went on to wonder *whether* she was going to marry him; then they wondered *why* she didn't marry him. From this they changed the venue, and began to wonder whether Paul Marchmont meant to marry her,—there was an essential difference in this new wonderment,—and next, why Paul Marchmont didn't marry her. And by this time Olivia's reputation was overshadowed by a terrible cloud, which had arisen no bigger than a man's hand,* in the first conjecturings of a few ignorant villagers.

People made it their business first to wonder about Mrs Marchmont, and then to set up their own theories about her; to which theories they clung with a stupid persistence, forgetting, as people generally do forget, that there might be some hidden clue, some secret key, to the widow's conduct, for want of which the cleverest reasoning respecting her was only so much groping in the dark.

Edward Arundel heard of the cloud which shadowed his cousin's name. Her father heard of it, and went to remonstrate with her, imploring her to come to him at Swampington, and to leave Marchmont Towers to the new lord of the mansion. But she only answered him with gloomy, obstinate reiteration, and almost in the same terms as she had answered Edward Arundel; declaring that she would stay at the Towers till her death; that she would never leave the place till she was carried thence in her coffin.

Hubert Arundel, always afraid of his daughter, was more than ever afraid of her now; and he was as powerless to contend against her sullen determination as he would have been to float up the stream of a rushing river.

So Olivia was talked about. She had scared away all visitors, after the ball at the Towers, by the strangeness of her manner and the settled gloom in her face; and she lived unvisited and alone in the gaunt stony mansion; and people said that Paul Marchmont was almost perpetually with her, and that she went to meet him in the painting-room by the river.

Edward Arundel sickened of his wearisome life, and no one helped him to endure his sufferings. His mother wrote to him imploring him to resign himself to the loss of his young wife, to return to Dangerfield, to begin a new existence, and to blot out the memory of the past.

'You have done all that the most devoted affection could prompt you to do,' Mrs Arundel wrote. 'Come back to me, my dearest boy. I gave you up to the service of your country because it was my duty to resign you then. But I cannot afford to lose you now; I cannot bear to see you sacrificing yourself to a chimera. Return to me; and let me see you make a new and happier choice. Let me see my son the father of little children who will gather round my knees when I grow old and feeble.'

'A new and happier choice!' Edward Arundel repeated the words with a melancholy bitterness. 'No, my poor lost girl; no, my blighted wife; I will not be false to you. The smiles of happy women can have no sunlight for me while I cherish the memory of the sad eyes that watched me when I drove away from Milldale, the sweet sorrowful face that I was never to look upon again.'

The dull empty days succeeded each other, and *did* resemble each other, with a wearisome similitude that well-nigh exhausted the patience of the impetuous young man. His fiery nature chafed against this miserable delay. It was so hard to have to wait for his vengeance. Sometimes he could scarcely refrain from planting himself somewhere in Paul Marchmont's way, with the idea of a hand-to-hand struggle in which either he or his enemy must perish.

Once he wrote the artist a desperate letter, denouncing him as an arch-plotter and villain; calling upon him, if his evil nature was redeemed by one spark of manliness, to fight as men had been in the habit of fighting only a few years before, with a hundred times less reason than these two men had for their quarrel.

'I have called you a villain and traitor; in India we fellows would kill each other for smaller words than those,' wrote the soldier. 'But I have no wish to take any advantage of my military experience. I may be a better shot than you. Let us have only one pistol, and draw lots for it. Let us fire at each other across a dinner-table. Let us do anything; so that we bring this miserable business to an end.'

Mr Marchmont read this letter slowly and thoughtfully, more than once; smiling as he read.

'He's getting tired,' thought the artist. 'Poor young man, I thought he would be the first to grow tired of this sort of work.'

He wrote Edward Arundel a long letter; a friendly but rather facetious letter; such as he might have written to a child who had asked him to jump over the moon. He ridiculed the idea of a duel, as something utterly Quixotic and absurd.

'I am fifteen years older than you, my dear Mr Arundel,' he wrote, 'and a great deal too old to have any inclination to fight with windmills; or to represent the windmill which a high-spirited young Quixote may choose to mistake for a villanous knight, and run his hot head against in that delusion. I am not offended with you for calling me bad names, and I take your anger merely as a kind of romantic manner you have of showing your love for my poor cousin. We are not enemies, and we never shall be enemies; for I will never suffer myself to be so foolish as to get into a passion with a brave and generous-hearted young soldier, whose only error is an unfortunate hallucination with regard to

'Your very humble servant,

'PAUL MARCHMONT.'

Edward ground his teeth with savage fury as he read this letter.

'Is there no making this man answer for his infamy?' he muttered. 'Is there no way of making him suffer?'

June was nearly over, and the year was wearing round to the anniversary of Edward's wedding-day, the anniversaries of those bright days which the young bride and bridegroom had loitered away by the trout-streams in the Hampshire meadows, when some most unlooked-for visitors made their appearance at Kemberling Retreat.

The cottage lay back behind a pleasant garden, and was hidden from the dusty high road by a hedge of lilacs and laburnums which grew within the wooden fence. It was Edward's habit, in this hot summer-time, to spend a great deal of his time in the garden; walking up and down the neglected paths, with a cigar in his mouth; or lolling in an easy chair on the lawn reading the papers. Perhaps the garden was almost prettier, by reason of the long neglect which it had suffered, than it would have been if kept in the trimmest order by the industrious hands of a skilful gardener. Everything grew in a wild and wanton luxuriance, that was very beautiful in this summer-time, when the earth was gorgeous with all manner of blossoms. Trailing branches from the espaliered apple-trees hung across the pathways, intermingled with roses that had run wild; and made 'bits'* that a landscape-painter might have delighted to copy. Even the weeds, which a gardener would have looked upon with horror, were beautiful. The wild convolvulus flung its tendrils into fantastic wreaths about the bushes of sweetbrier; the honeysuckle, untutored by the pruning-knife, mixed its tall branches with syringa and clematis; the jasmine that crept about the house had mounted to the very chimney-pots, and strayed in through the open windows; even the stable-roof was half hidden by hardy monthly roses that had clambered up to the thatch. But the young soldier took very little interest in this disorderly garden. He pined to be far away in the thick jungle, or on the burning plain. He hated the quiet and repose of an existence which seemed little better than the living death of a cloister.

The sun was low in the west at the close of a long midsummer day, when Mr Arundel strolled up and down the neglected pathways, backwards and forwards amid the long tangled grass of the lawn, smoking a cigar, and brooding over his sorrows.

He was beginning to despair. He had defied Paul Marchmont, and no good had come of his defiance. He had watched him, and there had been no result of his watching. Day after day he had wandered down to the lonely pathway by the river side; again and again he had reconnoitered the boat-house, only to hear Paul Marchmont's treble voice singing scraps out of modern operas as he worked at his easel; or on one or two occasions to see Mr George Weston, the surgeon, or Lavinia his wife, emerge from the artist's painting-room.

Upon one of these occasions Edward Arundel had accosted the surgeon of Kemberling, and had tried to enter into conversation with him. But Mr Weston had exhibited such utterly hopeless stupidity, mingled with a very evident terror of his brother-in-law's foe, that Edward had been fain to abandon all hope of any assistance from this quarter.

'I'm sure I'm very sorry for you, Mr Arundel,' the surgeon said, looking, not at Edward, but about and around him, in a hopeless, wandering manner, like some hunted animal that looks far and near for a means of escape from his pursuer,—'I'm very sorry for you— and for all your trouble—and I was when I attended you at the Black Bull—and you were the first patient I ever had there—and it led to my having many more—as I may say—though that's neither here nor there. And I'm very sorry for you, and for the poor young woman too—particularly for the poor young woman—and I always tell Paul so—and—and Paul—'

And at this juncture Mr Weston stopped abruptly, as if appalled by the hopeless entanglement of his own ideas, and with a brief 'Good evening, Mr Arundel,' shot off in the direction of the Towers, leaving Edward at a loss to understand his manner.

So, on this midsummer evening, the soldier walked up and down the neglected grass-plat,* thinking of the men who had been his comrades, and of the career which he had abandoned for the love of his lost wife.

He was aroused from his gloomy reverie by the sound of a fresh girlish voice calling to him by his name.

'Edward! Edward!'

Who could there be in Lincolnshire with the right to call to him thus by his Christian name? He was not long left in doubt. While he was asking himself the question, the same feminine voice cried out again.

'Edward! Edward! Will you come and open the gate for me, please? Or do you mean to keep me out here for ever?'

This time Mr Arundel had no difficulty in recognising the familiar tones of his sister Letitia, whom he had believed, until that moment, to be safe under the maternal wing at Dangerfield. And lo, here she was, on horseback at his own gate; with a cavalier hat and feathers overshadowing her girlish face; and with another young Amazon on a thorough-bred chestnut, and an elderly groom on a thorough-bred bay, in the background.

Edward Arundel, utterly confounded by the advent of such visitors, flung away his cigar, and went to the low wooden gate beyond which his sister's steed was pawing the dusty road, impatient of this stupid delay, and eager to be cantering stablewards through the scented summer air.

'Why, Letitia!' cried the young man, 'what, in mercy's name, has brought you here?'

Miss Arundel laughed aloud at her brother's look of surprise.

'You didn't know I was in Lincolnshire, did you?' she asked; and then answered her own question in the same breath: 'Of course you didn't, because I wouldn't let mamma tell you I was coming; for I wanted to surprise you, you know. And I think I have surprised you, haven't I? I never saw such a scared-looking creature in all my life. If I were a ghost coming here in the gloaming, you couldn't look more frightened than you did just now. I only came the day before yesterday—and I'm staying at Major Lawford's, twelve miles away from here—and this is Miss Lawford, who was at school with me at Bath. You've heard me talk of Belinda Lawford, my dearest, dearest friend? Miss Lawford, my brother; my brother, Miss Lawford. Are you going to open the gate and let us in, or do you mean to keep your citadel closed upon us altogether, Mr Edward Arundel?'

At this juncture the young lady in the background drew a little nearer to her friend, and murmured a remonstrance to the effect that it was very late, and that they were expected home before dark; but Miss Arundel refused to hear the voice of wisdom.

'Why, we've only an hour's ride back,' she cried; 'and if it should be dark, which I don't think it will be, for it's scarcely dark all night through at this time of year, we've got Hoskins with us, and Hoskins will take care of us. Won't you, Hoskins?' demanded the young lady, turning to the elderly groom.

Of course Hoskins declared that he was ready to achieve all that man could do or dare in the defence of his liege ladies, or something pretty nearly to that effect; but delivered in a vile Lincolnshire patois, not easily rendered in printer's ink.

Miss Arundel waited for no further discussion, but gave her hand to her brother, and vaulted lightly from her saddle.

Then, of course, Edward Arundel offered his services to his sister's companion, and then for the first time he looked in Belinda Lawford's face, and even in that one first glance saw that she was a good and beautiful creature, and that her hair, of which she had a great quantity, was of the colour of her horse's chestnut coat; that her eyes were the bluest he had ever seen, and that her cheeks were like the neglected roses in his garden. He held out his hand to her. She took it with a frank smile, and dismounted, and came in amongst the grass-grown pathways, amid the confusion of trailing branches and bright garden-flowers growing wild.

In that moment began the second volume of Edward Arundel's life. The first volume had begun upon the Christmas night on which the boy of seventeen went to see the pantomime at Drury Lane Theatre. The old story had been a long, sad story, full of tenderness and pathos, but with a cruel and dismal ending. The new story began to-night, in this fading western sunshine, in this atmosphere of balmy perfume, amidst these dew-laden garden-flowers growing wild.

But, as I think I observed before at the outset of this story, we are rarely ourselves aware of the commencement of any new section in our lives. It is only after the fact that we recognise the awful importance which actions, in themselves most trivial, assume by reason of their consequences; and when the action, in itself so unimportant, in its consequences so fatal, has been in any way a deviation from the right, how bitterly we reproach ourselves for that false step!

'I am so *glad* to see you, Edward!' Miss Arundel exclaimed, as she looked about her, critising her brother's domain; 'but you don't seem a bit glad to see me, you poor gloomy old dear. And how much better you look than you did when you left Dangerfield? only a little careworn, you know, still. And to think of your coming and burying yourself here, away from all the people who love you, you silly old darling! And Belinda knows the story, and she's so sorry for you. Ain't you, Linda? I call her Linda for short, and because it's prettier than *Be*-linda,' added the young lady aside to her brother, and with a contemptuous emphasis upon the first syllable of her friend's name.

Miss Lawford, thus abruptly appealed to, blushed, and said nothing.

If Edward Arundel had been told that any other young lady was acquainted with the sad story of his married life, I think he would have been inclined to revolt against the very idea of her pity. But although he had only looked once at Belinda Lawford, that one look seemed to have told him a great deal. He felt instinctively that she was as good as she was beautiful, and that her pity must be a most genuine and tender emotion, not to be despised by the proudest man upon earth.

The two ladies seated themselves upon a dilapidated rustic bench amid the long grass, and Mr Arundel sat in the low basket-chair in which he was wont to lounge a great deal of his time away.

'Why don't you have a gardener, Ned?' Letitia Arundel asked, after looking rather contemptuously at the flowery luxuriance around her.

Her brother shrugged his shoulders with a despondent gesture.

'Why should I take any care of the place?' he said. 'I only took it because it was near the spot where—where my poor girl—where I wanted to be. I have no object in beautifying it. I wish to Heaven I could leave it, and go back to India.'

He turned his face eastward as he spoke, and the two girls saw that half-eager, half-despairing yearning that was always visible in his face when he looked to the east. It was over yonder, the scene of strife, the red field of glory, only separated from him by a patch of purple ocean and a strip of yellow sand. It was yonder. He could almost feel the hot blast of the burning air. He could almost hear the shouts of victory. And he was a prisoner here, bound by a sacred duty,—by a duty which he owed to the dead.

'Major Lawford—Major Lawford is Belinda's papa; 33rd Foot—Major Lawford knew that we were coming here, and he begged me to ask you to dinner; but I said you wouldn't come, for I knew you had shut yourself out of all society—though the Major's the dearest creature, and the Grange is a most delightful place to stay at. I was down here in the midsummer holidays once, you know, while you were in India. But I give the message as the Major gave it to me; and you are to come to dinner whenever you like.'

Edward Arundel murmured a few polite words of refusal. No; he saw no society; he was in Lincolnshire to achieve a certain object; he should remain there no longer than was necessary in order for him to do so.

'And you don't even say that you're glad to see me!' exclaimed Miss Arundel, with an offended air, 'though it's six months since you were last at Dangerfield! Upon my word, you're a nice brother for an unfortunate girl to waste her affections upon!'

Edward smiled faintly at his sister's complaint.

'I am very glad to see you, Letitia,' he said; 'very, very glad.'

And indeed the young hermit could not but confess to himself that those two innocent young faces seemed to bring light and brightness with them, and to shed a certain transitory glimmer of sunshine upon the horrible gloom of his life. Mr Morrison had come out to offer his duty to the young lady—whom he had been intimate with from a very early period of her existence, and had carried upon his shoulder some fifteen years before—under the pretence of bringing wine for the visitors; and the stable-lad had been sent to a distant corner of the garden to search for strawberries for their refreshment. Even the solitary maid-servant had crept into the parlour fronting the lawn, and had shrouded herself behind the window-curtains, whence she could peep out at the two Amazons, and gladden her eyes with the sight of something that was happy and beautiful.

But the young ladies would not stop to drink any wine, though Mr Morrison informed Letitia that the sherry was from the Dangerfield cellar, and had been sent to Master Edward by his ma; nor to eat any strawberries, though the stable-boy, who made the air odorous with the scent of hay and oats, brought a little heap of freshly-gathered fruit piled upon a cabbage-leaf, and surmounted by a rampant caterpillar of the woolly species. They could not stay any longer, they both declared, lest there should be terror at Lawford Grange because of their absence. So they went back to the gate, escorted by Edward and his confidential servant; and after Letitia had given her brother a kiss, which resounded almost like the report of a pistol through the still evening air, the two ladies mounted their horses, and cantered away in the twilight.

'I shall come and see you again, Ned,' Miss Arundel cried, as she shook the reins upon her horse's neck; 'and so will Belinda—won't you, Belinda?'

Miss Lawford's reply, if she spoke at all, was quite inaudible amidst the clattering of the horses' hoofs upon the hard highroad.

CHAPTER XXVII

ONE MORE SACRIFICE

LETITIA ARUNDEL kept her word, and came very often to Kemberling Retreat; sometimes on horseback, sometimes in a little pony-carriage; sometimes accompanied by Belinda Lawford, sometimes accompanied by a younger sister of Belinda's, as chestnut-haired and blue-eyed as Belinda herself, but at the school-room and bread-and-butter period of life, and not particularly interesting. Major Lawford came one day with his daughter and her friend, and Edward and the half-pay officer* walked together up and down the grass-plat, smoking and talking of the Indian war, while the two girls roamed about the garden amidst the roses and butterflies, tearing the skirts of their riding-habits every now and then amongst the briers and gooseberry-bushes. It was scarcely strange after this visit that Edward Arundel should consent to accept Major Lawford's invitation to name a day for dining at the Grange; he could not, with a very good grace, have refused. And yet—and yet—it seemed to him almost a treason against his lost love, his poor pensive Mary,—whose face, with the very look it had worn upon that last day, was ever present with him,—to mix with happy people who had never known sorrow. But he went to the Grange nevertheless, and grew more and more friendly with the Major, and walked in the gardens—which were very large and old-fashioned, but most beautifully kept—with his sister and Belinda Lawford; with Belinda Lawford, who knew his story and was sorry for him. He always remembered *that* as he looked at her bright face, whose varying expression gave perpetual evidence of a compassionate and sympathetic nature.

'If my poor darling had had this girl for a friend,' he thought sometimes, 'how much happier she might have been!'

I dare say there have been many lovelier women in this world than Belinda Lawford; many women whose faces, considered artistically, came nearer perfection; many noses more exquisitely chiselled, and scores of mouths bearing a closer affinity to Cupid's bow; but I doubt if any face was ever more pleasant to look upon than the face of this blooming English maiden. She had a beauty that is sometimes wanting in perfect faces, and, lacking which, the most splendid loveliness will pall at last upon eyes that have grown weary of admiring; she had a charm for want of which the most rigidly classical profiles, the most exquisitely statuesque faces, have seemed colder and harder than the marble it was their highest merit to resemble. She had the beauty of goodness, and to admire her was to do homage to the purest and brightest attributes of womanhood. It was not only that her pretty little nose was straight and well-shaped, that her lips were rosy red, that her eyes were bluer than the summer heavens, and her chestnut hair tinged with the golden light of a setting sun; above and beyond such commonplace beauties as these, the beauties of tenderness, truth, faith, earnestness, hope and charity, were enthroned upon her broad white brow, and crowned her queen by right divine of womanly perfection. A loving and devoted daughter, an affectionate sister, a true and faithful friend, an untiring benefactress to the poor, a gentle mistress, a well-bred Christian lady; in every duty and in every position she bore out and sustained the impression which her beauty made on the minds of those who looked upon her. She was only nineteen years of age, and no sorrow had ever altered the brightness of her nature. She lived a happy life with a father who was proud of her, and with a mother who resembled her in almost every attribute. She led a happy but a busy life, and did her duty to the poor about her as scrupulously as even Olivia had done in the old days at Swampington Rectory; but in such a genial and cheerful spirit as to win, not cold thankfulness, but heartfelt love and devotion from all who partook of her benefits.

Upon the Egyptian darkness* of Edward Arundel's life this girl arose as a star, and by-and-by all the horizon brightened under her influence. The soldier had been very little in the society of women. His mother, his sister Letitia, his cousin Olivia, and John Marchmont's gentle daughter were the only women whom he had ever known in the familiar freedom of domestic intercourse; and he trusted himself in the presence of this beautiful and noble-minded girl in utter ignorance of any danger to his own peace of mind. He suffered himself to be happy at Lawford Grange; and in those quiet hours which he spent there he put away his old life, and forgot the stern purpose that alone held him a prisoner in England.

But when he went back to his lonely dwelling-place, he reproached himself bitterly for that which he considered a treason against his love.

'What right have I to be happy amongst these people?' he thought; 'what right have I to take life easily, even for an hour, while my darling lies in her unhallowed grave, and the man who drove her to her death remains unpunished? I will never go to Lawford Grange again.'

It seemed, however, as if everybody, except Belinda, was in a plot against this idle soldier; for sometimes Letitia coaxed him to ride back with her after one of her visits to Kemberling Retreat, and very often the Major himself insisted, in a hearty military fashion, upon the young man's taking the empty seat in his dog-cart, to be driven over to the Grange. Edward Arundel had never once mentioned Mary's name to any member of this hospitable and friendly family. They were very good to him, and were prepared, he knew, to sympathise with him; but he could not bring himself to talk of his lost wife. The thought of that rash and desperate act which had ended her short life was too cruel to him. He would not speak of her, because he would have had to plead excuses for that one guilty act; and her image to him was so stainless and pure, that he could not bear to plead for her as for a sinner who had need of men's pity, rather than a claim to their reverence.

'Her life had been so sinless,' he cried sometimes; 'and to think that it should have ended in sin! If I could forgive Paul Marchmont for all the rest—if I could forgive him for my loss of her, I would never forgive him for that.'

The young widower kept silence, therefore, upon the subject which occupied so large a share of his thoughts, which was every day and every night the theme of his most earnest prayers; and Mary's name was never spoken in his presence at Lawford Grange.

But in Edward Arundel's absence the two girls sometimes talked of the sad story.

'Do you really think, Letitia, that your brother's wife committed suicide?' Belinda asked her friend.

'Oh, as for that, there can't be any doubt about it, dear,' answered Miss Arundel, who was of a lively, not to say a flippant, disposition, and had no very great reverence for solemn things; 'the poor dear creature drowned herself. I think she must have been a little wrong in her head. I don't say so to Edward, you know; at least, I did say so once when he was at Dangerfield, and he flew into an awful passion, and called me hard-hearted and cruel, and all sorts of shocking

things; so, of course, I have never said so since. But really, the poor
dear thing's goings-on were so eccentric: first she ran away from her
stepmother and went and hid herself in a horrid lodging; and then
she married Edward at a nasty church in Lambeth, without so much
as a wedding-dress, or a creature to give her away, or a cake, or cards,
or anything Christian-like; and then she ran away again; and as her
father had been a super—what's its name?;—a man who carries
banners in pantomimes, and all that—I dare say she'd seen Mr
Macready as Hamlet, and had Ophelia's death in her head when she
ran down to the riverside and drowned herself. I'm sure it's a very
sad story; and, of course, I'm awfully sorry for Edward.'

The young lady said no more than this; but Belinda brooded over
the story of that early marriage,—the stolen honeymoon, the sudden
parting. How dearly they must have loved each other, the young
bride and bridegroom, absorbed in their own happiness, and forgetful of all the outer world! She pictured Edward Arundel's face as it
must have been before care and sorrow had blotted out the brightest
attribute of his beauty. She thought of him, and pitied him, with
such tender sympathy, that by-and-by the thought of this young
man's sorrow seemed to shut almost every idea out of her mind. She
went about all her duties still, cheerfully and pleasantly, as it was her
nature to do everything; but the zest with which she had performed
every loving office—every act of sweet benevolence, seemed lost to
her now.

Remember that she was a simple country damsel, leading a quiet
life, whose peaceful course was almost as calm and eventless as the
existence of a cloister; a life so quiet that a decently-written romance
from the Swampington book-club was a thing to be looked forward
to with impatience, to read with breathless excitement, and to brood
upon afterwards for months. Was it strange, then, that this romance
in real life—this sweet story of love and devotion, with its sad
climax,—this story, the scene of which lay within a few miles of her
home, the hero of which was her father's constant guest,—was it
strange that this story, whose saddest charm was its truth, should
make a strong impression upon the mind of an innocent and
unworldly woman, and that day by day and hour by hour she should,
all unconsciously to herself, feel a stronger interest in the hero of the
tale?

She was interested in him. Alas! the truth must be set down, even if it has to be in the plain old commonplace words. *She fell in love with him.* But love in this innocent and womanly nature was so different a sentiment to that which had raged in Olivia's stormy breast, that even she who felt it was unconscious of its gradual birth. It was not 'an Adam at its birth,' by-the-by. It did not leap, Minerva-like,* from the brain; for I believe that love is born of the brain oftener than of the heart, being a strange compound of ideality, benevolence, and veneration. It came rather like the gradual dawning of a summer's day,—first a little patch of light far away in the east, very faint and feeble; then a slow widening of the rosy brightness; and at last a great blaze of splendour over all the width of the vast heavens. And then Miss Lawford grew more reserved in her intercourse with her friend's brother. Her frank good-nature gave place to a timid, shrinking bashfulness, that made her ten times more fascinating than she had been before. She was so very young, and had mixed so little with the world, that she had yet to learn the comedy of life. She had yet to learn to smile when she was sorry, or to look sorrowful when she was pleased, as prudence might dictate—to blush at will, or to grow pale when it was politic to sport the lily tint. She was a natural, artless, spontaneous creature; and she was utterly powerless to conceal her emotions, or to pretend a sentiment she did not feel. She blushed rosy red when Edward Arundel spoke to her suddenly. She betrayed herself by a hundred signs; mutely confessing her love almost as artlessly as Mary had revealed her affection a twelvemonth before. But if Edward saw this, he gave no sign of having made the discovery. His voice, perhaps, grew a little lower and softer in its tone when he spoke to Belinda; but there was a sad cadence in that low voice, which was too mournful for the accent of a lover. Sometimes, when his eyes rested for a moment on the girl's blushing face, a shadow would darken his own, and a faint quiver of emotion stir his lower lip; but it is impossible to say what this emotion may have been. Belinda hoped nothing, expected nothing. I repeat, that she was unconscious of the nature of her own feeling; and she had never for a moment thought of Edward otherwise than as a man who would go to his grave faithful to that sad love-story which had blighted the promise of his youth. She never thought of him otherwise than as Mary's constant mourner; she never hoped that time would alter his feelings or wear out his constancy; yet she loved him, notwithstanding.

All through July and August the young man visited at the Grange, and at the beginning of September Letitia Arundel went back to Dangerfield. But even then Edward was still a frequent guest at Major Lawford's; for his enthusiasm upon all military matters had made him a favourite with the old officer. But towards the end of September Mr Arundel's visits suddenly were restricted to an occasional call upon the Major; he left off dining at the Grange; his evening rambles in the gardens with Mrs Lawford and her blooming daughters—Belinda had no less than four blue-eyed sisters, all more or less resembling herself—ceased altogether, to the wonderment of every one in the old-fashioned country-house.

Edward Arundel shut out the new light which had dawned upon his life, and withdrew into the darkness. He went back to the stagnant monotony, the hopeless despondency, the bitter regret of his old existence.

'While my sister was at the Grange, I had an excuse for going there,' he said to himself sternly. 'I have no excuse now.'

But the old monotonous life was somehow or other a great deal more difficult to bear than it had been before. Nothing seemed to interest the young man now. Even the records of Indian victories were 'flat, stale, and unprofitable.'* He wondered as he remembered with what eager impatience he had once pined for the coming of the newspapers, with what frantic haste he had devoured every syllable of the Indian news. All his old feelings seemed to have gone away, leaving nothing in his mind but a blank waste, a weary sickness of life and all belonging to it. Leaving nothing else—positively nothing? 'No!' he answered, in reply to these mute questionings of his own spirit,—'no,' he repeated doggedly, 'nothing.'

It was strange to find what a blank was left in his life by reason of his abandonment of the Grange. It seemed as if he had suddenly retired from an existence full of pleasure and delight into the gloomy solitude of La Trappe.* And yet what was it that he had lost, after all? A quiet dinner at a country-house, and an evening spent half in the leafy silence of an old-fashioned garden, half in a pleasant drawing-room amongst a group of well-bred girls, and only enlivened by simple English ballads, or pensive melodies by Mendelssohn. It was not much to forego, surely. And yet Edward Arundel felt, in sacrificing these new acquaintances at the Grange to the stern purpose of his life, almost as if he had resigned a second captaincy for Mary's sake.

CHAPTER XXVIII

THE CHILD'S VOICE IN THE PAVILION BY THE WATER

THE year wore slowly on. Letitia Arundel wrote very long letters to her friend and confidante, Belinda Lawford, and in each letter demanded particular intelligence of her brother's doings. Had he been to the Grange? how had he looked? what had he talked about? &c., &c. But to these questions Miss Lawford could only return one monotonous reply: Mr Arundel had not been to the Grange; or Mr Arundel had called on papa one morning, but had only stayed a quarter of an hour, and had not been seen by any female member of the family.

The year wore slowly on. Edward endured his self-appointed solitude, and waited, waited, with a vengeful hatred for ever brooding in his breast, for the day of retribution. The year wore on, and the anniversary of the day upon which Mary ran away from the Towers, the 17th of October, came at last.

Paul Marchmont had declared his intention of taking possession of the Towers upon the day following this. The twelvemonth's probation which he had imposed upon himself had expired; every voice was loud in praise of his conscientious and honourable conduct. He had grown very popular during his residence at Kemberling. Tenant farmers looked forward to halcyon days under his dominion; to leases renewed on favourable terms; to repairs liberally executed; to everything that is delightful between landlord and tenant. Edward Arundel heard all this through his faithful servitor, Mr Morrison, and chafed bitterly at the news. This traitor was to be happy and prosperous, and to have the good word of honest men; while Mary lay in her unhallowed grave, and people shrugged their shoulders, half compassionately, half contemptuously, as they spoke of the mad heiress who had committed suicide.

Mr Morrison brought his master tidings of all Paul Marchmont's doings about this time. He was to take possession of the Towers on the 19th. He had already made several alterations in the arrangement of the different rooms. He had ordered new furniture from Swampington,—another man would have ordered it from London; but Mr Marchmont was bent upon being popular, and did not despise even the good opinion of a local tradesman,—and by several other acts, insignificant enough in themselves, had asserted his ownership of the mansion which had been the airy castle of Mary Marchmont's day-dreams ten years before.

The coming-in of the new master of Marchmont Towers was to be, take it altogether, a very grand affair. The Chorley-Castle foxhounds were to meet at eleven o'clock, upon the great grass-plat, or lawn, as it was popularly called, before the western front. The county gentry from far and near had been invited to a hunting breakfast. Open house was to be kept all day for rich and poor. Every male inhabitant of the district who could muster anything in the way of a mount was likely to join the friendly gathering. Poor Reynard* is decidedly England's most powerful leveller. All differences of rank and station, all distinctions which Mammon raises in every other quarter, melt away before the friendly contact of the hunting-field. The man who rides best is the best man; and the young butcher who makes light of sunk fences, and skims, bird-like, over bullfinches* and timber, may hold his own with the dandy heir to half the countryside. The cook at Marchmont Towers had enough to do to prepare for this great day. It was the first meet of the season, and in itself a solemn festival. Paul Marchmont knew this; and though the Cockney artist of Fitzroy Square knew about as much of fox-hunting as he did of the source of the Nile,* he seized upon the opportunity of making himself popular, and determined to give such a hunting-breakfast as had never been given within the walls of Marchmont Towers since the time of a certain rackety Hugh Marchmont, who had drunk himself to death early in the reign of George III. He spent the morning of the 17th in the steward's room, looking through the cellar-book with the old butler, selecting the wines that were to be drunk the following day, and planning the arrangements for the mass of visitors, who were to be entertained in the great stone entrance-hall, in the kitchens, in the housekeeper's room, in the servants' hall, in almost every chamber that afforded accommodation for a guest.

'You will take care that people get placed according to their rank,' Paul said to the grey-haired servant. 'You know everybody about here, I dare say, and will be able to manage so that we may give no offence.'

The gentry were to breakfast in the long dining-room and in the western drawing-room. Sparkling hocks and Burgundies, fragrant

Moselles, champagnes of choicest brand and rarest bouquet, were to flow like water for the benefit of the country gentlemen who should come to do honour to Paul Marchmont's installation. Great cases of comestibles had been sent by rail from Fortnum and Mason's; and the science of the cook at the Towers had been taxed to the utmost, in the struggles which she made to prove herself equal to the occasion. Twenty-one casks of ale, every cask containing twenty-one gallons, had been brewed long ago, at the birth of Arthur Marchmont, and had been laid in the cellar ever since, waiting for the majority of the young heir who was never to come of age. This very ale, with a certain sense of triumph, Paul Marchmont ordered to be brought forth for the refreshment of the commoners.

'Poor young Arthur!' he thought, after he had given this order. 'I saw him once when he was a pretty boy with fair ringlets, dressed in a suit of black velvet. His father brought him to my studio one day, when he came to patronise me and buy a picture of me,—out of sheer charity, of course, for he cared as much for pictures as I care for foxhounds. *I* was a poor relation then, and never thought to see the inside of Marchmont Towers. It was a lucky September morning that swept that bright-faced boy out of my pathway, and left only sickly John Marchmont and his daughter between me and fortune.'

Yes; Mr Paul Marchmont's year of probation was past. He had asserted himself to Messrs Paulette, Paulette, and Mathewson, and before the face of all Lincolnshire, in the character of an honourable and high-minded man; slow to seize upon the fortune that had fallen to him, conscientious, punctilious, generous, and unselfish. He had done all this; and now the trial was over, and the day of triumph had come.

There has been a race of villains of late years very popular with the novel-writer and the dramatist, but not, I think, quite indigenous to this honest British soil; a race of pale-faced, dark-eyed, and all-accomplished scoundrels, whose chiefest attribute is imperturbability. The imperturbable villain has been guilty of every iniquity in the black catalogue of crimes; but he has never been guilty of an emotion. He wins a million of money at *trente et quarante*,* to the terror and astonishment of all Homburg;* and by not so much as one twinkle of his eye or one quiver of his lip does that imperturbable creature betray a sentiment of satisfaction. Ruin or glory, shame or triumph, defeat, disgrace, or death,—all are alike to the callous ruffian of the Anglo-Gallic novel. He smiles, and murders while he smiles, and smiles while he murders. He kills his adversary, unfairly, in a duel, and wipes his sword on a cambric handkerchief; and withal he is so elegant, so fascinating, and so handsome, that the young hero of the novel has a very poor chance against him; and the reader can scarcely help being sorry when retribution comes with the last chapter, and some crushing catastrophe annihilates the well-bred scoundrel.

Paul Marchmont was not this sort of man. He was a hypocrite when it was essential to his own safety to practice hypocrisy; but he did not accept life as a drama, in which he was for ever to be acting a part. Life would scarcely be worth the having to any man upon such terms. It is all very well to wear heavy plate armour, and a casque that weighs fourteen pounds or so, when we go into the thick of the fight. But to wear the armour always, to live in it, to sleep in it, to carry the ponderous protection about us for ever and ever! Safety would be too dear if purchased by such a sacrifice of all personal ease. Paul Marchmont, therefore, being a selfish and self-indulgent man, only wore his armour of hypocrisy occasionally, and when it was vitally necessary for his preservation. He had imposed upon himself a penance, and acted a part in holding back for a year from the enjoyment of a splendid fortune; and he had made this one great sacrifice in order to give the lie to Edward Arundel's vague accusations, which might have had an awkward effect upon the minds of other people, had the artist grasped too eagerly at his missing cousin's wealth. Paul Marchmont had made this sacrifice; but he did not intend to act a part all his life. He meant to enjoy himself, and to get the fullest possible benefit out of his good fortune. He meant to do this; and upon the 17th of October he made no effort to restrain his spirits, but laughed and talked joyously with whoever came in his way, winning golden opinions from all sorts of men;* for happiness is contagious, and everybody likes happy people.

Forty years of poverty is a long apprenticeship to the very hardest of masters,—an apprenticeship calculated to give the keenest possible zest to newly-acquired wealth. Paul Marchmont rejoiced in his wealth with an almost delirious sense of delight. It was his at last. At last! He had waited, and waited patiently; and at last, while his powers of enjoyment were still in their zenith, it had come. How often he had dreamed of this; how often he had dreamed of that which was to take place to-morrow! How often in his dreams he had seen the stone-built mansion, and heard the voices of the crowd doing him honour. He had felt all the pride and delight of possession to awake suddenly in the midst of his triumph, and gnash his teeth at the remembrance of his poverty. And now the poverty was a thing to be dreamt about, and the wealth was his. He had always been a good son and a kind brother; and his mother and sister were to arrive upon the eve of his installation, and were to witness his triumph. The rooms that had been altered were those chosen by Paul for his mother and maiden sister, and the new furniture had been ordered for their comfort. It was one of his many pleasures upon this day to inspect these apartments, to see that all his directions had been faithfully carried out, and to speculate upon the effect which these spacious and luxurious chambers would have upon the minds of Mrs Marchmont and her daughter, newly come from shabby lodgings in Charlotte Street.

'My poor mother!' thought the artist, as he looked round the pretty sitting-room. This sitting-room opened into a noble bed-chamber, beyond which there was a dressing-room. 'My poor mother!' he thought; 'she has suffered a long time, and she has been patient. She has never ceased to believe in me; and she will see now that there was some reason for that belief. I told her long ago, when our fortunes were at the lowest ebb, when I was painting landscapes for the furniture-brokers at a pound a-piece,—I told her I was meant for something better than a tradesman's hack; and I have proved it— I have proved it.'

He walked about the room, arranging the furniture with his own hands; walking a few paces backwards now and then to contemplate such and such an effect from a artistic point of view; flinging the rich stuff of the curtains into graceful folds; admiring and examining everything, always with a smile on his face. He seemed thoroughly happy. If he had done any wrong; if by any act of treachery he had hastened Mary Arundel's death, no recollection of that foul work arose in his breast to disturb the pleasant current of his thoughts. Selfish and self-indulgent, only attached to those who were neces-sary to his own happiness, his thoughts rarely wandered beyond the narrow circle of his own cares or his own pleasures. He was thoroughly selfish. He could have sat at a Lord Mayor's feast with a famine-stricken population clamouring at the door of the banquet-chamber. He believed in himself as his mother and sister had believed; and he considered that he had a right to be happy and prosperous, whosoever suffered sorrow or adversity.

Upon this 17th of October Olivia Marchmont sat in the little study looking out upon the quadrangle, while the household was busied with the preparations for the festival of the following day. She was to remain at Marchmont Towers as a guest of the new master of the mansion. She would be protected from all scandal, Paul had said, by the presence of his mother and sister. She could retain the apartments she had been accustomed to occupy; she could pursue her old mode of life. He himself was not likely to be very much at the Towers. He was going to travel and to enjoy life now that he was a rich man.

These were the arguments which Mr Marchmont used when openly discussing the widow's residence in his house. But in a private conversation between Olivia and himself he had only said a very few words upon the subject.

'You *must* remain,' he said; and Olivia submitted, obeying him with a sullen indifference that was almost like the mechanical submission of an irresponsible being.

John Marchmont's widow seemed entirely under the dominion of the new master of the Towers. It was as if the stormy passions which had arisen out of a slighted love had worn out this woman's mind, and had left her helpless to stand against the force of Paul Marchmont's keen and vigorous intellect. A remarkable change had come over Olivia's character. A dull apathy had succeeded that fiery energy of soul which had enfeebled and well-nigh worn out her body. There were no outbursts of passion now. She bore the miserable monotony of her life uncomplainingly. Day after day, week after week, month after month, idle and apathetic, she sat in her lonely room, or wandered slowly in the grounds about the Towers. She very rarely went beyond those grounds. She was seldom seen now in her old pew at Kemberling Church; and when her father went to her and remonstrated with her for her non-attendance, she told him sullenly that she was too ill to go. She *was* ill. George Weston attended her constantly; but he found it very difficult to administer to such a sickness as hers, and he could only shake his head despondently when he felt her feeble pulse, or listened to the slow beating of her heart. Sometimes she would shut herself up in her room for a month at a time, and see no one but her faithful servant Barbara, and Mr Weston—whom, in her utter indifference, she seemed to regard as a kind of domestic animal, whose going or coming were alike unimportant.

This stolid, silent Barbara waited upon her mistress with untiring patience. She bore with every change of Olivia's gloomy temper; she was a perpetual shield and protection to her. Even upon this day of preparation and disorder Mrs Simmons kept guard over the passage leading to the study, and took care that no one intruded upon her mistress. At about four o'clock all Paul Marchmont's orders had been given, and the new master of the house dined for the first time by himself at the head of the long carved-oak dining-table, waited upon in solemn state by the old butler. His mother and sister were to arrive by a train that would reach Swampington at ten o'clock, and one of the carriages from the Towers was to meet them at the station. The artist had leisure in the meantime for any other business he might have to transact.

He ate his dinner slowly, thinking deeply all the time. He did not stop to drink any wine after dinner; but, as soon as the cloth was removed, rose from the table, and went straight to Olivia's room.

'I am going down to the painting-room,' he said. 'Will you come there presently? I want very much to say a few words to you.'

Olivia was sitting near the window, with her hands lying idle in her lap. She rarely opened a book now, rarely wrote a letter, or occupied herself in any manner. She scarcely raised her eyes as she answered him.

'Yes,' she said; 'I will come.'

'Don't be long, then. It will be dark very soon. I am not going down there to paint; I am going to fetch a landscape that I want to hang in my mother's room, and to say a few words about—'

He closed the door without stopping to finish the sentence, and went out into the quadrangle.

Ten minutes afterwards Olivia Marchmont rose, and taking a heavy woollen shawl from a chair near her, wrapped it loosely about her head and shoulders.

'I am his slave and his prisoner,' she muttered to herself. 'I must do as he bids me.'

A cold wind was blowing in the quadrangle, and the stone pavement was wet with a drizzling rain. The sun had just gone down, and the dull autumn sky was darkening. The fallen leaves in the wood were sodden with damp, and rotted slowly on the swampy ground.

Olivia took her way mechanically along the narrow pathway leading to the river. Half-way between Marchmont Towers and the boathouse she came suddenly upon the figure of a man walking towards her through the dusk. This man was Edward Arundel.

The two cousins had not met since the March evening upon which Edward had gone to seek the widow in Paul Marchmont's painting-room. Olivia's pale face grew whiter as she recognised the soldier.

'I was coming to the house to speak to you, Mrs Marchmont,' Edward said sternly. 'I am lucky in meeting you here, for I don't want any one to overhear what I've got to say.'

He had turned in the direction in which Olivia had been walking; but she made a dead stop, and stood looking at him.

'You were going to the boat-house,' he said. 'I will go there with you.'

She looked at him for a moment, as if doubtful what to do, and then said,

'Very well. You can say what you have to say to me, and then leave me. There is no sympathy between us, there is no regard between us; we are only antagonists.'

'I hope not, Olivia. I hope there is some spark of regard still, in spite of all. I separate you in my own mind from Paul Marchmont. I pity you; for I believe you to be his tool.'

'Is this what you have to say to me?'

'No; I came here, as your kinsman, to ask you what you mean to do now that Paul Marchmont has taken possession of the Towers?'

'I mean to stay there.'

'In spite of the gossip that your remaining will give rise to amongst these country-people!'

'In spite of everything. Mr Marchmont wishes me to stay. It suits me to stay. What does it matter what people say of me? What do I care for any one's opinion—now?'

'Olivia,' cried the young man, 'are you mad?'

'Perhaps I am,' she answered, coldly.

'Why is it that you shut yourself from the sympathy of those who have a right to care for you? What is the mystery of your life?'

His cousin laughed bitterly.

'Would you like to know, Edward Arundel?' she said. 'You *shall* know, perhaps, some day. You have despised me all my life; you will despise me more then.'

They had reached Paul Marchmont's painting-room by this time. Olivia opened the door and walked in, followed by Edward. Paul was not there. There was a picture covered with green-baize upon the easel, and the artist's hat stood upon the table amidst the litter of brushes and palettes; but the room was empty. The door at the top of the stone steps leading to the pavilion was ajar.

'Have you anything more to say to me?' Olivia asked, turning upon her cousin as if she would have demanded why he had followed her.

'Only this: I want to know your determination; whether you will be advised by me—and by your father,—I saw my uncle Hubert this morning, and his opinion exactly coincides with mine,—or whether you mean obstinately to take your own course in defiance of everybody?'

'I do,' Olivia answered. 'I shall take my own course. I defy everybody. I have not been gifted with the power of winning people's affection. Other women possess that power, and trifle with it, and turn it to bad account. I have prayed, Edward Arundel,—yes, I have prayed upon my knees to the God who made me, that He would give me some poor measure of that gift which Nature has lavished upon other women; but He would not hear me, He would not hear me! I was not made to be loved. Why, then, should I make myself a slave for the sake of winning people's esteem? If they have despised me, I can despise them.'

'Who has despised you, Olivia?' Edward asked, perplexed by his cousin's manner.

'YOU HAVE!' she cried, with flashing eyes; 'you have! From first to last—from first to last!' She turned away from him impatiently. 'Go,' she said; 'why should we keep up a mockery of friendliness and cousinship? We are nothing to each other.'

Edward walked towards the door; but he paused upon the threshold, with his hat in his hand, undecided as to what he ought to do.

As he stood thus, perplexed and irresolute, a cry, the feeble cry of a child, sounded within the pavilion.

The young man started, and looked at his cousin. Even in the dusk he could see that her face had suddenly grown livid.

'There is a child in that place,' he said pointing to the door at the top of the steps.

The cry was repeated as he spoke,—the low, complaining wail of a child. There was no other voice to be heard,—no mother's voice soothing a helpless little one. The cry of the child was followed by a dead silence.

'There is a child in that pavilion,' Edward Arundel repeated.

'There is,' Olivia answered.

'Whose child?'

'What does it matter to you?'

'Whose child?'

'I cannot tell you, Edward Arundel.'

The soldier strode towards the steps, but before he could reach them, Olivia flung herself across his pathway.

'I will see whose child is hidden in that place,' he said. 'Scandalous things have been said of you, Olivia I will know the reason of your visits to this place.'

She clung about his knees, and hindered him from moving; half kneeling, half crouching on the lowest of the stone steps, she blocked his pathway, and prevented him from reaching the door of the pavilion. It bad been ajar a few minutes ago; it was shut now. But Edward had not noticed this.

'No, no, no!' shrieked Olivia; 'you shall trample me to death before you enter that place. You shall walk over my corpse before you cross that threshold.'

The young man struggled with her for a few moments; then he suddenly flung her from him; not violently, but with a contemptuous gesture.

'You are a wicked woman, Olivia Marchmont,' he said; 'and it matters very little to me what you do, or what becomes of you. I know now the secret of the mystery between you and Paul Marchmont. I can guess your motive for perpetually haunting this place.'

He left the solitary building by the river, and walked slowly back through the wood.

His mind—predisposed to think ill of Olivia by the dark rumours he had heard through his servant, and which had had a certain amount of influence upon him, as all scandals have, however baseless—could imagine only one solution to the mystery of a child's presence in the lonely building by the river. Outraged and indignant at the discovery he had made, he turned his back upon Marchmont Towers.

'I will stay in this hateful place no longer,' he thought, as he went back to his solitary home; 'but before I leave Lincolnshire the whole county shall know what I think of Paul Marchmont.'

END OF VOL. II

CHAPTER XXIX

CAPTAIN ARUNDEL'S REVENGE

EDWARD ARUNDEL went back to his lonely home with a settled purpose in his mind. He would leave Lincolnshire,—and immediately. He had no motive for remaining. It may be, indeed, that he had a strong motive for going away from the neighbourhood of Lawford Grange. There was a lurking danger in the close vicinage of that pleasant, old-fashioned country mansion, and the bright band of blue-eyed damsels who inhabited there.

'I will turn my back upon Lincolnshire for ever,' Edward Arundel said to himself once more, upon his way homeward through the October twilight; 'but before I go, the whole country shall know what I think of Paul Marchmont.'

He clenched his fists and ground his teeth involuntarily as he thought this.

It was quite dark when he let himself in at the old-fashioned half-glass door that led into his humble sitting-room at Kemberling Retreat. He looked round the little chamber, which had been furnished forty years before by the proprietor of the cottage, and had served for one tenant after another, until it seemed as if the spindle-legged chairs and tables had grown attenuated and shadowy by much service. He looked at the simple room, lighted by a bright fire and a pair of wax-candles in antique silver candlesticks. The red firelight flickered and trembled upon the painted roses on the walls, on the obsolete engravings in clumsy frames of imitation-ebony and tarnished gilt. A silver tea-service and a Sèvres china cup and saucer, which Mrs Arundel had sent to the cottage for her son's use, stood upon the small oval table: and a brown setter, a favourite of the young man's, lay upon the hearth-rug, with his chin upon his outstretched paws, blinking at the blaze.

As Mr Arundel lingered in the doorway, looking at these things, an image rose before him, as vivid and distinct as any apparition of Professor Pepper's* manufacture; and he thought of what that commonplace cottage-chamber might have been if his young wife had lived. He could fancy her bending over the low silver teapot,— the sprawling inartistic teapot, that stood upon quaint knobs like gouty feet, and had been long ago banished from the Dangerfield breakfast-table as utterly rococo and ridiculous. He conjured up the dear dead face, with faint blushes flickering amidst its lily pallor, and soft hazel eyes looking up at him through the misty steam of the tea-table, innocent and virginal as the eyes of that mythic nymph* who was wont to appear to the old Roman king. How happy she would have been! How willing to give up fortune and station, and to have lived for ever and ever in that queer old cottage, ministering to him and loving him!

Presently the face changed. The hazel-brown hair was suddenly lit up with a glitter of barbaric gold; the hazel eyes grew blue and bright; and the cheeks blushed rosy red. The young man frowned at this new and brighter vision; but he contemplated it gravely for some moments, and then breathed a long sigh, which was somehow or other expressive of relief.

'No,' he said to himself, 'I am *not* false to my poor lost girl; I do *not* forget her. Her image is dearer to me than any living creature. The mournful shadow of her face is more precious to me than the brightest reality.'

He sat down in one of the spindle-legged armchairs, and poured out a cup of tea. He drank it slowly, brooding over the fire as he sipped the innocuous beverage, and did not deign to notice the caresses of the brown setter, who laid his cold wet nose in his master's hand, and performed a species of spirit-rapping upon the carpet with his tail.

After tea the young man rang the bell, which was answered by Mr Morrison.

'Have I any clothes that I can hunt in, Morrison?' Mr Arundel asked.

His factotum stared aghast at this question.

'You ain't a-goin' to 'unt, are you, Mr Edward?' he inquired, anxiously.

'Never mind that. I asked you a question about my clothes, and I want a straightforward answer.'

'But, Mr Edward,' remonstrated the old servant, 'I don't mean no offence; and the 'orses is very tidy animals in their way; but if you're thinkin' of goin' across country,—and a pretty stiffish country too, as I've heard, in the way of bullfinches and timber,—neither of them 'orses has any more of a 'unter in him than I have.'

'I know that as well as you do,' Edward Arundel answered coolly; 'but I am going to the meet at Marchmont Towers to-morrow morning, and I want you to look me out a decent suit of clothes—that's all. You can have Desperado saddled ready for me a little after eleven o'clock.'

Mr Morrison looked even more astonished than before. He knew his master's savage enmity towards Paul Marchmont; and yet that very master now deliberately talked of joining in an assembly which was to gather together for the special purpose of doing the same Paul Marchmont honour. However, as he afterwards remarked to the two fellow-servants with whom he sometimes condescended to be familiar, it wasn't his place to interfere or to ask any questions, and he had held his tongue accordingly.

Perhaps this respectful reticence was rather the result of prudence than of inclination; for there was a dangerous light in Edward Arundel's eyes upon this particular evening which Mr Morrison never had observed before.

The factotum said something about this later in the evening.

'I do really think,' he remarked, 'that, what with that young 'ooman's death, and the solitood of this most dismal place, and the rainy weather,—which those as says it always rains in Lincolnshire ain't far out,—my poor young master is not the man he were.'

He tapped his forehead ominously to give significance to his words, and sighed heavily over his supper-beer.

The sun shone upon Paul Marchmont on the morning of the 18th of October. The autumn sunshine streamed into his bedchamber, and awoke the new master of Marchmont Towers. He opened his eyes and looked about him. He raised himself amongst the down pillows, and contemplated the figures upon the tapestry in a drowsy reverie. He had been dreaming of his poverty, and had been disputing a poor-rate* summons with an impertinent tax-collector in the dingy passage of the house in Charlotte Street, Fitzroy Square. Ah! that horrible house had so long been the only scene of his life, that it had grown almost a part of his mind, and haunted him perpetually in his sleep, like a nightmare of brick and mortar, now that he was rich, and had done with it for ever.

Mr Marchmont gave a faint shudder, and shook off the influence of the bad dream. Then, propped up by the pillows, he amused himself by admiring his new bedchamber.

It was a handsome room, certainly—the very room for an artist and a sybarite. Mr Marchmont had not chosen it without due consideration. It was situated in an angle of the house; and though its chief windows looked westward, being immediately above those of the western drawing-room, there was another casement, a great oriel window, facing the east, and admitting all the grandeur of the morning sun through painted glass, on which the Marchmont escutcheon was represented in gorgeous hues of sapphire and ruby, emerald and topaz, amethyst and aqua-marine. Bright splashes of these colours flashed and sparkled on the polished oaken floor, and mixed themselves with the Oriental gaudiness of a Persian carpet, stretched beneath the low Arabian bed, which was hung with ruby-coloured draperies that trailed upon the ground. Paul Marchmont was fond of splendour, and meant to have as much of it as money could buy. There was a voluptuous pleasure in all this finery, which only a parvenu could feel; it was the sharpness of the contrast between the magnificence of the present and the shabby miseries of the past that gave a piquancy to the artist's enjoyment of his new habitation.

All the furniture and draperies of the chamber had been made by Paul Marchmont's direction; but its chief beauty was the tapestry that covered the walls, which had been worked, two hundred and fifty years before, by a patient chatelaine of the House of Marchmont. This tapestry lined the room on every side. The low door had been cut in it; so that a stranger going into that apartment at night, a little under the influence of the Marchmont cellars, and unable to register the topography of the chamber upon the tablet of his memory, might have been sorely puzzled to find an exit the next morning. Most tapestried chambers have a certain dismal grimness about them, which is more pleasant to the sightseer than to the constant inhabitant; but in this tapestry the colours were almost as bright and glowing to-day as when the fingers that had handled the variegated worsteds were still warm and flexible. The subjects, too, were of a more pleasant order than usual. No mailed ruffians or drapery-clad barbarians menaced the unoffending sleeper with uplifted clubs, or horrible bolts, in the very act of being launched from ponderous crossbows; no wicked-looking Saracens, with ferocious eyes and copper-coloured visages, brandished murderous scimitars above their turbaned heads. No; here all was pastoral gaiety and peaceful delight. Maidens, with flowing kirtles and crisped yellow hair, danced before great waggons loaded with golden wheat. Youths, in red and purple jerkins, frisked as they played the pipe and tabor. The Flemish horses dragging the heavy wain were hung with bells and garlands as for a rustic festival, and tossed their untrimmed manes into the air, and frisked and gambolled with their awkward legs, in ponderous imitation of the youths and maidens. Afar off, in the distance, wonderful villages, very queer as to perspective, but all a-bloom with gaudy flowers and quaint roofs of bright-red tiles, stood boldly out against a bluer sky than the most enthusiastic pre-Raphaelite of to-day would care to send to the Academy in Trafalgar Square.*

Paul Marchmont smiled at the youths and maidens, the laden wagons, the revellers, and the impossible village. He was in a humour to be pleased with everything to-day. He looked at his dressing-table, which stood opposite to him, in the deep oriel window. His valet—he had a valet now—had opened the great inlaid dressing-case, and the silver-gilt fittings reflected the crimson hues of the velvet lining, as if the gold had been flecked with blood. Glittering bottles of diamond-cut glass, that presented a thousand facets to the morning light, stood like crystal obelisks amid the litter of carved-ivory brushes and Sèvres boxes of pomatum; and one rare hothouse flower, white and fragile, peeped out of a slender crystal vase, against a background of dark shining leaves.

'It's better than Charlotte Street, Fitzroy Square,' said Mr Marchmont, throwing himself back amongst the pillows until such time as his valet should bring him a cup of strong tea to refresh and invigorate his nerves withal. 'I remember the paper in my room: drab hexagons and yellow spots upon a brown ground. *So* pretty! And then the dressing-table: deal, gracefully designed; with a shallow drawer, in which my razors used to rattle like castanets when I tried to pull it open; a most delicious table, exquisitely painted in stripes, olive-green upon stone colour, picked out with the favourite brown. Oh, it was a most delightful life; but it's over, thank Providence; it's over!'

Mr Paul Marchmont thanked Providence as devoutly as if he had been the most patient attendant upon the Divine pleasure, and had never for one moment dreamed of intruding his own impious handiwork amid the mysterious designs of Omnipotence.

The sun shone upon the new master of Marchmont Towers. This bright October morning was not the very best for hunting purposes; for there was a fresh breeze blowing from the north, and a blue unclouded sky. But it was most delightful weather for the breakfast, and the assembling on the lawn, and all the pleasant preliminaries of the day's sport. Mr Paul Marchmont, who was a thorough-bred Cockney, troubled himself very little about the hunt as he basked in that morning light. He only thought that the sun was shining upon him, and that he had come at last—no matter by what crooked ways—to the realisation of his great day-dream, and that he was to be happy and prosperous for the rest of his life.

He drank his tea, and then got up and dressed himself. He wore the conventional 'pink,'* the whitest buckskins, the most approved boots and tops; and he admired himself very much in the cheval glass when this toilet was complete. He had put on the dress for the gratification of his vanity, rather than from any serious intention of doing what he was about as incapable of doing, as he was of becoming a modern Rubens or a new Raphael. He would receive his friends in this costume, and ride to cover, and follow the hounds, perhaps,— a little way. At any rate, it was very delightful to him to play the country gentleman; and he had never felt so much a country gentleman as at this moment, when he contemplated himself from head to heel in his hunting costume.

At ten o'clock the guests began to assemble; the meet was not to take place until twelve, so that there might be plenty of time for the breakfast.

I don't think Paul Marchmont ever really knew what took place at that long table, at which he sat for the first time in the place of host and master. He was intoxicated from the first with the sense of triumph and delight in his new position; and he drank a great deal, for he drank unconsciously, emptying his glass every time it was filled, and never knowing who filled it, or what was put into it. By this means he took a very considerable quantity of various sparkling and effervescing wines; sometimes hock, sometimes Moselle, very often champagne, to say nothing of a steady undercurrent of unpronounceable German hocks and crusted Burgundies. But he was not drunk after the common fashion of mortals; he could not be upon this particular day. He was not stupid, or drowsy, or unsteady upon his legs; he was only preternaturally excited, looking at everything through a haze of dazzling light, as if all the gold of his newly-acquired fortune had been melted into the atmosphere.

He knew that the breakfast was a great success; that the long table was spread with every delicious comestible that the science of a first-rate cook, to say nothing of Fortnum and Mason, could devise; that the profusion of splendid silver, the costly china, the hothouse flowers, and the sunshine, made a confused mass of restless glitter and glowing colour that dazzled his eyes as he looked at it. He knew that everybody courted and flattered him, and that he was almost stifled by the overpowering sense of his own grandeur. Perhaps he felt this most when a certain county magnate, a baronet, member of Parliament, and great landowner, rose,—primed with champagne, and rather thicker of utterance than a man should be who means to be in at the death, by-and-by,—and took the opportunity of— hum—expressing, in a few words,—haw—the very great pleasure which he—aw, yes—and he thought he might venture to remark,— aw—everybody about him—ha—felt on this most—arrah; arrah— interesting—er—occasion; and said a great deal more, which took a very long time to say, but the gist of which was, that all these country gentlemen were so enraptured by the new addition to their circle, and so altogether delighted with Mr Paul Marchmont, that they really were at a loss to understand how it was they had ever managed to endure existence without him.

And then there was a good deal of rather unnecessary but very enthusiastic thumping of the table, whereat the costly glass shivered, and the hothouse blossoms trembled, amidst the musical chinking of silver forks; while the foxhunters declared in chorus that the new owner of Marchmont Towers was a jolly good fellow, which—*i.e.*, the fact of his jollity—nobody could deny.

It was not a very fine demonstration, but it was a very hearty one. Moreover, these noisy fox-hunters were all men of some standing in the county; and it is a proof of the artist's inherent snobbery that to him the husky voices of these half-drunken men were more delicious than the sweet soprano tones of an equal number of Pattis*— penniless and obscure Pattis, that is to say—sounding his praises. He was lifted at last out of that poor artist-life, in which he had always been a groveller,—not so much for lack of talent as by reason of the smallness of his own soul,—into a new sphere, where everybody was rich and grand and prosperous, and where the pleasant pathways were upon the necks of prostrate slaves, in the shape of grooms and hirelings, respectful servants, and reverential tradespeople.

Yes, Paul Marchmont was more drunken than any of his guests; but his drunkenness was of a different kind to theirs. It was not the wine, but his own grandeur that intoxicated and besotted him.

These foxhunters might get the better of their drunkenness in half an hour or so; but his intoxication was likely to last for a very long time, unless he should receive some sudden shock, powerful enough to sober him.

Meanwhile the hounds were yelping and baying upon the lawn, and the huntsmen and whippers-in were running backwards and forwards from the lawn to the servants' hall, devouring snacks of beef and ham,—a pound and a quarter or so at one sitting; or crunching the bones of a frivolous young chicken,—there were not half a dozen mouthfuls on such insignificant half-grown fowls; or excavating under the roof of a great game-pie; or drinking a quart or so of strong ale, or half a tumbler of raw brandy, *en passant*; and doing a great deal more in the same way, merely to beguile the time until the gentlefolks should appear upon the broad stone terrace.

It was half-past twelve o'clock, and Mr Marchmont's guests were still drinking and speechifying. They had been on the point of making a move ever so many times; but it had happened every time that some gentleman, who had been very quiet until that moment, suddenly got upon his legs, and began to make swallowing and gasping noises, and to wipe his lips with a napkin; whereby it was understood that he was going to propose somebody's health. This had considerably lengthened the entertainment, and it seemed rather likely that the ostensible business of the day would be forgotten altogether. But at half-past twelve, the county magnate, who had bidden Paul Marchmont a stately welcome to Lincolnshire, remembered that there were twenty couple of impatient hounds scratching up the turf in front of the long windows of the banquet-chamber, while as many eager young tenant-farmers, stalwart yeomen, well-to-do butchers, and a herd of tag-rag and bobtail, were pining for the sport to begin;—at last, I say, Sir Lionel Boport remembered this, and led the way to the terrace, leaving the renegades to repose on the comfortable sofas lurking here and there in the spacious rooms. Then the grim stone front of the house was suddenly lighted up into splendour. The long terrace was one blaze of 'pink,' relieved here and there by patches of sober black and forester's green. Amongst all these stalwart, florid-visaged country gentlemen, Paul Marchmont, very elegant, very picturesque, but extremely unsportsmanlike, the hero of the hour, walked slowly down the broad stone steps amidst the vociferous cheering of the crowd, the snapping and yelping of impatient hounds, and the distant braying of a horn.

It was the crowning moment of his life; the moment he had dreamed of again and again in the wretched days of poverty and obscurity. The scene was scarcely new to him,—he had acted it so often in his imagination; he had heard the shouts and seen the respectful crowd. There was a little difference in detail; that was all. There was no disappointment, no shortcoming in the realisation; as there so often is when our brightest dreams are fulfilled, and the one great good, the all-desired, is granted to us. No; the prize was his, and it was worth all that he had sacrificed to win it.

He looked up, and saw his mother and his sisters in the great window over the porch. He could see the exultant pride in his mother's pale face; and the one redeeming sentiment of his nature, his love for the womankind who depended upon him, stirred faintly in his breast, amid the tumult of gratified ambition and selfish joy.

This one drop of unselfish pleasure filled the cup to the brim. He took off his hat and waved it high up above his head in answer to the shouting of the crowd. He had stopped halfway down the flight of steps to bow his acknowledgment of the cheering. He waved his hat, and the huzzas grew still louder; and a band upon the other side of the lawn played that familiar and triumphant march* which is supposed to apply to every living hero, from a Wellington just come home from Waterloo, to the winner of a boat-race, or a patent-starch proprietor newly elected by an admiring constituency.

There was nothing wanting. I think that in that supreme moment Paul Marchmont quite forgot the tortuous and perilous ways by which he had reached this all-glorious goal. I don't suppose the young princes smothered in the Tower were ever more palpably present in Tyrant Richard's memory than when the murderous usurper grovelled in Bosworth's miry clay, and knew that the great game of life was lost. It was only when Henry the Eighth took away the Great Seal that Wolsey was able to see the foolishness of man's ambition. In that moment memory and conscience, never very wakeful in the breast of Paul Marchmont, were dead asleep, and only triumph and delight reigned in their stead. No; there was nothing wanting. This glory and grandeur paid him a thousandfold for his patience and self-abnegation during the past year.

He turned half round to look up at those eager watchers at the window.

Good God! It was his sister Lavinia's face he saw; no longer full of triumph and pleasure, but ghastly pale, and staring at someone or something horrible in the crowd. Paul Marchmont turned to look for this horrible something the sight of which had power to change his sister's face; and found himself confronted by a young man,—a young man whose eyes flamed like coals of fire, whose cheeks were as white as a sheet of paper, and whose firm lips were locked as tightly as if they had been chiselled out of a block of granite.

This man was Edward Arundel,—the young widower, the handsome soldier,—whom everybody remembered as the husband of poor lost Mary Marchmont.

He had sprung out from amidst the crowd only one moment before, and had dashed up the steps of the terrace before any one had time to think of hindering him or interfering with him. It seemed to Paul Marchmont as if his foe must have leaped out of the solid earth, so sudden and so unlooked-for was his coming. He stood upon the step immediately below the artist; but as the terrace-steps were shallow, and as he was taller by half a foot than Paul, the faces of the two men were level, and they confronted each other.

The soldier held a heavy hunting-whip in his hand—no foppish toy, with a golden trinket for its head, but a stout handle of staghorn, and a formidable leathern thong. He held this whip in his strong right hand, with the thong twisted round the handle; and throwing out his left arm, nervous and muscular as the limb of a young gladiator, he seized Paul Marchmont by the collar of that fashionably-cut scarlet coat which the artist had so much admired in the cheval-glass that morning.

There was a shout of surprise and consternation from the gentlemen on the terrace and the crowd upon the lawn, a shrill scream from the women; and in the next moment Paul Marchmont was writhing under a shower of blows from the hunting-whip in Edward Arundel's hand. The artist was not physically brave, yet he was not such a cur as to submit unresistingly to this hideous disgrace; but the attack was so sudden and unexpected as to paralyse him—so rapid in its execution as to leave him no time for resistance. Before he had recovered his presence of mind; before he knew the meaning of Edward Arundel's appearance in that place; even before he could fully realise the mere fact of his being there,—the thing was done; he was disgraced for ever. He had sunk in that one moment from the very height of his new grandeur to the lowest depth of social degradation.

'Gentlemen!' Edward Arundel cried, in a loud voice, which was distinctly heard by every member of the gaping crowd, 'when the law of the land suffers a scoundrel to prosper, honest men must take the law into their own hands. I wished you to know my opinion of the new master of Marchmont Towers; and I think I've expressed it pretty clearly. I know him to be a most consummate villain; and I give you fair warning that he is no fit associate for honourable men. Good morning.'

Edward Arundel lifted his hat, bowed to the assembly, and then ran down the steps. Paul Marchmont, livid, and foaming at the mouth, rushed after him, brandishing his clenched fists, and gesticulating in impotent rage; but the young man's horse was waiting for him at a few paces from the terrace, in the care of a butcher's apprentice, and he was in the saddle before the artist could overtake him.

'I shall not leave Kemberling for a week, Mr Marchmont,' he called out; and then he walked his horse away, holding himself erect as a dart, and staring defiance at the crowd.

I am sorry to have to testify to the fickle nature of the British populace; but I am bound to own that a great many of the stalwart yeomen who had eaten game-pies and drunk strong liquors at Paul Marchmont's expense not half an hour before, were base enough to feel an involuntary admiration for Edward Arundel, as he rode slowly away, with his head up and his eyes flaming. There is seldom very much genuine sympathy for a man who has been horsewhipped; and there is a pretty universal inclination to believe that the man who inflicts chastisement upon him must be right in the main. It is true that the tenant-farmers, especially those whose leases were nearly run out, were very loud in their indignation against Mr Arundel, and one adventurous spirit made a dash at the young man's bridle as he went by; but the general feeling was in favour of the conqueror, and there was a lack of heartiness even in the loudest expressions of sympathy.

The crowd made a lane for Paul Marchmont as he went back to the house, white and helpless, and sick with shame.

Several of the gentlemen upon the terrace came forward to shake hands with him, and to express their indignation, and to offer any friendly service that he might require of them by-and-by,—such as standing by to see him shot, if he should choose an old-fashioned mode of retaliation; or bearing witness against Edward Arundel in a law-court, if Mr Marchmont preferred to take legal measures. But even these men recoiled when they felt the cold dampness of the artist's hands, and saw that *he had been frightened*. These sturdy, uproarious foxhunters, who braved the peril of sudden death every time they took a day's sport, entertained a sovereign contempt for a man who *could* be frightened of anybody or anything. They made no allowance for Paul Marchmont's Cockney education; they were not in the dark secrets of his life and knew nothing of his guilty conscience; and it was *that* which had made him more helpless than a child in the fierce grasp of Edward Arundel.

So one by one, after this polite show of sympathy, the rich man's guests fell away from him; and the yelping hounds and the cantering horses left the lawn before Marchmont Towers; the sound of the brass band and the voices of the people died away in the distance; and the glory of the day was done.

Paul Marchmont crawled slowly back to that luxurious bed-chamber which he had left only a few hours before, and, throwing himself at full length upon the bed, sobbed like a frightened child.

He was panic-stricken; not because of the horsewhipping, but because of a sentence that Edward Arundel had whispered close to his ear in the midst of the struggle.

'I know *everything*,' the young man had said; 'I know the secrets you hide in the pavilion by the river!'

CHAPTER XXX

THE DESERTED CHAMBERS

EDWARD ARUNDEL kept his word. He waited for a week and upwards, but Paul Marchmont made no sign; and after having given him three days' grace over and above the promised time, the young man abandoned Kemberling Retreat, for ever, as he thought, and went away from Lincolnshire.

He had waited; hoping that Paul Marchmont would try to retaliate, and that some desperate struggle, physical or legal,—he scarcely cared which,—would occur between them. He would have courted any hazard which might have given him some chance of revenge. But nothing happened. He sent out Mr Morrison to beat up information about the master of Marchmont Towers; and the factotum came back with the intelligence that Mr Marchmont was ill, and would see no one—'leastways' excepting his mother and Mr George Weston.

Edward Arundel shrugged his shoulders when he heard these tidings.

'What a contemptible cur the man is!' he thought. 'There was a time when I could have suspected him of any foul play against my lost girl. I know him better now, and know that he is not even capable of a great crime. He was only strong enough to stab his victim in the dark, with lying paragraphs in newspapers, and dastardly hints and innuendoes.'

It would have been only perhaps an act of ordinary politeness had Edward Arundel paid a farewell visit to his friends at the Grange. But he did not go near the hospitable old house. He contented himself with writing a cordial letter to Major Lawford, thanking him for his hospitality and kindness, and referring, vaguely enough, to the hope of a future meeting.

He despatched this letter by Mr Morrison, who was in very high spirits at the prospect of leaving Kemberling, and who went about his work with almost boyish activity in the exuberance of his delight. The valet worked so briskly as to complete all necessary arrangements in a couple of days; and on the 29th of October, late in the afternoon, all was ready, and he had nothing to do but to superintend the departure of the two horses from the Kemberling railway-station, under the guardianship of the lad who had served as Edward's groom.

Throughout that last day Mr Arundel wandered here and there about the house and garden that so soon were to be deserted. He was dreadfully at a loss what to do with himself, and, alas! it was not to-day only that he felt the burden of his hopeless idleness. He felt it always; a horrible load, not to be cast away from him. His life had been broken off short, as it were, by the catastrophe which had left him a widower before his honeymoon was well over. The story of his existence was abruptly broken asunder; all the better part of his life was taken away from him, and he did not know what to do with the blank and useless remnant. The ravelled threads of a once-harmonious web, suddenly wrenched in twain, presented a mass of inextricable confusion; and the young man's brain grew dizzy when he tried to draw them out, or to consider them separately.

His life was most miserable, most hopeless, by reason of its empti-ness. He had no duty to perform, no task to achieve. That nature must be utterly selfish, entirely given over to sybarite rest and self-indulgence, which does not feel a lack of something wanting these,—a duty or a purpose. Better to be Sisyphus* toiling up the mountain-side, than Sisyphus with the stone taken away from him, and no hope of ever reaching the top. I heard a man once—a bill-sticker, and not by any means a sentimental or philosophical person—declare that he had never known real prosperity until he had thirteen orphan grandchildren to support; and surely there was a universal moral in that bill-sticker's confession. He had been a drunkard before, perhaps,—he didn't say anything about that,—and a reprobate, it may be; but those thirteen small mouths clamoring for food made him sober and earnest, brave and true. He had a duty to do, and was happy in its performance. He was wanted in the world, and he was somebody. From Napoleon III, holding the destinies of civilised Europe in his hands, and debating whether he shall re-create Poland or build a new boulevard, to Paterfamilias in a Government office, working for the little ones at home,—and from Paterfamilias to the crossing-sweeper; who craves his diurnal halfpenny from busy citi-zens, tramping to their daily toil,—every man has his separate labour and his different responsibility. For ever and for ever the busy wheel of life turns round; but duty and ambition are the motive powers that keep it going.

Edward Arundel felt the barrenness of his life, now that he had taken the only revenge which was possible for him upon the man who had persecuted his wife. *That* had been a rapturous but brief enjoyment. It was over. He could do no more to the man; since there was no lower depth of humiliation—in these later days, when pillories and whipping-posts and stocks are exploded from our market-places—to which a degraded creature could descend. No; there was no more to be done. It was useless to stop in Lincolnshire. The sad suggestion of the little slipper found by the water-side was but too true. Paul Marchmont had not murdered his helpless cousin; he had only tortured her to death. He was quite safe from the law of the land, which, being of a positive and arbitrary nature, takes no cognisance of indefinable offences. This most infamous man was safe; and was free to enjoy his ill-gotten grandeur—if he could take much pleasure in it, after the scene upon the stone terrace.

The only joy that had been left for Edward Arundel after his retirement from the East India Company's service was this fierce delight of vengeance. He had drained the intoxicating cup to the dregs, and had been drunken at first in the sense of his triumph. But he was sober now; and he paced up and down the neglected garden beneath a chill October sky, crunching the fallen leaves under his feet, with his arms folded and his head bent, thinking of the barren future. It was all bare,—a blank stretch of desert land, with no city in the distance; no purple domes or airy minarets on the horizon. It was in the very nature of this young man to be a soldier; and he was nothing if not a soldier. He could never remember having had any other aspiration than that eager thirst for military glory. Before he knew the meaning of the word 'war,' in his very infancy, the sound of a trumpet or the sight of a waving banner, a glittering weapon, a sentinel's scarlet coat, had moved him to a kind of rapture. The unvarnished schoolroom records of Greek and Roman warfare had been as delightful to him as the finest passages of a Macaulay or a Froude, a Thiers or Lamartine.* He was a soldier by the inspiration of Heaven, as all great soldiers are. He had never known any other ambition, or dreamed any other dream. Other lads had talked of the bar, and the senate, and *their* glories. Bah! how cold and tame they seemed! What was the glory of a parliamentary triumph, in which words were the only weapons wielded by the combatants, compared with a hand-to-hand struggle, ankle deep in the bloody mire of a crowded trench, or a cavalry charge, before which a phalanx of fierce Afghans fled like frightened sheep upon a moor! Edward Arundel was a soldier, like the Duke of Wellington or Sir Colin Campbell,* —one writes the old romantic name involuntarily, because one loves it best,—or Othello.* The Moor's first lamentation when he believes that Desdemona is false, and his life is broken, is that sublime farewell to all the glories of the battle-field. It was almost the same with Edward Arundel. The loss of his wife and of his captaincy were blent and mingled in his mind and he could only bewail the one great loss which left life most desolate.

He had never felt the full extent of his desolation until now; for heretofore he had been buoyed up by the hope of vengeance upon Paul Marchmont; and now that his solitary hope had been realised to the fullest possible extent, there was nothing left,—nothing but to revoke the sacrifice he had made, and to regain his place in the Indian army at any cost.

He tried not to think of the possibility of this. It seemed to him almost an infidelity towards his dead wife to dream of winning honours and distinction, now that she, who would have been so proud of any triumph won by him, was for ever lost.

So, under the grey October sky he paced up and down upon the grass-grown pathways, amidst the weeds and briars, the brambles and broken branches that crackled as he trod upon them; and late in the afternoon, when the day, which had been sunless and cold, was melting into dusky twilight, he opened the low wooden gateway and went out into the road. An impulse which he could not resist took him towards the river-bank and the wood behind Marchmont Towers. Once more, for the last time in his life perhaps, he went down to that lonely shore. He went to look at the bleak unlovely place which had been the scene of his betrothal.

It was not that he had any thought of meeting Olivia Marchmont; he had dismissed her from his mind ever since his last visit to the lonely boat-house. Whatever the mystery of her life might be, her secret lay at the bottom of a black depth which the impetuous soldier did not care to fathom. He did not want to discover that hideous secret. Tarnished honour, shame, falsehood, disgrace, lurked in the obscurity in which John Marchmont's widow had chosen to enshroud her life. Let them rest. It was not for him to drag away the curtain that sheltered his kinswoman from the world.

He had no thought, therefore, of prying into any secrets that might be hidden in the pavilion by the water. The fascination that lured him to the spot was the memory of the past. He could not go to Mary's grave; but he went, in as reverent a spirit as he would have gone thither, to the scene of his betrothal, to pay his farewell visit to the spot which had been for ever hallowed by the confession of her innocent love.

It was nearly dark when he got to the riverside. He went by a path which quite avoided the grounds about Marchmont Towers,—a narrow footpath, which served as a towing-path sometimes, when some black barge crawled by on its way out to the open sea. To-night the river was hidden by a mist,—a white fog,—that obscured land and water; and it was only by the sound of the horses' hoofs that Edward Arundel had warning to step aside, as a string of them went by, dragging a chain that grated on the pebbles by the river-side.

'Why should they say my darling committed suicide?' thought Edward Arundel, as he groped his way along the narrow pathway. 'It was on such an evening as this that she ran away from home. What more likely than that she lost the track, and wandered into the river? Oh, my own poor lost one, God grant it was so! God grant it was by His will, and not your own desperate act, that you were lost to me!'

Sorrowful as the thought of his wife's death was to him, it soothed him to believe that death might have been accidental. There was all the difference betwixt sorrow and despair in the alternative.

Wandering ignorantly and helplessly through this autumnal fog, Edward Arundel found himself at the boat-house before he was aware of its vicinity.

There was a light gleaming from the broad north window of the painting-room, and a slanting line of light streamed out of the half-open door. In this lighted doorway Edward saw the figure of a girl,—an unkempt, red-headed girl, with a flat freckled face; a girl who wore a lavender-cotton pinafore and hob-nailed boots, with a good deal of brass about the leathern fronts, and a redundancy of rusty leathern bootlace twisted round the ankles.

The young man remembered having seen this girl once in the village of Kemberling. She had been in Mrs Weston's service as a drudge, and was supposed to have received her education in the Swampington union.*

This young lady was supporting herself against the half-open door, with her arms a-kimbo, and her hands planted upon her hips, in humble imitation of the matrons whom she had been wont to see lounging at their cottage-doors in the high street of Kemberling, when the labours of the day were done.

Edward Arundel started at the sudden apparition of this damsel.

'Who are you, girl?' he asked; 'and what brings you to this place?'

He trembled as he spoke. A sudden agitation had seized upon him, which he had no power to account for. It seemed as if Providence had brought him to this spot to-night, and had placed this ignorant country-girl in his way, for some special purpose. Whatever the secrets of this place might be, he was to know them, it appeared, since he had been led here, not by the promptings of curiosity, but only by a reverent love for a scene that was associated with his dead wife.

'Who are you, girl?' he asked again.

'Oi be Betsy Murrel, sir,' the damsel answered; 'some on 'em calls me "Wuk-us Bet;" and I be coom here to cle-an oop a bit.'

'To clean up what?'

'The paa-intin' room. There's a de-al o' moock aboot, and aw'm to fettle oop, and make all toidy agen t' squire gets well.'

'Are you all alone here?'

'All alo-an? Oh, yes, sir.'

'Have you been here long?'

The girl looked at Mr Arundel with a cunning leer, which was one of her 'wuk-us' acquirements.

'Aw've bin here off an' on ever since t' squire ke-ame,' she said. 'There's a deal o' cleanin' down 'ere.'

Edward Arundel looked at her sternly; but there was nothing to be gathered from her stolid countenance after its agreeable leer had melted away. The young man might have scrutinised the figure-head of the black barge creeping slowly past upon the hidden river with quite as much chance of getting any information out of its play of feature.

He walked past the girl into Paul Marchmont's painting-room. Miss Betsy Murrel made no attempt to hinder him. She had spoken the truth as to the cleaning of the place, for the room smelt of soapsuds, and a pail and scrubbing-brush stood in the middle of the floor. The young man looked at the door behind which he had heard the crying of the child. It was ajar, and the stone-steps leading up to it were wet, bearing testimony to Betsy Murrel's industry.

Edward Arundel took the flaming tallow-candle from the table in the painting-room, and went up the steps into the pavilion. The girl followed, but she did not try to restrain him, or to interfere with him. She followed him with her mouth open, staring at him after the manner of her kind, and she looked the very image of rustic stupidity.

With the flaring candle shaded by his left hand, Edward Arundel examined the two chambers in the pavilion. There was very little to reward his scrutiny. The two small rooms were bare and cheerless. The repairs that had been executed had only gone so far as to make them tolerably inhabitable, and secure from wind and weather. The furniture was the same that Edward remembered having seen on his last visit to the Towers; for Mary had been fond of sitting in one of the little rooms, looking out at the slow river and the trembling rushes on the shore. There was no trace of recent occupation in the empty rooms, no ashes in the grates. The girl grinned maliciously as Mr Arundel raised the light above his head, and looked about him. He walked in and out of the two rooms. He stared at the obsolete chairs, the rickety tables, the dilapidated damask curtains, flapping every now and then in the wind that rushed in through the crannies of the doors and windows. He looked here and there, like a man bewildered; much to the amusement of Miss Betsy Murrel, who, with her arms crossed, and her elbows in the palms of her moist hands, followed him backwards and forwards between the two small chambers.

'There was some one living here a week ago,' he said; 'some one who had the care of a——'

He stopped suddenly. If he had guessed rightly at the dark secret, it was better that it should remain for ever hidden. This girl was perhaps more ignorant than himself. It was not for him to enlighten her.

'Do you know if anybody has lived here lately?' he asked.

Betsy Murrel shook her head.

'Nobody has lived here—not that *oi* knows of,' she replied; 'not to take their victuals, and such loike. Missus brings her work down sometimes, and sits in one of these here rooms, while Muster Poll does his pictur' paa-intin'; that's all *oi* knows of.'

Edward went back to the painting-room, and set down his candle. The mystery of those empty chambers was no business of his. He began to think that his cousin Olivia was mad, and that her outbursts of terror and agitation had been only the raving of a mad woman, after all. There had been a great deal in her manner during the last year that had seemed like insanity. The presence of the child might have been purely accidental; and his cousin's wild vehemence only a paroxysm of insanity. He sighed as he left Miss Murrel to her scouring. The world seemed out of joint; and he, whose energetic nature fitted him for the straightening of crooked things, had no knowledge of the means by which it might be set right.

'Good-bye, lonely place,' he said; 'good-bye to the spot where my young wife first told me of her love.'

He walked back to the cottage, where the bustle of packing and preparation was all over, and where Mr Morrison was entertaining a select party of friends in the kitchen. Early the next morning Mr Arundel and his servant left Lincolnshire; the key of Kemberling Retreat was given up to the landlord; and a wooden board, flapping above the dilapidated trellis-work of the porch, gave notice that the habitation was to be let.

CHAPTER XXXI

TAKING IT QUIETLY

ALL the county, or at least all that part of the county within a certain radius of Marchmont Towers, waited very anxiously for Mr Paul Marchmont to make some move. The horse-whipping business had given quite a pleasant zest, a flavour of excitement, a dash of what it is the fashion nowadays to call 'sensation,' to the wind-up of the hunting-breakfast. Poor Paul's thrashing had been more racy and appetising than the finest olives that ever grew, and his late guests looked forward to a great deal more excitement and 'sensation' before the business was done with. Of course Paul Marchmont would do something. He *must* make a stir; and the sooner he made it the better. Matters would have to be explained. People expected to know the *cause* of Edward Arundel's enmity; and of course the new master of the Towers would see the propriety of setting himself right in the eyes of his influential acquaintance, his tenantry, and retainers; especially if he contemplated standing for Swampington at the next general election.

This was what people said to each other. The scene at the hunting-breakfast was a most fertile topic of conversation. It was almost as good as a popular murder, and furnished scandalous paragraphs *ad infinitum* for the provincial papers, most of them beginning, 'It is understood—,' or 'It has been whispered in our hearing that—,' or 'Rochefoucault* has observed that—.' Everybody expected that Paul Marchmont would write to the papers, and that Edward Arundel would answer him in the papers; and that a brisk and stirring warfare would be carried on in printer's-ink—at least. But no line written by either of the gentlemen appeared in any one of the county journals; and by slow degrees it dawned upon people that there was no further amusement to be got out of Paul's chastisement, and that the master of the Towers meant to take the thing quietly, and to swallow the horrible outrage, taking care to hide any wry faces he made during that operation.

Yes; Paul Marchmont let the matter drop. The report was circulated that he was very ill, and had suffered from a touch of brain-fever, which kept him a victim to incessant delirium until after Mr

Arundel had left the county. This rumour was set afloat by Mr Weston the surgeon; and as he was the only person admitted to his brother-in-law's apartment, it was impossible for any one to contradict his assertion.

The fox-hunting squires shrugged their shoulders; and I am sorry to say that the epithets, 'hound,' 'cur,' 'sneak,' and 'mongrel,' were more often applied to Mr Marchmont than was consistent with Christian feeling on the part of the gentlemen who uttered them. But a man who can swallow a sound thrashing, administered upon his own door-step, has to contend with the prejudices of society, and must take the consequences of being in advance of his age.

So, while his new neighbours talked about him, Paul Marchmont lay in his splendid chamber, with the frisking youths and maidens staring at him all day long, and simpering at him with their unchanging faces, until he grew sick at heart, and began to loathe all this new grandeur, which had so delighted him a little time ago. He no longer laughed at the recollection of shabby Charlotte Street. He dreamt one night that he was back again in the old bedroom, with the painted deal furniture, and the hideous paper on the walls, and that the Marchmont-Towers magnificence had been only a feverish vision; and he was glad to be back in that familiar place, and was sorry on awaking to find that Marchmont Towers was a splendid reality.

There was only one faint red streak upon his shoulders, for the thrashing had not been a brutal one. It was *disgrace* Edward Arundel had wanted to inflict, not physical pain, the commonplace punishment with which a man corrects his refractory horse. The lash of the hunting-whip had done very little damage to the artist's flesh; but it had slashed away his manhood, as the sickle sweeps the flowers amidst the corn.

He could never look up again. The thought of going out of this house for the first time, and the horror of confronting the altered faces of his neighhours, was as dreadful to him as the anticipation of that awful exit from the Debtor's Door,* which is the last step but one into eternity, must be to the condemned criminal.

'I shall go abroad,' he said to his mother, when he made his appearance in the western drawing-room, a week after Edward's departure. 'I shall go on the Continent, mother; I have taken a dislike to this place, since that savage attacked me the other day.'

Mrs Marchmont sighed.

'It will seem hard to lose you, Paul, now that you are rich. You were so constant to us through all our poverty; and we might be so happy together now.'

The artist was walking up and down the room, with his hands in the pockets of his braided velvet coat. He knew that in the conventional costume of a well-bred gentleman he showed to a disadvantage amongst other men; and he affected a picturesque and artistic style of dress, whose brighter hues and looser outlines lighted up his pale face, and gave a grace to his spare figure.

'You think it worth something, then, mother?' he said presently, half kneeling, half lounging in a deep-cushioned easy chair near the table at which his mother sat. 'You think our money is worth something to us? All these chairs and tables, this great rambling house, the servants who wait upon us, and the carriages we ride in, are worth something, are they not? they make us happier, I suppose. I know I always thought such things made up the sum of happiness when I was poor. I have seen a hearse going away from a rich man's door, carrying his cherished wife, or his only son, perhaps; and I've thought, "Ah, but he has forty thousand a year!" You are happier here than you were in Charlotte Street, eh, mother?'

Mrs Marchmont was a Frenchwoman by birth, though she had lived so long in London as to become Anglicised. She only retained a slight accent of her native tongue, and a good deal more vivacity of look and gesture than is common to Englishwomen. Her elder daughter was sitting on the other side of the broad fireplace. She was only a quieter and older likeness of Lavinia Weston.

'*Am* I happier?' exclaimed Mrs Marchmont. 'Need you ask me the question, Paul? But it is not so much for myself as for your sake that I value all this grandeur.'

She held out her long thin hand, which was covered with rings, some old-fashioned and comparatively valueless, others lately purchased by her devoted son, and very precious. The artist took the shrunken fingers in his own, and raised them to his lips.

'I'm very glad that I've made you happy, mother,' he said; 'that's something gained, at any rate.'

He left the fireplace, and walked slowly up and down the room, stopping now and then to look out at the wintry sky, or the flat expanse of turf below it; but he was quite a different creature to that which he had been before his encounter with Edward Arundel. The chairs and tables palled upon him. The mossy velvet pile of the new carpets seemed to him like the swampy ground of a morass. The dark-green draperies of Genoa velvet deepened into black with the growing twilight, and seemed as if they had been fashioned out of palls.

What was it worth, this fine house, with the broad flat before it? Nothing, if he had lost the respect and consideration of his neighbours. He wanted to be a great man as well as a rich one. He wanted admiration and flattery, reverence and esteem; not from poor people, whose esteem and admiration were scarcely worth having, but from wealthy squires, his equals or his superiors by birth and fortune. He ground his teeth at the thought of his disgrace. He had drunk of the cup of triumph, and had tasted the very wine of life; and at the moment when that cup was fullest, it had been snatched away from him by the ruthless hand of his enemy.

Christmas came, and gave Paul Marchmont a good opportunity of playing the country gentleman of the olden time. What was the cost of a couple of bullocks, a few hogsheads of ale, and a waggon-load of coals, if by such a sacrifice the master of the Towers could secure for himself the admiration due to a public benefactor? Paul gave *carte blanche* to the old servants; and tents were erected on the lawn, and monstrous bonfires blazed briskly in the frosty air; while the populace, who would have accepted the bounties of a new Nero fresh from the burning of a modern Rome, drank to the health of their benefactor, and warmed themselves by the unlimited consumption of strong beer.

Mrs Marchmont and her invalid daughter assisted Paul in his attempt to regain the popularity he had lost upon the steps of the western terrace. The two women distributed square miles of flannel and blanketing amongst greedy claimants; they gave scarlet cloaks and poke-bonnets to old women; they gave an insipid feast, upon temperance principles, to the children of the National Schools.* And they had their reward; for people began to say that this Paul Marchmont was a very noble fellow, after all, by Jove, sir and that fellow Arundel must have been in the wrong, sir; and no doubt Marchmont had his own reasons for not resenting the outrage, sir; and a great deal more to the like effect.

After this roasting of the two bullocks the wind changed

altogether. Mr Marchmont gave a great dinner-party upon New-Year's Day. He sent out thirty invitations, and had only two refusals. So the long dining-room was filled with all the notabilities of the district, and Paul held his head up once more, and rejoiced in his own grandeur. After all, one horsewhipping cannot annihilate a man with a fine estate and eleven thousand a year, if he knows how to make a splash with his money.

Olivia Marchmont shared in none of the festivals that were held. Her father was very ill this winter; and she spent a good deal of her time at Swampington Rectory, sitting in Hubert Arundel's room, and reading to him. But her presence brought very little comfort to the sick man; for there was something in his daughter's manner that filled him with inexpressible terror; and he would lie for hours together watching her blank face, and wondering at its horrible rigidity. What was it? What was the dreadful secret which had transformed this woman? He tormented himself perpetually with this question, but he could imagine no answer to it. He did not know the power which a master-passion has upon these strong-minded women, whose minds are strong because of their narrowness, and who are the bonden slaves of one idea. He did not know that in a breast which holds no pure affection the master-fiend Passion rages like an all-devouring flame, perpetually consuming its victim. He did not know that in these violent and concentrative natures the line that separates reason from madness is so feeble a demarcation, that very few can perceive the hour in which it is passed.

Olivia Marchmont had never been the most lively or delightful of companions. The tenderness which is the common attribute of a woman's nature had not been given to her. She ought to have been a great man. Nature makes these mistakes now and then, and the victim expiates the error. Hence comes such imperfect histories as that of English Elizabeth and Swedish Christina.* The fetters that had bound Olivia's narrow life had eaten into her very soul, and cankered there. If she could have been Edward Arundel's wife, she would have been the noblest and truest wife that ever merged her identity into that of another, and lived upon the refracted glory of her husband's triumphs. She would have been a Rachel Russell, a Mrs Hutchinson, a Lady Nithisdale, a Madame de Lavalette.* She would have been great by reason of her power of self-abnegation; and there would have been a strange charm in the aspect of this fierce nature attuned to harmonise with its master's soul, all the barbaric discords melting into melody, all the harsh combinations softening into perfect music; just as in Mr Buckstone's* most poetic drama we are bewitched by the wild huntress sitting at the feet of her lord, and admire her chiefly because we know that only that one man upon all the earth could have had power to tame her. To any one who had known Olivia's secret, there could have been no sadder spectacle than this of her decay. The mind and body decayed together, bound by a mysterious sympathy. All womanly roundness disappeared from the spare figure, and Mrs Marchmont's black dresses hung about her in loose folds. Her long, dead, black hair was pushed away from her thin face, and twisted into a heavy knot at the back of her head. Every charm that she had ever possessed was gone. The oldest women generally retain some traits of their lost beauty, some faint reflection of the sun that has gone down, to light up the soft twilight of age, and even glimmer through the gloom of death. But this woman's face retained no token of the past. No empty hull, with shattered bulwarks crumbled by the fury of fierce seas, cast on a desert shore to rot and perish there, was ever more complete a wreck than she was. Upon her face and figure, in every look and gesture, in the tone of every word she spoke, there was an awful something, worse than the seal of death. Little by little the miserable truth dawned upon Hubert Arundel. His daughter was mad! He knew this; but he kept the dreadful knowledge hidden in his own breast,—a hideous secret, whose weight oppressed him like an actual burden. He kept the secret; for it would have seemed to him the most cruel treason against his daughter to have confessed his discovery to any living creature, unless it should be absolutely necessary to do so. Meanwhile he set himself to watch Olivia, detaining her at the Rectory for a week together, in order that he might see her in all moods, under all phases.

He found that there were no violent or outrageous evidences of this mental decay. The mind had given way under the perpetual pressure of one set of thoughts. Hubert Arundel, in his ignorance of his daughter's secrets, could not discover the cause of her decadence; but that cause was very simple. If the body is a wonderful and complex machine which must not be tampered with, surely that still more complex machine the mind must need careful treatment. If such and such a course of diet is fatal to the body's health, may not some thoughts be equally fatal to the health of the brain? may not a monotonous recurrence of the same ideas be above all injurious? If by reason of the peculiar nature of a man's labour, he uses one limb or one muscle more than the rest, strange bosses rise up to testify to that ill usage, the idle limbs wither, and the harmonious perfection of Nature gives place to deformity. So the brain, perpetually pressed upon, for ever strained to its utmost tension by the wearisome succession of thoughts, becomes crooked and one-sided, always leaning one way, continually tripping up the wretched thinker.

John Marchmont's widow had only one set of ideas. On every subject but that one which involved Edward Arundel and his fortunes her memory had decayed. She asked her father the same questions—commonplace questions relating to his own comfort, or to simple household matters, twenty times a day, always forgetting that he had answered her. She had that impatience as to the passage of time which is one of the most painful signs of madness. She looked at her watch ten times an hour, and would wander out into the cheerless garden, indifferent to the bitter weather, in order to look at the clock in the church-steeple, under the impression that her own watch, and her father's, and all the time-keepers in the house, were slow.

She was sometimes restless, taking up one occupation after another, to throw all aside with equal impatience, and sometimes immobile for hours together. But as she was never violent, never in any way unreasonable, Hubert Arundel had not the heart to call science to his aid, and to betray her secret. The thought that his daughter's malady might be cured never entered his mind as within the range of possibility. There was nothing to cure; no delusions to be exorcised by medical treatment; no violent vagaries to be held in check by drugs and nostrums. The powerful intellect had decayed; its force and clearness were gone. No drugs that ever grew upon this earth could restore that which was lost.

This was the conviction which kept the Rector silent. It would have given him unutterable anguish to have told his daughter's secret to any living being; but he would have endured that misery if she could have been benefited thereby. He most firmly believed that she could not, and that her state was irremediable.

'My poor girl!' he thought to himself; 'how proud I was of her ten years ago! I can do nothing for her; nothing except to love and cherish her, and hide her humiliation from the world.'

But Hubert Arundel was not allowed to do even this much for the daughter he loved; for when Olivia had been with him a little more than a week, Paul Marchmont and his mother drove over to Swampington Rectory one morning and carried her away with them. The Rector then saw for the first time that his once strong-minded daughter was completely under the dominion of these two people, and that they knew the nature of her malady quite as well as he did. He resisted her return to the Towers; but his resistance was useless. She submitted herself willingly to her new friends, declaring that she was better in their house than anywhere else. So she went back to her old suite of apartments, and her old servant Barbara waited upon her; and she sat alone in dead John Marchmont's study, listening to the January winds shrieking in the quadrangle, the distant rooks calling to each other amongst the bare branches of the poplars, the banging of the doors in the corridor, and occasional gusts of laughter from the open door of the dining-room,—while Paul Marchmont and his guests gave a jovial welcome to the new year.

While the master of the Towers re-asserted his grandeur, and made stupendous efforts to regain the ground he had lost, Edward Arundel wandered far away in the depths of Brittany, travelling on foot, and making himself familiar with the simple peasants, who were ignorant of his troubles. He had sent Mr Morrison down to Dangerfield with the greater part of his luggage; but he had not the heart to go back himself—yet awhile. He was afraid of his mother's sympathy, and he went away into the lonely Breton villages, to try and cure himself of his great grief, before he began life again as a soldier. It was useless for him to strive against his vocation. Nature had made him a soldier, and nothing else; and wherever there was a good cause to be fought for, his place was on the battle-field.

CHAPTER XXXII

MISS LAWFORD SPEAKS HER MIND

MAJOR LAWFORD and his blue-eyed daughters were not amongst those guests who accepted Paul Marchmont's princely hospitalities. Belinda Lawford had never heard the story of Edward's lost bride as he himself could have told it; but she had heard an imperfect version of the sorrowful history from Letitia, and that young lady had informed her friend of Edward's animus against the new master of the Towers.

'The poor dear foolish boy will insist upon thinking that Mr Marchmont was at the bottom of it all,' she had said in a confidential chat with Belinda, 'somehow or other; but whether he was, or whether he wasn't, I'm sure I can't say. But if one attempts to take Mr Marchmont's part with Edward, he does get so violent and go on so, that one's obliged to say all sorts of dreadful things about Mary's cousin for the sake of peace. But really, when I saw him one day in Kemberling, with a black velvet shooting-coat, and his beautiful smooth white hair and auburn moustache, I thought him most interesting. And so would you, Belinda, if you weren't so wrapped up in that doleful brother of mine.'

Whereupon, of course, Miss Lawford had been compelled to declare that she was not 'wrapped up' in Edward, whatever state of feeling that obscure phrase might signify; and to express, by the vehemence of her denial, that, if anything, she rather detested Miss Arundel's brother. By-the-by, did you ever know a young lady who could understand the admiration aroused in the breast of other young ladies for that most uninteresting object, a *brother*? Or a gentleman who could enter with any warmth of sympathy into his friend's feelings respecting the auburn tresses or the Grecian nose of 'a sister'? Belinda Lawford, I say, knew something of the story of Mary Arundel's death, and she implored her father to reject all hospitalities offered by Paul Marchmont.

'You won't go to the Towers, papa dear?' she said, with her hands clasped upon her father's arm, her cheeks kindling, and her eyes filling with tears as she spoke to him; 'you won't go and sit at Paul Marchmont's table, and drink his wine, and shake hands with him? I know that he had something to do with Mary Arundel's death. He had indeed, papa. I don't mean anything that the world calls crime; I don't mean any act of open violence. But he was cruel to her, papa; he was cruel to her. He tortured her and tormented her until she—' The girl paused for a moment, and her voice faltered a little. 'Oh, how I wish that I had known her, papa,' she cried presently, 'that I might have stood by her, and comforted her, all through that sad time!'

The Major looked down at his daughter with a tender smile,—a smile that was a little significant, perhaps, but full of love and admiration.

'You would have stood by Arundel's poor little wife, my dear?' he said. 'You would stand by her *now*, if she were alive, and needed your friendship?'

'I would indeed, papa,' Miss Lawford answered resolutely.

'I believe it, my dear; I believe it with all my heart. You are a good girl, my Linda; you are a noble girl. You are as good as a son to me, my dear.'

Major Lawford was silent for a few moments, holding his daughter in his arms and pressing his lips upon her broad forehead.

'You are fit to be a soldier's daughter, my darling,' he said, 'or—or a soldier's wife.'

He kissed her once more, and then left her, sighing thoughtfully as he went away.

This is how it was that neither Major Lawford nor any of his family were present at those splendid entertainments which Paul Marchmont gave to his new friends. Mr Marchmont knew almost as well as the Lawfords themselves why they did not come, and the absence of them at his glittering board made his bread bitter to him and his wine tasteless. He wanted these people as much as the others,—more than the others, perhaps, for they had been Edward Arundel's friends; and he wanted them to turn their backs upon the young man, and join in the general outcry against his violence and brutality. The absence of Major Lawford at the lighted banquet-table tormented this modern rich man as the presence of Mordecai at the gate tormented Haman.* It was not enough that all the others should come if these stayed away, and by their absence tacitly testified to their contempt for the master of the Towers.

He met Belinda sometimes on horseback with the old grey-headed groom behind her, a fearless young amazon, breasting the January winds, with her blue eyes sparkling, and her auburn hair blowing away from her candid face: he met her, and looked out at her from the luxurious barouche in which it was his pleasure to loll by his mother's side, half-buried amongst soft furry rugs and sleek leopard-skins, making the chilly atmosphere through which he rode odorous with the scent of perfumed hair, and smiling over cruelly delicious criticisms in newly-cut reviews. He looked out at this fearless girl whose friends so obstinately stood by Edward Arundel; and the cold contempt upon Miss Lawford's face cut him more keenly than the sharpest wind of that bitter January.

Then he took counsel with his womankind; not telling them his thoughts, fears, doubts, or wishes—it was not his habit to do that—but taking *their* ideas, and only telling them so much as it was necessary for them to know in order that they might be useful to him. Paul Marchmont's life was regulated by a few rules, so simple that a child might have learned them; indeed I regret to say that some children are very apt pupils in that school of philosophy to which the master of Marchmont Towers belonged, and cause astonishment to their elders by the precocity of their intelligence. Mr Marchmont might have inscribed upon a very small scrap of parchment the moral maxims by which he regulated his dealings with mankind.

'Always conciliate,' said this philosopher. 'Never tell an unneces-sary lie. Be agreeable and generous to those who serve you. N.B. No good carpenter would allow his tools to get rusty. Make yourself master of the opinions of others, but hold your own tongue. Seek to obtain the maximum of enjoyment with the minimum of risk.'

Such golden saws as these did Mr Marchmont make for his own especial guidance; and he hoped to pass smoothly onwards upon the railway of life, riding in a first-class carriage, on the greased wheels of a very easy conscience. As for any unfortunate fellow-travellers pitched out of the carriage-window in the course of the journey, or left lonely and helpless at desolate stations on the way, Providence, and not Mr Marchmont, was responsible for *their* welfare. Paul had a high appreciation of Providence, and was fond of talking—very piously, as some people said; very impiously, as others secretly thought—about the inestimable Wisdom which governed all the affairs of this lower world. Nowhere, according to the artist, had the hand of Providence been more clearly visible than in this matter about Paul's poor little cousin Mary. If Providence had intended John Marchmont's daughter to be a happy bride, a happy wife, the prosperous mistress of that stately habitation, why all that sad business of old Mr Arundel's sudden illness, Edward's hurried journey, the railway accident, and all the complications that had thereupon arisen? Nothing would have been easier than for Providence to have prevented all this; and then he, Paul, would have been still in Charlotte Street, Fitzroy Square, patiently waiting for a friendly lift upon the high-road of life. Nobody could say that he had ever been otherwise than patient. Nobody could say that he had ever intruded himself upon his rich cousins at the Towers, or had been heard to speculate upon his possible inheritance of the estate; or that he had, in short, done any thing but that which the best, truest, most conscientious and disinterested of mankind should do.

In the course of that bleak, frosty January, Mr Marchmont sent his mother and his sister Lavinia to make a call at the Grange. The Grange people had never called upon Mrs Marchmont; but Paul did not allow any flimsy ceremonial law to stand in his way when he had a purpose to achieve. So the ladies went to the Grange, and were politely received; for Miss Lawford and her mother were a great deal too innocent and noble-minded to imagine that these pale-faced, delicate-looking women could have had any part, either directly or indirectly, in that cruel treatment which had driven Edward's young wife from her home. Mrs Marchmont and Mrs Weston were kindly received, therefore; and in a little conversation with Belinda about birds, and dahlias, and worsted work, and the most innocent subjects imaginable, the wily Lavinia contrived to lead up to Miss Letitia Arundel, and thence, by the easiest conversational short-cut, to Edward and his lost wife. Mrs Weston was obliged to bring her cambric handkerchief out of her muff when she talked about her cousin Mary; but she was a clever woman, and she had taken to heart Paul's pet maxim about the folly of *unnecessary* lies; and she was so candid as to entirely disarm Miss Lawford, who had a schoolgirlish notion that every kind of hypocrisy and falsehood was outwardly visible in a servile and slavish manner. She was not upon her guard against those practised adepts in the art of deception, who have learnt to make that subtle admixture of truth and falsehood which defies detection; like some fabrics in whose woof silk and cotton are so cunningly blended that only a practised eye can discover the inferior material.

So when Lavinia dried her eyes and put her handkerchief back in her muff, and said, betwixt laughing and crying,—

'Now you know, my dear Miss Lawford, you mustn't think that I would for a moment pretend to be sorry that my brother has come into this fortune. Of course any such pretence as that would be ridiculous, and quite useless into the bargain, as it isn't likely anybody would believe me. Paul is a dear, kind creature, the best of brothers, the most affectionate of sons, and deserves any good fortune that could fall to his lot; but I am truly sorry for that poor little girl. I am truly sorry, believe me, Miss Lawford; and I only regret that Mr Weston and I did not come to Kemberling sooner, so that I might have been a friend to the poor little thing; for then, you know, I might have prevented that foolish runaway match, out of which almost all the poor child's troubles arose. Yes, Miss Lawford; I wish I had been able to befriend that unhappy child, although by my so doing Paul would have been kept out of the fortune he now enjoys—for some time, at any rate. I say for some time, because I do not believe that Mary Marchmont would have lived to be old, under the happiest circumstances. Her mother died very young; and her father, and her father's father, were consumptive.'

Then Mrs Weston took occasion, incidentally of course, to allude to her brother's goodness; but even then she was on her guard, and took care not to say too much.

'The worst actors are those who over-act their parts.' That was another of Paul Marchmont's golden maxims.

'I don't know what my brother may be to the rest of the world,' Lavinia said; 'but I know how good he is to those who belong to him. I should be ashamed to tell you all he has done for Mr Weston and me. He gave me this cashmere shawl at the beginning of the winter, and a set of sables fit for a duchess; though I told him they were not at all the thing for a village surgeon's wife, who keeps only one servant, and dusts her own best parlour.'

And Mrs Marchmont talked of her son; with no loud enthusiasm, but with a tone of quiet conviction that was worth any money to Paul. To have an innocent person, some one not in the secret, to play a small part in the comedy of his life, was a desideratum with the artist. His mother had always been this person, this unconscious performer, instinctively falling into the action of the play, and shedding real tears, and smiling actual smiles,—the most useful assistant to a great schemer.

But during the whole of the visit nothing was said as to Paul's conduct towards his unhappy cousin; nothing was said either to praise or to exculpate; and when Mrs Marchmont and her daughter drove away, in one of the new equipages which Paul had selected for his mother, they left only a vague impression in Belinda's breast. She didn't quite know what to think. These people were so frank and candid, they had spoken of Paul with such real affection, that it was almost impossible to doubt them. Paul Marchmont might be a bad man, but his mother and sister loved him, and surely they were ignorant of his wickedness.

Mrs Lawford troubled herself very little about this unexpected morning call. She was an excellent, warm-hearted, domestic creature, and thought a great deal more about the grand question as to whether she should have new damask curtains for the drawing-room, or send the old ones to be dyed; or whether she should withdraw her custom from the Kemberling grocer, whose 'best black'* at four-and-sixpence was really now so very inferior; or whether Belinda's summer silk dress could be cut down into a frock for Isabella to wear in the winter evenings,—than about the rights or wrongs of that story of the horsewhipping which had been administered to Mr Marchmont.

'I'm sure those Marchmont-Towers people seem very nice, my dear,' the lady said to Belinda; 'and I really wish your papa would go and dine there. You know I like him to dine out a good deal in the winter, Linda; not that I want to save the housekeeping money,—only it is *so* difficult to vary the side-dishes for a man who has been accustomed to mess-dinners, and a French cook.'

But Belinda stuck fast to her colours. She was a soldier's daughter, as her father said, and she was almost as good as a son. The Major meant this latter remark for very high praise; for the great grief of his life had been the want of a boy's brave face at his fireside. She was as good as a son; that is to say, she was braver and more outspoken than most women; although she was feminine and gentle withal, and by no means strong-minded. She would have fainted, perhaps, at the first sight of blood upon a battle-field; but she would have bled to death with the calm heroism of a martyr, rather than have been false to a noble cause.

'I think papa is quite right not to go to Marchmont Towers, mamma,' she said; the artful minx omitted to state that it was by reason of her entreaties her father had stayed away. 'I think he is quite right. Mrs Marchmont and Mrs Weston may be very nice, and of course it isn't likely *they* would be cruel to poor young Mrs Arundel; but I *know* that Mr Marchmont must have been unkind to that poor girl, or Mr Arundel would never have done what he did.'

It is in the nature of good and brave men to lay down their masculine rights when they leave their hats in the hall, and to submit themselves meekly to feminine government. It is only the whippersnapper, the sneak, the coward out of doors who is a tyrant at home. See how meekly the Conqueror of Italy* went home to his charming Creole wife! See how pleasantly the Liberator of Italy* lolls in the carriage of his golden-haired Empress, when the young trees in that fair wood beyond the triumphal arch are green in the bright spring weather, and all the hired vehicles in Paris are making towards the cascade! Major Lawford's wife was too gentle, and too busy with her storeroom and her domestic cares, to tyrannise over her lord and master; but the Major was duly henpecked by his blue-eyed daughters, and went here and there as they dictated.

So he stayed away from Marchmont Towers to please Belinda, and only said, 'Haw,' 'Yes,' ''Pon my honour, now!' 'Bless my soul!' when his friends told him of the magnificence of Paul's dinners.

But although the Major and his eldest daughter did not encounter Mr Marchmont in his own house, they met him sometimes on the neutral ground of other people's dining-rooms, and upon one especial evening at a pleasant little dinner-party given by the rector of the parish in which the Grange was situated.

Paul made himself particularly agreeable upon this occasion; but in the brief interval before dinner he was absorbed in a conversation with Mr Davenant, the rector, upon the subject of ecclesiastical architecture,—he knew everything, and could talk about everything, this dear Paul,—and made no attempt to approach Miss Lawford. He only looked at her now and then, with a furtive, oblique glance out of his almond-shaped, pale-grey eyes; a glance that was wisely hidden by the light auburn lashes, for it had an unpleasant resemblance to the leer of an evil-natured sprite. Mr Marchmont contented himself with keeping this furtive watch upon Belinda, while she talked gaily with the Rector's two daughters in a pleasant corner near the piano. And as the artist took Mrs Davenant down to the dining-room, and sat next her at dinner, he had no opportunity of fraternising with Belinda during that meal; for the young lady was divided from him by the whole length of the table and, moreover, very much occupied by the exclusive attentions of two callow-looking officers from the nearest garrison-town, who were afflicted with extreme youth, and were painfully conscious of their degraded state, but tried notwithstanding to carry it off with a high hand, and affected the opinions of used-up fifty.

Mr Marchmont had none of his womankind with him at this dinner; for his mother and invalid sister had neither of them felt strong enough to come, and Mr and Mrs Weston had not been invited. The artist's special object in coming to this dinner was the conquest of Miss Belinda Lawford: she sided with Edward Arundel against him: she must be made to believe Edward wrong, and himself right; or she might go about spreading her opinions, and doing him mischief. Beyond that, he had another idea about Belinda; and he looked to this dinner as likely to afford him an opportunity of laying the foundation of a very diplomatic scheme, in which Miss Lawford should unconsciously become his tool. He was vexed at being placed apart from her at the dinner-table, but he concealed his vexation; and he was aggravated by the Rector's old-fashioned hospitality, which detained the gentlemen over their wine for some time after the ladies left the dining-room. But the opportunity that he wanted came nevertheless, and in a manner that he had not anticipated.

The two callow defenders of their country had sneaked out of the dining-room, and rejoined the ladies in the cosy countrified drawing-rooms. They had stolen away, these two young men; for they were oppressed by the weight of a fearful secret. *They couldn't drink claret!* No; they had tried to like it; they had smacked their lips and winked their eyes—both at once, for even winking with *one* eye is an accomplishment scarcely compatible with extreme youth—over vintages that had seemed to them like a happy admixture of red ink and green-gooseberry juice. They had perjured their boyish souls with hideous falsehoods as to their appreciation of pale tawny port, light dry wines, '42-ports, '45-ports, Kopke Roriz, Thompson and Croft's, and Sandemann's; when, in the secret recesses of their minds, they affected sweet and 'slab' compounds, sold by publicans, and facetiously called 'Our prime old port, at four-and-sixpence.' They were very young, these beardless soldiers. They liked strawberry ices, and were on the verge of insolvency from a predilection for clammy bath-buns, jam-tarts, and cherry-brandy. They liked gorgeous waistcoats; and varnished boots in a state of virgin brilliancy; and little bouquets in their button-holes; and a deluge of *millefleurs** upon their flimsy handkerchiefs. They were very young. The men they met at dinner-parties to-day had tipped them at Eton or Woolwich* only yesterday, as it seemed, and remembered it and despised them. It was only a few months since they had been snubbed for calling the Douro a mountain in Switzerland, and the Himalayas a cluster of islands in the Pacific, at horrible examinations, in which the cold perspiration had bedewed their pallid young cheeks. They were delighted to get away from those elderly creatures in the Rector's dining-room to the snug little back drawing-room, where Belinda Lawford and the two Misses Davenant were murmuring softly in the firelight, like young turtles in a sheltered dove-cote; while the matrons in the larger apartment sipped their coffee, and conversed in low awful voices about the iniquities of housemaids, and the insubordination of gardeners and grooms.

Belinda and her two companions were very polite to the helpless young wanderers from the dining-room; and they talked pleasantly enough of all manner of things; until somehow or other the conversation came round to the Marchmont-Towers scandal; and Edward's treatment of his lost wife's kinsman.

One of the young men had been present at the hunting-breakfast on that bright October morning, and he was not a little proud of his superior acquaintance with the whole business.

'I was the-aw, Miss Lawford,' he said. 'I on the tew-wace after bweakfast,—and a vewy excellent bweakfast it was, I ass-haw you; the still Moselle was weally admiwable, and Marchmont has some Medewa that immeasuwably surpasses anything I can indooce my wine-merchant to send me;—I was on the tew-wace, and I saw Awundel comin' up the steps, awful pale, and gwasping his whip; and I was a witness of all the west that occurred; and if I had been Marchmont I should have shot Awundel befaw he left the pawk, if I'd had to swing for it, Miss Lawford; for I should have felt, b' Jove, that my own sense of honaw demanded the sacwifice. Howevaw, Marchmont seems a vewy good fella; so I suppose it's all wight as far as he goes; but it was a bwutal business altogethaw, and that fella Awundel must be a scoundwel.'

Belinda could not bear this. She had borne a great deal already. She had been obliged to sit by very often, and hear Edward Arundel's conduct discussed by Thomas, Richard, and Henry, or anybody else who chose to talk about it; and she had been patient, and had held her peace, with her heart bumping indignantly in her breast, and passionate crimson blushes burning her cheeks. But she could *not* submit to hear a beardless, pale-faced, and rather weak-eyed young ensign—who had never done any greater service for his Queen and country than to cry 'SHUDDRUPH!'* to a detachment of raw recruits in a barrack-yard, in the early bleakness of a winter's morning—take upon himself to blame Edward Arundel, the brave soldier, the noble Indian hero, the devoted lover and husband, the valiant avenger of his dead wife's wrongs.

'I don't think you know anything of the real story, Mr Palliser,' Belinda said boldly to the half-fledged ensign. 'If you did, I'm sure you would admire Mr Arundel's conduct instead of blaming it. Mr Marchmont fully deserved the disgrace which Edward—which Mr Arundel inflicted upon him.'

The words were still upon her lips, when Paul Marchmont himself came softly through the flickering firelight to the low chair upon which Belinda sat. He came behind her, and laying his hand lightly upon the scroll-work at the back of her chair, bent over her, and said, in a low confidential voice,—

'You are a noble girl, Miss Lawford. I am sorry that you should think ill of me: but I like you for having spoken so frankly. You are a most noble girl. You are worthy to be your father's daughter.'

This was said with a tone of suppressed emotion; but it was quite a random shot. Paul didn't know anything about the Major, except that he had a comfortable income, drove a neat dog-cart, and was often seen riding on the flat Lincolnshire roads with his eldest daughter. For all Paul knew to the contrary, Major Lawford might have been the veriest bully and coward who ever made those about him miserable; but Mr Marchmont's tone as good as expressed that he was intimately acquainted with the old soldier's career, and had long admired and loved him. It was one of Paul's happy inspirations, this allusion to Belinda's father; one of those bright touches of colour laid on with a skilful recklessness, and giving sudden brightness to the whole picture; a little spot of vermilion dabbed upon the canvas with the point of the palette-knife, and lighting up all the landscape with sunshine.

'You know my father?' said Belinda, surprised.

'Who does not know him?' cried the artist. 'Do you think, Miss Lawford, that it is necessary to sit at a man's dinner-table before you know what he is? I know your father to be a good man and a brave soldier, as well as I know that the Duke of Wellington is a great general, though I never dined at Apsley House.* I respect your father, Miss Lawford; and I have been very much distressed by his evident avoidance of me and mine.'

This was coming to the point at once. Mr Marchmont's manner was candour itself. Belinda looked at him with widely-opened, wondering eyes. She was looking for the evidence of his wickedness in his face. I think she half-expected that Mr Marchmont would have corked eyebrows, and a slouched hat, like a stage ruffian. She was so innocent, this simple young Belinda, that she imagined wicked people must necessarily look wicked.

Paul Marchmont saw the wavering of her mind in that half-puzzled expression, and he went on boldly.

'I like your father, Miss Lawford,' he said; 'I like him, and I respect him; and I want to know him. Other people may misunderstand me, if they please. I can't help their opinions. The truth is generally strongest in the end; and I can afford to wait. But I can*not* afford to forfeit the friendship of a man I esteem; I cannot afford to be misunderstood by your father, Miss Lawford; and I have been very much pained—yes, very much pained—by the manner in which the Major has repelled my little attempts at friendliness.'

Belinda's heart smote her. She knew that it was her influence that had kept her father away from Marchmont Towers. This young lady was very conscientious. She was a Christian, too; and a certain sentence* touching wrongful judgments rose up against her while Mr Marchmont was speaking. If she had wronged this man; if Edward Arundel has been misled by his passionate grief for Mary; if she had been deluded by Edward's error,—how very badly Mr Marchmont had been treated between them! She didn't say anything, but sat looking thoughtfully at the fire; and Paul saw that she was more and more perplexed. This was just what the artist wanted. To talk his antagonist into a state of intellectual fog was almost always his manner of commencing an argument.

Belinda was silent, and Paul seated himself in a chair close to hers. The callow ensigns had gone into the lamp-lit front drawing-room, and were busy turning over the leaves—and never turning them over at the right moment—of a thundering duet which the Misses Davenant were performing for the edification of their papa's visitors. Miss Lawford and Mr Marchmont were alone, therefore, in that cosy inner chamber, and a very pretty picture they made: the rosy-cheeked girl and the pale, sentimental-looking artist sitting side by side in the glow of the low fire, with a background of crimson curtains and gleaming picture-frames; winter flowers piled in grim Indian jars; the fitful light flickering now and then upon one sharp angle of the high carved mantelpiece, with all its litter of antique china; and the rest of the room in sombre shadow. Paul had the field all to himself, and felt that victory would be easy. He began to talk about Edward Arundel.

If he had said one word against the young soldier, I think this impetuous girl, who had not yet learned to count the cost of what she did, would have been passionately eloquent in defence of her friend's brother—for no other reason than that he was the brother of her friend, of course; what other reason should she have for defending Mr Arundel?

But Paul Marchmont did not give her any occasion for indignation. On the contrary, he spoke in praise of the hot-headed young soldier who had assaulted him, making all manner of excuses for the young man's violence, and using that tone of calm superiority with which a man of the world might naturally talk about a foolish boy.

'He has been very unreasonable, Miss Lawford,' Paul said by-and-by; 'he has been very unreasonable, and has most grossly insulted me. But, in spite of all, I believe him to be a very noble young fellow, and I cannot find it in my heart to be really angry with him. What his particular grievance against me may be, I really do not know.'

The furtive glance from the long narrow grey eyes kept close watch upon Belinda's face as Paul said this. Mr Marchmont wanted to ascertain exactly how much Belinda knew of that grievance of Edward's; but he could see only perplexity in her face. She knew nothing definite, therefore; she had only heard Edward talk vaguely of his wrongs. Paul Marchmont was convinced of this; and he went on boldly now, for he felt that the ground was all clear before him.

'This foolish young soldier chooses to be angry with me because of a calamity which I was as powerless to avert, as to prevent that accident upon the South-Western Railway by which Mr Arundel so nearly lost his life. I cannot tell you how sincerely I regret the misconception that has arisen in his mind. Because I have profited by the death of John Marchmont's daughter, this impetuous young husband imagines—what? I cannot answer that question; nor can he himself, it seems, since he has made no definite statement of his wrongs to any living being.'

The artist looked more sharply than ever at Belinda's listening face. There was no change in its expression; the same wondering look, the same perplexity,—that was all.

'When I say that I regret the young man's folly, Miss Lawford,' Paul continued, 'believe me, it is chiefly on his account rather than my own. Any insult which he can inflict upon me can only rebound upon himself since everybody in Lincolnshire knows that I am in the right, and he in the wrong.'

Mr Marchmont was going on very smoothly; but at this point Miss Lawford, who had by no means deserted her colours, interrupted his easy progress.

'It remains to be proved who is right and who wrong, Mr Marchmont,' she said. 'Mr Arundel is the brother of my friend. I cannot easily believe him to have done wrong.'

Paul looked at her with a smile—a smile that brought hot blushes to her face; but she returned his look without flinching. The brave girl looked full into the narrow grey eyes sheltered under pale auburn lashes, and her steadfast gaze did not waver.

'Ah, Miss Lawford,' said the artist, still smiling, 'when a young man is handsome, chivalrous, and generous-hearted, it is very difficult to convince a woman that he can do wrong. Edward Arundel has done wrong. His ultra-quixotism has made him blind to the folly of his own acts. I can afford to forgive him. But I repeat that I regret his infatuation about this poor lost girl far more upon his account than on my own; for I know—at least I venture to think—that a way lies open to him of a happier and a better life than he could ever have known with my poor childish cousin Mary Marchmont. I have reason to know that he has formed another attachment, and that it is only a chivalrous delusion about that poor girl—whom he was never really in love with, and whom he only married because of some romantic notion inspired by my cousin John—that withholds him from that other and brighter prospect.'

He was silent for a few moments, and then he said hastily,—

'Pardon me, Miss Lawford; I have been betrayed into saying much that I had better have left unsaid, more especially to you. I——'

He hesitated a little, as if embarrassed; and then rose and looked into the next room, where the duet had been followed by a solo.

One of the Rector's daughters came towards the inner drawing-room, followed by a callow ensign.

'We want Belinda to sing,' exclaimed Miss Davenant. 'We want you to sing, you tiresome Belinda, instead of hiding yourself in that dark room all the evening.'

Belinda came out of the darkness, with her cheeks flushed and her eyelids drooping. Her heart was beating so fast as to make it quite impossible to speak just yet, or to sing either. But she sat down before the piano, and, with hands that trembled in spite of herself, began to play one of her pet sonatas.

Unhappily, Beethoven requires precision of touch in the pianist who is bold enough to seek to interpret him; and upon this occasion I am compelled to admit that Miss Lawford's fingering was eccentric, not to say ridiculous,—in common parlance, she made a mess of it; and just as she was going to break down, friendly Clara Davenant cried out,—

'That won't do, Belinda! We want you to sing, not to play. You are trying to cheat us. We would rather have one of Moore's melodies* than all Beethoven's sonatas.'

So Miss Lawford, still blushing, with her eyelids still drooping, played Sir John Stevenson's* simple symphony, and in a fresh swelling voice, that filled the room with melody, began:

> 'Oh, the days are gone when beauty bright
>   My heart's chain wove;
> When my dream of life, from morn till night,
>   Was love, still love!'

And Paul Marchmont, sitting at the other end of the room turning over Miss Davenant's scrapbook, looked up through his auburn lashes, and smiled at the beaming face of the singer. He felt that he had improved the occasion.

'I am not afraid of Miss Lawford now,' he thought to himself.

This candid, fervent girl was only another piece in the schemer's game of chess; and he saw a way of making her useful in the attainment of that great end which, in the strange simplicity of cunning, he believed to be the one purpose of *every* man's life,—Self-Aggrandisement.

It never for a moment entered into his mind that Edward Arundel was any more *real* than he was himself. There can be no perfect comprehension where there is no sympathy. Paul believed that Edward had tried to become master of Mary Marchmont's heritage; and had failed; and was angry because of his failure. He believed this passionate young man to be a schemer like himself; only a little more impetuous and blundering in his manner of going to work.

CHAPTER XXXIII

THE RETURN OF THE WANDERER

THE March winds were blowing amongst the oaks in Dangerfield Park, when Edward Arundel went back to the house which had never been his home since his boyhood. He went back because he had grown weary of lonely wanderings in that strange Breton country. He had grown weary of himself and of his own thoughts. He was worn out by the eager desire that devoured him by day and by night,—the passionate yearning to be far away beyond that low Eastern horizon line; away amid the carnage and riot of an Indian battle-field.

So he went back at last to his mother, who had written to him again and again, imploring him to return to her, and to rest, and to be happy in the familiar household where he was beloved. He left his luggage at the little inn where the coach that had brought him from Exeter stopped, and then he walked quietly homewards in the gloaming. The early spring evening was bleak and chill. The blacksmith's fire roared at him as he went by the smithy. All the lights in the queer latticed windows twinkled and blinked at him, as if in friendly welcome to the wanderer. He remembered them all: the quaint, misshapen, lop-sided roofs; the tumble-down chimneys; the low doorways, that had sunk down below the level of the village street, until all the front parlours became cellars, and strange pedestrians butted their heads against the flower-pots in the bedroom windows; the withered iron frame and pitiful oil-lamp hung out at the corner of the street, and making a faint spot of feeble light upon the rugged pavement; mysterious little shops in diamond-paned parlour win-dows, where Dutch dolls and stationery, stale gingerbread and pickled cabbage, were mixed up with wooden peg-tops, squares of yellow soap, rickety paper kites, green apples, and string; they were all familiar to him.

It had been a fine thing once to come into this village with Letitia, and buy stale gingerbread and rickety kites of a snuffy old pensioner of his mother's. The kites had always stuck in the upper branches of the oaks, and the gingerbread had invariably choked him; but with the memory of the kites and gingerbread came back all the freshness of his youth, and he looked with a pensive tenderness at the homely little shops, the merchandise flickering in the red firelight, that filled each quaint interior with a genial glow of warmth and colour.

He passed unquestioned by a wicket at the side of the great gates. The firelight was rosy in the windows of the lodge, and he heard a woman's voice singing a monotonous song to a sleepy child. Everywhere in this pleasant England there seemed to be the glow of cottage-fires, and friendliness, and love, and home. The young man sighed as he remembered that great stone mansion far away in dismal Lincolnshire, and thought how happy he might have been in this bleak spring twilight, if he could have sat by Mary Marchmont's side in the western drawing-room, watching the firelight and the shadows trembling on her fair young face.

It never had been; and it never was to be. The happiness of a home; the sweet sense of ownership; the delight of dispensing pleasure to others; all the simple domestic joys which make life beautiful,—had never been known to John Marchmont's daughter, since that early time in which she shared her father's lodging in Oakley Street, and went out in the cold December morning to buy rolls for Edward Arundel's breakfast. From the bay-window of his mother's favourite sitting-room the same red light that he had seen in every lattice in the village streamed out upon the growing darkness of the lawn. There was a half-glass door leading into a little lobby near this sitting-room. Edward Arundel opened it and went in, very quietly. He expected to find his mother and his sister in the room with the bay-window.

The door of this familiar apartment was ajar; he pushed it open, and went in. It was a very pretty room, and all the womanly litter of open books and music, needlework and drawing materials, made it homelike. The firelight flickered upon everything—on the pictures and picture-frames, the black oak panelling, the open piano, a cluster of snowdrops in a tall glass on the table, the scattered worsteds by the embroidery-frame, the sleepy dogs upon the hearth-rug. A young lady stood in the bay-window with her back to the fire. Edward Arundel crept softly up to her, and put his arm round her waist.

'Letty!'

It was not Letitia, but a young lady with very blue eyes, who blushed scarlet, and turned upon the young man rather fiercely; and then recognising him, dropped into the nearest chair and began to tremble and grow pale.

'I am sorry I startled you, Miss Lawford,' Edward said, gently; 'I really thought you were my sister. I did not even know that you were here.'

'No, of course not. I—you didn't startle me much, Mr Arundel; only you were not expected home. I thought you were far away in Brittany. I had no idea that there was any chance of your returning. I thought you meant to be away all the summer—Mrs Arundel told me so.'

Belinda Lawford said all this in that fresh girlish voice which was familiar to Mr Arundel; but she was still very pale, and she still trembled a little, and there was something almost apologetic in the way in which she assured Edward that she had believed he would be abroad throughout the summer. It seemed almost as if she had said: 'I did not come here because I thought I should see you. I had no thought or hope of meeting you.'

But Edward Arundel was not a coxcomb, and he was very slow to understand any such signs as these. He saw that he had startled the young lady, and that she had turned pale and trembled as she recognised him; and he looked at her with a half-wondering, half-pensive expression in his face.

She blushed as he looked at her. She went to the table and began to gather together the silks and worsteds, as if the arrangement of her work-basket were a matter of vital importance, to be achieved at any sacrifice of politeness. Then, suddenly remembering that she ought to say something to Mr Arundel, she gave evidence of the originality of her intellect by the following remark:

'How surprised Mrs Arundel and Letitia will be to see you!'

Even as she said this her eyes were still bent upon the skeins of worsted in her hand.

'Yes; I think they will be surprised. I did not mean to come home until the autumn. But I got so tired of wandering about a strange country alone. Where are they—my mother and Letitia?'

'They have gone down the village, to the school. They will be back to tea. Your brother is away; and we dine at three o'clock, and drink tea at eight. It is so much pleasanter than dining late.'

This was quite an effort of genius; and Miss Lawford went on sorting the skeins of worsted in the firelight. Edward Arundel had been standing all this time with his hat in his hand, almost as if he had been a visitor making a late morning call upon Belinda; but he put his hat down now; and seated himself near the table by which the young lady stood, busy with the arrangement of her work-basket.

Her heart was beating very fast, and she was straining her arithmetical powers to the uttermost, in the endeavour to make a very abstruse calculation as to the time in which Mrs Arundel and Letitia could walk to the village schoolhouse and back to Dangerfield, and the delay that might arise by reason of sundry interruptions from obsequious gaffers and respectful goodies, eager for a word of friendly salutation from their patroness.

The arrangement of the work-basket could not last for ever. It had become the most pitiful pretence by the time Miss Lawford shut down the wicker lid, and seated herself primly in a low chair by the fireplace. She sat looking down at the fire, and twisting a slender gold chain in and out between her smooth white fingers. She looked very pretty in that fitful firelight, with her waving brown hair pushed off her forehead, and her white eyelids hiding the tender blue eyes. She sat twisting the chain in her fingers, and dared not lift her eyes to Mr Arundel's face; and if there had been a whole flock of geese in the room, she could not have said 'Bo!' to one of them.

And yet she was not a stupid girl. Her father could have indignantly refuted any such slander as that against the azure-eyed Hebe who made his home pleasant to him. To the Major's mind Belinda was all that man could desire in the woman of his choice, whether as daughter or wife. She was the bright genius of the old man's home, and he loved her with that chivalrous devotion which is common to brave soldiers, who are the simplest and gentlest of men when you chain them to their firesides, and keep them away from the din of the camp and the confusion of the transport-ship.

Belinda Lawford was clever; but only just clever enough to be charming. I don't think she could have got through 'Paradise Lost,' or Gibbon's 'Decline and Fall,' or a volume by Adam Smith or McCulloch,* though you had promised her a diamond necklace when she came conscientiously to 'Finis.' But she could read Shakespeare for the hour together, and did read him aloud to her father in a fresh, clear voice, that was like music on the water. And she read Macaulay's 'History of England,' with eyes that kindled with indignation against cowardly, obstinate James, or melted with pity for poor weak foolish Monmouth, as the case might be. She could play Mendelssohn and Beethoven,—plaintive sonatas; tender songs, that had no need of words* to expound the mystic meaning of the music. She could sing old ballads and Irish melodies, that thrilled the souls of those who heard her, and made hard men pitiful to brazen Hibernian beggars in the London streets for the memory of that pensive music. She could read the leaders in the 'Times,' with no false quantities in the Latin quotations, and knew what she was reading about; and had her favourites at St Stephen's;* and adored Lord Palmerston,* and was liberal to the core of her tender young heart. She was as brave as a true Englishwoman should be, and would have gone to the wars with her old father, and served him as his page; or would have followed him into captivity, and tended him in prison, if she had lived in the days when there was such work for a high-spirited girl to do.

But she sat opposite Mr Edward Arundel, and twisted her chain round her fingers, and listened for the footsteps of the returning mistress of the house. She was like a bashful schoolgirl who has danced with an officer at her first ball. And yet amidst her shy confusion, her fears that she should seem agitated and embarrassed, her struggles to appear at her ease, there was a sort of pleasure in being seated there by the low fire with Edward Arundel opposite to her. There was a strange pleasure, an almost painful pleasure, mingled with her feelings in those quiet moments. She was acutely conscious of every sound that broke the stillness—the sighing of the wind in the wide chimney; the falling of the cinders on the hearth; the occasional snort of one of the sleeping dogs; and the beating of her own restless heart. And though she dared not lift her eyelids to the young soldier's face, that handsome, earnest countenance, with the chestnut hair lit up with gleams of gold, the firm lips shaded by a brown moustache, the pensive smile, the broad white forehead, the dark-blue handkerchief tied loosely under a white collar, the careless grey travelling-dress, even the attitude of the hand and arm, the bent head drooping a little over the fire,—were as present to her inner sight as if her eyes had kept watch all this time, and had never wavered in their steady gaze.

There is a second-sight that is not recognised by grave professors of magic—a second-sight which common people call Love.

But by-and-by Edward began to talk, and then Miss Lawford

found courage, and took heart to question him about his wanderings in Brittany. She had only been a few weeks in Devonshire, she said. Her thoughts went back to the dreary autumn in Lincolnshire as she spoke; and she remembered the dull October day upon which her father had come into the girl's morning-room at the Grange with Edward's farewell letter in his hand. She remembered this, and all the talk that there had been about the horsewhipping of Mr Paul Marchmont upon his own threshold. She remembered all the warm discussions, the speculations, the ignorant conjectures, the praise, the blame; and how it had been her business to sit by and listen and hold her peace, except upon that one never-to-be-forgotten night at the Rectory, when Paul Marchmont had hinted at something whose perfect meaning she had never dared to imagine, but which had, somehow or other, mingled vaguely with all her day-dreams ever since.

Was there any truth in that which Paul Marchmont had said to her? Was it true that Edward Arundel had never really loved his young bride?

Letitia had said as much, not once, but twenty times.

'It's quite ridiculous to suppose that he could have ever been in love with the poor, dear, sickly thing,' Miss Arundel had exclaimed; 'it was only the absurd romance of the business that captivated him; for Edward is really ridiculously romantic, and her father having been a supernumer—(it's no use, I don't think anybody ever did know how many syllables there are in that word)—and having lived in Oakley Street, and having written a pitiful letter to Edward, about this motherless daughter and all that sort of thing, just like one of those tiresome old novels with a baby left at a cottage-door, and all the *s*'s looking like *f*'s, and the last word of one page repeated at the top of the next page, and printed upon thick yellow-looking ribbed paper, you know. *That* was why my brother married Miss March-mont, you may depend upon it, Linda; and all I hope is, that he'll be sensible enough to marry again soon, and to have a Christianlike wedding, with carriages, and a breakfast, and two clergymen; and *I* should wear white glacé silk, with tulle puffings, and a tulle bonnet (I suppose I must wear a bonnet, being only a bridesmaid?), all showered over with clematis, as if I'd stood under a clematis-bush when the wind was blowing, you know, Linda.'

With such discourse as this Miss Arundel had frequently

entertained her friend; and she had indulged in numerous innuendoes of an embarrassing nature as to the propriety of old friends and schoolfellows being united by the endearing tie of sister-in-lawhood, and other observations to the like effect.

Belinda knew that if Edward ever came to love her,—whenever she did venture to speculate upon such a chance, she never dared to come at all near it, but thought of it as a thing that might come to pass in half a century or so—if he should choose her for his second wife, she knew that she would be gladly and tenderly welcomed at Dangerfield. Mrs Arundel had hinted as much as this. Belinda knew how anxiously that loving mother hoped that her son might, by-and-by, form new ties, and cease to lead a purposeless life, wasting his brightest years in lamentations for his lost bride: she knew all this; and sitting opposite to the young man in the firelight, there was a dull pain at her heart; for there was something in the soldier's sombre face that told her he had not yet ceased to lament that irrevocable past.

But Mrs Arundel and Letitia came in presently, and gave utterance to loud rejoicings; and preparations were made for the physical comfort of the wanderer,—bells were rung, lighted wax-candles and a glittering tea-service were brought in, a cloth was laid, and cold meats and other comestibles spread forth, with that profusion which has made the west country as proverbial as the north for its hospitality. I think Miss Lawford would have sat opposite the traveller for a week without asking any such commonplace question as to whether Mr Arundel required refreshment. She had read in her Hort's 'Pantheon'* that the gods sometimes ate and drank like ordinary mortals; yet it had never entered into her mind that Edward could be hungry. But she now had the satisfaction of seeing Mr Arundel eat a very good dinner; while she herself poured out the tea, to oblige Letitia, who was in the middle of the third volume of a new novel, and went on reading it as coolly as if there had been no such person as that handsome young soldier in the world.

'The books must go back to the club to-morrow morning, you know, mamma dear, or I wouldn't read at tea-time,' the young lady remarked apologetically. 'I want to know whether *he'll* marry Theodora or that nasty Miss St Ledger. Linda thinks he'll marry Miss St Ledger, and be miserable, and Theodora will die. I believe Linda likes love-stories to end unhappily. I don't. I hope if he *does* marry Miss St Ledger—and he'll be a wicked wretch if he does, after the *things* he has said to Theodora—I hope, if he does, she'll die—catch cold at a *déjeúner* at Twickenham, or something of that kind, you know; and then he'll marry Theodora afterwards, and all will end happily. Do you know, Linda, I always fancy that you're like Theodora, and that Edward's like *him*.'

After which speech Miss Arundel went back to her book, and Edward helped himself to a slice of tongue rather awkwardly, and Belinda Lawford, who had her hand upon the urn, suffered the teapot to overflow amongst the cups and saucers.

CHAPTER XXXIV

A WIDOWER'S PROPOSAL

FOR some time after his return Edward Arundel was very restless and gloomy: roaming about the country by himself, under the influence of a pretended passion for pedestrianism; reading hard for the first time in his life, shutting himself in his dead father's library, and sitting hour after hour in a great easy-chair, reading the histories of all the wars that have ever ravaged this earth—from the days in which the elephants of a Carthaginian ruler trampled upon the soldiery of Rome, to the era of that Corsican barrister's wonderful son,* who came out of his simple island home to conquer the civilised half of a world.

Edward Arundel showed himself a very indifferent brother; for, do what she would, Letitia could not induce him to join in any of her pursuits. She caused a butt to be set up upon the lawn; but all she could say about Belinda's 'best gold'* could not bring the young man out upon the grass to watch the two girls shooting. He looked at them by stealth sometimes through the window of the library, and sighed as he thought of the blight upon his manhood, and of all the things that might have been.

Might not these things even yet come to pass? Had he not done his duty to the dead; and was he not free now to begin a fresh life? His mother was perpetually hinting at some bright prospect that lay smiling before him, if he chose to take the blossom-bestrewn path that led to that fair country. His sister told him still more plainly of a prize that was within his reach, if he were but brave enough to stretch out his hand and claim the precious treasure for his own. But when he thought of all this,—when he pondered whether it would not be wise to drop the dense curtain of forgetfulness over that sad picture of the past,—whether it would not be well to let the dead bury their dead, and to accept that other blessing which the same Providence that had blighted his first hope seemed to offer to him now,—the shadowy phantom of John Marchmont arose out of the mystic realms of the dead, and a ghostly voice cried to him, 'I charged you with my daughter's safe keeping; I trusted you with her innocent love; I gave you the custody of her helplessness. What have you done to show yourself worthy of my faith in you?'

These thoughts tormented the young widower perpetually, and deprived him of all pleasure in the congenial society of his sister and Belinda Lawford; or infused so sharp a flavour of remorse into his cup of enjoyment, that pleasure was akin to pain.

So I don't know how it was that, in the dusky twilight of a bright day in early May, nearly two months after his return to Dangerfield, Edward Arundel, coming by chance upon Miss Lawford as she sat alone in the deep bay-window where he had found her on his first coming, confessed to her the terrible struggle of feeling that made the great trouble of his life, and asked her if she was willing to accept a love which, in its warmest fervour, was not quite unclouded by the shadows of the sorrowful past.

'I love you dearly, Linda,' he said; 'I love, I esteem, I admire you; and I know that it is in your power to give me the happiest future that ever a man imagined in his youngest, brightest dreams. But if you do accept my love, dear, you must take my memory with it. I cannot forget, Linda. I have tried to forget. I have prayed that God, in His mercy, might give me forgetfulness of that irrevocable past. But the prayer has never been granted; the boon has never been bestowed. I think that love for the living and remorse for the dead must for ever reign side by side in my heart. It is no falsehood to you that makes me remember her; it is no forgetfulness of her that makes me love you. I offer my brighter and happier self to you, Belinda; I consecrate my sorrow and my tears to her. I love you with all my heart, Belinda; but even for the sake of your love I will not pretend that I can forget her. If John Marchmont's daughter had died with her head upon my breast, and a prayer on her lips, I might have regretted her as other men regret their wives; and I might have learned by-and-by to look back upon my grief with only a tender and natural regret, that would have left my future life unclouded. But it can never be so. The poison of remorse is blended with that sorrowful memory. If I had done otherwise,—if I had been wiser and more thoughtful,—my darling need never have suffered; my darling need never have sinned. It is the thought that her death may have been a sinful one, that is most cruel to me, Belinda. I have seen her pray, with her pale earnest face uplifted, and the light of faith shining in her gentle eyes; I have seen the inspiration of God upon her face; and

I cannot bear to think that, in the darkness that came down upon her young life, that holy light was quenched; I cannot bear to think that Heaven was ever deaf to the pitiful cry of my innocent lamb.'

And here Mr Arundel paused, and sat silently, looking out at the long shadows of the trees upon the darkening lawn; and I fear that, for the time being, he forgot that he had just made Miss Lawford an offer of his hand, and so much of his heart as a widower may be supposed to have at his disposal.

Ah me! we can only live and die *once*. There are some things, and those the most beautiful of all things, that can never be renewed: the bloom on a butterfly's wing; the morning dew upon a newly-blown rose; our first view of the ocean; our first pantomime, when all the fairies were fairies for ever, and when the imprudent consumption of the contents of a pewter quart-measure in sight of the stage-box could not disenchant us with that elfin creature, Harlequin the graceful, faithful betrothed of Columbine the fair. The firstlings of life are most precious. When the black wing of the angel of death swept over agonised Egypt, and the children were smitten, offended Heaven, eager for a sacrifice, took the firstborn.* The young mothers would have other children, perhaps; but between those others and the mother's love there would be the pale shadow of that lost darling whose tiny hands *first* drew undreamed-of melodies from the sleeping chords, *first* evoked the slumbering spirit of maternal love. Amongst the later lines—the most passionate, the most sorrowful—that George Gordon Noel Byron wrote, are some brief verses that breathed a lament for the lost freshness, the never-to-be-recovered youth.

> 'Oh, could I feel as I have felt; or be what I have been;
> Or weep as I could once have wept!'*

cried the poet, when he complained of that 'mortal coldness of the soul,' which is 'like death itself.' It is a pity certainly that so great a man should die in the prime of life; but if Byron had survived to old age after writing these lines, he would have been a living anticlimax. When a man writes that sort of poetry he pledges himself to die young.

Edward Arundel had grown to love Belinda Lawford unconsciously, and in spite of himself; but the first love of his heart, the first fruit of his youth, had perished. He could not feel quite the same devotion, the same boyish chivalry, that he had felt for the innocent bride who had wandered beside him in the sheltered meadows near Winchester. He might begin a *new* life, but he could not live the *old* life over again. He must wear his rue with a difference* this time. But he loved Belinda very dearly, nevertheless; and he told her so, and by-and-by won from her a tearful avowal of affection.

Alas! she had no power to question the manner of his wooing. He loved her—he had said as much; and all the good she had desired in this universe became hers from the moment of Edward Arundel's utterance of those words. He loved her; that was enough. That he should cherish a remorseful sorrow for that lost wife, made him only the truer, nobler, and dearer in Belinda's sight. She was not vain, or exacting, or selfish. It was not in her nature to begrudge poor dead Mary the tender thoughts of her husband. She was generous, impulsive, believing; and she had no more inclination to doubt Edward's love for her, after he had once avowed such a sentiment, than to disbelieve in the light of heaven when she saw the sun shining. Unquestioning, and unutterably happy, she received her lover's betrothal kiss, and went with him to his mother, blushing and trembling, to receive that lady's blessing.

'Ah, if you knew how I have prayed for this, Linda!' Mrs Arundel exclaimed, as she folded the girl's slight figure in her arms.

'And I shall wear white glacé with pinked flounces, instead of tulle puffings, you sly Linda,' cried Letitia.

'And I'll give Ted the home-farm, and the white house to live in, if he likes to try his hand at the new system of farming,' said Reginald Arundel, who had come home from the Continent, and had amused himself for the last week by strolling about his estate and staring at his timber, and almost wishing that there was a necessity for cutting down all the oaks in the avenue, so that he might have something to occupy him until the 12th of August.*

Never was promised bride more welcome to a household than bright Belinda Lawford; and as for the young lady herself, I must confess that she was almost childishly happy, and that it was all that she could do to prevent her light step from falling into a dance as she floated hither and thither through the house at Dangerfield,—a fresh young Hebe in crisp muslin robes; a gentle goddess, with smiles upon her face and happiness in her heart.

'I loved you from the first, Edward,' she whispered one day to her lover. 'I knew that you were good, and brave, and noble; and I loved you because of that.'

And a little for the golden glimmer in his clustering curls; and a little for his handsome profile, his flashing eyes, and that distinguished air peculiar to the defenders of their country; more especially peculiar, perhaps, to those who ride on horseback when they sally forth to defend her. Once a soldier for ever a soldier, I think. You may rob the noble warrior of his uniform, if you will; but the *je ne sais quoi*, the nameless air of the 'long-sword, saddle, bridle,' will hang round him still.

Mrs Arundel and Letitia took matters quite out of the hands of the two lovers. The elderly lady fixed the wedding-day, by agreement with Major Lawford, and sketched out the route for the wedding-tour. The younger lady chose the fabrics for the dresses of the bride and her attendants; and all was done before Edward and Belinda well knew what their friends were about. I think that Mrs Arundel feared her son might change his mind if matters were not brought swiftly to a climax, and that she hurried on the irrevocable day in order that he might have no breathing time until the vows had been spoken and Belinda Lawford was his wedded wife. It had been arranged that Edward should escort Belinda back to Lincolnshire, and that his mother and Letitia, who was to be chief bridesmaid, should go with them. The marriage was to be solemnised at Hillingsworth church, which was within a mile and a half of the Grange.

The 1st of July was the day appointed by agreement between Major and Mrs Lawford and Mrs Arundel; and on the 18th of June Edward was to accompany his mother, Letitia, and Belinda to London. They were to break the journey by stopping in town for a few days, in order to make a great many purchases necessary for Miss Lawford's wedding paraphernalia, for which the Major had sent a bouncing cheque* to his favourite daughter.

And all this time the only person at all unsettled, the only person whose mind was ill at ease, was Edward Arundel, the young widower who was about to take to himself a second wife. His mother, who watched him with a maternal comprehension of every change in his face, saw this, and trembled for her son's happiness.

'And yet he cannot be otherwise than happy with Belinda Lawford,' Mrs Arundel thought to herself.

But upon the eve of that journey to London Edward sat alone with his mother in the drawing-room at Dangerfield, after the two younger ladies had retired for the night. They slept in adjoining apartments, these two young ladies; and I regret to say that a great deal of their conversation was about Valenciennes lace, and flounces cut upon the cross, moiré antique, mull muslin, glacé silk, and the last 'sweet thing' in bonnets. It was only when loquacious Letitia was shut out that Miss Lawford knelt alone in the still moonlight, and prayed that she might be a good wife to the man who had chosen her. I don't think she ever prayed that she might be faithful and true and pure; for it never entered into her mind that any creature bearing the sacred name of wife could be otherwise. She only prayed for the mysterious power to preserve her husband's affection, and make his life happy.

Mrs Arundel, sitting *tête-à-tête* with her younger son in the lamp-lit drawing-room, was startled by hearing the young man breathe a deep sigh. She looked up from her work to see a sadder expression in his face than perhaps ever clouded the countenance of an expectant bridegroom.

'Edward!' she exclaimed.

'What, mother?'

'How heavily you sighed just now!'

'Did I?' said Mr Arundel, abstractedly. Then, after a brief pause, he said, in a different tone, 'It is no use trying to hide these things from you, mother. The truth is, I am not happy.'

'Not happy, Edward!' cried Mrs Arundel; 'but surely you——?'

'I know what you are going to say, mother. Yes, mother, I love this dear girl Linda with all my heart; I love her most sincerely; and I could look forward to a life of unalloyed happiness with her, if—if there was not some inexplicable dread, some vague and most miserable feeling always coming between me and my hopes. I have tried to look forward to the future, mother; I have tried to think of what my life may be with Belinda; but I cannot, I cannot. I cannot look forward; all is dark to me. I try to build up a bright palace, and an unknown hand shatters it. I try to turn away from the memory of my old sorrows; but the same hand plucks me back, and chains me to the past. If I could retract what I have done; if I could, with any show of honour, draw back, even now, and not go upon this journey to Lincolnshire; if I *could* break my faith to this poor girl who loves me, and whom I love, as God knows, with all truth and earnestness, I would do so—I would do so.'

'Edward!'

'Yes, mother; I would do it. It is not in me to forget. My dead wife haunts me by night and day. I hear her voice crying to me, "False, false, false; cruel and false; heartless and forgetful!" There is never a night that I do not dream of that dark sluggish river down in Lincolnshire. There is never a dream that I have—however purposeless, however inconsistent in all its other details—in which I do not see *her* dead face looking up at me through the murky waters. Even when I am talking to Linda, when words of love for her are on my lips, my mind wanders away, back—always back—to the sunset by the boat-house, when my little wife gave me her hand; to the trout-stream in the meadow, where we sat side by side and talked about the future.'

For a few minutes Mrs Arundel was quite silent. She abandoned herself for that brief interval to complete despair. It was all over. The bridegroom would cry off; insulted Major Lawford would come post-haste to Dangerfield, to annihilate this dismal widower, who did not know his own mind. All the shimmering fabrics—the gauzes, and laces, and silks, and velvets—that were in course of preparation in the upper chambers would become so much useless finery, to be hidden in out-of-the-way cupboards, and devoured by misanthropical moths,—insect iconoclasts, who take a delight in destroying the decorations of the human temple.

Poor Mrs Arundel took a mental photograph of all the complicated horrors of the situation. An offended father; a gentle, loving girl crushed like some broken lily; gossip, slander; misery of all kinds. And then the lady plucked up courage and gave her recreant son a sound lecture, to the effect that this conduct was atrociously wicked; and that if this trusting young bride, this fair young second wife, were to be taken away from him as the first had been, such a calamity would only be a fitting judgment upon him for his folly.

But Edward told his mother, very quietly, that he had no intention of being false to his newly-plighted troth.

'I love Belinda,' he said; 'and I will be true to her, mother. But I cannot forget the past; it hangs about me like a bad dream.'

CHAPTER XXXV

HOW THE TIDINGS WERE RECEIVED IN LINCOLNSHIRE

THE young widower made no further lamentation, but did his duty
to his betrothed bride with a cheerful visage. Ah! what a pleasant
journey it was to Belinda, that progress through London on the way
to Lincolnshire! It was like that triumphant journey of last March,*
when the Royal bridegroom led his Northern bride through a surging sea of eager, smiling faces, to the musical jangling of a thousand
bells. If there were neither populace nor joy-bells on this occasion, I
scarcely think Miss Lawford knew that those elements of a triumphal progress were missing. To her ears all the universe was
musical with the sound of mystic joy-bells; all the earth was glad
with the brightness of happy faces. The railway-carriage,—the
commonplace vehicle,—frouzy with the odour of wool and morocco,
was a fairy chariot, more wonderful than Queen Mab's;* the white
chalk-cutting in the hill was a shining cleft in a mountain of silver;
the wandering streams were melted diamonds; the stations were
enchanted castles. The pale sherry, carried in a pocket-flask, and
sipped out of a little silver tumbler—there is apt to be a warm
flatness about sherry taken out of pocket-flasks that is scarcely agreeable to the connoisseur—was like nectar newly brewed for the gods;
even the anchovies in the sandwiches were like the enchanted fish in
the Arabian story. A magical philter had been infused into the
atmosphere: the flavour of first love was in every sight and sound.

Was ever bridegroom more indulgent, more devoted, than Edward
Arundel? He sat at the counters of silk-mercers for the hour
together, while Mrs Arundel and the two girls deliberated over crisp
fabrics unfolded for their inspection. He was always ready to be
consulted, and gave his opinion upon the conflicting merits of
peach-colour and pink, apple-green and maize, with unwearying
attention. But sometimes, even while Belinda was smiling at him,
with the rippling silken stuff held up in her white hands, and making
a lustrous cascade upon the counter, the mystic hand plucked him
back, and his mind wandered away to that childish bride who had
chosen no splendid garments for her wedding, but had gone with
him to the altar as trustfully as a baby goes in its mother's arms to the

cradle. If he had been left alone with Belinda, with tender, sympathetic Belinda,—who loved him well enough to understand him, and was always ready to take her cue from his face, and to be joyous or thoughtful according to his mood,—it might have been better for him. But his mother and Letitia reigned paramount during this antenuptial week, and Mr Arundel was scarcely suffered to take breath. He was hustled hither and thither in the hot summer noontide. He was taken to choose a dressing-case for his bride; and he was made to look at glittering objects until his eyes ached, and he could see nothing but a bewildering dazzle of ormolu and silver-gilt. He was taken to a great emporium in Bond Street to select perfumery, and made to sniff at divers essences until his nostrils were unnaturally distended, and his olfactory nerves afflicted with temporary paralysis. There was jewellery of his mother and of Belinda's mother to be reset; and the hymeneal victim was compelled to sit for an hour or so, blinking at fiery-crested serpents that were destined to coil up his wife's arms, and emerald padlocks that were to lie upon her breast. And then, when his soul was weary of glaring splendours and glittering confusions, they took him round the Park, in a whirlpool of diaphanous bonnets, and smiling faces, and brazen harness, and emblazoned hammer-cloths, on the margin of a river whose waters were like molten gold under the blazing sun. And then they gave him a seat in an opera-box, and the crash of a monster orchestra, blended with the hum of a thousand voices, to soothe his nerves withal.

But the more wearied this young man became with glitter, and dazzle, and sunshine, and silk-mercer's ware, the more surely his mind wandered back to the still meadows, and the limpid trout-stream, the sheltering hills, the solemn shadows of the cathedral, the distant voices of the rooks high up in the waving elms.

The bustle of preparation was over at last, and the bridal party went down to Lincolnshire. Pleasant chambers had been prepared at the Grange for Mr Arundel and his mother and sister; and the bridegroom was received with enthusiasm by Belinda's blue-eyed younger sisters, who were enchanted to find that there was going to be a wedding and that they were to have new frocks.

So Edward would have been a churl indeed had he seemed otherwise than happy, had he been anything but devoted to the bright girl who loved him.

Tidings of the coming wedding flew like wildfire through

Lincolnshire. Edward Arundel's romantic story had elevated him into a hero; all manner of reports had been circulated about his devotion to his lost young wife. He had sworn never to mingle in society again, people said. He had sworn never to have a new suit of clothes, or to have his hair cut, or to shave, or to eat a hot dinner. And Lincolnshire by no means approved of the defection implied by his approaching union with Belinda. He was only a commonplace widower, after all, it seemed; ready to be consoled as soon as the ceremonious interval of decent grief was over. People had expected something better of him. They had expected to see him in a year or two with long grey hair, dressed in shabby raiment, and, with his beard upon his breast, prowling about the village of Kemberling, baited by little children. Lincolnshire was very much disappointed by the turn that affairs had taken. Shakesperian aphorisms were current among the gossips at comfortable tea-tables; and people talked about funeral baked meats, and the propriety of building churches* if you have any ambitious desire that your memory should outlast your life; and indulged in other bitter observations, familiar to all admirers of the great dramatist.

But there were some people in Lincolnshire to whom the news of Edward Arundel's intended marriage was more welcome than the early May-flowers to rustic children eager for a festival. Paul Marchmont heard the report, and rubbed his hands stealthily, and smiled to himself as he sat reading in the sunny western drawing-room. The good seed that he had sown that night at the Rectory had borne this welcome fruit. Edward Arundel with a young wife would be very much less formidable than Edward Arundel single and dis-contented, prowling about the neighbourhood of Marchmont Towers, and perpetually threatening vengeance upon Mary's cousin.

It was busy little Lavinia Weston who first brought her brother the tidings. He took both her hands in his, and kissed them in his enthusiasm.

'My best of sisters,' he said, 'you shall have a pair of diamond earrings for this.'

'For only bringing you the news, Paul?'

'For only bringing me the news. When a messenger carries the tidings of a great victory to his king, the king makes him a knight upon the spot. This marriage is a victory to me, Lavinia. From to-day I shall breathe freely.'

'But they are not married yet. Something may happen, perhaps, to prevent——'

'What should happen?' asked Paul, rather sharply. 'By-the-bye, it will be as well to keep this from Mrs John,' he added, thoughtfully; 'though really now I fancy it matters very little what she hears.'

He tapped his forehead lightly with his two slim fingers, and there was a horrible significance in the action.

'She is not likely to hear anything,' Mrs Weston said; 'she sees no one but Barbara Simmons.'

'Then I should be glad if you would give Simmons a hint to hold her tongue. This news about the wedding would disturb her mistress.'

'Yes, I'll tell her so. Barbara is a very excellent person. I can always manage Barbara. But oh, Paul, I don't know what I'm to do with that poor weak-witted husband of mine.'

'How do you mean?'

'Oh, Paul, I have had such a scene with him to-day—such a scene! You remember the way he went on that day down in the boat-house when Edward Arundel came in upon us unexpectedly? Well, he's been going on as badly as that to-day, Paul,—or worse, I really think.'

Mr Marchmont frowned, and flung aside his newspaper, with a gesture expressive of considerable vexation.

'Now really, Lavinia, this is too bad,' he said; 'if your husband is a fool, I am not going to be bored about his folly. You have managed him for fifteen years: surely you can go on managing him now without annoying *me* about him? If Mr George Weston doesn't know when he's well off; he's an ungrateful cur, and you may tell him so, with my compliments.'

He picked up his newspaper again, and began to read. But Lavinia Weston, looking anxiously at her brother's face, saw that his pale auburn brows were contracted in a thoughtful frown, and that, if he read at all, the words upon which his eyes rested could convey very little meaning to his brain.

She was right; for presently he spoke to her, still looking at the page before him, and with an attempt at carelessness.

'Do you think that fellow would go to Australia, Lavinia?'

'Alone?' asked his sister.

'Yes, alone of course,' said Mr Marchmont, putting down his

paper, and looking at Mrs Weston rather dubiously. 'I don't want you to go to the Antipodes; but if—if the fellow refused to go without you, I'd make it well worth your while to go out there, Lavinia. You shouldn't have any reason to regret obliging me, my dear girl.'

The dear girl looked rather sharply at her affectionate brother.

'It's like your selfishness, Paul, to propose such a thing,' she said, 'after all I've done——!'

'I have not been illiberal to you, Lavinia.'

'No; you've been generous enough to me, I know, in the matter of gifts; but you're rich, Paul, and you can afford to give. I don't like the idea that you're so willing to pack me out of the way now that I can be no longer useful to you.'

Mr Marchmont shrugged his shoulders.

'For Heaven's sake, Lavinia, don't be sentimental. If there's one thing I despise more than another, it is this kind of mawkish sentimentality. You've been a very good sister to me; and I've been a very decent brother to you. If you have served me, I have made it answer your purpose to do so. I don't want you to go away. You may bring all your goods and chattels to this house to-morrow, if you like, and live at free quarters here for the rest of your existence. But if George Weston is a pig-headed brute, who can't understand upon which side his bread is buttered, he must be got out of the way somehow. I don't care what it costs me; but he must be got out of the way. I'm not going to live the life of a modern Damocles,* with a blundering sword always dangling over my head, in the person of Mr George Weston. And if the man objects to leave the country without you, why, I think your going with him would be only a sisterly act towards me. I hate selfishness, Lavinia, almost as much as I detest sentimentality.'

Mrs Weston was silent for some minutes, absorbed in reflection. Paul got up, kicked aside a footstool, and walked up and down the room with his hands in his pockets.

'Perhaps I might get George to leave England, if I promised to join him as soon as he was comfortably settled in the colonies,' Mrs Weston said, at last.

'Yes,' cried Paul; 'nothing could be more easy. I'll act very liberally towards him, Lavinia; I'll treat him well; but he shall not stay in England. No, Lavinia; after what you have told me to-day, I feel that he must be got out of the country.'

Mr Marchmont went to the door and looked out, to see if by

chance any one had been listening to him. The coast was quite clear. The stone-paved hall looked as desolate as some undiscovered chamber in an Egyptian temple. The artist went back to Lavinia, and seated himself by her side. For some time the brother and sister talked together earnestly.

They settled everything for poor henpecked George Weston. He was to sail for Sydney immediately. Nothing could be more easy than for Lavinia to declare that her brother had accidentally heard of some grand opening for a medical practitioner in the metropolis of the Antipodes. The surgeon was to have a very handsome sum given him, and Lavinia would *of course* join him as soon as he was settled. Paul Marchmont even looked through the 'Shipping Gazette' in search of an Australian vessel which should speedily convey his brother-in-law to a distant shore.

Lavinia Weston went home armed with all necessary credentials. She was to promise almost anything to her husband, provided that he gave his consent to an early departure.

CHAPTER XXXVI

MR WESTON REFUSES TO BE TRAMPLED UPON

UPON the 30th of June,* the eve of Edward Arundel's wedding-day, Olivia Marchmont sat in her own room,—the room that she had chiefly occupied ever since her husband's death,—the study looking out into the quadrangle. She sat alone in that dismal chamber, dimly lighted by a pair of wax-candles, in tall tarnished silver candlesticks. There could be no greater contrast than that between this desolate woman and the master of the house. All about him was bright and fresh, and glittering and splendid; around her there was only ruin and decay, thickening dust and gathering cobwebs,—outward evidences of an inner wreck. John Marchmont's widow was of no importance in that household. The servants did not care to trouble themselves about her whims or wishes, nor to put her rooms in order. They no longer curtseyed to her when they met her, wandering— with a purposeless step and listless feet that dragged along the ground—up and down the corridor, or out in the dreary quadrangle. What was to be gained by any show of respect to her, whose brain was too weak to hold the memory of their conduct for five minutes together?

Barbara Simmons only was faithful to her mistress with an unvarying fidelity. She made no boast of her devotion; she expected neither fee nor reward for her self-abnegation. That rigid religion of discipline which had not been strong enough to preserve Olivia's stormy soul from danger and ruin was at least all-sufficient for this lower type of woman. Barbara Simmons had been taught to do her duty, and she did it without question or complaint. As she went through rain, snow, hail, or sunshine twice every Sunday to Kemberling church,—as she sat upon a cushionless seat in an uncomfortable angle of the servants' pew, with the sharp edges of the woodwork cutting her thin shoulders, to listen patiently to dull rambling sermons upon the hardest texts of St Paul,—so she attended upon her mistress, submitting to every caprice, putting up with every hardship; because it was her duty so to do. The only relief she allowed herself was an hour's gossip now and then in the housekeeper's room; but she never alluded to her mistress's infirmities, nor would it have been safe for any other servant to have spoken lightly of Mrs John Marchmont in stern Barbara's presence.

Upon this summer evening, when happy people were still lingering amongst the wild flowers in shady lanes, or in the dusky pathways by the quiet river, Olivia sat alone, staring at the candles.

Was there anything in her mind; or was she only a human automaton, slowly decaying into dust? There was no speculation in those large lustreless eyes, fixed upon the dim light of the candles. But, for all that, the mind was not a blank. The pictures of the past, for ever changing like the scenes in some magic panorama, revolved before her. She had no memory of that which had happened a quarter of an hour ago; but she could remember every word that Edward Arundel had said to her in the Rectory-garden at Swampington,—every intonation of the voice in which those words had been spoken.

There was a tea-service on the table: an attenuated little silver teapot; a lopsided cream-jug, with thin worn edges and one dumpy little foot missing; and an antique dragon china cup and saucer with the gilding washed off. That meal, which is generally called social, has but a dismal aspect when it is only prepared for one. The solitary teacup, half filled with cold, stagnant tea, with a leaf or two floating upon the top, like weeds on the surface of a tideless pond; the tea-spoon, thrown askew across a little pool of spilt milk in the tea-tray,—looked as dreary as the ruins of a deserted city.

In the western drawing-room Paul was strolling backwards and forwards, talking to his mother and sisters, and admiring his pictures. He had spent a great deal of money upon art since taking possession of the Towers, and the western drawing-room was quite a different place to what it had been in John Marchmont's lifetime.

Etty's* divinities smiled through hazy draperies, more transparent than the summer vapours that float before the moon. Pearly-complexioned nymphs, with faces archly peeping round the corner of soft rosy shoulders, frolicked amidst the silver spray of classic fountains. Turner's* Grecian temples glimmered through sultry summer mists; while glimpses of ocean sparkled here and there, and were as beautiful as if the artist's brush had been dipped in melted opals. Stanfield's* breezy beaches made cool spots of freshness on the wall, and sturdy sailor-boys, with their hands up to their mouths and their loose hair blowing in the wind, shouted to their comrades upon the decks of brown-sailed fishing-smacks. Panting deer upon dizzy

crags, amid the misty Highlands, testified to the hand of Landseer.*
Low down, in the corners of the room, there lurked quaint cottage-
scenes by Faed and Nichol. Ward's* patched and powdered beaux and
beauties,—a Rochester, in a light perriwig; a Nell Gwynne, showing
her white teeth across a basket of oranges; a group of *Incroyables*,*
with bunches of ribbons hanging from their low topboots, and two
sets of dangling seals at their waists—made a blaze of colour upon
the walls: and amongst all these glories of to-day there were prim
Madonnas and stiff-necked angels by Raphael and Tintoretto; a
brown-faced grinning boy by Murillo* (no collection ever was complete without that inevitable brown-faced boy); an obese Venus, by
the great Peter Paul;* and a pale Charles the First, with martyrdom
foreshadowed in his pensive face, by Vandyke.*

Paul Marchmont contemplated his treasures complacently, as he
strolled about the room, with his coffee-cup in his hand; while his
mother watched him admiringly from her comfortable cushioned
nest at one end of a luxurious sofa.

'Well, mother,' Mr Marchmont said presently, 'let people say
what they may of me, they can never say that I have used my money
badly. When I am dead and gone, these pictures will remain to speak
for me; posterity will say, "At any rate the fellow was a man of taste."
Now what, in Heaven's name, could that miserable little Mary have
done with eleven thousand a year, if—if she had lived to enjoy it?'

The minute-hand of the little clock in Mrs John Marchmont's study
was creeping slowly towards the quarter before eleven, when Olivia
was aroused suddenly from that long reverie, in which the images of
the past had shone upon her across the dull stagnation of the present
like the domes and minarets in a Phantasm City gleaming athwart
the barren desert-sands.

She was aroused by a cautious tap upon the outside of her window. She got up, opened the window, and looked out. The night was
dark and starless, and there was a faint whisper of wind among the
trees.

'Don't be frightened,' whispered a timid voice; 'it's only me,
George Weston. I want to talk to you, Mrs John. I've got something
particular to tell you—awful particular; but *they* mustn't hear it; *they*
mustn't know I'm here. I came round this way on purpose. You can
let me in at the little door in the lobby, can't you, Mrs John? I tell

you, I must tell you what I've got to tell you,' cried Mr Weston, indifferent to tautology in his excitement. 'Do let me in, there's a dear good soul. The little door in the lobby, you know; it's locked, you know, but I dessay the key's there.'

'The door in the lobby?' repeated Olivia, in a dreamy voice.

'Yes, *you* know. Do let me in now, that's a good creature. It's awful particular, I tell you. It's about Edward Arundel.'

Edward Arundel! The sound of that name seemed to act upon the woman's shattered nerves like a stroke of electricity. The drooping head reared itself erect. The eyes, so lustreless before, flashed fire from their sombre depths. Comprehension, animation, energy returned; as suddenly as if the wand of an enchanter had summoned the dead back to life.

'Edward Arundel!' she cried, in a clear voice, which was utterly unlike the dull deadness of her usual tones.

'Hush,' whispered Mr Weston; 'don't speak loud, for goodness gracious sake. I dessay there's all manner of spies about. Let me in, and I'll tell you everything.'

'Yes, yes; I'll let you in. The door by the lobby—I understand; come, come.'

Olivia disappeared from the window. The lobby of which the surgeon had spoken was close to her own apartment. She found the key in the lock of the door. The place was dark; she opened the door almost noiselessly, and Mr Weston crept in on tiptoe. He followed Olivia into the study, closed the door behind him, and drew a long breath.

'I've got in,' he said; 'and now I am in, wild horses shouldn't hold me from speaking my mind, much less Paul Marchmont.'

He turned the key in the door as he spoke, and even as he did so glanced rather suspiciously towards the window. To his mind the very atmosphere of that house was pervaded by the presence of his brother-in-law.

'O Mrs John!' exclaimed the surgeon, in piteous accents, 'the way that I've been trampled upon. *You've* been trampled upon, Mrs John, but you don't seem to mind it; and perhaps it's better to bring oneself to that, if one can; but I can't. I've tried to bring myself to it; I've even taken to drinking, Mrs John, much as it goes against me; and I've tried to drown my feelings as a man in rum-and-water. But the more spirits I consume, Mrs John, the more of a man I feel.'

Mr Weston struck the top of his hat with his clenched fist, and stared fiercely at Olivia, breathing very hard, and breathing rum-and-water with a faint odour of lemon-peel.

'Edward Arundel!—what about Edward Arundel?' said Olivia, in a low eager voice.

'I'm coming to that, Mrs John, in due c'course,' returned Mr Weston, with an air of dignity that was superior even to hiccough. 'What I say, Mrs John,' he added, in a confidential and argumentative tone, 'is this: *I won't be trampled upon!*' Here his voice sank to an awful whisper. 'Of course it's pleasant enough to have one's rent provided for, and not to be kept awake by poor's-rates, Mrs John; but, good gracious me! I'd rather have the Queen's taxes and the poor-rates following me up day and night, and a man in possession* to provide for at every meal—and you don't know how contemptuous a man in possession can look at you if you offer him salt butter, or your table in a general way don't meet his views—than the conscience I've had since Paul Marchmont came into Lincolnshire. I feel, Mrs John, as if I'd committed oceans of murders. It's a miracle to me that my hair hasn't turned white before this; and it would have done it, Mrs J., if it wasn't of that stubborn nature which is too wiry to give expression to a man's sufferings. O Mrs John, when I think how my pangs of conscience have been made game of,—when I remember the insulting names I have been called, because my heart didn't happen to be made of adamant,—my blood boils; it boils, Mrs John, to that degree, that I feel the time has come for action. I have been put upon until the spirit of manliness within me blazes up like a fiery furnace. I have been trodden upon, Mrs John; but I'm not the worm they took me for. To-day they've put the finisher upon it.' The surgeon paused to take breath. His mild and rather sheep-like countenance was flushed; his fluffy eyebrows twitched convulsively in his endeavours to give expression to the violence of his feelings. 'To-day they've put the finisher upon it,' he repeated. 'I'm to go to Australia, am I? Ha! ha! we'll see about that. There's a nice opening in the medical line, is there? and dear Paul will provide the funds to start me! Ha! ha! two can play at that game. It's all brotherly kindness, of course, and friendly interest in my welfare—that's what it's *called*, Mrs J. Shall I tell you what it *is*? I'm to be got rid of; at any price, for fear my conscience should get the better of me, and I should speak. I've been made a tool of, and I've been trampled upon; but they've been *obliged* to trust me. I've got a conscience, and I don't suit their views. If I hadn't got a conscience, I might stop here and have my rent and taxes provided for, and riot in rum-and-water to the end of my days. But I've a conscience that all the pineapple rum in Jamaica wouldn't drown, and they're frightened of me.'

Olivia listened to all this with an impatient frown upon her face. I doubt if she knew the meaning of Mr Weston's complaints. She had been listening only for the one name that had power to transform her from a breathing automaton into a living, thinking, reasoning woman. She grasped the surgeon's wrist fiercely.

'You told me you came here to speak about Edward Arundel,' she said. 'Have you been only trying to make a fool of me?'

'No, Mrs John; I have come to speak about him, and I come to you, because I think you're not so bad as Paul Marchmont. I think that you've been a tool, like myself; and they've led you on, step by step, from bad to worse, pretty much as they have led me. You're Edward Arundel's blood-relation, and it's your business to look to any wrong that's done him, more than it is mine. But if you don't speak, Mrs John, I will. Edward Arundel is going to be married.'

'Going to be married!' The words burst from Olivia's lips in a kind of shriek, and she stood glaring hideously at the surgeon, with her lips apart and her eyes dilated. Mr Weston was fascinated by the horror of that gaze, and stared at her in silence for some moments. 'You are a madman!' she exclaimed, after a pause; 'you are a madman! Why do you come here with your idiotic fancies? Surely my life is miserable enough without this!'

'I ain't mad, Mrs John, any more than'—Mr Weston was going to say, 'than you are;' but it struck him that, under existing circumstances, the comparison might be ill-advised—'I ain't any madder than other people,' he said, presently. 'Edward Arundel is going to be married. I have seen the young lady in Kemberling with her pa; and she's a very sweet young woman to look at; and her name is Belinda Lawford; and the wedding is to be at eleven o'clock to-morrow morning at Hillingsworth Church.'

Olivia slowly lifted her hands to her head, and swept the loose hair away from her brow. All the mists that had obscured her brain melted slowly away, and showed her the past as it had really been in all its naked horror. Yes; step by step the cruel hand had urged her on from bad to worse; from bad to worse; until it had driven her *here*.

It was for *this* that she had sold her soul to the powers of hell. It was for *this* that she had helped to torture that innocent girl whom a dying father had given into her pitiless hand. For this! for this! To find at last that all her iniquity had been wasted, and that Edward Arundel had chosen another bride—fairer, perhaps, than the first. The mad, unholy jealousy of her nature awoke from the obscurity of mental decay, a fierce ungovernable spirit. But another spirit arose in the next moment. CONSCIENCE, which so long had slumbered, awoke and cried to her, in an awful voice, 'Sinner, whose sin has been wasted, repent! restore! It is not yet too late.'

The stern precepts of her religion came back to her. She had rebelled against those rigid laws, she had cast off those iron fetters, only to fall into a worse bondage; only to submit to a stronger tyranny. She had been a servant of the God of Sacrifice, and had rebelled when an offering was demanded of her. She had cast off the yoke of her Master, and had yielded herself up the slave of sin. And now, when she discovered whither her chains had dragged her, she was seized with a sudden panic, and wanted to go back to her old master.

She stood for some minutes with her open palms pressed upon her forehead, and her chest heaving as if a stormy sea had raged in her bosom.

'This marriage must not take place,' she cried, at last.

'Of course it mustn't,' answered Mr Weston; 'didn't I say so just now? And if you don't speak to Paul and prevent it, I will. I'd rather you spoke to him, though,' added the surgeon thoughtfully, 'because, you see, it would come better from you, wouldn't it now?'

Olivia Marchmont did not answer. Her hands had dropped from her head, and she was standing looking at the floor.

'There shall be no marriage,' she muttered, with a wild laugh. 'There's another heart to be broken—that's all. Stand aside, man,' she cried; 'stand aside, and let me go to *him*; let me go to him.'

She pushed the terrified surgeon out of her pathway, and locked the door, hurried along the passage and across the hall. She opened the door of the western drawing-room, and went in.

Mr Weston stood in the corridor looking after her. He waited for a few minutes, listening for any sound that might come from the western drawing-room. But the wide stone hall was between him and that apartment; and however loudly the voices might have been uplifted, no breath of them could have reached the surgeon's ear. He waited for about five minutes, and then crept into the lobby and let himself out into the quadrangle.

'At any rate, nobody can say that I'm a coward,' he thought complacently, as he went under a stone archway that led into the park. 'But what a whirlwind that woman is! O my gracious, what a perfect whirlwind she is!'

CHAPTER XXXVII

'GOING TO BE MARRIED'

PAUL MARCHMONT was still strolling hither and thither about the room, admiring his pictures, and smiling to himself at the recollection of the easy manner in which he had obtained George Weston's consent to the Australian arrangement. For in his sober moments the surgeon was ready to submit to anything his wife and brother-in-law imposed upon him; it was only under the influence of pineapple rum that his manhood asserted itself. Paul was still contemplating his pictures when Olivia burst into the room; but Mrs Marchmont and her invalid daughter had retired for the night, and the artist was alone,—alone with his own thoughts, which were rather of a triumphal and agreeable character just now; for Edward's marriage and Mr Weston's departure were equally pleasant to him.

He was startled a little by Olivia's abrupt entrance, for it was not her habit to intrude upon him or any member of that household; on the contrary, she had shown an obstinate determination to shut herself up in her own room, and to avoid every living creature except her servant Barbara Simmons.

Paul turned and confronted her very deliberately, and with the smile that was almost habitual to him upon his thin pale lips. Her sudden appearance had blanched his face a little; but beyond this he betrayed no sign of agitation.

'My dear Mrs Marchmont, you quite startle me. It is so very unusual to see you here, and at this hour especially.'

It did not seem as if she had heard his voice. She went sternly up to him, with her thin listless arms hanging at her side, and her haggard eyes fixed upon his face.

'Is this true?' she asked.

He started a little, in spite of himself; for he understood in a moment what she meant. Some one, it scarcely mattered who, had told her of the coming marriage.

'Is what true, my dear Mrs John?' he said carelessly.

'Is this true that George Weston tells me?' she cried, laying her thin hand upon his shoulder. Her wasted fingers closed involuntarily upon the collar of his coat, her lips contracted into a ghastly smile, and a sudden fire kindled in her eyes. A strange sensation awoke in the tips of those tightening fingers, and thrilled through every vein of the woman's body,—such a horrible thrill as vibrates along the nerves of a monomaniac, when the sight of a dreadful terror in his victim's face first arouses the murderous impulse in his breast.

Paul's face whitened as he felt the thin finger-points tightening upon his neck. He was afraid of Olivia.

'My dear Mrs John, what is it you want of me?' he said hastily. 'Pray do not be violent.'

'I am not violent.'

She dropped her hand from his breast. It was true, she was not violent. Her voice was low; her hand fell loosely by her side. But Paul was frightened of her, nevertheless; for he saw that if she was not violent, she was something worse—she was dangerous.

'Did George Weston tell me the truth just now?' she said.

Paul bit his nether-lip savagely. George Weston had tricked him, then, after all, and had communicated with this woman. But what of that? She would scarcely be likely to trouble herself about this business of Edward Arundel's marriage. She must be past any such folly as that. She would not dare to interfere in the matter. She could not.

'Is it true?' she said ; '*is* it? Is it true that Edward Arundel is going to be married to-morrow?'

She waited, looking with fixed, widely-opened eyes at Paul's face.

'My dear Mrs John, you take me so completely by surprise, that I——'

'That you have not got a lying answer ready for me,' said Olivia, interrupting him. 'You need not trouble yourself to invent one. I see that George Weston told me the truth. There was reality in his words. There is nothing but falsehood in yours.'

Paul stood looking at her, but not listening to her. Let her abuse and upbraid him to her heart's content; it gave him leisure to reflect, and plan his course of action; and perhaps these bitter words might exhaust the fire within her, and leave her malleable to his skilful hands once more. He had time to think this, and to settle his own line of conduct while Olivia was speaking to him. It was useless to deny the marriage. She had heard of it from George Weston, and she might hear of it from any one else whom she chose to interrogate. It was useless to try to stifle this fact.

'Yes, Mrs John,' he said, 'it is quite true. Your cousin, Mr Arundel, is going to marry Belinda Lawford; a very lucky thing for us, believe me, as it will put an end to all questioning and watching and suspicion, and place us beyond all danger.'

Olivia looked at him, with her bosom heaving, her breath growing shorter and louder with every word he spoke.

'You mean to let this be, then?' she said, when he had finished speaking.

'To let what be?'

'This marriage. You will let it take place?'

'Most certainly. Why should I prevent it?'

'Why should you prevent it?' she cried fiercely; and then, in an altered voice, in tones of anguish that were like a wail of despair, she exclaimed, 'O my God! my God! what a dupe I have been; what a miserable tool in this man's hands! O my offended God! why didst Thou so abandon me, when I turned away from Thee, and made Edward Arundel the idol of my wicked heart?'

Paul sank into the nearest chair, with a faint sigh of relief.

'She will wear herself out,' he thought, 'and then I shall be able to do what I like with her.'

But Olivia turned to him again while he was thinking this.

'Do you imagine that *I* will let this marriage take place?' she asked.

'I do not think that you will be so mad as to prevent it. That little mystery which you and I have arranged between us is not exactly child's play, Mrs John. We can neither of us afford to betray the other. Let Edward Arundel marry, and work for his wife, and be happy; nothing could be better for us than his marriage. Indeed, we have every reason to be thankful to Providence for the turn that affairs have taken,' Mr Marchmont concluded, piously.

'Indeed!' said Olivia; 'and Edward Arundel is to have another bride. He is to be happy with another wife; and I am to hear of their happiness, to see him some day, perhaps, sitting by her side and smiling at her, as I have seen him smile at Mary Marchmont. He is to be happy, and I am to know of his happiness. Another baby-faced girl is to glory in the knowledge of his love; and I am to be quiet—I am to be quiet. Is it for this that I have sold my soul to you, Paul Marchmont? Is it for this I have shared your guilty secrets? Is it for this I have heard *her* feeble wailing sounding in my wretched feverish slumbers, as I have heard it every night, since the day she left this house? Do you remember what you said to me? Do you remember *how* you tempted me? Do you remember how you played upon my misery, and traded on the tortures of my jealous heart? "He has despised your love," you said: "will you consent to see him happy with another woman?" That was your argument, Paul Marchmont. You allied yourself with the devil that held possession of my breast, and together you were too strong for me. I was set apart to be damned, and you were the chosen instrument of my damnation. You bought my soul, Paul Marchmont. You shall not cheat me of the price for which I sold it. You shall hinder this marriage!'

'You are a madwoman, Mrs John Marchmont, or you would not propose any such thing.'

'Go,' she said, pointing to the door; 'go to Edward Arundel, and do something, no matter what, to prevent this marriage.'

'I shall do nothing of the kind.'

He had heard that a monomaniac was always to be subdued by indomitable resolution, and he looked at Olivia, thinking to tame her by his unfaltering glance. He might as well have tried to look the raging sea into calmness.

'I am not a fool, Mrs John Marchmont,' he said, 'and I shall do nothing of the kind.'

He had risen, and stood by the lamp-lit table, trifling rather nervously with its elegant litter of delicately-bound books, jewel-handled paper-knives, newly-cut periodicals, and pretty fantastical toys collected by the women of the household.

The faces of the two were nearly upon a level as they stood opposite to each other, with only the table between them.

'Then *I* will prevent it!' Olivia cried, turning towards the door.

Paul Marchmont saw the resolution stamped upon her face. She would do what she threatened. He ran to the door and had his hand upon the lock before she could reach it.

'No, Mrs John,' he said, standing at the door, with his back turned to Olivia, and his fingers busy with the bolts and key. In spite of himself, this woman had made him a little nervous, and it was as much as he could do to find the handle of the key. 'No, no, my dear Mrs John; you shall not leave this house, nor this room, in your present state of mind. If you choose to be violent and unmanageable, we will give you the full benefit of your violence, and we will give you a better sphere of action. A padded room will be more suitable to your present temper, my dear madam. If you favour us with this sort of conduct, we will find people more fitted to restrain you.'

He said all this in a sneering tone that had a trifling tremulousness in it, while he locked the door and assured himself that it was safely secured. Then he turned, prepared to fight out the battle somehow or other.

At the very moment of his turning there was a sudden crash, a shiver of broken glass, and the cold night-wind blew into the room. One of the long French windows was wide open, and Olivia Marchmont was gone.

He was out upon the terrace in the next moment; but even then he was too late, for he could not see her right or left of him upon the long stone platform. There were three separate flights of steps, three different paths, widely diverging across the broad grassy flat before Marchmont Towers. How could he tell which of these ways Olivia might have chosen? There was the great porch, and there were all manner of stone abutments along the grim façade of the house. She might have concealed herself behind any one of them. The night was hopelessly dark. A pair of ponderous bronze lamps, which Paul had placed before the principal doorway, only made two spots of light in the gloom. He ran along the terrace, looking into every nook and corner which might have served as a hiding-place; but he did not find Olivia.

She had left the house with the avowed intention of doing something to prevent the marriage. What would she do? What course would this desperate woman take in her jealous rage? Would she go straight to Edward Arundel and tell him——?

Yes, this was most likely; for how else could she hope to prevent the marriage?

Paul stood quite still upon the terrace for a few minutes, thinking. There was only one course for him. To try and find Olivia would be next to hopeless. There were half-a-dozen outlets from the park. There were ever so many different pathways through the woody labyrinth at the back of the Towers. This woman might have taken any one of them. To waste the night in searching for her would be worse than useless.

There was only one thing to be done. He must countercheck this desperate creature's movements.

He went back to the drawing-room, shut the window, and then rang the bell.

There were not many of the old servants who had waited upon John Marchmont at the Towers now. The man who answered the bell was a person whom Paul had brought down from London.

'Get the chestnut saddled for me, Peterson,' said Mr Marchmont. 'My poor cousin's widow has left the house, and I am going after her. She has given me very great alarm to-night by her conduct. I tell you this in confidence; but you can say as much to Mrs Simmons, who knows more about her mistress than I do. See that there's no time lost in saddling the chestnut. I want to overtake this unhappy woman, if I can. Go and give the order, and then bring me my hat.'

The man went away to obey his master. Paul walked to the chimneypiece and looked at the clock.

'They'll be gone to bed at the Grange,' he thought to himself. 'Will she go there and knock them up, I wonder? Does she know that Edward's there? I doubt that; and yet Weston may have told her. At any rate, I can be there before her. It would take her a long time to get there on foot. I think I did the right thing in saying what I said to Peterson. I must have the report of her madness spread everywhere. I must face it out. But how—but how? So long as she was quiet, I could manage everything. But with her against me, and George Weston—oh, the cur, the white-hearted villain, after all that I've done for him and Lavinia! But what can a man expect when he's obliged to put his trust in a fool?'

He went to the window, and stood there looking out until he saw the groom coming along the gravel roadway below the terrace, leading a horse by the bridle. Then he put on the hat that the servant had brought him, ran down the steps, and got into the saddle.

'All right, Jeffreys,' he said; 'tell them not to expect me back till to-morrow morning. Let Mrs Simmons sit up for her mistress. Mrs John may return at any hour in the night.'

He galloped away along the smooth carriage-drive. At the lodge he stopped to inquire if any one had been through that way. No, the woman said; she had opened the gates for no one. Paul had expected no other answer. There was a footpath that led to a little wicket-gate opening on the high-road; and of course Olivia had chosen that way, which was a good deal shorter than the carriage-drive.

CHAPTER XXXVIII

THE TURNING OF THE TIDE

IT was past two o'clock in the morning of the day which had been appointed for Edward Arundel's wedding, when Paul Marchmont drew rein before the white gate that divided Major Lawford's garden from the high-road. There was no lodge, no pretence of grandeur here. An old-fashioned garden surrounded an old-fashioned red-brick house. There was an apple-orchard upon one side of the low white gate, and a flower-garden, with a lawn and fish-pond, upon the other. The carriage-drive wound sharply round to a shallow flight of steps, and a broad door with a narrow window upon each side of it.

Paul got off his horse at the gate, and went in, leading the animal by the bridle. He was a Cockney, heart and soul, and had no sense of any enjoyments that were not of a Cockney nature. So the horse he had selected for himself was anything but a fiery creature. He liked plenty of bone and very little blood in the steed he rode, and was contented to go at a comfortable, jog-trot, seven-miles-an-hour pace, along the wretched country roads.

There was a row of old-fashioned wooden posts, with iron chains swinging between them, upon both sides of the doorway. Paul fastened the horse's bridle to one of these, and went up the steps. He rang a bell that went clanging and jangling through the house in the stillness of the summer night. All the way along the road he had looked right and left, expecting to pass Olivia; but he had seen no sign of her. This was nothing, however; for there were byways by which she might come from Marchmont Towers to Lawford Grange.

'I must be before her, at any rate,' Paul thought to himself, as he waited patiently for an answer to his summons.

The time seemed very long to him, of course; but at last he saw a light glimmering through the mansion windows, and heard a shuffling foot in the hall. Then the door was opened very cautiously, and a woman's scared face peered out at Mr Marchmont through the opening.

'What is it?' the woman asked, in a frightened voice.

'It is I, Mr Marchmont, of Marchmont Towers. Your master knows me. Mr Arundel is here, is he not?'

'Yes, and Mrs Arundel too; but they're all abed.'

'Never mind that; I must see Major Lawford immediately.'

'But they're all abed.'

'Never mind that, my good woman; I tell you I must see him.'

'But won't to-morrow morning do? It's near three o'clock, and to-morrow's our eldest miss's weddin'-day; and they're all abed.'

'I *must* see your master. For mercy's sake, my good woman, do what I tell you! Go and call up Major Lawford,—you can do it quietly,—and tell him I must speak to him at once.'

The woman, with the chain of the door still between her and Mr Marchmont, took a timid survey of Paul's face. She had heard of him often enough, but had never seen him before, and she was rather doubtful as to his identity. She knew that thieves and robbers resorted to all sorts of tricks in the course of their evil vocation. Mightn't this application for admittance in the dead of the night be only a part of some burglarious plot against the spoons and forks, and that hereditary silver urn with lions' heads holding rings in their mouths for handles, the fame of which had no doubt circulated throughout all Lincolnshire? Mr Marchmont had neither a black mask nor a dark-lantern,* and to Martha Philpot's mind these were essential attributes of the legitimate burglar; but he might be bur-glariously disposed, nevertheless, and it would be well to be on the safe side.

'I'll go and tell 'em,' the discreet Martha said civilly; 'but perhaps you won't mind my leaving the chain oop. It ain't like as if it was winter,' she added apologetically.

'You may shut the door, if you like,' answered Paul; 'only be quick and wake your master. You can tell him that I want to see him upon a matter of life and death.'

Martha hurried away, and Paul stood upon the broad stone steps waiting for her return. Every moment was precious to him, for he wanted to be beforehand with Olivia. He had no thought except that she would come straight to the Grange to see Edward Arun-del; unless, indeed, she was by any chance ignorant of his whereabouts.

Presently the light appeared again in the narrow windows, and this time a man's foot sounded upon the stone-flagged hall. This time, too, Martha let down the chain, and opened the door wide enough for Mr Marchmont to enter. She had no fear of burglarious marauders now that the valiant Major was at her elbow.

'Mr Marchmont,' exclaimed the old soldier, opening a door leading into a little study, 'you will excuse me if I seem rather bewildered by your visit. When an old fellow like me is called up in the middle of the night, he can't be expected to have his wits about him just at first. (Martha, bring us a light.) Sit down, Mr Marchmont; there's a chair at your elbow. And now may I ask the reason——?'

'The reason I have disturbed you in this abrupt manner. The occasion that brings me here is a very painful one; but I believe that my coming may save you and yours from much annoyance.'

'Save us from annoyance! Really, my dear sir, you——'

'I mystify you for the moment, no doubt,' Paul interposed blandly; 'but if you will have a little patience with me, Major Lawford, I think I can make everything very clear,—only too painfully clear. You have heard of my relative, Mrs John Marchmont,—my cousin's widow?'

'I have,' answered the Major, gravely.

The dark scandals that had been current about wretched Olivia Marchmont came into his mind with the mention of her name, and the memory of those miserable slanders overshadowed his frank face.

Paul waited while Martha brought in a smoky lamp, with the half-lighted wick sputtering and struggling in its oily socket. Then he went on, in a calm, dispassionate voice, which seemed the voice of a benevolent Christian, sublimely remote from other people's sorrows, but tenderly pitiful of suffering humanity, nevertheless.

'You have heard of my unhappy cousin. You have no doubt heard that she is—mad?'

He dropped his voice into so low a whisper, that he only seemed to shape this last word with his thin flexible lips.

'I have heard some rumour to that effect,' the Major answered; 'that is to say, I have heard that Mrs John Marchmont has lately become eccentric in her habits.'

'It has been my dismal task to watch the slow decay of a very powerful intellect,' continued Paul. 'When I first came to Marchmont Towers, about the time of my cousin Mary's unfortunate elopement with Mr Arundel, that mental decay had already set in. Already the compass of Olivia Marchmont's mind had become reduced to a monotone, and the one dominant thought was doing its ruinous work. It was my fate to find the clue to that sad decay; it was my fate very speedily to discover the nature of that all-absorbing thought which, little by little, had grown into monomania.'

Major Lawford stared at his visitor's face. He was a plain-spoken man, and could scarcely see his way clearly through all this obscurity of fine words.

'You mean to say you found out what had driven your cousin's widow mad?' he said bluntly.

'You put the question very plainly, Major Lawford. Yes; I discovered the secret of my unhappy relative's morbid state of mind. That secret lies in the fact, that for the last ten years Olivia Marchmont has cherished a hopeless affection for her cousin, Mr Edward Arundel.'

The Major almost bounded off his chair in horrified surprise.

'Good gracious!' he exclaimed; 'you surprise me, Mr Marchmont, and—and—rather unpleasantly.'

'I should never have revealed this secret to you or to any other living creature, Major Lawford, had not circumstances compelled me to do so. As far as Mr Arundel is concerned, I can set your mind quite at ease. He has chosen to insult me very grossly; but let that pass. I must do him the justice to state that I believe him to have been from first to last utterly ignorant of the state of his cousin's mind.'

'I hope so, sir; egad, I hope so!' exclaimed the Major, rather fiercely. 'If I thought that this young man had trifled with the lady's affection; if I thought——'

'You need think nothing to the detriment of Mr Arundel,' answered Paul, with placid politeness, 'except that he is hot-headed, obstinate, and foolish. He is a young man of excellent principles, and has never fathomed the secret of his cousin's conduct towards him. I am rather a close observer,—something of a student of human nature,—and I have watched this unhappy woman. She loves, and has loved, her cousin Edward Arundel; and hers is one of those concentrative natures in which a great passion is nearly akin to a monomania. It was this hopeless, unreturned affection that embittered her character, and made her a harsh stepmother to my poor cousin Mary. For a long time this wretched woman has been very quiet; but her tranquillity has been only a deceitful calm. To-night the storm broke. Olivia Marchmont heard of the marriage that is to take place to-morrow; and, for the first time, a state of melancholy mania developed into absolute violence. She came to me, and attacked me upon the subject of this intended marriage. She accused me of having plotted to give Edward Arundel another bride; and then, after exhausting herself by a torrent of passionate invective against me, against her cousin Edward, your daughter,—every one concerned in to-morrow's event,—this wretched woman rushed out of the house in a jealous fury, declaring that she would do something—no matter what—to hinder the celebration of Edward Arundel's second marriage.'

'Good Heavens!' gasped the Major. 'And you mean to say——'

'I mean to say, that there is no knowing what may be attempted by a madwoman, driven mad by a jealousy in itself almost as terrible as madness. Olivia Marchmont has sworn to hinder your daughter's marriage. What has not been done by unhappy creatures in this woman's state of mind? Every day we read of such things in the newspapers—deeds of horror at which the blood grows cold in our veins; and we wonder that Heaven can permit such misery. It is not any frivolous motive that brings me here in the dead of the night, Major Lawford. I come to tell you that a desperate woman has sworn to hinder to-morrow's marriage. Heaven knows what she may do in her jealous frenzy! She *may* attack your daughter.'

The father's face grew pale. His Linda, his darling, exposed to the fury of a madwoman! He could conjure up the scene: the fair girl clinging to her lover's breast, and desperate Olivia Marchmont swooping down upon her like an angry tigress.

'For mercy's sake, tell me what I am to do, Mr Marchmont!' cried the Major. 'God bless you, sir, for bringing me this warning! But what am I to do? What do you advise? Shall we postpone the wedding?'

'On no account. All you have to do is to keep this wretched woman at bay. Shut your doors upon her. Do not let her be admitted to this house upon any pretence whatever. Get the wedding over an hour earlier than has been intended, if it is possible for you to do so, and hurry the bride and bridegroom away upon the first stage of their wedding-tour. If you wish to escape all the wretchedness of a public scandal, avoid seeing this woman.'

'I will, I will,' answered the bewildered Major. 'It's a most awful situation. My poor Belinda! Her wedding-day! And a mad woman to attempt—Upon my word, Mr Marchmont, I don't know how to thank you for the trouble you have taken.'

'Don't speak of that. This woman is my cousin's widow: any shame of hers is disgrace to me. Avoid seeing her. If by any chance she does contrive to force herself upon you, turn a deaf ear to all she may say. She horrified me to-night by her mad assertions. Be prepared for anything she may declare. She is possessed by all manner of delusions, remember, and may make the most ridiculous assertions. There is no limit to her hallucinations. She may offer to bring Edward Arundel's dead wife from the grave, perhaps. But you will not, on any account, allow her to obtain access to your daughter.'

'No, no—on no account. My poor Belinda! I am very grateful to you, Mr Marchmont, for this warning. You'll stop here for the rest of the night? Martha's beds are always aired. You'll accept the shelter of our spare room until tomorrow morning?'

'You are very good, Major Lawford; but I must hurry away directly. Remember that I am quite ignorant as to where my unhappy relative may be wandering at this hour of the night. She may have returned to the Towers. Her jealous fury may have exhausted itself; and in that case I have exaggerated the danger. But, at any rate, I thought it best to give you this warning.'

'Most decidedly, my dear sir; I thank you from the bottom of my heart. But you'll take something—wine, tea, brandy-and-water— eh?'

Paul had put on his hat and made his way into the hall by this time. There was no affectation in his eagerness to be away. He glanced uneasily towards the door every now and then while the Major was offering hospitable hindrance to his departure. He was very pale, with a haggard, ashen pallor that betrayed his anxiety, in spite of his bland calmness of manner.

'You are very kind. No; I will get away at once. I have done my duty here; I must now try and do what I can for this wretched woman. Good night. Remember; shut your doors upon her.'

He unfastened the bridle of his horse, mounted, and rode away slowly, so long as there was any chance of the horse's tread being heard at the Grange. But when he was a quarter of a mile away from Major Lawford's house, he urged the horse into a gallop. He had no spurs; but he used his whip with a ruthless hand, and went off at a tearing pace along a narrow lane, where the ruts were deep.

He rode for fifteen miles; and it was grey morning when he drew rein at a dilapidated five-barred gate leading into the great, tenant-less yard of an uninhabited farmhouse. The place had been unlet for some years; and the land was in the charge of a hind* in Mr March-mont's service. The hind lived in a cottage at the other extremity of the farm; and Paul had erected new buildings, with engine-houses and complicated machinery for pumping the water off the low-lying lands. Thus it was that the old farmhouse and the old farmyard were suffered to fall into decay. The empty sties, the ruined barns and outhouses, the rotting straw, and pools of rank corruption, made this tenantless farmyard the very abomination of desolation. Paul Marchmont opened the gate and went in. He picked his way very cautiously through the mud and filth, leading his horse by the bridle till he came to an outhouse, where he secured the animal. Then he crossed the yard, lifted the rusty latch of a narrow wooden door set in a plastered wall, and went into a dismal stone court, where one lonely hen was moulting in miserable solitude.

Long rank grass grew in the interstices of the flags. The lonely hen set up a roopy cackle, and fluttered into a corner at sight of Paul Marchmont. There were some rabbit-hutches, tenantless; a dove-cote, empty; a dog-kennel, and a broken chain rusting slowly in a pool of water, but no dog. The courtyard was at the back of the house, looked down upon by a range of latticed windows, some with closed shutters, others with shutters swinging in the wind, as if they had been fain to beat themselves to death in very desolation of spirit.

Mr Marchmont opened a door and went into the house. There were empty cellars and pantries, dairies and sculleries, right and left of him. The rats and mice scuttled away at sound of the intruder's footfall. The spiders ran upon the damp-stained walls, and the dis-turbed cobwebs floated slowly down from the cracked ceilings and tickled Mr Marchmont's face.

Farther on in the interior of the gloomy habitation Paul found a great stone-paved kitchen, at the darkest end of which there was a rusty grate, in which a minimum of flame struggled feebly with a maximum of smoke. An open oven-door revealed a dreary black cavern; and the very manner of the rusty door, and loose, half-broken handle, was an advertisement of incapacity for any homely hospitable use. Pale, sickly fungi had sprung up in clusters at the corners of the damp hearthstone. Spiders and rats, damp and cobwebs, every sign by which Decay writes its name upon the dwelling man has deserted, had set its separate mark upon this ruined place.

Paul Marchmont looked round him with a contemptuous shudder. He called 'Mrs Brown! Mrs Brown!' two or three times, each time waiting for an answer; but none came, and Mr Marchmont passed on into another room.

Here at least there was some poor pretence of comfort. The room was in the front of the house, and the low latticed window looked out upon a neglected garden, where some tall foxgloves reared their gaudy heads amongst the weeds. At the end of the garden there was a high brick wall, with pear-trees trained against it, and dragon's-mouth and wallflower waving in the morning-breeze.

There was a bed in this room, empty; an easy-chair near the window; near that a little table, and a *set of Indian chessmen*. Upon the bed there were some garments scattered, as if but lately flung there; and on the floor, near the fireplace, there were the fragments of a child's first toys—a tiny trumpet, bought at some village fair, a baby's rattle, and a broken horse.

Paul Marchmont looked about him—a little puzzled at first; then with a vague dread in his haggard face.

'Mrs Brown!' he cried, in a loud voice, hurrying across the room towards an inner door as he spoke.

The inner door was opened before Paul could reach it, and a woman appeared; a tall, gaunt-looking woman, with a hard face and bare, brawny arms.

'Where, in Heaven's name, have you been hiding yourself, woman?' Paul cried impatiently. 'And where's—your patient?'

'Gone, sir.'

'Gone! Where?'

'With her stepmamma, Mrs Marchmont—not half an hour ago. As it was your wish I should stop behind to clear up, I've done so, sir; but I did think it would have been better for me to have gone with——'

Paul clutched the woman by the arm, and dragged her towards him.

'Are you mad?' he cried, with an oath. 'Are you mad, or drunk? Who gave you leave to let that woman go? Who——?'

He couldn't finish the sentence. His throat grew dry, and he gasped for breath; while all the blood in his body seemed to rush into his swollen forehead.

'You sent Mrs Marchmont to fetch my patient away, sir,' exclaimed the woman, looking frightened. 'You did, didn't you? She said so!'

'She is a liar; and you are a fool or a cheat. She paid you, I dare say! Can't you speak, woman? Has the person I left in your care, whom you were paid, and paid well, to take care of,—have you let her go? Answer me that.'

'I have, sir,' the woman faltered,—she was big and brawny, but there was that in Paul Marchmont's face that frightened her not-withstanding,—'seeing as it was your orders.'

'That will do,' cried Paul Marchmont, holding up his hand and looking at the woman with a ghastly smile; 'that will do. You have ruined me; do you hear? You have undone a work that has cost me— O my God! why do I waste my breath in talking to such a creature as this? All my plots, my difficulties, my struggles and victories, my long sleepless nights, my bad dreams,—has it all come to this? Ruin, unutterable ruin, brought upon me by a mad-woman!'

He sat down in the chair by the window, and leaned upon the table, scattering the Indian chessmen with his elbow. He did not weep. That relief—terrible relief though it be for a man's breast— was denied him. He sat there with his face covered, moaning aloud. That helpless moan was scarcely like the complaint of a man; it was rather like the hopeless, dreary utterance of a brute's anguish; it sounded like the miserable howling of a beaten cur.

revenge

CHAPTER XXXIX

BELINDA'S WEDDING–DAY

THE sun shone upon Belinda Lawford's wedding–day. The birds were singing in the garden under her window as she opened her lattice and looked out. The word lattice is not a poetical licence in this case; for Miss Lawford's chamber was a roomy, old-fashioned apartment at the back of the house, with deep window-seats and diamond-paned casements.

The sun shone, and the roses bloomed in all their summer glory. ''Twas in the time of roses,' as gentle-minded Thomas Hood* so sweetly sang; surely the time of all others for a bridal morning. The girl looked out into the sunshine with her loose hair falling about her shoulders, and lingered a little looking at the familiar garden, with a half-pensive smile.

'Oh, how often, how often,' she said, 'I have walked up and down by those laburnums, Letty!' There were two pretty white-curtained bedsteads in the old-fashioned room, and Miss Arundel had shared her friend's apartment for the last week. 'How often mamma and I have sat under the dear old cedar, making our poor children's frocks! People say monotonous lives are not happy: mine has been the same thing over and over again; and yet how happy, how happy! And to think that we'—she paused a moment, and the rosy colour in her cheeks deepened by just one shade; it was so sweet to use that simple monosyllable 'we' when Edward Arundel was the other half of the pronoun,—'to think that we shall be in Paris to-morrow!'

'Driving in the Bois,'* exclaimed Miss Arundel; 'and dining at the Maison Dorée, or the Café de Paris. Don't dine at Meurice's, Linda; it's dreadfully slow dining at one's hotel. And you'll be a young married woman, and can do anything, you know. If I were a young married woman, I'd ask my husband to take me to the Mabille, just for half an hour, with an old bonnet and a thick veil. I knew a girl whose first-cousin married a cornet in the Guards, and they went to the Mabille one night. Come, Belinda, if you mean to have your back-hair done at all, you'd better sit down at once and let me commence operations.'

Miss Arundel had stipulated that, upon this particular morning, she was to dress her friend's hair; and she turned up the frilled sleeves of her white dressing-gown, and set to work in the orthodox manner, spreading a network of shining tresses about Miss Lawford's shoulders, prior to the weaving of elaborate plaits that were to make a crown for the fair young bride. Letitia's tongue went as fast as her fingers; but Belinda was very silent.

She was thinking of the bounteous Providence that had given her the man she loved for her husband. She had been on her knees in the early morning, long before Letitia's awakening, breathing out innocent thanksgiving for the happiness that overflowed her fresh young heart. A woman had need to be country-bred, and to have been reared in the narrow circle of a happy home, to feel as Belinda Lawford felt. Such love as hers is only given to bright and innocent spirits, untarnished even by the knowledge of sin.

Downstairs Edward Arundel was making a wretched pretence of breakfasting *tête-à-tête* with his future father-in-law.

The Major had held his peace as to the unlooked-for visitant of the past night. He had given particular orders that no stranger should be admitted to the house, and that was all. But being of a naturally frank, not to say loquacious disposition, the weight of this secret was a very terrible burden to the honest half-pay soldier. He ate his dry toast uneasily, looking at the door every now and then, in the perpetual expectation of beholding that barrier burst open by mad Olivia Marchmont.

The breakfast was not a very cheerful meal, therefore. I don't suppose any ante-nuptial breakfast ever is very jovial. There was the state banquet—*the* wedding breakfast—to be eaten by-and-by; and Mrs Lawford, attended by all the females of the establishment, was engaged in putting the last touches to the groups of fruit and confectionery, the pyramids of flowers, and that crowning glory, the wedding-cake.

'Remember the Madeira and still Hock are to go round first, and then the sparkling; and tell Gogram to be particular about the corks, Martha,' Mrs Lawford said to her confidential maid, as she gave a nervous last look at the table. 'I was at a breakfast once where a champagne-cork hit the bridegroom on the bridge of his nose at the very moment he rose to return thanks; and being a nervous man, poor fellow,—in point of fact, he was a curate, and the bride was the rector's daughter, with two hundred a year of her own,—it quite overcame him, and he didn't get over it all through the breakfast. And now I must run and put on my bonnet.'

There was nothing but putting on bonnets, and pinning lace-shawls, and wild outcries for hairpins, and interchanging of little feminine services, upon the bedroom floor for the next half-hour.

Major Lawford walked up and down the hall, putting on his white gloves, which were too large for him,—elderly men's white gloves always are too large for them,—and watching the door of the citadel. Olivia must pass over a father's body, the old soldier thought, before she should annoy Belinda on her bridal morning.

By-and-by the carriages came round to the door. The girl brides-maids came crowding down the stairs, hustling each other's crisped garments, and disputing a little in a sisterly fashion; then Letitia Arundel, with nine rustling flounces of white silk ebbing and flowing and surging about her, and with a pleased simper upon her face; and then followed Mrs Arundel, stately in silver-grey moiré, and Mrs Lawford, in violet silk,—until the hall was a show of bonnets and bouquets and muslin.

And last of all, Belinda Lawford, robed in cloud-like garments of spotless lace, with bridal flowers trembling round her hair, came slowly down the broad old-fashioned staircase, to see her lover loiter-ing in the hall below.

He looked very grave; but he greeted his bride with a tender smile. He loved her, but he could not forget. Even upon this, his wedding-day, the haunting shadow of the past was with him: not to be shaken off.

He did not wait till Belinda reached the bottom of the staircase. There was a sort of ceremonial law to be observed, and he was not to speak to Miss Lawford upon this special morning until he met her in the vestry at Hillingsworth church; so Letitia and Mrs Arundel hustled the young man into one of the carriages, while Major Lawford ran to receive his daughter at the foot of the stairs.

The Arundel carriage drove off about five minutes before the vehicle that was to convey Major Lawford, Belinda, and as many of the girl bridesmaids as could be squeezed into it without detriment to lace and muslin. The rest went with Mrs Lawford in the third and last carriage. Hillingsworth church was about three-quarters of a mile from the Grange. It was a pretty irregular old place, lying in a little nook under the shadow of a great yew-tree. Behind the square

Norman tower there was a row of poplars, black against the blue summer sky; and between the low gate of the churchyard and the grey, moss-grown porch, there was an avenue of good old elms. The rooks were calling to each other in the topmost branches of the trees as Major Lawford's carriage drew up at the churchyard gate.

Belinda was a great favourite amongst the poor of Hillingsworth parish, and the place had put on a gala-day aspect in honour of her wedding. Garlands of honeysuckle and wild clematis were twined about the stout oaken gate-posts. The school-children were gathered in clusters in the churchyard, with their pinafores full of fresh flowers from shadowy lanes and from prim cottage-gardens,—bright homely blossoms, with the morning dew still upon them.

The rector and his curate were standing in the porch waiting for the coming of the bride; and there were groups of well-dressed people dotted about here and there in the drowsy-sheltered pews near the altar. There were humbler spectators clustered under the low ceiling of the gallery—tradesmen's wives and daughters, radiant with new ribbons, and whispering to one another in delighted anticipation of the show.

Everybody round about the Grange loved pretty, genial Belinda Lawford, and there was universal rejoicing because of her happiness.

The wedding party came out of the vestry presently in appointed order: the bride with her head drooping, and her face hidden by her veil; the bridesmaids' garments making a fluttering noise as they came up the aisle, like the sound of a field of corn faintly stirred by summer breezes.

Then the grave voice of the rector began the service with the brief preliminary exordium; and then, in a tone that grew more solemn with the increasing solemnity of the words, he went on to that awful charge which is addressed especially to the bridegroom and the bride:

'I require and charge you both, as ye will answer at the dreadful day of judgment, when the secrets of all hearts shall be disclosed, that if either of you know any impediment, why ye may not be lawfully joined together in matrimony, ye do now confess it. For be ye well assured——'

The rector read no further; for a woman's voice from out the dusky shadows at the further end of the church cried 'Stop!'

There was a sudden silence; people stared at each other with scared faces, and then turned in the direction whence the voice had come. The bride lifted her head for the first time since leaving the vestry, and looked round about her, ashy pale and trembling.

'O Edward, Edward!' she cried, 'what is it?'

The rector waited, with his hand still upon the open book. He waited, looking towards the other end of the chancel. He had no need to wait long: a woman, with a black veil thrown back from a white, haggard face, and with dusty garments dragging upon the church-floor; came slowly up the aisle.

Her two hands were clasped upon her breast, and her breath came in gasps, as if she had been running.

'Olivia!' cried Edward Arundel, 'what, in Heaven's name—'

But Major Lawford stepped forward, and spoke to the rector.

'Pray let her be got out of the way,' he said, in a low voice. 'I was warned of this. I was quite prepared for some such disturbance.' He sank his voice to a whisper. *'She is mad!'* he said, close in the rector's ear.

The whisper was like whispering in general,—more distinctly audible than the rest of the speech. Olivia Marchmont heard it.

'Mad until to-day,' she cried; 'but not mad to-day. O Edward Arundel! a hideous wrong has been done by me and through me. Your wife—your wife—'

'My wife! what of her? She—'

'She is alive!' gasped Olivia; 'an hour's walk from here. I came on foot. I was tired, and I have been long coming. I thought that I should be in time to stop you before you got to the church; but I am very weak. I ran the last part of the way—'

She dropped her hands upon the altar-rails, and seemed as if she would have fallen. The rector put his arm about her to support her, and she went on:

'I thought I should have spared her this,' she said, pointing to Belinda; 'but I can't help it. *She* must bear her misery as well as others. It can't be worse for her than it has been for others. She must bear—'

'My wife!' said Edward Arundel; 'Mary, my poor sorrowful darling—alive?'

Belinda turned away, and buried her face upon her mother's shoulder. She could have borne anything better than this.

His heart—that supreme treasure, for which she had rendered up thanks to her God—had never been hers after all. A word, a breath, and she was forgotten; his thoughts went back to that other one. There was unutterable joy, there was unspeakable tenderness in his tone, as he spoke of Mary Marchmont, though *she* stood by his side, in all her foolish bridal finery, with her heart newly broken.

'O mother,' she cried, 'take me away! take me away, before I die!'

Olivia flung herself upon her knees by the altar-rails. Where the pure young bride was to have knelt by her lover's side this wretched sinner cast herself down, sunk far below all common thoughts in the black depth of her despair.

'O my sin, my sin !' she cried, with clasped hands lifted up above her head. 'Will God ever forgive my sin? will God ever have pity upon me? Can He pity, can He forgive, such guilt as mine? Even this work of to-day is no atonement to be reckoned against my wickedness. I was jealous of this other woman; I was jealous! Earthly passion was still predominant in this miserable breast.'

She rose suddenly, as if this outburst had never been, and laid her hand upon Edward Arundel's arm.

'Come !' she said; 'come!'

'To her—to Mary—my wife?'

They had taken Belinda away by this time; but Major Lawford stood looking on. He tried to draw Edward aside; but Olivia's hand upon the young man's arm held him like a vice.

'She is mad,' whispered the Major. 'Mr Marchmont came to me last night, and warned me of all this. He told me to be prepared for anything; she has all sorts of delusions. Get her away, if you can, while I go and explain matters to Belinda. Edward, if you have a spark of manly feeling, get this woman away.'

But Olivia held the bridegroom's arm with a tightening grasp.

'Come!' she said; 'come! Are you turned to stone, Edward Arundel? Is your love worth no more than this? I tell you, your wife, Mary Marchmont, is alive. Let those who doubt me come and see for themselves.'

The eager spectators, standing up in the pews or crowding in the narrow aisle, were only too ready to respond to this invitation.

Olivia led her cousin out into the churchyard; she led him to the gate where the carriages were waiting. The crowd flocked after them; and the people outside began to cheer as they came out. That cheer was the signal for which the school-children had waited; and they set to work scattering flowers upon the narrow pathway, before they looked up to see who was coming to trample upon the rosebuds and jessamine, the woodbine and syringa. But they drew back, scared and wondering, as Olivia came along the pathway, sweeping those tender blossoms after her with her trailing black garments, and leading the pale bridegroom by his arm.

She led him to the door of the carriage beside which Major Lawford's gray-haired groom was waiting, with a big white satin favour pinned upon his breast, and a bunch of roses in his button hole. There were favours in the horses' ears, and favours upon the breasts of the Hillingsworth tradespeople who supplied bread and butcher's meat and grocery to the family at the Grange. The bell-ringers up in the church-tower saw the crowd flock out of the porch, and thought the marriage ceremony was over. The jangling bells pealed out upon the hot summer air as Edward stood by the churchyard-gate, with Olivia Marchmont by his side.

'Lend me your carriage,' he said to Major Lawford, 'and come with me. I must see the end of this. It may be all a delusion; but I must see the end of it. If there is any truth in instinct, I believe that I shall see my wife—alive.'

He got into the carriage without further ceremony, and Olivia and Major Lawford followed him.

'Where is my wife?' the young man asked, letting down the front window as he spoke.

'At Kemberling, at Hester Jobson's.'

'Drive to Kemberling,' Edward said to the coachman,—'to Kemberling High Street, as fast as you can go.'

The man drove away from the churchyard-gate. The humbler spectators, who were restrained by no niceties of social etiquette, hurried after the vehicle, raising white clouds of dust upon the high road with their eager feet. The higher classes lingered about the churchyard, talking to each other and wondering.

Very few people stopped to think of Belinda Lawford. 'Let the stricken deer go weep.'* A stricken deer is a very uninteresting object when there are hounds in full cry hard by, and another deer to be hunted.

'Since when has my wife been at Kemberling?' Edward Arundel asked Olivia, as the carriage drove along the high road between the two villages.

'Since daybreak this morning.'

'Where was she before then?'

'At Stony-Stringford Farm.'

'And before then?'

'In the pavilion over the boat-house at Marchmont.'

'My God! And—'

The young man did not finish his sentence. He put his head out of the window, looking towards Kemberling, and straining his eyes to catch the earliest sight of the straggling village street.

'Faster!' he cried every now and then to the coachman; 'faster!'

In little more than half an hour from the time at which it had left the churchyard-gate, the carriage stopped before the little carpenter's shop. Mr Jobson's doorway was adorned by a painted representation of two very doleful-looking mutes standing at a door; for Hester's husband combined the more aristocratic avocation of undertaker with the homely trade of carpenter and joiner.

Olivia Marchmont got out of the carriage before either of the two men could alight to assist her. Power was the supreme attribute of this woman's mind. Her purpose never faltered; from the moment she had left Marchmont Towers until now, she had known neither rest of body nor wavering of intention.

'Come,' she said to Edward Arundel, looking back as she stood upon the threshold of Mr Jobson's door; 'and you too,' she added, turning to Major Lawford,—'follow us, and *see* whether I am MAD.'

She passed through the shop, and into that prim, smart parlour in which Edward Arundel had lamented his lost wife.

The latticed windows were wide open, and the warm summer sunshine filled the room.

A girl, with loose tresses of hazel-brown hair falling about her face, was sitting on the floor, looking down at a beautiful fair-haired nursling of a twelvemonth old.

The girl was John Marchmont's daughter; the child was Edward Arundel's son. It was *his* childish cry that the young man had heard upon that October night in the pavilion by the water.

'Mary Arundel,' said Olivia, in a hard voice, 'I give you back your husband.'

The young mother got up from the ground with a low cry, tottered forward, and fell into her husband's arms.

'They told me you were dead! They made me believe that you

were dead!' she said, and then fainted on the young man's breast. Edward carried her to a sofa and laid her down, white and senseless; and then knelt down beside her, crying over her, and sobbing out inarticulate thanksgiving to the God who had given his lost wife back to him.

'Poor sweet lamb!' murmured Hester Jobson; 'she's as weak as a baby; and she's gone through so much a'ready this morning.'

It was some time before Edward Arundel raised his head from the pillow upon which his wife's pale face lay, half hidden amid the tangled hair. But when he did look up, he turned to Major Lawford and stretched out his hand.

'Have pity upon me,' he said. 'I have been the dupe of a villain. Tell your poor child how much I esteem her, how much I regret that—that—we should have loved each other as we have. The instinct of my heart would have kept me true to the past; but it was impossible to know your daughter and not love her. The villain who has brought this sorrow upon us shall pay dearly for his infamy. Go back to your daughter; tell her everything. Tell her what you have seen here. I know her heart, and I know that she will open her arms to this poor ill-used child.'

The Major went away very downcast. Hester Jobson bustled about bringing restoratives and pillows, stopping every now and then in an outburst of affection by the slippery horsehair couch on which Mary lay.

Mrs Jobson had prepared her best bedroom for her beloved visitor, and Edward carried his young wife up to the clean, airy chamber. He went back to the parlour to fetch the child. He carried the fair-haired little one up-stairs in his own arms; but I regret to say that the infant showed an inclination to whimper in his newly-found father's embrace. It is only in the British Drama that newly discovered fathers are greeted with an outburst of ready-made affection. Edward Arundel went back to the sitting-room presently, and sat down, waiting till Hester should bring him fresh tidings of his wife. Olivia Marchmont stood by the window, with her eyes fixed upon Edward.

'Why don't you speak to me?' she said presently. 'Can you find no words that are vile enough to express your hatred of me? Is that why you are silent?'

'No, Olivia,' answered the young man, calmly. 'I am silent,

because I have nothing to say to you. Why you have acted as you have
acted,—why you have chosen to be the tool of a black-hearted
villain,—is an unfathomable mystery to me. I thank God that your
conscience was aroused this day, and that you have at least hindered
the misery of an innocent girl. But why you have kept my wife
hidden from me,—why you have been the accomplice of Paul
Marchmont's crime,—is more than I can even attempt to guess.'

'Not yet?' said Olivia, looking at him with a strange smile. 'Even
yet I am a mystery to you?'

'You are, indeed, Olivia.'

She turned away from him with a laugh.

'Then I had better remain so till the end,' she said, looking out
into the garden. But after a moment's silence she turned her head
once more towards the young man. 'I will speak,' she said; 'I *will*
speak, Edward Arundel. I hope and believe that I have not long to
live, and that all my shame and misery, my obstinate wickedness, my
guilty passion, will come to an end, like a long feverish dream. O
God, have mercy on my waking, and make it brighter than this
dreadful sleep! I loved you, Edward Arundel. Ah! you start. Thank
God at least for that. I kept my secret well. You don't know what that
word "love" means, do you? You think you love that childish girl
yonder, perhaps; but I can tell you that you don't know what love is.
I know what it is. I have loved. For ten years,—for ten long, dreary,
desolate, miserable years, fifty-two weeks in every year, fifty-two
Sundays, with long idle hours between the two church services—I
have loved you, Edward. Shall I tell you what it is to love? It is to
suffer, to hate, yes, to hate even the object of your love, when that
love is hopeless; to hate him for the very attributes that have made
you love him; to grudge the gifts and graces that have made him
dear. It is to hate every creature on whom his eyes look with greater
tenderness than they look on you; to watch one face until its familiar
lines become a perpetual torment to you, and you cannot sleep
because of its eternal presence staring at you in all your dreams. It is
to be like some wretched drunkard, who loathes the fiery spirit that
is destroying him, body and soul, and yet goes on, madly drinking,
till he dies. Love! How many people upon this great earth know the
real meaning of that hideous word! I have learnt it until my soul
loathes the lesson. They will tell you that I am mad, Edward, and
they will tell you something near the truth; but not quite the truth.

My madness has been my love. From long ago, when you were little
more than a boy—you remember, don't you, the long days at the
Rectory? *I* remember every word you ever spoke to me, every sentiment you ever expressed, every look of your changing face—you
were the first bright thing that came across my barren life; and I
loved you. I married John Marchmont—why, do you think?—
because I wanted to make a barrier between you and me. I wanted to
make my love for you impossible by making it a sin. So long as my
husband lived, I shut your image out of my mind as I would have
shut out the Prince of Darkness,* if he had come to me in a palpable
shape. But since then—oh, I hope I have been mad since then; I hope
that God may forgive my sins because I have been mad!'

Her thoughts wandered away to that awful question which had
been so lately revived in her mind—Could she be forgiven? Was it
within the compass of heavenly mercy to forgive such a sin as hers?

CHAPTER XL

MARY'S STORY

ONE of the minor effects of any great shock, any revolution, natural or political, social or domestic, is a singular unconsciousness, or an exaggerated estimate, of the passage of time. Sometimes we fancy that the common functions of the universe have come to a dead stop during the tempest which has shaken our being to its remotest depths. Sometimes, on the other hand, it seems to us that, because we have endured an age of suffering, or half a lifetime of bewildered joy, the terrestrial globe has spun round in time to the quickened throbbing of our passionate hearts, and that all the clocks upon earth have been standing still.

When the sun sank upon the summer's day that was to have been the day of Belinda's bridal, Edward Arundel thought that it was still early in the morning. He wondered at the rosy light all over the western sky, and that great ball of molten gold dropping down below the horizon. He was fain to look at his watch, in order to convince himself that the low light was really the familiar sun, and not some unnatural appearance in the heavens.

And yet, although he wondered at the closing of the day, with a strange inconsistency his mind could scarcely grapple with the idea that only last night he had sat by Belinda Lawford's side, her betrothed husband, and had pondered, Heaven only knows with what sorrowful regret, upon the unknown grave in which his dead wife lay.

'I only knew it this morning,' he thought; 'I only knew this morning that my young wife still lives, and that I have a son.'

He was sitting by the open window in Hester Jobson's best bedroom. He was sitting in an old-fashioned easy-chair, placed between the head of the bed and the open window,—a pure cottage window, with diamond panes of thin greenish glass, and a broad painted ledge, with a great jug of homely garden-flowers standing on it. The young man was sitting by the side of the bed upon which his newly-found wife and son lay asleep; the child's head nestled on his mother's breast, one flushed cheek peeping out of a tangled confusion of hazel-brown and babyish flaxen hair.

The white dimity curtains overshadowed the loving sleepers. The pretty fluffy knotted fringe—neat Hester's handiwork—made fantastical tracery upon the sunlit counterpane. Mary slept with one arm folded round her child, and with her face turned to her husband. She had fallen asleep with her hand clasped in his, after a succession of fainting-fits that had left her terribly prostrate.

Edward Arundel watched that tender picture with a smile of ineffable affection.

'I can understand now why Roman Catholics worship the Virgin Mary,' he thought. 'I can comprehend the inspiration that guided Raphael's hand when he painted the Madonna de la Chaise. In all the world there is no picture so beautiful. From all the universe he could have chosen no subject more sublime. O my darling wife, given back to me out of the grave, restored to me,—and not alone restored! My little son! my baby-son! whose feeble voice I heard that dark October night. To think that I was so wretched a dupe! to think that my dull ears could hear that sound, and no instinct rise up in my heart to reveal the presence of my child! I was so near them, not once, but several times,—so near, and I never knew—I never guessed!'

He clenched his fists involuntarily at the remembrance of those purposeless visits to the lonely boat-house. His young wife was restored to him. But nothing could wipe away the long interval of agony in which he and she had been the dupe of a villainous trickster and a jealous woman. Nothing could give back the first year of that baby's life,—that year which should have been one long holiday of love and rejoicing. Upon what a dreary world those innocent eyes had opened, when they should have looked only upon sunshine and flowers, and the tender light of a loving father's smile!

'O my darling, my darling!' the young husband thought, as he looked at his wife's wan face, upon which the evidence of all that past agony was only too painfully visible,—'how bitterly we two have suffered! But how much more terrible must have been your suffering than mine, my poor gentle darling, my broken lily!'

In his rapture at finding the wife he had mourned as dead, the young man had for a time almost forgotten the villainous plotter who had kept her hidden from him. But now, as he sat quietly by the bed upon which Mary and her baby lay, he had leisure to think of Paul Marchmont.

What was he to do with that man? What vengeance could he

wreak upon the head of that wretch who, for nearly two years, had condemned an innocent girl to cruel suffering and shame? To shame; for Edward knew now that one of the most bitter tortures which Paul Marchmont had inflicted upon his cousin had been his pretended disbelief in her marriage.

'What can I do to him?' the young man asked himself. '*What* can I do to him? There is no personal chastisement worse than that which he has endured already at my hands. The scoundrel! the heartless villain! the false, cold-blooded cur! What can I do to him? I can only repeat that shameful degradation, and I *will* repeat it. This time he shall howl under the lash like some beaten hound. This time I will drag him through the village-street, and let every idle gossip in Kemberling see how a scoundrel writhes under an honest man's whip. I will—'

Edward Arundel's wife woke while he was thinking what chastisement he should inflict upon her deadly foe; and the baby opened his round innocent blue eyes in the next moment, and sat up, staring at his new parent.

Mr Arundel took the child in his arms, and held him very tenderly, though perhaps rather awkwardly. The baby's round eyes opened wider at sight of those golden absurdities dangling at his father's watch-chain, and the little pudgy hands began to play with the big man's lockets and seals.

'He comes to me, you see, Mary!' Edward said, with naïve wonder.

And then he turned the baby's face towards him, and tenderly contemplated the bright surprised blue eyes, the tiny dimples, the soft moulded chin. I don't know whether fatherly vanity prompted the fancy, but Edward Arundel certainly did believe that he saw some faint reflection of his own features in that pink and white baby-face; a shadowy resemblance, like a tremulous image looking up out of a river. But while Edward was half-thinking this, half-wondering whether there could be any likeness to him in that infant countenance, Mary settled the question with womanly decision.

'Isn't he like you, Edward?' she whispered. 'It was only for his sake that I bore my life all through that miserable time; and I don't think I could have lived even for him, if he hadn't been so like you. I used to look at his face sometimes for hours and hours together, crying over him, and thinking of you. I don't think I ever cried except when he was in my arms. Then something seemed to soften my heart, and the tears came to my eyes. I was very, very, very ill, for a long time before my baby was born; and I didn't know how the time went, or where I was. I used to fancy sometimes I was back in Oakley Street, and that papa was alive again, and that we were quite happy together, except for some heavy hammer that was always beating, beating, beating upon both our heads, and the dreadful sound of the river rushing down the street under our windows. I heard Mr Weston tell his wife that it was a miracle I lived through that time.'

Hester Jobson came in presently with a tea-tray, that made itself heard, by a jingling of teaspoons and rattling of cups and saucers, all the way up the narrow staircase.

The friendly carpenter's wife had produced her best china and her silver teapot,—an heirloom inherited from a wealthy maiden aunt of her husband's. She had been busy all the afternoon, preparing that elegant little collation of cake and fruit which accompanied the tea-tray; and she spread the lavender-scented table-cloth, and arranged the cups and saucers, the plates and dishes, with mingled pride and delight.

But she had to endure a terrible disappointment by-and-by; for neither of her guests was in a condition to do justice to her hospitality. Mary got up and sat in the roomy easy-chair, propped up with pillows. Her pensive eyes kept a loving watch upon the face of her husband, turned towards her own, and slightly crimsoned by that rosy flush fading out in the western sky. She sat up and sipped a cup of tea; and in that lovely summer twilight, with the scent of the flowers blowing in through the open window, and a stupid moth doing his best to beat out his brains against one of the diamond panes in the lattice, the tortured heart, for the first time since the ruthless close of that brief honeymoon, felt the heavenly delight of repose.

'O Edward!' murmured the young wife, 'how strange it seems to be happy!'

He was at her feet, half-kneeling, half-sitting on a hassock of Hester's handiwork, with both his wife's hands clasped in his, and his head leaning upon the arm of her chair. Hester Jobson had carried off the baby, and these two were quite alone, all in all to each other, with a cruel gap of two years to be bridged over by sorrowful memories, by tender words of consolation. They were alone, and they could talk quite freely now, without fear of interruption; for although in purity and beauty an infant is first cousin to the angels, and although I most heartily concur in all that Mr Bennett and Mr Buchanan* can say or sing about the species, still it must be owned that a baby *is* rather a hindrance to conversation, and that a man's eloquence does not flow quite so smoothly when he has to stop every now and then to rescue his infant son from the imminent peril of strangulation, caused by a futile attempt at swallowing one of his own fists.

Mary and Edward were alone; they were together once more, as they had been by the trout-stream in the Winchester meadows. A curtain had fallen upon all the wreck and ruin of the past, and they could hear the soft, mysterious music that was to be the prelude of a new act in life's drama.

'I shall try to forget all that time,' Mary said presently; 'I shall try to forget it, Edward. I think the very memory of it would kill me, if it was to come back perpetually in the midst of my joy, as it does now, even now, when I am so happy—so happy that I dare not speak of my happiness.'

She stopped, and her face drooped upon her husband's clustering hair.

'You are crying, Mary!'

'Yes, dear. There is something painful in happiness when it comes after such suffering.'

The young man lifted his head, and looked in his wife's face. How deathly pale it was, even in that shadowy twilight; how worn and haggard and wasted since it had smiled at him in his brief honeymoon. Yes, joy is painful when it comes after a long continuance of suffering; it is painful because we have become sceptical by reason of the endurance of such anguish. We have lost the power to believe in happiness. It comes, the bright stranger; but we shrink appalled from its beauty, lest, after all, it should be nothing but a phantom.

Heaven knows how anxiously Edward Arundel looked at his wife's altered face. Her eyes shone upon him with the holy light of love. She smiled at him with a tender, reassuring smile; but it seemed to him that there was something almost supernal in the brightness of that white, wasted face; something that reminded him of the countenance of a martyr who has ceased to suffer the anguish of death in a foretaste of the joys of Heaven.

'Mary,' he said, presently, 'tell me every cruelty that Paul

Marchmont or his tools inflicted upon you; tell me everything, and I will never speak of our miserable separation again. I will only punish the cause of it,' he added, in an undertone. 'Tell me, dear. It will be painful for you to speak of it; but it will be only once. There are some things I must know. Remember, darling, that you are in my arms now, and that nothing but death can ever again part us.'

The young man had his arms round his wife. He felt, rather than heard, a low plaintive sigh as he spoke those last words.

'Nothing but death, Edward; nothing but death,' Mary said, in a solemn whisper. 'Death would not come to me when I was very miserable. I used to pray that I might die, and the baby too; for I could not have borne to leave him behind. I thought that we might both be buried with you, Edward. I have dreamt sometimes that I was lying by your side in a tomb, and I have stretched out my dead hand to clasp yours. I used to beg and entreat them to let me be buried with you when I died; for I believed that you were dead, Edward. I believed it most firmly. I had not even one lingering hope that you were alive. If I had felt such a hope, no power upon earth would have kept me prisoner.'

'The wretches!' muttered Edward between his set teeth; 'the dastardly wretches! the foul liars!'

'Don't, Edward; don't, darling. There is a pain in my heart when I hear you speak like that. I know how wicked they have been; how cruel—how cruel. I look back at all my suffering as if it were some one else who suffered; for now that you are with me I cannot believe that miserable, lonely, despairing creature was really me, the same creature whose head now rests upon your shoulder, whose breath is mixed with yours. I look back and see all my past misery, and I cannot forgive them, Edward; I am very wicked, for I cannot forgive my cousin Paul and his sister—yet. But I don't want you to speak of them; I only want you to love me; I only want you to smile at me, and tell me again and again and again that nothing can part us now—but death.'

She paused for a few moments, exhausted by having spoken so long. Her head lay upon her husband's shoulder, and she clung a little closer to him, with a slight shiver.

'What is the matter, darling?'

'I feel as if it couldn't be real.'

'What, dear?'

'The present—all this joy. O Edward, is it real? Is it—is it? Or am I only dreaming? Shall I wake presently and feel the cold air blowing in at the window, and see the moonlight on the wainscot at Stony Stringford? Is it all real?'

'It is, my precious one. As real as the mercy of God, who will give you compensation for all you have suffered; as real as God's vengeance, which will fall most heavily upon your persecutors. And now, darling, tell me,—tell me all. I must know the story of these two miserable years during which I have mourned for my lost love.'

Mr Arundel forgot to mention that during those two miserable years he had engaged himself to become the husband of another woman. But perhaps, even when he is best and truest, a man is always just a shade behind a woman in the matter of constancy.

'When you left me in Hampshire, Edward, I was very, very miserable,' Mary began, in a low voice; 'but I knew that it was selfish and wicked of me to think only of myself. I tried to think of your poor father, who was ill and suffering; and I prayed for him, and hoped that he would recover, and that you would come back to me very soon. The people at the inn were very kind to me. I sat at the window from morning till night upon the day after you left me, and upon the day after that; for I was so foolish as to fancy, every time I heard the sound of horses' hoofs or carriage-wheels upon the high-road, that you were coming back to me, and that all my grief was over. I sat at the window and watched the road till I knew the shape of every tree and housetop, every ragged branch of the hawthorn-bushes in the hedge. At last—it was the third day after you went away—I heard carriage-wheels, that slackened as they came to the inn. A fly stopped at the door, and oh, Edward, I did not wait to see who was in it,—I never imagined the possibility of its bringing anybody but you. I ran down-stairs, with my heart beating so that I could hardly breathe; and I scarcely felt the stairs under my feet. But when I got to the door—O my love, my love!—I cannot bear to think of it; I cannot endure the recollection of it—'

She stopped, gasping for breath, and clinging to her husband; and then, with an effort, went on again:

'Yes; I will tell you, dear; I must tell you. My cousin Paul and my stepmother were standing in the little hall at the foot of the stairs. I think I fainted in my stepmother's arms; and when my consciousness came back, I was in our sitting-room,—the pretty rustic room, Edward, in which you and I had been so happy together.

'I must not stop to tell you everything. It would take me so long to speak of all that happened in that miserable time. I knew that something must be wrong, from my cousin Paul's manner; but neither he nor my stepmother would tell me what it was. I asked them if you were dead; but they said, "No, you were not dead." Still I could see that something dreadful had happened. But by-and-by, by accident, I saw your name in a newspaper that was lying on the table with Paul's hat and gloves. I saw the description of an accident on the railway, by which I knew you had travelled. My heart sank at once, and I think I guessed all that had happened. I read your name amongst those of the people who had been dangerously hurt. Paul shook his head when I asked him if there was any hope.

'They brought me back here. I scarcely know how I came, how I endured all that misery. I implored them to let me come to you, again and again, on my knees at their feet. But neither of them would listen to me. It was impossible, Paul said. He always seemed very, very kind to me; always spoke softly; always told me that he pitied me, and was sorry for me. But though my stepmother looked sternly at me, and spoke, as she always used to speak, in a harsh, cold voice, I sometimes think she might have given way at last and let me come to you, but for him—but for my cousin Paul. He could look at me with a smile upon his face when I was almost mad with my misery; and he never wavered; he never hesitated.

'So they took me back to the Towers. I let them take me; for I scarcely felt my sorrow any longer. I only felt tired; oh, so dreadfully tired; and I wanted to lie down upon the ground in some quiet place, where no one could come near me. I thought that I was dying. I believe I was very ill when we got back to the Towers. My stepmother and Barbara Simmons watched by my bedside, day after day, night after night. Sometimes I knew them; sometimes I had all sorts of fancies. And often—ah, how often, darling!—I thought that you were with me. My cousin Paul came every day, and stood by my bedside. I can't tell you how hateful it was to me to have him there. He used to come into the room as silently as if he had been walking upon snow; but however noiselessly he came, however fast asleep I was when he entered the room, I always knew that he was there, standing by my bedside, smiling at me. I always woke with a shuddering horror thrilling through my veins, as if a rat had run across my face.

'By-and-by, when the delirium was quite gone, I felt ashamed of myself for this. It seemed so wicked to feel this unreasonable antipathy to my dear father's cousin; but he had brought me bad news of you, Edward, and it was scarcely strange that I should hate him. One day he sat down by my bedside, when I was getting better, and was strong enough to talk. There was no one besides ourselves in the room, except my stepmother, and she was standing at the window, with her head turned away from us, looking out. My cousin Paul sat down by the bedside, and began to talk to me in that gentle, compassionate way that used to torture me and irritate me in spite of myself.

'He asked me what had happened to me after my leaving the Towers on the day after the ball.

'I told him everything, Edward—about your coming to me in Oakley Street; about our marriage. But, oh, my darling, my husband, he wouldn't believe me; he wouldn't believe. Nothing that I could say would make him believe me. Though I swore to him again and again—by my dead father in heaven, as I hoped for the mercy of my God—that I had spoken the truth, and the truth only, he wouldn't believe me; he wouldn't believe. He shook his head, and said he scarcely wondered I should try to deceive him; that it was a very sad story, a very miserable and shameful story, and my attempted falsehood was little more than natural.

'And then he spoke against you, Edward—against you. He talked of my childish ignorance, my confiding love, and your villainy. O Edward, he said such shameful things; such shameful, horrible things! You had plotted to become master of my fortune; to get me into your power, because of my money; and you had not married me. You had *not* married me; he persisted in saying that.

'I was delirious again after this; almost mad, I think. All through the delirium I kept telling my cousin Paul of our marriage. Though he was very seldom in the room, I constantly thought that he was there, and told him the same thing—the same thing—till my brain was on fire. I don't know how long it lasted. I know that, once in the middle of the night, I saw my stepmother lying upon the ground, sobbing aloud and crying out about her wickedness; crying out that God would never forgive her sin.

'I got better at last, and then I went downstairs; and I used to sit sometimes in poor papa's study. The blind was always down, and none of the servants, except Barbara Simmons, ever came into the room. My cousin Paul did not live at the Towers; but he came there every day, and often stayed there all day. He seemed the master of the house. My stepmother obeyed him in everything, and consulted him about everything.

'Sometimes Mrs Weston came. She was like her brother. She always smiled at me with a grave compassionate smile, just like his; and she always seemed to pity me. But she wouldn't believe in my marriage. She spoke cruelly about you, Edward; cruelly, but in soft words, that seemed only spoken out of compassion for me. No one would believe in my marriage.

'No stranger was allowed to see me. I was never suffered to go out. They treated me as if I was some shameful creature, who must be hidden away from the sight of the world.

'One day I entreated my cousin Paul to go to London and see Mrs Pimpernel. She would be able to tell him of our marriage. I had forgotten the name of the clergyman who married us, and the church at which we were married. And I could not tell Paul those; but I gave him Mrs Pimpernel's address. And I wrote to her, begging her to tell my cousin all about my marriage; and I gave him the note unsealed.

'He went to London about a week afterwards; and when he came back, he brought me my note. He had been to Oakley Street, he said; but Mrs Pimpernel had left the neighbourhood, and no one knew where she was gone.'

'A lie! a villainous lie!' muttered Edward Arundel. 'Oh, the scoundrel! the infernal scoundrel!'

'No words would ever tell the misery of that time; the bitter anguish; the unendurable suspense. When I asked them about you, they would tell me nothing. Sometimes I thought that you had forgotten me; that you had only married me out of pity for my loneliness; and that you were glad to be freed from me. Oh, forgive me, Edward, for that wicked thought; but I was so very miserable, so utterly desolate. At other times I fancied that you were very ill, helpless and unable to come to me. I dared not think that you were dead. I put away that thought from me with all my might; but it haunted me day and night. It was with me always like a ghost. I tried to shut it away from my sight; but I knew that it was there.

'The days were all alike,—long, dreary, and desolate; so I scarcely know how the time went. My stepmother brought me religious books, and told me to read them; but they were hard, difficult books, and I couldn't find one word of comfort in them. They must have been written to frighten very obstinate and wicked people, I think. The only book that ever gave me any comfort, was that dear Book I used to read to papa on a Sunday evening in Oakley Street. I read that, Edward, in those miserable days; I read the story of the widow's only son* who was raised up from the dead because his mother was so wretched without him. I read that sweet, tender story again and again, until I used to see the funeral train, the pale, still face upon the bier, the white, uplifted hand, and that sublime and lovely counten- ance, whose image always comes to us when we are most miserable, the tremulous light upon the golden hair, and in the distance the glimmering columns of white temples, the palm-trees standing out against the purple Eastern sky. I thought that He who raised up a miserable woman's son chiefly because he was her only son, and she was desolate without him, would have more pity upon me than the God in Olivia's books: and I prayed to Him, Edward, night and day, imploring Him to bring you back to me.

'I don't know what day it was, except that it was autumn, and the dead leaves were blowing about in the quadrangle, when my step- mother sent for me one afternoon to my room, where I was sitting, not reading, not even thinking—only sitting with my head upon my hands, staring stupidly out at the drifting leaves and the gray, cold sky. My stepmother was in papa's study, and I was to go to her there. I went, and found her standing there, with a letter crumpled up in her clenched hand, and a slip of newspaper lying on the table before her. She was as white as death, and she was trembling violently from head to foot.

'"See," she said, pointing to the paper; "your lover is dead. But for you he would have received the letter that told him of his father's illness upon an earlier day; he would have gone to Devonshire by a different train. It was by your doing that he travelled when he did. If this is true, and he is dead, his blood be upon your head; his blood be upon your head!"

'I think her cruel words were almost exactly those. I did not hope for a minute that the horrible lines in the newspaper were false. I thought they must be true, and I was mad, Edward—I was mad; for utter despair came to me with the knowledge of your death. I went to my own room, and put on my bonnet and shawl; and then I went out of the house, down into that dreary wood, and along the narrow path-way by the river-side. I wanted to drown myself; but the sight of the black water filled me with a shuddering horror. I was frightened, Edward; and I went on by the river, scarcely knowing where I was going, until it was quite dark; and I was tired, and sat down upon the damp ground by the brink of the river, all amongst the broad green flags and the wet rushes. I sat there for hours, and I saw the stars shining feebly in a dark sky. I think I was delirious, for sometimes I knew that I was there by the water side, and then the next minute I thought that I was in my bedroom at the Towers; sometimes I fancied that I was with you in the meadows near Winchester, and the sun was shining, and you were sitting by my side, and I could see your float dancing up and down in the sunlit water. At last, after I had been there a very, very long time, two people came with a lantern, a man and a woman; and I heard a startled voice say, "Here she is; here, lying on the ground!" And then another voice, a woman's voice, very low and frightened, said, "Alive!" And then two people lifted me up; the man carried me in his arms, and the woman took the lantern. I couldn't speak to them; but I knew that they were my cousin Paul and his sister, Mrs Weston. I remember being carried some distance in Paul's arms; and then I think I must have fainted away, for I can recollect nothing more until I woke up one day and found myself lying in a bed in the pavilion over the boat-house, with Mr Weston watching by my bedside.

'I don't know how the time passed; I only know that it seemed endless. I think my illness was rheumatic fever, caught by lying on the damp ground nearly all that night when I ran away from the Towers. A long time went by—there was frost and snow. I saw the river once out of the window when I was lifted out of bed for an hour or two, and it was frozen; and once at midnight I heard the Kemberling church-bells ringing in the New Year. I was very ill, but I had no doctor; and all that time I saw no one but my cousin Paul, and Lavinia Weston, and a servant called Betsy, a rough country girl, who took care of me when my cousins were away. They were kind to me, and took great care of me.'

'You did not see Olivia, then, all this time?' Edward asked eagerly.

'No; I did not see my stepmother till some time after the New Year began. She came in suddenly one evening, when Mrs Weston was with me, and at first she seemed frightened at seeing me. She spoke to me kindly afterwards, but in a strange, terror-stricken voice; and she laid her head down upon the counterpane of the bed, and sobbed aloud; and then Paul took her away, and spoke to her cruelly, very cruelly—taunting her with her love for you. I never understood till then why she hated me: but I pitied her after that; yes, Edward, miserable as I was, I pitied her, because you had never loved her. In all my wretchedness I was happier than her; for you had loved me, Edward—you had loved me!'

Mary lifted her face to her husband's lips, and those dear lips were pressed tenderly upon her pale forehead.

'O my love, my love!' the young man murmured; 'my poor suffering angel! Can God ever forgive these people for their cruelty to you? But, my darling, why did you make no effort to escape?'

'I was too ill to move ; I believed that I was dying.'

'But afterwards, darling, when you were better, stronger,—did you make no effort then to escape from your persecutors?'

Mary shook her head mournfully.

'Why should I try to escape from them?' she said. 'What was there for me beyond that place? It was as well for me to be there as anywhere else. I thought you were dead, Edward; I thought you were dead, and life held nothing more for me. I could do nothing but wait till He who raised the widow's son should have pity upon me, and take me to the heaven where I thought you and papa had gone before me. I didn't want to go away from those dreary rooms over the boat-house. What did it matter to me whether I was there or at Marchmont Towers? I thought you were dead, and all the glories and grandeurs of the world were nothing to me. Nobody ill-treated me; I was let alone. Mrs Weston told me that it was for my own sake they kept me hidden from everybody about the Towers. I was a poor disgraced girl, she told me; and it was best for me to stop quietly in the pavilion till people had got tired of talking of me, and then my cousin Paul would take me away to the Continent, where no one would know who I was. She told me that the honour of my father's name, and of my family altogether, would be saved by this means. I replied that I had brought no dishonour on my dear father's name; but she only shook her head mournfully, and I was too weak to dispute with her. What did it matter? I thought you were dead, and that the world was finished for me. I sat day after day by the window; not looking out, for there was a Venetian blind that my cousin Paul had nailed down to the window-sill, and I could only see glimpses of the water through the long, narrow openings between the laths. I used to sit there listening to the moaning of the wind amongst the trees, or the sounds of horses' feet upon the towing-path, or the rain dripping into the river upon wet days. I think that even in my deepest misery God was good to me, for my mind sank into a dull apathy, and I seemed to lose even the capacity of suffering.

'One day,—one day in March, when the wind was howling, and the smoke blew down the narrow chimney and filled the room,—Mrs Weston brought her husband, and he talked to me a little, and then talked to his wife in whispers. He seemed terribly frightened, and he trembled all the time, and kept saying, "Poor thing; poor young woman!" but his wife was cross to him, and wouldn't let him stop long in the room. After that, Mr Weston came very often, always with Lavinia, who seemed cleverer than he was, even as a doctor; for she dictated to him, and ordered him about in everything. Then, by-and-by, when the birds were singing, and the warm sunshine came into the room, my baby was born, Edward; my baby was born. I thought that God, who raised the widow's son, had heard my prayer, and had raised you up from the dead; for the baby's eyes were like yours, and I used to think sometimes that your soul was looking out of them and comforting me.

'Do you remember that poor foolish German woman who believed that the spirit of a dead king came to her in the shape of a blackbird? She was not a good woman, I know, dear; but she must have loved the king very truly, or she never could have believed anything so foolish. I don't believe in people's love when they love "wisely," Edward: the truest love is that which loves "too well."*

'From the time of my baby's birth everything was changed. I was more miserable, perhaps, because that dull, dead apathy cleared away, and my memory came back, and I thought of you, dear, and cried over my little angel's face as he slept. But I wasn't alone any longer. The world seemed narrowed into the little circle round my darling's cradle. I don't think he is like other babies, Edward. I think he has known of my sorrow from the very first, and has tried in his mute way to comfort me. The God who worked so many miracles, all separate tokens of His love and tenderness and pity for the sorrows of mankind, could easily make my baby different from other children, for a wretched mother's consolation.

'In the autumn after my darling's birth, Paul and his sister came for me one night, and took me away from the pavilion by the water to a deserted farmhouse, where there was a woman to wait upon me and take care of me. She was not unkind to me, but she was rather neglectful of me. I did not mind that, for I wanted nothing except to be alone with my precious boy—your son, Edward; your son. The woman let me walk in the garden sometimes. It was a neglected garden, but there were bright flowers growing wild, and when the spring came again my pet used to lie on the grass and play with the buttercups and daisies that I threw into his lap; and I think we were both of us happier and better than we had been in those two close rooms over the boat-house.

'I have told you all now, Edward, all except what happened this morning, when my stepmother and Hester Jobson came into my room in the early daybreak, and told me that I had been deceived, and that you were alive. My stepmother threw herself upon her knees at my feet, and asked me to forgive her, for she was a miserable sinner, she said, who had been abandoned by God; and I forgave her, Edward, and kissed her; and you must forgive her too, dear, for I know that she has been very, very wretched. And she took the baby in her arms, and kissed him,—oh, so passionately!—and cried over him. And then they brought me here in Mr Jobson's cart, for Mr Jobson was with them, and Hester held me in her arms all the time. And then, darling, then after a long time you came to me.'

Edward put his arms round his wife, and kissed her once more. 'We will never speak of this again, darling,' he said. 'I know all now; I understand it all. I will never again distress you by speaking of your cruel wrongs.'

'And you will forgive Olivia, dear?'

'Yes, my pet, I will forgive—Olivia.'

He said no more, for there was a footstep on the stair, and a glimmer of light shone through the crevices of the door. Hester Jobson came into the room with a pair of lighted wax-candles, in white crockery-ware candlesticks. But Hester was not alone; close behind her came a lady in a rustling silk gown, a tall matronly lady, who cried out,—

'Where is she, Edward? Where is she? Let me see this poor ill-used child.'

It was Mrs Arundel, who had come to Kemberling to see her newly-found daughter-in-law.

'Oh, my dear mother,' cried the young man, 'how good of you to come! Now, Mary, you need never again know what it is to want a protector, a tender womanly protector, who will shelter you from every harm.'

Mary got up and went to Mrs Arundel, who opened her arms to receive her son's young wife. But before she folded Mary to her friendly breast, she took the girl's two hands in hers, and looked earnestly at her pale, wasted face.

She gave a long sigh as she contemplated those wan features, the shining light in the eyes, that looked unnaturally large by reason of the girl's hollow cheeks.

'Oh, my dear,' cried Mrs Arundel, 'my poor long-suffering child, how cruelly they have treated you!'

Edward looked at his mother, frightened by the earnestness of her manner; but she smiled at him with a bright, reassuring look.

'I shall take you home to Dangerfield with me, my poor love,' she said to Mary; 'and I shall nurse you, and make you as plump as a partridge, my poor wasted pet. And I'll be a mother to you, my motherless child. Oh, to think that there should be any wretch vile enough to—But I won't agitate you, my dear. I'll take you away from this bleak horrid county by the first train to-morrow morning, and you shall sleep to-morrow night in the blue bedroom at Dangerfield, with the roses and myrtles waving against your window; and Edward shall go with us, and you shan't come back here till you are well and strong; and you'll try and love me, won't you, dear? And, oh, Edward, I've seen the boy! and he's a *superb* creature, the very *image* of what you were at a twelvemonth old; and he came to me, and smiled at me, almost as if he knew I was his grandmother; and he has got FIVE teeth, but I'm *sorry* to tell you he's cutting them crossways, the top first instead of the bottom, Hester says.'

'And Belinda, mother dear?' Edward said presently, in a grave undertone.

'Belinda is an angel,' Mrs Arundel answered, quite as gravely. 'She has been in her own room all day, and no one has seen her but her mother; but she came down to the hall as I was leaving the house this evening, and said to me, "Dear Mrs Arundel, tell him that he must not think I am so selfish as to be sorry for what has happened. Tell him that I am very glad to think his young wife has been saved." She put her hand up to my lips to stop my speaking, and then went back again to her room; and if that isn't acting like an angel, I don't know what is.'

CHAPTER XLI

'ALL WITHIN IS DARK AS NIGHT'

PAUL MARCHMONT did not leave Stony-Stringford Farmhouse till dusk upon that bright summer's day; and the friendly twilight is slow to come in the early days of July, however a man may loathe the sunshine. Paul Marchmont stopped at the deserted farmhouse, wandering in and out of the empty rooms, strolling listlessly about the neglected garden, or coming to a dead stop sometimes, and standing stock-still for ten minutes at a time, staring at the wall before him, and counting the slimy traces of the snails upon the branches of a plum-tree, or the flies in a spider's web. Paul Marchmont was afraid to leave that lonely farmhouse. He was afraid as yet. He scarcely knew what he feared, for a kind of stupor had succeeded the violent emotions of the past few hours; and the time slipped by him, and his brain grew bewildered when he tried to realise his position.

It was very difficult for him to do this. The calamity that had come upon him was a calamity that he had never anticipated. He was a clever man, and he had put his trust in his own cleverness. He had never expected to be *found out*.

Until this hour everything had been in his favour. His dupes and victims had played into his hands. Mary's grief, which had rendered her a passive creature, utterly indifferent to her own fate,—her peculiar education, which had taught her everything except knowledge of the world in which she was to live,—had enabled Paul Marchmont to carry out a scheme so infamous and daring that it was beyond the suspicion of honest men, almost too base for the comprehension of ordinary villains.

He had never expected to be found out. All his plans had been deliberately and carefully prepared. Immediately after Edward's marriage and safe departure for the Continent, Paul had intended to convey Mary and the child, with the grim attendant whom he had engaged for them, far away, to one of the remotest villages in Wales.

Alone he would have done this; travelling by night, and trusting no one; for the hired attendant knew nothing of Mary's real position. She had been told that the girl was a poor relation of Paul's, and that her story was a very sorrowful one. If the poor creature had strange fancies and delusions, it was no more than might be expected; for she had suffered enough to turn a stronger brain than her own. Everything had been arranged, and so cleverly arranged, that Mary and the child would disappear after dusk one summer's evening, and not even Lavinia Weston would be told whither they had gone.

Paul had never expected to be found out. But he had least of all expected betrayal from the quarter whence it had come. He had made Olivia his tool; but he had acted cautiously even with her. He had confided nothing to her; and although she had suspected some foul play in the matter of Mary's disappearance, she had been certain of nothing. She had uttered no falsehood when she swore to Edward Arundel that she did not know where his wife was. But for her accidental discovery of the secret of the pavilion, she would never have known of Mary's existence after that October afternoon on which the girl left Marchmont Towers.

But here Paul had been betrayed by the carelessness of the hired girl who acted as Mary Arundel's gaoler and attendant. It was Olivia's habit to wander often in that dreary wood by the water during the winter in which Mary was kept prisoner in the pavilion over the boat-house. Lavinia Weston and Paul Marchmont spent each of them a great deal of their time in the pavilion; but they could not be always on guard there. There was the world to be hoodwinked; and the surgeon's wife had to perform all her duties as a matron before the face of Kemberling, and had to give some plausible account of her frequent visits to the boat-house. Paul liked the place for his painting, Mrs Weston informed her friends; and he was *so* enthusiastic in his love of art, that it was really a pleasure to participate in his enthusiasm; so she liked to sit with him, and talk to him or read to him while he painted. This explanation was quite enough for Kemberling; and Mrs Weston went to the pavilion at Marchmont Towers three or four times a week without causing any scandal thereby.

But however well you may manage things yourself, it is not always easy to secure the careful co-operation of the people you employ. Betsy Murrel was a stupid, narrow-minded young person, who was very safe so far as regarded the possibility of any sympathy with, or compassion for, Mary Arundel arising in her stolid nature; but the stupid stolidity which made her safe in one way rendered her dangerous in another. One day, while Mrs Weston was with the hapless young prisoner, Miss Murrel went out upon the water-side to converse with a good-looking young bargeman, who was a connexion of her family, and perhaps an admirer of the young lady herself; and the door of the painting-room being left wide open, Olivia Marchmont wandered listlessly into the pavilion—there was a dismal fascination for her in that spot, on which she had heard Edward Arundel declare his love for John Marchmont's daughter—and heard Mary's voice in the chamber at the top of the stone steps.

This was how Olivia had surprised Paul's secret; and from that hour it had been the artist's business to rule this woman by the only weapon which he possessed against her,—her own secret, her own weak folly, her mad love of Edward Arundel and jealous hatred of the woman whom he had loved. This weapon was a very powerful one, and Paul used it unsparingly.

When the woman who, for seven-and-twenty years of her life, had lived without sin; who from the hour in which she had been old enough to know right from wrong, until Edward Arundel's second return from India, had sternly done her duty,—when this woman, who little by little had slipped away from her high standing-point and sunk down into a morass of sin; when this woman remonstrated with Mr Marchmont, he turned upon her and lashed her with the scourge of her own folly.

'You come and upbraid me,' he said, 'and you call me villain and arch-traitor, and say that you cannot abide this, your sin; and that your guilt, in keeping our secret, cries to you in the dead hours of the night; and you call upon me to undo what I have done, and to restore Mary Marchmont to her rights. Do you remember what her highest right is? Do you remember that which I must restore to her when I give her back this house and the income that goes along with it? If I restore Marchmont Towers, I must restore to her *Edward Arundel's love*! You have forgotten that, perhaps. If she ever re-enters this house, she will come back to it leaning on his arm. You will see them together—you will hear of their happiness; and do you think that *he* will ever forgive you for your part of the conspiracy? Yes, it is a conspiracy, if you like; if you are not afraid to call it by a hard name, why should I fear to do so? Will he ever forgive you, do you think, when he knows that his young wife has been the victim of a senseless, vicious love? Yes, Olivia Marchmont; any love is vicious which is given unsought, and is so strong a passion, so blind and unreasoning a folly, that honour, mercy, truth, and Christianity are trampled down before it. How will you endure Edward Arundel's contempt for you? How will you tolerate his love for Mary, multiplied twenty-fold by all this romantic business of separation and persecution?

'You talk to me of my sin. Who was it who first sinned? Who was it who drove Mary Marchmont from this house,—not once only, but twice, by her cruelty? Who was it who persecuted her and tortured her day by day and hour by hour, not openly, not with an uplifted hand or blows that could be warded off, but by cruel hints and innuendoes, by unwomanly sneers and hellish taunts? Look into your heart, Olivia Marchmont; and when you make atonement for your sin, I will make restitution for mine. In the meantime, if this business is painful to you, the way lies open before you: go and take Edward Arundel to the pavilion yonder, and give him back his wife; give the lie to all your past life, and restore these devoted young lovers to each other's arms.'

This weapon never failed in its effect. Olivia Marchmont might loathe herself, and her sin, and her life, which was made hideous to her because of her sin; but she *could* not bring herself to restore Mary to her lover-husband; she could not tolerate the idea of their happiness. Every night she grovelled on her knees, and swore to her offended God that she would do this thing, she would render this sacrifice of atonement; but every morning, when her weary eyes opened on the hateful sunlight, she cried, 'Not to-day—not to-day.'

Again and again, during Edward Arundel's residence at Kemberling Retreat, she had set out from Marchmont Towers with the intention of revealing to him the place where his young wife was hidden; but, again and again, she had turned back and left her work undone. She *could* not—she could not. In the dead of the night, under pouring rain, with the bleak winds of winter blowing in her face, she had set out upon that unfinished journey, only to stop midway, and cry out, 'No, no, no—not to-night; I cannot endure it yet!'

It was only when another and a fiercer jealousy was awakened in this woman's breast, that she arose all at once, strong, resolute, and undaunted, to do the work she had so miserably deferred. As one poison is said to neutralise the evil power of another, so Olivia Marchmont's jealousy of Belinda seemed to blot out and extinguish her hatred of Mary. Better anything than that Edward Arundel should have a new, and perhaps a fairer, bride. The jealous woman had always looked upon Mary Marchmont as a despicable rival. Better that Edward should be tied to this girl, than that he should rejoice in the smiles of a lovelier woman, worthier of his affection. *This* was the feeling paramount in Olivia's breast, although she was herself half unconscious how entirely this was the motive power which had given her new strength and resolution. She tried to think that it was the awakening of her conscience that had made her strong enough to do this one good work; but in the semi-darkness of her own mind there was still a feeble glimmer of the light of truth, and it was this that had prompted her to cry out on her knees before the altar in Hillingsworth church, and declare the sinfulness of her nature.

Paul Marchmont stopped several times before the ragged, untrimmed fruit-trees in his purposeless wanderings in the neglected garden at Stony Stringford, before the vaporous confusion cleared away from his brain, and he was able to understand what had happened to him.

His first reasonable action was to take out his watch; but even then he stood for some moments staring at the dial before he remembered why he had taken the watch from his pocket, or what it was that he wanted to know. By Mr Marchmont's chronometer it was ten minutes past seven o'clock; but the watch had been unwound upon the previous night, and had run down. Paul put it back in his waistcoat-pocket, and then walked slowly along the weedy pathway to that low latticed window in which he had often seen Mary Arundel standing with her child in her arms. He went to this window and looked in, with his face against the glass. The room was neat and orderly now; for the woman whom Mr Marchmont had hired had gone about her work as usual, and was in the act of filling a little brown earthenware teapot from a kettle on the hob when Paul stared in at her.

She looked up as Mr Marchmont's figure came between her and the light, and nearly dropped the little brown teapot in her terror of her offended employer.

But Paul pulled open the window, and spoke to her very quietly. 'Stop where you are,' he said; 'I want to speak to you. I'll come in.'

He went into the house by a door, that had once been the front and principal entrance, which opened into a low wainscoted hall. From this room he went into the parlour, which had been Mary Arundel's apartment, and in which the hired nurse was now preparing her breakfast. 'I thought I might as well get a cup of tea, sir, whiles I waited for your orders,' the woman murmured, apologetically; 'for bein' knocked up so early this morning, you see, sir, has made my head *that* bad, I could scarcely bear myself; and——'

Paul lifted his hand to stop the woman's talk, as he had done before. He had no consciousness of what she was saying, but the sound of her voice pained him. His eyebrows contracted with a spasmodic action, as if something had hurt his head.

There was a Dutch clock in the corner of the room, with a long pendulum swinging against the wall. By this clock it was half-past eight.

'Is your clock right?' Paul asked.

'Yes, sir. Leastways, it may be five minutes too slow, but not more.'

Mr Marchmont took out his watch, wound it up, and regulated it by the Dutch clock.

'Now,' he said, 'perhaps you can tell me clearly what happened. I want no excuses, remember; I only want to know what occurred, and what was said—word for word, remember.'

He sat down but got up again directly, and walked to the window; then he paced up and down the room two or three times, and then went back to the fireplace and sat down again. He was like a man who, in the racking torture of some physical pain, finds a miserable relief in his own restlessness.

'Come,' he said; 'I am waiting.'

'Yes, sir; which, begging your parding, if you wouldn't mind sitting still like, while I'm a-telling of you, which it do remind me of the wild beastes in the Zoological, sir, to that degree, that the boil, to which I am subjeck, sir, and have been from a child, might prevent me bein' as truthful as I should wish. Mrs Marchmont, sir, she come before it was light, *in* a cart, sir, which it was a shaycart,* and made comfortable with cushions and straw, and suchlike, or I should not have let the young lady go away in it; and she bring with her a respectable, homely-looking young person, which she call Hester Jobling or Gobson, or somethink of that sound like, which my memory is treechrous, and I don't wish to tell a story on no account; and Mrs Marchmont she go straight up to my young lady, and she shakes her by the shoulder; and then the young woman called Hester, she wakes up my young lady quite gentle like, and kisses her and cries over her; and a man as drove the cart, which looked a small trades- man well-to-do, brings his trap round to the front-door,—you may see the trax of the wheels upon the gravel now, sir, if you disbelieve me. And Mrs Marchmont and the young woman called Hester, between 'em they gets my young lady up, and dresses her, and dresses the child; and does it all so quick, and overrides me to such a degree, that I hadn't no power to prevent 'em; but I say to Mrs Marchmont, I say: "Is it Mr Marchmont's orders as his cousin should be took away this morning?" and she stare at me hard, and say, "Yes;" and she have allus an abrumpt way, but was abrumpter than ordinary this morning. And, oh sir, bein' a poor lone woman, what was I to do?'

'Have you nothing more to tell me?'

'Nothing, sir; leastways, except as they lifted my young lady into the cart, and the man got in after 'em, and drove away as fast as his horse would go; and they had been gone two minutes when I began to feel all in a tremble like, for fear as I might have done wrong in lettin' of 'em go.'

'You have done wrong,' Paul answered, sternly; 'but no matter. If these officious friends of my poor weak-witted cousin choose to take her away, so much the better for me, who have been burdened with her long enough. Since your charge has gone, your services are no longer wanted. I shan't act illiberally to you, though I am very much annoyed by your folly and stupidity. Is there anything due to you?'

Mrs Brown hesitated for a moment, and then replied, in a very insinuating tone,—

'Not *wages*, sir; there ain't no *wages* doo to me,—which you paid me a quarter in advance last Saturday was a week, and took a receipt, sir, for the amount. But I have done my dooty, sir, and had but little sleep and rest, which my 'ealth ain't what it was when I answered your advertisement, requirin' a respectable motherly person, to take charge of a invalid lady, not objectin' to the country—which I freely tell you, sir, if I'd known that the country was a rheumatic old place like this, with rats enough to scare away a regyment of soldiers, I would not have undertook the situation; so any present as you might think sootable, considerin' all things, and——'

'That will do,' said Paul Marchmont, taking a handful of loose money from his waistcoat-pocket; 'I suppose a ten-pound note would satisfy you?'

'Indeed it would, sir, and very liberal of you too——'

'Very well. I've got a five-pound note here, and five sovereigns. The best thing you can do is to get back to London at once; there's a train leaves Milsome Station at eleven o'clock—Milsome's not more than a mile and a half from here. You can get your things together; there's a boy about the place who will carry them for you, I suppose?'

'Yes, sir; there's a boy by the name of William.'

'He can go with you, then; and if you look sharp, you can catch the eleven-o'clock train.'

'Yes, sir; and thank you kindly, sir.'

'I don't want any thanks. See that you don't miss the train; that's all you have to take care of.'

Mr Marchmont went out into the garden again. He had done something, at any rate; he had arranged for getting this woman out of the way.

If—if by any remote chance there might be yet a possibility of keeping the secret of Mary's existence, here was one witness already got rid of.

But was there any chance? Mr Marchmont sat down on a rickety old garden-seat, and tried to think—tried to take a deliberate survey of his position.

No; there was no hope for him. Look which way he could, there was not one ray of light. With George Weston and Olivia, Betsy Murrel the servant-girl, and Hester Jobson to bear witness against him, what could he hope?

The surgeon would be able to declare that the child was Mary's son, her legitimate son, sole heir to that estate of which Paul had taken possession.

There was no hope. There was no possibility that Olivia should waver in her purpose; for had she not brought with her two witnesses—Hester Jobson and her husband?

From that moment the case was taken out of her hands. The honest carpenter and his wife would see that Mary had her rights.

'It will be a glorious speculation for them,' thought Paul Marchmont, who naturally measured other people's characters by a standard derived from an accurate knowledge of his own.

Yes, his ruin was complete. Destruction had come upon him, swift and sudden as the caprice of a madwoman—or—the thunderbolt of an offended Providence. What should he do? Run away, sneak away by back-lanes and narrow footpaths to the nearest railway-station, hide himself in a third-class carriage going London-wards, and from London get away to Liverpool, to creep on board some emigrant vessel bound for New York?

He could not even do this, for he was without the means of getting so much as the railway-ticket that should carry him on the first stage of his flight. After having given ten pounds to Mrs Brown, he had only a few shillings in his waistcoat-pocket. He had only one article of any great value about him, and that was his watch, which had cost fifty pounds. But the Marchmont arms were emblazoned on the outside of the case; and Paul's name in full, and the address of Marchmont Towers, were ostentatiously engraved inside, so that any attempt to dispose of the watch must inevitably lead to the identification of the owner.

Paul Marchmont had made no provision for this evil day. Supreme in the consciousness of his own talents, he had never imagined discovery and destruction. His plans had been so well arranged. On the very day after Edward's second marriage, Mary and her child would have been conveyed away to the remotest district in Wales; and the artist would have laughed at the idea of danger. The shallowest schemer might have been able to manage this poor broken-hearted girl, whose many sorrows had brought her to look upon life as a thing which was never meant to be joyful, and which was only to be endured patiently, like some slow disease that would be surely cured in the grave. It had been so easy to deal with this ignorant and gentle victim that Paul had grown bold and confident, and had ignored the possibility of such ruin as had now come down upon him.

What was he to do? What was the nature of his crime, and what penalty had he incurred? He tried to answer these questions; but as his offence was of no common kind, he knew of no common law which could apply to it. Was it a felony, this appropriation of another person's property, this concealment of another person's existence; or was it only a conspiracy, amenable to no criminal law; and would he be called upon merely to make restitution of that which he had spent and wasted? What did it matter? Either way, there was nothing for him but ruin—irretrievable ruin.

There are some men who can survive discovery and defeat, and begin a new life in a new world, and succeed in a new career. But Paul Marchmont was not one of these. He could not stick a hunting-knife and a brace of revolvers in his leathern belt, sling a game-bag across his shoulders, take up his breech-loading rifle, and go out into the backwoods of an uncivilised country, to turn sheep-breeder, and hold his own against a race of agricultural savages. He was a Cockney, and for him there was only one world—a world in which men wore varnished boots and enamelled shirt-studs with portraits of La Montespan or La Dubarry,* and lived in chambers in the Albany,* and treated each other to little dinners at Greenwich and Richmond, or cut a grand figure at a country-house, and collected a gallery of art and a museum of *bric à brac*. This was the world upon the outer edge of which Paul Marchmont had lived so long, looking in at the brilliant inhabitants with hungry, yearning eyes through all the days of his poverty and obscurity. This was the world into which he had pushed himself at last by means of a crime.

He was forty years of age; and in all his life he had never had but one ambition,—and that was to be master of Marchmont Towers. The remote chance of that inheritance had hung before him ever since his boyhood, a glittering prize, far away in the distance, but so brilliant as to blind him to the brightness of all nearer chances. Why should he slave at his easel, and toil to become a great painter? When would art earn him eleven thousand a year? The greatest painter of Mr Marchmont's time lived in a miserable lodging at Chelsea. It was before the days of the 'Railway Station' and the 'Derby Day;'* or perhaps Paul might have made an effort to become that which Heaven never meant him to be—a great painter. No; art was only a means of living with this man. He painted, and sold his pictures to his few patrons, who beat him down unmercifully, giving him a small profit upon his canvas and colours, for the encouragement of native art; but he only painted to live.

He was waiting. From the time when he could scarcely speak plain, Marchmont Towers had been a familiar word in his ears and on his lips. He knew the number of lives that stood between his father and the estate, and had learned to say, naïvely enough then,—

'O pa, don't you wish that Uncle Philip and Uncle Marmaduke and Cousin John would die soon?'

He was two-and-twenty years of age when his father died; and he felt a faint thrill of satisfaction, even in the midst of his sorrow, at the thought that there was one life the less between him and the end of his hopes. But other lives had sprung up in the interim. There was young Arthur, and little Mary; and Marchmont Towers was like a caravanserai* in the desert, which seems to be farther and farther away as the weary traveller strives to reach it.

Still Paul hoped, and watched, and waited. He had all the instincts of a sybarite, and he fancied, therefore, that he was destined to be a rich man. He watched, and waited, and hoped, and cheered his mother and sister when they were downcast with the hope of better days. When the chance came, he seized upon it, and plotted, and succeeded, and revelled in his brief success.

But now ruin had come to him, what was he to do? He tried to make some plan for his own conduct; but he could not. His brain reeled with the effort which he made to realise his own position.

He walked up and down one of the pathways in the garden until a quarter to ten o'clock; then he went into the house, and waited till Mrs Brown had departed from Stony-Stringford Farm, attended by the boy, who carried two bundles, a bandbox, and a carpet-bag.

'Come back here when you have taken those things to the station,' Paul said; 'I shall want you.'

He watched the dilapidated five-barred gate swing to after the departure of Mrs Brown and her attendant, and then went to look at his horse. The patient animal had been standing in a shed all this time, and had had neither food nor water. Paul searched amongst the empty barns and outhouses, and found a few handfuls of fodder. He took this to the animal, and then went back again to the garden,—to that quiet garden, where the bees were buzzing about in the sunshine with a drowsy, booming sound, and where a great tabby-cat was sleeping stretched flat upon its side, on one of the flower-beds.

Paul Marchmont waited here very impatiently till the boy came back.

'I must see Lavinia,' he thought. 'I dare not leave this place till I have seen Lavinia. I don't know what may be happening at Hillings-worth or Kemberling. These things are taken up sometimes by the populace. They may make a party against me; they may—'

He stood still, gnawing the edges of his nails, and staring down at the gravel-walk.

He was thinking of things that he had read in the newspapers,—cases in which some cruel mother who had illused her child, or some suspected assassin who, in all human probability, had poisoned his wife, had been well-nigh torn piece-meal by an infuriated mob, and had been glad to cling for protection to the officers of justice, or to beg leave to stay in prison after acquittal, for safe shelter from honest men and women's indignation.

He remembered one special case in which the populace, unable to get at a man's person, tore down his house, and vented their fury upon unsentient bricks and mortar.

Mr Marchmont took out a little memorandum book, and scrawled a few lines in pencil:

'I am here, at Stony-Stringford Farmhouse,' he wrote. 'For God's sake, come to me, Lavinia, and at once; you can drive here yourself. I want to know what has happened at Kemberling and at Hillingsworth. Find out everything for me, and come.

P. M.'

It was nearly twelve o'clock when the boy returned. Paul gave him this letter, and told the lad to get on his own horse, and ride to Kemberling as fast as he could go. He was to leave the horse at Kemberling, in Mr Weston's stable, and was to come back to Stony-Stringford with Mrs Weston. This order Paul particularly impressed upon the boy, lest he should stop in Kemberling, and reveal the secret of Paul's hiding-place.

Mr Paul Marchmont was afraid. A terrible sickening dread had taken possession of him, and what little manliness there had ever been in his nature seemed to have deserted him to-day.

Oh, the long dreary hours of that miserable day! the hideous sunshine, that scorched Mr Marchmont's bare head, as he loitered about the garden!—he had left his hat in the house; but he did not even know that he was bareheaded. Oh, the misery of that long day of suspense and anguish! The sick consciousness of utter defeat, the thought of the things that he might have done, the purse that he might have made with the money that he had lavished on pictures, and decorations, and improvements, and the profligate extravagance of splendid entertainments. This is what he thought of, and these were the thoughts that tortured him. But in all that miserable day he never felt one pang of remorse for the agonies that he had inflicted upon his innocent victim; on the contrary, he hated her because of this discovery, and gnashed his teeth as he thought how she and her young husband would enjoy all the grandeur of Marchmont Towers,—all that noble revenue which he had hoped to hold till his dying day.

It was growing dusk when Mr Marchmont heard the sound of wheels in the dusty lane outside the garden-wall. He went through the house, and into the farmyard, in time to receive his sister Lavinia at the gate. It was the wheels of her pony-carriage he had heard. She drove a pair of ponies, which Paul had given her. He was angry with himself as he remembered that this was another piece of extravagance,—another sum of money recklessly squandered, when it might have gone towards the making of a rich provision for this evil day.

Mrs Weston was very pale; and her brother could see by her face that she brought him no good news. She left her ponies to the care of the boy, and went into the garden with her brother.

'Well, Lavinia?'

'Well, Paul, it is a dreadful business,' Mrs Weston said, in a low voice.

'It's all George's doing! It's all the work of that infernal scoundrel!' cried Paul, passionately. 'But he shall pay bitterly for——'

'Don't let us talk of him, Paul; no good can come of that. What are you going to do?'

'I don't know. I sent for you because I wanted your help and advice. What's the good of your coming if you bring me no help?'

'Don't be cruel, Paul. Heaven knows, I'll do my best. But I can't see what's to be done—except for you to get away, Paul. Everything's known. Olivia stopped the marriage publicly in Hillingsworth Church; and all the Hillingsworth people followed Edward Arundel's carriage to Kemberling. The report spread like wildfire; and, oh Paul, the Kemberling people have taken it up, and our windows have been broken, and there's been a crowd all day upon the terrace before the Towers, and they've tried to get into the house, declaring that they know you're hiding somewhere. Paul, Paul, what are we to do? The people hooted after me as I drove away from the High Street, and the boys threw stones at the ponies. Almost all the servants have left the Towers. The constables have been up there trying to get the crowd off the terrace. But what are we to do, Paul? what are we to do?'

'Kill ourselves,' answered the artist savagely. 'What else should we do? What have we to live, for? You have a little money, I suppose; I have none. Do you think I can go back to the old life? Do you think I can go back, and live in that shabby house in Charlotte Street, and paint the same rocks and boulders, the same long stretch of sea, the same low lurid streaks of light,—all the old subjects over again,—for the same starvation prices? Do you think I can ever tolerate shabby clothes again, or miserable make-shift dinners,—hashed mutton, with ill-cut hunks of lukewarm meat floating about in greasy slop called gravy, and washed down with flat porter fetched half an hour too soon from a public-house,—do you think I can go back to *that*? No; I have tasted the wine of life: I have lived; and I'll never go back to the living death called poverty. Do you think I can stand in that passage in Charlotte Street again, Lavinia, to be bullied by an illiterate tax-gatherer, or insulted by an infuriated baker? No, Lavinia; I have made my venture, and I have failed'

'But what will you do, Paul?'

'I don't know,' he answered, moodily.

This was a lie. He knew well enough what he meant to do: he would kill himself.

That resolution inspired him with a desperate kind of courage. He would escape from the mob; he would get away somewhere or other quietly and there kill himself. He didn't know how, as yet; but he would deliberate upon that point at his leisure, and choose the death that was supposed to be least painful.

'Where are my mother and Clarissa?' he asked presently.

'They are at our house; they came to me directly they heard the rumour of what had happened. I don't know how they heard it; but every one heard of it simultaneously, as it seemed. My mother is in a dreadful state. I dared not tell her that I had known it all along.'

'Oh, of course not,' answered Paul, with a sneer; 'let me bear the burden of my guilt alone. What did my mother say?'

'She kept saying again and again, "I can't believe it. I can't believe that he could do anything cruel; he has been such a good son."'

'I was not cruel,' Paul cried vehemently; 'the girl had every comfort. I never grudged money for her comfort. She was a miserable, apathetic creature, to whom fortune was almost a burden rather than an advantage. If I separated her from her husband—bah!—was that such a cruelty? She was no worse off than if Edward Arundel had been killed in that railway accident; and it might have been so.'

He didn't waste much time by reasoning on this point. He thought of his mother and sisters. From first to last he had been a good son and a good brother.

'What money have you, Lavinia?'

'A good deal; you have been very generous to me, Paul; and you shall have it all back again, if you want it. I have got upwards of two thousand pounds altogether; for I have been very careful of the money you have given me.'

'You have been wise. Now listen to me, Lavinia. I *have* been a good son, and I have borne my burdens uncomplainingly. It is your turn now to bear yours. I must get back to Marchmont Towers, if I can, and gather together whatever personal property I have there. It isn't much—only a few trinkets, and suchlike. You must send me some one you can trust to fetch those to-night; for I shall not stay an hour in the place. I may not even be admitted into it; for Edward Arundel may have already taken possession in his wife's name. Then you will have to decide where you are to go. You can't stay in this part of the country. Weston must be liable to some penalty or other for his share in the business, unless he's bought over as a witness to testify to the identity of Mary's child. I haven't time to think of all this. I want you to promise me that you will take care of your mother and your invalid sister.'

'I will, Paul; I will indeed. But tell me what you are going to do yourself, and where you are going?'

'I don't know,' Paul Marchmont answered, in the same tone as before; 'but whatever I do, I want you to give me your solemn promise that you will be good to my mother and sister.'

'I will, Paul; I promise you to do as you have done.'

'You had better leave Kemberling by the first train to-morrow morning; take my mother and Clarissa with you; take everything that is worth taking, and leave Weston behind you to bear the brunt of this business. You can get a lodging in the old neighbourhood, and no one will molest you when you once get away from this place. But remember one thing, Lavinia: if Mary Arundel's child should die, and Mary herself should die childless, Clarissa will inherit

Marchmont Towers. Don't forget that. There's a chance yet for you: it's far away, and unlikely enough; but it *is* a chance.'

'But you are more likely to outlive Mary and her child than Clarissa is,' Mrs Weston answered, with a feeble attempt at hopefulness; 'try and think of that, Paul, and let the hope cheer you.'

'Hope!' cried Mr Marchmont, with a discordant laugh. 'Yes; I'm forty years old, and for five-and-thirty of those years I've hoped and waited for Marchmont Towers. I can't hope any longer, or wait any longer. I give it up; I've fought hard, but I'm beaten.'

It was nearly dark by this time, the shadowy darkness of a midsummer's evening; and there were stars shining faintly out of the sky.

'You can drive me back to the Towers,' Paul Marchmont said. 'I don't want to lose any time in getting there; I may be locked out by Mr Edward Arundel if I don't take care.'

Mrs Weston and her brother went back to the farmyard. It was sixteen miles from Kemberling to Stony Stringford; and the ponies were steaming, for Lavinia had come at a good rate. But it was no time for the consideration of horseflesh. Paul took a rug from the empty seat, and wrapped himself in it. He would not be likely to be recognised in the darkness, sitting back in the low seat, and made bulky by the ponderous covering in which he had enveloped himself. Mrs Weston took the whip from the boy, gathered up the reins, and drove off. Paul had left no orders about the custody of the old farmhouse. The boy went home to his master, at the other end of the farm; and the night-winds wandered wherever they listed through the deserted habitation.

CHAPTER XLII

'THERE IS CONFUSION WORSE THAN DEATH'

THE brother and sister exchanged very few words during the drive between Stony Stringford and Marchmont Towers. It was arranged between them that Mrs Weston should drive by a back-way leading to a lane that skirted the edge of the river, and that Paul should get out at a gate opening into the wood, and by that means make his way, unobserved, to the house which had so lately been to all intents and purposes his own.

He dared not attempt to enter the Towers by any other way; for the indignant populace might still be lurking about the front of the house, eager to inflict summary vengeance upon the persecutor of a helpless girl.

It was between nine and ten o'clock when Mr Marchmont got out at the little gate. All here was very still; and Paul heard the croaking of the frogs upon the margin of a little pool in the wood, and the sound of horses' hoofs a mile away upon the loose gravel by the water-side.

'Good night, Lavinia,' he said. 'Send for the things as soon as you go back; and be sure you send a safe person for them.'

'O yes, dear; but hadn't you better take any thing of value yourself?' Mrs Weston asked anxiously. 'You say you have no money. Perhaps it would be best for you to send me the jewellery, though, and I can send you what money you want by my messenger.'

'I shan't want any money—at least I have enough for what I want. What have you done with your savings?'

'They are in a London bank. But I have plenty of ready money in the house. You must want money, Paul?'

'I tell you, no; I have as much as I want.'

'But tell me your plans, Paul; I must know your plans before I leave Lincolnshire myself. Are *you* going away?'

'Yes.'

'Immediately?'

'Immediately.'

'Shall you go to London?'

'Perhaps. I don't know yet.'

'But when shall we see you again, Paul? or how shall we hear of you?'

'I'll write to you.'

'Where?'

'At the Post-office in Rathbone Place. Don't bother me with a lot of questions to-night Lavinia; I'm not in the humour to answer them.'

Paul Marchmont turned away from his sister impatiently, and opened the gate; but before she had driven off, he went back to her.

'Shake hands, Lavinia,' he said; 'shake hands, my dear; it may be a long time before you and I meet again.'

He bent down and kissed his sister.

'Drive home as fast as you can, and send the messenger directly. He had better come to the door of the lobby, near Olivia's room. Where is Olivia, by-the-bye? Is she still with the stepdaughter she loves so dearly?'

'No; she went to Swampington early in the afternoon. A fly was ordered from the Black Bull, and she went away in it.'

'So much the better,' answered Mr Marchmont. 'Good night, Lavinia. Don't let my mother think ill of me. I tried to do the best I could to make her happy. Good-bye.'

'Good-bye, dear Paul; God bless you!'

The blessing was invoked with as much sincerity as if Lavinia Weston had been a good woman, and her brother a good man. Perhaps neither of those two was able to realise the extent of the crime which they had assisted each other to commit.

Mrs Weston drove away; and Paul went up to the back of the Towers, and under an archway leading into the quadrangle. All about the house was as quiet as if the Sleeping Beauty and her court had been its only occupants.

The inhabitants of Kemberling and the neighbourhood were an orderly people, who burnt few candles between May and September; and however much they might have desired to avenge Mary Arundel's wrongs by tearing Paul Marchmont to pieces, their patience had been exhausted by nightfall, and they had been glad to return to their respective abodes, to discuss Paul's iniquities comfortably over the nine-o'clock beer.

Paul stood still in the quadrangle for a few moments, and listened. He could hear no human breath or whisper; he only heard the sound of the corn-crake in the fields to the right of the Towers, and the distant rumbling of wagon-wheels on the high-road. There was a glimmer of light in one of the windows belonging to the servants' offices,—only one dim glimmer, where there had usually been a row of brilliantly-lighted casements. Lavinia was right, then; almost all the servants had left the Towers. Paul tried to open the half-glass door leading into the lobby; but it was locked. He rang a bell; and after about three minutes' delay, a buxom country-girl appeared in the lobby carrying a candle. She was some kitchenmaid or dairymaid or scullerymaid, whom Paul could not remember to have ever seen until now. She opened the door, and admitted him, dropping a curtsey as he passed her. There was some relief even in this. Mr Marchmont had scarcely expected to get into the house at all; still less to be received with common civility by any of the servants, who had so lately obeyed him and fawned upon him.

'Where are all the rest of the servants?' he asked.

'They're all gone, sir; except him as you brought down from London,—Mr Peterson,—and me and mother. Mother's in the laundry, sir; and I'm scullerymaid.'

'Why did the other servants leave the place?'

'Mostly because they was afraid of the mob upon the terrace, I think; sir; for there's been people all the afternoon throwin' stones, and breakin' the windows; and I don't think as there's a whole pane of glass in the front of the house, sir; and Mr Gormby, sir, he come about four o'clock, and he got the people to go away, sir, by tellin' 'em as it wern't your property, sir, but the young lady's, Miss Mary Marchmont,—leastways, Mrs Airendale,—as they was destroyin' of; but most of the servants had gone before that, sir, except Mr Peterson; and Mr Gormby gave orders as me and mother was to lock all the doors, and let no one in upon no account whatever; and he's coming to-morrow mornin' to take possession, he says; and please, sir, you can't come in; for his special orders to me and mother was, no one, and you in particklar.'

'Nonsense, girl!' exclaimed Mr Marchmont, decisively; 'who is Mr Gormby, that he should give orders as to who comes in or stops out? I'm only coming in for half an hour, to pack my portmanteau. Where's Peterson?'

'In the dinin'-room, sir; but please, sir, you mustn't——'

The girl made a feeble effort to intercept Mr Marchmont, in

accordance with the steward's special orders; which were, that Paul should, upon no pretence whatever, be suffered to enter the house. But the artist snatched the candlestick from her hand, and went towards the dining-room, leaving her to stare after him in amazement.

Paul found his valet Peterson, taking what he called a snack, in the dining-room. A cloth was spread upon the corner of the table; and there was a fore-quarter of cold roast-lamb, a bottle of French brandy, and a decanter half-full of Madeira before the valet.

He started as his master entered the room, and looked up, not very respectfully, but with no unfriendly glance.

'Give me half a tumbler of that brandy, Peterson,' said Mr Marchmont.

The man obeyed; and Paul drained the fiery spirit as if it had been so much water. It was four-and-twenty hours since meat or drink had crossed his dry white lips.

'Why didn't you go away with the rest?' he asked, as he set down the empty glass.

'It's only rats, sir, that run away from a falling house. I stopped, thinkin' you'd be goin' away somewhere, and that you'd want me.'

The solid and unvarnished truth of the matter was, that Peterson had taken it for granted that his master had made an excellent purse against this evil day, and would be ready to start for the Continent or America, there to lead a pleasant life upon the proceeds of his iniquity. The valet never imagined his master guilty of such besotted folly as to be *un*prepared for this catastrophe.

'I thought you might still want me, sir,' he said; 'and wherever you're going, I'm quite ready to go too. You've been a good master to me, sir; and I don't want to leave a good master because things go against him.'

Paul Marchmont shook his head, and held out the empty tumbler for his servant to pour more brandy into it.

'I am going away,' he said; 'but I want no servant where I'm going; but I'm grateful to you for your offer, Peterson. Will you come upstairs with me? I want to pack a few things.'

'They're all packed, sir. I knew you'd be leaving, and I've packed everything.'

'My dressing-case?'

'Yes, sir. You've got the key of that.'

'Yes; I know, I know.'

Paul Marchmont was silent for a few minutes, thinking. Everything that he had in the way of personal property of any value was in the dressing-case of which he had spoken. There was five or six hundred pounds worth of jewellery in Mr Marchmont's dressing-case; for the first instinct of the *nouveau riche* exhibits itself in diamond shirt-studs, cameo rings, malachite death's-heads with emerald eyes; grotesque and pleasing charms in the form of coffins, coal-scuttles, and hobnailed boots; fantastical lockets of ruby and enamel; wonderful bands of massive yellow gold, studded with diamonds, wherein to insert the two ends of flimsy lace cravats. Mr Marchmont reflected upon the amount of his possessions, and their security in the jewel-drawer of his dressing-case.

The dressing-case was furnished with a Chubb's lock, the key of which he carried in his waistcoat-pocket. Yes, it was all safe.

'Look here, Peterson,' said Paul Marchmont; 'I think I shall sleep at Mrs Weston's to-night. I should like you to take my dressing-case down there at once.'

'And how about the other luggage, sir,—the portmanteaus and hat-boxes?'

'Never mind those. I want you to put the dressing-case safe in my sister's hands. I can send here for the rest to-morrow morning. You needn't wait for me now. I'll follow you in half an hour.'

'Yes, sir. You want the dressing-case carried to Mrs Weston's house, and I'm to wait for you there?'

'Yes; you can wait for me.'

'But is there nothing else I can do, sir?'

'Nothing whatever. I've only got to collect a few papers, and then I shall follow you.'

'Yes, sir.'

The discreet Peterson bowed, and retired to fetch the dressing-case. He put his own construction upon Mr Marchmont's evident desire to get rid of him, and to be left alone at the Towers. Paul had, of course, made a purse, and had doubtless put his money away in some very artful hiding-place, whence he now wanted to take it at his leisure. He had stuffed one of his pillows with bank-notes, perhaps; or had hidden a cash-box behind the tapestry in his bedchamber; or had buried a bag of gold in the flower-garden below the terrace. Mr Peterson went upstairs to Paul's dressing-room, put his hand through the strap of the dressing-case, which was very heavy, went downstairs again, met his master in the hall, and went out at the lobby-door.

Paul locked the door upon his valet, and then went back into the lonely house, where the ticking of the clocks in the tenantless rooms sounded unnaturally loud in the stillness. All the windows had been broken; and though the shutters were shut, the cold night-air blew in at many a crack and cranny, and well-nigh extinguished Mr Marchmont's candle as he went from room to room looking about him.

He went into the western drawing-room, and lighted some of the lamps in the principal chandelier. The shutters were shut, for the windows here, as well as elsewhere, had been broken; fragments of shivered glass, great jagged stones, and handfuls of gravel, lay about upon the rich carpet,—the velvet-pile which he had chosen with such artistic taste, such careful deliberation. He lit the lamps and walked about the room, looking for the last time at his treasures. Yes, *his* treasures. It was he who had transformed this chamber from a prim, old-fashioned sitting-room—with quaint japanned cabinets, shabby chintz-cushioned cane-chairs, cracked Indian vases, and a faded carpet—into a saloon that would have been no discredit to Buckingham Palace or Alton Towers.*

It was he who had made the place what it was. He had squandered the savings of Mary's minority upon pictures that the richest collector in England might have been proud to own; upon porcelain that would have been worthy of a place in the Vienna Museum or the Bernal Collection.* He had done this, and these things were to pass into the possession of the man he hated,—the fiery young soldier who had horsewhipped him before the face of wondering Lincolnshire. He walked about the room, thinking of his life since he had come into possession of this place, and of what it had been before that time, and what it must be again, unless he summoned up a desperate courage—and killed himself.

His heart beat fast and loud, and he felt an icy chill creeping slowly through his every vein as he thought of this. How was he to kill himself? He had no poison in his possession,—no deadly drug that would reduce the agony of death to the space of a lightning-flash. There were pistols, rare gems of choicest workmanship, in one of the buhl-cabinets* in that very room; there were both fowling-piece and ammunition in Mr Marchmont's dressing-room: but the artist was not expert with the use of firearms, and he might fail in the attempt to blow out his brains, and only maim or disfigure himself hideously. There was the river,—the black, sluggish river: but then, drowning is a slow death, and Heaven only knows how long the agony may seem to the wretch who endures it! Alas! the ghastly truth of the matter is that Mr Marchmont was afraid of death. Look at the King of Terrors how he would; he could not discover any pleasing aspect under which he could meet the grim monarch without flinching.

He looked at life; but if life was less terrible than death, it was not less dreary. He looked forward with a shudder to see—what? Humiliation, disgrace, perhaps punishment,—life-long transporta- tion, it may be; for this base conspiracy might be a criminal offence, amenable to criminal law. Or, escaping all this, what was there for him? What was there for this man even then? For forty years he had been steeped to the lips in poverty, and had endured his life. He looked back now, and wondered how it was that he had been patient; he wondered why he had not made an end of himself and his obscure troubles twenty years before this night. But after looking back a little longer, he saw the star which had illumined the darkness of that miserable and sordid existence, and he understood the reason of his endurance. He had hoped. Day after day he had got up to go through the same troubles, to endure the same humiliations: but every day, when his life had been hardest to him, he had said, 'To-morrow I may be master of Marchmont Towers.' But he could never hope this any more; he could not go back to watch and wait again, beguiled by the faint hope that Mary Arundel's son might die, and to hear by- and-by that other children were born to her to widen the great gulf betwixt him and fortune.

He looked back, and he saw that he had lived from day to day, from year to year, lured on by this one hope. He looked forward, and he saw that he could not live without it.

There had never been but this one road to good fortune open to him. He was a clever man, but his was not the cleverness which can transmute itself into solid cash. He could only paint indifferent pic- tures; and he had existed long enough by picture-painting to realise the utter hopelessness of success in that career.

He had borne his life while he was in it, but he could not bear to go back to it. He had been out of it, and had tasted another phase of existence; and he could see it all now plainly, as if he had been a spectator sitting in the boxes and watching a dreary play performed upon a stage before him. The performers in the remotest provincial theatre believe in the play they are acting. The omnipotence of passion creates dewy groves and moonlit atmospheres, ducal robes and beautiful women. But the metropolitan spectator, in whose mind the memory of better things is still fresh, sees that the moonlit trees are poor distemper daubs, pushed on by dirty carpenters, and the moon a green bottle borrowed from a druggist's shop, the ducal robes threadbare cotton velvet and tarnished tinsel, and the heroine of the drama old and ugly.

So Paul looked at the life he had endured, and wondered as he saw how horrible it was.

He could see the shabby lodging, the faded furniture, the miserable handful of fire struggling with the smoke in a shallow grate, that had been half-blocked up with bricks by some former tenant as badly off as himself. He could look back at that dismal room, with the ugly paper on the walls, the scanty curtains flapping in the wind which they pretended to shut out; the figure of his mother sitting near the fireplace, with that pale, anxious face, which was a perpetual complaint against hardship and discomfort. He could see his sister standing at the window in the dusky twilight, patching up some worn-out garment, and straining her eyes for the sake of economising in the matter of half an inch of candle. And the street below the window,— the shabby-genteel street, with a dingy shop breaking out here and there, and children playing on the doorsteps, and a muffin-bell jingling through the evening fog, and a melancholy Italian grinding 'Home, sweet Home!' in the patch of lighted road opposite the pawnbroker's. He saw it all; and it was alike—sordid, miserable, hopeless.

Paul Marchmont had never sunk so low as his cousin John. He had never descended so far in the social scale as to carry a banner at Drury Lane, or to live in one room in Oakley Street, Lambeth. But there had been times when to pay the rent of three rooms had been next kin to an impossibility to the artist, and when the honorarium of a shilling a night would have been very acceptable to him. He had drained the cup of poverty to the dregs; and now the cup was filled again, and the bitter draught was pushed once more into his unwilling hand.

He must drink that, or another potion,—a sleeping-draught, which is commonly called Death. He must die! But how? His coward heart sank as the awful alternative pressed closer upon him. He must die!—to night,—at once,—in that house; so that when they came in the morning to eject him, they would have little trouble; they would only have to carry out a corpse.

He walked up and down the room, biting his finger-nails to the quick, but coming to no resolution, until he was interrupted by the ringing of the bell at the lobby-door. It was the messenger from his sister, no doubt. Paul drew his watch from his waistcoat-pocket, unfastened his chain, took a set of gold-studs from the breast of his shirt, and a signet-ring from his finger; then he sat down at a writing-table, and packed the watch and chain, the studs and signet-ring, and a bunch of keys, in a large envelope. He sealed this packet, and addressed it to his sister; then he took a candle, and went to the lobby. Mrs Weston had sent a young man who was an assistant and pupil of her husband's—a good-tempered young fellow, who willingly served her in her hour of trouble. Paul gave this messenger the key of his dressing-case and packet.

'You will be sure and put that in my sister's hands,' he said.

'O yes, sir. Mrs Weston gave me this letter for you; sir. Am I to wait for an answer?'

'No; there will be no answer. Good night.'

'Good night, sir.'

The young man went away; and Paul Marchmont heard him whistle a popular melody as he walked along the cloistered way and out of the quadrangle by a low archway commonly used by the tradespeople who came to the Towers.

The artist stood and listened to the young man's departing footsteps. Then, with a horrible thrill of anguish, he remembered that he had seen his last of humankind—he had heard his last of human voices: for he was to kill himself that night. He stood in the dark lobby, looking out into the quadrangle. He was quite alone in the house; for the girl who had let him in was in the laundry with her mother. He could see the figures of the two women moving about in a great gaslit chamber upon the other side of the quadrangle—a building which had no communication with the rest of the house. He was to die that night; and he had not yet even determined how he was to die.

He mechanically opened Mrs Weston's letter: it was only a few lines, telling him that Peterson had arrived with the portmanteau and dressing-case, and that there would be a comfortable room prepared for him. 'I am so glad you have changed your mind, and are coming to me, Paul,' Mrs Weston concluded. 'Your manner, when we parted to-night, almost alarmed me.'

Paul groaned aloud as he crushed the letter in his hand. Then he went back to the western drawing-room. He heard strange noises in the empty rooms as he passed by their open doors, weird creaking sounds and melancholy moanings in the wide chimneys. It seemed as if all the ghosts of Marchmont Towers were astir to-night, moved by an awful prescience of some coming horror.

Paul Marchmont was an atheist; but atheism, although a very pleasant theme for a critical and argumentative discussion after a lobster-supper and unlimited champagne, is but a poor staff to lean upon when the worn-out traveller approaches the mysterious portals of the unknown land.

The artist had boasted of his belief in annihilation; and had declared himself perfectly satisfied with a materialistic or pantheistic arrangement of the universe, and very indifferent as to whether he cropped up in future years as a summer-cabbage, or a new Raphael; so long as the ten stone or so of matter of which he was composed was made use of somehow or other, and did its duty in the great scheme of a scientific universe. But, oh! how that empty, soulless creed slipped away from him now, when he stood alone in this tenantless house, shuddering at strange spirit-noises, and horrified by a host of mystic fears—gigantic, shapeless terrors—that crowded in his empty, godless mind, and filled it with their hideous presence!

He had refused to believe in a personal God. He had laughed at the idea that there was any Deity to whom the individual can appeal, in his hour of grief or trouble, with the hope of any separate mercy, any special grace. He had rejected the Christian's simple creed, and now—now that he had floated away from the shores of life, and felt himself borne upon an irresistible current to that mysterious other side, what did he *not* believe in?

Every superstition that has ever disturbed the soul of ignorant man lent some one awful feature to the crowd of hideous images uprising in this man's mind:—awful Chaldean gods and Carthaginian goddesses, thirsting for the hot blood of human sacrifices, greedy for hecatombs of children flung shrieking into fiery furnaces, or torn limb from limb by savage beasts; Babylonian abominations; Egyptian Isis and Osiris; classical divinities, with flaming swords and pale impassible faces, rigid as the Destiny whose type they were; ghastly Germanic demons and witches.—All the dread avengers that man, in the knowledge of his own wickedness, has ever shadowed for himself out of the darkness of his ignorant mind, swelled that ghastly crowd, until the artist's brain reeled, and he was fain to sit with his head in his hands, trying, by a great effort of the will, to exorcise these loathsome phantoms.

'I must be going mad,' he muttered to himself. 'I am going mad.'

But still the great question was unanswered—How was he to kill himself?

'I must settle that,' he thought. 'I dare not think of anything that may come afterwards. Besides, what *should* come? I *know* that there is nothing. Haven't I heard it demonstrated by cleverer men than I am? Haven't I looked at it in every light, and weighed it in every scale— always with the same result? Yes; I know that there is nothing *after* the one short pang, any more than there is pain in the nerve of a tooth when the tooth is gone. The nerve was the soul of the tooth, I suppose; but wrench away the body, and the soul is dead. Why should I be afraid? One short pain—it will seem long, I dare say— and then I shall lie still for ever and ever, and melt slowly back into the elements out of which I was created. Yes; I shall lie still—and be *nothing*.'

Paul Marchmont sat thinking of this for a long time. Was it such a great advantage, after all, this annihilation, the sovereign good of the atheist's barren creed? It seemed to-night to this man as if it would be better to be anything—to suffer any anguish, any penalty for his sins, than to be blotted out for ever and ever from any conscious part in the grand harmony of the universe. If he could have believed in that Roman Catholic doctrine of purgatory, and that after cycles of years of suffering he might rise at last, purified from his sins, worthy to dwell among the angels, how differently would death have appeared to him! He might have gone away to hide himself in some foreign city, to perform patient daily sacrifices, humble acts of self-abnegation, every one of which should be a new figure, however small a one, to be set against the great sum of his sin.

But he could not believe. There is a vulgar proverb which says,

'You cannot have your loaf and eat it;' or if proverbs would only be grammatical, it might be better worded, 'You cannot eat your loaf, and have it to eat on some future occasion.' Neither can you indulge in rationalistic discussions or epigrammatic pleasantry about the Great Creator who made you, and then turn and cry aloud to Him in the dreadful hour of your despair: 'O my God, whom I have insulted and offended, help the miserable wretch who for twenty years has obstinately shut his heart against Thee!' It may be that God would forgive and hear even at that last supreme moment, as He heard the penitent thief upon the cross; but the penitent thief had been a sinner, not an unbeliever, and he *could* pray. The hard heart of the atheist freezes in his breast when he would repent and put away his iniquities. When he would fain turn to his offended Maker, the words that he tries to speak die away upon his lips; for the habit of blasphemy is too strong upon him; he can *blague** upon all the mighty mysteries of heaven and hell, but he *cannot* pray.

Paul Marchmont could not fashion a prayer. Horrible witticisms arose up between him and the words he would have spoken—ghastly *bon mots*, that had seemed so brilliant at a lamp-lit dinner-table, spoken to a joyous accompaniment of champagne-corks and laughter. Ah, me! the world was behind this man now, with all its pleasures; and he looked back upon it, and thought that, even when it seemed gayest and brightest, it was only like a great roaring fair, with flaring lights, and noisy showmen clamoring for ever to a struggling crowd.

How should he die? Should he go upstairs and cut his throat?

He stood before one of his pictures—a pet picture; a girl's face by Millais,* looking through the moonlight, fantastically beautiful. He stood before this picture, and he felt one small separate pang amid all his misery as he remembered that Edward and Mary Arundel were now possessors of this particular gem.

'They sha'n't have it,' he muttered to himself; 'they sha'n't have *this*, at any rate.'

He took a penknife from his pocket, and hacked and ripped the canvas savagely, till it hung in ribbons from the deep gilded frame.

Then he smiled to himself, for the first time since he had entered that house, and his eyes flashed with a sudden light.

'I have lived like Sardanapalus* for the last year,' he cried aloud; 'and I will die like Sardanapalus!'

There was a fragile piece of furniture near him,—an *étagère** of marqueterie work, loaded with costly *bric à brac*, Oriental porcelain, Sèvres and Dresden, old Chelsea and crown Derby cups and saucers, and quaint teapots, crawling vermin in Pallissy ware, Indian monstrosities, and all manner of expensive absurdities, heaped together in artistic confusion. Paul Marchmont struck the slim leg of the *étagère* with his foot, and laughed aloud as the fragile toys fell into a ruined heap upon the carpet. He stamped upon the broken china; and the frail cups and saucers crackled like eggshells under his savage feet.

'I will die like Sardanapalus!' he cried; 'the King Arbaces shall never rest in the palace I have beautified.

> "Now order here
> Faggots, pine-nuts, and wither'd leaves, and such
> Things as catch fire with one sole spark;
> Bring cedar, too, and precious drugs, and spices,
> And mighty planks, to nourish a tall pile;
> Bring frankincense and myrrh, too; for it is
> For a great sacrifice I build the pyre."*

I don't think much of your blank verse, George Gordon Noel Byron. Your lines end on lame syllables; your ten-syllable blank verse lacks the fiery ring of your rhymes. I wonder whether Marchmont Towers is insured? Yes, I remember paying a premium last Christmas. They may have a sharp tussle with the insurance companies though. Yes, I will die like Sardanapalus—no, not like him, for I have no Myrrha to mount the pile and cling about me to the last. Pshaw! a modern Myrrha would leave Sardanapalus to perish alone, and be off to make herself safe with the new king.'

Paul snatched up the candle, and went out into the hall. He laughed discordantly, and spoke in loud ringing tones. His manner had that feverish excitement which the French call exaltation. He ran up the broad stairs leading to the long corridor, out of which his own rooms, and his mother's and sister's rooms, opened.

Ah, how pretty they were! How elegant he had made them in his reckless disregard of expense, his artistic delight in the task of beautification! There were no shutters here, and the summer breeze blew in through the broken windows, and stirred the gauzy muslin curtains, the gay chintz draperies, the cloudlike festoons of silk and lace.

Paul Marchmont went from room to room with the flaring candle in his hand; and wherever there were curtains or draperies about the windows, the beds, the dressing-tables, the low lounging-chairs, and cosy little sofas, he set alight to them. He did this with wonderful rapidity, leaving flames behind him as he traversed the long corridor, and coming back thus to the stairs. He went downstairs again, and returned to the western drawing-room. Then he blew out his candle, turned out the gas, and waited.

'How soon will it come?' he thought.

The shutters were shut, and the room was quite dark.

'Shall I ever have courage to stop till it comes?'

Paul Marchmont groped his way to the door, double-locked it, and then took the key from the lock.

He went to one of the windows, clambered upon a chair, opened the top shutter, and flung the key out through the broken window. He heard it strike jingling upon the stone terrace and then bound away, Heaven knows where.

'I shan't be able to go out by the door, at any rate,' he thought.

It was quite dark in the room, but the reflection of the spreading flames was growing crimson in the sky outside. Mr Marchmont went away from the window, feeling his way amongst the chairs and tables. He could see the red light through the crevices of the shutters, and a lurid patch of sky through that one window, the upper half of which he had left open. He sat down, somewhere near the centre of the room, and waited.

'The smoke will kill me,' he thought. 'I shall know nothing of the fire.'

He sat quite still. He had trembled violently while he had gone from room to room doing his horrible work; but his nerves seemed steadier now. Steadier! why, he was transformed to stone! His heart seemed to have stopped beating; and he only knew by a sick anguish, a dull aching pain, that it was still in his breast.

He sat waiting and thinking. In that time all the long story of the past was acted before him, and he saw what a wretch he had been. I do not know whether this was penitence; but looking at that enacted story, Paul Marchmont thought that his own part in the play was a mistake, and that it was a foolish thing to be a villain.

When a great flock of frightened people, with a fire-engine out of order, and drawn by whooping men and boys, came hurrying up to the Towers, they found a blazing edifice, which looked like an enchanted castle—great stone-framed windows vomiting flame; tall chimneys toppling down upon a fiery roof; molten lead, like water turned to fire, streaming in flaming cataracts upon the terrace; and all the sky lit up by that vast pile of blazing ruin. Only salamanders, or poor Mr Braidwood's* own chosen band, could have approached Marchmont Towers that night. The Kemberling firemen and the Swampington firemen, who came by-and-by, were neither salamanders nor Braidwoods. They stood aloof and squirted water at the flames, and recoiled aghast by-and-by when the roof came down like an avalanche of blazing timber, leaving only a gaunt gigantic skeleton of red-hot stone where Marchmont Towers once had been.

When it was safe to venture in amongst the ruins—and this was not for many hours after the fire had burnt itself out—people looked for Paul Marchmont; but amidst all that vast chaos of smouldering ashes, there was nothing found that could be identified as the remains of a human being. No one knew where the artist had been at the time of the fire, or indeed whether he had been in the house at all; and the popular opinion was, that Paul had set fire to the mansion, and had fled away before the flames began to spread.

But Lavinia Weston knew better than this. She knew now why her brother had sent her every scrap of valuable property belonging to him. She understood now why he had come back to her to bid her good-night for the second time, and press his cold lips to hers.

CHAPTER XLIII

'DEAR IS THE MEMORY OF OUR WEDDED LIVES'

MARY and Edward Arundel saw the awful light in the sky, and heard the voices of the people shouting in the street below, and calling to one another that Marchmont Towers was on fire.

The young mistress of the burning pile had very little concern for her property. She only kept saying, again and again, 'O Edward! I hope there is no one in the house. God grant there may be no one in the house!'

And when the flames were highest, and it seemed by the light in the sky as if all Lincolnshire had been blazing, Edward Arundel's wife flung herself upon her knees, and prayed aloud for any unhappy creature that might be in peril.

Oh, if we could dare to think that this innocent girl's prayer was heard before the throne of an Awful Judge, pleading for the soul of a wicked man!

Early the next morning Mrs Arundel came from Lawford Grange with her confidential maid, and carried off her daughter-in-law and the baby, on the first stage of the journey into Devonshire. Before she left Kemberling, Mary was told that no dead body had been found amongst the ruins of the Towers; and this assertion deluded her into the belief that no unhappy creature had perished. So she went to Dangerfield happier than she had ever been since the sunny days of her honeymoon, to wait there for the coming of Edward Arundel, who was to stay behind to see Richard Paulette and Mr Gormby, and to secure the testimony of Mr Weston and Betsy Murrel with a view to the identification of Mary's little son, who had been neither registered nor christened.

I have no need to dwell upon this process of identification, registration, and christening, through which Master Edward Arundel had to pass in the course of the next month. I had rather skip this dry-as-dust business, and go on to that happy time which Edward and his young wife spent together under the oaks at Dangerfield—that bright second honeymoon season, while they were as yet houseless; for a pretty villa-like mansion was being built on the Marchmont property, far away from the dank wood and the dismal river, in a pretty pastoral little nook, which was a fair oasis amidst the general dreariness of Lincolnshire.

I need scarcely say that the grand feature of this happy time was THE BABY. It will be of course easily understood that this child stood alone amongst babies. There never had been another such infant; it was more than probable there would never again be such a one. In every attribute of babyhood he was a twelvemonth in advance of the rest of his race. Prospective greatness was stamped upon his brow. He would be a Clive or a Wellington, unless indeed he should have a fancy for the Bar and the Woolsack, in which case he would be a little more erudite than Lyndhurst, a trifle more eloquent than Brougham.* All this was palpable to the meanest capacity in the very manner in which this child crowed in his nurse's arms, or choked himself with farinaceous food, or smiled recognition at his young father, or performed the simplest act common to infancy.

I think Mr Sant* would have been pleased to paint one of those summer scenes at Dangerfield—the proud soldier-father; the pale young wife; the handsome, matronly grandmother; and, as the mystic centre of that magic circle, the toddling flaxen-haired baby, held up by his father's hands, and taking caricature strides in imitation of papa's big steps.

To my mind, it is a great pity that children are not children for ever—that the pretty baby-boy by Sant, all rosy and flaxen and blue-eyed, should ever grow into a great angular pre-Raphaelite hobada-hoy,* horribly big and out of drawing. But neither Edward nor Mary nor, above all, Mrs Arundel were of this opinion. They were as eager for the child to grow up and enter for the great races of this life, as some speculative turf magnate who has given a fancy price for a yearling, and is pining to see the animal a far-famed three-year-old, and winner of the double event.

Before the child had cut a double-tooth Mrs Arundel senior had decided in favour of Eton as opposed to Harrow, and was balancing the conflicting advantages of classical Oxford and mathematical Cambridge; while Edward could not see the baby-boy rolling on the grass, with blue ribbons and sashes fluttering in the breeze, without thinking of his son's future appearance in the uniform of his own regiment, gorgeous in the splendid crush of a levee at St James's.*

How many airy castles were erected in that happy time, with the baby for the foundation-stone of all of them! *The* BABY! Why, that definite article alone expresses an infinity of foolish love and admiration. Nobody says *the* father, the husband, the mother; it is 'my' father, my husband, as the case may be. But every baby, from St Giles's to Belgravia, from Tyburnia to St Luke's,* is 'the' baby. The infant's reign is short, but his royalty is supreme, and no one presumes to question his despotic rule.

Edward Arundel almost worshipped the little child whose feeble cry he had heard in the October twilight, and had *not* recognised. He was never tired of reproaching himself for this omission. That baby-voice *ought* to have awakened a strange thrill in the young father's breast.

That time at Dangerfield was the happiest period of Mary's life. All her sorrows had melted away. They did not tell her of Paul Marchmont's suspected fate; they only told her that her enemy had disappeared, and that no one knew whither he had gone. Mary asked once, and once only, about her stepmother; and she was told that Olivia was at Swampington Rectory, living with her father, and that people said she was mad. George Weston had emigrated to Australia, with his wife, and his wife's mother and sister. There had been no prosecution for conspiracy; the disappearance of the principal criminal had rendered that unnecessary.

This was all that Mary ever heard of her persecutors. She did not wish to hear of them; she had forgiven them long ago. I think that in the inner depths of her innocent heart she had forgiven them from the moment she had fallen on her husband's breast in Hester's parlour at Kemberling, and had felt his strong arms clasped about her, sheltering her from all harm for evermore.

She was very happy; and her nature, always gentle, seemed sublimated by the sufferings she had endured, and already akin to that of the angels. Alas, this was Edward Arundel's chief sorrow! This young wife, so precious to him in her fading loveliness, was slipping away from him, even in the hour when they were happiest together—was separated from him even when they were most united. She was separated from him by that unconquerable sadness in his heart, which was prophetic of a great sorrow to come.

Sometimes, when Mary saw her husband looking at her, with a mournful tenderness, an almost despairing love in his eyes, she would throw herself into his arms, and say to him:

'You must remember how happy I have been, Edward. O my darling! promise me always to remember how happy I have been.'

When the first chill breezes of autumn blew among the Dangerfield oaks, Edward Arundel took his wife southwards, with his mother and the inevitable baby in her train. They went to Nice, and they were very quiet, very happy, in the pretty southern town, with snow-clad mountains behind them, and the purple Mediterranean before.

The villa was building all this time in Lincolnshire. Edward's agent sent him plans and sketches for Mrs Arundel's approval; and every evening there was some fresh talk about the arrangement of the rooms, and the laying-out of gardens. Mary was always pleased to see the plans and drawings, and to discuss the progress of the work with her husband. She would talk of the billiard-room, and the cosy little smoking-room; and the nurseries for the baby, which were to have a southern aspect, and every advantage calculated to assist the development of that rare and marvellous blossom, and she would plan the comfortable apartments that were to be specially kept for dear grandmamma, who would of course spend a great deal of her time at the Sycamores—the new place was to be called the Sycamores. But Edward could never get his wife to talk of a certain boudoir opening into a tiny conservatory, which he himself had added on to the original architect's plan. He could never get Mary to speak of this particular chamber; and once, when he asked her some question about the colour of the draperies, she said to him, very gently,—

'I would rather you would not think of that room, darling.'

'Why, my pet?'

'Because it will make you sorry afterwards.'

'Mary, my darling——'

'O Edward! you know,—you must know, dearest,—that I shall never see that place?'

But her husband took her in his arms, and declared that this was only a morbid fancy, and that she was getting better and stronger every day, and would live to see her grandchildren playing under the maples that sheltered the northern side of the new villa. Edward told his wife this, and he believed in the truth of what he said. He could not believe that he was to lose this young wife, restored to him after so many trials. Mary did not contradict him just then; but that night, when he was sitting in her room reading by the light of a shaded lamp after she had gone to bed,—Mary went to bed very early, by order of the doctors, and indeed lived altogether according to medical *régime*,—she called her husband to her.

'I want to speak to you, dear,' she said; 'there is something that I must say to you.'

The young man knelt down by his wife's bed.

'What is it, darling?' he asked.

'You know what we said to-day, Edward?'

'What, darling? We say so many things every day—we are so happy together, and have so much to talk about.'

'But you remember, Edward,—you remember what I said about never seeing the Sycamores? Ah! don't stop me, dear love,' Mary said reproachfully, for Edward put his lips to hers to stay the current of mournful words,—'don't stop me, dear, for I must speak to you. I want you to know that *it must be*, Edward darling. I want you to remember how happy I have been, and how willing I am to part with you, dear, since it is God's will that we should be parted. And there is something else that I want to say, Edward. Grandmamma told me something—all about Belinda. I want you to promise me that Belinda shall be happy by-and-by; for she has suffered so much, poor girl! And you will love her, and she will love the baby. But you won't love her quite the same way that you loved me, will you, dear? because you never knew her when she was a little child, and very poor. She has never been an orphan, and quite lonely, as I have been. You have never been *all the world* to her.'

The Sycamores was finished by the following midsummer, but no one took possession of the newly-built house; no brisk upholsterer's men came, with three-foot rules and pencils and memorandum-books, to take measurements of windows and floors; no waggons of splendid furniture made havoc of the gravel-drive before the principal entrance. The only person who came to the new house was a snuff-taking crone from Stanfield, who brought a turn-up bedstead, a Dutch clock, and a few minor articles of furniture, and encamped in a corner of the best bedroom.

Edward Arundel, senior, was away in India, fighting under Napier and Outram; and Edward Arundel, junior, was at Dangerfield, under the charge of his grandmother.

Perhaps the most beautiful monument in one of the English cemeteries at Nice is that tall white marble cross and kneeling figure, before which strangers pause to read an inscription to the memory of Mary, the beloved wife of Edward Dangerfield Arundel.

THE EPILOGUE

FOUR years after the completion of that pretty stuccoed villa, which seemed destined never to be inhabited, Belinda Lawford walked alone up and down the sheltered shrubbery-walk in the Grange garden in the fading September daylight.

Miss Lawford was taller and more womanly-looking than she had been on the day of her interrupted wedding. The vivid bloom had left her cheeks; but I think she was all the prettier because of that delicate pallor, which gave a pensive cast to her countenance. She was very grave and gentle and good; but she had never forgotten the shock of that broken bridal ceremonial in Hillingsworth Church.

The Major had taken his eldest daughter abroad almost immediately after that July day; and Belinda and her father had travelled together very peacefully, exploring quiet Belgian cities, looking at celebrated altar-pieces in dusky cathedrals, and wandering round battle-fields, which the intermingled blood of rival nations had once made one crimson swamp. They had been nearly a twelve-month absent, and then Belinda returned to assist at the marriage of a younger sister, and to hear that Edward Arundel's wife had died of a lingering pulmonary complaint at Nice.

She was told this: and she was told how Olivia Marchmont still lived with her father at Swampington, and how day by day she went the same round from cottage to cottage, visiting the sick; teaching little children, or sometimes rough-bearded men, to read and write and cipher; reading to old decrepid pensioners; listening to long histories of sickness and trial, and exhibiting an unwearying patience that was akin to sublimity. Passion had burnt itself out in this woman's breast, and there was nothing in her mind now but remorse, and the desire to perform a long penance, by reason of which she might in the end be forgiven.

But Mrs Marchmont never visited anyone alone. Wherever she went, Barbara Simmons accompanied her, constant as her shadow. The Swampington people said this was because the Rector's daughter was not quite right in her mind; and there were times when she forgot where she was, and would have wandered away in a purposeless manner, Heaven knows where, had she not been accompanied by her faithful servant. Clever as the Swampington people and the Kemberling people might be in finding out the business of their neighbours, they never knew that Olivia Marchmont had been consentient to the hiding-away of her stepdaughter. They looked upon her, indeed, with considerable respect, as a heroine by whose exertions Paul Marchmont's villainy had been discovered. In the hurry and confusion of the scene at Hillingsworth Church, nobody had taken heed of Olivia's incoherent self-accusations: Hubert Arundel was therefore spared the misery of knowing the extent of his daughter's sin.

Belinda Lawford came home in order to be present at her sister's wedding; and the old life began again for her, with all the old duties that had once been so pleasant. She went about them very cheerfully now. She worked for her poor pensioners, and took the chief burden of the housekeeping off her mother's hands. But though she jingled her keys with a cheery music as she went about the house, and though she often sang to herself over her work, the old happy smile rarely lit up her face. She went about her duties rather like some widowed matron who had lived her life, than a girl before whom the future lies, mysterious and unknown.

It has been said that happiness comes to the sleeper—the meaning of which proverb I take to be, that Joy generally comes to us when we least look for her lovely face. And it was on this September afternoon, when Belinda loitered in the garden after her round of small duties was finished, and she was free to think or dream at her leisure, that happiness came to her,—unexpected, unhoped-for, supreme; for, turning at one end of the sheltered alley, she saw Edward Arundel standing at the other end, with his hat in his hand, and the summer wind blowing amongst his hair.

Miss Lawford stopped quite still. The old-fashioned garden reeled before her eyes, and the hard-gravelled path seemed to become a quaking bog. She could not move; she stood still, and waited while Edward came towards her.

'Letitia has told me about you, Linda,' he said; 'she has told me how true and noble you have been; and she sent me here to look for a wife, to make new sunshine in my empty home,—a young mother to smile upon my motherless boy.'

Edward and Belinda walked up and down the sheltered alley for a long time, talking a great deal of the sad past, a little of the fair-seeming future. It was growing dusk before they went in at the old-fashioned half-glass door leading into the drawing-room, where Mrs Lawford and her younger daughters were sitting, and where Lydia, who was next to Belinda, and had been three years married to the Curate of Hillingsworth, was nursing her second baby.

'Has she said "yes"?' this young matron cried directly; for she had been told of Edward's errand to the Grange. 'But of course she has. What else could she say, after refusing all manner of people, and giving herself the airs of an old-maid? Yes, um pressus Pops, um Aunty Lindy's going to be marriedy-pariedy,' concluded the Curate's wife, addressing her three-months-old baby in that peculiar patois which is supposed to be intelligible to infants by reason of being unintelligible to everybody else.

'I suppose you are not aware that my future brother-in-law is a major?' said Belinda's third sister, who had been struggling with a variation by Thalberg,* all octaves and accidentals, and who twisted herself round upon her music-stool to address her sister. 'I suppose you are not aware that you have been talking to Major Arundel, who has done all manner of splendid things in the Punjab? Papa told us all about it five minutes ago.'

It was as much as Belinda could do to support the clamorous felicitations of her sisters, especially the unmarried damsels, who were eager to exhibit themselves in the capacity of bridesmaids; but by-and-by, after dinner, the Curate's wife drew her sisters away from that shadowy window in which Edward Arundel and Belinda were sitting, and the lovers were left to themselves.

That evening was very peaceful, very happy, and there were many other evenings like it before Edward and Belinda completed that ceremonial which they had left unfinished more than five years before.

The Sycamores was very prettily furnished, under Belinda's superintendence; and as Reginald Arundel had lately married, Edward's mother came to live with her younger son, and brought with her the idolised grandchild, who was now a tall, yellow-haired boy of six years old.

There was only one room in the Sycamores which was never tenanted by any one of that little household except Edward himself, who kept the key of the little chamber in his writing-desk, and only allowed the servants to go in at stated intervals to keep everything bright and orderly in the apartment.

The shut-up chamber was the boudoir which Edward Arundel had planned for his first wife. He had ordered it to be furnished with the very furniture which he had intended for Mary. The rosebuds and butterflies on the walls, the guipure* curtains lined with pale blush-rose silk, the few chosen books in the little cabinet near the fireplace, the Dresden breakfast-service, the statuettes and pictures, were things he had fixed upon long ago in his own mind as the decorations for his wife's apartment. He went into the room now and then, and looked at his first wife's picture—a crayon sketch taken in London before Mary and her husband started for the South of France. He looked a little wistfully at this picture, even when he was happiest in the new ties that bound him to life, and all that is brightest in life.

Major Arundel took his eldest son into this room one day, when young Edward was eight or nine years old, and showed the boy his mother's portrait.

'When you are a man, this place will be yours, Edward,' the father said. '*You* can give your wife this room, although I have never given it to mine. You will tell her that it was built for your mother, and that it was built for her by a husband who, even when most grateful to God for every new blessing he enjoyed, never ceased to be sorry for the loss of his first love.'

And so I leave my soldier-hero, to repose upon laurels that have been hardly won, and secure in that modified happiness which is chastened by the memory of sorrow. I leave him with bright children crowding round his knees, a loving wife smiling at him across those fair childish heads. I leave him happy and good and useful, filling his place in the world, and bringing up his children to be wise and virtuous men and women in the days that are to come. I leave him, above all, with the serene lamp of faith for ever burning in his soul, lighting the image of that other world in which there is neither marrying nor giving in marriage, and where his dead wife will smile upon him from amidst the vast throng of angel faces—a child for ever and ever before the throne of God!

THE END

APPENDIX

The Time-Scheme of *John Marchmont's Legacy*

The action of the novel covers the period 1838–55.

1838	(29 December) Edward Arundel, aged 17, visits a London theatre and sees John Marchmont, who has been his mathematics teacher at a private academy two years earlier. (Marchmont has been at Cambridge 'seven or eight years' earlier, has been widowed at the age of 24, and has taught for three years before being dismissed from the academy.) The next day Edward visits Marchmont's home and meets Mary, aged 8. (Later evidence indicates that she was born in July 1830. Edward was born in 1821, Olivia in 1819, Paul in 1806; Braddon is frequently inconsistent in making later references to the ages of her characters.)
1839	At the beginning of the year Edward goes to a private tutor to prepare for the army examinations.
1840	Now 18, he enters a cavalry regiment and goes to India, leaving his Devon home on 31 January and sailing from Southampton on 2 February. (On contemporary events in Anglo–Indian history, see note on pp. 493–4.)
1843	Between the end of Ch. 4 and the beginning of Ch. 5 three and a half years pass, so it is now the summer of 1843. John Marchmont has come into his inheritance 'within the last six months', having first learned about it in January. It emerges that Marmaduke Marchmont has died of apoplexy on 30 December 1837; the heir to the estate has been killed in a shooting accident on 1 September 1838; Philip Marchmont has died 'at the close of the year '43', which must be an error for ''42'.
	(July) Edward, now 21, returns from India and visits Marchmont Towers. He is stated (p. 56) as now being 24 (and Mary 13), but this must be an error (Mary's age is consistent with earlier indications). He later goes to Devon, but returns to Lincolnshire after six weeks and is there in November. In December John Marchmont marries Olivia; later, the will dated 4 February 1844 is said to have been made 'exactly two months after John's marriage', but elsewhere 'the first week of December' is said to be one week

before the wedding. Edward has left Marchmont Towers the day before the wedding, and soon afterwards returns to India.

1844   John and Olivia return from their brief honeymoon in January.

1845–6   'Nearly two years' pass. By 'late in the autumn' John is sinking fast. 'Soon after the funeral' Mary and Olivia go to Scarborough, returning to Marchmont Towers 'in the early spring' (of 1846).

1848   Another two years pass; Mary's seventeenth birthday in July 1847 has come and gone, and John Marchmont has been dead 'nearly three years'; it is now June 1848. Edward returns to England (he is said to have been away for five years, but it must be somewhat less, since he did not leave England until the end of 1843 or beginning of 1844). He pays a visit to Marchmont Towers.

After Mary's flight from Marchmont Towers in July (at the end of Volume 1), Edward visits her daily in Oakley Street, Lambeth, 'for a little more than a fortnight'. They marry on an 'August morning': it must be at the very beginning of August, since the railway accident in the middle of the month takes place 'within a fortnight' of the wedding. They are spending their honeymoon in Hampshire on 14 August when Edward leaves to go to his sick father in Devon and is injured in a railway accident. Paul Marchmont learns of Mary's whereabouts on 15 August and exchanges letters with Edward's mother at the end of the month, by which time Edward is lying seriously ill at his Devon home.

Three months elapse between Chs. 5 and 6 of Volume II (Chs. 19–20 of the present edition). In November Edward travels to Marchmont Hall and learns that Mary has disappeared on 17 October. (Her age is correctly given as 18.) It emerges that on that day Paul has sent Olivia a newspaper cutting wrongly reporting Edward's death.

1849   'Early in the new year' Edward settles at Kemberling Retreat, having retired from the service of the East India Company. In the next few months he hears news of British victories in India: 'Every mail brought some new record of triumph and glory.' He visits Olivia to enquire whether there is any truth in the rumour that she is intending to marry.

According to Mary's later statement, she is visited in her imprisonment by the Westons in March, and her baby is born 'when the birds were singing': this must be in mid-May or thereabouts, since the baby was presumably conceived in the early August of 1848. During July and August Edward pays frequent visits to the Grange, where his sister Letitia is a guest of the Lawfords; she returns to Devon 'at the beginning of September'. In the autumn Mary is moved from the pavilion to the farmhouse. 17 October is the first anniversary of Mary's supposed death. Paul takes possession of Marchmont Towers. Edward hears a child's cry from the pavilion near the river. On 18 October Edward horsewhips and denounces Paul in public. On the 30th he leaves Lincolnshire and goes to Brittany.

1850   In March Edward returns to his family home in Devon, and in 'early May' proposes to Belinda Lawford. The wedding is arranged for 1 July. After the ceremony has been stopped, Edward and Mary are reunited. In the autumn Edward and his wife and child travel to Nice, where Mary dies (date unspecified).

1851   By midsummer the new house is completed, but by this time Edward has returned to India.

1855   In September he returns and marries Belinda; it is now 'more than five years' since his failed attempt to do so.

EXPLANATORY NOTES

6 *Montague Square*: correctly 'Montagu Square', it is situated in the London Borough of St Marylebone, and was a fashionable address at this time. (This and several other notes are greatly indebted to information kindly supplied by Professor Andrew Sanders.)

 demi-toilettes: half-evening or dinner dress, as opposed to full dress (French).

 valse à deux temps: French phrase meaning 'waltz in two-time (duple time)', and seemingly paradoxical, since waltzes are in triple time; the phrase, however, refers to the number of steps taken by the dancer to each bar of the music. This type of waltz, popular in the mid-nineteenth century, was faster and livelier than the usual kind.

 scena: extract from an opera or other dramatic vocal composition (Italian).

9 *pantomime*: in the nineteenth-century English theatre, a full-length serious drama (here a 'tragedy') was often followed by a shorter and lighter production; a pantomime involved broad comedy and spectacular effects.

 half-price: the time, part of the way through the programme, at which people were admitted to a theatre at a reduced rate.

 supernumeraries: actors who have no lines to speak.

11 *Euclid*: Greek mathematician of the third century BC whose *Elements* was still the standard textbook of geometry in the nineteenth century.

15 *blue-fire*: 'blue light used on the stage for weird effect' (*OED*).

16 *Perigord pies*: meat pies flavoured with truffles (Perigord is a district of south-west France famous for truffles).

 Fortnum and Mason: famous grocer's shop in Piccadilly, still in business.

17 *Léotard*: Jules Léotard was a famous French acrobat who gave his name to the garment worn by gymnasts.

 Olmar: stage name of James Chadwick (d. 1885), circus performer.

18 *Belgravian*: in Belgravia, then and now a fashionable and expensive district of Central London, situated south-west of Hyde Park Corner.

20 *dip-candles*: small candles made by dipping a wick into melted tallow.

 New Cut: working-class neighbourhood in Lambeth, South London; according to Peter Cunningham's *Handbook of London* (1850), it was 'chiefly inhabited by general dealers, fixture dealers and furniture brokers'.

22 *Palestine and Julienne or Hare and Italian*: kinds of soup.

Row: Rotten Row, a track in Hyde Park, London, popular in the nineteenth century for those taking exercise or seeking fresh air on horseback or in carriages.

penny papers: cheap newspapers became possible only after the abolition of the newspaper tax in 1855.

23 *cabriolet*: two-wheeled horse-drawn carriage with a large hood.

27 *preux chevalier*: valiant knight (French).

32 *TRDL*: Theatre Royal, Drury Lane.

34 *Tyburnia*: the London district once referred to as Tyburnia, a middle-class neighbourhood also known as Bayswater, extended from Marble Arch (the approximate site of Tyburn, celebrated until 1783 as a place of public execution) to Paddington Station.

Dr Fell: an allusion to a well-known rhyme, based on an epigram by the Roman poet Martial and said to have been composed by Thomas Brown (1663–1704) while an undergraduate at Christ Church, Oxford (Dr John Fell was Dean of Christ Church and became a well-known patron of the Oxford University Press). The rhyme survives in various versions, one of which runs:

> I do not love thee, Doctor Fell,
> The reason why I cannot tell;
> But this alone I know full well,
> I do not love thee, Doctor Fell.

Basil: Wilkie Collins's novel appeared in 1852; a revised version was published in 1862, the year before *John Marchmont's Legacy*.

David Copperfield: Dickens's novel had appeared in 1850.

35 *wear a silk gown*: 'to take silk' is still an expression applied to a barrister who becomes a Queen's Counsel.

transpontine: literally, 'across the bridge'; here, on the south and less fashionable side of the River Thames.

37 *examinations*: after the Crimean War competitive recruitment to the army had become more stringent; the Staff College at Camberley had been established in 1858.

Aristophanes . . . Calderon de la Barca: Aristophanes (*c*.448–*c*.380 BC), Greek writer of comedies; Pedro Calderón de la Barca (1500–81), Spanish dramatist.

38 *Clive*: Robert Clive (1725–74), soldier and Indian administrator.

39 *Afghanistan*: see note on ''39' below.

40 *Bolan Pass*: goes through the Brahui range of mountains in what is now Pakistan.

'39: the First Afghan War had in fact broken out in October 1838, when Britain acted to limit the influence of Russia in the region, seen as posing a threat to British interests in India. Fighting had continued throughout

1839 and Afghan forces had surrendered in November 1840. War broke out again in November 1841, when British army officers were massacred in an Afghan uprising; the Second Afghan War ended on 1 January 1842 with the British capitulation at Kabul. Edward Arundel would not have landed in India earlier than March 1840 (see 'The Time-Scheme of *John Marchmont's Legacy*', p. 489), so he would have been in that part of the world for the later stages of the First Afghan War and the whole of the Second.

40 *Cornelia*: a Roman lady popularly known as 'the mother of the Gracchi', and a byword for maternal pride: when another lady showed off her jewels, she is said to have remarked, pointing to her sons: 'These are my jewels.'

The young Queen: Victoria had come to the throne in 1837 at the age of 18.

44 *Castle of Otranto*: Horace Walpole's novel *The Castle of Otranto* was published in 1764.

giant helmet: at the beginning of Walpole's novel (see previous note), Conrad, the son of Prince Manfred, is crushed to death on his wedding day by a giant helmet that falls from a statue.

45 *chariots, barouches, chaises, phaetons*: a chariot was a light four-wheeled carriage with seats at the back; a barouche a four-wheeled closed carriage with seats for four people inside; a chaise an open carriage for one or two persons; a phaeton a light, four-wheeled, open carriage drawn by two horses.

46 *own-man*: valet or personal servant to a gentleman.

48 *Alnaschar*: in the *Arabian Nights*, a poor and simple man who dreams of becoming rich and marrying the Vizier's daughter.

49 *Ash Wednesday*: the first day of Lent. In the Book of Common Prayer the Epistle for the day (Joel 2: 12) calls for 'fasting, and . . . weeping, and . . . mourning'.

fettled: warmed.

52 *'The Fields'*: Lincoln's Inn Fields, one of the centres of the legal profession.

hammer-cloths: coverings for the driver's seat in a family coach.

53 *Brown-George wigs*: a brown wig of a kind worn in the second half of the eighteenth century and said to have been favoured by George III.

56 *'swell'*: stylishly dressed (Eric Partridge's *Dictionary of Slang and Unconventional English* dates the appearance of the word in this sense from *c*.1812).

58 *Dost Mohammed Khan*: (1793–1863), ruler of Afghanistan, who long pursued a pro-Russian, anti-British policy.

59 *tucker*: piece of lace or other material worn inside or around the top of a woman's bodice in the seventeenth and eighteenth centuries.

Rubens . . . Lely: Sir Peter Paul Rubens (1577–1640), worked at various times as a court painter and produced many portraits; he also became famous for his depictions of mythological subjects with generously-proportioned female figures. Diego Velasquez (1599–1660), Spanish painter noted for his royal portraits. 'Vandyke' is the Anglicized spelling of the name of Sir Anthony van Dyck (1599–1641), who came from Flanders to England in 1632 and painted Charles I and others. Hans Holbein (1497–1543), German painter, also came to England and is well known for his portraits of Henry VIII. Sir Peter Lely (1618–80), Dutch portraitist who worked for Charles I and Charles II.

stomacher: 'ornamental covering for the chest, often covered with jewels, formerly worn by women under the lacing of the bodice' (*OED*).

60 *gig*: light two-wheeled carriage.

62 *Conrad . . . Medora*: in Byron's poem *The Corsair* (1814), Conrad is a pirate chief loved by Medora, who dies of grief after receiving a false report of his death.

Lurleis: the Lorelei (usual spelling) is a large rock close to the Rhine and possessing a famous echo; in German legend (the basis of poems by Heine and other romantic writers) it is the home of a siren who lures boatmen to their death.

69 *Judith*: in the apocryphal Book of Judith, she cuts off the head of the Assyrian general Holofernes.

Magdalene: a woman, mentioned in all four gospels, who 'wiped [Jesus's] feet with her hair' (John 11: 2); she is usually identified with the unnamed 'sinner', a repentant prostitute, who performs a similar action in Luke 7: 38–9.

70 *newly married*: the young Victoria married Prince Albert of Saxe-Coburg-Gotha on 10 February 1840. He had died on 14 December 1861, so his death was still fresh in the minds of Braddon and the first readers of this novel.

77 *[chapter-title]*: in the serial version, this chapter was titled 'Temptation'. The substituted title seems to echo the repeated complaint of the speaker in Tennyson's poem 'Mariana' (published in 1830) that 'My life is dreary'. (On other Tennysonian elements in the novel, see Introduction, p. xxi.)

St Swithin: St Swithin's Day (15 July) has a popular meteorological significance, the belief long being current that if it rained on that day it would rain for the next forty days.

78 *Pallas Athenë*: in Greek mythology, the daughter of Zeus, king of the gods; she is often portrayed brandishing a spear.

jesuitical: a derogatory reference to the Jesuits, members of the Society of Jesus, founded by Ignatius Loyola in 1533. 'Owing to the casuistical principles maintained by many of its leaders, the name Jesuit acquired an opprobrious signification, and a *Jesuit* or *Jesuitical person* means (secondarily) a deceiver, a prevaricator, etc.' (*Brewer's Dictionary of Phrase and Fable*).

85 *Vincennes*: suburb of Paris whose medieval castle was formerly used as a prison.

86 *skeleton clock*: one in which the works are visible through a glass cover.

90 *Bill Sykes'*: the ruffian in Dickens's *Oliver Twist* (1838), whose name is properly spelled 'Sikes', is loved by the prostitute Nancy.

99 *ruined walls*: Macbeth's castle was traditionally placed at Dunsinane in the Scottish Highlands.

100 *barmecide feast*: proverbial phrase, originating in one of the stories of the *Arabian Nights*, meaning an illusion that ends in disappointment.

Dutch metal: malleable alloy of copper and zinc, beaten into thin leaves to produce a cheap substitute for gold leaf.

Princes Street: the long and handsome main street of Edinburgh.

nipping and eager airs: the first of several allusions to Shakespeare's *Hamlet*, here to Act I, scene iv, line 2.

modern Athens: familiar phrase referring to Edinburgh.

Calton Hill: well-known landmark in Edinburgh.

Melrose and Abbotsford: beauty spots in the south-east Lowlands of Scotland, much favoured by tourists then and now. Melrose possesses the fine ruins of a Cistercian abbey; Abbotsford is the site of the mansion built in Scottish Baronial style by Sir Walter Scott in 1817.

105 *Lucy Ashton or Amy Robsart*: characters in novels by Sir Walter Scott, respectively *The Bride of Lammermoor* (1819) and *Kenilworth* (1821).

106 *Hertz or Schubert*: 'Hertz' is perhaps an error for 'Herz', referring to the Viennese pianist and composer Henri Herz (1806–88); Franz Schubert (1797–1828), a much more enduring Viennese composer, produced almost every kind of musical composition, including much piano music.

108 *She suffered, and was still*: the phrase 'to suffer and be still' appears in the poem 'Madeline: A Domestic Tale' (1828) by Felicia Hemans, and was taken up by a number of subsequent writers as well as by Braddon.

110 *Mr Reuter's*: Reuters, the famous news agency, the first of its kind, was established in London in 1851 by a German telegrapher, Baron Paul von Reuter.

Printing-house Square: then the address in London of *The Times* newspaper.

116 *Juggernaut*: originally, in Hindu mythology, one of the names of Krishna, it was applied to an idol conveyed through the streets in an annual procession in Orissa, when devotees would fling themselves under the wheels of the 'chariot' carrying it.

117 *Brocken*: the Brocken is the highest peak of the Hartz range of moun-

tains in Germany. In popular belief, the site of a Witches' Sabbath on Walpurgis Night (see e.g. Goethe, *Faust, Part 1*, 'Walpurgis-Night').

118 *flys*: light carriages available for hire.

121 *Tennyson's Moated Grange*: the figure portrayed in Tennyson's lyric 'Mariana', published in 1830, lives in a 'moated grange'—a phrase borrowed by Tennyson from Shakespeare's *Measure for Measure*.

126 *ticket-of-leave*: permission for a convict to be set free, under certain restrictions, before the expiry of the sentence.

130 *Semiramis . . . Boadicea*: Semiramis was a legendary queen of Assyria and founder of Babylon; Boadicea (d. AD 62), queen of the Iceni tribe, led a revolt against the Roman occupation of Britain.

131 *Charles Kingsley*: well-known novelist (1819–75) who also wrote and lectured on a wide variety of subjects, including natural history and geology.

132 *Mendelssohn's wordless songs*: Felix Mendelssohn-Bartholdy (1809–47), German composer, whose 'Lieder ohne Worte' (Songs without Words) is a series of forty-eight piano pieces published between 1830 and 1845, very popular with Victorian players and listeners.

136 *Dinah Morris*: Methodist preacher in George Eliot's *Adam Bede* (1859).

140 *pegtops*: 'trousers very wide in the hips and narrow at the ankles' (*OED*, which dates the appearance of the term from 1858).

le genre: fashionable (French).

143 *arrière-pensée*: ulterior motive (French).

153 *Jacob*: 'And Jacob served seven years for Rachel'—but when he claimed his wife he was told to serve 'yet seven other years' (Genesis 29: 20,27), hence the 'fourteen' referred to.

154 *Napier*: Sir Charles Napier (1782–1853) served in India from 1841 to 1851, becoming commander-in-chief of the army there.

156 *bullion*: the likely meaning here seems to be 'a fringe made of twists of gold or silver thread' (*OED*).

158 *Titania*: fairy queen in Shakespeare's *A Midsummer Night's Dream*.

159 *Sutlej*: river flowing through Tibet, India, and Pakistan.

160 *Florizel and Perdita . . . Paul and Virginia*: the first young couple appear in Shakespeare's *The Winter's Tale*, the last in Bernardin de Saint-Pierre's novel *Paul et Virginie* (1787).

164 *Abigail*: traditional term for a lady's maid, from David's handmaid in the Old Testament (1 Samuel 25: 24–8).

165 *Fra Diavolo*: opera by the French composer Auber, produced in 1829.

168 *whipper-in*: huntsman's assistant, employed to control the pack of hounds.

169 *a Mrs Fry or a Mrs Brownrigg*: Elizabeth Fry (1780–1845), Quaker

preacher and noted prison reformer; Elizabeth Brownrigg, hanged for murder in 1767.

173 *Ophelia*: the sentence refers closely to the passage describing the death by drowning of Ophelia in Shakespeare's *Hamlet* (IV. vii. 167–84).

175 *Bayard*: Pierre du Terrail, Chevalier de Bayard (1475–1524), whose character and conduct led to his being regarded as the model of knightly virtues: the famous phrase 'chevalier sans peur et sans reproche' (knight without fear and without reproach) was applied to him.

176 *parliamentary train*: train carrying passengers at a fare of not more than one penny per mile; railway companies were required by statute to run such trains at least once daily in each direction on their lines.

178 *patent theatre*: one established or licensed by royal 'letters patent' (i.e. open letters granting some privilege, often for a fixed period).

180 *creases . . . best fresh*: 'creases' presumably suggests an uneducated pronunciation of 'cresses' (i.e. watercress); 'best fresh' appears to be a popular term for butter of good quality.

181 *Macready . . . Miss Faucit*: W. C. Macready (1793–1873) was one of the leading Shakespearean actors and theatre managers of his day; Helena Faucit (1817–98), one of the most admired actresses of the period, often played opposite him. The play referred to cannot readily be identified.

182 *live a fortnight*: period of residence necessary in order to qualify for marriage in a given parish.

Bedlam: the Hospital of St Mary of Bethlehem, which from the sixteenth century had served as a lunatic asylum (the name is a corruption of 'Bethlehem').

184 *long vacation*: summer recess during which the lawcourts would not sit; during this period wealthy lawyers might well go to Yorkshire or Scotland ('northern wanderings') for shooting holidays.

185 *spencer*: short double-breasted overcoat.

186 *hack cab*: hackney carriage, i.e. one available for hire.

187 *virtù*: love or knowledge of the fine arts (Italian).

196 *Aeolian harp*: stringed instrument producing musical sounds as a result of the action of the wind.

201 *hegira*: originally, the flight of Mohammed from Mecca to Medina in 622; hence, the Mohammedan era, which is dated from that event.

Macbeth: see *Macbeth*, II. ii. 54.

205 *statute of lunacy*: legal process by which an individual was declared insane.

206 *palki*: Hindi word for 'palanquin', a covered litter carried on the shoulders of four men.

208 *Hebe . . . Clotho . . . Atropos*: in Greek mythology, Hebe is the daughter of Zeus and cupbearer to the gods ('nectar' being the divine drink); Clotho and Atropos are two of the three Fates who preside over human destiny.

211 *screw*: an old horse of poor quality, which might be expected to lose its footing easily.

Berlin wool-work: needlework using 'Berlin wool', a type of fine, dyed wool.

212 *vouée au blanc*: literally, 'dedicated to the white' (French)—i.e. destined for one of the orders of nuns.

217 *boluses*: large pills.

gallipots: small earthenware pots used by apothecaries to hold ointments, etc.

218 *hollands*: gin, originally of Dutch manufacture.

219 *pipe or recorder*: another allusion to *Hamlet*: the Prince asks Rosencrantz and Guildenstern, who are trying to manipulate him, 'Do you think I am easier to be played on than a pipe?' (III. ii. 393–4).

221 *Baal*: false god referred to in the Old Testament.

225 *pocket-pistol*: small container holding liquid.

226 *'Bradshaw': Bradshaw's Guide*: the famous railway timetable, was started in 1839 by a Manchester printer, George Bradshaw.

230 *Lancet*: a leading medical journal, founded in 1823 (and still published).

232 *hartshorn, sal volatile*: smelling-salts, ammoniac substances used to revive one suffering from faintness and often carried in small bottles or flasks by ladies.

238 *Outram*: Sir James Outram (1803–63) had a distinguished military career in India and played a notable role during the Indian Mutiny. He was popularly known as 'the Bayard of the East' and 'the Bayard of the Indian Army' (see note on p. 175 above).

240 *vestal sister*: in Ancient Rome, the vestal virgins tended the sacred fire in the Forum; loss of their virginity caused them to be put to death, hence they became synonymous with chastity.

243 *star of the morning*: Lucifer (literally light-bearer) is a name applied both to Venus, the morning star, and to Satan. Braddon probably has in mind Milton's allusions to the latter in *Paradise Lost* (x. 425–6 and elsewhere).

256 *sacque*: loose gown, also a silk train attached to such a gown.

260 *Turneresque*: in the style of the painter J. M. W. Turner (see note on p. 397 below).

261 *meerschaum*: kind of tobacco-pipe.

269 *buried cities of Italy*: excavations at Pompeii had begun in 1748.

274 *Canaanitish woman*: see Matthew 15: 22–8.

ller . . . thieves: an allusion to Jesus's parable of the Good Samaritan (e 10: 30–7).

y: strong cotton material, striped and patterned, used for ...heets.

282 *Ireland*: the reference is to the famine of 1845.

   Sikhs: there were campaigns against the Sikhs in 1834, 1845–6 and 1848–9; the context suggests that the reference here is to the brief Anglo- Sikh War that broke out on 11 December 1845 and was concluded with a British victory on 28 January 1846.

283 *Apothecaries' Hall*: in Water Lane, Blackfriars. It was built in 1670 to rehouse the Worshipful Company of Apothecaries after the Great Fire of London. Both the building and the Company, which functioned as a medical college and an examining body licensing apothecaries to practise, still survive.

284 *davenport*: small and elegant writing-table with drawers.

287 *HEICS*: Honourable East India Company Service.

294 *levanted*: disappeared, absconded (the word carries implications of cheating or other disreputable behaviour).

299 *recovered*: common nineteenth-century usage for 'recovered from'.

   penny-a-liner: derogatory term for a journalist or hack-writer for the popular press.

300 *Voltaire . . . Encyclopaedia*: Voltaire (1694–1778), the leading figure of the French Enlightenment, was one of the contributors to the *Encyclo- pédie*, published between 1751 and 1780, which expounded the most advanced intellectual and scientific ideas of its day and represented the spirit of rationalism.

305 *no bigger than a man's hand*: this popular phrase originates in the Old Testament story of Elijah (1 Kings 18: 44).

308 *'bits'*: colloquial term used by artists to signify 'pleasant or pretty "pieces" of scenery' suitable for artistic treatment (Eric Partridge, *Dictionary of Slang and Unconventional English*).

309 *grass-plat*: lawn ('plat' is a variant of 'plot').

315 *half-pay officer*: one who has retired on a pension.

316 *Egyptian darkness*: Exodus 10: 21 refers to 'darkness over the land of Egypt'.

319 *Minerva-like*: Minerva, the Roman goddess of wisdom, known to the Greeks as Pallas Athenë (see note on p. 78 above), is supposed to have sprung from the brain of Jupiter.

320 *'flat, stale, and unprofitable'*: slightly misquoted from *Hamlet*, I. ii. 133, which has 'stale, flat, and unprofitable').

   La Trappe: the Cistercian abbey at Soligny La Trappe in France was the home of the monks popularly known as Trappists and associated with a life of great austerity that included a vow of silence.

322 *Reynard*: traditional name for the fox.

bullfinches: high quickset hedges with a ditch on one side.

the source of the Nile: J. H. Speke's *Journal of the Discovery of the Source of the Nile* was published in 1863.

323 *trente et quarante*: card game played by gamblers, also known as *rouge-et-noir*.

Homburg: Prussian town and well-known spa, much frequented by English visitors.

324 *golden opinions . . . men*: quotes Shakespeare's *Macbeth*, I. vii. 33.

332 *Professor Pepper*: John Pepper (1821–1900), chemist, inventor, and author of works on popular science, exhibited in America and Australia an invention known as 'Pepper's Ghost', by which the apparition of an actor could be produced on stage. A book on the subject by Henry Dircks appeared in 1863, the year of Braddon's novel.

333 *mythic nymph*: according to an ancient myth, the nymph Egeria gave instruction to Numa Pompilius, the second king of Rome.

334 *poor-rate*: local tax levied for the relief of the poor.

336 *the Academy in Trafalgar Square*: the Royal Academy of Arts was housed in the National Gallery, Trafalgar Square, until 1867, when it moved to its present home at Burlington House, Piccadilly.

337 '*pink*': the term used for the scarlet coat traditionally worn by a huntsman.

338 *Pattis*: Adelina Patti (1843–1919), the great Italian soprano, had made her London debut in 1861 and was still only 20 when Braddon's novel appeared.

340 *march*: presumably 'Hail, the Conquering Hero' from Handel's *Judas Maccabaeus*.

345 *Sisyphus*: in Greek legend, Sisyphus was punished in the underworld for his earthly misdeed by being compelled everlastingly to roll a huge stone to the top of a hill, whereupon it rolled down again.

346 *Macaulay . . . Froude . . . Thiers . . . Lamartine*: notable English and French historians. Lord Macaulay (1800–59) was a celebrated historian, critic, poet and politician; J. A. Froude (1818–94) published a *History of England* between 1856 and 1869; Louis Thiers (1797–1877) was a French statesman and historian; Alphonse de Lamartine (1790–1869), French Romantic poet, became a statesman and historian.

347 *the Duke of Wellington or Sir Colin Campbell*: military heroes. Wellington (1769–1852), soldier and statesman, was the hero of the Peninsular Campaign and Waterloo and also served in India. Campbell (1792–1863) commanded the British forces in India during the Mutiny and was responsible for the relief of Lucknow.

347 *Othello*: the allusion that follows is to Shakespeare's *Othello*, III. iii. 394 ff.

349 *union*: workhouse.

352 *Rochefoucault*: François, Duke of La Rochefoucauld (1613–80), French writer remembered for his witty and often cynical epigrams collected as *Maximes* (1665).

353 *Debtors' Door*: in Newgate Prison; it is referred to in Dickens's *Great Expectations*, ch. 20 (1861) ('out of which culprits came to be hanged').

355 *National Schools*: popular name for the elementary schools under the control of the Church of England, founded by the National Society for the Education of the Poor in the Principles of the Established Church, founded in 1811.

356 *Elizabeth . . . Christina*: two outstanding queens, Elizabeth I of England (1533–1603) and Christina of Sweden (1626–89).

a Rachel Russell, a Mrs Hutchinson, a Lady Nithisdale, a Madame de Lavalette: historical ladies, all notable for their courage in their husbands' hour of need. Rachel, Lady Russell (1636–1723), was the wife of Lord Russell, who was accused of complicity in a plot, imprisoned in the Tower of London, and executed for high treason; she assisted during his trial and made strenuous efforts to secure his release. 'Mrs Hutchison' is probably Lucy, wife of the Puritan John Hutchison who was one of the judges responsible for sentencing Charles I to death; when he was later imprisoned in the Tower she 'exerted all her influence with her royalist relatives to save the life of her husband' (*DNB*), whose biography she later wrote. Winifred Maxwell, later the Countess of Nithsdale (correct spelling) (d. 1749), was the wife of the fifth Earl of Nithsdale, a Scottish Jacobite imprisoned in the Tower and sentenced to death; after vainly petitioning George I for her husband's life, she assisted his escape, dressed in women's clothes, on the night before the execution in 1716, and later wrote an account of this adventure. Madame de Lavalette, actually another Countess and a niece of the Empress Josephine, was the wife of one of Napoleon's generals; condemned to die in 1815, he made his escape by exchanging clothes with his wife.

357 *Buckstone*: John Buckstone (1802–79), actor-manager and prolific (but now forgotten) dramatist.

361 *Mordecai . . . Haman*: in the Old Testament Book of Esther, the Jew Mordecai refused to bow down to Haman, the king's favourite: 'when Haman saw Mordecai in the king's gate . . . he was filled with wrath against Mordecai' (Esther 5: 9).

365 *'best black'*: presumably a superior variety of tea (an expensive item in the nineteenth century).

366 *Conqueror of Italy*: Giuseppe Garibaldi (1807–82), who after liberating Sicily and Naples retired to his country home.

Liberator of Italy: Napoleon III (1808–73), who had married Eugénie in 1853.

368 *millefleurs*: perfume distilled from flowers.

Woolwich: this London suburb was in the nineteenth century a busy town possessing a number of military and naval establishments, including a Royal Military Academy.

369 '*SHUDDRUPH!*': presumably a version of the command 'Shoulder arms!'

370 *Apsley House*: mansion at Hyde Park Corner, London, formerly the home of the Duke of Wellington (see note on p. 347 above) and now a museum.

a certain sentence: there are many biblical references to judgement; Braddon may possibly be thinking of Matthew 7: 2 ('For with what judgement ye judge, ye shall be judged').

373 *Moore's melodies*: the Irish poet Thomas Moore (1779–1852) published a series of *Irish Melodies* between 1801 and 1834 that included many popular lyrics.

Stevenson: Sir John Stevenson (?1760–1833), composer, whose settings of Moore's *Irish Melodies* (see previous note) were once well known.

378 *Adam Smith or McCulloch*: the celebrated economist (1723–90), best known for his *The Wealth of Nations* (1776). John McCulloch (1789–1864), political economist and statistician, the author of *Principles of Political Economy* (1825) and other works.

379 *songs . . . words*: see note on p. 132 above.

St Stephen's: a name for the British Parliament (until 1834 the House of Commons sat in the Chapel of St Stephen's in the Palace of Westminster).

Lord Palmerston: twice Prime Minister between 1855 and his death in 1865. Earlier, as Foreign Secretary, Palmerston had been a highly controversial figure: in 1850, the date now reached by Braddon's story, a vote of censure on his foreign policy was carried in the House of Lords but defeated by the Commons.

381 *Hort's 'Pantheon'*: William Jillard Hort, *The New Pantheon; or, an Introduction to the Mythology of the Ancients, in A Question and Answer; Compiled for the Use of Young Persons* (1854).

383 *Carthaginian ruler . . . Corsican barrister's wonderful son*: respectively Hannibal and Napoleon.

'best gold': in archery, the bull's-eye or 'gilt centre of a target' (*OED*).

385 *firstborn*: 'the Lord slew all the first-born in the land of Egypt' (Exodus 13: 15).

'Oh, could I feel . . .': from Byron's 'Stanzas for Music', dated 1815, beginning 'There's not a joy the world can give . . .'.

386 *wear his rue with a difference*: adapted from the mad Ophelia's remark in *Hamlet*, IV. vi. 182 that 'you must wear your rue with a difference'.

12th of August: the beginning of the season for grouse-shooting.

387 *bouncing cheque*: not in the modern sense of a cheque that is not honoured by the bank, but a generous or handsome one.

390 *last March*: the Prince of Wales (later Edward VII) had married Princess Alexandra of Denmark on 5 March 1863.

Queen Mab's: the chariot of 'the fairies' midwife' is described in detail by Mercutio in a famous passage in Shakespeare's *Romeo and Juliet*, I. iv. 55 ff.

392 *funeral baked meats . . . building churches*: more references to *Hamlet* (I. ii. 180 and II. i. 140).

394 *Damocles*: according to an ancient story, Damocles was invited to a feast by the tyrant Dionysius the Elder of Syracuse, but could not enjoy it because a sword was suspended by a single hair just above his head.

396 *30th of June*: both the serial and the first edition have '31st of June', presumably as a result of a printer's error that went uncorrected.

397 *Etty's*: William Etty (1787–1849) specialized in painting female nudes ('divinities . . . nymphs').

Turner's: the large output of J. M. W. Turner (1775–1851) includes both classical subjects and seascapes.

Stanfield: Clarkson Stanfield (1793–1867), Irish marine painter.

398 *Landseer*: Sir Edwin Landseer (1802–73), well known for his sentimental depictions of animals; some of his work, including his celebrated *The Stag at Bay*, has a Highland setting.

Faed . . . Ward's: Thomas Faed (1826–1900) painted scenes of humble Scottish life. 'Nichol' is perhaps Andrew Nicholl (1804–86), Irish landscape painter. Edward Ward (1816–79), a historical painter who specialized in subjects from the seventeenth and eighteenth centuries.

Incroyables: extravagantly dressed dandies of the French Directory period following the Revolution (French).

Raphael . . . Murillo: Raphael was one of the greatest painters (1483–1520) of the Italian Renaissance, well known for his religious subjects. Jacopo Tintoretto (1518–94), famous Venetian painter. Bartolomé Murillo (1617–82), Spanish painter: a well-known example of his depictions of smiling beggar-boys picturesquely garbed in rags is in the National Gallery, London.

Peter Paul: Rubens (see note on p. 59 above).

Vandyke: see note on p. 59 above.

400 *man in possession*: bailiff's man who moves into a debtor's household to ensure that goods under distraint are not removed.

411 *a dark lantern*: one with a device whereby the light could be concealed.

416 *hind*: farm servant.

419 *Hood*: Thomas Hood (1799–1845), whose lyrics and humorous poems were once very popular. The line, slightly misquoted, is from his ballad beginning 'It was not in the winter . . .'.

 Bois: the Bois de Boulogne, a park in Paris and a fashionable place of exercise for the well-to-do.

425 *'Let the stricken deer go weep'*: *Hamlet*, III. ii. 287.

429 *Prince of Darkness*: Satan.

434 *Mr Bennett and Mr Buchanan*: William Bennett (1820–95) published many poems and songs from 1850. Presumably Robert Buchanan (1841–1901), who later became well known as a poet, novelist, and dramatist, though his first volume appeared only in 1863.

440 *the widow's only son*: the reference is to one of the miracles performed by Christ (see Luke 7: 12).

443 *'wisely . . . too well'*: the allusion is to the hero's dying speech in Shakespeare's *Othello* (v. ii. 343).

452 *shaycart*: cart used for pleasure ('shay' is a corruption of 'chaise').

456 *La Montespan or La Dubarry*: the Marquise de Montespan (1641–1707), famous for her beauty and wit, was the mistress of Louis XIV; the Comtesse du Barry (1741–93) was the favourite of Louis XV.

 Albany: then and now, expensive and exclusive apartments in Piccadilly.

 'Railway Station' . . . *'Derby Day'*: large and crowded canvases, painted in 1862 and 1858 respectively, by W. P. Frith (1819–1909), who became the richest artist of his day. In 1865 he painted a portrait of Braddon, now in the National Portrait Gallery.

457 *caravanserai*: originally in Middle Eastern countries a kind of inn or halting-place for caravans of camels crossing the desert.

468 *Alton Towers*: large country house in Staffordshire, built in the early nineteenth century in the Gothic style.

 Bernal Collection: a collection of works of art 'from the Byzantine period to Louis Seize', assembled by Ralph Bernal (d. 1854) and displayed at 93 Eaton Square, London. It was sold by auction in 1855 for more than £70,000.

 buhl-cabinets: articles of furniture in which the woodwork is elaborately inlaid with brass, ivory, and other decorative materials.

474 *blague*: talk jokingly or disrespectfully (French).

 Millais: John Everett Millais (1829–96), English painter, associated with the Pre-Raphaelites and well known for his depictions of literary subjects.

 Sardanapalus: Greek name of an Assyrian king mentioned in the Old

Testament; by extension, an extravagant and self-indulgent tyrant. (See also note below on p. 475.)

475 *étagère*: set of open shelves (French).

'*Now order here . . . pyre*': quoted from Byron's tragedy *Sardanapalus* (1821), v. i.

477 *Mr Braidwood*: James Braidwood (1800–61), superintendent of the London Fire Brigade, was killed in a fire near London Bridge.

479 *Lyndhurst . . . Brougham*: Lord Lyndhurst (1772–1863), distinguished lawyer and Tory politician, was Lord Chancellor ('the Woolsack') under three governments; Lord Brougham (1778–1868) was a Liberal politician, law reformer, and noted orator.

Mr Sant: James Sant (1820–1916), genre painter and portraitist.

hobadahoy: variant form of 'hobbledehoy', a clumsy, awkward young person, especially one who is growing rapidly but is not yet adult.

a levee at St James's: a reception held by the Queen at St James's Palace.

480 *from St Giles's to Belgravia, from Tyburnia to St Luke's*: from the poorest to the wealthiest or most respectable areas of London. St Giles's was a notorious slum in the neighbourhood of St Martin's Lane; Belgravia was (and still is) a fashionable and expensive district south-west of Hyde Park Corner. According to Professor Andrew Sanders, 'The contrast between Tyburnia and St Luke's is between bourgeois Bayswater and the socially very mixed area of Shoreditch around St Luke's church in Old Street (mixed, that is, from the lower middle class downwards, and decidedly in favour of the latter)'.

486 *Thalberg*: Sigismond Thalberg (1812–71), Swiss-German pianist and composer.

487 *guipure*: a kind of lace.

TROLLOPE IN OXFORD WORLD'S CLASSICS

ANTHONY TROLLOPE

An Autobiography

Ayala's Angel

Barchester Towers

The Belton Estate

The Bertrams

Can You Forgive Her?

The Claverings

Cousin Henry

Doctor Thorne

Doctor Wortle's School

The Duke's Children

Early Short Stories

The Eustace Diamonds

An Eye for an Eye

Framley Parsonage

He Knew He Was Right

Lady Anna

The Last Chronicle of Barset

Later Short Stories

Miss Mackenzie

Mr Scarborough's Family

Orley Farm

Phineas Finn

Phineas Redux

The Prime Minister

Rachel Ray

The Small House at Allington

La Vendée

The Warden

The Way We Live Now

THE OXFORD SHERLOCK HOLMES

The Oxford World's Classics Website

www.worldsclassics.co.uk

- Information about new titles
- Explore the full range of Oxford World's Classics
- Links to other literary sites and the main OUP webpage
- Imaginative competitions, with bookish prizes
- Peruse *Compass*, the Oxford World's Classics magazine
- Articles by editors
- Extracts from Introductions
- A forum for discussion and feedback on the series
- Special information for teachers and lecturers

www.worldsclassics.co.uk

American Literature

British and Irish Literature

Children's Literature

Classics and Ancient Literature

Colonial Literature

Eastern Literature

European Literature

History

Medieval Literature

Oxford English Drama

Poetry

Philosophy

Politics

Religion

The Oxford Shakespeare

A complete list of Oxford Paperbacks, including Oxford World's Classics, OPUS, Past Masters, Oxford Authors, Oxford Shakespeare, Oxford Drama, and Oxford Paperback Reference, is available in the UK from the Academic Division Publicity Department, Oxford University Press, Great Clarendon Street, Oxford OX2 6DP.

In the USA, complete lists are available from the Paperbacks Marketing Manager, Oxford University Press, 198 Madison Avenue, New York, NY 10016.

Oxford Paperbacks are available from all good bookshops. In case of difficulty, customers in the UK can order direct from Oxford University Press Bookshop, Freepost, 116 High Street, Oxford OX1 4BR, enclosing full payment. Please add 10 per cent of published price for postage and packing.